The Adversary

Volume IV of The Saga of Pliocene Exile

Julian May

A Del Rey Book

BALLANTINE BOOKS • NEW YORK

For three masterly twig benders—
    Julia Feilen May, mother
    Norma Olson, teacher
    Ruth Davies, neighbor
        in gratitude.

I am the dark-avised, the widower, the inconsolable,
The Prince of Aquitaine before his ruined tower:
My only star is dead; and now my jewel-studded lute
Will only bear the blackened sun of Melancholia...

My forehead is red yet with the kiss of the queen;
I have dreamed in the grotto where the siren swims.
And twice I have crossed the Acheron, triumphant...

El Desdichado, Gérard de Nerval

LOGE:
They are hastening on to their end,
They who imagine themselves so firmly enduring.
I'm almost ashamed to share in their dealings!
How strongly I'm tempted to change myself again
Into licking flames, consuming the ones who once tamed me,
Rather than blindly passing away with the blind,
Were they ever so splendidly godlike!
That's not such a bad idea...
I'll think it over.
Who knows what I'll do?

Das Rheingold, Richard Wagner

CONTENTS

SYNOPSIS, *The Galactic Milieu and the Pliocene Exile* • xi

PROLOGUE • 1

PART I • *The Subsumption* • 17

PART II • *The Convergence* • 159

PART III • *Nightfall* • 311

APPENDIXES • 461

Map of Northwestern Europe

During the Pliocene Epoch • 462

Map of Western Mediterranean Region

During the Pliocene Epoch,

After the Gibraltar Rupture • 464

Map of the Monte Rosa Massif

During the Pliocene Epoch • 467

Some Aspects of Hyperspatial

Translation and D-Jumping • 469

SYNOPSIS

THE GALACTIC MILIEU

AND THE PLIOCENE EXILE

THE GREAT INTERVENTION OF 2013 OPENED HUMANITY'S WAY to the stars. By the year 2110, when the action of the first volume in this saga began, Earthlings were fully accepted members of a benevolent confederation of planet colonizers, the Coadunate Galactic Milieu, who shared high technology and the capability of performing advanced mental operations known as metafunctions. Genes for the five principal metapsychic abilities—farsensing, coercion, creativity, psychokinesis, and redaction, or healing—had been part of human heredity from time immemorial; but the mental powers were at first only rarely manifest, remaining mostly latent until evolutionary pressure resulted in increasing numbers of operant human metapsychics' being born late in the twentieth century.

The five founding races of the Galactic Milieu had observed the slow metapsychic development of humanity for tens of thousands of years. But it was not until a small group of beleaguered pioneer operants broadcast a desperate telepathic appeal that the Milieu finally intervened in Earthly affairs. After some debate, the galactic confederation decided to admit Earthlings into the Milieu "in advance of their psychosocial maturation" because of the vast mental potential of humanity, which might eventually exceed that of any other race.

In the hectic years following the Great Intervention, the mundane problems of humanity seemed all but solved. Poverty, disease, and ignorance were wiped out. With the help of the nonhumans, people from Earth colonized more than 700 new planets that had already been surveyed and found suitable.

Earthlings also learned how to speed the development of their metapsychic powers through special training and genetic engineering. However, even though the number of humans with operant metafunctions increased with each generation, in 2110 the majority of the population was still "normal"—that is, possessing metafunctions that were either meager to the point of nullity or else latent, unusable because of psychological barriers or other factors. Most of the day-to-day socioeconomic activities of the Human Polity of the Milieu were carried on by "normals," but human metapsychics did occupy privileged positions in government, in the sciences, and in other areas where high mental powers were valuable to the Milieu as a whole.

At only one period between the Great Intervention and 2110 did it seem that the admission of humanity to the Milieu had been a mistake: This was in 2083, during the brief Metapsychic Rebellion. Instigated by a group of Earth-based humans led by Marc Remillard, this attempted coup narrowly missed destroying the entire Milieu organization. The Rebellion was suppressed by loyalist humans, who included Marc's own brother, Jack, and steps were taken to insure that such a disaster never would occur again.

A hundred or so battered survivors of the Rebellion managed to evade retribution by following Marc Remillard through a unique escape hatch: a one-way time-gate leading into Earth's Pliocene Epoch, six million years in the past. Eventually the Rebels settled on Ocala Island, in a part of North America that would one day be called Florida. Well equipped with sophisticated Milieu gadgetry, they lived in isolation for twenty-seven years while their leader made a futile search of the Pliocene galaxy with his artificially enhanced farsenses, seeking another planet inhabited by metapsychics with high technology. Marc Remillard never gave up his dream of human domination of the galaxy—not even when his old allies despaired and their children openly opposed the plan.

In the Galactic Milieu, six million years into the future, the crushing of the Metapsychic Rebellion signaled the start of a new Golden Age for humanity. Human metapsychics achieved Unity—assimilation into a near-mystical mental fellowship of the Galactic Mind. Nonmetas on the planet Earth and its hundreds of interstellar colonies enjoyed unlimited lebensraum, energy sufficiency, the challenges of settling and exploiting new worlds, and citizenship in a splendid galaxy-wide civilization. But even Golden Ages have their misfits: in this case, humans who, for one reason or another, were temperamentally unsuited to the rather structured social environment of the Milieu. These malcontents chose to exile themselves by passing through the time-gate that led to an Earth six million years younger.

The time-gate was discovered in 2034, during the heady years of the scientific knowledge explosion subsequent to the Great Intervention. But since the time-warp opened only backward (anything attempting to return became six million years old and usually crumbled to dust), and since it had a fixed focus (a point in France's Rhône River Valley), its discoverer concluded that it was a useless oddity without practical application.

After the death of the time-gate discoverer in 2041, his widow, Madame Angélique Guderian, learned that her husband had been mistaken. The fair numbers of malcontents in the developing Human Polity of the Milieu were willing to pay handsomely to be transported to a simpler world without rules. Geologists and paleontologists knew that the Pliocene Epoch was an idyllic period just before the dawn of rational life on our planet. Romantics and rugged individualists from almost all of Earth's ethnic groups eventually discovered Madame's "underground railroad" to the Pliocene, which operated out of a quaint French inn located outside the metropolitan center of Lyon.

From 2041 until 2106, the rejuvenated Madame Guderian transported clients from the Milieu to the Pliocene Exile, a presumed natural paradise. After suffering belated qualms of conscience about the fate of the time-travelers, Madame herself passed into the Pliocene, and operation of her clandestine service was taken over by the Human Polity in a quasi-official manner. The time-gate was a convenient glory hole for dissidents.

By 2110, when the gate into the Pliocene Exile had been operating for nearly seventy years, some 100,000 human timefarers had passed through it into an unknown destiny.

On 25 August 2110, eight persons, making up that week's "Group Green," were transported to Exile. These three women and five men would play key roles in a drama that would affect not only the Pliocene world, but ultimately that of the Milieu itself.

Group Green discovered, as other time-travelers had before them, that the natural paradise of Pliocene Europe was under the control of a humanoid race from the Duat Galaxy, a starwhirl many millions of light-years away from our own part of the universe. The exotics were also exiled, having been driven from their home because of their barbarous battle-religion.

The dominant exotic faction, the Tanu, were tall and handsome. In spite of a thousand-year sojourn on Earth, there were still less than 20,000 of them because their reproduction was inhibited by solar radiation. Antagonistic to the Tanu and outnumbering them by at least four to one were their ancient foes, the Firvulag. Often called the Little People, these exotics were mostly of short stature, although there were plenty of humansized and even gigantic individuals among them. They reproduced quite well on Earth but were short-lived compared to the Tanu.

Tanu and Firvulag constituted a dimorphic race—the former metapsychically latent, and the latter possessed of operant metafunctions, mostly limited in power. The Tanu, with their higher technology, had long ago developed mind-amplifying devices, called golden torcs, that raised them to operancy. Use of the torcs had its price, however: A certain percentage of Tanu children proved incompatible with it and died of the "black-torc" syndrome, in spite of the efforts of the grieving adults. These black-torc tragedies exacerbated the already serious problem of low birthrate among the Tanu.

The Firvulag, tougher and cruder than their resplendent kin, did not require torcs in order to exercise their metafunctions.

The leaders and great heroes among the Little People were the mental equals of the Tanu; but most Firvulag were weaker. Stubborn and conservative, for most of their stay on Earth they had resisted the notion of acting in metaconcert—that is, using a multimind operational mode. The Tanu had experimented with this technique, although they never attained the efficiency achieved by metapsychics in the Galactic Milieu.

For most of the thousand years that Tanu and Firvulag resided on Pliocene Earth (which they called the Many-Colored Land), they were fairly evenly matched in the ritual wars fought as part of their battle-religion. The greater finesse and technology of the Tanu tended to counterbalance the superior numbers of the ferociously obstinate Firvulag. The advent of time-traveling humanity was to change the situation drastically.

Early on, the Tanu gained control of the fixed-focus time-gate and took prisoner all the newly arrived humans, enslaving them. The astounding discovery was made that human germ plasm was compatible with that of the Tanu. The meaning behind this paradox was immaterial to the Tanu; they were delighted to be able to use their human slaves in breeding, since Tanu-human hybrids tended to have unusual physical and mental strength. The time-travelers also proved to be a valuable technological resource, enhancing the rather decadent science establishment of the Tanu by injecting the expertise of the greatly advanced Galactic Milieu. It had been strictly forbidden for time-travelers to carry sophisticated weaponry back to the Pliocene (a restriction that was often honored in the breach), and the Tanu were conservative in the types of military hardware that they permitted their human serfs to build. Nevertheless, it was human ingenuity that eventually gave the Tanu almost complete ascendency over the Firvulag—who never mated with humans and generally despised them.

Most of the enslaved time-travelers actually lived quite well under the benevolent overlordship of the Tanu. Rough work was done by small ramapithecine apes who were, ironically, part of the direct hominid line that would climax in Homo sapiens six million years in the future. The ramas wore tiny gray torcs that compelled obedience; they had been used in largely abortive breeding experiments by the Tanu prior to the arrival of time-traveling humans.

Certain human slaves were also fitted with collarlike torcs.

Those who occupied positions of trust or were engaged in vital pursuits wore gray torcs similar to those fitted to the ramas. These did not amplify the mind, but did allow telepathic communication with the Tanu, who were also able to administer punishment or reward through the device. Luckier humans, who showed evidence of metapsychic latencies when tested, were given silver torcs. These were similar to the golden collars worn by the Tanu, making latent metafaculties operant. The silver torcs contained control circuits, however, and disobedience brought swift and excruciating punishment. Silver-torc humans were accepted as conditional citizens of the Tanu kingdom, and under certain circumstances the silvers might be granted golden torcs and full freedom. For humans as well as for Tanu the torcs were potentially hazardous. Occasionally an incompatible human torc wearer would be driven insane or killed outright by the device. Pathological reactions were especially likely among humans without significant metapsychic latencies.

The eight members of Group Green were to be mind-tested by Tanu overlords immediately upon their arrival in the Pliocene, as were all time-travelers. Five of them were "normal," that is, possessing latencies far below the threshold of potential operancy. These were Claude Majewski, an elderly paleontologist; Sister Amerie Roccaro, a physician and burnt-out priest; Stein Oleson, a herculean planet-crust driller, Richard Voorhees, a disgraced starship captain; and Bryan Grenfell, an anthropologist who had followed his lover, Mercy Lamballe, into the Pliocene.

The other three members of Group Green were anything but "normal." Aiken Drum, a charming young criminal, showed very strong latencies and was fitted with a silver torc. Felice Landry, a disturbed young athlete, knew that she also possessed extremely powerful latent metafaculties; but for reasons of her own, she refused to cooperate with the Tanu overlords and was able to postpone being tested.

The eighth and most unusual member of Group Green was Elizabeth Orme. In the Milieu, she had been a fully operant Grand Master metapsychic, an honored teacher. Through a brain trauma she had apparently lost her awesome powers of farsensing and redaction and reverted to the "normal" state. In despair at having been shut out of the metapsychic Unity she had rejoiced in, Elizabeth elected to pass into the Pliocene. There she would be among others like herself, since no operants were allowed to undertake time-travel.

To her horror, Elizabeth discovered that the shock of temporal translation had begun the restoration of her lost powers. Convalescent, at first terrified and then consumed with rage at the irony of her situation, Elizabeth heard the Tanu overlord Creyn tell her that a "wonderful life" awaited her in the Many-Colored Land. As the only torcless operant, she would be considered a unique treasure: The Tanu King himself would be her consort . . .

That evening, two caravans set out from the Tanu Castle Gateway. Group Green had been split in half. Bound north for the city of Finiah on the Proto-Rhine was a sizable mob of normal humans destined to become ordinary slaves and brood stock. These included Claude, Sister Amerie, Richard, and Felice—who had confided to her friends that she planned not only to escape, but also to "take" the entire Tanu race!

The southbound caravan was much smaller. En route to the Tanu capital of Muriah in the Mediterranean Basin were the Tanu overlord Creyn, Elizabeth, Aiken Drum, two other silver-torced humans named Sukey Davies and Raimo Hakkinen, the gigantic driller Stein, who had been fitted with a gray torc in preparation for life as a gladiator, and the untorced anthropologist Bryan Grenfell, whose expertise was strangely valued by the Tanu and who looked forward to finding his lost lover somewhere in Muriah.

The caravan bound for Finiah was soon involved in a prisoner revolt, engineered by the erstwhile professional athlete, Felice. Abnormally strong, with powerful coercive latencies that let her mind-control animals, Felice had smuggled a small steel dagger past the searchers at Castle Gateway. Working with Richard, the starship captain, and two men named Yoshimitsu and Tatsuji who were costumed as samurai, Felice engineered the killing of the female overlord Epone as well as the entire prisoner escort of gray-torc human troops.

One group of freed prisoners elected to follow Basil Wimborne, a mountain climber and former Oxford don, who felt the best plan of escape lay beyond Lac de Bresse in the Jura

highlands. Claude, the old paleontologist, convinced his three
Group Green friends that they would be safer fleeing into the
heavily forested Vosges Mountains rather than risking a long
lake voyage to the Jura. A long course was taken by the surviving Japanese, Yoshimitsu, who headed north hoping to reach
the sea.

Claude, Richard, Amerie, and Felice fled deep into the
Vosges. Eventually they were contacted by a ragtag group of
free outlaw humans, fugitives from Tanu settlements, who called
themselves Low-lives. The Lowlife leader was none other than
Madame Angélique Guderian, former keeper of the time-gate
and the ultimate author of Pliocene humanity's degradation.
She wore a golden torc, the gift of the Firvulag, who had formed
a shaky alliance with the Lowlives against their mortal foe, the
Tanu.

A great manhunt had been mounted by the Tanu after the
prisoner revolt. Basil Wimborne and most of his contingent
were recaptured and sent to Finiah. Its city-lord, Velteyn, led
a Flying Hunt himself over the Vosges in search of the other
escapees; but they were safe with Madame and her Lowlives,
listening incredulously to the old woman's scheme for freeing
humanity from the Tanu yoke, which would utilize the rather
reluctant cooperation of the exotic Firvulag.

Hundreds of kilometers east of the Rhine River lay the so-
called Ship's Grave. There the titanic space-going organism
who had carried both Tanu and Firvulag from the Duat Galaxy
to our own had plunged to Earth, creating a huge crater. Tanu
and Firvulag passengers in the Ship, led by its spouse, a woman
named Brede, had escaped from the dying organism in small
flying machines before it impacted. Later the two groups of
exotics had left the flyers parked around the rim of the crater
after their two greatest heroes, Shining Lugonn of the Tanu
and Sharn the Atrocious of the Firvulag, fought a ritual battle
in honor of the defunct Ship. Ceremoniously entombed within
one of the flyers—which were presumed to be still at the crater
after a thousand years—was the body of Lugonn, together with
his laserlike weapon, the Spear.

Madame proposed to lead an expedition of Lowlives to the
Ship's Grave crater and retrieve this Spear for use against the
very Tanu who held it sacred. And if the flyers were still
operational, as seemed likely, the expedition would attempt to

bring one back to participate in a joint Lowlife-Firvulag attack on Finiah, a Tanu stronghold.

After many vicissitudes, this first phase of Madame Guderian's great plan for the liberation of Pliocene humanity was successful. The Tanu were forced to abandon Finiah, thus losing their only barium mine, which had produced an element vital in the making of all torcs. Felice, who showed increasing symptoms of a severe psychosis, obtained a golden torc for herself from the ruins of Finiah. The mental amplifier unlocked the stupendous powers of coercion, psychokinesis, and creativity that had been latent in her brain, and fueled the girl's fierce desire for revenge upon the Tanu.

The next phase of Madame's plan involved an infiltration of the torc factory in the Tanu capital, Muriah, and a parallel operation that had as its objective the permanent closing of the time-gate.

Madame and ten other conspirators, including Felice, Claude, Sister Amerie, and Basil Wimborne—who had been rescued during the fall of Finiah—now set out on a long trip south. They took with them the laserlike Spear of Lugonn. Its energies had been totally discharged during the Finiah operation, but they hoped that their clever Group Green companion, Aiken Drum, would be able to recharge it when they appealed to him for assistance down in the Tanu capital.

Aiken—together with Elizabeth, Bryan, Stein, and the other privileged captives—had encountered an utterly different face of the Many-Colored Land upon arriving in Muriah some weeks past. They were presented to the Tanu aristocracy at a lavish feast, where they were treated at first like honored guests instead of slaves.

Elizabeth was told by Thagdal, the King, that she would first be initiated into Tanu ways by Brede Shipspouse, the enigmatic guardian of both exotic races. When this was accomplished, she and the King would found a new dynasty of torcless, fully operant Tanu-human hybrids. (Queen Nontusvel seemed entirely agreeable to this plan, in spite of the fact that her own large brood of powerful adult children would undoubtedly be overshadowed by Elizabeth's offspring.)

Bryan the anthropologist was ordered to make a study of the impact of humanity upon the Tanu socioeconomy. King

Thagdal believed that human genes and human innovation had been a boon to the Tanu, and he expected Bryan's survey to vindicate his policy encouraging interbreeding and the adoption of certain human inventions. A minority Tanu faction, headed by Nodonn Battlemaster, the most powerful son of Nontusvel and heir presumptive, maintained that the exotic culture was being poisoned by human influences.

As the "welcoming" banquet progressed, it became clear that a grim fate was in store for Stein Oleson, the brawny ex-driller who had been befriended by the trickster youth, Aiken Drum. Stein was put up for auction as a kind of gladiator; to save him from certain death, Aiken himself impudently put in his own bid for Stein. The Tanu throng was stunned when the head of the Farsensor Guild, Mayvar Kingmaker, not only endorsed Aiken's bid but also took him for her protégé. Mayvar was well aware that the young man, who wore a golden suit all covered with pockets, possessed enormous latent mindpowers that were only beginning to come fully operant as a result of the triggering action of his silver torc.

Deeply shaken by a glimpse into Aiken's mind and by Mayvar's embrace of the youth (she was not called "kingmaker" for nothing), Thagdal accepted Aiken's bid for Stein. After a period of training, Aiken would be obliged to rid the kingdom of a certain Firvulag monster, Delbaeth.

In the weeks that followed, Aiken was tutored by Mayvar in the exercise of his fast-developing metafunctions. He became fully operant without a torc—although this fact was concealed from the other Tanu by Mayvar. He successfully disposed of Delbaeth and, with Stein as his henchman, became cautiously allied with the human President of the Coercer Guild, Sebi-Gomnol, who had plans of his own for advancing human domination of the Tanu kingdom.

The untorced anthropologist, Bryan Grenfell, carried out his cultural survey—but scarcely paid attention to the import of the growing body of data, because he was once more under the spell of his long-lost love, Mercy Lamballe. This woman had arrived in the Pliocene shortly before Group Green. A latent metapsychic with extraordinary creative powers, Mercy had become the latest consort of the formidable Nodonn Battlemaster and was completely converted to the Tanu cause. Nodonn and his siblings of the Host of Nontusvel encouraged

Mercy to entice Bryan, so that the anthropologist's survey could be used against the King and Gomnol.

Meanwhile, Elizabeth was under the protection of the mysterious Brede Shipspouse, after having been subjected to inept attacks by Nodonn and the Host, who saw her as a dynastic threat. Safe inside Brede's room without doors, a sophisticated force-field secure against physical and mental penetration, Elizabeth confided her despair and hopelessness to the exotic woman. The Shipspouse, maternally concerned with both the Tanu and Firvulag races, perceived Elizabeth as one who might lead them (as Brede apparently could not) out of their barbarous battle-culture into a truly civilized society of the mind. Elizabeth declined this role of spiritual motherhood. She did, however, use her Milieu training to lift Brede into metapsychic operancy, and the two briefly enjoyed a limited Unity. This was broken when Brede insisted that she foresaw Elizabeth assuming the guardian role and the human woman violently rejected the responsibility.

Around the beginning of October, the entire Many-Colored Land prepared for the annual ritual war, the Grand Combat, by means of a month-long Truce. Up north, Madame Guderian and her band of saboteurs made use of the peace to implement their plans. Madame and Claude, the old paleontologist, went into hiding close by the time-gate. They planned to wait until the others—including Felice, Sister Amerie, Basil, and a Native American leader named Peopeo Moxmox Burke—reached Muriah and readied a strike against the torc factory inside Coercer Guild headquarters. The attacks against time-gate and factory would be made simultaneously.

Felice and the other southbound saboteurs at first hoped to use the Spear to destroy the factory. They summoned Aiken Drum to their hiding place and gave him the weapon, which he promised to recharge and return to them. Actually, Aiken had no intention of aiding his former compatriots. Encouraged by both Mayvar and Gomnol, he aspired to become King of the Many-Colored Land by defeating Nodonn in the upcoming Grand Combat. He warned his confederate Gomnol to protect the torc factory against the saboteurs; then he flew north, disguised as a bird, in order to thwart Claude and Madame's attempt to close the time-gate. In this he failed. Sacrificing

themselves, the elderly couple carried a warning back in time
to the Milieu authorities, and the time-gate operation was suspended.

The saboteurs infiltrating the torc factory were surprised by
a force of Tanu knights, members of the Host of Nontusvel,
who had been sent by Nodonn. Of the surviving humans, Felice
was turned over to Culluket the Interrogator for torture, while
Sister Amerie, Chief Burke, and Basil were thrown into a
dungeon to await death during the Grand Combat. The human
Lord Coercer, Gomnol, was mind-blasted to death by the Host
in a subterfuge, and the blame was put on Felice.

As the time of the Grand Combat approached, a number of
crises reached a critical stage. Aiken, deprived of his powerful
ally, Gomnol, found himself endangered by Stein. The big
crust driller had been imprisoned with Sukey, now his wife,
and his sanity was beginning to totter because of the unhealthy
effect of the gray torc he wore. There was a chance that Stein
might inadvertently reveal that Aiken conspired against the
Tanu.

Resisting the temptation to kill his friend, Aiken asked Mayvar to get Stein and Sukey out of Muriah, beyond range of the
Host's mental snooping. Mayvar agreed, then went to a meeting
of the clandestine Tanu Peace Faction. This group hoped that
Aiken would succeed in his bid for the kingship and bring a
new era of peace and civilization to the Many-Colored Land.
Among the peacelovers was Minanonn the Heretic, once Tanu
Battlemaster, who had been forced into exile deep in the Pyrénées.

Brede Shipspouse let Elizabeth leave the room without doors
when she saw that the human metapsychic was determined to
live a life free of responsibility. Elizabeth agreed to take Stein
and Sukey away with her in her three-place hot-air balloon.
She awaited arrival of the pair on a mountaintop above Muriah.
Creyn the redactor fetched them from prison—but he could
not help bringing Felice, too, whom he had found unconscious
and near death in an adjoining cell, in hopes that Elizabeth
would give up her place in the balloon to the tortured young
athlete.

Elizabeth was trapped by her own altruism, even though
convinced that the Shipspouse had planned this to forestall her

escape. Finally, Elizabeth sent Felice, Stein, and Sukey away in the balloon, and she returned to the room without doors, where she withdrew into a fiery mental cocoon that isolated her from Brede and all other minds.

The time of the Grand Combat had come. Virtually the entire population of Tanu and Firvulag—together with large numbers of human slaves, assembled on the White Silver Plain below Muriah for the ceremonies and the ritual war. Aiken was appointed by Mayvar to be a leader in the Combat; he had attracted many adherents among the Tanu and hybrid warriors. In a preliminary contest, Mercy overcame Aluteyn Craftsmaster to become the new President of the Creator Guild.

Hundreds of kilometers west of the White Silver Plain, the three escaping balloonists were enacting a drama that would ultimately affect the fate of the unsuspecting combatants.

In his torture of Felice, Culluket the Interrogator had unwittingly duplicated a drastic mind-altering technique that Elizabeth had used on Brede to raise her to operancy; now Felice had gone operant, too, and no longer needed a torc to exercise her metapsychic powers. These powers—at least the destructive aspects of psychokinesis and creativity—were greater than those of any other person in the world. The girl's incipient psychosis had similarly burgeoned under the torture; her thirst for revenge against the Tanu was now inextricably merged with a darker sadomasochistic element of her sick mind. Compelling Stein, the former planet-crust driller, to help her, Felice began to blast the narrow Gibraltar isthmus with bolts of psychoenergy. She intended to admit the Atlantic waters into the nearly empty basin of the Pliocene Mediterranean and down the Grand Combat participants.

As the madwoman smote the earth with her mindbolts, the rocky barrier neared the breaking point. But Felice weakened before the job was complete. In her extremity of hatred she prayed for help from whatever powers of darkness might exist—and the assistance came from *somewhere*. A final titanic burst of psychoenergy opened the Gibraltar Gate and a cascade of seawater thundered into the dry Mediterranean, heading toward the White Silver Plain below the Tanu capital of Muriah.

Felice was flung from the balloon by the final concussion. Quite insane, she assumed the shape of a monstrous raven.

Stein and Sukey soared away on the stormwinds and ultimately landed in a remote part of France.

The prescient Brede Shipspouse knew about the catastrophe. She appeared to Amerie, Basil, and Chief Burke in their prison cell, healed them, and took them to a room within the Redactor Guild complex, high on the Mount of Heroes above Muriah. There Elizabeth lay in her self-induced coma. Brede instructed the trio to guard Elizabeth, "the most important person in the world," and to wait until the following morning, when they would know what had to be done.

Meanwhile, the Grand Combat was reaching its climax. For the first time in forty years, the Firvulag were holding their own. The stubbornly conservative Little People had previously refused to emulate human tactics, as the Tanu had done; but the Firvulag-Lowlife victory at Finiah had opened the eyes of their generals, Sharn and Ayfa, and inspired them to innovation. In the mêlée phase of Combat scoring, the Firvulag were only slightly behind the Tanu. The finale of the ritual war, in which individual champions met hand to hand, would decide the victor.

The rivalry between Aiken and Nodonn divided the loyalty of the Tanu forces. At a war feast prior to the Heroic Encounters, Nodonn tried to discredit Aiken by producing Bryan Grenfell and the latter's adverse study of humanity's impact upon the Many-Colored Land. This aggravated the split between traditionalist Tanu and those loyal to Aiken. The Encounters were won by Firvulag heroes in an upset. Only a victory by Aiken over ogreish Firvulag general, Pallol One-Eye, could save the day for the Tanu. Aiken told Nodonn and the traditionalists that he could lick the monster if he were allowed to fight in a human way. This was finally permitted. Aiken conquered Pallol and the Tanu were declared overall winners of the Grand Combat.

Heartbroken and bitter over their narrow loss, most of the Firvulag left the White Silver Plain. Only their royalty remained for the award ceremony and its intriguing anticlimax, a duel between Aiken and Nodonn for the battlemastership (and ultimately the kingship) of the Tanu. Virtually the entire flower and chivalry of the Tanu were gathered as witnesses. Brede herself was there to see Mayvar Kingmaker bestow upon Aiken his Tanu name: He was called Lugonn, after the Shining Hero who had fallen at the Ship's Grave a thousand years before, and he was invested with the sacred Spear, now recharged and ready for use again. Nodonn took up a similar weapon, the Sword, which had once belonged to a Firvulag hero.

The two rivals squared off and began their duel just as the cataclysmic flood from the encroaching Atlantic swept over the White Silver Plain.

The mind-cries of the thousands of drowning people roused Elizabeth, and she and her three human companions looked out upon devastated Muriah and a submerged White Silver Plain. Not all of the combatants and spectators of the last Grand Combat died, however. Most of the Firvulag, already en route home in their boats, survived. Some Tanu were cast ashore by the flood wave or managed to use their metapsychic powers to save themselves. Humans and hybrids in fair numbers swam to safety. Wounded Tanu knights who had retired to Redactor House, together with many members of that guild who attended them, were secure from the floodwaters. Aluteyn Craftsmaster and a rabble of craven knights floated to safety aboard the vessel in which they were to have been incinerated. Aiken Drum rode the flood inside a ceremonial cauldron and later rescued Mercy.

But more than half of the glorious Tanu, who were especially vulnerable to immersion, perished. Profoundly shocked and torn from her self-centered despair, Elizabeth finally undertook the guardian role that the dead Brede bequeathed to her, and coordinated the evacuation of Muriah with the help of Chief Burke, Basil, Sister Amerie, and the powerful redactors Dionket and Creyn.

The Postdiluvium saw an entirely new balance of power take form in the Many-Colored Land. Sharn and Ayfa became co-monarchs of the Firvulag and inaugurated unprecedented reforms, including the domestication of animals, the utilization of contraband Milieu weapons, and experiments in metaconcerted mind-offensives. The Firvulag throne patched up a long-standing schism with the mutant Howlers, granted them the franchise, and encouraged the Howler lord Sugoll to resettle the abandoned Firvulag city of Nionel.

After leading the multiracial band of refugees from Muriah

to safety, Elizabeth retired to a stronghold on Black Crag in southern France to meditate on her new role and its implications. Creyn the Redactor was among those who chose to attend her. Dionket and certain peace-loving Tanu, Firvulag, and humans went into the remote Pyrénées to join Minanonn the Heretic.

Felice, now completely insane, lived in an eyrie on Mount Mulhacén in southern Spain and frequently shape-shifted into the form of a giant raven. Her cave contained an immense trove of scavenged golden torcs and also the Spear of Lugonn, which she had retrieved from the deepening New Sea. Felice was obsessed with the idea of finding Culluket the Interrogator, whom she called her "Beloved." She also felt persecuted by the "devils" who had helped her breach the Gibraltar Gate.

Felice's devil voices were by no means imaginary. Far away in North America lay the Ocala Island settlement of the Metapsychic Rebellion survivors. Twenty-seven years earlier, the fleeing Rebels had forced their way into Madame Guderian's establishment and passed through the time-gate into the Pliocene, taking with them a great store of equipment. When their leader, Marc Remillard, discovered that Europe was under the control of exotics, he withdrew beyond the Atlantic. The Tanu who tried to stop him were badly beaten in a skirmish, and the incident was expunged from Tanu history.

For most of the intervening years, Marc Remillard had devoted himself to his star-search, hoping to find another world with advanced mentalities. His companions eventually dwindled to forty-three, and there were now, in addition, thirty-two mature children and a handful of third-generation youngsters living on the island, vegetating or chaffing in idleness according to their individual temperaments.

For years the adult children of the Rebels had watched events in the Many-Colored Land as a respite from boredom, yearning hopelessly for the sophisticated Milieu that their parents had tried to dominate. When Felice sent out her telepathic appeal at Gibraltar, the children prevailed upon Marc and the other elders to join them in assisting her, linking in a metaconcert to channel a psychocreative blast through Felice. Ever since the Flood, ringleaders among the rebel children had been importuning Felice telepathically, but she was terrified by the voice of the "devils" and refused to respond. Marc and most of the members of his generation dismissed the European catastrophe as a moment's diversion, but their children believed that the postdiluvial chaos in the Many-Colored Land afforded them a unique opportunity to escape from their dead-end existence in the Pliocene.

In Europe, the rising star in the devastated Tanu kingdom was none other than the incorrigible Aiken Drum, who now styled himself Aiken-Lugonn Battlemaster and presided as usurper over Nodonn's former city of Goriah in Brittany. Mercy, bowing to expediency and believing that her beloved Nodonn was dead, assisted Aiken in his bid to take over the vacant Tanu throne and promised to marry him at the Grand Loving festivities in May.

Many surviving Tanu—including most of the Tanu-human hybrids—flocked to the banner of the metapowerful youth. The conservatives rallied around Celadeyr of Afaliah, one of the few surviving fullblooded battle heroes.

Culluket the Interrogator attached himself to Aiken as a sort of Grand Vizier—not only because he perceived the human upstart as the main chance, but also in hopes that Aiken could protect him from the madwoman Felice, still searching relentlessly for her "Beloved."

During the winter rainy season, Firvulag forces began a systematic series of attacks upon outlying Tanu cities and Lowlife villages—this in spite of an armistice that had been proclaimed in the aftermath of the Flood. The Firvulag monarchs Sharn and Ayfa blamed the raids on renegade Howlers and stoutly maintained that they were in favor of Aiken's pacification scheme. This involved the abolition of the Grand Combat (and the other fighting between Firvulag and Tanu) and the substitution of a nonlethal "Grand Tourney" in its place. This would be celebrated on the Firvulag Field of Gold outside Nionel—traditional alternate to the Tanu White Silver Plain, which had been disused for the forty years of Tanu supremacy in the Combat. The Firvulag artisans crafted a new trophy, the Singing Stone, to take the place of the Sword of Sharn, presumed lost in the Flood.

In order to cement the new Tanu-Firvulag Entente, it was planned that Firvulag royalty would for the first time attend the Tanu Grand Loving festival in Goriah as honored guests of Aiken and Mercy. When certain Tanu nobles showed a reluctance to attend this event, suspecting that Aiken would take the occasion to proclaim himself king, the usurper gathered his forces and undertook a "progress" in order to intimidate the vacillators. The progress was ultimately successful, but stubborn old Celadeyr of Afaliah capitulated only after Aiken defeated him in a mental duel.

At about the same time that Aiken began his progress, early in April, the Rebel children in Ocala finally managed to contact Felice. They made extravagant promises to the madwoman and she agreed to meet with them if they came to Europe. The children planned to use Felice's awesome power for their own ends—which ultimately included building a new time-warp device that would give them access to the Milieu. Ringleaders among the younger generation included Marc's son, Hagen, and daughter, Cloud. The formidable Marc was at first utterly opposed to the plan. A two-way time-gate, he said, would allow Milieu authorities access to *him*. The children swore that they would destroy the Pliocene gate after passing through, so that their elders would remain secure. In an attempt to temporize, Marc agreed to let Cloud, three other young people, and his own contemporary Owen Blanchard sail to Europe to meet with Felice. He forbade Hagen to go, telling his only son he was needed to assist in the star-search. Hagen, who had long feared and envied his powerful father, now actively hated Marc and schemed to escape his dominance.

Back in Goriah, Mercy gave birth to Agraynel, her child by King Thagdal, and mourned the loss of Nodonn. She agreed to marry Aiken even though she did not love him and knew that the young man's infatuation for her was deeply tinged with fear—and even menace.

Unknown to Mercy, Nodonn was not dead. Cast up by the flood upon the distant Isle of Kersic (Corsica-Sardinia), he was rescued by Huldah, a simple-minded woman of Firvulag-human ancestry, and her malevolent grandfather, Isak. After lying unconscious for nearly five months, Nodonn awoke. He discovered to his horror that he was paralyzed and bereft of one hand, and that Huldah had been using him as a helpless love object while she tended him. With his telepathic calls muted by the cave rock around him, Nodonn endured Huldah's devotion and Isak's mockery.

Freeliving Lowlife humans, in the forests adjacent to the Firvulag capital, High Vrazel, had set up iron-mining villages shortly after the fall of Finiah. The "blood-metal" was poisonous to both exotic races, and humans hoped to secure their own independence by forging iron weapons. A metallurgical engineer, Tony Wayland, who had enjoyed a privileged position in Finiah under the Tanu, was forced by Lowlife captors to work in the mines. He ran away, together with an eccentric companion, Dougal, hoping to gain both sanctuary and restored privileges from Aiken Drum. Instead, Tony and Dougal were taken by Howlers to refurbished Nionel just in time for the Firvulag Grand Loving.

In Goriah, Aiken returned from his progress exhausted in mind and body. Securing a portable force-field to screen himself against attempts on his life, he showed Mercy an enormous cache of contraband Milieu armament and other equipment that Nodonn had secreted in the dungeon of the Castle of Glass. He fully expected the visiting Firvulag nobles to attempt assassination during the upcoming Grand Loving.

On 27 April the boat bearing Cloud Remillard and her confederates arrived at the mouth of the Río Genil in Spain. Vaughn Jarrow, one of the Rebel children, infuriated Felice by killing dolphins. She annihilated him and mortally wounded the boat's skipper, Jillian Morgenthaler. Calmed by the elderly Rebel Owen Blanchard, Felice nearly fell into a trap that would have put her under control of the North Americans. She was saved by a telepathic warning from Elizabeth, who urged her to come to Black Crag for treatment of her mental illness.

Felice finally agreed and flew away in raven guise, leaving the shaken Cloud, Owen, and Elaby Gathen wondering what to do next. Marc was inaccessible, locked away in cerebro-energetic equipment scrutinizing distant stars. It seemed obvious that the only course left was to make a friendly approach to Aiken Drum.

The usurper of Goriah was busy with other affairs, however. As a preliminary to the Tanu celebration, he took King Sharn on a Flying Hunt in which the Firvulag ruler barely escaped a

fierce plesiosaur. Sharn suspected (correctly) that Aiken had
set him up. Later, Sharn and his stalwarts did their metaconcerted best to mind-blast Aiken, but they were not yet skilled
enough to harm him.

The Grand Loving of Tanu shocked the straitlaced Firvulag
visitors. There were murmurings about an upcoming Nightfall
War—presumably a resumption of the ancient conflict of Tanu
and Firvulag in the Duat Galaxy, which had been interrupted
by Brede's offer of exile a thousand years ago.

On May Day, Aiken married Mercy. Having impressed or
intimidated the majority of Tanu, he proclaimed himself king
with the blessing of Elizabeth, and named a new High Table
that included both his friends and certain former enemies. Among
the latter were Celadeyr of Afaliah and Kuhal Earthshaker, a
blood-brother to Nodonn being nursed back to health after
rescue by Celadeyr.

Simultaneously, the Grand Loving of Firvulag took place
in the Howler city of Nionel. Humiliation of the Howler brides
was averted when they were chosen in the Bridal Dance by
love-starved Lowlife males, who could not see the true monstrous shapes behind the attractive feminine illusions. Among
the bewitched were Tony and Dougal, who awoke the next
morning to find that they were wed to devoted she-goblins.

In the cave on Kersic, Huldah celebrated the Grand Loving
by dressing the paralyzed Nodonn in his glass armor and embracing him. Wicked old Isak spied on the couple. Nodonn's
disgust and fury were so intense that he regained his strength,
thrust away Huldah, and killed the wretched old man. He would
have slain the woman as well, but Isak had tauntingly ordered
him to "look inside" her before doing so.

Exerting his farsight, Nodonn discovered that Huldah was
pregnant with his son. Here in the cave, shielded from sublethal
solar radiation that had rendered him all but sterile for some
800 years, Nodonn had engendered the heir he had so long
desired. Sparing Huldah, he told her to care for the child when
it was born and wait for his instructions. Then he left the cave
and sent out a telepathic call to Mercy, informing her that he
was alive.

In Ocala, Hagen Remillard had finally worked up the courage to defy his terrible father. While Marc continued his futile

star-search, Hagen and the rest of the Rebel children and grand-children fled the island, heading for Europe after disabling pursuit. Marc "returned" on 16 May with a premonition of what had happened four days previous. Some of his old cronies were in favor of blasting the fleeing children, eliminating the threat of a two-way time-gate once and for all. Marc refused to consider this and proposed another plan. In a week or so, when conditions were favorable, the children would be forced off course onto the African shore, giving their parents time to repair their own damaged ships and go after them. In the mean-time, Marc had a plan to forestall any attempt by Cloud to deal independently with Aiken. With luck, he would be able to neutralize the newly crowned King altogether...

Concealing his identity, Marc farspoke Aiken and revealed a knowledge of the King's impending expedition into Spain. With Felice undergoing redaction by Elizabeth, Aiken hoped to hunt out the mad-woman's lair and retrieve the invaluable Spear of Lugonn—which was not only a useful weapon but also the ancient authority symbol of Tanu kingship. Marc of-fered to reveal the exact location of the lair and also pledged the mental assistance of his people. No one knew when Felice would leave Black Crag. If she caught Aiken attempting to rob her, he'd need all the help he could get.

Aiken shrewdly deduced the identity of the unknown far-speaker. Not trusting Marc, he was nevertheless eager to use a sophisticated metaconcert program that the rebel leader of-fered—provided that a fail-safe living "fuse" (in the person of the luckless Culluket) was inserted in the multimind structure to shield Aiken from Marc's direct mental influence.

Having concluded the agreement with Marc, Aiken set off for Spain with an army of his strongest metapsychics, planning to rendezvous with Cloud Remillard and her companions, and with an auxiliary force led by the conservative Celadeyr of Afaliah.

Mercy accompanied Aiken. She forced Culluket to accom-pany her on a secret flight to Celadeyr's camp and there broke the news that Nodonn was alive. Celadeyr was overjoyed, as was the convalescent Kuhal Earthshaker. Mercy had not dared previously to broadcast the news telepathically because she feared that Culluket, a powerful redactor who hated his brother Nodonn, would betray her to Aiken. But now...Culluket wryly admitted he had undergone an about-face—since Aiken had designated him willy-nilly for the "fuse" role, which was likely to be fatal.

Mercy urged the others to abandon Aiken and fly with her to distant Var-Mesk, where Nodonn was hiding. Aluteyn pointed out that they had given Aiken their oath of fealty; it would be dishonorable for them to desert their companions so late in the game. No . . . they would have to go ahead with the raid on Felice's lair. If they survived, *then* would be the time to rally round Nodonn!

On 2 June, with Aiken's force poised for the rush to Mount Mulhacén, Elizabeth made her culminating attempt to purge Felice's mind of the pathological factors responsible for her psychosis. Against the advice of the wiser Dionket, who had been Lord Healer of the Tanu, she believed that once Felice was sane, she would give up her megalomaniacal power fantasies and become a tremendous force for good. At great personal danger, Elizabeth accomplished the psychic drainage. Felice awoke with her mind free of anomalies—only to laugh at Elizabeth's altruistic proposals and fly happily from Black Crag seeking her own pleasure.

Her first stop was the Lowlife Village of Hidden Springs. There Sister Amerie, whom Felice loved, was celebrating a solitary Mass in thanksgiving for a safe homecoming. Felice demanded that the nun abandon her vocation and come away with her. When Amerie refused, Felice exerted her psychic force. Amerie was killed. Felice then coolly set her sights on her other love, Culluket the Interrogator. Failing to find him in a swift inspection of several Tanu cities, she headed for her lair to spend the night.

She discovered the mountain hideaway buried under tons of fallen rock—Aiken's work. Incandescent with fury, she went after the despoiler and his fleeing force, who were in boats racing down the Río Genil. Aiken and his technicians were working madly to fix the laser-like Spear, knowing it would provide the margin of safety if Felice should attack.

Marc's enhanced farsight saw Felice approaching and he gave warning. Aiken assumed the executive position in the metaconcert and expelled an immense blast of psychoenergy. (Large as this blast was, it was safely *below* the potential maximum for the structure. Aiken had discovered during his previous use of the metaconcert, when he zapped Felice's lair, that attempting to channel the full output through his bare brain would very likely kill him. And this might be exactly what the wily Marc had planned.)

As the reverberations of the blast against Felice died away, Aiken heard Marc's farspoken voice say: *I think you got her*. A split second later, the King's elation turned to stark terror. He heard an agonized telepathic shout from Marc: *GOD NO SHE D-JUMPED!* There was an unintelligible image, a pause, and then the farspoken voice of Marc urging Aiken to hit Felice again.

The metaconcert, with its thousands of linked minds, faltered, then steadied. Something had gone terribly wrong—but Aiken realized that if he didn't strike Felice with every bit of psychoenergy at his disposal, she would surely destroy them all. In desperation, he flung the entire load of psychoenergy at her. The shock sent him falling into oblivion.

He awoke to discover Elizabeth, Dionket, and Creyn attending him. He had nearly died, but they had saved him. In anticipation of such a disaster, Elizabeth had asked Minanonn to fly her and the other two redactors to Spain, where they had observed the encounter with Felice and its aftermath.

Felice had vanished. The mental blast had triggered an enormous rockfall into the river, burying part of Aiken's fleet and altering the course of the Genil. Cull was gone, and the Craftsmaster, and Mercy, and some ninety others. The rest were safe—and awaiting the recovery of their King.

It hardly seemed possible to Aiken that Mercy could be dead. Her body had not been recovered. But there was the testimony of Celadeyr, who claimed to have seen her die, and Mercy's empty silver-and-emerald helmet. Still deathly weak, Aiken returned to Goriah to recuperate. He attempted to farspeak Marc Remillard in North America, but received no reply.

Some time passed. A force of Lowlives led by Basil Wimborne traveled once again to the Ship's Grave crater. There they rendered no less than twenty-nine of the exotic aircraft operational. The rest were destroyed. According to plan, twenty-seven of the flyers were brought to a secret hiding place on the slopes of Monte Rosa—which during Pliocene times exceeded Mount Everest in height. Chief Burke hoped that this region would be inaccessible to Aiken and the Firvulag alike.

The other two flyers brought the Lowlife expedition back to the Vosges Mountains. They were concealed in the Vale of Hyenas, not far from Nionel, where it was planned to adapt them for defensive purposes.

In the small Tanu city of Var-Mesk on the shore of the New Sea, Celadeyr of Afaliah finally met with Nodonn. He brought with him Mercy—who, of course, was not dead at all. There was a tender reunion between Nodonn and his former wife. Since there was no time to heal Nodonn's missing hand, Mercy furnished him with one made of silver to take the place of a wooden prosthesis old Isak had carved, back on Kersic. Regretfully, Nodonn told Mercy that she would have to return to Aiken while he himself accompanied Celadeyr to Afaliah and set about gathering an opposition force of conservatives. It was necessary that Mercy keep them informed of Aiken's movements. Aiken was too metapowerful for any of the Tanu to keep track of by means of ordinary farsensing. After a brief happy interlude, the lovers parted.

Mercy came back to Aiken with a story of having had amnesia. The King seemed to believe her; but he was much changed from the fun-loving trickster who had come to the Many-Colored Land the previous August. There was a somber air about him, and he still had not fully recovered from the terrible effects of the fight against Felice. Together, Aiken and Mercy supervised preparations for the Grand Tourney, which would be held at the end of October in place of the abolished Combat.

Meanwhile, in Afaliah, Nodonn and Celadeyr passed the word to all traditionalist Tanu that the designated heir of the late King Thagdal was alive and ready to challenge the human usurper. Nodonn's brother Kuhal Earthshaker regained his strength almost completely after an innovative Skin treatment shared with Cloud Remillard. Cloud, attracted to Kuhal and now alone in the Many-Colored Land (her brother and the others were slowly making their way north on land from their landing site in western Africa), became converted to the traditionalist cause. Nodonn had promised his cooperation in a temporary reopening of the time-gate if the Rebel children subsequently destroyed it completely.

Marc's fate was still a mystery. He had not responded to Cloud's attempts at farsensing, nor had any of the other old Rebels back in Ocala. Cloud concluded that her father must have been attacked by Felice in an unusual metapsychic maneuver, the dimensional-jump, or translocation. This was essentially a mind-powered hyperspace trip—the kind of operation performed by Brede's Ship when it had transported the exotics from the Duat Galaxy to this one. D-jumping was a rare but recognized metafaculty in the Galactic Milieu. Felice could have tracked Marc along his farsense beam and done considerable harm. Cloud and Hagen suspected that Marc had survived, since he was encased in the armor of the cerebroenergetic equipment that provided artificial augmentation of his mind. But once he left the armor's protection, his injuries would surely require treatment in Ocala's regeneration tank. This would explain why Marc had been incommunicado for nearly three months . . .

Up north in the Howler city of Nionel, Tony Wayland the metallurgist and his friend Dougal once more made plans to join Aiken Drum. Abandoning their devoted goblin brides, the pair set off through the jungle, only to stumble by accident into the Vale of Hyenas, where they were captured by the Lowlives working on the two exotic aircraft. As known deserters from the Iron Villages and possible traitors, Tony and Dougal were to be sent to Hidden Springs under guard, for trial by Chief Burke. En route, the party was fallen upon by Firvulag regulars. Dougal escaped, the escorting Lowlives were killed, and craven Tony saved his life by babbling to the Firvulag about the aircraft.

Hustled off to High Vrazel, Tony repeated his tale to King Sharn and Queen Ayfa. He was then turned over to an ogress, the Dreadful Skathe, while the Firvulag monarchs pondered on ways to use his intelligence. They were aware that Nodonn was assembling forces down in Afaliah and that he had in his possession the sacred Sword of Sharn, which had once been wielded by the Firvulag King's own ancestor in the Nightfall War and which would have to be in the possession of his successor in any renewal of hostilities. Nodonn was as yet far too weak to attack Aiken in Goriah—even using the Sword. After all, Aiken had the Spear.

But if Nodonn had the advantage of aircraft...

Sharn and Ayfa decided to tell Nodonn about the two flyers (which the Firvulag were incapable of using themselves) hidden in the Vale of Hyenas, in exchange for the Sword—if and when Nodonn conquered the usurper. Nodonn would be honor-bound to carry out his part of the bargain, and there undoubtedly were, among Tanu First Comers, a few surviving pilots.

The proposal was made and accepted. On 24 August, four Tanu and Cloud Remillard invaded the Vale of Hyenas, sub-duing Basil and his crew. With one aircraft commanded by Thufan Thunderhead, an experienced Tanu pilot, and the other flown by Celadeyr, who had had a bit of flight training, Nodonn led 400 Tanu knights in an air assault on Goriah.

Mercy knew they were coming. In order to prevent Aiken from using the cache of Milieu arms against Nodonn, she pre-vailed upon a human psychokinetic specialist, Sullivan-Tonn, whose young wife, Olone, was infatuated with Aiken. Mercy and Sullivan broke into the dungeon storage room, and she used her creative power to disrupt the chamber's insulating lining, embedding all of the equipment in a spongelike mass pervaded with bubbles of poisonous gas.

Aiken confronted them as they fled from the dungeon. The Nonborn King disposed of Sullivan, then took Mercy to their bed for a final, fatal embrace. As she died, his brain assimilated all the powers that had been hers.

In the small hours, Nodonn and his knights attacked the forewarned Aiken. The trickster brought down the aircraft, and one planeload of invading Tanu perished. The 200 led by No-donn and Celadeyr and Kuhal Earthshaker attained the Castle of Glass and engaged Aiken's forces in a pitched battle. Aiken had been able to muster only a skeleton army of defenders, but most of these were equipped with Milieu weapons such as laser carbines and stun-guns. They gained the upper hand.

Nodonn came upon Mercy's body, now nothing but a form composed of gray ash, still wearing its golden torc. At the same moment that he told Mercy farewell, Nodonn heard Aiken's voice commanding him to come out of the castle for their final encounter.

Hovering in midair, the pair took up the duel that had been interrupted by the Flood so many months ago. Nodonn was the principal aggressor, blasting Aiken with the photon weapon as well as with his mind's energies. Aiken seemed barely to defend himself, hiding instead inside a psychocreative bubble. Those in the castle left off their fighting to watch the fantastic conflict.

When it seemed that Aiken's force-shield was weakening, Nodonn gambled everything on two final strokes that drained the Sword. The little human disappeared in a blinding globe of light . . . but when it dissipated, he was still there, unshielded, alive, and ready to put an end to it. The witnesses had seen Nodonn do his utmost. Now it was Aiken's turn.

Disdainfully, the power of the Nonborn King sent both Sword and Spear hurtling away. Using only his mind, Aiken struck. As Mercy had gone, so went Nodonn—his mind subsumed, his body reduced to ash, his blackened silver hand falling toward the sea, only to be caught up and borne aloft in triumph by Aiken.

Across the Atlantic on Ocala Island, Marc Remillard had been watching. Now he was prepared to put his own plans into action.

It was 25 August. Exactly one year before, Aiken and the other members of Group Green had passed through the time-gate into the Pliocene.

Now read the fourth and final volume of The Saga of Pliocene Exile, which begins with a flashback to the time of the great fight with Felice at the Río Genil—and then picks up the main thread of the chronicle immediately after Aiken's victory over Nodonn.

PROLOGUE

1

IT HAD HAPPENED, JUST AS ELIZABETH HAD KNOWN IT WOULD; and there was no metapsychic prolepsis involved in the foretelling, only logic and inevitability, given those protagonists: Aiken Drum, Felice Landry, and Marc Remillard.

The last reverberations of the great psychocreative blast had dissipated. The four observers still hung high above Spain, out of range, inside the protective bubble spun by the mind of Minanonn the Heretic.

"Felice is surely dead," he observed.

"Her thoughts and her image are snuffed out." Creyn was noncommittal.

"Which proves nothing," muttered Dionket Lord Healer.

Elizabeth's ranging farsenses, so much more powerful than those of the three Tanu, could provide no positive reassurance at that high altitude. Felice, if she lived, was buried beneath the enormous landslide. "I think it's safe for us to descend," she said. "We must take the risk. There are casualties needing help..."

A swift warning passed between Dionket and Minanonn: Maintain your shield at maximum strength Brother!

The three exotic men and the human woman felt no flow of air as they glided down through smoke-layered twilight. They were isolated from the stench of the burning jungle, the steam rising from the diverted Río Genil, the dust still roiling up from the rockfall that had pushed the river from its bed and overwhelmed part of Aiken's flotilla.

"So many dead and wounded at the margin of the landslide," the Heretic mourned. "There lies Artigonn, my late sister's son. And Aluteyn Craftsmaster, may Tana grant him peace! He would not abjure the ancient battle-religion, even though his heart rejected it."

"I see the King." Dionket's farsight showed a vision of Aiken flung up on a gravel bank downstream, his body in its golden suit stiffened, his heart stopped and mind contracted to a screaming nub.

"You and Creyn go to him," Elizabeth said. The four touched down upon a great flat rock crusted with burnt vegetation, an island amid foaming dirty water. "You'll be able to keep him alive until I come. There are plenty of uninjured survivors. The majority escaped harm, I think. Organize rescue parties for the wounded. Minanonn and I will join you . . . after I find out what happened to Felice." After I search this place where she fell, a meteor self-consummate; and how my mind still shrinks from the memory of her mind's last cry: agony and regret, to be sure—but *triumph*?

"The monster is dead, as Minanonn said. And the Goddess be thanked!" Creyn's face was crimson-lit by flames. "Let us go. Lord Healer." Borne by Dionket's psychokinesis, the two redactors vanished into the murk.

Elizabeth and Minanonn stood on the charred ruin of the islet, the protective sphere of psychoenergy now extinguished. All around them half-submerged trees thrust from the water, trailing broken lianas in the debris-laden current. A few were still afire. In others, terrified monkeys and other jungle creatures shrieked and hooted piteously.

Elizabeth's eyes were closed, her mind searching again, exerting itself to the utmost in order to farsense underground. Drifting bits of ash and soot settled onto her hair and jumpsuit. Minanonn towered beside her, a bearded blond giant wearing a tunic with a triskelion badge. Under one arm he carried a cubic container that measured perhaps half a meter along the edge. It was made of a dark exotic substance with fragile patterns on its surface, filaments of red and silver that glowed in the deepening night like wisps of interstellar gas. The box held the powerful force-field projector that Brede Shipspouse had called the room without doors.

Elizabeth searched.

A body clad in broken glass armor drifted past on the wreck of a pneumatic barge. Somewhere in the rockfall on the right, lost in lurid shadows, a partially buried warrior woman sent out a telepathic plea for aid.

Soon Sister, the ex-Battlemaster reassured her. And his mind-voice lifted to encourage others: *Soon help will come.*

Elizabeth searched.

Had Felice really been killed? Had she flashed into extinction at the climax of the gigantomachy, taking Culluket with her? Reconstitute the memory; dissect and analyze it. Resolve the paradoxes by forcing on the critical moment of the girl's rematerialization after her split-second leap to North America, her dimensional translation. Aiken Drum, in the extreme of desperation, had called up the full force of his metaconcert. In replay, Elizabeth saw the slow crawl of psychoenergy vouchsafed to the King by the thousands of linked minds—and the diabolical augmentation by Marc just as the mental blast was about to pass through the helpless conduit of Felice's Beloved.

Yes! Inexperienced though she was in the ways of offensive metafunction, Elizabeth saw how the Angel of the Abyss had planted this from the very beginning: the elimination of two great minds that threatened his schemes, and the coincidental death of the third, beneath contempt.

But Culluket, the unwilling mental fuse, was the key.

In memory Elizabeth saw Felice still poised within the synchronicity of the translation threshold, not yet fully emerged from her time-violating d-jump, seeing the mortal danger to her Beloved. Knowing instinctively how to thwart it and what the price would be.

The girl had inserted herself into the metaconcert structure, invading the hapless conductor before his mind could disrupt. She had taken into herself the soul-bursting volume of energy, freely absorbing the entire quotient of destruction and thereby being transformed into an incandescent new Duality.

The King, hanging senseless in the flashover, was cut free—his body momentarily dead, his mind wrecked: Both were susceptible of healing. Not so the body of Culluket the Interrogator Beloved, which was gone beyond saving along with the mortal form of Felice. Only their fused minds remained, bound together in a tiny speck of matter transmuted from the psychic energies by an indomitable will.

Deep under thousands of tons of steaming rock at a shallow ford in the Río Genil, a tiny thing like a ruby cylinder burned whitely at the core...

"I've found Felice." Elizabeth opened her eyes, transmitted the image of Minanonn. "And Cull, too."

Elizabeth! They *live*?

You might call it that. Or suspension. Or limbo.

Such a state beyond understanding.

Not myunderstanding! I have been. [Fiery cocoon image.]

Tana—! You humans. But Cull...

...is there of this freechoice. Lifeclinging.

Suffering withoutend!

Alive nonetheless in pseudoUnity.

Lovetravesty! Abomination!

Minanonn they are damned soulmates I tried to save her yes how I tried and thought I had foolishpride but she *will* be her own Center and centripetency refusing grace determined to burn as are Cull & Mark & O God sometimes I think even I...

Elizabeth your thoughts are riddles.

I know. Ignore them.

How can you compare yourself to others? I am simpleman warrior enlightened unto peace but still child before you & MarcAbaddon. If you two share sin it is one beyond myken. But Cull! He was Thagdalson mybrother. I knew his temptation. Unlike poor Aluteyn & somany others he knew truth but mocked it aloof alone outside intheend bored to death afraid of death *personifying* death.

Now doomed to crave it. Enclosing her fire.

I mourn my poor brother.

As I mourn Felice.

We can only pray and sing the Song for them.

Something else I must do with your help. [Image.]

Goddess! Surely no chance resuscitation?!

We dare not risk it.

...So this why you bring roomwithoutdoors!

Room programmed to my aura alone by Brede before her death. Once activated it admits me and no other. Not Aiken not even Marc. Understand! None must needle with this terrible Duality hoping to revive and use it! I must make for it a dark temenos tabernaculum sanctuary inviolate where it will burn unmolested.

How long?

God knows.

It will be . . . secure within?

No energy no matter no mind can break into this forcefield from outside. Room gravomagneticpowered enduring as long as Earth. Or until I myself return to enter and deactivate.

Then Duality safeimprisoned.

Not quite.

?

You forget. Those inside room always free exit themselves.

But—how? Surely it never could! Look at thing Elizabeth. Microscopic weakglowing at extinctionedge!

But refusing death.

Then we never free of threat?

Peace myfriend. I feel (perhaps Shipspouse would say know!) that this thing will never again menace ManyColoredLand.

Yours the dangerous judgment Lady.

This time I have no doubts.

. . . If you leave roomwithoutdoors here you deprive yourself of its protection. You will be vulnerable at Black Crag—

Enough Minanonn. Help me now. Use your psychokinetic power to uncover the Duality for a moment so that I can erect its tomb. Then we must hurry to Aiken—

Heal him and you heal nemesis.

Nevertheless I will. I owe him too much. He undertook the job I shirked.

2

THE MIDDLE-AGED MAN WITH THE PROMINENT JAW AND THE unobtrusive apparatus clamped to his skull tended to his simple gardening chores. Inside the observatory, the other inhabitants of Ocala Island were rallying round their ruined leader in a battle that strained the very planetary aether. It was almost like the good old days!

They had known better than to invite *him* to join them.

"Poor wand'ring one," sang Alexis Manion in a plaintive tone. "Dee-dah-dah d'hum-dum DAH-hah." He swept up a dead palm warbler and deposited it into the wheeled cart that trundled behind him, obedient to his irrepressible PK function. "Oh, yes, I have surely strayed. I am a disgrace to villainy." Humming, wearing the abstractly intoxicated smile of the docilated, he shuffled along the path. The gardens around Marc Remillard's star-search observatory simmered in late afternoon sun but there was heavy shade beneath the macrophyllas. Their blossoms, wide as dinnerplates against whorls of meter-long leaves, gave off a cloying scent that overwhelmed the subtler perfume of the granadilla vines. He tidied up a section of the white coquina walk that was littered with zapped butterflies. (Common heliconians, alas. Nothing suitable for his collection.) Then he tsked in sympathy as he spied another victim of the observatory's robot defenses: a crumpled male golden egret, gorgeous in mating plumage, that had fallen close to the building wall.

A thought slowly formed in Manion's electronically dulled brain. He squinted up into the sun dazzle at the narrow parapet around the open observatory dome, where the barrels of the X-lasers protruded in a glittering cheval-de-frise. Yes! There was the female egret's body as well, caught in the angle of the pendentive. Poor birdie lovers! Still, if one had to go . . .

"And if you remain callous and obdurate, I," he caroled, "Shall perish as they did and you will know why." A mental nudge sent the corpse tumbling down. He consigned it to the bin. "Though I probably shall not exclaim as I die—"

Alex. Come at once.

"Oh, willow," he whispered, carefully closing the lid. "Tit-willow—"

Quickly dammit!

"Titwillow."

The coercive power of Steinbrenner, clutching at Manion's mind, failed to get a grip on the docilated, preprogrammed mush. There were telepathic epithets.

Manion smiled his sad idiot smile (so at odds with the set of his jaw) and restored push broom and dustpan to their brackets on the side of the cart. He took up a pair of clippers. Overhead, the laser array lost its sparkle as the power was switched off. A cormorant winged above the slowly closing dome with impunity and soared out over Lake Serene. Manion waved at it, then began to snip spent blooms from a cluster of pink laelias nestled in the crotch of a gumbo-limbo tree. He stared a new song:

> *My boy, you may take it from me,*
> *That of all the afflictions accurst*
> *With which a man's saddled*
> *And hampered and added,*
> *A diffident nature's the worst!*

Now people were rushing from the observatory into the garden. There was a wild mélange of farspoken thought:

It's that goddam docilator Steinbrenner go *fetch* him—
Right. Pat comealong help coldturkey letdown.
Affirm hurryhurry!
SHEWASHERERIGHTTHEREYESMONSTERFELICE
WASHEREODIDYOUSEEWASITILLUSIONOCHRISTNO-
REALDIDN'TYOUSEE—
Laura you&Dorsey get tank ready Keoghs bring bodytrans-
porter.
Affirm/Affirm/Affirmaffirm.
GODBLANCHARDDIEDDIDYOUFEELITFUCKHIM
WHATABOUTMONSTERFELICEDIDSHEFUSEMARC
WHOTHEHELLKNOWSITWASADJUMPDJUMPCHIL-
DRENWHATABOUTTHEMARETHEYSAFESHUTUP
OGODISMARCDEADISFELICEDEADORDIDSHESUB-
SUMEMARCYOUFUCKINGIDIOTSHUTUPONOSHUTUP
ONOTHEGENESMENTALMANTHEGENESMARCMARC
SHUTUPSHUTUP—
SHUT UP!
DJUMPDJUMPSHECOULDHAVEFUSEDSUBSUMED   it
was a d-jump I tell you . . .
Silence!
. . . .
Jordy you can't be certain.
It was a d-jump.
You don't dare divest until we confirm her excursion.
That's why they're bringing Manion you fool!
THE GENES. O GOD THE GENES.
Damn genes! *The children*!
GathenDalembertWarshawVanWyk STAY. Everybodyelse GO.
Must know children can't push me out
damn Marc damn genes damn all of you . . .
*Steinbrenner when you get Manion out docilator put Helayne
IN*.
Affirm.

Oblivious, Alexis Manion pottered among the orchids. And
there came big Jess Steinbrenner, archquack and babykiller,
all reeking with adrenalin overload! And pretty Pat Castellane,
her steel eyes weeping! Amazing. Manion sang out:

If you wish in the world to advance,
Your merits you're bound to enhance.
You must stir it and stump it,
And blow your own trumpet,
Or trust me, you haven't a chance!

The two of them pounced on Manion and tore off the docilator headpiece. He staggered, convulsing, as the Florida landscape melted into concentric expanding shells of color. They held him while his muscles bucked and spasmed. Pat's redactive douche calmed while Jeff's numbed the recollection of anguish; and at last his brain settled into its normal rhythm and he could stand alone.

Trembling, with blood trickling down his chin from his bitten tongue, he forced their hands away with his psychokinesis. The social aspect of his mind was so tattered that he was unable to contain the malicious satisfaction that welled up as he discovered why they had come.

"*Felice* nailed him?" Manion began to laugh. Steinbrenner's coercion lashed out to no effect. Docilated, Manion had been barely biddable; free, he was a rock of intransigeance. "Let the bastard boil in his own devil-rig!"

"Alex, it's not just Marc!" Patricia cried. She took one of Manion's hands. Her skin was icy in spite of the June heat. "We're all in danger. And the children. The metaconcert operation—we don't know what's happened. Owen Blanchard is dead, and Ragner Gathen's son and God knows how many others in Europe. We don't know about Felice. Marc's data input to the computer cut off at the moment of the d-jump—"

In spite of himself, Manion found his interest aroused. "Her mind generated a real upsilon-field? Barebrained?"

"We think so. She seemed to appear right there in the observatory and . . . attack Marc in some way through the cerebroenergetic equipment."

Manion chuckled. "Well, well. What a nasty surprise."

Patricia was drawing him along the white pathway toward the observatory entrance. Some twenty of the veteran Rebels were standing about exuding an emotional farrago to chill the blood.

Steinbrenner's thought was thunderous. *Go to the lodge!*
Go to your homes! Anywhere away from here. He's alive and
we'll have him safe in the regen tank as soon as Diarmid &
Deirdre get here with transport. NOW GET OUT.

With much mental murmuring, the people began to disperse.
Manion was lost in his own thoughts, animosity vanished
in the face of an intriguing problem. "A d-jump! Now when
was the last time we tried to confirm one at the IDFS? 2067?
Yes . . . an adolescent from one of the black worlds. Engong,
was it? But he only translated across two kilometers and we—"

Patricia interrupted. "You're going to have to confirm the
event with a retrospective dynamic-field analysis. Kramer can't
hack it and we must confirm Felice's excursion. Listen to me,
Alex!" Her anxiety flamed out at him. Her mind displayed the
terrible possibility. "We think Marc's still alive inside the CE
rig. But the scanner's nearly burnt out and we have no conscious
communication from him. We don't dare open the armor—"

Manion nodded. His smile was gone. "Until you confirm
that the person inside is Marc Remillard. Yes. An interesting
point."

They entered the observatory at the same time that Peter
Dalembert and Ragnar Gathen were hustling Helayne Strangford out. Steinbrenner handed over the docilator.

Helayne's powerful, crazed mind latched onto Manion.
"Don't help them, Alex! Let Marc die in that damned cerebroenergetic enhancer of his! Then we'll be sure that the children
aren't—"

The voice fell abruptly silent. Patricia urged Manion inside.
It was dark with the dome closed, the temperature at least ten
degrees cooler. Only a handful of the senior Rebels remained.
In the center of the chamber was the hydraulic lift cylinder
with the recliner carriage lowered. On it, gleaming under a
small spotlight but opaque to the mind's eye, was a mass of
black cerametal armor. Alexis Manion shrugged free of Castellane and approached the sinister form.

"So you miscalculated again, did you?"

The display screen and the loudspeaker that normally provided communication with the hidden CE operator remained
mute. Manion strolled to the vital-signs monitor and studied
the readouts, then looked over the offerings of the crippled

brain-scanner. There was no identifiable pattern to the sub-perceptual emanations coming from the bulky mass of armor, only the assurance that inside, someone or something was alive.

"Are you Marc Remillard in there?" Manion inquired archly. "Or little Felice?"

"That what you're going to find out for us, Alex," said Jordan Kramer. He stood at the main console of the computer with Van Wyk dithering behind him. The Keoghs had finally arrived with the first-aid unit. Warshaw helped them to position it next to the carriage.

"You'd trust me?" Manion swept the minds of his fellow magnates with a mocking fillip. "Marc didn't. That's why he zombied me."

Gerrit Van Wyk said, "We have to trust you, Alex. Analyzing this damn event is beyond my competence, or Jordy's. Only you can tell us whether Felice jumped back to Europe after she zapped Marc. If she's still here—if she subsumed Marc and we open that rig and let her out—she could wipe out Ocala!"

Manion hummed "Here's a How-De-Do." He frowned as he examined a screenful of dubious probability graphics prominently labeled: EVENT UNCONFIRMED.

"Whoever is inside that armor,'" Patricia said, "is gravely injured. If you force us to let Marc die, then I'm going to kill you, too, Alex."

"Perhaps I'd be grateful, Pat."

Kramer held out the commander mouthpiece. "We know you care deeply about the children, Alex. Marc wants to save them, but we don't know what his plans are. Without him, we have only one option to prevent the reopening of the time-gate. An ugly one."

"Suppose I lie to you about the analysis?" Manion retorted. "Let Felice cook our collective goose if she's in there? Then I'd be certain that the kids get their chance."

The frustration and fury of the other ex-conspirators impinged on the mental screen of the dynamic-field specialist. Uselessly.

Van Wyk's control, always precarious, began to falter. His mind cried out: He might lie he might! He did before we never twigged when he&kids planned damned Feliceploy firstplace—

Suddenly weary, Manion said, "Oh, shut up, Gerry." He took the computer microphone from Kramer's hand and began to speak rapidly.

The others fell back. Psychic tension drained away, leaving dullness leavened by faint hope. As the multicolored probability edifices formed and reformed smoothly on the visual display, Manion whistled "I Am the Captain of the Pinafore" through his teeth. Finally he froze an elaborate construct and simultaneously shot a blast of mathematical esoterica at the minds of Kramer and Van Wyk.

"There you have it. Explicit enough even for you two Scheissphysiker. A single dimensional translation confirmed, together with the rubberband-effect withdrawal hypersnap. Your overmodulated hell-load must have finished Felice off. Probably the Little King as well. The PC equivalent was in the seven hundreds, for Christ's sake."

"We had vague intraconcert perception of *some* kind of mental fusion," Cordelia Warshaw insisted.

"Felice never fused to Marc," Manion stated. "For my money, the damn girl's dead as mutton." He addressed himself again to the command mouthpiece, erasing the analysis and calling up a heavy artificial i-mode carrier. It was tuned to a certain mental signature with a precision none of the others could have achieved.

"You there in the armor! Do you hear me?"

The all but worthless scanner showed that someone inside the black mass did.

"Tell these fools who you are. I've called up an EK ident. All we need is one conscious thought sequence."

From the speaker came a crackling stutter. The visual flickered. The analytical display said: ID UNCONFIRMED.

Patricia Castellane took the microphone. "Marc, it's Pat. Communicate with us. Use either the mechanism or your farsense. We must know whether your mind is still integral. Please, Marc!"

The speaker rustled, a breath stirring dry leaves. The screen said: ZH? JE? [PHONEME AMBIGUOUS]

And the analysis: ID UNCONFIRMED.

Dr. Warshaw, working at the backup terminal said, "We need more than that."

"Marc, we want to help you," said Patricia. "Just speak to us."

A buzz fading to a hiss. ZH? JE? SS? [[PHONEMES AMBIGUOUS]

ID UNCONFIRMED.

"Ask him for his name," said Warshaw.

As if speaking to a young child, Patricia asked, "Quel est ton nom, chéri?"

JE SU? SOO? SÜ? JE SUIS = "I AM." [FRENCH-AMERICAN DIALECT]

"Ton nom! Quel est ton nom, mon ange d'abîme?"

JE SUIS LE TÉNÉBREUX = "I AM THE DARK ONE." [FIGURATE USAGE? CF. POEM 'EL DESDICHADO' BY GÉRARD DE NERVAL (PSEUD. LABRUNIE, GÉRARD, 1808–1855).]

"Gotcha!" exclaimed the psychotactician. The metallic accents hung in the air. On the screen the glowing words persisted, and confirmation of the mental signature shone in the lower righthand corner:

IMS POSITIVE: REMILLARD, MARC ALAIN KENDALL 3-6Ø2-437-121-Ø15M.

Gerrit Van Wyk was blubbering. Ragnar Gathen turned away, expelling a great sigh. Diarmid Keogh and his mute sister exchanged lightning thoughts with Steinbrenner and readied the cephalic envelope of the emergency life-support equipment.

JE SUIS LE TÉNÉBREUX LE VEUF L'INCONSOLÉ LE PRINCE D'AQUITAINE À LA TOUR ABOLIE ABOLIE ABOLIE CYNDIA MY GOD CYNDIA DON'T—

Alexis Manion laughed. Patricia Castellane gave an inarticulate cry and dropped the command microphone. Pseudo-speech reverberated into the dark-domed chamber:

MA SEULE ÉTOILE EST MORTE! CYNDIA...MON LUTH CONSTELLÉ PORTE LE SOLEIL NOIR... J' AIDEUX FOIS VAINQUEUR TRAVERSÉ L'ACHERON FOR NOTHING. THE BITCH IS DEAD JACK. SHE'S RUINED ME BUT SHE'S DEAD.

Diarmid Keogh's PK hastily scooped up the fallen mouthpiece. He cut off the armor audio, letting the screen continue its mad flickerings, and initiated the divestment routine. The

helmet hoist sent down its cables. Clamps latched onto the
massive blind casque. Its dogs clicked open and it rotated a
quarter turn. Liquid seeped from the juncture with the body
casing, then gushed out in a small flood. The dermal lavage
drainage had failed and Marc might be drowning.

Steinbrenner swore. "Activate the damned hoist! But easy.
God knows what's under there—"

Images!

They poured forth as the thought-opaque helmet lifted and
the operator's head was uncovered: sights and sounds and feelings and smells and tastes, normal and distorted, concrete and
fragmentary, evanescent and smashing. Memories. Hallucinations. Terrors. Ecstasies. The archetypal ragbag of the deep
unconscious: mental cacophony, nightmare broadcast fortissis-
simo, wide-open emotional stops shrillingblaringhissing above
bourbon thunder-bellow. The whole wrapped in a web of incandescent pain.

Marc stop! they all screamed, crushed by the hurricane.

There was silence.

The head above the cerametal collar lifted slightly. Deepest
gray eyes opened, showing enormous pupils. The silver-streaked
curls dripped greenish fluid onto the forehead, where it mingled
with blood from tiny wounds stitched by the withdrawn cerebral
electrodes.

"They're all dead," he said in a normal voice. *[Images:
Snow Christmas lights sleigh Dobbin Cantique de Noël brass
plaque Mount Washington dim in blizzard mad old man holding
longhaired cat.]*

Patricia came closer. "Who is dead? Felice and Aiken Drum?"

"Cyndia and Jack and Diamond." The familiar smile lifted
one side of his generous mouth. The bruised-looking eyelids
closed. *[Images: Blue-white scintillating point of disaster.
Mindwhisper: It's finished BigBrother now you must magnify
too like it or not adieu dear Marc scent white pine fading
gemlight crash of Unity triumphant.]*

"No significant trauma above the neck seal," Steinbrenner
was saying. "The carotid circulatory shunts are intact and the
helmet apparatus seems undamaged. Negative the cephenvel-
ope, ready the body bag. You getting any joy on the deep-
redact, Diarmid?"

"He seems to be sustaining his autonomic system consciously." Keogh shook his head. "Very bad, Jeff. Deirdre says there's metabolic evidence of severe external trauma to the trunk and limbs. You know he's self-rejuvenating—able to handle any ordinary injury. But this time the angiogenetic programming is faltering from overload."

"We've got to get this body armor off," Steinbrenner said, "and see just what—"

"Wait," said Marc distinctly. His eyes opened again. *[Overwhelming scent of pine.]*

Steinbrenner and the two Keoghs froze.

"I'm sustaining refrigeration . . . lavage . . . in lower-body casing. When I exit the rig . . . I must go switch-off to sustain my vitals. No communication. But first I must tell you—"

"Let us help!" they all exclaimed.

"No. Listen. Our experiment was a . . . qualified success. Felice is gone. Unfortunately, Aiken Drum is not. He's badly damaged. No doubt his healers will put him together again in due course, as mine will me."

"But what happened to you?" Patricia cried.

[Images: Blazing female shape materializing in midair. Armored form high on its carriage wrapped in astral fire from the neck down. Refrigeration and life-support laboring inside the ultradense cerametal as the demonic power seeps through the impermeable, attacks the inhumanly strengthened body within. Femoral circulatory shunts and neuroceptors burned away, the entire sustenance load shifted to the carotids. Iceblood and chemical amniotic fluid preserving internal organs, major skeletal units, and musculature. Psychocreative torch of the frustrated monstermind playing over vulnerable body surface, burning away all dermal elements to a depth of four millimeters, destroying hands and feet and external genitalia utterly. Then, unable to complete the Jackforming, forced to withdraw.]

The genes!

"Safe. Don't worry. Three months in the tank and I'll be as good as I ever was."

The brain!

"I diverted my entire creative flux to my head the instant that she struck. My brain was saved . . . most of it. Managed to force her out of the armor. Episode . . . took less than half a second. Fortunately, shock is delayed in such cases. I was able to retain control of the metaconcert until we funneled the final blast. Then . . . diverted all energies to self-sustenance."

The eyes in their cavernous orbits glazed and the watchers flinched from a new transmission of agony. Marc's mind steadied. The old magnetism and reassurance flowed out to touch each one of them with confident warmth.

"Don't worry! Even this disaster . . . this d-jump has been *valuable*. I learned . . . but I'll show you when I wake up. Meanwhile, get everything ready to go to Europe. Jordy and Peter . . . I'm counting on you and your people to repair this CE rig. Dismantle it . . . power supply, computer, auxiliaries, the spare suit for armor, everything! Salvage Kyllikki . . . get this equipment set up on board. Use the small sigmas so that the children and Aiken Drum can't farsense you clearly. My plan . . . destroy deep geological structure of timegate site, thus . . . interfere with geomagnetic input to tau-field. Old Guderian himself wrote that this input was critical to the focus of the time-warp. Advantage of this plan . . . we need not confront the children directly, nor Aiken Drum. And solution is permanent. Can't say more now. Trust me."

"We do," said Patricia.

Again that smile *[pine pine pine]*. And pain.

Marc's farspeech was laughing, shouting. You aren't born yet Mental Man I'm free of you!

Then he was speaking rationally, aloud, concentrating entirely upon Patricia Castellane. "Keep a close watch on me while I'm floating, Pat. We all know the regen tank has its quirks and crotchets. I don't want to wake up with extra fingers or toes . . . or anything else."

"I'll see to it," she whispered. "Now let me take you down. Out of the pain."

Painpinepainpine.

[Images: Adolescent boy opening baby's blanket to see rosy perfection. Mama he's all right Papa was wrong after all wasn't he Yes dear wrong wrong wrong. Pine roses cancerous degeneration stink smoke guttering vigil candle consummatum est young Jack.]

"Thank you, Pat. No. I must go alone. Au 'voir." The eyes closed. The mental projections faded.

Marc Remillard had withdrawn into his abyss.

PART I

THE

SUBSUMPTION

1

SUMMER FOG.

It leached all color and substance from the world, leaving only grays. Lead gray tombstone gray cobweb gray mouse gray ash gray snot gray dust gray corpse gray. It was unheard-of that there be fog at that time of the year, late August. So it had to be still another portent—as dire a one as the death of the One-Handed Warrior. There were many who said that the fog had its origin in the supercooled ashes of the hero: each molecule of his scattered body accreting water vapor, each tiny relic drawing to itself the air's own tears to fashion this wide-spreading shroud over the Many-Colored Land.

(The less morbidly poetic decided that the fog was a meteorological freak, perhaps a belated consequent of the Flood refilling the Empty Sea. Ah . . . but they had not been there in Goriah, watching the duel at dawn from the battlements of the Castle of Glass!)

The fog rolled over Armorica from the Strait of Redon to the dense jungles of the Upper Laar, south beyond the Gulf of Aquitaine and the marshes of Bordeaux. It brimmed the Paris Basin swamps and the Hercynian Forest and flowed eastward to the Vosges, the Jura, the very foothills of the High Helvetides. By afternoon its south-moving front had poured through the Cantabrian passes into central Koneyn. Paradoxically growing in volume, it buried the low Sierra Morena, seeped into the embayment of the Guadalquivir, and only halted at the snow-dusted Betic crest, lapping the slopes of Veleta and Alcazaba and blasted, empty Mulhacén.

Bland, energy sapping, it masked the sun and stifled sound and left the vegetation dripping sadly. Forest animals hid. Chilled birds and insects slept. The great herds of the Pliocene steppes crowded together on the heights, nostrils quivering and eyes wide and ears pricked, paralyzed because their senses gave no input but misty uncertainty.

It was the day the Nonborn King had his great victory. The day Queen Mercy-Rosmar and Nodonn Battlemaster died.

In the aftermath, the King returned to his castle, carrying the trophy.

The knights and retainers came rushing to meet him, exultant and mind-shouting, eager to proclaim the triumph. But they fell back dismayed when he dropped the silver hand in the courtyard and stood there silent and empty-eyed, his mind guarded—yet clearly changed in some terrible way, full to the bursting point rather than drained, as might have been expected.

Those who were closest to him, the great heroes Bleyn and Alberonn, prevailed on him to withdraw from the tumult. But he would not go to his own bedchamber (it was not until much later that they knew why), and so Bleyn said, "Let us take you then to my apartments, where my lady Tirone Heartsinger will attempt to help you with her healing power."

The King went with them and did not resist as they removed his dulled glass armor and laid him on a cot in a secluded retiring room. There were no bodily wounds; but even though he maintained his mental shield, they were aware of how swollen his psyche was, how it threatened to overflow and escape from the small body that confined it.

"What has happened?" Tirone asked him, fearful and overawed. But he would not reply. She said, "If I am to help you, High King, you must open to me at least a little, and tell me what manner of strange disability afflicts you."

He only shook his head.

Tirone made a helpless gesture to her husband and Alberonn. She said to the King, "Would you prefer that we leave you, then? Is there nothing we can do?"

He spoke at last. "Not for me. But take care of our people and oversee the mopping-up operations. I'll rest here. At twenty-one hundred hours, I'll deal with the prisoners. Farspeak the other High Table members and tell them to be ready."

"Surely that can wait," Alberonn protested.

"No," said the King.

The three of them prepared to go. Tirone said, "I will remain outside in case you need me. The best thing you can do now is sleep."

The Nonborn King smiled at her. "It would be best . . . but the two of them won't let me."

They did not understand, but only touched him with reassurance and loyal deference and then went away, thinking that he was alone.

The relief column crept along the Great South Road above Sayzorask, twenty wagons loaded with contraband Milieu matériel, 200 Tanu knights, an equal number of humans belonging to the King's Own Elite Golds, and 500 gray-torcs serving in the capacity of men-at-arms, teamsters, lackeys, and logistics personnel. The travelers without farsight (and this included most of the human golds, who had received their torcs as honorariums from the King, irrespective of any metapsychic latency) had their vision limited to a little over two meters, a scant chaliko length. Not that you had much of a chance of seeing the fellows ahead of you, not with the caravan in extended order the way it had been all morning, with each pair of riders or wagon with its escort seeming to clump along in damp isolation. The column was strung out to minimize problems with the pack of guardian bear-dogs. Ever since they had departed Sayzorask the willful brutes had been acting up—spooking the stock by getting underfoot, slavering and yowling and rolling their yellow eyes and resisting attempts by the coercers to force them back into their proper stations on the flank.

"Bad ions in the air," the gold-torc Yoshimitsu Watanabe diagnosed. "The fog's made the amphicyons hypersensitive to metapsychic vibes. I can almost feel something myself lurking on the mental fringes . . . I had a dog back in Colorado, a forty-five-kilo Akita who used to go backpacking with me in the Rockies. Acted like this sometimes when really foul weather was moving in. Berzerko, you know? Primitive dogs, Akitas. I learned to listen up good when old Inu told me to get out of the high country."

"Hey—you think *we're* in for a storm, chief?" Sunny Jim Quigley, driving a huge-wheeled Conestoga with the precious infrared spotter and its power supply and auxiliary robotics, was nothing but a hooded silhouette. Only his voice was clear, amplified telepathically by his gray torc.

"Storm?" Yosh shrugged. "Who can say? My experience with Pliocene climate is limited. You're the native."

"The Paris swamps were nothin' like this here," Jim said. "Half a desert on these slopes 'bove the Rhône, jungle in the bottoms. But it sure's hell got cold of a sudden. Could be the rainy season'll come early."

"That's all we'd bloody well need," grunted Vilkas, who rode a chaliko to the right of the wagon. "As if it hasn't been tough enough hauling this damn equipment all the way from Goriah overland. By the time we get it to Bardelask, the damn spooks'll be thicker on the ground than roaches in a garbage dump! I've seen it all before and I know. The Firvulag plan to pick off the little cities first. That's why they hit Burask— why they're sniping at Bardelask and putting the blame on renegade Howlers. Once the little cities fall, they'll make a move on vulnerable big ones like Roniah. And His Exalted Shininess can't do a friggerty thing about it!"

"Aw, Vilkas," Jim demurred. "The King's sending us, i'n't he? We get this IR spotterscope set up in Bardelask, ain'no spook gone be able t' sneak up under illusion-cover. We got 'nuff good stuff in the other wagons t' fix Lady Armida's people so's the Famorel mob won't dare poke snout outa the Alps. Ain'at right, chief?"

"That's King Aiken-Lugonn's strategy." Yosh guided his chaliko closer to the wagon, frowning. His golden torc was warm beneath the clammy mastodon-hide plates of his nodowa, the throat-piece of his ornate samurai-style armor. He could "hear" the Tanu members of the column whispering anxiously among themselves on their private mental wavelength, incomprehensible to the human golds. What was happening?

Vilkas was still beefing bitterly. "If the King is so worried about Bardelask, why didn't he fly this junk to the city himself—or have that fat sod Sullivan-Tonn do it—instead of sending us on this three-week slog?"

"What good the spotterscope be, 'thout Yoshi-sama to set 'er up?" Sunny Jim asked reasonably. "And the weapons 'thout Lord Anket and Lord Raimo and the elites who know how t'use 'em? Shoo-oo!"

Yoshi beware! came Anket's mind-shout. Bear-dogs crazy! Maybe sabrecats—maybe Foe—maybe Tanaknowswhat—

"Heads up!" the samurai cried to his companions, and at the same moment Vilkas broke into vicious swearing as his chaliko reared. Something big and black hurtled out of the soup. A single amphicyon zigged to avoid the claws of Vilkas' chaliko and disappeared under the bed of the high-wheeled wagon. Another pair, whoofing and shambling, approached the wagon from Yosh's side, intent on using the same shelter. A bedlam of howls and snarling broke out. The four giraffids in the hitch plunged and squealed. Beneath the lurching vehicle the bear-dogs, weighing nearly 200 kilos each, thrashed and fought and banged against the enormous wheels.

"Look out!" Jim yelled, hauling back on the reins. "We'll get upset!"

Vilkas jabbed futilely at the furry bodies with the butt of his long lance. His curses were lost in the tumult. Jim clung for his life as the wagon heaved like a lifeboat on the high seas and the valuable cargo thumped the side panels.

Two Tanu coercers and an operant human gold, their glass armor glowing fuzzy blue in the swirling fog, galloped up on their chalikos. But their mental efforts were unavailing in the face of the bear-dogs' frenzy.

Move back! Yosh ordered. He unsheathed his Husqvarna and now thumbed it to widest angle. The stun-gun sizzled, sweeping the ground with its beam. There were throttled yelps and moans. One massive shape lashed out in a final paroxysm, shattering the right front wheel of the Conestoga.

Suddenly, it was very quiet.

A tall form, luminous violet, the trappings of his mount shining with the same eerie light, materialized out of featureless opacity. It was Ochal the Harper, grandson of the ruler of Bardelask and leader of the relief column.

He silenced Yosh's attempts at explanation and the excuses of the coercer knights. "I have found the source of the madness—and the sense of unease that has plagued us all morning." He pointed to the east. "Out there. On the opposite bank of the Rhône. Behold!"

His powerful farsense projected a vision. For the shorter-sighted people in the train, it was as if the mysterious fog had abruptly become transparent, and the bottomland forest beyond the river as well.

Pouring out of one of the steep tributary valleys that formed corridors into the Alps came an army, arrogant in strength. It quick-marched through the ghostly farseen jungle casting no shadows, its members dark and numberless as a horde of predatory ants, unidentifiable until Ochal's mental eye magnified them and proved them to be Firvulag. They were some four kilometers away, not generating illusion-camouflage as was their usual custom, perhaps trusting in the fog to conceal them— or perhaps not caring whether or not they were detected. They came, giants and dwarfs and medium-sized warriors clad in obsidian battle-dress, bearing their traditional arms and holding standards draped with festoons of gilded skulls. As they marched they hummed a war chant with notes far beyond the threshold of audibility for Tanu or humans.

But the bear-dogs heard.

The track that the Firvulag army followed led straight into the Rhône bottomland, intersecting the narrow east-bank trail to Bardelask, not half a day's march upstream.

There were at least 8000 warriors.

"It's the main host of Mimee of Famorel," said Ochal, letting the terrible picture fade. "Now the raids and the pretense of Howler responsibility for the outrages committed against my grandmother's city are at an end. The Little People violate the Armistice openly! Doubtless the death of Nodonn Battlemaster served to embolden them."

One of the Tanu coercers said, "This is the opening offensive in that conflict that certain of us feared to be inevitable. I cannot speak its name! But we all know Celadeyr's prediction. Tana have mercy!"

Ochal said, "I have already farspoken Lady Armida. My kinfolk, although hopelessly outnumbered, will defend the city to the end."

"Shoo!" breathed Jim. "Never saw so many spooks in my life!"

"Compared to the army that hit Burask, it's a skeleton crew," Vilkas growled. "But it'll do. Bardelask's doomed—and the best damn brewery in the Pliocene along with it! Now we'll drink nothing but plonk and jungle juice."

Yosh sat slumped in the saddle. "Well, Ochal—our infrared eyeball system and load of Milieu arms aren't worth a mousefart to Bardy now."

The farsenor leader nodded grim agreement. He addressed the entire column on the command mode:

Companions! There is no way we can reach my home city before the Firvulag do. They would surely fall upon us as we attempted to cross the Rhône to the Bardelask docks. I have bespoken the King, pleading with him to allow us to die with my Exalted Grandmother. But for strategic reasons, he has forbidden it—

"God save Aiken Drum!" muttered Vilkas.

—so we must regroup, then return at once to Sayzorask. Our King has told me that the futuristic equipment we carry must be safeguarded from the Foe at all costs. We will wait in Sayzorask for his orders . . .

"And with our luck," came Vilkas' sotto voce snarl, "we'll end up marching on Famorel itself."

Ignoring him, Ochal addressed Yosh. "Have this wagon repaired as quickly as possible while I inspect the rest of the column. There's small chance of the Foe crossing the river to engage us, but we must not present an overly tempting target by lingering. They doubtless know that we're here—and they may suspect what we carry."

Yosh gave the Tanu salute. Ochal the Harper beckoned mentally to the waiting coercer knights, and the glowing purple shape and the three blue ones faded away into the fog. Their departure revealed how much darker it had become. Sunset was less than an hour away and the miasma seemed thicker than ever.

Yosh slipped the Husky back into its sheath. "Well, let's go on with it. Unpack a spotlight, Vilkas, and we'll study the damage."

As the Lithuanian complied, Jim slid cautiously down and soothed the four helladotheria in the team. They stamped their feet and swiveled their tufted ears. When the solar-powered lantern went on, Jim hunkered down and inspected the broken wheel. "Too bad we can't make *our* armor glow from mindpower, like Lord Ochal an' the other op'rants. Be handy in a sitch-ashun like this."

"You don't glow unless you got the power," said Vilkas. "The psychoactive microbes sandwiched in the glass armor laminations don't light up for grunts like you and me." He paused, then added pointedly, "*Or* for golds like Lord Yoshimitsu, who aren't genuine latents."

"But who nevertheless earned their privileges," Yosh said.

"If the King had kept his promise, all of us humans would be wearing gold!" The Lithuanian's voice was bitter.

Jim looked up at Vilkas and winked. "Hey—*I* like my gray torc just fine. Specially on lonely nights!" To Yosh he said, "Chief, we gone need a PK-head to lift this sumbitch wagon outa the dirt. A human—not some Tanu 'ristocat who'll screw up. And you'd best bespeak ol' Maggers to bring us a spare wheel."

Yosh nodded. "Get the team unhitched. I'll ask Lord Raimo to give us a hand."

He guided his chaliko back behind the wagon a few meters, dismounted, and said, "Matte, Kiku. Good girl." The great animal was like a dappled statue in the vaporous dusk. Standing on tiptoe, Yosh opened a saddlebag and took out the kawanawa, a stout rope joined to a set of wickedly sharp gang hooks.

Returning to the wagon, he summoned Vilkas and indicated the stunned bear-dogs still bunched under the canted bed. "We'll have to drag these brutes away and finish them off. One of those hellads that Jim's uncoupling can do the hauling. But you'll have to crawl under and make fast."

Vilkas gronaed. His tans had been fresh that morning and his bronze and green-glass cuirass and greaves freshly polished. For an instant, he hesitated, a mutinous protest on the tip of his tongue. And then he felt the faintest pulse of electricity in the metal at his throat.

"Yes, Yoshi-sama."

"Thank you, Vilkas." Yosh turned away to deal with the hellad while Vilkas dropped to his knees in the bloody dust and crept under the Conestoga with the hook end of the rope. The stunned and badly slashed brutes were all in a tangle. One had voided with the shock of the stun-beam. Retching, Vilkas sank the big barbs into the creature's shoulder.

"Ready?" Yosh sang out.

"Ready." Without the slave-torc's amplification, the Lithuanian's reply would have been inaudible. Fortunately for him, his samurai master was unable to decipher the deeper nuances of the telepathic message.

Vilkas hauled himself out from under the wagon as the rope tightened and the first amphicyon body began to move. Standing, he cursed with revulsion. Bloody mud and excrement stained his arms and legs.

Jim tried to sympathize. "Wot th' hey, guy—leastways we ain' fightin' for our lives upriver at Bardy-Town. Things could be lots worse."

"They will be. Just wait!"

Yosh reappeared out of the fog leading the draft hellad. "Monku, monku, monku," he chided, handing the hooks back to Vilkas. "That's enough bitching. Down you go again, my man. I'll program extra goodies for you on the torc tonight to compensate."

"Thank you, Yoshi-sama." Vilkas' manner was completely civil. He ducked back under the wagon, took a firm grip on the kawa-nawa, and drove the daggerlike points into the throat of the next bear-dog.

2

THE CONVOY OF FOURPLEX MODULAR ATVs, ITS NUMBER
reduced to fifteen after the disaster with the fright hauler back
in the Rif Mountains, crept along in the brassy African sunset
enveloped in dust, ion-defiant midges, and anticipatory elation.

The Mediterranean rim was less than 90 kilometers away.
And the Great Waterfall.

For more than two months, ever since they had dared to
leave the camp on the Moroccan shore to which they had been
diverted by their elders, the runaway adult children of Ocala
Island had fled northeast by north toward that landmark that
had somehow become symbolic of their guilt and daring. They
had crossed more than 1500 kilometers of Pliocene wilderness—swamps and jungles, waterless desert, and most recently
the Rif Range—and now rolled through the sere hills and scrub
thickets covering the upper extremity of the broken Gibraltar
Isthmus. Logic had told the expedition's leader, Hagen Remillard, to bear farther east on a more direct course to the
flooded Mediterranean Basin, which they would have to cross
in order to rendezvous with Cloud in Afaliah. But logic faltered
before the irresistible glamour of the Waterfall. How could

they pass it by? They had shared in its creation when they joined minds with their parents and helped mad Felice admit the western ocean waters into the Empty Sea. To view it was a psychological imperative.

The five youngsters of Ocala's meager third generation, called the Cubs, were even more eager than their parents. When a towering column of vapor signaling the cascade finally appeared on the horizon, the little ones dissolved into a frenzy of fidgeting. It became evident that none of them would be able to sleep that night without first beholding the marvel; so Hagen decided to forgo the usual sunset bivouac and press on. There would be plenty of moonlight to illumine the scene.

Hagen regretted his impulse when Phil Overton caved in to the winsome coercion of his four-year-old, Calinda, who had been begging to sit with her father in the leading ATV. Brokenhearted protests from the other Cubs, both vocal and excruciatingly telepathic, were inevitable. In spite of Hagen's objections, nothing would do but that all of the little ones transfer to the command module. Diane Manion traded places with Nial Keogh and swore to Hagen that she would use every erg of her redactive metafunction to keep the Cubs under control, and the complaisant Overton was demoted from navigator to assistant babysitter. But the closer they came to the Waterfall, the more disorderly the children became.

"Daddy, turn on the peep-sweep again!" Calinda pleaded. "This time, I *know* we'll be able to scan the falls!"

"The peep-sweep! The peep-sweep!" chanted Joel Strangford and Riki Teichmann, who were four-and-a-half and five. They tussled with each other, trying to get closer to the cockpit's terrain holo display, and shoved little Hope Dalembert to the deck in the process. She began to wail.

"Meatheads!" The indictment of six-year-old Davey Warshaw was pitying. "A TSL can't see a hole in the ground when there are hills in the way."

"It can too! It can too!"

"Only if the refractive angle's right," Davey sneered. "And it's not. You think the Gibraltar Gate's some little bitty thing like a dry wadi or a sandpit that the peep can analog? Hah!"

"Then farsense it for us, Mr. Smarty!" Calinda demanded.

Although incapable of such a feat, Davey used his imagination to conjure a vision that stunned the other Cubs to silence:

a planetary orb cleft like a gigantic melon, with a fountain of water gushing into outer space.

Gently, Diane Manion emended the picture. "It's more likely to look like this, dear."

All the Cubs squealed in disappointment.

"But that's just a *little* waterfall," Riki protested. "Like in my Nana's book about the old World. Niagara. *Our* waterfall's bigger than any in the whole world that ever was!"

Calinda's lip thrust out. "Don't want to see a little waterfall. Hagen—you said it would be *humongous.*"

"Humongous," repeated little Hope Dalembert, through tears.

"Phil, Phil, turn on the peep-sweep!" Joel cried, and the others chimed in, swarming over the hapless Overton and crowding Hagen at the command console until he fended them off with his PK and uttered a simultaneous mental expostulation:

All of you be quiet!

Miraculously, they were.

Aloud, Hagen said, "Now listen, you Cubs. We're almost there. I think I sense something! You might, too, if you just pipe down for a damn minute . . ."

The whine of the turbine as the ATV labored toward the top of a ridge. The crunch and snap of flattened brush. The hum of the faltering environmental conditioner. Outside, an off-key serenade of dwarf hyenas hidden in the dusk-purpled chaparral.

And then, a sound that was no sound. An atmospheric stirring so profound that it could not be detected by auditory nerves.

"Daddy, there's something in my throat," Calinda whispered. *"I taste a noise."*

Phil swept her onto his lap before her apprehension could grow, and Diane was swift to mind-comfort the three smaller children. But Davey Warshaw, mature in wisdom, was jubilant.

"That's it! That's the Great Waterfall! Faster, Hagen—drive faster!"

The son of Abaddon gave a short laugh and advanced the throttle. An obstructing scrub oak threatened, and instead of turning aside, he zapped it. The Cubs shrieked as they charged ahead through swirling resinous steam and flying woodchips. The solar-powered turbine of the ATV howled at the steepening grade and climbed higher and higher toward the evening sky.

The peculiar subsonic vibration intensified to a singing in the bone. Even the adults felt the large cartilages of their throats thrill to its enormous note. Hope Dalembert whimpered and hid her face in Diane's breast; but the four other Cubs, wide-eyed, strained with ineffective juvenile farsight to discover what lay ahead. The vehicle finally crested the ridge, bumped over summit outcroppings, and slowed to a halt on a narrow windswept plateau.

The ATV and the height on which it stood shivered in never-ending thunder. The sound was not painful to the ear; the frequency was too low, too nearly palpable. The adults and children sat motionless for a long minute. Then Davey had the hatch open and was clambering out, and Phil Overton took Calinda and Joel while Diane kept tight hold on the hands of Riki and Hope.

Hagen, left alone in the cockpit, took brief note of the stupendous landform being plotted on the graphic display of the terrain scanner. He remarked to the empty aether: "We're finally here, Papa. It's your scene as much as Felice's and ours. Would you like to commandeer my eyes?"

Nothing.

Hagen laughed. "Did she kill you, then? Did a raw-talent crazy finish off the Milieu's challenger? What a tacky ending that would be. Not at all what my Oedipal fantasy anticipated."

Nothing.

"You won't stop us from reopening the time-gate," he whispered. "You *let* us get away from Ocala. You could have blasted us, and you didn't. I know you, Papa! You don't dare stop us. And it's not only the guilt—but the tempting elegance of the wheel come full-circle that you won't be able to resist . . ."

Nothing.

Hagen stifled soliloquy and let thunder fill his skull. His hands worked automatically to kill the vehicle systems and then he went outside to join the others.

They were on a land's end beneath an indigo sky. The full moon of late August was well risen above the eastern horizon. On their left a wide sluiceway stretched toward the Atlantic, and on the right was a monstrous chasm, the new Gulf of Alborán, with its distant floor of starless black water. Joining these two like a silver curtain stretching into infinite night, its hem frothing in the sump of the world, was the grandest waterfall Earth had ever known.

Hagen's instruments had mapped its dimensions: 9.7 kilometers wide and 822 meters high, with a flow ever-increasing as erosion widened and deepened the Gibraltar cut. The Great Waterfall would live for less than a hundred years, for in that time it would fill the entire Pliocene Mediterranean Basin.

One by one the other vehicles of the convoy reached the plateau and came to a standstill. Their occupants alighted and gathered near the cliff edge—twenty-eight men and women and five little children. Normal speech was impossible and mental converse seemed superfluous. It was enough to look, and to memorize.

They might have stayed there for hours, but at last the moonlight dimmed and the breeze grew dank. A wall of heavy fog pushed out from Europe and obliterated the spectacle.

Calinda Overton's small mind-voice said: I think it's over.

And Hagen said: Yes. The nice part is.

Many of the adults laughed then, to cover other emotions. Those who were parents spoke of bedtime. Nial Keogh, ever practical, pointed out the campsite he had taken note of while the rest of them had thought only of racing ahead to see the wonder. Mind-chattering in dull reaction, the children and grandchildren of Rebellion straggled back to the ATVs. Only Hagen stayed alone on the plateau with the command module, after sending Phil and Diane and the Cubs off with the others.

He waited in the thickening fog until midnight, when far-sensing conditions were optimal, then groped cautiously northeastward beyond the Betic Cordillera to the Tanu citadel of Afaliah. When he was certain he had identified its concentration of life-aura, he refined his thought-beam to the slenderest possible needle, tuned it to the intimate mode of his sister, and called.

HAGEN: Do you hear?

CLOUD: Yes. Where are you.

HAGEN: [Image.]

CLOUD: !!So that's It! No wonder the Flood destroyed Muriah. It seems incredible that mindpower alone was responsible. Felice—

HAGEN: —and her devils!

CLOUD: Hagen, we *had* to.

HAGEN: You rationalize after the fact, Marcdaughter.

CLOUD: I thought you were coming to have Diane work on that damn Hamletesquerie. You're becoming a great bore.

HAGEN: You and Papa combined couldn't shrink me. Why expect better of her?

CLOUD: She loves you, stupid. It helps immeasurably in redaction.

HAGEN: Ah, yes. I should have remembered you and your Tanu darling—

CLOUD: Damn you and your can of cranial worms, brother.

HAGEN: Shall we postpone the pleasantries? What happened in Goriah?

CLOUD: [Cinematic event replay.]

HAGEN: Total fiasco. So much for our projected alliance with Nodonn! Nice for you that your lad Kuhal survived . . . I guess we revert to our original Aiken Drum scenario, then. He won't be as easy to manipulate as Nodonn would have been, but we'll probably muddle through. Who knows? The kid might be having his own doubts by now about his future as King of the Elves. He may just decide that our plan to return to the Milieu has a subtle appeal—

CLOUD: *Hagen, Papa's coming.*

HAGEN: Oh, shit. When?

CLOUD: He was vague. He farspoke me this morning, after Aiken won his duel with Nodonn. He had been watching.

HAGEN: He would.

CLOUD: He said he'd come to Europe just as soon as modifications of the cerebroenergetic enhancer were completed. He's bringing it—and the master computer, and the X-laser array from the observatory.

HAGEN: Good God—*how*?

CLOUD: They raised Walter Saastamoinen's four-masted schooner. That seventy-meter brute is big enough to carry half the apparatus on Ocala.

HAGEN: Damn—I told Veikko he should have scuttled her in deeper water or blown her up! Sentimental ass. Let me think . . . she'd take at least a month to get here loaded.

CLOUD: Papa's furious that you started the overland trek.

HAGEN: Did he threaten any long-distance mind-blast?

CLOUD: No. He was very restrained. He just told me to warn you not to attempt any contact with Aiken Drum—or else face dire consequences.

HAGEN: ?? Strange that he didn't farspeak me himself . . .

CLOUD: The CE rig is down for reinstallation on the boat—

HAGEN: Hell, babe, he has plenty of watts to bespeak me in broad daylight, with nothing but the ol' naked gray. Or—? !!! [Image.]

CLOUD: We were right about Felice's d-jump. She rode down his peripheral and scragged him horribly. Fire-flayed him from the neck down—

HAGEN: [Hastily suppressed image.]

CLOUD: [Pain.] He's been floating in the regeneration tank since June.

HAGEN: Cloudie, what if Felice did *more* than broil his bod? What if she cooked his brain, too? What if he pasted himself together again as well as he could—healed his worst body injuries, but didn't dare stay in the soup long enough for a complete neural refit? Hell—that could take eight, nine months easy!

CLOUD: If his metafaculties are crippled, it would explain—

HAGEN: You bet your sweet life it would. He'd speak you rather than me on i-mode because you're more farsensitive. Chances are, he can't crank up anything approaching his normal armamentarium! And if he's unable to handle a full-zorch creative metaconcert, then there's no more danger of his nailing us with a long-distance psychozap! Oh, Cloudie, baby—this could be our big break! He's going to have to fight fair! Get really close to us if he hopes to coerce or mind-blast. Let him try, with Aiken Drum and his mob of exotics on our side—

CLOUD: When Papa farspoke me he said . . . he said he would do his best to work things out for us. If we could only trust him!

HAGEN: [Expletive.]

CLOUD: He should *know* that we wouldn't let the Milieu authorities come back to the Pliocene for him.

HAGEN: Wouldn't we? . . .

CLOUD: You—you—*he loves us*!

HAGEN: His bloody inhuman brand of love—! He loved Mama,

and we know what he did to her. Didn't you ever wonder why?

CLOUD: This is all—

HAGEN: In the Ocala library. Ever notice that the computer entries on the Metapsychic Rebellion are all baldfaced and frank about most aspects of the conflict—except for the bottom line, the goal of the whole damn thing! Why did they have to fight for God's sake? The Rebel objective: "The fostering of Mental Man and the assurance that he will take his rightful place in the Coadunate Milieu." What the hell kind of war motivation is that?

CLOUD: Papa and his people wanted the Human Polity to dominate—

HAGEN: Not that simple! There was something else. You have to pick it up from hints in the other data entries. Subliminal boojum hints as skittish as those things you almost, but not quite, see out of the corner of your eye! Papa's Rebellion had something to do with *us*. With human children. He planned to do something so terrible that his own wife felt justified in trying to murder him—and the Milieu declared war on him after a hundred thousand years of unbroken peace.

CLOUD: It's over. Finished long ago.

HAGEN: Sister dear, *it hasn't happened yet*.

CLOUD: Stop it Hagen stop it! The important thing—the only thing—is for us to get away! Away from him, away from this miserable primitive world where our minds are all alone and hopeless. We can't lose sight of that goal for any reason.

HAGEN: . . . Well?

CLOUD: We must take a chance and contact Aiken Drum. You must come to Afaliah with all speed. It shouldn't take long, now that you've reached the Mediterranean. Sail to the neck of the Balearic Peninsula. There's a very good track called the Aven Road that leads directly to Afaliah. Once you arrive, we can arrange a meeting. Kuhal says . . . he suggested to me a certain bargaining factor that might assure Aiken's cooperating with us. We farspoke together just after Aiken defeated Nodonn. Kuhal didn't want me to lose hope.

HAGEN: Well, what's his idea?

CLOUD: [Image.]

HAGEN: ! I'll be damned. Right there in Afaliah?

CLOUD: They're in the dungeon. There's no one left here to contest my authority over them, so I've been squeezing all day with the help of the local chief redactor. We've almost got it.

HAGEN: Aiken Drum'll kiss our asses to get hold of this!

CLOUD: Don't talk like a fool. Even with this information as a trade-off, we'll have to be extremely careful dealing with him. Aiken's dangerous, Hagen. Perhaps more dangerous now than Papa.

HAGEN: Bullshit.

CLOUD: In the Goriah duel, Aiken stood up to everything that Nodonn could throw at him—including that photon-cannon Spear. But there was something else. As he killed Nodonn and Queen Mercy, he subsumed their metapsychic complexus.

HAGEN: Say *what*?

CLOUD: [Image.] A very obscure phenomenon. I remember that the Poltroyan entry in the computer mentioned it in connection with some ancestor-worship thing. It's very abstruse. Never fully documented among humans. But it seems Aiken did it. The whole Castle of Glass in Goriah is buzzing with the news. How useful the powers will be to him remains to be seen. Kuhal says some Tanu believe the subsumption may kill Aiken.

HAGEN: Wishful thinking ... Listen, Cloud, we'll have to get his cooperation somehow. We can't fight him for the timegate site, and building the Guderian device will mean batting about from one end of Europe to the other gathering raw materials. To say nothing of conscripting Milieu-trained technicians to work out the trickier bits in building the thing. Our only hope of success depends upon cultivating the goodwill of this brain-gobbling little Dracula. Or coercing him into helping us.

CLOUD: More than *that* depends on Aiken.

HAGEN: ?

CLOUD: Kuhal. He and the surviving invaders were taken. They're imprisoned in Goriah now, incommunicado under a sigma-field, charged with high treason. The penalty for that is death.

3

"YOU ARE SUMMONED TO JUDGMENT," COMMANDER CONgreve announced.

The 129 survivors of Nodonn's defeated little army came together and formed a silent double file with Kuhal Earthshaker and Celadeyr of Afaliah at the head. Having been warned by the smirking human lackeys who brought them supper, the Tanu knights were wearing their glass armor, cleaned up as well as they could manage. They glowed in splendid defiance—creator cyan and coercer sapphire and psychokinetic rose-gold, with the few combatants farsensors in the company resembling statues carved from shining amethyst.

A squad of Congreve's human troopers marched in carrying covered baskets. At a mental command they passed down the lines of prisoners, distributing sets of crystal chains. Each insurgent freely bound himself or herself with the symbol of submission to Tanu, manacles about gauntleted wrists, the central snap-link fastened to the golden torc.

"We are ready," said Kuhal. Magnificent in halide radiance, he towered over the human commandant of the Goriah garrison. He eyed the twenty-second-century weapon Congreve carried, incongruous against his exotic parade armor. "And you will not require *that*."

37

"The sacred chains bind us in honor," growled old Celadeyr.

Congreve's mental aspect was glacial. "So did your oath of fealty to King Aiken-Lugonn, which you swore at the Grand Loving! Follow me." He turned, lifting the Matsushita laser carbine to a ceremonial port arms, and led the way from the detention barracks into the outer ward of the Castle of Glass.

Fog swathed the heavily damaged façade. Even though it was less than sixteen hours after the failed attack, much of the debris had already been cleared away. Piles of translucent blocks and the downed tools of workers indicated that repairs were in progress. The faerie lighting of the towers was only a violet-and-gold blur tonight, with the overall effect oddly mutilated since the great spire of the castle had been blasted away by Nodonn.

The prisoners passed through the scorched ruin of the main gate and into the central keep. Most of the corridors had been cleaned up, and only an occasional melt-scar or boarded casement remained as souvenirs of the desperate fighting that had taken place.

The knights marched along bearing their chains proudly, their metapsychic luminosity overwhelming the lesser light of the oil-fueled wall sconces. At length they came into the main audience chamber of the Goriah citadel, which the usurper had caused to be almost completely refurbished. The floor was tiled in gold and midnight-purple. Pillars of twisted amber glass supported a high vaulted ceiling spangled with tiny starlike lamps. The dais was the only bright place in the room. Behind it shone the precious-metal sunburst of Nodonn Battlemaster, retained by the usurper because a solar disk had also been the traditional heraldic cognizance of the first-coming Lugonn. But the ornamental sun-face was blank now, its apollonian smile gone along with recollections of drifting ashes and a tarnished silver hand tumbling out of the dawn sky.

In the place of honor stood a black-marble throne, surrounded by twenty lesser seats, all empty. On the throne sat a little human eating an apple: the Nonborn King of the Many-Colored Land. He had evidently just come in out of the mist, for he wore a Tanu-style stormsuit of golden leather still glistening with beads of moisture. Its visored hood was thrown back and the neck open. Aiken-Lugonn's throat was bare. He required no artificial stimulus to mental operancy.

The prisoners came before the dais and waited while Congreve made his brief telepathic announcement and then retired with the guard detail to the shadows in the rear of the hall.

The King munched his apple and let his gaze rove over the depleted battle-company. He had no metapsychic nimbus. In fact, his appearance was peculiarly wan, with only his dark red hair and brows and the eyes like little chunks of jet giving life to his face.

Kuhal Earthshaker spoke to Celadeyr on the intimate mode:

So he lives Celo . . . Alas for the rumor that he choked in the Devouring!

Not that one. But he does look psychodyspeptic.

Both Nodonn and Mercy-Rosmar—! To subsume either would have been beyond the power of our mightiest legendary heroes. What are we to make of a being who assimilates *two* such minds? Perhaps it is the final confirmation that he is indeed the Adversary.

I didn't need any confirmation. Only you younger ones doubted.

Not true Celo. The Craftsmaster didn't believe it. Nor does Lady Morna-Ia. I know that even my brother Nodonn himself doubted as his end approached . . .

He believed.

He doubted. Who knew Nodonn as I did—unless perhaps my lost mind-twin Fian Skybreaker! Nodonn was the eldest son of my father Thagdal and mother Nontusvel and I served him for three hundred and eighty-five years as Second Lord Psychokinetic. Aiken Drum the Adversary—? Nonsense. Nodonn hated and feared this parentless wariangle as a Lowlife upstart and adventurer. But he never accepted him as the ultimate Foe.

Tchah! Even the Firvulag know the bastard for what he is! Why do you think the Little People connived with us—showed us the aircraft in return for our promise to return Sharn's Sword? The Adversary's coming foreshadows the Nightfall War, and they cannot fight the last battle without their sacred Sword. O Kuhal believe! Nodonn never doubted. You are the doubter! And I know why. That North American woman is to blame— the one Boduragol paired you with in the healing—

Old fool. Were it not for Cloud I would still be half a mind.

You still are. The wrong half! All your Tanu instincts your racial soul died with Fian—

Wretchedoldman STOP! Not you not anyone may fault my courage in this doomed undertaking! Nor my loyalty to Nodonn and our battle-religion. This matter of the Adversary is beside the point as we stand here flagrant traitors brought to judgment.

...Ah yes. Your pardon Brother Earthshaker. I am a defeated dotard and should bethink me of Tanu's imminent peace rather than some mythical apocalypse...But I have seen fulfilled so many portents that puzzled us ancients by their absence during that conflict at Void's Edge a thousand years agone in the old Duat Galaxy. Now we have seen the engulfing waters! The monstrous carrion-bird Morigel! The One-Handed Warrior leading the battle-company against all custom! The summer fog! So there remains only the last dread epiphany...that baleful mindstar heralding the fall of Night...I tell you Kuhal that soon the war will rage in which no warrior can tell friend from foe. And finally there will be a tearing asunder of the earth and high heaven as the Adversary triumphs.

Celo—

And he is *here*.

Aiken Drum had come to the front of the dais, nibbling the last bits from his fruit. He flicked the apple core over his right shoulder and it vanished. At the same moment a double-lever steel boltcutter appeared in his right hand.

"Do you know what this is?" His voice was quiet. The deadly bloodmetal tool gleamed as he raised it nigh. "It's iron. You Tanu thought that there was no way to remove a torc without killing the wearer. Well, you were wrong. There are two ways—and using this thing is one of them. When you cut off a torc with an iron tool it hurts like the fires of hell. It may even drive you mad. But most healthy adult Tanu live through it, even though all of your wonderful metapsychic powers fall back into latency...and you become as mentally impotent as the lowest bareneck human."

The prisoners glowed more brightly.

Aiken's face was expressionless. He turned his back on them, and then suddenly his telepathic voice clanged on the declamatory mode:

LET THE HIGH TABLE GATHER FOR THE JUDGMENT.

Above certain of the twenty seats reserved for the Most Exalted Ones, faces were materializing—the farsent simulacra of the ruling council of the Many-Colored Land: Morna-Ia Kingmaker, Bleyn the Champion, Alberonn Mindeater and his wife Eadnar, Condateyr Fulminator of Roniah, Sibel Longtress, Neyal of Sasaran, the human Estella-Sirone of Darask, and Lomnovel Brainburner of Sayzorask.

Celadeyr's intimate thought was aghast: So few!

And Kuhal's sardonic: Our own seats are empty Celo. And likewise those of Thufan of Tarasiah and Diarmet of Geroniah who perished when the aircraft fell. And the seat of poor Moreyn Glasscrafter who poisoned himself with ferrous sulfate when the usurper flamed victorious. And Queen Mercy's place! And the seats of those who perished at the Río Genil—Artigonn and the Craftsmaster and my brother the Interrogator. Let me see . . . the Second Redactor's position was vacant. Who is the missing twentieth? I have it. Armida the Formidable Lady of Bardelask. No doubt she has more important matters to occupy her.

Celo said: Nine percent. A quorum. Enough to condemn. Ylahayll the lot!

Aiken said: *DELIBERATE! WHAT IS YOUR JUDGMENT OF THIS COMPANY?*

The nine spectral heads said: *They are guilty of high treason. WHAT IS THE PENALTY UNDER TANU LAW?*

The heads: *Confinement under Chain of Silence until the next Grand Combat. Then life-offering to our compassionate Goddess in the Great Retort.*

The little man grinned. "Too bad," he said in his normal voice. "I've abolished the Combat, as we all know. It's to be a Grand Tourney this Hallowe'en. And cooking criminals in a glass oven would spoil the tone of the festivities."

He turned to face the prisoners, hefting the boltcutter.

"We've heard the High Table opinion. Now I'm going to ask you for yours! . . . But first, a few relevant bits of data to help your cogitation.

"*One*: Make no mistake—Nodonn Battlemaster is dead and so is Queen Mercy-Rosmar. I've subsumed portions of their mentalities. I'll leave it to your imagination to decide just what *that* means . . .

"*Two*: Sharn and Ayfa have not only broken the Armistice,

they're stomping on the bits. You've noticed that Armida the Formidable didn't appear to judge you. Right this minute her city of Bardelask is under attack by eight thousand Firvulag regulars. Armida and her people are fighting for their lives and they're going to lose. The relief force I sent didn't arrive in time.

"*Three*: Condateyr's spies have information that Roniah will be next on the hit-list. Unless we can keep the city secure until the Truce starts a month from now, we are in very deep trouble indeed! Because the late Lord Bormol of Roniah was a collector of smuggled Milieu artifacts just like his equally defunct brother, Osgeyr of Burask, and we all know what happened when Burask fell. The Little People nicked a fair-sized cache of contraband high-technology weapons that they're using right now to zap down the walls of Bardelask. But if the Firvulag get their gnomish hands on *Bormol's* stash it will be all hell out for noon, dear enemies—because Condateyr says that his late leader's illicit arms dump is ten times the size of Osgeyr's! If we can't safeguard Roniah, we'll have to destroy the stuff to keep it alway from Sharn and Ayfa."

The radiance of the chained knights had undergone a chilled diminution. Old Celadeyr's mouth was working furiously. "To hell with anything that corrupts the battle's glory!" he shouted. "Destroy the Lowlife gadgetry right now or you are no Tanu king! Where's your sense of honor?"

Aiken said, "Perhaps you'd better ask King Sharn and Queen Ayfa that question. And their viceroy, Mimee of Famorel, who's investing Bardelask... While you're at it, make certain that *their* idea of a Nightfall War is the same as yours."

The old hero's face inside his open helmet was as pale and hard as limestone. His mental barrier trembled, preparing for another explosive eruption.

Kuhal intervened. "Nodonn informed me that the greatest store of futuristic weapons is right here in the souterrain of the castle. Or did Queen Mercy-Rosmar succeed in destroying them?"

"She merely rendered them unusable," Aiken said. "Nodonn wasn't a traditionalist ass like Celo. He planned to use the Milieu weapons himself later, putting down any human opposition to his takeover. Right now, the entire storage area is buried in a sticky mess of poison-filled foam. We've sent to

Rocilan for a Milieu-trained chemist. He's the best one in the Many-Colored Land, and you Tanu had him torced with silver and supervising a bloody candy factory!" Aiken's golliwog grin was wry. "He's not looking forward to his new job, even though I promised him an instant promotion to gold."

"If what you say about the Firvulag is true," Kuhal ventured, "we totter on the verge of ruin—"

"*I* totter," Aiken corrected. He gesticulated at the nine projections of the High Table members. "*They* totter! The Tanu High Kingdom that you cheese-brains say you love totters! But you don't have to stick around for the debacle. Oh, no. You can choose death if you like. Not next November in the damned Retort, but tomorrow morning, quick and clean in front of the Matsu carbines of Congreve's guard. By all tenets of Tanu law, you stand condemned. But this is a new era, and I say that the lot of you are going to pass judgment on yourselves...and choose your own punishment."

Confused and astonished, the minds of the prisoners buzzed on the intimate mode.

"There's something else you should know," Aiken said. "Elizabeth farspoke me a piece of intelligence earlier this evening. The human operant that we've known as Abaddon is ready to leave North America. He's coming here."

"The starmind out of the western morning," said Celadeyr in a dead voice.

Aiken was silent.

"You have told us that one of our options is clean death," Kuhal said. "And is *that* another?" He nodded at the steel boltcutter in Aiken's hand. "Mental castration as the price of liberty?"

"What good would you be to me then?" inquired the King softly. "I only showed you the iron to...encourage attitude adjustment."

"Kuhal, nothing has changed—" Celadeyr began.

The Earthshaker interrupted. "I am your senior in rank, Celo, even if your junior in years. I claim the right to be spokesman for all of us." His mind encompassed those of the other chained knights: Do you agree battle-companions?

We agree.

And you Celadeyr of Afaliah?

I—I yield to your authority.

Kuhal Earthshaker lifted his arms. The crystal links made two glittering curves from his wrists to his throat. His form burned with rose-gold luminescence.

"I pass judgment, then, upon this company. We are guilty of breaking our oath of fealty. Guilty of supporting a Pretender. Guilty of taking up arms against our lawful Sovereign. Our lives are forfeit and you may do with us as you will, King Aiken-Lugonn. But know that we now submit to you utterly and beg mercy, and if you condescend, we pledge our minds and bodies to your service without reservation. And thou, Tana, witnesseth."

The little man sighed.

The glass chains fell to the floor with a musical clash.

"You're free." The King turned about, went to the black throne, and sat himself down on the hard stone seat. He leaned forward, and abruptly his coercive grip held Kuhal like a beetle on a pin.

"Fine sentiments are all very well. But we Lowlives tend to think that actions speak louder than words! I want proof of your born-again righteousness. No weaseling, no horse trading, no quid pro quo power brokering between you traditionalists and me. Do you understand me, Earthshaker?"

"I understand, High King."

Aiken smiled. His coercion softened. "Then we'll get down to serious business. Where have you hidden the rest of those aircraft?"

4

GASPING FOR BREATH, HALTING EVERY FIFTY PACES OR SO TO rest his swollen ankle and thudding heart, Brother Anatoly Gorchakov O.F.M. made his way up the fogbound mountain.

What a pity that the bandits had taken his chaliko! Chalikos never lost their way, no matter how dark the night or exiguous the trail. With a mount he would have reached the lodge four or five hours ago. He'd be dry, warm, and fed, perhaps even beginning to lay the groundwork for the mission. But the chaliko, a handsome animal that had been the gift of Lomnovel of Sayzorask, had proved an irresistible temptation to the four footpads back on the Great South Road. Anatoly's reasoned plea that he needed the mount in order to carry on the Lord's work was greeted with merry laughter—and four vitredur lances pricking at his neck.

"Blessed are the poor," said the bandit chieftain with a sententious grin. "We're just helping to keep you holy, padre. Now hit the dirt."

Anatoly sighed and slid out of the high saddle. Thirty years as a circuit rider in Pliocene Europe had made him sensitive to the more obscure manifestations of the divine will. If he had to travel the last 50 kilometers of his journey on foot, then fiat voluntas tua. On the other hand . . .

"You'll never sell the beast, you know," he said. "White chalikos are a reserved breed. You even try to ride him into a town, the first gray-torc patrol you meet will tie your guts into a bowknot."

"Cutch!" exclaimed a younger bandit who was missing two front teeth.

Thinking he was being reviled with some ethnic obscenity, Brother Anatoly snapped, "Watch your mouth, pizdosos."

The leader of the gang was all affability. "No, no, padre! Cutch. Catechutannic acid, a dye you make from the bark of spine-bushes. A swab-down with that'll turn this nag from Exalted white to wild-chaliko brown slick as a whistle. By the time we get him down to the Amalizan auction, his claws'll be roughed up and the saddle marks blurred. And so he doesn't act too tame for the stock inspector, we'll put a little ginger up him at the last."

The gap-toothed ruffian giggled and explained this last strat-agem in disgusting detail while the others rifled Anatoly's bag-gage. They decided to let him keep the woolen habit and sandals he was wearing, a pouch with hardtack and dry salami, his small spare waterskin, and finally—after the friar's sternest rebuke—the quartz-halogen lantern. This last was grudgingly conceded when Anatoly told them that he was bound for the Montagne Noire wilderness, where the high humidity made it impossible to keep a night fire going and some source of light was needed to ward off prowling man-eaters. In a final mag-nanimous gesture, the bandit chief cut Anatoly a sturdy hiking staff. Thus minimally equipped, the friar continued on his way.

For the better part of three days he traveled through dense rain forest along a boisterous little river. The only hostile wild-life he encountered was a patriarchal sable antelope, which fortunately stood its ground on the opposite bank of the river. With increasing altitude, the jungle merged into conifer forest and then opened onto long vistas of moorland split by rocky ridges. Anatoly saw herds of ibex with massive horns like scimitars, and sometimes he was followed by curious little chamois as he toiled up the steepening trail.

When Black Crag itself finally came into view, jutting stark among spruce-clad mountains, his heart lifted. There, if God willed, he would fulfill the promise made more than four months ago to the other priest, the troubled one who had been struck by his own tough-mindedness when they met so briefly in the refugee camp at Castle Gateway and together conceived the mission . . .

. . . but now, lost in the fog, with night closing in, he asked himself: "Was I an arrogant old osloyeb to think I might succeed where she failed? What if I never even find the place? What if I get there—and the bodyguard of Tanu mind-benders sends me off with a flea in my ear?"

He had eaten his last scraps of food for breakfast. Hunger and fatigue made him dizzy and he stumbled many times as he traversed a rubble-strewn slope, which was devoid of any semblance of shelter. The fog was metamorphosing into a chill drizzle. His left ankle, which he had turned early in the afternoon when the mist thickened abruptly, was now so puffed that the strap of his sandal had disappeared into discolored flesh.

Where could the damned trail be?

He switched on the lantern and cast about, the yellow beam seeming almost semisolid in the murk. He prayed, "Archangel Rafe, patron of travelers, help me spot that perishing trail-marker!"

And there it was: three stacked rocks, light against the graphitic shale and, as a bonus, a pile of old chaliko dung, sure sign that some other wayfarer had passed this spot. Brother Anatoly blessed the Lord, the marker, and the dung. His ankle throbbed, he was benighted and hypothermic and famished enough to eat shoe leather—but at least he was no longer lost.

Fastening the lantern to his cincture, he gripped the staff and plodded on. The trail continued to rise, twisting among rock slabs as black as ink. He came to a fork. Right or left? He shrugged and turned right, onto the wider section of path. The butter-colored cone of lamplight shone on wet gravel, on tumbled chunks of gneiss, one a treacherous slickensides incline, and on . . . nothing.

"Mat' chestnaya!" yelled the priest. He teetered and clung to the staff, which skidded into a small fissure and wedged tight. Just one more step would have taken him over the precipice edge. Only the lantern's warning had saved him, and the bandit-gift staff.

He rested on his knees, trembling in terror and relief. Cracked shale pressed through his soaked robe like dull knives, but his unrejuvenated old bones were so chilled that he felt hardly any pain. Head bowed, he mumbled an Ave in the old tongue. Somewhere down below, a mountain stream seethed and roared and wind was rising. He looked up and saw a nearly full moon racing amid rags of cloud. The fog was dissipating—or perhaps he had simply climbed high enough to top it—and in a few minutes he had a clear view of a deep coombe threaded by a silvery torrent. The opposite wall was in heavy shadow and above it rose a ridge that culminated in a great moonlit eminence shaped roughly like an old-fashioned papal tiara. Black Crag.

Anatoly climbed to his feet and lifted the lantern high. They could probably see him! He was well out in the open, away from any screening mass of rock, and the guardian farsensors might have been watching him for hours as he picked his way along the fog-shrouded slope. Perhaps they had even given the warning.

In a voice raised only slightly against the wind, he said, "Good evening! I am Brother Anatoly Severinovich Gorchakov of the Order of Friars Minor. I've been sent with an important message. May I come ahead?"

Was it only the wind—or were spectral metasenses plucking at him, feeling him out? Was exotic scrutiny viewing him with Olympian benevolence—or preparing to flick him off like some intrusive gnat?

Was there no one up there at all, and was he simply a silly old crank with a rumbling stomach and fast-dwindling strength?

He clutched staff and lantern and stood there swaying. Then he saw it, farther into the ravine, on his side of the stream: a tiny red light. And then a white one springing into being just beyond it, and another red one, and then many others, alternately red and white, red and white—a dotted line leading toward the head of the valley, undoubtedly illuminating the continuation of the trail. Anatoly gasped. More lights were zigzagging up the valley's far wall, pricking out a series of ascending switchbacks that snaked to the very summit of the crag. And up there, perched in lofty isolation and glowing like a basket of red-hot coals was a great structure resembling an alpine chalet. The lodge, just as Sister Roccaro had said.

Anatoly switched off his lantern. The last shreds of the Summer Fog were gone and the mountainside lay luminous under the moon. As suddenly as they had appeared, the panorama of faerie lights and the enchanted dwelling on the crag vanished. All that remained was a single little red beacon not a dozen meters away that indicated the correct turning back at the fork of the trail. Anatoly limped toward it. Before he reached the juncture the red light winked out and a white one, farther along, came on.

"Very kind of you, I'm sure," he said. "Still, it may take me a while. You'll keep the tea water hot, won't you? And perhaps save me a sandwich?"

The white star shone steadily. Except for the wind sighing among the rocks, it was very quiet.

"Here I come, then," said Brother Anatoly, and resumed his interrupted journey.

Minds still linked, Elizabeth and Creyn returned from their latest metapsychic range of Ocala Island. But instead of disengaging, they waited, hands lightly clasped across the oak table, to see if the thing would happen again. They were both turned toward the western windows. The sky beyond the balcony railing was now an extravagant blaze of stars, barely challenged by the high-riding moon.

Creyn said: It manifests.

Elizabeth said: Yes. Just like the other two times. Perhaps a bit more leisurely in the coalescence. More sure of itself.

Creyn said: It *is* a simulacrum isn't it?

Elizabeth said: Pray God yes friend. Let us attempt a finer analysis.

A silhouette was materializing outside, blotting out the stars. It was the figure of a tall human male, apparently no more than seven meters away from them on the other side of the leaded window panes. Their linked farsense concentrated into a lancet-probe and explored with superlative delicacy. Were there actual molecules present—or was the thing merely a psychocreative simulacrum, a projected image no more substantial than the holograms of a Tri-D or the "sendings" broadcast by the Tanu and Firvulag? The probe was defeated by an aetheric phenomenon more subtle than a mental screen, a dynamicfield manifestation unfamiliar to Elizabeth, more absorptive than reflective.

Creyn said: He's bluffing. He must be.

Elizabeth said: Psychological warfare. Softening up before the real confrontation damn him.

The man on the balcony wore a dark and glistening garment with a diagonal fastening, virtually skintight from neck to toe. Obscure embellishments, apparently of a technical nature, studded it in the region of the collarbone and the groin. The neck and head were bare and the curly hair stood out oddly from the scalp, almost like tendrils. The man's features were unmistakable and he seemed to be looking at them.

To make certain that he heard, Elizabeth spoke on the distance-spanning intimate mode:

Why not communicate with us Marc instead of playing games?

The image was not quite motionless. The hair stirred and one corner of the mouth lifted by a millimeter. Tonight, unlike on the previous two visitations, the body was haloed in a faintly luminescent complex of mechanical gadgetry; around the head was a brighter nimbus of half-visible components and a hint of great flex-lines and cables trailing off into the night sky.

Creyn said: Obviously the cerebroenergetic apparatus is again fully operational.

Elizabeth said: They must have been tinkering with it the first two tries. Or perhaps his injuries forced him to utilize unfamiliar neural circuits—

Did the head nod, ever so fractionally?

Can you hear us on shortrange conversational Marc?

The smile broadened.

Elizabeth said: Well that's a relief. We're quite tired out from spying on you and your children and Aiken and Nodonn's invaders and the Firvulag. It's been a very wearying thirty-six hours . . . We missed you last night. Were you too engrossed in watching the Great Duel to bother visiting us? . . . Whom were you cheering for? It was quite a setback for your bewildering offspring but no doubt they'll come up with a new scheme in due course . . . What do they *really* want in Europe Marc? It's obvious they have a deeper motive than simply snipping the paternal apron strings and seeking their fortune on barbarian shores. I can't see you coming hotfoot after them for anything as mundane as that . . . Your preparations must be nearly complete for the voyage by now. Even with the sigma-fields erected over the Kyllikki we can tell you've managed to stow a remarkable quantity of matériel aboard her . . . Will you set sail soon? . . . Quite a lot of mysterious whispering on the intimate mode wafting up from Africa during the last few weeks. What do you suppose the children are up to? . . .

The eyes of the phantom, sunken in deep orbits, blinked slowly. His quirked smile had faded.

Elizabeth said: Marc you have no idea how you're complicating my job as de facto dirigent of Pliocene Earth. I doubt that Brede's plan for my godmothering her people took you and your meddling young into account . . . I've told Aiken about your travel preparations and he's quite upset. He takes his kingly duties rather seriously and I suspect that he'll resist any impertinencies with all his newly acquired might. Do you take my meaning? No doubt you witnessed the two metafunctional subsumptions he pulled off. I'm hard to impress these days— but I must admit to a definite bogglement at *that* little ploy.

Were the eyes a trifle narrower, the mouth more tight?

Elizabeth said: I want to forestall any violent confrontation between you and Aiken. Let me mediate. I could prevent disastrous miscalculations on *both* your parts . . . Aiken is no longer the metaprodigal prankster you dealt with before you went into the tank. He's changed vastly since June. In outlook as well as in aggressive potential! He debugged the metaconcert program you gave him and he's been drilling his golds in the technique. These torc-augmented mentalities may be crude but they can amount to a respectable potential when stacked. If Aiken gathers enough people together and acquires full use of the powers he subsumed he'll be more than a match for you . . . Consider carefully before you act. Advise your hothead children to do the same. We can have peace Marc! Won't you at least talk to me about it? . . .

The shape out on the balcony was dissolving into a star-punctured wraith even as she persisted in her futile pleading. She shifted from the short-range to the distance-spanning mode, calling Marc's name, then broke off. The vision shimmered and disappeared without a trace.

The mental linkage between Elizabeth and Creyn severed.

She exclaimed, "Damn the man for his arrogance! *Damn* him!" She lowered her head onto her arms and burst into tears.

Creyn the Redactor came to her and knelt beside her chair. She found herself clinging to him while pent-up anxiety and exasperation poured out of her; the old temptation to withdraw loomed more ominously than ever before.

The Tanu's mind was discreetly closed. There was only his enormous physical presence, the strong embracing arms, the chest warm and superhumanly broad, the steady exotic heartbeat.

When she stopped weeping, she said, "I'm a bloody idiot."

"The release is good for you. Very human. Very Tanu, too, for that matter."

"I've done the best I could. When I woke up after the Flood at Redactor House and took this job on, I really intended to do my best. Back in the Milieu, the job of dirigent—planetary overseer, that is—traditionally went to the person who didn't want it. And God knows, that's me! But . . . I'm bungling it, Creyn. Can't you see? All of you think that a Grand Master Farsensor and Redactor should be a metapsychic wizard, an all-wise demigoddess. But I was only a *teacher* back in the Milieu, not a trained administrator or a socioeconomic analyst. How can I be the ombudsman and arbiter for a crazy mixed bag of factions like this? . . . And now this wretched galactic Napoleon coming at me from his North American Elba! . . . Brede called me the most important woman in the world. What arrant nonsense! Look at the terrible mistake I made with Felice. I had no idea how to deal with a dangerous personality like her. Aiken's successful intervention was entirely his own idea . . . And soon he'll be coming here, wanting me to help reintegrate his mind. The subsumption has given him a case of mental indigestion that could lead to a breakdown if he doesn't get help soon. What shall I do? If I integrate those faculties he stole, he might turn into another Felice. If I let him fall apart, Marc or his children will have a free hand! I don't know how to handle situations as complex as this, Creyn. I'm wrong for the job. A dirigent in the Milieu has a vast support organization— the enforcing arm of the Magistratum, all the resources of the Concilium to advise, the Unity to strengthen and give solace. *But I'm alone*."

He said, It would help if you could love us.

She shrank from him. As always when he dared approach this dangerous ground, the mental wall sprang up.

He said, You could learn make a beginning with one who loved you.

Creynmyfriend no I don't can't no...

He spoke aloud. "It's the way of both our races to need the beloved other. Not to strive alone. You know that I've loved you almost from the first time we met in Castle Gateway. Neither of us was a willing solitary then. It was the death of your Lawrence as much as the apparent loss of your meta-functions that drove you to exile. And I myself was widowed scarcely a year when you came to us. I could only stand back then, watching you being used, a pawn of the Great Ones. But later... when I was able to serve you, to help on the exodus from Aven, to assist you here at Black Crag... in all my life I've never been happier. My heart aches to share it with you."

The walls were high and adamant, but she had her arms tightly around him. He said, "Listen to what your body says. Neither Tanu nor human is mere disembodied mind. You knew love's dual expression once, back in the Milieu with your husband, and it helped you to love the thousands of children you taught. Now you live in another world... but you can learn to love again."

She spoke gently. "You're the dearest friend I have. I know what you're offering, what you hope to do for me, even though you know I don't love you in a sexual way. But it can't work—"

"It has for others, in your world as well as mine." His mind-tone reflected wistful self-mockery. "And we redactors aren't without skill in such matters."

"Oh, my dear." Her head lifted and they drew apart. The tears had started again; impulsively, she showed him a glimpse of burning memory. "If it could only be so simple! But you said it yourself: I *did* love once. If only I hadn't already known a real marriage in the Unity..."

"Is the gulf so great?" he cried. "Am I so far beneath you—so inferior?"

She wept, completely sealed in.

He said, "You raised Brede to operancy, even started to

initiate her. Do the same for me. In time we could forge a Unity of our own!" He was no longer holding her but standing upright, a towering red-robed figure with rubies and moon-stones gleaming in his belt and a golden torc around his neck.

"Brede wasn't a Tanu." Elizabeth's voice was dull. Slowly she rose from her chair and went to the fireplace where the logs of stone-pine had fallen apart and were fitfully aglow. Using the hook of the poker, she pulled them back together, then worked the leather bellows until a few small flames sprang up. "Brede belonged to a more resilient race. In some ways more human than yours; in other ways, less. She was incredibly old and this gave her mind a monumental fund of endurance. And she was the Shipspouse! Her mate left her a special legacy that engendered the mind-expanding ordeal that we shared. *Shared*, Creyn!"

He nodded. "My own pain is not sufficient . . ."

"I don't know any way to strengthen you so that you could survive the ascent to operancy. So that *I* could survive it with you. Can you understand what I'm trying to tell you, my dear? Look into me very carefully. What an adult latent like yourself would have to go through in order to open those new mental channels—"

"I'd suffer anything to make you love me!"

"You'd *die*. I'm incompetent! It's beyond me! I can't make you operant any more than I can save poor Mary-Dedra's black-torc baby. Don't you think I would set *all* your minds free if I could? If I only could . . ."

Somehow she was clinging to him again and they stood at the eastern windows. He said: Don't give up Elizabeth. Don't be tempted by the fire. Endure. If you can't love then be consoled by the devotion of those who need you. Pray for a resolution.

Elizabeth laughed out loud. "Brede waited fourteen thousand years to die. Will I have to wait six million?"

His long fingers touched her swollen eyelids, drying tears and leaving coolness. "Turn your thoughts. Look at the stars and compose yourself. Downstairs they're waiting for us, and have been for hours."

"Poor Minanonn. I don't know what to tell *him*, either."

In spite of herself, she found her eyes drawn to the sky.

"How strange! That tight grouping of very small stars, down near the horizon. I wonder if they could possibly be the Pleiades? It was a funny little cluster four hundred light-years from my home planet of Denali, and the same distance from the Old World—from Earth. We colonists were very sentimental about it."

"We and the Firvulag have a similar symbolic constellation that we call the Trumpet. See there? Just above your Pleiades. Our galaxy is so remote that it is invisible, even in the telescopes brought by time-travelers to this Many-Colored Land. But we know that Duat lies out beyond the mouthpiece star of the Trumpet, uncounted light-years from Earth."

His arm was around her shoulder. He drew her toward the alcove opposite the fireplace where the force-field projector called the room without doors had formerly been installed. Now the little niche was empty except for another pair of gifts from the Shipspouse: a picture of a barrel-spiral galaxy trailing two great arms, and hovering in front of it, an abstract sculpture of a female figure.

He said, "We trust—Minanonn and I and the rest of the Peace Faction—that Tana is truly caring. That there is a greater evolution than that of the physical universe, of body, of mind. That there is an All toward which creation yearns, which each generation perceives ever more clearly, and in doing so, approaches. Those following the old battle-religion see the all in All as achievable only in death and annihilation. Hence their myth of the Nightfall War, which we thought would first engulf our tiny breakaway group of Tanu and Firvulag, and later destroy all the rest of the Duat worlds as well."

She said, "Brede spoke of it, and its being rooted in the torcs. She told me how the ancestral Tanu introduced the torc technology to the other Duat races, and how this was eventually seen by her as a metapsychic catastrophe, dooming the Mind of your galaxy to a dead end. And her intuitive insight was correct, Creyn. The torc—*any* artificial mind enhancement that becomes a permanent crutch—is an intrinsic bar to Unity. Marc Remillard and his people proved that in the Milieu."

He said, "Those of us who trust believe that even this terrible paradox, the dead end of the Duat Mind, fits somehow in the greater pattern—and will be resolved."

Elizabeth turned her back on the statue and the star-whirl and moved to the fire. She took a bronze poker and jabbed half-heartedly at the embers. A few sparks flew.

"I don't think Brede took that view. In the end, she came to believe that the evolution of the Duat Mind could continue only in your merging with the human race. I think she may have envisioned some relict Pliocene population eventually mating with primitive Homo sapiens—planting metapsychic seeds in the huge, marvelous, empty Neanderthaler brains. Voilà! Instant Cro-Magnon. The really funny thing is, the modern type of human *did* appear with suspicious suddenness, and leaped to metapsychic operancy in a paltry fifty thousand years or so."

She thrust emphatically at the dying fire. The logs, reduced almost entirely to charcoal, crumbled to bits. His voice was flat and her mind tightly sealed. "If this is what you'd call the masterplan of a compassionate God, then your faith is more cold-blooded than mine, Creyn. We humans will have climbed to Unity using the doomed Mind of Duat as a stepping-stone. Have you seen the army ants bridge a stream in the jungle? Thousands of them link together and willingly drown so their luckier fellows cross over without getting wet feet."

"Elizabeth, the people in Duat *don't know.*"

"But I do." She carefully replaced the poker. "And I don't think I can bear it. Not that, not any of it."

"You only toy with despair," he insisted.

"I know. Sister Amerie used to say that one twits the Holy Spirit only at one's peril—but she couldn't quite break me of the habit." Elizabeth smiled brightly. "Shall we go downstairs and take care of our intelligence briefing?"

When the big door to the lodge's grand salon banged open, there was instant uproar. Elizabeth and the Peace Faction conferees, deeply engrossed in their mind-meld, were so taken aback that they did nothing. That left the friar free to elude Mary-Dedra and Godal the Steward and the other two Tanu retainers, who had chased him up from the kitchen and who lacked the PK or coercive ability that would have restrained the old man in the first place. He barged right into the salon with the pursuers shouting and clutching at him and uttering telepathic apologies and belated pleas for help.

"Hold!" bellowed Minanonn, rising from the depths of the sofa like fulminating Jupiter.

The entire quintet of intruders froze in midcry.

"Who in the world—" Elizabeth began.

Minanonn released his coercive grip on the Black Crag people, who pulled themselves together. The elderly human male in the tattered Franciscan habit remained completely paralyzed, balanced on one foot and with hands raised and clenched. His eyes were alive and glittering.

"We'd welcomed him," said Mary-Dedra indignantly. "Helped him to find the place, then dried him and gave him a nice supper!"

"He seemed harmless enough," said Godal the Steward, "until Dedra let slip that Elizabeth had come down at last to meet with you Exalted Ones—"

"And at that, the silly old coot yelled something about his mission," Mary-Dedra said, "and came charging up here before we knew what we were about! Now, if you please, we'll be chucking him out the front gate."

Dionket the Healer said, "First, we'd better hear what he wants."

"Let him speak, Minnie," said Peredeyr Firstcomer.

"But keep a firm hold on the rest of him," said Meyn the Unsleeping.

The friar, still immobile from the neck down, licked his lips and cleared his throat. He fixed his eyes on Leilani-Tegveda the Fairbrowed and said, "Am I addressing the Grand Master Elizabeth Orme?"

"I am she," said a much less imposing woman who wore a severe black gown.

The paralyzed priest looked somewhat relieved. In spite of his ludicrous posture, he spoke with dignity. "My name is Anatoly Severinovich Gorchakov and I am a brother of the Order of Friars Minor. Your friend Amerie Roccaro has sent me to be your spiritual adviser."

Elizabeth stared at him, speechless.

"You can turn me loose now," Brother Anatoly told Minanonn. "I'll go back peaceably to my supper and you can get on with your conference." He said to Elizabeth, "I just wanted you to know that I'll be waiting when you're ready for me."

Minanonn looked at Elizabeth, who nodded.

The coercive grip faded. Anatoly lowered his foot, unclenched his hands, and resettled his rope belt. He managed a rather sketchy sign of the cross. "When you're ready," he repeated, then turned and walked out the door.

5

THE VERY FIRST VISIT OF THE GHASTLY HOURI TO TONY WAYland had come closest to being the final one.

Half-mad with fear and still befuddled by his interrogation at the hands of Their Awful Majesties Sharn and Ayfa, Tony had been certain that only torture and death awaited him. He was astonished but not inclined to ask questions when the seductive creature entered his cell in the dungeon at High Vrazel. Perhaps she was there to provoke him to fresh treasons against humanity; perhaps she was merely the Firvulag equivalent of a last cigarette for the condemned. Whatever . . . she was lissome and lubricious, more or less humanly proportioned, and although her coal-black skin and scarlet hair and écu betrayed her exotic origins, he never would have suspected the truth. He had already embraced her, and was well on the way to the point of no return, when doom was averted in a most unlikely way.

Karbree the Worm, the giant who had captured him, came tramping into the dungeon and hammered on the cell's wooden door with both mailed fists, bellowing:

"Skathe! I know you're in there, you snaggle-cunt rama-fucker! Ha-ha! Bad luck for you, comrade! We're off to Goriah *right now*."

This demonic charivari having deflated all Tony's amorous aspirations, the houri leaped off him with a screech of rage and cursed the laughing monster on the other side of the door.

"Don't blame me, sweeting," Karbree cooed. A slitted green eye glinted in the door's peephole. "It was Sharn and Ayfa's decision. They want emissaries on the spot as soon as possible after Nodonn fries the brains of the Lowlife usurper. We're to press him for the return of our sacred Sword before he manages to think of some reason to repudiate the bargain he made with us. The royals command that we leave High Vrazel within the hour—so forget that unholy experiment of yours, and get your ass armored and hopping!"

The houri leaned over Tony, curtaining him in glorious hair. Her hands caressed his pectorals. "Later, dear Tonee," she whispered, letting one blood-red fingernail trace a line from his sternum to his navel. He felt the cell whirl about him. She kissed him with lips that tasted of strawberries, and for one split second he believed she was his abandoned goblin wife and cried:

"Rowane, don't go!"

Then the illusion vanished and he uttered a sob of horror.

Standing over him, her head grazing the stone ceiling, was the appalling ogress official called the Dreadful Skathe. She grinned, showing a mouthful of tusks like crooked ivory daggers.

"Pretty good, was I?" She chucked Tony under the chin. Her fist was ham-sized, and the tickling finger had a talon that would have done credit to a firebacked eagle. "Let's see now," the monster mused. "I don't see any reason why we can't take you with us. We'll be traveling fast and light on this fucking royal mission, but you can ride pillion. We'll find our magic moment somewhere along the way."

For more than two sleepless days, the Firvulag heroes and their human superumerary traveled west, halting only to exchange ruined chalikos for fresh ones. The news of Nodonn's defeat reached them at Burask, and the original mission was aborted. Hoping to resume her interrupted experiment, Skathe booked an expensive suite at the best hotel in town, which had been the local pleasure dome when Burask belonged to the Tanu. But Tony only gave a woozy sneer when the houri reappeared, said, "Not bloody likely," and collapsed and slept like a dead man.

Skathe cursed human fragility roundly and reassumed her gigantic shape. There were ways to rouse Tony, and other droll experiments besides the amatory sort that he might be encouraged to participate in as a prelude to the ultimate diversion. But no sooner had the ogress begun to rehearse the possibilities than she felt her brain tingle. The fur-covered bed with Tony snoring on it wavered and grew dim, and a vision of Queen Ayfa of the Firvulag took its place.

Skathe, my Great Captain! came the farspoken voice of the Monarch.

"I am here, Your Appalling Highness."

Up to your old vulgar tricks, I see—while princes perish and worlds quake and omens and portents proliferate like hoobies in a mulch pile! Well, you can forget about playing games. Momentous deeds are pending—battles!—and you're going to be there.

"Your obedient vassal, Sovereign of the Heights and Depths."

That's better . . . I want you and the Worm to ride hell-for-leather to Bardelask. With Nodonn dead and the Trickster slightly the worse for wear, we have a perfect opportunity to launch a decisive assault. The town's well softened by raids and ripe for the kill. We've ordered Mimee of Famorel to march on it—and you and the Worm are to hightail it on down there and act as official observers. Sharn and I want an honest report, not one of the Birdbrain's usual self-serving pieces of bombastic bullshit. You know these male generals! Stuff their dispatches with endless accounts of glorious derring-do, and stint the casualty reports and unit efficiency ratings and loot inventories. This will be the first field action for the Famorel host in more than fifty years. They did well enough in the Last Grand Combat with the general staff keeping a close eye on them—but I want to be certain that they're fully committed to the new ways.

"Arms united, minds united!" Skathe interposed smartly, quoting the new Firvulag victory slogan.

Save that bumf for the troops—not that they'll need much encouragement, what with Bardelask's having the biggest brewery in the Many-Colored Land . . .

"Now that's what I call a strategic objective!"

You keep a clear head—and that goes for the Worm, too. Or else! Just remember that we'll be counting on Famorel to guard our south flank when we make our big move on Roniah next month. This Bardelask action is just a piddling little skirmish, but it's a perfect opportunity for performance evaluation. Do a good job. Once the battle's won and you've sent your reports in, I don't care how much beer guzzling or Lowlife futtering you do. Now get moving—and Slitsal!

The warrior-ogress saluted the fading vision. "Slitsal, High Queen!" Then she threw Tony over her shoulder and headed for the hotel stables.

Ten hours later, the two Great Captains of the Firvulag and their unconscious captive reached a certain derelict Tanu fort on the River Saône, after having been slowed only slightly by a thick fog that rolled in over the Côte d'Or. There, by prearrangement, they took delivery of a confiscated riverboat and its detorced human pilot. The Firvulag regulars who had seen to the procurement of the boat loaded the heroes' baggage while Tony stood groggily on the fort dock wondering where he was.

The boat's skipper, a homely beanpole of a woman, proved unexpectedly mettlesome in spite of her lost gray torc and the fact that both her ankles were chained to a twenty-seven-kilo anchor that she was obliged to hold in her arms. She spat at Krabee's spurred feet when he told her that she was to take them to Bardelask, and said, "Fat chance. Go take a flying fuck."

The Worm's ophidian eyes crinkled in good humor. "Don't be unreasonable, Lowlife. Your alternative is a melancholy one—a diving lesson with that large piece of polymer-clad lead preceding you to the bottom of the Saône."

"I might as well die now as later," she retorted. "Everyone knows what happens to humans captured by you fiends. Rape, dismemberment, and then watching bits of yourself being gobbled up before your dying eyes. No thanks, ogre. You can drown me now."

"You've listened to too many Tanu lies, dear," said Skathe.

She propelled Tony up the gangplank and eased him into a comfortable seat. "Ask this chap. Nobody's eaten *him*."

"Not yet," said the woman.

Tony snapped wide-awake.

Skathe croaked merrily. "Just propaganda. Fairy tales. My, what a lovely boat!"

Karbree drew himself up. His obsidian armor, inset with hundreds of green beryls and chased with gold, gleamed splendidly in the swirling mist. "Do you know who we are, Lowlife? Heroes of the Grand Combat! Peaceful emissaries of the Firvulag Court!"

"You're spooks, and spooks eat people," the skipper insisted. "At least, the giant ones do—and you qualify on that point with knobs on, big buddy."

Karbree smote his breastplate with a ringing clang. "On my honor as a member of the Gnomish Council—I, Karbree the Worm, swear that you will be unharmed if you cooperate! Pilot the three of us to Bardelask speedily, get us past the Tanu marine patrol at Roniah and through the four stretches of rapids, and we will set you free in your own boat when we arrive safe at our destination."

The baggage was all stowed and dwarf troopers stood ready at the bow and stern lines. Karbree smiled, held out a hand to the skipper, and said, "Let me carry your anchor into the wheelhouse."

The woman chewed her lower lip. "Well . . ."

"Such a well-kept craft," Skathe said. "She must be very fast. How long will it take for us to make the trip, dear?"

"I can get you to Bardy-Town inside of twenty-six hours. Less if this puke blows away and I can shoot the rapids at speed."

"Wonderful," said the ogress. "Let's be off."

"All right, it's a deal." The skipper marched up the gangplank with Karbree solicitously bearing the anchor, and a few minutes later they were on their way.

In the calm stretch of water below Roniah, when deepening night and the fog transformed the plass-roofed boat into a gently rocking womb, Tony dozed again and it seemed that the terrible creature who held him in thrall was not a Firvulag she-warrior at all, but his own Howler bride, Rowane.

"I didn't want to leave you," he mumbled. "It's just that I'm not too strong these days. If only they hadn't robbed me of my silver torc, it would have been all right. Forgive me for going away. Forgive me . . ."

She said, "But you didn't go, darling Tonee. You're right here with me. You don't have to be afraid. Just love me the way you used to do."

"I can't, without the torc. That's the trouble." But Rowane—or was it the scarlet-haired houri?—was tantalizingly insistent, and he was trying to remember a danger, and pushing at her, and thrashing about on some couch that was much too narrow, and when his sleep-drugged eyes opened and he finally saw—

"Aaugh!" he screamed, and threw a wild punch. He fell off the slippery leather couch and landed flat on his face. Fortunately, the deck of the pneumatic craft was quite resilient.

"Everything all right back there?" came the amused voice of Karbree from the forward cabin.

"No!" said Skathe. "Mind your own business, Worm."

The houri lifted Tony and sat him back on the couch. The only light was a greenish glow from some redundant instrumentation in the stern. This had the unfortunate effect of turning the succubus's hair from scarlet to muddy gray. Cuddling up to him, she began to kiss the angle of his jaw and stroke his spine.

He flinched. "Please don't. I'd like my clothes back."

Her fingernails nipped his earlobe. The kisses skittered down his chest like light-footed insects. "*I'd* like something else!"

But he was shivering and pulled away. "You have a lot to learn about human men. You really can't make me, you know. I have to be in the mood. Which at this moment I emphatically am not."

"Are you frightened, poor baby? There's no need to be. After our little experiment, I promise to let you go. Just . . . cooperate a little! Our people have always been very prejudiced against alliances with you humans. But lately there have been rumors—from the Howler women at Nionel who took human mates—that you were something special."

In spite of himself, Tony felt a prideful chauvinistic stirring. "There's a certain allure," he ventured primly, "in novelty."

"Exactly! So what's wrong? This body I'm wearing doesn't

appeal to you? Let me try another! You had a Howler wife, so I thought you'd go for something kinky. But I could be a human wench just as easily. Or... since you were a silver-torc, how about a domineering blonde with wraparound breasts—"

"*Please!*" Tony edged away.

The houri's expression became calculating. "What did you mean, about not being strong enough since you lost the torc? You're not burned out, are you?"

"Of course not! It's just—well, you see, when humans experience sex with you exotic women—that is, when we *have* the torc, most of us are able to carry on—uh—more efficiently. Whereas without it—and even with it, if one proves incompatible—I mean, there's a danger—a certain inhibiting factor takes over—"

"Ah-*ha!*" said Skathe.

There was a meditative silence. Feeling about in the dark, Tony found his pants and shirt. The houri made no move to stop him, and he gratefully slipped into his clothes, simultaneously slithering to the far end of the couch. The monster did not follow, but she never took her eyes off him.

Finally she said, "You have no significant metapsychic powers. Why did the Tanu give you a silver torc, then? For your prowess in the pleasure dome?"

Tony bridled. "Certainly not. I was a very important person in Finiah. As a metallurgical engineer, my professional skills were highly valued. I was in charge of the entire barium extraction operation."

"Interesting. That mine was our principal target, you know. Madame Guderian pointed out to us that without a barium supply, the Tanu were unable to manufacture new torcs."

Tony had the distinct feeling that he might have said too much. He hastened to add, "The mine's completely buried in lava, you know. Not the remotest chance of its ever being opened again. Not in a million years."

"Or six," said Skathe.

Tony kept very quiet. The houri's body was melting, lengthening. The Dreadful Skathe looked down at him and asked quietly, "Why did you come through the time-gate, Tony?"

"Well... it was very commonplace, really. My lover told me she was leaving me for another chap, my immediate superior. We three worked together in the same facility, you see, and there was no question of *their* leaving. The situation became quite unbearable."

"So you ran away."

"Actually, I tipped the pair of them into an eight-hundred-meganewton forging press."

The monster's eyes bugged. "Té's titties!"

"It passed as an accident at the time, but I knew that the Milieu's forensic redactors would catch up with me sooner or later. It seemed the sensible thing to leg it."

Skathe patted Tony on the head. "You know, I *like* you."

"Then why not turn me loose? I'm never going to be any good for your experiment. Aside from being scared to death of you, I'm so tired that I could sleep for a week, and devilishly hungry besides."

"Are you, by damn!" She exploded in great gusts of laughter that brought Karbree to the compartment door. "Sling that hamper of food and drink in here, Worm!" She tipped a wink to Tony. "After you've eaten, get some rest. Strap into one of the soft seats so you won't be bothered by the rapids. I've got business to attend to down in Bardelask, but when that's over— we'll see about letting you go."

Again, Tony dreamed. But this time it was about Finiah, flaming and devastated, with bodies heaped in the streets and Firvulag monstrosities gathering for their final assault on the palace gate, and Lord Velteyn and his Flying Hunt poised in the smoke, their brave battle cries ringing in his mind while he, Tony, hacked his way through a horde of Lowlife invaders, wielding an aquamarine sword.

But he hadn't.

Even as the dream scenario unfolded, Tony knew it for falsehood. He had never even suspected that Finiah was under attack until the ragtag Hidden Springs troops broke into the pleasure dome, dispatched his Tanu bedmate with an iron-studded mace, and hustled him off to judgment. Dream-Tony, defying his contradiction, fought on until the moment that the sleeper opened his eyes to reality—to lurid smoke clouds rolling above the boat's bubbletop roof, to martial shouts and screams faintly heard, to the unmistakable battle-reek that smote his nostrils and shocked him into alertness.

He was alone in the after cabin of the boat. It was moored in the midst of papyrus plants so tall and densely crowded that he could see no details of the region on either side. The view forward was less restricted and he could see a dock area with devastated buildings ablaze; and when the air cleared momentarily he caught sight of a Tanu citadel with scorched walls and broken towers and a single defiant blue beacon against the lowering sky. Pulses of multicolored lights sparked fitfully behind the fortress windows. There were random small explosions that uncannily resembled heavy-caliber rifle fire.

This, beyond a doubt, was Bardelask. And it seemed as though the battle was nearly over. *How long had he been asleep?*

Wondering if the monsters had abandoned him, he began to make his way forward. And then he heard indeterminate soft noises and muttered speech coming from up there, and a sudden burst of choked laughter. Tony stood stock-still.

"Marvelous. Terrific!" The voice was that of Karbree the Worm.

"No turn-on like a good bit of warfare," Skathe agreed. "Just enough to whet the old lower appetites."

Karbree giggled hideously. "Still say you should have taken yours, too. *Any* which way."

"My turn's coming, cockie. I have my own style."

"You watched me, I get to watch you. Fair's fair."

"Shares on your leftovers, then," Skathe demanded.

The Worm growled, then waxed jovial. "Oh, why the hell not? Here—try these toes." There came a distinct crunch.

Tony felt his guts transmute into a frigid lump. Fee fie . . . *Tanu lies!* . . . for fum . . . *propaganda, on my honor as a member of the Gnomish Council* . . .

Somebody emitted a colossal belch. Somebody else vented a replete sigh. The voices of the Firvulag seemed to recede to a great distance.

"Great little battle, all right," said Karbree. "Discipline in the ranks pretty well fell apart after the brewery was taken, but you can't expect miracles."

Skathe murmured assent. "I'll give old Mimee the Bird high marks for the main action, though. And I thought his special forces did particularly well, considering the small number of high-technology weapons we were able to send to Famorel."

A guffaw broke from the Worm. "And didn't the Exalted Lady Armida look surprised when Anduvor Doubletarse put that steel-jacketed bullet into her gizzard! Pity the body fell into the main fermentation vat. Contaminated the whole batch." The ogres chortled in reminiscence. There was a loud splash, followed by a number of small ones. Tidying up time, no doubt. Karbree uttered a huge yawn.

"Why not catch a little zizz?" Skathe said. "I've got a lot of female-type preliminaries I want to enjoy before getting around to my own main event. Tease my miminy-piminy poppet before letting him have his little souvenir of Bardelask. Keep him begging. Take my time in the buildup. But you'll be waked up when the real fun starts—no fear!"

Energized at last by sheer panic. Tony spun wildly about and staggered toward the stern. There was no way he could escape overboard. Abaft the wheelhouse, the boat was still securely roofed over, the plass panels held in place by stubborn little clips. To hide then . . . but the big deck hatches wouldn't budge, and the lockers were too small to hold him, and the pedestals of the benches were already stuffed with marine paraphernalia. It would be hopeless to hide in the head; the she-monster could rip the door off its hinges in an instant. There remained only the pile of baggage jumbled in the stern sheets— all manner of bags and pouches and dispatch boxes and map cases, most unstrapped and scattering their contents in a jumble on the deck. He could burrow into the heap and—

"Tonee, are you awake?"

He froze, partially concealed behind an enormous leather armor case. The houri came slinking along the passage. He saw her enter, sable-skinned, crowned with the flowing mane of luscious scarlet, holding something aloft in one hand, something that shone metallic by the light of the burning city.

"I've brought you a wonderful present, darling—just what you needed! We're going to have the greatest fun with my little experiment—"

She paused, frowning. "Tonee, are you going to be tiresome?"

He shrank down, tried in desperation to creep into the capacious leather box with its compartments and supportive loops, and then felt, held in a kind of open scabbard, something slender, hard, and longer than his arm. He drew it out, not believing his eyes. The monsters had carried other arms, of course, but this—

"Come out of there at once," she hissed, brandishing the gift angrily. Tony saw at last what it was.

A torc. But not one of silver. It was gold.

He peeked over the top of the armor case and grinned. "Just fooling, luv!" His hands, out of sight, fumbled inexpertly. But there had been that long-ago holiday on barbarous Assiniboia, and these classic pieces were all of a type, after all.

The Dreadful Skathe chuckled, pranced toward him in a parody of a nautch-dance, enticing as a black widow spider on the verge of its fatal embrace. Tony came slowly to his feet, keeping the thing pointed at the deck until the last possible moment. Then as she held the torc high and safe, he swept up the archaic Rigby .470 elephant rifle and shot her in the face.

The explosion and the fierce recoil sent him reeling. He saw the ogress fall with the rear half of her skull blown away and the bulkhead behind her suddenly turned to the color of her hair.

The other Firvulag came roaring down the passage, wearing his illusory guise of a limbless winged dragon with saucer-sized green eyes and fangs dripping venom. But the Rigby was a double-barreled weapon, and Karbree died as ignominiously as the female hero had done.

Like a man still spellbound, Tony picked up the golden torc and fastened it about his neck. He said to himself, "Rowane."

And then he heard the hissing and gurgling and realized he had not got off scot-free after all. There was a price to be paid when one banged about on a pneumatic boat with a high-powered rifle—but it was, under the circumstances, reasonable enough.

6

THE PROTECTIVE SPHERE OF PSYCHOCREATIVE FORCE CARRYING
the King and the chemist hung poised above the foamy mass
that had surged out of the subterranean storage area and partially
filled the stairwell. Embedded in the goop were countless plass-
sheathed packages and container pods.

"Rather like a devil's Nesselrode pudding," the chemist
observed. At his silver-torc initiation, the Tanu had dubbed
him Wex-Velitokal, which was only slightly less ungainly than
his original name of Ethelbert Anketell Milledge-Wexler; but
the exotic penchant for nicknames having come to the rescue,
he was now known to one and all as Bert Candyman, and had
so introduced himself to the King without the slightest trace of
embarrassment.

"Queen Mercy-Rosmar made this mess out of the wall in-
sulation," Aiken said. "Her purpose was to prevent me from
using any of these weapons or other contraband Milieu equipment against Nodonn and his invaders—but not to ruin the
matériel beyond retrieval. She succeeded very well in the first
instance. The bubbles of that sticky foam are filled with poison
gas. Any ordinary human poking around in it is an instant

goner. A Tanu unshielded by creativity becomes a candidate for six weeks in Skin."

"Can you filch a sample for me and pop it into here?" Bert Candyman held out a device about the size of a pocket AV recorder, with a tiny hopper open at the top. "This will analyze the constituents for us in half a sec."

Aiken nodded. A small bubble materialized above the deadly suds and scooped up a portion. It oozed through the superficies of the greater sphere enveloping the two men and disappeared into the analyzer. Bert snapped the hopper shut and studied the diminutive visual display.

"Beastly ingenious, Her Late Majesty. She simply unzipped a fairly standard polyurethane molecule. Broke up the original insulating material into its constituent tolylene diisocyanate and poly(oxypropylene)triol. She heated this foul glop and injected groundwater from the castle sumps, then diddled around a bit further with the isocyanate to generate the hydrogen cyanide gas."

"How do we get rid of it?"

"Well, a talented metapsychic creator might simply reverse the process—"

The King's face was expressionless. "How *else*?"

"The likeliest solvent would be acetone. Effective, and harmless to the fluorocarbon thermoplastic of the equipment wrappings. I don't suppose you have a few thousand liters stashed away somewhere?"

Aiken laughed bitterly. "There's probably a gadget buried down there that would make as much as we need in five minutes—if we could only identify it. But the Queen destroyed the inventory-control computer, so it's all one big high-tech grab bag now. I probably wouldn't know an acetone cooker from a robot bartender if you set the two pods in front of me."

"Ah. Well! We can make acetone from scratch, too, of course. Not particularly difficult. Hardly on a par with my last project—perfecting a pickling process that would yield a pecan flavor in the walnuts we utilize in the brandied buttercream chocolates—"

Aiken blinked. The chemist broke off his genial digression as though a bullwhip had been snapped in front of his face.

"You make pyroligneous acid from hog-fuel—hardwood chips, that is. Treat it with quicklime. Your stonemasons should

have plenty of that on hand. Then distill the slurry to make
calcium acetate. A modicium of further heating yields the acetone by fractional distillation. A straightforward industrial operation."

The two of them were wafting upward. "How long to make
what we'll need?" Aiken asked. Their feet touched stone and
the sphere of mental force flattened as it pushed the invisible
gas away from the tightly closed door.

"Give me carte blanche on supplies and personnel, and I'll
have the solvent ready in three weeks. The actual decontami-
nation operation may take longer unless you have protective
clothing with oxygen apparatus for the workers. The acetone
wash will remove the foam, but there's still the cyanide to
contend with."

The small man in the golden leather storm-suit and the
chemist dressed in the elegant turquoise robes of the Creator
Guild emerged into the safe atmosphere of the castle's grand
foyer. The door to the deadly storage area clanged shut.

"You're not thinking like a metapsychic, Candyman," the
King chided, "but that's not surprising, since your own talents
run more to the intellectual than the physical." They walked
rapidly down a corridor, and Aiken continued. "You will have
at your service—and I mean, prepared to do whatever dirty
work this dirty job requires—a cadre of very special assistants.
They'll use their mindpower to build your apparatus, to prepare
the raw materials, to expedite things in whatever manner you
command. They'll protect themselves mentally while they swab
down the contaminated stuff—pod by pod, package by package—so you needn't worry about safety gear. They can protect
you as well as themselves. What's more, they'll work without
sleeping for a week. It's easy, if you're a Tanu stalwart."

Aiken opened the door to a small antechamber. Several
dozen Tanu wearing knightly mufti waited there. As the King
entered they rose and placed right hands to their golden torcs
in the gesture of fealty. Their protective mental barriers were
down. All of them were either creators or psychokinetics, and
their status was such that the human chemist stepped back,
overawed, and would have abased himself in the customary
manner of silver-torcs if the King had not subliminally restrained him.

A slight smile twitched at the King's lips as he made introductions. "Here are Kuhal Earthshaker and Celadeyr of Afaliah and certain of their followers. They'll be your principal helpers on the job, but you can have as many others in addition as you might require."

Bert Candyman could only nod wordlessly as the former High Table members and the other noble Tanu made humble mental obeisance to him. And then the King seemed to look into his soul with devouring black eyes, and the torc at his throat warmed and *changed*—and by the mind-whispers of the exotics Bert knew that it had become free gold.

Aiken said, "You have seven days to produce that solvent and decontaminate the Milieu weapons and the other matériel. Work as though the fate of the Many-Colored Land depended upon you."

"Does it?" the shaken chemist asked, and the perplexed Tanu minds seemed to echo the question, and ready scores of others.

But those hot eyes held a warning, and the Tanu hesitated, and a moment later the King was gone.

AIKEN: Ochal! How goes it?

OCHAL THE HARPER: Well enough, High King. We of the vanguard are just crossing the River Galegaar, and we'll reach Calamosk shortly. There we will remount for the final sprint. We should arrive in Afaliah less than ten hours from now.

AIKEN: Kaleidoscopic. Your advance party should get there handily before the North Americans . . . But here's the bad news. They had a stiff tailwind on the New Sea yesterday, and Morna-Ia farsighted Hagen's ATVs approaching the Neck of Aven just before midnight.

OCHAL: Tana's teeth, what rotten luck! The supply wagons and the bulk of our forces can't get to Afaliah until more than forty hours after us. If the futuristic vehicles of the North Americans make a dash for the city up the Old Aven Road, we're for it!

AIKEN: Quite possibly. I don't think we can trust Cloud Remillard to honor her promise—not if she's backed up by her brother and his bunch, armed to the teeth with Milieu weapons. *She* says this crew of junior rebels has no ambition to take over the Many-Colored Land, but there's no way I can get the truth of it until I brain-ream the lot of them in person.

OCHAL: What shall we do then, High King?

AIKEN: Your advance party is too small and too lightly armed to risk attempting a stand in Afaliah. Carry on as we planned—be the courtly diplomatist until Cloud takes you to meet Wimborne and the other prisoners. Then spring it on her that you're taking them to Calamosk—and run. Without her brother to back her up, and with Kuhal Earthshaker still in my hands, Cloud won't dare use her aggressive redaction on you.

OCHAL: You will have the reinforcements meet us in Calamosk?

AIKEN: I think the timing will jibe. It's quite likely that Hagen Remillard will be tempted to follow you, and I don't doubt that he has the firepower advantage. But my guess is that these North American kids will recognize the stalemate and hold back, rather than risk killing the Wimborne group in an all-out blitz on Calamosk. That'll be my cue to talk sweet reason with 'em!

OCHAL: You will bring your Flying Hunt to Koneyn, High King?

AIKEN: In time. But count on seeing Me in Calamosk in two or three days! Just remember that I'm relying on you, Harper. *Don't let anything happen to Basil's Bastards.*

SHARN!

Aikenladdiebuck! How YOU? Longtimenothink! Bloodybleatingbastard whatfuck BARDELASK?

Nownownownow . . . MimeeFamorelViceroy ownhook distantHighVrazel beyondMycontrol Armisticeviolator let oldgrievance vs. ArmidaFormidable(maysherestGoddesspeaceful) overrule royalpolicy just wait till Ayfa&I gethold MimeeBirdbrainhotspur—

BAT SHIT.

Aiken! Lad! You don't seriously think We'd encourage lawless excusions against You? Breaking Our Royal Word?

Bet yourballs I do.

. . .I swear on My Honor as Monarch of the Heights and Depths Father of All Firvulag—

Put a bung in it! I know verywell what yourword worth given humanbeing. [Colorful obscene image.] And don't

think not wise to stunt you pulled fingering Low-
lives&aircraft for Nodonn!

>Well ladomyheart there you got me cold . . . I was tempted
beyondstrength thoughtofSWORD fell like ripepompel-
mous into fiendBattlemastertrap—

Morelikely wholething youridea. Well you backed wrong-
starter KingScorpionGlitterguts and screwed self royally! I
had planned nicefriendly surprise GrandTourney but now—

>No! You *didn't*! O Té damme to uttermostchasm!

—now I'll be drawn&quartered&liverfriedwithonions before I let you get perfidioushooks on Sword.

>Lad . . . KingAikenLugonn . . . BrotherSovereign . . . it was
just a terrible MISUNDERSTANDING.

[Pitying laughter.]

>No really! I'll prove it! Force Mimee withdraw Barde-
lask—

Dammit Sharn RoyalAssholeness place smoking *ruin* Ar-
mida&knights *dead* whatflaminggood withdrawal?

>Well . . . reparations then.

Roniah.

>?

Roniah soddinghypocrite. Call it off.

>??

Abort your planned strike against Roniah with High-
Vrazelregulars scheduled lastweek September.

>As Té is my Witness—

OKAY THE HUNT FLIES TONIGHT.

>No wait I'll check perhaps Medor or Betularn or Fafnor
conspired circumvent authority—

Save yourdamnface anywhichway but hands *off* Roniah!

>Checko. You just rest easy.

[Pained laughter.]

>??? (!) Aiken we can be friends. ManyColoredLand big-
enough for all. And about the Sword . . . You know it's
sacred to mypeople. It belonged myown sainted great-
greatgrandsire SharnAtrocious. Give it back to us Aiken.
We'll keep the peace. I *swear*.

No finaldecision until postTourney. Consider Sword security goodbehavior.

>Agreed! I knew you'd be reasonable lad! I'll use your-

promise Swordgift keep hotheads inline let 'em save
energy for Tourney! Great idea! Wait till you see wonderful SingingStone—
[Weariness.] Good night Sharn.
Good night Aiken.

Good night . . .
For the first time in nearly a week, Aiken came to the royal
apartments.

The golden doors were back on their hinges and there remained no traces of the damage done by the invaders. He had
commanded that all things that had belonged to Queen Mercy-
Rosmar should be removed. And now as he passed through
the silent sitting room with its balcony overlooking the moonlit
sea, he noted that certain paintings and pieces of sculpture and
potted plants were gone, and the loom where she had woven
soft shawls from the wool of the sheep she herself had brought
to the Pliocene, and the water dish of her great white dog, and
the carved cabinet with the stoppered flasks of special herbs,
and a certain blue rug, and the embroidered cushions from the
rattan lounge seats. In her dressing room the closets gaped open
and empty. The vases held no flowers. Her jewel cases were
gone, and the cosmetics, and even the scent of her perfume.
Her chaise with its Milieu-style reading lamp had been removed, and the cases with her page-books and plaques and the
audiovisual recordings of the medieval pageants and the operas
and the plays and the travelogs of Old Earth that she had shared
with him, a callow boy from a colonial planet, on the nights
last winter when the rains lashed the Castle of Glass and they
planned together how he would seize the throne . . .

She was gone. She remained. And the other as well.

Standing there in the empty dressing room he seemed surrounded by leftover laughter. He burned. His brain and his
body seemed hideously swollen, straining the seams of the
golden storm-suit he had insisted on wearing even when the
Summer Fog was long gone. He found himself saying: If only
you'd loved me! Or if I hadn't! And remembering: "When I'm
gone, you'll find no other. Fatal Fool! How will you do it,
Amadán-na-Briona?"

He had done it as his instincts drove him, taking both of
them in a rage of fear and envy and terrible love, gorging

himself on the coveted power, the vitality.

It was the only way, his mind screamed.

He found himself standing in the royal bath, reflected in the mirrored walls, a manikin in shining gold leather, reduplicated to infinity. He put both hands to his ears, pressing the stormsuit's hood tightly against his skull with all his superhuman strength. The coarser agony swamped anguish. He cried, "You belong to Me!"

And it was all right.

One little man staring at himself in a jeweled mirror. The familiar onxy-and-gold bathroom, with the small fountain playing in the cool end of the great sunken tub and the warm end steaming invitingly. Baskets of heavy-scented yellow orchids. A lumpish moon spying on him through the glazed skylight. Piles of purple towels and his yellow-silk dressing gown and amethyst-studded espadrilles. A pitcher of iced mead and a crystal tumbler, just as his telepathic orders to the silver domestics had specified.

It was all right.

He studied his reflected face, pale and woeful in the crested hood. The lips were tight-shut in reaction to his involuntary shout, the nose cruelly sharpened. He had thought that the fever would manifest itself physically. He had worn the tough gilded hide of the storm-suit to conceal his condition from the others: the gross swelling, the incandescence. He knew that when he took the suit off, the consequences of his gluttony and lust would be shamefully manifest.

But it seemed to be all right.

He unfastened the hood, pulled it away. His head was sweatplastered, the dark auburn hair almost as black as his eyes. He kicked off the boots, opened the wrists and ankles, threw away the belt, finally unzipped the suit from throat to crotch and stepped out of it. His body was wiry, corded with muscle, scantily haired. There were faint pressure marks from the seams of the tight suit, but otherwise he was ordinary, and quiescent. What he had been so afraid of finding was gone. If it had ever existed.

He gave a great shout of laughter and dived into the steaming pool.

It *was* all right.

* * *

Later, as he sat on the balcony drinking mead and watching the owls, Olone came. She was as tall as a young tree, with blonde hair floating loose in the sea breeze, and she sent tentative coercive emanations stealing into his mind, feather-touching the erotic triggers.

"No," he told her.

"I'm sorry, my King." She was wearing a translucent gown without a sash that fell from her shoulders like silvery water. "I only thought to help you in your need."

"And what else?" he inquired softly. His own coercive-redactive probe went into her so subtly that she was without suspicion, intent on her artless maneuvering.

"I wanted to tell you how glad I am. That you won. That both of the traitors are dead—and Tonn with them! I am yours forever if you want me."

Aiken laughed very gently.

She stood proud before him, one hand resting on her abdomen. "And I have conceived your child."

"So have sixty-seven other Tanu women. I'm the King."

"I thought you'd be pleased!" she cried.

He sipped his drink, gaze veiled, mind inspecting her proud young ego. "I know what you thought, Oly. What you *think*. When I believed that Mercy was dead, when I was drained and weakened after the fight with Felice, you gave me great comfort and helped heal me. I'm grateful for that, and I'm happy that you carry one of my sons. But don't ever think you can manipulate Me, Coercive Sister."

Frantic mental walls crashed into place. She backed toward the balcony door. "My King, forgive me—"

"Poor Oly. Your ambition is a futile one, and mortally dangerous. I've had enough of queens for now."

"I—I was foolish and presumptuous. Don't hurt me!"

He was reassuring. "Not if you accept that I've changed."

She hesitated. Her fear dissipated and her aspect softened as she realized that he was not angry but amused, and sad. "Shall I leave Goriah, then?"

"Of course not. And just because we don't share a bed, don't think that I've lost my fondness for you. You're a marvelous randy Tanu lass, and we'll share sweet houghmagandy anon. But not now. You can give us a wee kiss, though!"

She burst out laughing and flew to him, and kissed him first

with caution and then with full passion. And he held her lightly
as she surrendered to ecstatic relief, and her mind confessed,
and he forgave. Later, she sat on the floor at his feet and said,
"Is it true? That you've swallowed the minds of Nodonn and
the Queen in the manner of the legendary heroes of our lost
Duat world? And if you bedded me now, with the conquering
fire still investing your mind, then I'd be taken, too?"

He tried to explain. "Elizabeth says that what I did—and
you must believe that it was done without my conscious volition—was to subsume the metapsychic attributes of Mercy
and Nodonn. I know nothing about your Duat legends. I certainly didn't eat two people alive, and I didn't drain their souls
and imprison them inside my head—"

"—even though you were afraid that you had," Olone whispered.

"Dear Oly. You're nobody's fool. Is my royal indisposition
the talk of the castle?"

"We know that you do not sleep. That you are deeply troubled."

"Don't you think I have reason to be? You know how the
Firvulag have broken the peace accords."

"Will there be war?" She had both hands clenched tightly
against her belly.

"If there's a war, I'll win it."

Her eagerness was desperate. "Has—has the subsumption
made you very strong, then? So strong that Sharn and Ayfa
will not dare to come against us?"

Had it? Would the stolen powers be his to use?

Aye, there was the rub! Not yet, that was certain. The
subsumption had been an appalling trauma; he had not dared
to reveal the full extent of his dysfunction to anyone except
Elizabeth. Only she knew that he was able to perform only the
simplest metapsychic operations with reliable competence—
that he was barely able to fly, that he could not begin to generate
the psychokinetic power needed to lift his 400 mounted Hunt
knights, that he could no longer conjure up mighty bolts of
mental energy or create a laser-deflecting mindscreen. The new
powers he had taken over from Nodonn and Mercy were there
inside him, crowding and disrupting his own metafunctions.
But he was unable to energize them efficiently. The existing
neural pathways were inadequate. He would have to form new

ones capable of bearing the increased load, just as he had modified other aspects of his cortical operation after the Felice affair, incorporating the metaconcert program and the novel techniques for aggression vouchsafed him by Abaddon. That had taken time. So would the fullness of the subsumption—if he did not go mad in the process, as Elizabeth had warned he might. In the meantime, he would have to bluff and stall and cajole and bamboozle. And hold fast to the Milieu armaments and seize those ancient flying machines that Basil Wimborne and his crew had hidden away in the Alps—

"I will never reveal your secret, my King. Rely on me."

"What?" Lost in his reverie, he had forgotten Olone and her question, secure (he thought) behind the mental defenses that still retained most of their old effectiveness. But she had risen and stood now before him, respiring compassion.

"I will never tell."

She had guessed. Sensitive and anxious for their unborn child, clever and self-serving and fearful and thoroughly in love with him, Olone knew.

"Aiken, it's all right. You'll find a way. You must. You're our King."

"Yes," he said desolately, and leaned back in the chair, and closed his eyes and his mind, and waited until she went away.

Still later, he paced along the parapet, moving from block to block of the castle, up the towers and across the flying bridges and in and out of the partially repaired bastions—dark now, with the periodic lights-out in effect. He greeted the night watch as he prowled, and they reassured him that all was well. With the inner demons coming alive in the predawn hours, he went up into the great broken spire where the beacon had shone, where he and Mercy had watched the meteors, in order to check the rebuilding job. The workers had reached the penultimate landing and would be topping off within another day or two. He stood on the new floor of dusty glass blocks with the wind whipping his silk robe and humming through the narrow embrasures. A large chunk of the western wall was still out and he had a stunning view over the Strait of Redon.

What was *he* up to these days?

Had he set sail yet?

"And can I farsense you?" Aiken inquired softly. He could mindspeak well enough over several hundred kilometers, and this morning he had viewed the devastation of Bardelask quite clearly. Farsensing, unlike the "muscle" metafaculties, was more a matter of adroitness than strength. It even had its own auxiliary neural circuitry integrating it with the physical senses, and this was much less vulnerable than the faculties that functioned holographically.

Why not give it a shot? It was night, the optimal time for a long-distance effort, and he sure as hell knew the mental signature!

He would simply observe. Not attempt communication.

Leaning against the half-finished wall, he put his head into an embrasure that would provide the proper inclination. Then he relaxed, let his mental vision range out, following the curvature of Pliocene Earth, skimming lightly over the unobstructive Atlantic waters on wide beam. Lightly . . . lightly . . . diffused and soft, minimally powered, skating above incipient pain . . . range . . . range . . . range.

Ha. North America.

Now, very charily, close her up. Narrow the beam. Sweep southward along the teeming lagoons of Georgia, cross Apalachee Channel, and find Ocala Island. See its dots of human life-aura. And the *one* . . .

Pain. But concentrate the beam anyhow, scanning the south end of the island and the big bay that Cloud Remillard had said was shielded from the worst of the hurricane winds by the scattered atolls of the Still-Vexed Bermoothes. There they would moor the boat.

Severe pain. The big four-masted schooner Kyllikki, trig and handy and utilitarian. Deep in the water. Loaded. Elizabeth had said that they put a sigma-field umbrella over her at quayside, but there was none now. She rode at anchor in forty meters of salt water, and no portable sigma could overcome such a power drain.

Excruciating pain. Now seek him out. All the ex-Rebels were on that ship, waiting for dawn. He was sitting alone on the afterdeck under the midnight sky, wearing stagged white dungarees and a black singlet.

Marc Remillard smiled at Aiken Drum. The vision of him was dim, minuscule. But his voice sounded as though he was there on the windy tower in Goriah.

"As you can see, we're ready to sail. It's quite a wrench, after more than twenty-seven years. Some of us were very reluctant to leave here."

Then why?

"Ah, I quite forgot!" The smile widened. "You don't really have the full picture, do you? What our errant children told you ... well, we must make allowances. But it's time you knew the truth, King Aiken-Lugonn. My son Hagen and daughter Cloud and the rest of their contemporaries have come to Europe with only one objective. To reopen the time-gate. From the Pliocene side."

Not possible!

Marc's laugh was rueful. "From my point of view, I could hope you were right. But I'm afraid that it's quite possible—given the construction of a very intricate piece of apparatus. Our rebellious young took with them complete schematics for the Guderian device, together with certain manufacturing equipment and what specialized components they could find here. They hope to prevail on you to provide Milieu-trained technicians and raw materials, as well as access to the time-gate site. For my part, I would suggest that you hold off giving them your whole-hearted cooperation until you consider the consequences most carefully."

Open ... gate ... RETURN ...

"The children hope, as they quaintly put it, to 'return home' to the Milieu. You can imagine my own thoughts on this subject."

The sun was hovering just below the eastern hills of Armorica. Its plasma-generated roar filled the aether, making farsensed concentration hideously painful to Aiken's mind. The gulf was widening, the vision fading beyond recall. He heard the voice clearly until the end, however:

"Think about it, Aiken. An open time-gate leading back to the Galactic Milieu—and, of course, its concomitant: the reopening of the original gate leading from the Milieu to the Pliocene. Do you want that, King Aiken-Lugonn? Do *you* want to go home again?"

The wind whistled about the broken tower. Aiken's head

throbbed as though it would burst. Blinded, he slid to his knees and pressed his forehead against the cool glass blocks.

When the sun was full up and he heard the voices of the approaching workers on the staircase below, he pulled himself together. A saving cloak of invisibility was still within his powers. He conjured the illusion and slipped back into his own apartments. There he went to the closet where his old suit of many pockets hung. He opened the compartment below the right knee and took out a book-plaque that he had stowed away in there one year and one week ago. It was entitled

THE GUDERIAN TAU-FIELD GENERATOR
Theory and Practical Application

"Do I want to go home?" he asked himself.

He sat down on the edge of the big round bed in the morning sun and began reading page one.

7

IT WAS NOT SO MUCH THE GIANT SPIDERS THEMSELVES AS THEIR feeding habits that finally caused Mr. Betsy to crack.

On the ninth day of their incarceration in the communal cell, he awoke to the all too familiar tickle of one of the things running over his hand. He mewled in revulsion and pulled himself up in his straw nest, patting his wig back into place—and then spotted the odious creature still lurking not half a meter away, close by the snoring medievalist, Dougal. The spider saw Betsy, too, for it reared up, twiddled its pedipalps with conspicuous insolence, and emitted a crackling purr. It was coal-black and hairy and had a body the size of a peach.

"Disgusting brute!" Betsy hissed. He adjusted his crumpled ruff. Dawnlight from the slot-window overlooking the gorge weakly illuminated the dungeon's squalor. All about lay the hunched or sprawled forms of that little band of technicians, pilots, and adventurers known as Basil's Bastards, betrayed into the hands of Nodonn Battlemaster by a mysterious operant woman, robbed of the aircraft that were to have insured the freedom of Lowlife humanity. Basil himself had been removed from the cell days ago, presumably to be sent to the torturers.

Keeping a wary eye on the spider, Betsy bent to untie the scarf that bound his farthingale skirts tightly about his ankles. He had learnt to sleep that way early on, since the cell was alive with mice, the legitimate prey of the giant spiders. Betsy was well aware—as had been generations of full-skirted women before him—of the havoc the little mammals could wreak if they ran up your legs. Perhaps he should have welcomed the presence of the spiders, for the mice bit and the spiders didn't; but instead he loathed them. They were too calculating, too agile in pursuit of their victims, and the mice screeched in such a heart-rending fashion when they were caught and whisked away to the lairs up in the dungeon ceiling. After the predators had drunk their fill of rodent bodily fluids, they dropped sad little web-wrapped carcasses on the prisoners below.

Betsy, with his elaborate Elizabethan costume, was by far the most vulnerable target.

And now *this* spider had the temerity to challenge him! He threw a few bits of straw at it but it refused to retreat, standing its ground near Dougal's bandaged ginger head. Betsy felt about in the heavy shadows for a more substantial missile, but there was nothing handy. The spider waved its legs mockingly. With some effort, Betsy struggled to stand upright, and then saw to his dismay that there was a long tear all along the side of the hoopskirt, exposing the frame. Muttering darkly, he shook the costume to settle it into place.

Three packaged mouse bodies dropped out of his petticoats into the straw.

"You—you ugly *monster*!" the former rhocraft engineer shrieked. He tore off a red-heeled brocade slipper and pitched it overhand with all his strength. It missed the spider, which sprang onto Dougal's face. The husky medievalist opened his eyes and screamed blue murder, whacking at his beard with open hands and kicking the straw in all directions. "Away, you scullion, you rampallion, you fustilarian! *Aaach*—the whoreson's fanged me!"

The other twenty prisoners were coming awake in varying degrees of alertness. As they tumbled from their pallets they disturbed other questing arachnids, and it seemed as if the dungeon was suddenly alive with the scuttling things. They ran about like the disembodied hands of black demons, and wild-eyed Dougal in his fake chainmail howled and sucked one thumb and crashed to the floor with a doleful cry. "Then, venom, to thy . . . work," he whispered. His eyes closed.

"Bloody hell!" exclaimed the appalled Betsy. The medievalist writhed slightly.

"It got Dougal!" Clifford gasped. He pointed a trembling finger at the surgeon, Magnus Bell. "And you said they were harmless . . ."

"But they are," Bell protested. He had knelt to take the medievalist's pulse. "He's only hysterical."

All around them, the walls and floor seemed to crawl. But it was a tangible enemy at last, not a mysterious human woman who tricked and mind-blasted them, who clamped the gray torcs of slavery around their necks and threw them into a Tanu dungeon.

Phronsie Gillis' clarion contralto rang out. "What're we waiting for, mates? Let's *get* the mothers!"

Basil's Bastards were galvanized. They locked on to the target and roared into a counterattack. Betsy wielded his slipper. Phronsie and Ookpik and Taffy Evans and Nirupam slammed at the spiders with loose boots, wooden cups, and plates. Farhat and Pongo Warburton stomped. Bengt hammered the creatures with his bare fists. The zany technician Cisco Briscoe snapped his belt like a whip, to sick-making effect. They cursed, whooped, chased, and tripped over one another, all the while taking a fearful toll of invertebrate life. Only a handful of the Bastards were noncombatants: Miss Wang cowered against one wall, trying not to throw up; Philippe the ultrafastidious curled his lip and stood aloof; and the Tibetan physician Thongsa piped out futile admonitions:

"I beg of you! Stop! Have respect! The life-form is physically unprepossessing, but it serves a useful purpose in the local ecology!"

"Bugger the ecology," croaked Stan Dziekonski, who had captained a dreadnought in the Metapsychic Rebellion. He jumped on a spider with both feet.

Dimitri Anastos knelt beside Magnus, holding the water bucket while the medic swabbed Dougal's bite. "You're sure he's not dying?"

"Aslan!" groaned the knight. "Shall I abide in this dull world, which in thy absence is no better than a sty?"

"Take it easy, big fella," Magnus said. "You'll live, all right."

"Kill!" Mr. Betsy smote the arachnid foe right and left, using his ichor-smeared slipper. "Kill!"

The dungeon door clanked, squalled, and flew open with a resounding crash. Six gold-torc human troopers armed with Husqvarna stun-guns marched in, followed by a brilliantly glowing Tanu farsensor knight whose glass cuirass was emblazoned with a harp motif. In the corridor brandishing naked swords were other stalwarts who shone coercer blue and psychokinetic rose-gold, as well as more nonoperant humans carrying Milieu weapons.

The farsensor lifted a commanding hand. Constrained by their gray torcs, Basil's Bastards were instantly mute and submissive.

The Tanu smiled on them. "I am Ochal the Harper, and I bring you greetings and affirmations of goodwill from King Aiken-Lugonn. Rejoice—for your unjust imprisonment is at an end! We are here to take you away from this place and transport you with the utmost speed to Calamosk, where the King himself will meet with you. Follow us now to the courtyard, where your leader, Basil Wimborne, awaits you." He turned and left the cell.

Their minds released, the Bastards looked at one another in numb disbelief. One of the Husky-toting troopers cocked a thumb. "Come on, hop it! Or we might *all* end up in the soup."

The Bastards began to laugh. They put on their footgear, gathered up their meager possessions, and began to file out, the able-bodied assisting the halt. Betsy was the last to leave, having wiped his slippers as well as he could on the straw and resettled his bedraggled wig. Two troopers of the rear guard stood on either side of the dungeon door, grinning, and presented arms as the reincarnation of Good Queen Bess the First swept grandly past.

The door swung shut. When the metallic boom had died away the great cell was utterly silent. Among the welter of black bodies in the straw a few kicked brokenly, then were still.

After a time the mice crept out and discovered that the Jubilee was upon them.

* * *

It was a dream, Hagen Remillard told himself. It had to be a dream...

The linked ATVs bobbed at anchor in the Mediterranean shallows south of Aven's neck, waiting for first light and the land race to Afaliah. Hagen had taken the night watch, sure that he wouldn't sleep after his sister told him of the gold-torc force that would certainly arrive at the citadel ahead of him. Would this advance guard of the Nonborn King present him with some impossible ultimatum? Would it threaten the captive pilots and technicians who might be so crucial to his plans?

Brooding over the contingencies kept Hagen alert throughout most of the night. But around the dead hour, 0400, when human vital energies burn lowest with the depletion of blood sugar, even a metapsychic tended to falter. The mind's eye glazed and looked inward to a world of shadows, to memories and fearful imaginings concretized in nightmare...

Trudi takes his hand and leads him along an unfamiliar path to a place where the soil is churned and raw and a new building thrusts up huge against the morning sky, sparkling and humming. He begins to whimper as they go inside and the terrible ineffabilities threaten (he is only three and his metapsychic receptors are untrained and clumsy), and the nurse says, "Hush. It's all right. We must say 'Welcome back' to Papa."

They walk on a strange slick floor into dim coolness, and grownups crowd tall about him, ignoring his weak telepathic queries, mind-whispering of matters incomprehensible:

Starsearch... Lylmik? ... MADNESS! ... Goddam he did it!

1700 lightyear scan first try!
And back with brains nonfried—

Can't believe he got rig work bloodyjungle.
NevergetMEusefuckinghellrigMarcMad2yearsrecover nowstartallover—

Get that imbecile out of here.
But how long a starsearch?
MADNESS! MADNESS!

We've got nothing but time sweetheart.
6,000,000 friggerty years.
It'll work... starsearch... rescue us! ... new beginning...

coadunation . . . coerce them or appeal altruismethic . . .
 MADNESS!

   Mental Man . . . we still may know Him!
The kid you booby.
   Oh . . .

    Let Hagen upfront to see.
    Let him see!
    Let him see!

MADNESS! LET THE CHILD SEE THE MADNESS THAT
BROUGHT US TO THIS EXILE! LET HIM SEE HIS OWN
FUTURE . . .

It was only a dream. A dream of an enormous captive thing,
a brain shucked from its body. Glad to be! Energized artificially, scorning true Unity, glorying in loneness.

In the dream, Trudi lifted him to see the thing, and said,
"It's your Papa." The three-year-old boy screamed and tried
to run away.

Only a dream. That was why he didn't try to run now as
he saw the thing again, outside the cockpit windscreen of the
modular combine. It seemed to be resting on the impeller access
hatch, between the twin housings of the sonic disruptors. A
hulking form, dully gleaming, having the rough shape of a
man. Power-cables and armored horses sprouted from its blind
head and melted into the graying sky.

In his dream, Hagen arose from his seat at the navigation
console, opened the cockpit door, and stepped outside. He
seemed to float toward the phantom CE rig on the foredeck,
and as he approached, it became transparent, and the operator
in his pressure-envelope coverall extended his arms, bending
down, and smiled at the frightened three-year-old.

"It's only me. It's only Papa."

But he held back, knowing he could not risk the embrace,
even in the dream aware that the real body of a man wearing
that armor would be refrigerated to a point near absolute zero,
almost completely divorced from the transcendent brain.

"I think I finally understand," Hagen said. "Jack was your
model. It wasn't possible for you to permanently modify yourself. You were too old for a successful adaptation. But you
were determined to be more than Mental Man's brother."

"I would have been his father," Marc said. "And I would

have lived content, seeing you and the others command the stars I gave you."

"No longer human."

"You would never have remembered."

"Go away!" the three-year-old cried. "Don't touch me. Don't look at me!" The nurse held him and stopped him from running away, but he buried his face in her long skirt and wept, refusing to look again at his father. The others mind-whispered, and then the walls closed gently about him, and he was lifted and carried away . . .

He woke standing on the empty foredeck in the dawn breeze, and went to look at the hatch where the illusion had stood. There were two great circular indentations in the plass, as if it had supported a tremendous weight.

Yosh wedged his face more firmly into the hooded viewer of the infrared spotterscope and said, "Now we're finally cooking." Servo motors whined and the machine and its operator spun slowly in a 360-degree scan. "Terrific. Perfect emplacement, up here in the beacon tower. Must have a coarse range of seventy, eighty kloms, Calamosk being on a hill. Nearly halfway to Afaliah clearview-wise before we smack into those hills the other side of the Opaar. Oh, this baby was made for steppes."

"How she do on the fine-tune, chief?" inquired Sunny Jim. He and Vilkas were sitting in the shade and drinking beer after having spent a sweaty two hours deploying the solar-collection panels of the power supply.

"Working," Yosh muttered. "Yes, here we go, sauntering down the Great South Road at . . . four-one-three-one-two-pip-six-one, a herd of hippies, taking to the freeway, the lazy scuts. Good thing this Pliocene doesn't run to high-speed surface transit. You'd need HIPPARION CROSSING warning signs every fifty meters."

Vilkas set down his big covered stein, wiped his moustache with the back of his hand, and sighed in a martyred fashion. "Will we have to hook up the remote right away, or can it wait until after chow?"

"What do *you* think?" Yosh grinned at his two ashigaru briefly, then vanished again into the viewer. Vilkas groaned. In a muffled voice, Yosy went on. "What's more, we're going to have to string cables instead of slave-transmit, and cobble up something to match the brain-detected board with this red eyeball and the weapons batteries. Sorry, men. This piece of junk must be forty years old if it's a day, and the zappers are even older. You'd think some turkey would have smuggled in more up-to-date stuff by now."

"Could be they did." Vilkas peered gloomily into his empty stein. "But who's to know? The Tanu lords who had contraband dumps kept mum about their collections. No swap meets or comparing goodies. King Thagdal would have had their heads on a pike if he found out they were holding out on him. All important Milieu gadgetry coming through the time-gate was supposed to be the property of the Crown. And things like guns were supposed to be destroyed." He gave a bark of ironic laughter.

"Lucky for us they wasn't!" Jim nodded at the newly installed cluster of medium-sized laser weapons. "We'ns wouldn' have a hope 'n hell 'gainst this North 'merican gang if all we fielded was glass blades 'n' brainpower. Those zappers—shoo! Never saw nothin' like this yere in the swamp!"

"They're junk," said Yosh flatly. "So antiquated, it's pitiful. Supposed to have a range of ten kloms and they go plasmatic at seven! God, what I wouldn't give for some modern field-jacketed beam blasters—or even an old-time X-ray job."

Jim regarded him open-mouthed. "Shoo, boss—what a place that 'ere Galactic Mil-yew must be!"

Yosh and Vilkas eyed each other. The robotics engineer asked, "Were your parents time-travelers, Jim?"

"Gran'parents," said the young man. "We lived two whole gen'rations free there in Stilt Town, after the Firvulag abandoned Nionel. Not even Howlers wanted the Paree Basin." He giggled. "Which was fine by us!"

Vilkas was staring at his boots. "Would you go back to the swamp if you had the chance, kid? Go home?"

"An' eat smews 'n' bulrush roots and hog-deer?" Jim snorted. "Not this chile. You can keep ol' Paree." He snapped two fingers against his gray torc, making the metal ring. "*This* is livin'!"

"Jesus," said Vilkas softly.

Yosh was back inside the spotterscope, both hands manipulating the controls. "Last test. Plug in one of those zappers and let's see how she tracks on semiauto."

Jim went to pay out a thin cable from one of the weapons in the tower battery while Vilkas cleared the orifice and powered up. When the gun was mated to the scanning device, both gray-torcs said: *Ready Yoshi-sama.*

Servos tilted the spotter, putting Yosh comfortably onto his back in the bucket seat. The electronically linked weapon tracked along in parallel as Yosh searched the sky. "Close range. That's what we got and that's what we'll use. Gonna zap me a bird. Just one small bird. The Rocky Mountain Audubon Society'd ride me out of town on a rail if they knew, but I need a warm bod to target this sucker. And . . . and . . . ah-ah! We got us a falcon conformation coming up on Cal-City at range one-one-six-seven-pip-oh-four . . . chotto matte! Dammit, he jinked! Definite falcon. Aureate. Male. Ready again—"

"Chief—don't!" Jim cried. "Don't shoot!"

Yosh looked out of the scope, forehead furrowed in annoyance. "What the hell?"

"Them gold falcons—it's bad luck to kill 'em! You shoot one, you get th' shit o' the worl' dump on you!"

"Oh, for God's sake," exclaimed Yosh.

"Please, chief," Jim begged.

Yosh gave him a disgusted grimace and returned to the scanner. He swiveled round to the south, down near the bank of the River Ybaar. "How about a goddam guinea hen in a goddam mudwallow?"

"Zap away," said Jim cheerily.

The laser spoke a truncated sizzling yelp. Yosh relaxed in his seat and sighed. "So much for that. Unplug the gun, and we'll get downstairs—" He froze as his golden torc transmitted a hail.

Yoshi do you hear?

(He did . . . and he knew that mind-voice.) I hear High King!

I'm coming. You have spotterscope ready?

Just finished but unremote and unconnex guns—

Nevermind that. Won't need after all. Stay tower. Wait Me. Tell NO ONE I come.

Yes High King.

Vilkas and Jim had been gathering up the tool kits and testing gear. Neither had noticed Yosh's abstraction. The Lithuanian said, "If we're going to hook this eye to the brain-board, we'll have to cannibalize MP interfacers from something."

"Forget it," Yosh said. "The King's coming. There's a change in plan." He was frowning as he reoriented the spotter to scan the sky northeast of Calamosk. "He wants us to stay right here, and tell no one else that he's on the way."

"Hey—great!" Jim cried. "He bringin' the Flyin' Hunt t' roust out them oversea sumbitches?"

Yosh kept silent as he studied the scope readout. "He can't be. I'd get a whacking body-read—and there's nothing out there. Nothing!"

"A land force?" Vilkas ventured.

"How c'd he keep a lan' march secret?" scoffed Jim. "Course he'd fly!"

"Oh, my God," said Yosh. He lifted a drained face from the viewer and pressed the neutralization stud. Stiffly, he climbed from the seat. His samurai armor, discarded for the installation work, lay in a neat pile. A well-known telepathic signal set Jim and Valkas scurrying to assist him in donning it. They were puzzled by the perspiration that had broken out on their master's brow and the faint tremor in his cheek muscles. Through their gray torcs they perceived a hint of the mental turmoil that Yosh was doing his best to hide.

Artless Jim was solicitous. "Gee, boss—you feelin' all right?"

"I'm fine. But listen . . . do you remember Clarty Jock telling us how to hide our private thoughts if we were afraid some Tanu with redactive powers was snooping in our minds?"

"I remember," said Vilkas. "Not tha'   needed *him* to tell me."

"'Think of a song, over 'n' over,'" Jim rehearsed obediently. "I allus think o' one Gran'daddy useta sing:

> *We are the virgin mountaineers,*
> *With lots of hair upon our ears—*

Yosh interrupted him. "When the King arrives, *hide your thoughts.*"

"But why, chief?"

Yosh settled his daisho and nodachi swords while Vilkas tied on the collarlike nodowa (cut low to show the prestigious golden torc) and Jim held out the elaborate helmet with its crescent-moon horns. "Never mind why. You'll know when the King gets here."

The three of them stood at attention, facing east. There was a tiny speck in the cloudless afternoon sky, obviously approaching, and Jim and Vilkas tensed. But then they saw that it was only a bird, perhaps some kind of hawk, with yellow and black feathers. It glided low over the tower and the long piece of straw it clutched in its talons was clearly visible.

Look out, Yosh whispered telepathically to his minions.

The bird floated down. It was not a hawk but an aureate falcon, and when it touched the parapet it changed into King Aiken-Lugonn holding his great golden-glass Spear in one gloved hand.

"Hi," said the King, pushing up the face-shield of his storm suit. "You boys got the spotterscope ready?"

Yosh saluted and gestured wordlessly at the device. Jim mumbled, "We are the virgin mountaineers!"

Aiken raised one quizzical eyebrow. "Never would have guessed it." He turned his back on them and climbed into the seat of the scanning device. "Don't bother with instructions. I've used these things before." He looked south. "Yes . . . here comes Ochal the Harper and his riders—and I presume the extra bodies are the coveted Basil's Bastards." One finger rapped the mode-select into ultimate range. "And zooming up behind them, clearing the hills, we have fifteen all-terrain vehicles driving flat-out."

Vilkas and Jim were staring at one another in mingled shock and apprehension. Yosh stood calmly at the King's shoulder and said, "How can we assist you?"

Aiken climbed out of the spotterscope and motioned for Yosh to take his place. Jim was quick to catch the kabuto that his master whipped from his head and flung away.

"I'm going to entrust the three of you with a state secret," Aiken said. His eyes were burning coals in a paper-white countenance. "I won't threaten you—but if you tell anyone what kind of chicane I pull here this afternoon, there's a good chance my throne will fall. And you along with it, of course."

"We are your slaves," said Yosh. Even in the embrace of the big spotterscope, he managed a solemn bow. Vilkas and Jim shuffled their feet and licked their lips.

Aiken said, "The North American vehicles are certain to catch up with Ochal's group before they get within range of Calamosk's defenses. I realized this as I farsensed them while flying in. So *I'll* have to do something."

"Hell—ever'body thought you'd bring the Flyin' Hunt!" Jim said. Vilkas kicked him in the ankle.

"I couldn't carry the Hunt," Aiken told him quietly. "I barely have strength enough to fly—and maintain the bird illusion. If I overfly that enemy ATV column and attack it with the Spear, I won't have enough watts left to generate a psycho-creative shield against their weapons. I have a portable sigma-field generator, but using it makes flying even more difficult, and chances are that those North Americans have guns that will go through a small sigma like an axe through a muskmelon. So I'm going to try something different, and you'll help me with this scanner. I'll ascend to a high altitude with the Spear. *Very* high. You, Yosh, will zero in precisely fifty meters in front of the lead ATV and farspeak the coordinates to me." He blinked, anticipating the engineer's question. "No, I can't use my own farsense to aim. I'm incapable of a precise focus at sixty kilometers. Besides, I'll need what residual mind-wattage I have left to screw up *their* scanners. I'll probably have to use the Spear more than once, so you must be ready to refocus whenever I give the order. Is that clear?"

"Yes, High King. It would be best if you could wait until the target is within forty-five kilometers. The scanner may not be reliable at extreme range."

"Good thinking. I'll hold off as long as I can."

Jim cried, "But what *happened*? Kee-rist, Y'r Maj'sty! How we gone lick this bunch—how we gone lick the *Firvulag*—if you got no powers left?"

Aiken smiled and tapped the crested hood of his golden suit. "I still have my full quotient of low cunning, Jim boy. The ordinary little gray cells that got me banished to the Pliocene in the first place. Didn't you ever wonder why they threw me out of the Milieu? Because I was a menace, that's why! There are brains and there are brains. Mine may be a trifle shy of metapsychic firepower at the moment, but not to worry. I'll recover soon enough. Meanwhile, I'll find other ways to rise to the occasion."

* * *

Cloud gripped the edge of the command console with taut concentration. "We're going to catch them! Estimated convergence eleven-point-four minutes!"

"Shall we man the sonic disruptors?" Phil Overton asked Hagen.

"No, you idiot. When we get clear line of sight—no trees, no bloody antelopes or anything stampeding in the way—we put up the sigmas. Then deploy in echelon off-road and chase until we're within stun range. Knock down their chalikos, close in and deliver a low-power lullaby to the folks, then scoop 'em up."

"We could hit the animals at longer range with the disruptors or the zappers," Phil said.

"And maybe kill some pilot or technician our lives may depend upon when Papa comes after us!" Hagen snapped. "No disruptors, dammit, and no photon arms, either. Those are only for use against troops from Calamosk."

"We'll have to leave slots in the sigmas to navigate and shoot Huskies through," Nial Keogh said. "They could nail us if they're sharp. Use psychozap in a bouncing ball-lightning effect."

"We'll risk it," said Hagen. "You and the other heavy PK-heads will have to watch out for metafoolery. Now farspeak the others and advise them. We won't go echelon until the terrain's suitable. I'm going to call for max speed to close the gap. Hang onto your teeth."

The whining turbos rose to a howl. The fourplex vehicles charged along the crudely graded track, bouncing and veering and raising a monumental plume of dust. "Got 'em on the TSL monitor," said Veikko Saastamoinen. "Closeup farsight, too. They know we're here, but they don't look worried."

Hagen scowled. "Hear anything?"

"Screened six ways from Sunday. The torcers have a blanket on the whole outfit. What I wouldn't give for your old man's metaconcert program! Funnel a mind-blast through me, we could drill every one of that bottle-armored lot right between the ears."

"The King's got that program," Cloud said, "in case you've forgotten."

The fleeing chaliko riders were crossing a dry streambed

and racing through a narrow line of poplar trees on the opposite bank. With the ATV safety governors on override, the vehicles were careering along at a speed that threatened to send them out of control.

"You've got to slow down!" Cloud exclaimed. "The others are—"

From the sky came a brief green flash. Dirt fountained up in an opaque brown blossom and an explosion smote their brains at the same time as a farspoken roar:

STOP YOUR VEHICLES. DO NOT ATTEMPT ERECT SIGMAS OR I ZAP LEADER.

Veikko screamed and clapped both hands to his skull. Hagen wrestled with the brakes and the vehicle slewed crazily off the track into the stony veldt, rocking and plowing furrows with its deflectors as it tilted far onto its left side and nearly turned turtle.

There was a second explosion born from an emerald firebar, and this time the beam hit less than fifteen meters in front of them. Hagen cursed as he brought the vehicle to a halt.

DO NOT MOVE. DO NOT ERECT SIGMAS OR I ZAP.

Nial Keogh was speaking calmly into the microphone of the RF com, checking on the others. Veikko, his sensitive mind overwhelmed by the volume of the vibrant mental shout, had fallen to the cockpit floor and was curled in a fetal ball, clawlike hands over his ears. The TSL display showed only multicolored snow.

Cloud and Hagen looked at each other with bleak comprehension. The first game of the match was over. But at least their father was not the winner.

Cloud spoke on Aiken's intimate mode: We've stopped. May I come out on the bridge and parley?

There was a third explosion behind the last vehicle of the train, and godlike laughter.

YOU FOOLS. I'VE BEEN WATCHING YOU FOR HOURS. I COULD HAVE FRIED YOUR BRAINS THE MOMENT YOU SET FOOT ON MY MANY-COLORED LAND. AND YOU THINK YOU CAN PARLEY?

Cloud said: We have a proposition that may interest you. We really intend no harm to your kingdom.

I KNOW YOUR PROPOSAL. I KNOW YOU HOPE TO REOPEN THE TIME-GATE.

We will . . . pay for your help.
HOW?

Hagen's face was puzzled. He and Phil Overton had been hurriedly conferring and now he covertly told his sister: Something funny that not psychocreativeblast but photoncannontype!

ANSWER ME! OR MY METAPSYCHIC POWER WILL ANNIHILATE YOU!

"The Wizard of Oz," Phil Overton said. "But with a giga-class zapper. Not quite a bluff—but we may have maneuvering room."

Hagen said: I am Marc Remillard's son. We'll pay for your cooperation by working with you to overcome our mutual enemy—whom we know a great deal better than you do. Without our help he will destroy you as he will probably destroy us.

HE TELLS ME YOU ARE THE ENEMY!

Hagen said: And has he told you that he's learned to d-jump?

There was a long silence. Finally the thunder-voice said:

WAIT WHERE YOU ARE FOR THREE HOURS. THEN COME UP TO CALAMOSK WITH YOUR VEHICLE TOPS OFF AND YOUR ARMAMENTS DEMOUNTED—AND WE'LL ALL HAVE TEA.

8

BASIL WIMBORNE AND HIS CREW OF BASTARDS CAME AGAIN to the citadel of Calamosk, which they had visited earlier that year under far different circumstances. Then, during the worst of the rainy season, Basil had served as one of the leaders of the refugee army retreating from the flood-ravaged Aven Peninsula. The little cadre that later became the Bastards had formed an impromptu staff under himself, Chief Burke, Sister Amerie, and Elizabeth. After the throng of displaced people had been driven away from Afaliah by the implacable Celadeyr, they had approached the smaller city anticipating an even ruder dismissal by its arriviste human master, Sullivan-Tonn. Instead, they found that Sullivan and his young Tanu fiancée had been freshly ousted by Aluteyn Craftsmaster and a rabble of renegade knights from the Great Retort. Calamosk was battered and provision-short after the siege, but Aluteyn had given the refugees whatever could be spared before advising them to press on farther north to more prosperous regions.

Riding into Calamosk behind Ochal the Harper, Basil and his Bastards noted certain changes. The colorwashed half-timbered cottages that had once sheltered bareneck human townsfolk were now nearly all empty. Weeds grew among the street cobbles and there was abundant dust lying about, and neglected heaps of animal droppings. The stone planters and public gardens were untended and suffering from the summer drought.

Because he had once worn a golden torc, Basil alone among the contingent rescued from the dungeon was experienced enough in the use of the mind-enhancer to speak telepathically on the Tanu mode. He now asked Ochal:

What has happened? The city looks so shabby so unlike the other Tanu cities I have seen since the Flood.

Ochal said: The ramas. Those who have not died have fled into the wilderness. It is a result of the fighting the mental strife the turmoil attending the Craftsmaster's takeover. Ramas are peaceloving creatures with sensitive and fragile minds. Wearing torcs they react to manifestations of extreme emotionality in adverse ways fleeing the malign aetheric vibrations if possible and suffering acute psychosomatic disorders if restrained. Not only Calamosk but my own lamented Bardelask and even Goriah itself have experienced this flight of the ramas. The High King has naturally ordered that replacement apes be sent to the capital. But Calamosk has had to initiate a complete new breeding program.

Basil said: Hard luck for the local nobs needing domestics.

Ochal said: Many gray-torc humans are still faithful nay eager to serve . . . and even numbers of barenecks.

Basil: Those who were too timid or too prudent to go the Lowlife route—or too wise to rush up to Goriah hoping the King would give them golden torcs!

Ochal: [Laughter.] That has been a problem in more cities than Calamosk. King Aiken-Lugonn has had to depart considerably from his original hope of offering instant citizenship to any human who requested it.

Basil: Mm. His instincts were generous—

Ochal: But fortunately for the good order of the High Kingdom they were overruled by his innate pragmatism. Ah! . . . We arrive at last.

The caravan came into the forecourt of the central citadel, where there were numerous torced humans of every station as well as civilian and fully armed Tanu. None of the neglect evident in the city's outer purlieus affected the castle environs. Human servitors ran up to assist the dismounting of the new arrivals, and Basil and his Bastards were attended every bit as solicitously as their escort. The Elite Guard of human golds stood by, however, their Milieu-style weapons at the ready.

Ochal said to Basil, "Here's a great honor for you—the City-Lord himself come down to bid you welcome."

Basil inclined his head respectfully as a Tanu creator wearing a short tunic and aquamarine half-armor came sweeping up. "Parthol Swiftfoot," said he, by way of introduction. He briefly tapped the pleasure-circuitry of the Bastards' gray torcs, precipitating a startled reaction among those who were metapsychically unsophisticated. "My personal felicitations! King's most anxious to meet you."

"And we, him," said Basil. *Calm*, he told his friends. *Keep calm!*

"Suppose we clean you up a bit first, eh?" Parthol winked. "Old Celo's dungeon—not exactly a health resort."

Basil managed a dry laugh. "You're very considerate, Lord Parthol."

"Follow me! Nice surprise waiting!" And the Tanu was off, with Basil and the others tumbling along in his wake (for a Tanu stalwart can easily cover two meters at a stride). He pointed out noteworthy improvements in the citadel defenses instituted by his predecessor, the late Aluteyn, as he led them through the barbican, across the inner ward, and up an ornate white-marble ramp into the palatial keep.

"You were . . . one of the Craftsmaster's companions in adversity?" Basil said breathlessly.

Parthol chortled. "Fellow jailbird, you mean! Quite right. Old Thagdal slung me into the Retort for murder. Decapitated my mother-in-law, Coventone Petrifactrix, on a Royal Hunt up in the Dark Mountains. No one would believe I mistook her for a Firvulag. Can't think why."

They passed down a series of marble staircases into the bowels of the castle, where torches in silver holders illuminated corridors paved in pink and black tiles. A certain anxiety radiated from Basil and the Bastards at this descent. "Not the dungeon this time!" Parthol reassured them. They came to a huge black door with silver fittings, guarded by statuesque human females in silver-lustre armor. Grinning expectantly, the City-Lord of Calamosk gestured, causing the portal to open, and motioned for the visitors to follow him inside.

The Bastards began whispering and elbowing one another. Somebody unloosed an incredulous whistle. They had come into a complex of vaulted and pillared connecting chambers that seemed to combine features of a sumptuous Turkish bath with the decor of a fin-de-siècle Hungarian whorehouse. There were dripping crystal chandeliers, baroque divans in veil-curtained alcoves, and a fantastic gilt-and-jasper steam room, the walls of which were adorned with Paphian mosaics.

"Amusing, isn't it?" Parthol remarked to Basil. "Your lamented compatriot Sullivan-Tonn had it installed during his brief tenure and we decided to keep it. Ingenious race, you humans—if those depictions are a fair sampling of your Old World sexual mores."

Basil cleared his throat diffidently. "Some of the mosaics have—uh—a folkloric derivation. The centaurs and the mermaids, for example, and the—uh—more heroically proportioned individuals."

"Oh? What a pity. Still, I'd wondered why we didn't get any of those coming through the time-gate." He broadcast a brief order on the command mode and a jolly-looking Polynesian couple in flowered lava-lavas trotted in bearing trays of carnations. They wore silver torcs, and as they passed the flowers to the bemused Bastards, they seemed to radiate comfortable reassurance.

"Salote and Malietoa will see to your comfort," Parthol said. "We're a bit short-handed, so you'll have to scrub one another's backs, but I think you'll enjoy your ablutions. Try the bubble bath! That Sullivan thought of the damnedest things. And when that's done, you can have fresh clothes. I'm proud to say that Calamosk boasts a really first-rate tailoring moduplex—a Halston 2100. Make any type of apparel you like."

Mr. Betsy, who had been savoring his carnation, let out a great sigh of rapture.

Parthol beamed at the Elizabethan in the sadly dilapidated finery. "We're a bit short of Milieu fabrics since the time-gate closed—not much of a selection in nebulin or dacolite or repelvel—but you'll find some very nice linen and fine cotton; and I'm quite certain there's at least twenty ells of tourmaline silk brocade left, and you might fancy silver lace for that collar thingy of yours."

Phronsie Gillis smothered a wicked simper. "And I'll just

have me some silk knickers from the scraps!" Betsy ignored her.

Parthol Swiftfoot said to Basil, "I'll come to fetch you in a couple of hours. You won't try to escape or hide or anything tedious like that, will you? Not to put too fine a point on it— you *are* all wearing gray torcs. We could track you down easily. At least wait until you've heard what the High King has to say before you begin plotting and scheming."

"Very well," said Basil. "We'll wait."

As the Bastards finished King Aiken-Lugonn's high tea, the noncommittal chit-chat slowly faded to silence and all eyes turned to the small figure of the monarch. He was sitting in front of the unlit hearth of the presence room on a throne of gilded oak; his guests had had to make do with tufted floor cushions and most now lounged on these, leaving only a few of the recalcitrantly suspicious and Mr. Betsy standing. The King was wearing his golden storm-suit without the hood; a simple circlet of black glass rested on his dark red hair. He drank minted iced tea from a Waterford tumbler and then chewed the cubes as the stillness grew and the Bastards stared.

"How many of you," the King said at last, "would like to go back through the time-gate to the Galactic Milieu?"

Pandemonium.

Aiken smiled and raised a hand. An appalling blast of coercion struck every mind dumb. "Sorry about that, but we don't have much time to spare. More guests will be arriving very shortly to join our little party. Among them will be the lady who clapped you all into the Afaliah slammer after helping to steal your aircraft—Cloud Remillard."

"Remillard!" exclaimed the minds and voices of the Bastards.

"I see that a bell has rung," the King remarked. His smile was grim. "Yes, she's his daughter. Marc Remillard and his ex-Rebels have been living in North America for twenty-seven years, mostly minding their own business. But not any longer. It seems the Rebels had children, and the kids decided that they'd had enough of the old folks' domination, and so they packed up and blew the homestead and came *here*. Cloud was first, with a handful of others. Later her brother Hagen came with all the rest of the second generation."

"Good God," said Basil. "It's incredible! Marc Remillard was alleged to have perished in the Rebellion, together with his top confederates."

Aiken shrugged. "Madame Guderian had a lot to answer for. I don't know if she let 'em go through willingly, or if they coerced her. Probably the latter. They brought contraband galore."

"Oh, Your Majesty, never mind that!" cried little Miss Wang passionately. "Tell us more about reopening the time-gate—and going back!"

"Not possible," Dimitri Anastos told her. "It's a one-way warp, Milieu to Pliocene."

"Not," said Aiken, "if you build a second Guderian tau-field generator *here*. Which is what Marc Remillard's children and their friends propose to do."

"To go home!" cried Miss Wang. "To undo the terrible error! To leave this awful place and live once again in the tranquillity of the Milieu—"

"Oh, I dunno," said Phronsie Gillis, pulling a dubious face. "This exile has its hairy moments, but by and large I dig it. *You* feel like boogying back, Bets?"

Mr. Betsy uttered a hollow chuckle. "Surely you jest."

"The Milieu is a benevolent despotism! To hell with it!" said Pushface.

"Speak for yourself, joker," Chazz said. "I'd be at the head of the queue for a return ticket."

"How many of you," Aiken asked, "would go back?"

Eleven hands rose—and then a twelfth, from an eagle-beaked man who said, "Me too, King—if you and the friggerty Angel of the Abyss are planning a little war."

Phronsie Gillis gave him a thunderous scowl. "Any war that features ol' Marc the Paramount Badass Grand Master won't be little, Nazir! More likely it'll be terminal to the Pliocene Earth, and the Milieu'll end up never been born!"

"No, that can't happen," Dimitri interjected with pedantic insistence. "Contrary to popular superstition, so-called alternate universes or parallel space-time lattices are impossible. One does not kill one's own grandfather and subsequently vanish! No action here in the Pliocene can alter the primary reality of which the Milieu—and all future events, for that matter—is a manifestation. According to the universal field theory—"

"Stuff it, Dimitri," said Mr. Betsy.

A wrangle broke out, which Aiken cut off with another coercive slap. "Those of you who would go. How many are able to pilot the Tanu aircraft?"

Miss Wang, Phillipe, Bengt Sandvik, Farhat, Pongo Warburton, and Clifford raised their hands.

"How many pilots would stay here?"

Hands went up from Mr. Betsy, Taffy Evans, Thongsa, Pushface, and Stan Dziekonski.

The King fixed Mr. Betsy with a ruminative eye. "Just what *did* you do back in the Galactic Milieu?"

Betsy drew himself up in an attitude of stubborn hauteur. Basil quickly said, "Dr. Hudspeth was a researcher and test pilot with Boeing's Commercial Rhocraft Division."

"I'll be gormed," murmured the Nonborn King. His gaze roamed over the rest of the assembled crew and the adventurers stiffened, feeling redactive probes invading their memories, trying in vain to shut the mental windows that the gray torcs had opened into their brains.

"An Oxford don who climbs mountains," Aiken mused wonderingly. "A third engineer on a tramp starfreighter ... a surgeon who did one microtomy operation too many ... an upsilon-field generator designer for G-Dyn Cumberland ... an egg-bus maintenance mechanic ... an Eskimo electronics engineer ... too bad there's no metallurgist ..."

When the King withdrew his scrutiny, Basil said, "Sir, we have been told that you bear us no ill will. Your deputy, Ochal the Harper, described you as a just and worthy ruler—given a few human eccentricities."

Aiken laughed.

Basil continued persistently. "You have tantalized us with visions of a return to the Milieu and frightened us by suggesting that the Pliocene might be the scene of a renewed Metapsychic Rebellion. You have rummaged in our brains in a desultory fashion, and I presume that you will interrogate us more stringently in good time, in order to learn the location of the other exotic flying machines—"

"Oh, I know that," Aiken said. "Cloud Remillard told me."

"Then tell us what you intend to do with us," the don demanded. "Are we to remain enslaved? Are we mere pawns in your dealings with the young Rebels?"

Aiken leaned back in the throne of intricately carved and gilded wood. It was a trophy, stolen centuries ago from the Firvulag by some Tanu Hunt, and the back was surmounted by a shining lion guardant with chrysoberyl eyes. Ignoring Basil's questions, the King pointed to a man who stood apart from the rest, whose dreaming face was framed by a ginger beard and who wore a surtout of crimson over a chainmail shirt.

"You aren't one of Basil's Bastards," Aiken said. "Who are you?"

"Only a madman," said Dougal, "seeking the savior."

"Dougal's quite harmless," said Basil.

"Mad?" The King seemed puzzled. "Is that why I can't probe your brain?"

"Perhaps," said Dougal. "Or there might be another reason."

Aiken lifted one eyebrow. "And would you like to go home to the Galactic Milieu, Sir Dougal the Mad?"

"Sire—I am, as thou, at war 'twixt will and will not."

"Ah," said the King. He arose from the throne and went to the long table where the food and drink were arrayed. He helped himself to more iced tea from a faceted crystal urn and began to poke through the plates of cakes, biscuits, and finger sandwiches. He said, "The adult children of Marc Remillard's Rebels have defied parental authority by coming to Europe. The elders are on their way here via windjammer, hell-bent to stop the kids from building the Guderian device."

"If it were done when 'tis done," said Dougal, "then 'twere well it were done quickly."

Aiken blinked at him, then said, "Cloud and Hagen originally intended to make a pact with Nodonn. Now, of course, they've set their sights on Me. They want not only the exotic aircraft, but the lot of you to fly and maintain them. The fleet is to be used for toting them and their equipment about as they gather materials for the time-warper. I understand some of the rarer elements will have to be located through aerial surveys, then mined and refined on the spot."

"And you intend to cooperate," Basil stated.

Aiken popped a square of shortbread into his mouth and munched it up. "I have strategic reason for doing so. And I want you to help me to help these young Rebels."

"It's Hobson's choice we have," Taffy complained, "collared with these fuckin' torcs!"

Aiken sipped his tea with bowed head. "Alas, my friends—I face a certain dilemma there. Try to appreciate my position. I want this time-gate built and so do about half of you . . . so you say. But what if those who *don't* want to return to the Milieu get sick and tired of the gate-building scheme and do a flit—or perhaps scarper with some of the aircraft? That could jeopardize the entire operation. We have too few pilots and ground-crew folks as it is, and I'd hate to lose any of you." He smiled in a winning fashion.

"You intend to keep us torced, then," said Basil.

"Until the time-gate's finished. But I promise that you won't be coerced or punished through them if you behave reasonably. Now how does that strike you?"

"We'll end up having to fight off that monster, Marc Remillard!" Mr. Betsy cried. "When he arrives with his pack of metapsychic felons, those of us piloting the aircraft will face heaven knows what kind of mechanical and mental zappery!"

"We'll have weapons of our own, and we also have some sigmas that can be installed on the ships," Aiken said. "And there are such things as mental screens against mind-blasts."

"I'm sure *I* wouldn't know," the rhocraft engineer retorted.

Aiken grinned. "I keep forgetting. You don't know Me very well." He set down the tea tumbler and strolled back to the throne, where he struck a pose. "Let me give you a small demonstration of what it takes to be King of the Many-Colored Land."

He stood quietly for a moment, eyes closed. Then the lids lifted and his mind's fire seemed to look out through the deep orbits. His hair stood out, lit by dancing sparks, and the glass coronet shone with an inner fluorescence. A webwork of crawling violet and amber lightnings poured down from his shoulders to his feet, sheathing his body as though he had become a living electrode. The web coalesced into a blazing nimbus, and about his head was a veritable mane of golden flames, reflecting off the gilt-wood carving of the lion above the throne. He lifted both hands and held miniature suns, and seemed to grow in stature until he towered incandescent against the ceiling beams and threatened to ignite the Firvulag trophy banners hung there.

Waves of coercion and psychocreative force oscillated in the room. The Bastards' minds seemed filled with crashing sonorities. They were transfixed, enthralled by the apotheosis.

Only Dougal retained the power of movement. He reeled forward and dropped to his knees. His face was contorted with pain and joy and tears flowed down his cheeks. "It's you!" he cried. "It's *you!*"

The brief flash of uncanny power shut off as though it had been only inadvertently manifested. The little man in the golden leather suit stood there, leaning casually against the throne, his aspect quite normal.

"Not to brag," said Aiken, "but Marc Remillard may discover a nasty surprise if he attempts to invade this continent. Remember that his power during the Metapsychic Rebellion rested in a vast assemblage of minds, which he directed in aggressive metaconcert. Here in the Pliocene he's handicapped. A lot of his old cronies are worn out. Others are unreliable—or their metafunctions aren't suited to offense. It seems very likely that if he comes against Me, he'll have to come alone. His people will try to help him, but their efforts will be piddling compared to the kind of fighting that went on during the Rebellion. We can lick 'em—and we can build that gate! The job will be easier if you help. Will you?"

Dougal had both hands pressed to the leonine charge embroidered on his new surtout. Still weeping, he spoke in a low voice. "Before, with your glory masked, I did not know you. None of us did. But now I see you, Aslan, come to save Narnia just as I prayed. You will not abandon us to pass through the dread doorway. You will not let the dream die—"

"Be quiet," said the King sharply; and although he withheld his coercive power, the mad medievalist subsided, sinking down with his face to the marble floor. Aiken stepped around him to survey the others.

"Will you help me freely?" he asked, and his voice was strangely dulled.

There was a brief pause. "Yes," said Basil at last. "Those of us who would stay in the Pliocene will cooperate for the sake of our friends who wish to leave."

Aiken sighed. "Thank you." Behind the Bastards, the doors of the grand salon opened. Parthol Swiftfoot stood there, this time attired in full armor that blazed blue-green in the dusk. Beside him was Ochal the Harper. Their minds said:

You summoned us High King.

"These friends are to be conducted to rooms where they can rest," Aiken said aloud. He turned to Basil. "Tomorrow, we'll confer about an aircraft salvage expedition to the Alps. My Deputy Lord Psychokinetic, Bleyn the Champion, will lead you. You'll leave as soon as possible."

"As you like, sir." Basil inclined his head slightly and sent a brief telepathic image to the others. Those who were still sitting arose. The Bastards began to drift toward the doors.

Dougal roused and climbed to his feet. He pulled a linen mouchoir out of one mailed sleeve and blew his nose. The dreamy look was gone as he eyed the King and said, "If you plan to whip up Guderian's Gazebo from scratch, Aslan, take my advice and get hold of my old master, Tony Wayland. I mean, extruding that bloody niobiumdysprosium wire for the tau-generator alone will call for world-class boffinry, to say nothing of refining the stuff from ores. Tony ran the barium works in Finiah . . . Really knows his metallic stuff, old Tony."

Aiken was urgent. "Where is he now?"

Dougal rolled his eyes heavenward. "Alas! He was nobbled by wicked dwarfs in the Vosges woodland, and only I escaped to tell the tale!"

Aiken shot a telepathic instruction to Parthol, who came up and put a gently coercive hand on Dougal's shoulder and suggested, "Why don't you come along and tell me all about it?"

Dougal suffered himself to be guided toward the door, but as it was closing, he said over his shoulder, "And thou, Aslan, in thine own hand bear the power to cancel his captivity . . . a parlous exchange, yet necessary, I ween." And he was gone.

Aiken shook his head and the expression he showed to Ochal was almost helpless. "I suppose Parthol will make sense of it. Creator ingenuity . . . but dammit, Occy, there's something uncanny about that big gomeril."

"I sensed it too, High King." Thinly veiled anxiety hovered behind his social screen. "Is it well with you? We could have the North Americans wait longer—"

"No. There isn't time. Dougal was right . . . 'twere well it were done quickly."

"They have followed our instructions with complete docility and await your pleasure. Would you believe that they've brought five tiny toddlers along with them?"

"I'm ready to believe almost anything these days," Aiken remarked. "You got the big sigma from Hagen Remillard without any hassle?"

"Yoshi is supervising its installation up in the gallery right now, High King."

"Good." Aiken strode to the throne and dropped into it. "We want to be damn sure no unauthorized parties eavesdrop on this next little confab."

"Do you have any other commands?"

Aiken waved a hand. "Just get some grays in here to spiffy up the tea table, then bring on the Children of Rebellion."

Ochal saluted and would have withdrawn, but the King suddenly said, "Do you remember the night I first came to Muriah—King Thagdal's crazy feast, and the show-and-tell we newcomers put on so you could bid for our services?"

"I remember, High King." Ochal's mouth twitched. "What a wild affair that was! And now I see that it was your opening move in the great game."

Aiken seemed to be staring into the far distance. "There was a little human redactor woman, a silver, who sang. Do you remember?"

"I hear her still in memory, Shining One."

Please, said Aiken.

And later, when the North Americans came apprehensively into the sigma-sheltered salon to meet the terrible King of the Many-Colored Land, they saw a little man sitting on a large lion-crested throne, and at his feet a faerie knight enarmed in amethyst, singing and playing "All Through the Night" on a jewel-starred harp.

When he was certain that the silver-torc castellan and his minions were gone, Basil Wimborne went out onto the balcony of his bedroom, located the Pliocene Polaris, and oriented himself as best he could. The massif of the Flaming Mountains lay between Calamosk and Black Crag and his farsensing ability, even when he was wearing gold, had been only meager. But Elizabeth was a Grand Master, and there was a chance she would hear his feeble gray call.

He closed his eyes, placed his fingers on the warm metal about his neck, and channeled all his psychic energy into the hail:

ELIZABETH...

    Basil! O mydear mydear we thought you dead.

CloudRemillard&Nodonn took Bastards&all in aircraft Afaliah.

    But you safe? And others?

Safe now yes. With Aiken Calamosk, You know RebelChildren come?

    Yes. And I know theirfather won't be far behind.

Aiken&Children plan use us&aircraft. We agreed.

    But Basil...since you wear gray I presume the others do also and you have been forced to cooperate. There is danger. Aiken will make enemy of Marc by allying with Children. You will be caught in metapsychic quarrel. Better perhaps that I demand Aiken free you—

Elizabeth don't you know?

    ?

Why Children come ally with Aiken?

    ...To escape parents flex muscles mingle other minds— *To open time-gate from this side.*

    ...

Elizabeth?...Elizabeth?

    Yes, Basil. How they plan do this?

Build Guderiandevice. They can if Aiken helps.

    Marc will do utmost prevent it.

Children 5tons Milieu weapons + aircraft hope win. Aiken says Marcweaker him.

    My God.

What do? WHAT? We giveup aircraft Lowlifefreedomhope doomed—Elizabeth help us tell us what do!

    I don't know Basil I must consider so many factors now *this* be patient obey Aiken for now I'll contact you via intimode thoughtbeam after I have time think time think O God *an open gate!*

Elizabeth do one thing.

    Yes Basil?

Tell PeopeoMoxmoxBurke HiddenSprings.

    ...Verywell. But there is little chance his people can get to aircraft hidden Alps ahead Aikensponsored group—

Nonono DON'T ask him try that! No. Tell him opengate.
Help him resolve inaction/dilemma/fear.

Peo fear? *Peo?*

Elizabeth you meditated BlackCrag long while we waited
hoping advice. None. Aircraftscheme seemed onlyhope protect Lowlives Firvulag&Aiken freedomthreat. Peo wanted
use aircraft invade Roniah obtain Milieuweaponry for de-
terrent. We almost ready go when Nodonn came.
Now . . . what now? What hope? Can you not advise?

Basil I don't know what Aiken plans or Marc. Firvulag
will continue brushfirewar pattern at least until Truce. I
cannot advise Peo anymore than you. Not yet.

Tell him opengate.

Open gate . . . You think Peo weary struggle would return
Milieu?

He might. Others certainly would now aircrafthope gone.

And you Basildear would you go?

I have not climbed my mountain.

Ah. Pliocene Everest. I remember.

Peo must know opengate. All humans must. To decide.
Even you.

. . .

Forgive me Elizabeth. I will wait your call. Goodbye.

Goodbye Basil.

9

NO BREATH OF AIR STIRRED IN THE NURSERY, FOR EVEN THOUGH the sun had set, stagnant summer air still pressed upon the chalet like a fat sweaty hand. Elizabeth, standing at the open window and rapt in farsensing, was oblivious, her bare arms stiffly extended, pale and sheened with moisture. As if to armor herself for the ordeal, she had dressed in a beltless Tanu gown of black peau de cygne with a yoke and pendant ribands of jewel-encrusted scarlet: Brede's colors.

The waiting lengthened. Minanonn endured imperturbably, lost in his own thoughts; but Brother Anatoly's indignation grew along with his physical discomfort as the suffering baby wailed. Finally Mary-Dedra lifted the child from his waterbed basket and held him against her shoulder, rocking, torc to torc, sharing the pain she could not diminish.

Anatoly could bear it no longer. He sprang up from his stool in the corner of the room and went to Minanonn. "This is monstrous," he whispered. "You're a coercer. Help that poor woman and her child! At least take the baby down out of his pain—"

"He must be fully alert for the procedure. Dedra understands."

"Then get on with it!" the priest blurted. "What's Elizabeth playing at, for heaven's sake? Call her back here!"

"She would not have responded to the farspoken summons if it had not been important," Minanonn said. "Calm yourself and remember your own duty."

Stung, Anatoly turned away from the exotic and hurried to Mary-Dedra. It was she who had requested his presence at the operation, not the aloof Grand Master, who had barely acknowledged his existence since he had taken up residence in the chalet eight days earlier. The former Maribeth Kelly-Dakin, who had been a gold-torc protegée of Mayvar Kingmaker, now served as executive housekeeper of Black Crag. As Anatoly laid a hand on her hybrid baby's head, she managed to smile.

"I'm glad of the delay, Brother. It'll be even worse for poor Brendan when Elizabeth and Minanonn start. That's why I asked you to be here. For my sake."

Anatoly withdrew his hand from the child convulsively, as if he had been burned. "But if he's a black-torc—" he started to say, and then caught himself and expostulated, "Elizabeth and the redactors should be doing their best to *ease* his pain—not aggravate it with some hellish experiment! Dedra, how can you let them do this?"

The woman closed her eyes and tears started from beneath the lids. The child wailed in grating monotony, clinging to his mother. He was beautiful, blond, and long-limbed; only the unnatural flush about his extremities and the hot blisters beneath his miniature golden torc betrayed his impending fate.

Dedra said, "You don't understand, Brother. Brendan presents a unique opportunity for Elizabeth. Perhaps it's providential—or at least synchronicitous!—that he should have failed to adapt to the torc. The syndrome afflicts other babies, too, you know. But all of the others except Brendan are pureblooded Tanu." Her eyes opened and held those of the old priest. "You've been here in the Pliocene for a long time. Surely you know about the problem."

"If they didn't torc the children in the first place, there'd *be* no maladaptation!"

"And no metapsychic powers." Dedra's tear-streaked face was amazingly ironic. "I never realized what the metas had when I lived in the Milieu. When I came here, and the Tanu tests showed I had strong latencies, and they said they were giving me a torc—I was afraid. Now, I would rather die than give it up."

"And this is the price," Anatoly said, nodding at the child. "Was it worth it, Dedra?"

She lifted her chin. "Somewhere, millions of light-years away, there's a whole galaxy full of torced people who think it's worth it. Why don't you judge *them*, Brother?"

"I'm sorry I was so crude." He shrugged. "I was never much of a theologian—just a poor fool of an apparatchik from Yakutsk who decided in a rash moment to make the Pliocene my parish . . . But tell me why you think little Brendan's case is a unique opportunity."

"Hybrid children aren't supposed to go black-torc. Neither are offspring of the Thagdal. Brendan's both"—her arms tightened about the whimpering infant—"and you can see that he's got the damned syndrome in spades. We don't know why. Elizabeth tried to help Tanu black-torc babies when she lived in Muriah, but she had no success. Her failure was as much due to the exotic circuitry of their minds as to the complexity of the problem. But my Brendan, with his hybrid mind, is more familiar territory. Elizabeth has been mullocking about in him ever since he came down with the sickness a month ago, trying things."

Dedra's eyes shut again and fresh tears came. Brother Anatoly looked at his sandaled feet and waited for her to compose herself. Finally she said, "Poor Brendan is special in another way. Most black-torc children die of the thing within two or three weeks. My baby's tougher. Hybrids often are."

"Then there is hope?"

The baby wailed more loudly and Dedra swayed, rocking him. She had turned toward Elizabeth, who still stood at the window, facing the distant Pyrénées, pink with alpenglow above the haze-blurred landscape of Haut Languedoc.

"My Brendan was so strong, so perfect," Dedra crooned. "Never sick a day, all through the exodus from Aven when we were cold and wet and half-starved and bedeviled by mosquitoes and biting midges and Lord Celadeyr's heartless brutes. He was a marvel, my Brendan! Walking at seven months, farspeaking me no matter what part of the lodge I was in. If any baby can survive black-torc, he will—and then perhaps others like him." She kissed the blond curls nestling at her shoulder. The child's crying had diminished to hiccoughing sobs. "If Brendan dies, then at least we will have tried. The knowledge we gain will have repaid his pain and mine."

"But, Dedra, he's too young to *choose*," Anatoly protested.

"I choose for him." She lay the child back on his waterbed, took a soft cloth, and wiped his face. "It's my right. I know what's best for my own child."

The priest shrank from the sudden cold sensation that clutched his vitals. How many times, as an executive assistant in the Siberian Primacy, had he heard this same argument put forth by fellow clerics who sided with the elitists advocating forced evolution, with the elder Remillards and the others who maintained that virtually any means—even potentially fatal or crippling experimentation with immature minds—was justified if it promoted the supereminence of metapsychic humanity. In those days, human moralists had been divided on the question; but there had been no doubts at all among the disapproving exotic ethical arbiters of the Milieu. Three years after Anatoly set off on his mission through the time-gate, he learned that the controversy had culminated in the Metapsychic Rebellion.

Minanonn came out of the shadows and stood over the baby's bed, stern and majestic in cerulean robes. He said to Mary-Dedra, "What Brother Anatoly is saying to you echoes the philosophy of my own Peace Faction. Difficult though it may be, we must surrender ourselves to the divine will. The only peace is that of Tana."

Dedra was scathing. "*You* don't believe I should simply let Brendan die in peace! If you did, you wouldn't be helping Elizabeth in this new procedure!"

"She asked me to help," said the former Battlemaster, "and I do so willingly at this point, in the hope that the child may be cured. But I would not abet you in continuing treatments that would prolong his pain if there were not a good chance of ultimate success. It is unjust to force an innocent to suffer so terribly—even for his own good, or for the greater good of his fellows."

"You should have been a Jesuit!" said Dedra to Minanonn. And to Anatoly, "As for you, Brother, I asked you here to

pray for us, not to preach. So if you're going to, get busy!"
The baby, startled by her vehemence, began to cry again.

Anatoly heroically held his temper, lowered his head, and
muttered, "Lord God, bless this mother and her child and relieve their suffering. Lead us not into temptation, but deliver
us from evil."

"Find a better prayer," Elizabeth said coldly, coming up
behind him. "You're too late with that one—both for Dedra
and for me." As the priest shrank back, white-faced, Elizabeth's
mind added covertly to Minanonn: *And perhaps too late for
the Many-Colored Land as well.*

Minanonn said: Elizabeth ... will you tell me what por-
tends?

Elizabeth said: I've talked to Basil and the King and done
some heavy scanning to confirm what they said. Aiken and the
young North Americans have agreed to work together in an
attempt to reopen the time-gate from the Pliocene side. Marc
Remillard is en route to Europe with his confederates determined to do his utmost to prevent it.

Minanonn said: Tana have mercy it could lead to Nightfall.

The old Franciscan priest was gaping at Elizabeth. She
seemed as beautiful and as inaccessible as an image of Athena,
in her flowing black silk dress and ruby-studded yoke. Her
long hair, unbound, had formed into loose curls in the high
humidity. Smiling slightly, she said aloud, "You came to pray
for us, Brother. Do so now. Show us how we should put our
trust in divine grace instead of in ourselves."

And the priest thought: You ice-hearted bitch! No wonder
poor Amerie gave up on you ...

He was about to stomp out of the room, abandoning them
to their inhuman machinations, when he felt a peculiar soothing
touch invading his mind. Torcless, he nevertheless knew that
it could only be Minanonn's own strength entering him, irresistible as the tide, bearing him up and promising cooperation.
Somehow (the exotic seemed to say) we are akin. Both of us
are destined to influence this awful woman in a crucial way ...

Well, so be it. And ne bzdi, Anatoly Severinovich!

He said, "There's an old prayer from the Sunday Missal
that's become a favorite of mine. It seems almost to have been
written with us Pliocene exiles in mind:

Eternal Father, reaching from end to end of the universe
and ordering all things with your mighty arm,
for you, time is the unfolding of truth that already is,
the unveiling of beauty that is yet to be.
Your Son, our Omega, has saved us in history
so that, transcending time, he might free us from death.
May his presence among us lead to the vision of limitless
    truth
and reveal to us the beauty of your love.

And now I'm going to leave you here to do what you think
you have to do. I think I'll wander down to the spring before
it gets too dark. It might be cooler there, and I think mushrooms
may be coming up. Can't resist those 'shrooms. It's the Siberian
in me."

He laid his hand on the baby's head and blessed him. Mary-
Dedra said, "May I come with you, Brother?"

"Suit yourself," said Anatoly, "but don't expect me to share."
He held the nursery door open and the two of them went out.

Elizabeth and Minanonn, linked, seemed to be suspended
within a vast glowing fabric, a vinelike tangle that penetrated
as well as surrounded them. The analog of the infant mind was
multidimensional, surreally colored, athrob with sickly vitality.
Bursts of hectic energy zipped along the conjoined strands in
apparently random paths, like meteoric mice hurtling to and
fro in a maze of crystalline tubes.

Now press *this* way, Elizabeth directed Minanonn. Now
that. Good! And as I open here, where I must cauterize, dam
back the surge that will arise, lest it trigger an epileptic seizure,
aggravating the dysfunction . . .

And so the two manipulators worked, reaming and weaving,
forming fresh junctures and bypassing others, refashioning the
neural tapestry so that the errant mental energies might function
in harmony with other aspects of the baby's mind, rather than
ramping and warring to the death.

Strength. That had been the breakthrough. When Elizabeth
had previously attempted this procedure together with Dionket
and Creyn, fellow redactors, she had been hopelessly balked
by the intractability of the immature will. The baby "refused"
to learn the thought-revisions that might save him, his young
mind incapable of responding to subtlety. Nevertheless, Eliz-

abeth had remained confident that her redactive salvage program *would* work, if only it could be imposed. And so she had gambled, designing a new configuration that included a powerful coercer—Minanonn—and sacrificing finesse for the cruder but practicable technique utilizing main strength.

Together, they pounded and bored, spliced and cut. And it worked. But it was taking too long.

She signaled a pause, for they had finally completed a section of rechannelization in the cerebral commissures, the fibers connecting the right and left hemispheres. It was an operation that Elizabeth had adjudged critical, and if it succeeded it would at least vindicate the basic design of the salvage program.

The two of them seemed to hover within a webwork shot with speeding lights. Elizabeth directed Minanonn to hold off from his damming function so that the new channels could be tested; and then with her redaction precisely tuned, she stimulated a certain region of the right cortex.

The entire mental hologram responded, swelling into a lattice of glorious, consonant light. For one brief moment, the baby owned a normal mind . . . *and more*. Then it was as before.

Elizabeth withdrew, dragging Minanonn with her.

"Did you see!" she gasped out loud.

"Almighty Tana—it was magnificent. But what was it?" He had been lying on a couch with his head close to the baby's basket while Elizabeth sat in a chair beside them. Now he pulled himself up, trembling and so drenched in perspiration that the blue silk of his robe clung to almost every contour of his herculean frame.

"My program," Elizabeth whispered. She reached out to the baby, who whimpered fretfully and plucked at his torc with swollen little fingers. At her touch he subsided and breathed easily.

"It's working, then?" Minanonn asked. "We'll be able to cure him?"

Elizabeth seemed frozen except for her hand, which caressed the front fastening knob of the infant's torc. Minanonn repeated his questions and she said, "I don't know if we'll be able to cure him. We're working so slowly . . . it's taking a tremendous toll of your coercive strength. But the program itself—" She lifted her head and met his gaze. "Minanonn, just for an instant, the baby went operant."

He stared, uncomprehending.

"That beautiful flash of harmonious function," she said. "He was bypassing the old torc-generated neural circuitry completely, using *more* than the fresh channels we'd opened. He slipped into true operant metafunction."

The Heretic was sitting on the edge of the couch now, and as he listened his fingers went to the gold at his own throat. "The baby's mind functioned metapsychically without the torc? As yours does, and that of the King?"

She nodded. "When I designed this salvage program, I naturally based it upon human paradigms—metapsychic patterns similar to those imposed upon the young children I taught back in the Milieu. A certain percentage of human offspring are potentially operant—but metafaculties almost never develop optimally unless the young mind is trained. The process is rather like learning to talk. Oral communication is an immensely complicated business that we tend to take for granted, but a child won't learn it unless his brain receives the proper input, preferably at a very early age when volition is very strong. Gaining full access to one's spectrum of metafunctions also depends largely upon education—although under special circumstances the process can become virtually instinctive. There's a lot we still don't know—especially about repressive factors that tend to keep a person nonoperant in spite of strong latencies."

"As happened with Felice."

"And Aiken," she agreed. "The two of them eventually did attain operancy, but by very different routes. Felice's painful breakthrough was similar to the procedure I used on Brede Shipspouse. But Aiken's . . . As I said, there are things we don't know. It seems that, occasionally, persons with exceptionally great latencies can raise themselves by mental bootstraps to the higher level. Certainly the pre-Intervention human metas were almost all self-taught. But once our race was inducted into the Milieu, we depended upon preceptive techniques taught to us by the exotics. For example, we laid the groundwork for childhood metapsychic education by telepathic interaction between mother and fetus."

Minanonn uttered a weak laugh. "With our torcs, things are much simpler!"

"Simplest doesn't equate with best." Her tone was sharp. "Babies wouldn't need to learn to walk if you cut off their legs and grafted their bodies to efficient motorized carts!"

His head drooped. "You're right, of course. I'm not thinking too clearly." He scrubbed the sweat from his brow with the back of one great hand. "Goddess, but I'm tired. Toward the last, I was afraid I'd let you down. We finished that segment just in time."

"You did very well," she reassured him. But even as she spoke she slid an adroit lancet-probe into his mind, and was shocked at the profundity of his fatigue. She herself was drained, but the Tanu hero, unused to husbanding his strength during prolonged and concentrated actions, seemed to have strained his coercive faculty almost to the breaking point. The digital clock on the nursery wall showed that they had been working for nearly eight hours. It was past two in the morning. "You're going to have to rest now," she told him. "What we did was very hard work."

"You don't have to tell me that!" He rose shakily from the couch and looked down on the child, who had drifted off to sleep. "I feel as though I'd just fought a Grand Combat single-handed. But *he* was the only antagonist."

"The minds of children are far less fragile than those of adults. It's a survival thing."

He sighed, and managed a rueful smile. "Well, I'm game to work him over again tomorrow night if you are."

"Minanonn—" She hesitated, then laid a hand on his enormous forearm. "We'd better wait a while longer. Three days."

His blond brows shot up, and then his eyes brightened in alarm and comprehension. "That bad, eh?"

She nodded. "It's not your fault. You're one of the finest coercers I know. But the job is fiendishly difficult. The concentrated small-scale thrusting—"

Minanonn said to the baby, "Oh, you tough little beggar. More than a match for a worn-out warrior like me." He moved toward the door and asked Elizabeth, "Shall I tell Mary-Dedra to come?"

"Not yet. I want to reexamine the redacted regions of the child's brain first, while he's still quiet. Good night, Minanonn. And thank you."

When he had gone she resumed her seat beside the little bed and studied the commissures with her deep-seeing eye. The baby's pain was temporarily in abeyance; but was he really improved? His fever was still high and there were new blisters forming in the neck area. Tough, Brendan might be—nevertheless, he was still very likely doomed. The bludgeon technique of mind alteration had been effective, but it was much too slow.

If only Minanonn were stronger, Elizabeth lamented. She was sure that the redactor-coercer configuration was the correct one in this case. Strength. That was the key . . .

The baby slept. Strong little Brendan, whose unfolding mind had fought the torc instead of adapting. Were the children who succumbed always the fighters, always the ones hovering closest to natural operancy? Aiken Drum in the fullness of young adulthood had resisted his torc and conquered it. *How?* But Aiken would not know, being, as he was, a natural talent, inexperienced in metapsychic analysis. And even though he was by far the greatest coercer in Europe, she did not dare ask him to assist her in the child's redaction. Aiken was too badly damaged himself, too near dissolution.

She slumped back in the chair, brooding, and felt a welcome cool breeze brush her bare shoulders. If only the wretched hot weather would break and an honest thunderstorm recharge the atmosphere with negative ions. Then she might be able to make sense of it. Not only solve the problem of the black-torc babies but the greater question as well, her own mountain of challenge, erected by Brede.

The wind intensified and she let herself luxuriate in it, reaching back to lift her hair. "Oh, that's wonderful," she murmured.

"I'm glad you like it. I wish I could manage the storm for you, but the range is too extreme."

She whirled about, galvanized by astonishment, then froze to see Marc Remillard watching her from just outside the open window. This time, the cross-sectional halo effect of the mind-enhancing equipment was reduced to an indistinct shimmer and his body, suspended in midair, seemed completely material. She could see the play of muscle beneath the tight black pressure-suit as he lifted his right hand, palm forward, in the familiar Milieu metapsychic greeting that invited physical as well as mental touch.

No! she cried in instinctive revulsion, leaping from the chair and backing away.

A fresh wave of chill air emanated from him. He smiled sadly, one side of his mouth lifted slightly higher than the other. The hand dropped slowly to his side.

"You're really here," she stated, rather than asked.

"As you see, Grand Master."

"It's a genuine hyperspatial translation? By mind-power alone?"

"The cerebroenergetic enhancer assists me in generating the upsilon-field, but I do the actual d-jump—and the return, of course—under my own steam."

"I presume you learned the program from Felice. Did she injure you seriously in the process?"

Instead of replying, he demanded, "Where is she? I've been unable to farsense her aura, even with the CE rig augmenting my search faculties to the maximum."

Elizabeth showed him the site of the girl's tomb alongside the Río Genil, the impervious globe of the room without doors buried deep in the rockfall. "Felice is beyond your reach, Marc. You'll have to look for another partner."

The shadowed eyes seemed to twinkle. "You've left yourself vulnerable, Grand Master."

She stood straight. "Why don't you come inside and do your worst? We've learned a few things in the Milieu since your damned Rebellion! All metas learn self-defensive maneuvers to forestall the kind of coercive manipulation you and your confederates used. And for Grand Masters, there's a last recourse against mind-violation that I'd almost welcome using at this point."

"Perhaps I'd better stay where I am. For both our sakes. The CE rig persists in following me through hyperspace like Mary's little lamb. Unless your chalet has reinforced floors, I might prove a perilous guest in more ways than one."

Fascinated in spite of herself, she asked, "Do you mean that the machine will stay behind, once the translation program is properly edited?"

"Oh, yes. And the coverall, too, if I wished." He made a Gallic gesture. "However, I'll retain it to spare you the sight of my scars."

"What do you want?" she asked, tiring of the verbal fencing.

He nodded at the sleeping baby. "His problem interests me. It's not unlike certain matters that once occupied me . . . au temps perdu."

"I'm sure Brother Anatoly would agree."

He laughed. "You feel a certain affinity?"

"For another member of the Frankenstein Club? Oh, yes. But I'm a comparative amateur in meddling with the course of human evolution. I lack your self-assurance as well as your paramount qualifications. Take this black-torc business—I'm bungling it and the baby will likely die, but I can't help feeling that it would be for the best. If I save Brendan and the others like him, what future would they have in this poor damned land? I don't need Brede's clairvoyance to foresee what's going to happen when you get to Europe. There will be a war over the time-gate site."

"Not if Aiken cooperates with me instead of with my son. *You* could show Aiken where his best interests lie."

She laughed bitterly. "You're a fool if you think I can exert that kind of influence. Aiken does as he pleases. If he's decided to help your children escape from you, nothing I say or do will deter him."

The hovering dark shape drifted nearer, sending a wash of chill air ahead. Hastily, Elizabeth covered the baby.

"Your protestations of helplessness lack conviction," Marc said. "Perhaps you have your own reasons for encouraging the building of a Pliocene time-gate."

"And what about your motive for preventing it?" she retorted. "Are you really so afraid that the Magistratum will come after you? Or is it that you would prefer to see your children dead rather than lose them to the Unity you couldn't accept?"

"You misjudge me," he said. "I love them. Everything I've done has been for them. For all human children. For Mental Man crying to be born—"

"Let it be, Marc!" she cried. "It's over—it has been, for more than twenty-seven years! Humanity chose the other way, not yours!" A great weariness oppressed her and she felt her eyes sting. The strong mental walls she had erected against the commanding presence of the Milieu's challenger wavered, weakened. She was vulnerable and he knew it—but he forbore. She whispered, "Let your children go. The Millieu will welcome them. Turn your ship around and return to North America. I'll do my utmost to insure that the Pliocene side of the time-gate is permanently closed, so that you and the other Rebels will be left unmolested."

"How will you do that?" he asked. "By going back to the Milieu yourself?"

She turned her head away. "Leave us alone, Marc. Don't destroy our little world."

"Poor Grand Master. It's a difficult rôle you've chosen. Almost as lonely as mine." The sound of his voice intensified and she looked up, startled, to see that he was actually standing on the broad sill of the window. There was no longer any trace of ghostly machinery surrounding him. As in a dream, Elizabeth watched him step down and walk slowly to the infant's wicker bed, leaving wet footprints on the parquet floor. The exudation of cold air was no longer apparent. He was fully materialized, divorced from the mind-enhancing equipment. One gloved hand gripped the rim of the baby basket and she heard the fibers creak. His gray eyes beneath their heavy winged brows held hers.

"Show me the program you're using in the child's redaction. Quickly! I can't sustain this stasis for more than a few minutes."

Her mind had gone numb, beyond fear. She summoned the program and displayed it.

"Very ingenious. Is it entirely your own construct?"

"No. Great chunks of it come from the preceptive courses I used when teaching children at the Metapsychic Institute on Denali."

"Redactive science has come a long way since my day . . . I would judge that this program of yours is fully capable of effecting a cure."

"It's too slow." Her admission was starkly clinical. "At the rate I was going with Minanonn, the procedure would take more than twelve hundred hours. The baby would almost certainly die before we could finish."

"All you need do is magnify the coercive loading. At that minute focus, the child's mind can endure ten times the pressure Minanonn delivers." He had gone into the small brain, scrutinizing, testing. The baby stirred and exhaled a soft cooing sound, smiling in his sleep.

Elizabeth said, "I can only utilize a single auxiliary mind in this configuration. Phasing in a coercive metaconcert is out of the question."

"I was thinking of something quite different." Marc withdrew his redactive faculty and took two steps backward. "We would have to wait until Manion and Kramer and I solve the problem of maintaining my translation in stasis—holding off the rubberband effect that tends to pull me back to the takeoff point of the jump. We couldn't risk that happening in mid-redaction. Even with a maximum feed of coercion, it will still take more than a hundred hours to finish the little chap off."

"Finish him?" Elizabeth's voice was a faltering whisper.

Marc's mind engaged hers on the intimate mode: Together we could heal him completely. With certain emendations of your program we might even raise him to permanent operancy.

"Work with *you*? But I could never—"

"You could never trust me?" The asymmetrical smile was self-mocking. He tapped the side of his head and greenish drops flew from his dripping hair to splatter the window frame. "I'm barebrained at this end of the d-jump, Elizabeth. There would be no danger to you if we use the program exactly as formulated—coercer-inferior, with you retaining executive function. You'd be quite safe from . . . diabolical influence."

He seemed to step outside into the night. The semitransparent cerebroenergetic equipment reformed about his levitant body and he began to recede rapidly; but his mental voice was distinct:

I want to do this. Let me help you.

She asked, "How long do you think it will take you to solve the stasis problem?" And thought: Am I mad? Am I actually taking his proposal seriously—willing to trust him?

He said: I'll need at least a week. Pehpaps a bit longer. Can you keep the child alive that long?

"Minanonn and I can continue the procedure. If no complications turn up, the baby should survive. I think . . ."

And a fading ironic comment: Perhaps Brother Anatoly can storm heaven.

Then the starry sky was empty and the infant wailed—hungry, cold, and in need of changing.

10

THE FORMER MR. JUSTICE BURKE, STRIPPED TO BREECHCLOUT
and mocassins, knelt spraddle-legged in the canoe hidden in
the reeds and waited for the waterbuck to slosh a meter or so
nearer, within positive dub-shot range. This time he couldn't
miss.

The sun above the marshland of the Upper Moselle valley
was a brass porthole into hell. Sweat trickled from beneath
Burke's headband into his eyes, blurring the approaching antelope. He blinked slowly, breathed in shallow pants, held the
taut bowstring against his cheek. His kishkas were contorted
in a frightful ache; his skull pounded; his cramped hamstrings
added their pangs to the hangover's anguish. Then he saw that
the buckthorn arrowshaft was warped—and this final evidence
of incompetence wrung an unvoiced "Gevalt!" from his re-
buking aboriginal conscience. He shifted aim in a futile attempt
to compensate, and let fly.

The arrow nicked the waterbuck across the withers. The
animal leaped, floundering in hock-deep water. Partially chewed
plants drooled from its mouth. Peopeo Moxmox Burke of the
Wallawalla whipped another arrow into position and shot again,

wide of the mark. The antelope bounded off in a series of great splashes. Frightened mallards took to the air ahead of it and a pied swan, hooting, exploded up from a patch of sawgrass. Then it was quiet except for Burke's muttered curses.

He lowered the bow and let it drop onto the canoe bottom. Taking up the paddle, he dug in deeply and sent the boat shooting out of the natural blind into open water, heading for the thin shade of taxodium cypress. After he had moored to one of the half-submerged knee-roots, he took a long drink from his skin bota. Something seemed to twang behind his eyeballs. He drank again and his sight cleared. Grunting, he worked himself into a comfortable position and began to examine the rest of the arrows.

Almost all of them were off true.

He picked up the bow. The laminations of yew wood were separating as the cement succumbed to decay. The twisted sinew of the bowstring was frayed and weak. Even the buckskin quiver was spotted with mildew and gaping at the seams. Small wonder that he hadn't managed to take a single antelope! The bow and arrows, like the rest of his Native American paraphernalia, had lain neglected on the shelf of his wigwam for long months during his southern adventures. Since his return to Hidden Springs, he had been too busy planning countermeasures against the encroaching Firvulag to take time to hunt.

What in the world had been in his mind this morning, prompting this primitivist folly?

He had flung himself out of Marialena Torrejon's bed, abruptly awake, with the ringing declaration that there would take place that night a great feast—an official celebration of the great news!—and he, freeleader of the Lowlives, would provide game for the entrée.

"You want *another* party?" Marialena asked blearily, disentangling her plump limbs from the linen sheets. "Hombre, que te jodas! I've got a head like an exploding volcano after last night—"

He only grinned owlishly. The village had gone into a frenzy of jubilation when he announced that Nodonn's coup had failed and Basil and the Bastards were safe. "But I didn't tell you all of Elizabeth's news, bubeleh. I wanted to save it! We'll have a really big feast—a monster barbecue, you hear me? I'll bring you six antelope to roast. Afterwards I'll tell you and the rest of the people the biggest news since the Flood!"

"Loco indio," she mumbled fondly. "No me importa dos cojones." She came squirming toward him. "Look, it's nice and cool now. You don't really want to go hunting. Lucien and the kids can get game for your feast. Vamos a pichar, mi corazón, mi porra de azúcar—"

She made a grab for him, but he was already out the door of her hut, buck-naked in the dawn (and still well shickered, if the truth be told), aflame with atavistic masculine instincts that were, at least for now, more imperative than sex. He stumbled to his wigwam and got dressed—not in the chino cargo pants and sturdy boots that had been his customary garb ever since the exodus from Muriah, but in his old breechclout and moccasins. When he rummaged about for hunting equipment he shoved aside the modern plass-and-metal compound bow, deadly and dependable, and the iron-tipped vitredur arrows that had slain so many exotic antagonists. He took up instead the gear he had chosen to carry through the time-gate many years earlier, when he still cherished a dream of returning to tribal ways.

Peopeo Moxmox, noble savage and late Justice of the Washington State Supreme Court, sat in his canoe and laughed. The craft was not made of bark but of decamole, that marvel of Milieu technology, and he would deflate it and tuck it into a waist-pouch when the day's comedy ended. He suddenly remembered the tag good old Saul Mermelstein used to tease him with when he was a fledgling lawyer in Salt Lake City: "Lo, the poor Indian, whose soul proud science never taught to stray..." But he had, he had! And nowhere more than in the primeval Pliocene.

He fingered the warped shaft of an arrow, turning it so that the carefully chipped obsidian point glittered in the sun. Somewhere back in the wigwam was a shaft straightener, a simple gadget no primitive huntsman would be without. But on the other hand, vitredur arrows were indestructible, with self-fletching and a wide assortment of interchangeable heads. Some of them even had built-in transponders for tracking wounded game and easy retrieval.

Apple Injun!

"So why *did* I come out here today?" he inquired of the world at large. "Why ask, Burke? You hopeless shmegeggeh!"

An unseen crocodilian choofed and a warbler sang. Two blue butterflies twirled in a mating dance above the gleaming water. He caught a whiff of vanilla essence in the still, hot air and looked up to see a spray of exquisite tiny orchids growing from a cleft in the bark of the cypress. Burke reached out and touched it. He was very glad he had come, glad he had killed nothing.

After a while he consulted his wrist chronograph, a thing as handsome (and nonaboriginal) as his golden torc. The time was coming up on 1600 hours, and he had left a note for Denny Johnson, asking to be met at the river trail with chalikos and plenty of game bags for the antelopes . . .

Grinning, he untied the painter and stroked out into the lagoon toward the mainstream of the Moselle. The swan reappeared, majestic in black-and-white plumage, and glided tamely after the canoe. As Burke left it behind and the ripples of his wake subsided, the bird seemed poised in the center of a peat-dark mirror, superimposed upon a reflection of itself. Clumps of emerald grasses topped by feathery plumes framed it against the deeper green of the jungle. Staring back over his shoulder, Burke caught his breath. He would remember this—and so much more.

Then the canoe grounded on a mudbar. Setting aside the paddle, he boosted the craft over into the river backwater, stood up, and began to pole stoutly upstream. He hoped that Denny himself would be waiting. There would be salutary jibes to endure, but as they rode back to Hidden Springs he could break the news about the time-gate. And they could discuss ways and means for a Lowlife capture of Castle Gateway.

Lowlife prisoners from Iron Maiden and Haut Fourneauville numbering sixty or seventy were armed and ready in their big wooden cage. Their position was one of strength, partially sheltered behind granite outcroppings at the crest of the small ridge. There was no way they could be surprised or outflanked, no chance that the Firvulag might overwhelm them by resorting to the traditional massed assault or bogeyman tactics. The Lowlife miners, veterans of many a skirmish in the beleaguered Iron Villages, would only be bested by mind-power.

Up in the royal observation post on a nearby height, King Sharn chewed his lower lip as he watched the first company

of stalwart gnomes, led by Pingol the Horripilant, begin their
advance. Curses and catcalls came from the defending prisoners, but they held their fire. Some experienced fighter must
have taken on the leadership, imparting a modicum of discipline
to the demoralized crew. Their yells subsided, then rose afresh
as a second and smaller contingent of Firvulag, warrior ogresses
under Fouletot Blackbreast, started up the ravine on the left
shoulder of the ridge. This route provided more shelter for the
attackers, but was considerably steeper. To Sharn and Ayfa,
watching the maneuvers from their vantage point half a kilometer away, the two assault forces looked like separate swarms
of jet-black beetles, serrated pikes and standards waving like
antennae under the blazing sun, creeping up on a gigantic
exposed picnic basket.

"I still think it was a mistake to arm the prisoners with iron,"
Sharn said. "Just one scratch, and it's curtains for our folks."

"They've got to get used to the hazard," Ayfa retorted brutally. "Do you think Roniah will be defended with glass swords
and bronze battle-axes? By rights, those prisoners should have
stunners and laser carbines as well as arrows tipped with the
blood metal. That's what our troops will be up against in a
real battle. Look what happened to Mimee's outfit at Bardelask."

"Hell, they won, didn't they?"

"Only because the Bardy-Town defenders were vastly outnumbered and ran out of arrows. And if Aiken Drum's supply
train had arrived with the futuristic weaponry, it would have
been Goddess-Bless-Me-ere-I-Sleep!" The Queen frowned at
the Firvulag forces creeping up the hill. "Our lads and lasses
have to understand that *mind-power* is the only sure way to
victory. Concerted mind-power—not our usual higgledy-pig-
gledy uncoordinated individual efforts. That's why Betularn
White Hand set up these maneuvers to give the Lowlives the
tactical advantage—and why he put gonzo youngsters like
Fouletot and Pingol in command of this first demonstration."

"Let's hope the prisoners put up a good fight," Sharn said,
shading his eyes to peer at the now silent cage. "Be a pity if
they funked out."

Ayfa snickered. "Betularn gave them his personal assurance
that if they managed to hold off our troops until sunset, we'd
set them free."

The King guffawed in appreciation of the jest. "Poor dolts! They never seem to learn that the solemn word of a Firvulag holds only when given to another Firvulag or a Tanu—not to a Lowlife. I mean, how can you make a pact of honor with a nonperson?"

"But they keep falling for it," Ayfa observed, shaking her sable-helmed head in wonderment. "Even the biggest Lowlife of them all!"

The King leaned forward in his seat, scowling. "Pingol's bunch is getting too damn close to the cage. Why doesn't he call up the defensive screen? Any minute now those prisoners— *Té's tushie!*"

At the monarch's exclamation of dismay a hail of iron-tipped missiles exploded from the cage and rained upon the frontal assault force. There were scattered screeches and wails and a tardy telepathic command. A sparkling barrier of mental energy sprang raggedly into existence, flickering here and there as some dwarf belatedly linked into the defensive metaconcert. The Lowlives bellowed in derision and sent off salvo after salvo of arrows. Most of Pingol's company held their ground and concentrated on shoring up the mind-shield, which steadied into a translucent bubble-section three or four meters high that hovered just ahead of the forward ranks. Even at a distance, Sharn and Ayfa could hear the sinister tinkle of iron points striking this barrier and falling away.

Well done! the King broadcast, by way of encouragement. He rose up and assumed his guise of a monstrous scorpion. A handful of gnomes raised a pro forma cheer, but most of them had all they could do to keep the great protective umbrella erected. For others, motionless on the rocks in tumbled and broken attitudes, the mental shelter had come too late.

"They didn't act together, and the screen's too widespread," Ayfa noted, glowering her disapproval. "And that turd-head Pingol waited much too long before giving the command—"

"Here come the big girls!" Sharn exclaimed.

Fouletot's ogresses were swarming up the defile to the left of the cage, a businesslike little screen protecting them in the steep terrain. A dozen or so of the giant exotics, perhaps one-fifth of the total force, fell back from the others and gathered into a close formation. An instant later a gout of blue flame soared up from their midst like a shot from a Roman candle. It arced high above the ridge and fell onto the cage roof, where it sank slowly through the heavy gridwork to the accompaniment of hideous Lowlife screams. Coils of greasy smoke seeped out around the rocks. After a brief pause, a furious shower of arrows descended upon the ogresses. One fell, howling, and the survivors hastened to expand their screen.

Downslope in front of the cage, the gnomish force was redeploying. A desultory discharge of arrows fell on them, to be mostly deflected by their mental screen. This was now much more compact and efficient, generated by a semicircle of creative stalwarts who slowly advanced up the hill. Only the occasional missile penetrated, but these were sufficient to bring death with the slightest wound. The humans inside the cage jeered and screamed at the top of their lungs every time an exotic fell.

Now Pingol's fighters left off waving their halberds and skull-draped standards and formed three bodies in close array behind the moving shield. Suddenly three glowing balls of energy, almost white beneath the harsh sun, flew up in cometlike trajectories and converged upon the cage. The structure burst actively into flame and the prisoners inside shrieked and leaped about, batting at the blazing timbers with their garments and dousing the more stubborn flames with their scant supply of drinking water. The storm of arrows abated only slightly, and within minutes was thicker than ever.

The smaller force of ogresses had attained a rocky platform, a stratum of denser rock that capped the top of the ravine about fifty meters below the end of the cage. The ledge was very narrow, little more than a sharp lip strewn with slippery scree from the precipitous slope above. Rather than attempting this, they strung out in a cordon, maintaining the mind-screen umbrella. At a farspoken signal, each warrior extended her black-glass sword and opened a slit in the screen. From the points of the weapons flowed individual corruscating rays that united, just before striking the cage, into a thick, twisted flash of lightning. It hit the cage squarely, and at the same time a blast of thunder reached the ears of Sharn and Ayfa and caused them to blink, so that they missed the beginning of Pingol's charge—then shouted in delight at the sight of the gnomes, still in their disciplined trifid formation preceded by the shielders, racing up the hill and bombarding the cage with a fusillade of small psychocreative bursts.

"Beautiful!" shouted Sharn, lashing about with his scorpion tail. He knocked over the refreshment table, but neither he nor the Queen seemed to notice that they were jumping up and down in a mess of spilled beer, hooby mushrooms, Danish cucumbers, slices of black melon, eel à la Flamande, and candied malmignattes.

Ayfa cried: *Smite the Lowlife bastards! Arms united, minds united!*

And the Firvulag soldiery responded: *Yllahayl the Foe!*

The thunderbolt generated by Fouletot Blackbreast and her platoon had knocked that end of the cage to flinders at the same time that it killed numbers of human defenders outright. The survivors now began to scramble out onto the rocks, brandishing their bows and arrows, long knives, and small tomahawks, ready to engage the advancing Firvulag hand to hand. More fireballs popped up from the dwarf attackers. The ogresses got off one last streak of lightning, completing the demolition of the cage. Then humans and exotics mingled in combat, the Lowlives diving under shaky mental screens or shooting arrows in high parabolas so that the missiles might strike the rear ranks of the enemy. Discipline among the exotics wavered, then collapsed. Both officers and troops forgot about working in metaconcert and reverted to the traditional fighting form. They bawled out the old battle cries, shape-shifted into monstrous apparitions, and fell upon the outnumbered Lowlives. Dwarfs hacked and flailed with serrated obsidian blades. Ogres thrust about, impaling bodies with barbed lances—or even snatched up disarmed humans to rend them limb from limb. The tumult reverberated throughout the fastness of Grand Ballon mountain. Plumes of smoke and steam rose as the odd stalwart remembered orders and used mental energy to annihilate the foe.

Sharn and Ayfa, wearing their normal shapes and saying nothing, watched. The blinding disk of the sun descended behind the towers of High Vrazel and a cool wind swept away some of the carnage stench. Carrion birds circled and began to descend. Finally there settled over the rocky battleground a great stillness, and in the minds of the King and Queen rang the simultaneous farspoken voices of Pingol and Fouletot:

High King and High Queen—we proclaim a victory in Té's name!

All the dwarfs and ogres and middling monsters came together on the foreslope beneath the devastated cage, and with weapons and standards raised on high, shouted: "Praise and glory to Té, Goddess of Battles! And to Sharn and Ayfa, High King and High Queen! And to the Great Captains Pingol and Fouletot—and to all of *us*! Arms united! Minds united! *Slitsal! Slitsal! Slitsal!*"

Hearts full, the co-monarchs made the ritual response and declared the maneuvers at a triumphant end. After that they stood for some time watching as the stretcher bearers and healers and morticians and inspectors and talleymen and salvors and the other homely technicians of war's aftermath did their work. The mock battle had cost twenty-two Firvulag lives; only three were wounded. Every last human prisoner had been slain.

Sharn said, "It was well done. The other captains will profit by this demonstration to the death, and subsequent maneuvers can be bloodless."

"They'll jolly well have to be, now that the Iron Villages are nearly abandoned," Ayfa said. "We're smack out of prisoners—unless we want to unleash Monolokee the Scunnersome on Fort Rusty."

"Not yet. Mopping up the Vosges Lowlives can wait until truce time. We'll have to concentrate on important business during the next three weeks. There's the Tourney practice in addition to the Nightfall preliminaries. And Roniah."

The Queen retrieved a golden goblet from the floor, tapped a fresh keg of beer, and resumed her seat. "Still planning to make a big deal of it? Full-scale assault, with Mimee and all?"

Sharn was still staring down at the battlefield, ham-sized fists resting on his ceremonially armored hips. "After seeing that we can really use metaconcert—I'm inclined to change the plan. Since Bardelask, the balance of terror has tipped nicely to our side; we won't need to labor the point at Roniah. As for Mimee, let him loot Bardelask and withdraw, so we seem to be caving in to Aiken's demands. Meanwhile, we take a force of stalwarts and infiltrate carefully along the east bank of the Saône, then make a lightning stab at the citadel from the river side after drifting down in decamole boats. Condateyr would never dream that we'd attempt a water invasion. Too unprecedented for the hidebound Little People! We whip in there fast as weasels, hit 'em with mind-power and blood-metal and high-tech zappers, raid the Milieu weapons cache—and streak out with the loot before the garrison can even pull its socks up." He turned around and grinned at his wife. "And if we strike just before the Truce, Aiken won't have any comeback."

"But the kid will be pissed to the wide, and he'll know who to blame—"

"True, but the High Table won't let him violate the Truce by mounting a counterstrike. He's constrained by his adopted Tanu ethics in dealing with *us*—but we're free to treat *him* like any other Lowlife!"

Ayfa considered for a moment. "It would be easy to disguise our people as Lowlives for the Roniah action. A little shape-shifting wouldn't drain much energy from the offensive meta-concert. And the deception would be enhanced by our use of iron and futuristic weapons. Of course, we'd have to carry away our deaders and be careful not to leave any incriminating equipment behind."

"I like it!" exclaimed Sharn. He picked up his own goblet, gave it a perfunctory wipe with the brocade table-runner, and held it out to Ayfa for filling. After taking a long pull, he studied the jewel-eyed skull of the late Velteyn of Finiah and remarked, "This chap here was really our first fruits of Nightfall, Ayfa. It all began at Finiah, with that first victory after so many years of ignominy—and was well and truly launched during the Last Grand Combat, even though we were robbed of our rightful triumph. The first event lifted our hearts; the second confirmed our resolution." He looked upon the orange-haired ogress tenderly. "I've commanded Mimee to send up the skull of Lady Armida of Bardelask to make a new matching goblet for you."

She lowered her eyes, feeling a sentimental tear steal down her cheek, and then could not help but say, "Before the rains come, we might even have a whole set!"

Sharn roared in appreciation. The two royals toasted each other and refilled the goblets. Sharn said, "Too bad Aiken's such a shrimp. His skull's barely big enough for an eggcup."

"We can take turns at breakfast," said his wife. "By the way—what did he want this morning?"

The King waved a dismissive paw. "Some drivel about reparations for Bardelask, to be debited against the Grand Tourney prizes. I agreed to everything he asked for. Why not? We can take it all back after Nightfall! . . . He came up with one matter that was a puzzler, though. Do we know anything about a Lowlife named Tony Wayland?"

"He was that chap the Worm captured. The one who spilled the beans about the aircraft hidden in the Vale of Hyenas."

Sharn smacked the edge of the table. "That's right. I'd forgotten. Well—Aiken wants us to give the creature back. He claims this Tony is the bosom buddy of a great friend of his. Even offered to knock off a goodly portion of the reparation if we fork him over right away."

Ayfa scowled as she swirled the dregs of her beer. "Oh, he did, did he? Something stinks here, vein of my heart. Skathe took a fancy to Tony. When I sent her and Karbree down to oversee the Bardelask operation, they carried the Lowlife along. And they died, Skathe and the Worm, in a most mysterious way . . ."

The King nodded. "Lowlife treachery written all over the murders. Mimee was at a loss to account for it. The city was already taken when the half-sunken boat and the bodies were found. So you think this Tony might have—"

"Who knows?" The Queen's face within her lunetted helmet wore a terrible expression. "Have Mimee keep an eye out for him. Pass the word to the other Little People in the South. If this Lowlife did kill my friend Skathe and the Worm, let's not be in too much of a hurry to give him back to the Tanu."

"Well," said the King, "Aiken didn't specify condition of merchandise."

Ayfa leaned over and kissed his bearded cheek. "You always understand."

"Always!" he repeated, catching the gleam in her eye. He set down his goblet on the table and gently detached hers from her hand. Then the two monstrous armored forms came together, and the sun-gilded rocks echoed with the clashing consummation.

Secure in his redoubt of peanut sacks, Tony Wayland watched from the loft of a dockside warehouse as the looting of Bardelask wound down to its fatal finale.

The last packtrains loaded with goods were gathering along the quayside road. Gangs of human captives, half-dead after almost a week of forced labor, now brought up the few remaining treasures to be gleaned from the buildings along the wharf: kegs of oil, alcohol, and dyestuffs, bales of rare leathers, loaf sugar, silken cordage and fabric, coffee beans in jute sacks, and cases of processed spices and precious strawberry jam.

Fortunately for Tony, the Firvulag did not care for peanuts. And after eating little else for six days, he was getting thoroughly sick of the worthy legume himself.

Through his golden torc, he could hear the dispirited telepathic speech of the gray-torced prisoners. (Anyone torced with gold or silver had been summarily slain.) From Tony's point of view, there was good news. Instead of holding Bardelask and using it as a base for harrying shipping on the Rhône, the invaders had been ordered to withdraw. The leader of the Famorel Host, a malignant gnome named Mimee whose illusory aspect was that of a flightless roc, had exploded in a paroxysm of avian rage at being deprived of this additional source of booty, and had snapped off the heads of twenty-two helpless grays before recovering his self-possession. Somewhat later, Tony learned that Mimee had suffered a second fit of pique when King Sharn canceled Famorel's participation in a projected assault on Roniah. This piece of intelligence helped Tony make up his mind to travel north, not south, when it was safe to leave his hiding place among the goobers.

Meanwhile, he used the time to get reacquainted with his torc.

The golden collar that the late Skathe had given him contained mind-expanding components precisely similar to those in the silver torc he had worn in Finiah. Unlike the silver, however, the golden torc had no slave-circuitry binding him to Tanu control, nor the tracking device that would enable gold-torced persons to locate him with minimal exertion of farsense. Wearing gold, Tony was free—but once again possessed of the wonderful powers that had made life so satisfying back in lost Finiah.

The enhancement of his modest psychocreative faculty gave him the ability to perform numerous small but useful energy-manipulative acts. He could extract water from the air for drinking, and remove it from his clammy clothing when the river mist enveloped his hiding place at night. He could roast the peanuts in their shells. When it was safe, he could strike a small light without recourse to a permamatch. He could zap fleas or other tiny vermin that dared to infest his person. When the loft grew stifling hot during the day, he could whistle up a cool breeze. If he became bored, the magic collar provided autoerotic amusement. It eased the pangs of physical fatigue, made injuries unnoticeable, sent him into refreshing sleep in a trice, woke him if any medium-to-large life-form approached within fifteen meters of his hiding place, banished anxieties, and cleared his head for fruitful planning. With it, he could speak, hear, and dimly see with his metasenses over a range of some 300 kilometers. (This last talent was none too common among silvers; but Tony had had eleven years of practice.) Since Finiah was a bit of a backwater, it had amused him to "collect" the mental signatures of certain Tanu notables whom he met at social occasions in the pleasure dome. Later, he would spy on them during their peregrinations in the open air. To his regret, he could not farsense through stone walls, but it had been diverting to see what the exotics got up to al fresco. Hunts were the least of it!

Now, as Tony waited for the Firvulag to evacuate Bardelask, he began to wonder which, if any, of his old silver-torc comrades might have survived the destruction of Finiah. Where were they now—old Yevgeny and Stendal, cocky Liem and stolid Tiny Tim, Luscious Lisette and Agnes Virgin-Martyr? Now he could call them . . . and for an hour or so, he did. But the signatures broadcast into the aether evoked not a single response. His friends of yore were either detorced or dead, lost in the chaos of changing times. He had no desire to farspeak his former Tanu associates, not even those who had called themselves his Creative Siblings. The exotics wouldn't care about him, a single human outcast among thousands of others. They had troubles of their own these days, poor devils—and not a few of them human-caused.

There was Dougal. Mad but loyal, he had been some kind of friend. But Dougal had worn no torc, and by now he was probably maggot-meat in the Hercynian Forest, where Karbree the Worm's patrol had ambushed them. No . . . there was only one living soul left in the Many-Colored Land who might care if Tony Wayland lived or died.

Or did she hate him by now? It would serve him right.

His eyes misted in self-pity and he leaned his head back against the crunchy peanut-sack pillow. Outside the warehouse were the noises of guttural Firvulag commands, whips cracking, hellads and chalikos snorting and blowing, the jingle of harness, the thump and thud of loading. It was hot and humid and tedious—time to call upon the torc's solace.

Then he heard an exotic's rage-filled roar. A human shriek bubbled and then stilled. Tony switched to the gray band and heard:

Damndamndamn *look* at poorWerner!

Poor sod should know better use figureeight hitch loose load like that bound spill—

But to pull his tongue out?

His fault for lipping Spook.

MaryMother he's bleeding death!

Sowhat? Weall be dead soon.

Lookoutlookout here come 3 Jabberwocks OChrist with zappers—

Sickened, Tony shut them out. There was nothing he could do to help the poor doomed bastards. Wails sounded outside, and curses, and a certain word barked out loudly in the Firvulag language. Then came sizzling chirps from Matsu carbines, one note after another in precise rhythm, until the human babble was stilled.

Tony let the torc's bright comfort cover him. He saw himself crossing the Rhône in a stolen boat, traveling cautiously north on the Great Road, surviving by his wits and the cachet of mental gold. Once the Truce began, the track north of Roniah would be mobbed with sports lovers of all three races, peacefully heading up to the Grand Tourney. It would be safe to travel openly then. He would go up the Saône trail, pass Firvulag-held Burask (harmless in Truce time), and finally voyage down the Nonol to the only sanctuary left to him—the city with toadstool domes that gleamed like El Dorado, the city hemmed with meadows and linked to the tournament Field of Gold by a rainbow bridge. The city of monsters, the city of friends. He would go home to Nionel and Rowane.

Rapt in the fantasy, he held her and knew joy. Later he woke to find that the sun had set and it was much cooler. Except for the distant howls of hyenas and the squeaking of rats in the warehouse, Bardelask was utterly silent.

Tony stood up, brushed peanut shells from his clothes, and went confidently down the loft ladder. Outisde on the quay he found what he was afraid he would find. But there was also a stout little wherry, complete with oars, tied up below the devastated ship chandler's shop. After a brief foray for items that the Firvulag had thought too insignificant for looting, Tony was ready to cast off. The boat floated on the placid Ysaar and there was no need to row. The current would carry him to the confluence with the Rhône, less than a kilometer away, and he could camp on the opposite bank of the larger river and start out for home in the morning.

11

AIKEN: GREETINGS, ELIZABETH.

ELIZABETH: Hello and congratulations! I see you're ready to leave Calamosk with the all-terrain vehicles. You've been very adroit in handling the young North Americans.

AIKEN: They've swallowed my bluff, if that's what you mean. And for the moment, they're willing to accept my authority. Hagen Remillard suspects something fishy might be going on, but he can't quite put his finger on what it is.

ELIZABETH: He's tried to probe you?

AIKEN: That's his sister's gig . . . but no, they've been discreet so far. Still sniffing me out.

ELIZABETH: Are you heading directly back to Goriah now?

AIKEN: All of us except the expedition to the Alps. They'll split from our caravan at the Amalizan crossroads. Sail across Lac Provençal and then head into the mountains along the trail behind Darask. They'll approach Monte Rosa via the Italian back door. Bleyn's on his way down from Goriah to lead the expedition and Ochal the Harper will be his second. I'm sending seven of the fifteen fourplex ATVs, with ten of Hagen's nontechnical people as drivers. Basil and his Bastards will go, of course—all except one guy named Dimitri Anastos, who's some kind of hotshot u-field

142

engineer. Hagen thought he might come in handy on the time-gate project. I'm filling out the expedition with thirty-odd Tanu and elite golds, armed to the teeth. Those aircraft are the family jewels, babe. Time-gate or no time-gate, I'll be truly snookered if I don't get my hands on them in time to counter Marc and the Firvulag. You could help the expedition, if you would.

ELIZABETH: Routemaking?

AIKEN: Primarily. The Darask people say that nobody knows the territory east of the Maritimes. To the north is Famorel, of course. The expedition wants to avoid an encounter with Mimee's forces at all costs. If you could keep an eye out, steer them away from hostiles, show them the fastest routes for the ATVs, you'd save lives.

ELIZABETH: Of course. I'll be glad to.

AIKEN: [Relief.] I was afraid it might be against one of your damn principles.

ELIZABETH: I can't assist you in *aggression*, Aiken. This is nothing of the sort. Your acquisition of the aircraft may prevent war.

AIKEN: It better.

ELIZABETH: Will you begin work immediately on the Guderian device?

AIKEN: I've got Alberonn and Lady Morna-la tracking down likely technicians and other boffin types right now. They'll assemble the personnel in Goriah. I wish I could hide the project away in some secret spot where Marc wouldn't be able to find it—but I wouldn't trust Hagen out of my sight, and there are some other specimens among those young rascals who make *him* look like Sir Galahad. Oh, we're getting along famously.

ELIZABETH: Do you really think it will be possible to build the taufield generator?

AIKEN: These North Americans brought a hell of a lot of stuff with them—components, manufacturing apparatus, gadgets galore. And we'll probably find more useful items in the Goriah store that Kuhal and Celo mopped up for me. They're finishing the new inventory now. The most difficult raw material will be some rare-earth element Hagen says we'll have to mine in Fennoscandia. Even with an aerial survey, it'll be the devil's own job to locate the ores. None of the

Tanu are familiar with that northern country.

ELIZABETH: You should enlist Sugoll's help.

AIKEN: ?

ELIZABETH: Numbers of his people lived in that region prior to the Howler ingathering. Some may still remain. I know that many mutants were keen miners of jewels and precious metals. If you described these rare-earth minerals to them, they might be able to expedite your survey.

AIKEN: Great idea. I'll farspeak Sugoll, spin him some yarn—

ELIZABETH: Tell him the truth. About everything.

AIKEN: You don't think he'd . . . oh, my God, *no*!

ELIZABETH: All peace-loving persons in the Many-Colored Land must know about the time-gate. And have the option to choose.

AIKEN: [Laughter.] Oh, Woman! I can just see it. Nine or ten thousand hobgoblins pouring out of the gate into twenty-second-century France! There goes the neighborhood! The Milieu would have to find a spare planet or something.

ELIZABETH: You could be dirigent.

AIKEN: Who said I was returning?

ELIZABETH: Aren't you? I took it for granted.

AIKEN: Take yourself for granted, sweets. The gate project is a long, long shot at a murky target. I have plenty of other troubles to keep me amused. Such as regaining my own sanity and powers before that damned Abaddon lands in Europe.

ELIZABETH: Aiken . . . I thought you knew about Marc's d-jumping ability. [Image.] He came here. To Black Crag. He doesn't have the faculty under control yet, but it won't be long before he's able to teleport anywhere in the world.

AIKEN: Then Hagen was telling the truth. I hoped he had it wrong—that Marc was only pulling some sophisticated bilocation stunt with his augmented farsenses and creativity.

ELIZABETH: He materialized inside my chalet.

AIKEN: Jesus! Did he threaten you?

ELIZABETH: No.

AIKEN: I can give you a sigma generator. Hagen doesn't think Marc will be able to d-jump through its force-field.

ELIZABETH: Thank you, but no. I must deal with Marc in my own way.

AIKEN: You have a way? Nice! I wish I could say the same. We've been hiding under Hagen's big SR-35 sigma for our conferences here so Marc couldn't farpeep or join the party— and I'll use the thing in Goriah to shield the Guderian project. But the King can't live permanently inside a friggerty silver fishbowl . . . When Marc gets his act together, he'll put the screws on me proper. And I'm scared, sweets. When he finds out about the gate project, he'll try to burn me— and maybe succeed.

ELIZABETH: He's much weaker than he was before. Felice injured both his body and his brain.

AIKEN: That's what Hagen and Cloud said. But they didn't know how seriously his barebrain wattage had been diminished. Even if he's ninety percent wrecked, he's probably more than a match for Me right now! . . . Not to mention the help he'll get from *them*.

ELIZABETH: [Concern.] Them. You're not talking about the Remillard children and their friends, or the older Rebels—

AIKEN: [Quiet laughter.]

ELIZABETH: . . . There's been no improvement in your subsumption?

AIKEN: I'm losing ground, if anything.

ELIZABETH: Symptoms?

AIKEN: I haven't slept since the fight with Nodonn. Ten perishing days. I can barely fly, let alone carry anything. My creativity is shot except for illusion making. The redaction is just about wiped out. I can still coerce. (Wouldn't you know?) I can farsense, but it hurts like hell.

ELIZABETH: I never would have known. You have a very deceptive psychosurface.

AIKEN: [Desperate weariness.] You mean, dear lady, that I am *tricky*. It may be my last bastion of survival. If I don't get some help soon, I'll be stark raving mad before Truce.

ELIZABETH: Oh, Aiken.

AIKEN: Well? I'm ready. Say the word, and I'll come.

ELIZABETH: To Black Crag—?

AIKEN: Unless you've learned to deep-redact at distance. The ATV train leaves Calamost within the hour. It'll take us less than two days to reach the Amalizan cutoff where we rendezvous with Bleyn and split off the Alpine expedition. Black Crag is only eighty kloms from there as the golden falcon flies. I think I can just about make it. Say—on the evening of September fifth.

ELIZABETH: Aiken . . . I'm expecting Marc to return here. It wouldn't be safe for you to come. Not even with the sigma. He mustn't . . . I don't dare . . .

AIKEN: [Anger + fear.] Maybe you think I'm joking about my mental state! Well, I'm not. During the day when I'm busy it's not so bad. But every night they get bigger, more out of control. They're doing it that way so the last joke will be on me. I won't just die, I'll die *ridiculous*!

ELIZABETH: I don't understand. You say you're experiencing hallucinations now along with the metapsychic weakening and the pain?

AIKEN: It's not a delusion! It's real [image] real grotesque I'm so ashamed it can't be happening [image] not to Me and Mine they're dead there's no way they can be doing it [image] making me swell and burn and drain away again [image] and again [image] not real or real it doesn't matter because it's ruining me Me me *ELIZABETH HELP ME!!* [Supremely obscene montage abruptly cut off.]

ELIZABETH: Yes. Of course I'll help. I'll come to you.

AIKEN: Come?

ELIZABETH: Be easy, dear. I'll come. Minanonn will bring me— and Dionket and Creyn as well. We'll help you.

AIKEN: Alone. Come alone. (Nobody must know! Nobody must know!)

ELIZABETH: I'll need help, just as I did when I redacted you on the Río Genil, after the battle with Felice. Trust me.

AIKEN: You'll really come?

ELIZABETH: Yes. Now listen to me. We'll need a secure place. We don't want to use the sigma. The thing is a virtual beacon to a long-distance farsensor and Marc mustn't suspect that I'm working on you.

AIKEN: (Nobody must know! Him above all! Humiliation! Ridicule! A jest on the jester!)

ELIZABETH: There are more important reasons for secrecy. I can only help you to set up a skeletal structure for your reintegration. A mental framework for you to mount the subsumed faculties on.

AIKEN: I won't be cured . . . ?

ELIZABETH: You'll be freed of distressing symptoms if the

redaction succeeds, able to reestablish your metafaculties by yourself. You'll heal, just as you did after the Río Genil. But you don't want your enemies to know your weakness.

AIKEN: (Nobody must know the shame.)

ELIZABETH: Listen. I've asked Minanonn, and he says there's a suitable place about twenty kilometers southwest of the trails junction. [Image.] It's a disused Firvulag cave, abandoned centuries ago when the Little People withdrew from southern France.

AIKEN: Yes. I see. You want to meet me there?

ELIZABETH: Try to be inside the cave before sundown on the fifth. Marc seems to do his d-jumping by night to minimize solar interference with the upsilon-field.

AIKEN: *They* grow at night, too. Even if I sleep under the sigma.

ELIZABETH: You'll be better soon.

AIKEN: *Are you sure?*

ELIZABETH: No, I'm not. What you did—the subsumption—is unprecedented. But I'm going to do my best to help you.

AIKEN: Please. Please. Try anything. Oh Elizabeth they're so freakish so enormous and now It's bigger than all the rest of my body controlling me punishing me making me Its slave making me hate It because I used It I didn't know it would happen didn't think why how I did it—

ELIZABETH: Tell yourself it's only a delusion. A dream. Not real.

AIKEN: Not happening to my body?

ELIZABETH: No, dear. Be easy. Wait for me in the cave. It will be all right. (Please let it be.)

AIKEN: Yes. I told myself that.

ELIZABETH: Goodbye, Aiken. (Goodbye poor demigodling, poor rampant Loki, poor priapic Fool, poor Mentu-Ra with the fiery mentule, poor Ithyphallikos. Now we both know what a terrible thing it is to live the myth of our own choosing.)

The storm, racing along the front of the Pyrénées, came into view shortly after Minanonn carried Elizabeth, Dionket, and Creyn over the valley of the Proto-Aude to the Great South Road. Anvil-headed cloud cells formed a long rank from the Gulf of Lions into the angry sunset. They were filmy white at their stratospheric tops and purplish black below, tinged with lurid brushstrokes of copper on their western flanks, where the lowering sun still sulked. Lightning flickered in their hearts and beneath the gray-curtained bases. A low rumble of thunder became almost continuous as Minanonn bore his passengers farther south.

"Don't worry," the former Battlemaster reassured Elizabeth. "We'll be at the cave ahead of the rain."

"It will mean an end to this awful heat wave, at any rate," she said.

"Has it seriously distressed you?" Dionket asked in surprise. "I found it pleasant myself. Reminiscent of Duat. We could have used a bit more humidity, though, to make it genuinely homelike."

"You First Comers!" Creyn said, amused. "Nostalgic for the ancestral hellhole."

"Nonsense, lad," said Minanonn. "Duat was much more comfortable than this planet. A soft haze to temper the sun's glare, never these prolonged droughts for part of the year and half drowning the rest. On Duat, the rains came fairly uniformly all year round. And the temperature was rarely low enough to chill, even at aphelion."

"He speaks of the Tanu motherlands, of course," Dionket explained. "We lived in the equatorial regions and the Firvulag at the poles, where the really high mountains were. Ghastly country, that of the Foe. Constant winter."

"No changing seasons at all?" Elizabeth asked.

"None to speak of," said the Lord Healer. "Our planetary axis had a minimal tilt."

"A stiff-necked world," Creyn observed, "like the peoples it bred. Fortunately, the spawn of Duat's daughter-planets proved more flexible. It was they who engendered the peaceful galactic federation that rejected Duat's attempt—*our* attempt—to reintroduce the ancient battle-religion."

"Brede told me something of your history," Elizabeth said. Her gaze was fixed on the looming line of thunderheads. "At the time of your exile, were the Duat colonies the only planets in your galaxy that had an interstellar socioeconomy?"

"The only planets," Dionket said, "but not the only people. There were the Ships."

"The Ships." Elizabeth's voice was tinged with wonder. "They seem incredible, even though I have Brede's glass model.

How could highly intelligent life-forms evolve in a void?"

"There is no void," said the Lord Healer. "The space between the stars is pervaded by matter and energy. All of the organic molecules necessary for the generation of life are present in the clouds of dust that drift through the galaxies. This one, as well as the star-whirl of Duat that is its sister."

Elizabeth was silent. The surrounding air had attained a supernatural clarity. Even without exerting her farsensing eye, she seemed able to detect each separate leaf on the jungle trees, each tuft of dry grass between the ruts of the dusty road, each pebble and grasshopper and rock-rose of the arid verge. She finally said, "We had seven hundred eighty-four human planets in our Milieu, including Old Earth. How many worlds were daughter-colonies of Duat at the time of your exile?"

"More than eleven thousand four hundred," Dionket replied. "Even with the attrition from the Galactic Civil War, the total population approached one hundred fifteen billion."

"Half that of our Milieu," Elizabeth mused, "and yet more than adequate for coadunation of the Galactic Mind, if you had not followed the dead end of the golden torcs."

"So you say."

Minanonn addressed Elizabeth with a certain bluff impatience. "My mind is a simple one, suited to porter duties and other tasks requiring more brawn than subtlety. Nevertheless, I hope that someday you will explain to me exactly what this 'coadunation' might be—and why we Tanu are so deprived not to have it! In our Peace Faction, we enjoy a fellowship that is both consoling and stimulating. Can your Unity be so much greater?"

"Perhaps you'll find out for yourselves," Elizabeth said faintly. An image formed in her mind that made the three exotic men gasp.

"A time-gate to the Milieu?" Dionket's question was incredulous.

"And we might be permitted to pass through?" cried Minanonn.

Elizabeth said, "If the device can be built—and operated without danger to the Milieu itself—then all persons of goodwill in the Many-Colored Land will have the option of passing through. You know how skeptical I have been about Brede's calling me the 'most important woman in the world.'

Well . . . lately I've wondered whether she might have seen me in the rôle of time-gate shepherdess. Certainly it would make more sense than my merely serving as dirigent to a continent full of barbarian hordes and exiled Milieu malcontents."

"You would go back?" Creyn asked. "Leading us?"

"If it seems right that I should." But the old uncertainty was plain beneath the ambiguity.

"How will you *know*?" Creyn asked.

She said, "It's premature to think too deeply about it now. Too many things could go wrong. The gate may never reopen—we may find ourselves in the Nightfall War at last!—if we can't help Aiken regain his mental strength."

Minanonn said, "We approach the caravan camp. Render us invisible to casual surveillance, Lord Healer."

"It is done," said Dionket.

They flew over an area of prairie between two streams. Scattered about were open groves of silverleaf poplar and ash. The all-terrain vehicles of the North Americans were parked in a tidy circle, surrounded by a more casual collection of Tanu pavilions and tethered chalikos.

"I see Bleyn's forces have arrived," Minanonn remarked. He asked Elizabeth, "Can you farsense the King's presence below?"

She exerted her metafaculty. "He's safely gone. Would you like a closeup view of the newcomers?"

When the three assented she showed them a group gathered beneath a large dining pavilion. Supper was being served. Two long tables were separated from the others by a distinct psychic veil. At the head of one sat a burly young man in his late twenties who scowled as he listened to a slighter, foxy-faced companion. "Hagen Remillard," Elizabeth noted. "Except for the dark blond hair and a somewhat shorter stature, he bears a rather strong physical resemblance to his father. The mental resemblance is not so strong." She showed them Cloud, who headed the second table, then panned the other twenty-seven adults and five little children.

"All of them are so young," Creyn said. "Are their minds exceptional?"

Elizabeth said, "I know very little about them as yet, except for what Aiken has told me about the Remillards. As to their metafaculties—they're all fully operant, but only imperfectly trained by their parents and the other ex-Rebels. Considering their heritage, they probably represent a wide spectrum of talent and strength. I wouldn't be surprised if the majority were quite formidable. Let's not forget that they helped Felice to blast open Gibraltar."

"And drown thousands of people," Minanonn added tonelessly.

The exotics studied the innocent-appearing diners. A young black man at Cloud's table was regaling his companions with a funny story. Parents wiped the messy chins of children and admonished breaches of etiquette. A plumpish brunette was teased by her tablemates for taking two pieces of Calamosk torte.

Dionket said, "And the Unity of your Milieu is a goal so precious to them, that even such a terrible means seemed justified?"

"Their nurture," Elizabeth said, "can hardly have been ideal, from an ethical standpoint."

"If we are barbarians," Minanonn murmured, "what are they?"

"Children," Elizabeth replied. "Adult children."

"And your Milieu," Dionket said. "Would it welcome these youthful mass murderers?"

"It will accept any mind prepared to seek maturity—which is always a very painful process with ample opportunity for atonement. And the Milieu will know who strives sincerely and who does not. There is no deceiving the Unity...not anymore."

The campsite was falling behind them. They flew now over foothills thickly clad with climax forest. To the west, the sky had become wholly dark except for the lightning. Thunder had swelled from a growl to a full tympanic rumble punctuated with heavier booming peals. Irregular gusts of wind rippled the treetops.

Minanonn pointed ahead and magnified the view for the others. "The cave lies there, on the side of that hill. The entrance is well concealed."

They descended into the wildly swaying jungle and landed on a slope where a rill flowed over mossy rocks and tangled lianas hung from huge sweetgum trees. The cleft in the rock was unobtrusive. As they came to it on foot, they saw that the

web of a handsome black-and-yellow spider stretched across
the cave entrance like some gossamer gate. The Heretic lifted
the creature with his PK and sent it scurrying into the under-
growth. "The royal sentinel," he suggested with a wintry smile.
"And you will note that we have arrived before the rain."

They stepped into what seemed to be a blind-ended chamber,
clogged with rubble and dried leaves. But Minannon led them
confidently into it, and at the rear they turned sharply into
darkness. Their guide raised two fingers and kindled a steady
yellow flame, lighting the way into a tortuous passage so low
and narrow that the Tanu men had to move at an awkward
crouch. As they descended, the tunnel widened and its walls
glistened with seepage. The air washed back and forth in sinister
rhythm and carried a metallic-oniony odor.

Finally they reached a cul-de-sac where the dark rock was
richly veined with red and orange minerals. Set into the wall
was a door of rotting wood. Faded Firvulag ideographs were
barely visible on a tarnished plaque mounted low, where gnomish eyes might have conveniently read it.

Minanonn had to stoop. "Quicksilver Cave," he translated.
"This is the place." He cocked his massive head alertly. "Listen!"

They strained their metafaculties, but it seemed that a psychic
void lay behind the crumbling planks. The only audible sounds
were water dripping and stones crunching underfoot.

Minannon put his hand to the latch and slowly extinguished
his metapsychic torch. A flickering illumination shone through
cracks in the door.

"Keep up your guard, Coercive Brother," Dionket cautioned.

The door swung wide without a sound. They looked down
a shallow flight of steps into a pillared chamber hewn in living
rock. At its center was a sunken area that seemed to be floored
with a mirror at least five meters square. Light streamed obliquely
out of an alcove on the right, throwing a shadow onto an
otherwise featureless gray wall.

The shadow of a monster.

It swayed back and forth so that its dimensions were constantly changing and its true size was impossible to estimate.
The shadow was enormous. The body was humanoid but grotesquely thick, with a bloated belly, protruding buttocks, and

incongruously slender legs. It had immense breasts with pointed nipples, which it seemed to be supporting with pipestem arms. From the broad shoulders sprang three elongate necks that intertwined like the bodies of pythons. The heads were less easily distinguished. One seemed to be birdlike, a second leonine, and the third reptilian, with multiple fangs and a forked tongue.

"Great Goddess!" Creyn whispered. "What can it be? It's not a Firvulag or a Howler throwing that shadow. We'd sense their aura. What . . . what's it *doing?* Tana—is it growing some monstrous tail?"

"No," said Dionket. "It's not a tail."

There was a sound, a soft animal cry from three disparate throats, forced out in a series of grunts timed to the writhing of the creature's body. The sound swelled in volume as the contortions became more and more frenzied. Something columnar thrust from the lower torso, stiff as a tree trunk and nearly three times the breadth of the legs. The creature staggered, overbalanced by the weight, and the thing grew to shoulder height and above, throbbing, while the spidery hands tried in vain to support it and the spine arched and the three heads twisted and howled a demonic trio. The knees collapsed and the shadow-body leaned backward over its heels, still pumping its hips. The breasts jutted toward the chamber ceiling, as did the overwhelming member, which seemed to have grown longer than all the rest of the body. The animal cries were deafening as the shadow organs attained their culmination, and then the picture was obliterated in a triple gush of blazing white light. A dwindling three-note moan echoed from pillar to pillar. The shadow had vanished. The chamber was dark except for a fitful golden glow emanating from the general direction of the original bright light.

"A chimaera," said Elizabeth softly. "Come." And she hurried down the steps.

Beware! cried Minanonn's mind, and he flung a mental shield ahead of her. But she turned back and shook her head. The giant coercer let his barrier fall. He and his fellows drew close to form a protective cordon about Elizabeth as she went quickly across the chamber, past the big sunken mirror, and into the alcove on the right. There was complete silence except for their footsteps. The aether was empty.

They entered the subsidiary chamber and found a meta-activated jewel-lantern, dim as a dying ember, standing on the floor. Lying on his face in front of it was Aiken Drum. His body was normal and so was his face, which was turned toward them. His eyes were open and he breathed through slightly open lips.

He had been wearing his golden storm-suit. The strong leather was split in every seam and lay in rags on his pallid skin.

Elizabeth knelt beside him, lifted the scraps of his crested hood away, and touched his cheek. The faintest of smiles appeared.

"You did come," he said. "*Now* it's going to be all right."

Aiken dreamed.

He stood on the mirror, which reached from horizon to horizon, and above him was a brilliant night sky splashed with the Sagittarius Arm of the Milky Way as seen from his former home planet of Dalriada. Looking down, he saw reflected stars, his own naked body and wondering face, and peering over his shoulders—

With a startled exclamation he looked up and behind him. Nothing. Nobody. But when he looked down again the two of them were back, austere and faintly disapproving in their expressions.

A man and a woman he had never seen before. He dark-haired, with snapping black eyes, a prominent nose, and a mouth compressed to a tight line. She with dark red frizzy hair, a high brow, and tiny regular features too stern to be beautiful.

"Where have you been?" he scolded them. They exchanged glances, looked back at him with dubious, fractional smiles, then vanished. Bitter reproach welled up in him. He heard some small creature squalling, and the sing-song mockery of children, and his own powerful adult voice shouting vicious obscenities.

Under his feet, the mirror undulated like mercury, became fluid. He sank into it and found himself standing in the middle of a rather ordinary landscape: short grass with a few scattered flowers, the edge of a forest a stone's throw away...

He stooped to pick up a stone to throw. There was lettering on the smooth white surface:

I WAS NOT, I CAME TO BE.
I WAS, I AM NOT: THAT IS ALL.
AND WHO SHALL SAY MORE WILL LIE.
I SHALL NOT BE.

There was a whole line of the stones, half hidden in the grass. He picked up another, but there were no words on it. He hesitated, put both stones back into place, and studied the lineup uneasily. It seemed to mark a boundary, one that it might be extremely dangerous to cross. Staring at the stones and his own feet, he discovered that he was shod in his good old golden boots with the stash compartments, and wearing the suit of many pockets, each one containing some useful item for a prudent wayfarer.

"Why the hell not?" he asked himself saucily, and stepped over the boundary, confident once again.

He was swimming for his life.

Salt water filled his mouth and nose and strangled him. He struggled upward toward a green light that steadily became more golden, and burst onto the surface, coughing and choking, so weak that he knew he would sink again in only a moment.

But something was bobbing nearby, drawing closer. He saw it was a cauldron, a vessel of salvation, and he kicked feebly and beat the water with his hands, and in that way swam a few strokes and reached for one of the handgrips mounted below the kettle rim.

A dragon reared up from inside and struck at him. Its fangs narrowly missed his questing hand. A drop of flying venom struck him in the left eye and he screamed with the burning pain of it and sank back. Immediately the hurt was soothed, and he let himself relax and drift in the warm darkening waters . . . the waters that meant death.

No! he cried. Fury electrified him. Pain returned. Again he broke through into the air and found himself floating beside the golden Kral. But this time when Mercy darted at him, open-mouthed, he seized her and squeezed the dragon's neck and smashed the fangs against the rim again and again until the reptile was broken and bloody. Then he climbed into the bowl, safe.

Mayvar the Hag leaned over him and kissed the burnt blind

eye. It was healed. Then she took him into her lap to nurse him, and the baby nestled down, content at last, and drank and slept.

He was on a plain of sparkling salt, wearing his gold-lustre armor.

The antagonist was nowhere to be seen. The coward! Where was he hiding? Why didn't he come out and fight?

Gripping his photonic Spear, he searched the glaring flatland through slitted eyes. A shadow raced toward him and he looked up, into the sun.

The golden eagle stooped, talons ready, and plummeted straight for his face. His visor was full open and he shrieked as the claws raked his right eye and the bird shrilled in triumph. He fell heavily onto his back. Blood was welling uncontrollably and the sky was red, as was the relentless sun. He knew he would lie there, half-blind and parched and stricken, until he died. The eagle wheeled high out of reach and he roasted in his armor under aloof and pitiless light, impotent.

But there was still the Spear.

With his last strength he lifted the glass lance, thumbed its highest power setting, and triggered the shot full in the face of the solar disk. Light drowned light. The patriarchal bird tumbled from a sky gone suddenly indigo. When it struck the salt it was a man in dulled glass armor holding a broken Sword.

In mortal agony, Aiken inched toward the unmoving form of the Battlemaster, feeling his own life ebbing through his torn eyesocket. He stretched a trembling hand to the cracked helmet of his enemy and opened it.

The face inside was that of Stein Oleson.

With his mind spinning, Aiken slumped over the chest of the titanic knight. Beneath the glass cuirass with its sun-face blazon a heart was still beating. Astonished, revitalized, Aiken pulled himself up. He saw that the giant was smiling. His gauntleted hand lifted, proffering the broken Sword in a gesture of fealty. Aiken took it and felt life surge back into him. His sight cleared. He leaned over the dying man and kissed him on the mouth.

It was deep night on the mirror.

From out of the quicksilver pool came the three-headed hermaphrodite, pulling itself onto the gleaming shore. The chimaera was no longer a threatening monstrosity. Even though it was still both male and female, the bodily distortions were gone and the limbs well-filled and proportionate. It stood poised in the starlight, graceful and tall. The central lion head was erect and proud; the dragon and the eagle faced it, slightly bowed. The radiance of the Sagittarius Arm gave it a reflection, not a shadow, that extended across the mirror of the quicksilver pool. Aiken saw that the reflection was himself.

"But what does it *mean*?" he exclaimed, rather testily.

"You are born," Elizabeth said.

He thought about that for a while. "On Dalriada, they called me a psychopath."

"You were. A suffering soul. Incomplete. Lacking eros. A freak and a cripple, almost inevitably damned. You were intelligent and charming and utterly self-centered. It was impossible for you to love anyone but yourself, even though you gave the illusion of caring when it suited you."

"They were going to lock me away—or kill me!"

"You were a menace, a liability to a structured society. You saved yourself by coming here. Your silver torc rechanneled the aberrant psychic energies. You were reassured and began to change when you saw you were able to exert genuine power."

"In the Milieu, that would have been impossible."

"There, your ambition didn't fit. But this Many-Colored Land is a simpler world. You were even able to love here. And you dared to do it unselfishly, twice. You reached a species of mental integration. But that wasn't enough. Not for you! You were drawn toward Mercy, and driven to challenge Nodonn. You wanted to be more than a powerful, successful person: You wanted to be King. And so, instinctively, you were drawn to two extraordinary minds—and you subsumed their attributes in an attempt to fulfill your ambition. Before the subsumption, you knew you were inadequate."

"But I tricked them into believing that I wasn't!"

"Yes. But you couldn't fool yourself. Look at the illusory bodies you wore: butterfly, dragonfly, nighthawk, golden falcon. Each one more potent than the last but still winged, elusive, flyaway. You were a counterfeit King, royal without being noble."

"Cock of the rock."

"With the ambition to rule a world . . . This is why you committed the act of surpassing chutzpah: in spite of the mortal danger, subsuming those very metafaculties that might support true kingship. You were like a man living in a fine large home who nevertheless craves a palace. So one day your dream is accomplished and all the necessary building materials are delivered—"

"Burying and damn near destroying the original house! I see."

"Most of this redaction you've done yourself. Dionket and Creyn and I helped you—I guided and they sustained—but the psychic insights that now provide a solid foundation are your own. Your palace is by no means complete, but now you have the blueprints for construction and the means to assemble the parts into a harmonious whole."

"How long is it going to take to finish?"

"It may take years, or happen in an instant."

"You better pray for the latter, babe, for all our sakes! . . . One last thing, though, that I still don't understand. Why a *lion*?"

"You'll have to discover for yourself what it signifies in your own psyche, Aiken. It's obviously a kingly animal—but it has no wings. Sometimes it destroys its own young—and sometimes it defends the pride to the death."

"You mean, I can *still* blow it."

"You're a human being, dear, and you still have to face up to many choices. You can undoubtedly fail. The Trickster archetype is a strange one, not commonly personified. Perhaps it's just as well! You see, the Trickster is a person we simultaneously admire and fear. We know that he can hit and run— victimize us. But he also has the saving gift of laughter that enables us to abide in the midst of life's pain. He takes our pain onto himself, as a great psychologist once said. And that may help you to understand where the lion image fits. If you accept it as an integral part of your self, you can no longer be fugitive Mercurius, dashing about as the spirit wills. You'll have to relinquish some of the laughter and take pain in defending the pride; perhaps even lay down your life."

"Ha! It's the hyenas that better look out!"

Elizabeth had to laugh. "Oh, my dear. Go get 'em, Hermes Trismegistos—thrice-mighty leader."

"You can count on it," said the King.

THE END OF PART ONE

PART II

THE

CONVERGENCE

1

DURING THE FIRST FOUR YEARS OF THE REBELS' EXILE, WHEN resolution was still strong and optimism ran so high that some of the Ocala settlers dared to have children, appropriate technology was all the rage. There was really no necessity for roughing it, since the former scientists, military specialists, and planetary administrators had brought a vast collection of Milieu equipment with them. Nevertheless, low-tech achievement flourished as the exiles worked to turn their island into a home. Once they had recovered from their mental and physical wounds, most of the Rebels set about to develop one or more frontier skills.

For Walter Saastamoinen, who had been Deputy Chief Starfleet Operations (Strategy) under Ragnar Gathen, the vocational choice was a foregone conclusion. He took up the trade of his ancestors—shipbuilding. With the help of his former aide, Roy Marchand, and a dozen others (plus the elegantly complete data supplied by the computer library), Walter built a seventy-meter four-masted sailing vessel that would become the principal freighter for the colony, transporting everything from minerals to Megahippus horses from the Antilles and the North and South

American mainland to Ocala's first settlement at the head of Manchineel Bay.

She was named Kyllikki, after an enchantress in a Finnish epic, and her lines followed those of the old Pacific timber haulers, capacious but trim. She had a clipper bow figureheaded with a blonde witch, a long platformed bowsprit, a sweeping sheer, and a neatly tucked up counter stern. Her masts, the trunks of great longleaf pines from the virgin forests of Georgia, rose thirty-five meters above the black-mahogany deck and had a sportive rake.

When it came time to rig her, Walter's companions, full of romantic fancies about legendary windjammers, wanted to fit her with a full suit of square sails. The master shipbuilder pointed out that squareriggers required large crews, agile and fearless enough to climb the shrouds and swarm about the yards in all kinds of weather—not excluding the violent line squalls and all too frequent hurricanes that infested Floridian waters. A fore-and-aft rig, while not quite so speedy or spectacular, could be worked from the deck, even by a gang of tyros. Furthermore, it lent itself to the installation of powered winches for hoisting and hauling and fully automatic reefing devices. Practicality and Walter's superior coercive faculty won out, and Kyllikki became a four-poster gaff schooner navigable by a crew of six.

When the charms of simple technology paled and Ocala enjoyed a brief spurt of highly sophisticated manufacturing, Kyllikki acquired a solar-powered auxiliary engine that drove a pair of retractable cycloidal impeller rotors, similar to those in the all-terrain vehicles that the Rebels had originally brought with them from the Milieu. The schooner traveled widely to satisfy the need for exotic raw materials; she even served for a time as a floating drill-platform and as a pumping station for the big marine-ion concentrator. But then ambition declined among the castaways as the years became decades and Marc's star-search was perceived as fruitless by more and more of the former Rebels. Kyllikki shared in the creeping malaise, being converted into a party boat for bored degenerates. She chased whales up the Mississippi Embayment, carried nostalgic fun seekers to Pliocene New England, embarked on diving expeditions along the Spanish Main, transported cargoes of ferocious fauna to the Zoo Island hunting preserve in the Bermoothes, and took part in the disastrous Costa Rican Volcano-Teasing Operation. Finally, and most memorably, the great schooner carried a large party of Rebels and their adolescent children on an epic tour of the Antarctic Islands. Walter's wife, Solange Forester, had been one of the twenty-odd people who elected to end their lives in the "clean white silence" of the glacier-crowned south.

When Walter returned to Florida, he made his son Veikko a present of Kyllikki and retreated into alcohol. But the young man made scant use of the enormous toy, and when the Children of Rebellion finally decided to flee Ocala, Veikko was secretly relieved when Hagen ordered that the schooner be scuttled. Veikko took her to Sun Key Hole, fully intending to sink her in eighty fathoms. Then he thought of the cargo of memories she still carried, the loving care that Walter still lavished on her during his rare sober hours, and his maudlin protestations that one day soon he would straighten out and take them all sailing again. Veikko brought the ship back to Ocala and opened her petcocks on the eastern side of Manchineel Bay, so that she lay softly on coral sand in the shallows with her tall masts awash at low tide.

It was from this inadequate grave that Marc Remillard had her raised, refitted, and made ready for the punitive voyage to Europe. Of all the motley sailing craft, sunken or still afloat, that constituted Ocala's small fleet, only Kyllikki had a hold deep enough to admit installation of Marc's cerebroenergetic enhancer. She was a key factor in his plans, as was her master.

Walter, rehabilitated with cruel efficiency by Jeff Steinbrenner, had wept as he piloted the schooner out of Manchineel Bay for the last time, outward bound for the Gulf Stream and the forbidden East Passage. His fellow Rebels were touched by what they thought was a display of sentiment. No one dreamed of intruding upon his mind at such a moment. If they had, they would have heard his heart's cry to the fugitive younger generation on the opposite side of the Atlantic. Walter's telepathic powers were too weak to reach them, but he still had to attempt a warning, coupled with bitter reproach:

If only you'd had the courage to kill the ship! If only you had done what I now lack the guts to do! Then your dream might have had a chance of success . . . But we're coming after you now in Kyllikki. We'll stop you from opening the gate.

Marc says you children can be peaceably restrained, but most of us fear for the worst. Run away, Veikko! Take Irena with you and whoever else will listen. Hide! Beware! Because Kyllikki's coming and she's carrying death.

The mental anguish of the ship's master went unnoticed by the other forty-two people on board. For the most of them, the first week of the voyage was a time of respite and tranquillity, a chance to recover from frantic weeks of preparation and the final tearing up of roots. It was a time to deny fear and squelch renewed doubts. Walter's crew kept busy with shakedown routine while the passengers dozed on sundrenched decks, lounged in the stern watching flying fishes skitter in the creamy wake, or perched in one of the crow's nests under a cobalt sky while frigatebirds wheeled overhead and the full spread of solarpanel sail thrummed in a smart breeze. During those brief idyllic days, the tired old Rebels attempted to purge their minds of all thought—leaving that to Marc and the ten surviving magnates who were his intimates—and instead merged themselves with the entity who seemed more alive than any of them: the tall ship running strong on a sparkling ocean.

On 7 September, when they were a little more than 400 kilometers southwest of Bermuda, the wind freshened and the sky turned lead-gray. Kyllikki raced close-reefed through increasingly heavy seas and the passengers stayed below, paying little attention to Walter's assurance that no really severe weather was in the offing, only a chain of minor tropical disturbances. A mood of dejection prevailed as the schooner endured intervals of nasty chop, through which she punched, hammering and shaking. Then came thundersqualls—and shorter tempers. When the sun condescended to shine, the sea heaved with great queasy rollers while the veering wind blew fits and starts. The prologue to genuine disaster was a near gale under dreary torn scud, the remnant of a moribund hurricane, before which Kyllikki plunged and ramped, more often than not hove down nearly on her ear.

Those of the passengers who had not surrendered to seasickness were rendered lethargic and irritable at the continued close confinement, the unsettling motion, and above all, the noise. Timbers creaked and groaned, winch motors squealed in the adjustment of sail, marching breakers hissed along the hull, the wind howled, the auxiliary engine powering the rotors cut in and out as Ragnar and the engineers worked to isolate some obscure malfunction, and the great ship's masts, spars, and rigging vibrated in a hundred inharmonious notes. It seemed that the magical barque of earlier days had suffered a sea change into a floating torture chamber. As the dirty weather prolonged itself into a fourth night, the barometer of morale aboard Kyllikki reached its nadir.

Patricia Castellane found herself alone in the grand saloon, whence all but she had fled. Supper, if she wanted it, would be a scratch affair; both Alonzo Jarrow and Charisse Buckmaster were prostrate with mal de mer and no one had volunteered to take over their culinary duties. Patricia decided she was not hungry. She tried to watch a Tri-D of Wagner's "Flying Dutchman," but its stormy cadences only made her feel worse. So she turned the lamps low, huddled in a gyro-lounge reading a classic thiller by Desmond Bagley, and sipped hot buttered rum. The ship was heeled far to starboard, so that below-sheer portlights on that side of the saloon were fully underwater. She could see phosphorescent froth swirling by on the other side of the thick glass. The sight of it and the mélange of noises were so mesmerizing that she finally dozed off—only to start wide-awake as someone gripped her shoulder and an urgent telepathic voice said:

Pat! Wake up—we need your help!

It was Cordelia Warshaw, looking like a soaked and bedraggled elderly child in stormgear three sizes too large for her. With her was Steve Vanier, a former tactical analyst who was Walter Saastamoinen's second mate. His mind was shut tight as an oyster and his face bore a grimace of combined pain and fury. He held his right wrist against his chest with his left hand. A trickle of blood seeped down the front of his gloyello coat and dripped into the fresh pool of water on the saloon carpet.

"It's Helayne Strangford," said Cordelia, thrusting a weatherproof jacket and sou'wester hat at Patricia. "She had a knife, and she got onto the bridge and attacked Steve at the helm."

"Must have had some dope squirreled away after all, the crazy bitch," said Steve. "Walter fought her off. She was raving about saving the children. Wanted to wreck the ship."

"Oh, God," said Patricia.

Cordelia said, "Now she's climbed up to the jiggermast

crow's nest and says she'll jump. You know what a strong coercer she is. I don't think we'll be able to stop her. Tried to call the other magnates to help but only Steinbrenner responded."

"Fat fucking good he is," Steve muttered. He had been fumbling behind the bar and now downed a huge swallow of vodka from the bottle. "Ah, Jesus—that helps."

"Call Marc!" said Patricia.

Cordelia uttered a trilling little laugh. "As usual, he's gone. Before he learned to d-jump, it was only his mind that wandered. Now he abandons us body *and* soul!"

Steve said, "Walter tried to raise Marc as soon as Strangford broke in. Kramer said he's been on the hop for more than two hours."

"I'll see what I can do," Patricia said.

"And you get to sick bay," Cordelia told Steve. "Wake those damn Keoghs out of whatever seventh heaven they're floating in. Tell them what Steinbrenner said about possible cut tendons in your wrist."

Still cradling the bottle, the mate staggered into the forward passage while the two women headed aft. All of the cabin doors were shut and this part of the ship seemed deserted. Bracing themselves against the excessive heel, they came to the modified stern hold containing the accommodation for the CE rig and its auxiliaries. The armored door that provided sole access was dogged shut from the opposite side. Patricia exerted her farspeech to penetrate the metal.

Jordy! Gerrit! It's Pat. Let me in. Emergency!

Cordelia took a big torch from the pocket of her oilskin jacket and banged on the door. A tentative glimmer of farsense stole out after a few moments and flicked over them. Then there were clicks and a grudging crack opened. Jordan Kramer peered out, his face like a thundercloud.

"What the devil is it? Marc has gone extraplanetary and we're at a tricky point in the stasis monitoring—"

Patricia shoved the mental image at him. "Helayne's broken loose. We need Marc."

Kramer groaned. "Damn that woman to hell! If we didn't need her input so badly for the offensive metaconcert, I'd say let her jump!"

"Can you retrieve Marc? Patricia persisted.

"Not a chance. He's independent now. The rubberband effect is finally neutralized. There's no telling when he'll return. Why don't you call out the other coercers and put together a concert—"

"Mostly everyone seems to be seasick, asleep, or otherwise switch-off," Cordelia said. "Those of us who were topside when Helayne went berserk got almost zip response from a general hail. Steinbrenner came, and Boom-Boom Laroche. Besides them, there's Walter and Roy and Nannie Fox, who had the watch with me and Steve—and now Pat."

Kramer looked harried. "Well, there's nothing Van Wyk or I can do. We're neither of us coercers, and we have to monitor the equipment." He started to close the door.

"Then give us Manion!" Patricia demanded. "If we take off the docilator, his PK will probably be strong enough to override her and scoop her in."

"Not on your life!" Kramer shouted. "We're keeping that bastard right in here brain-wrapped until Marc is safely home. Let him out—? God—you'd have two crazies on the loose instead of just one!"

Knowing it was hopeless, Patricia pleaded, "Alex would want to help Helayne. You know they used to be—"

"Oh, yes, I know very well," retorted the psychophysicist. "And I know just what would happen after Manion got his old flame fitted with *his* docilator. He'd skunk the lot of you, smash the powerplant, and strand Marc in the gray limbo!" The door slammed shut.

Wasting no more time, the two women turned and ran for the after companionway. On deck, the rain had stopped and a crescent moon was intermittently visible through broken clouds. Kyllikki, on autopilot, drove along under minimal canvas. Black waves with glowing crests leaped and stretched chaotically as the wind died. Walter, Roy Marchand, and Nanomea Fox were gathered at the foot of the jiggermast, which arose from the low sterncastle structure. Standing away from them, clinging to the rail, were Jeff Steinbrenner and Guy Laroche. Nanomea held a spotlight on the wildly gyrating crow's nest. Roy carried a stun-gun and Laroche had a laser carbine slung over his shoulder.

Cordelia said: Here's Pat. She was the only one who'd help.

Walter said: Helayne's still there ducked down out of sight in bucket.

Patricia said: No chance stun?

Roy said: Masts grounded hellandgone besides her creativity sufficient shield. Boom-Boom has zapper burn her if she threatens—

Patricia said: Negative negative! We NEED Helayne! I direct metaconcert okay?

The others said: Right.

Patricia said: Ready—COME IN.

Their minds meshed, following the lead of the one-time dirigent of Okanagon. The combined coercive faculty reached out to the crazed mind aloft and enclosed it in a net of mental energy. And tightened . . .

They all screamed. An overpowering mind-thrust, like a white-hot blade, split the metaconcert asunder. High in the air a ghostly face leaned over the rim of the crow's nest bucket. Helayne Strangford's telepathic laughter rang in their brains.

Patricia said: We want to help you Helayne. Please come down.

LetHIMbegmewhydidn'tHecomewhere'sHEhidingneverlet Him-hurtchildren—

Patricia said: Marc doesn't want to hurt the children.

Othersdo! YOUsteeleyedmetagroupie! YOUcuteGranny Cordelia! YOU Jeffbabykiller! YouwantkillchildrensoI killYOU!

Patricia said: Come with me to Marc Helayne. He'll see that nobody harms the children. He promised. You know you can trust Marc.

Trust . . . oooh I did. We all did. In the Milieu during Rebellion and even in defeat. Trusted Marc followed Marc loved Marc. BUT HE LIED.

Patricia said: Marc doesn't lie.

HedoeshedoesHEDOES. Said he'd never leave us. NEVER. BUT HE GOES.

Patricia said: Helayne he always comes back to us.

He lies says destroying time gates site prevent children escape! MustkillchildrenprotectHIMSELF. ButIstopIknowhowstop. KillYOU! KillHIM!

A knife flashed in the spotlight. Helayne clung to the upper crosstrees and slowly climbed onto the rim of the bucket. Her flowing silk pajamas crackled in the wind like pennants.

FlydownkillyouALL!

Patricia said: You can't fly Helayne. If you jump you'll die. Chris and Leila will feel guilty. Little Joel will cry for his Nana. Don't jump. Come down and let us help you.

DarlingChris . . . darlingLeila . . . preciousJoel. HewantskillthembutIknowhowstop. Kill the other minds. Deprive devil-angelexecutor of metaconcertcooperators make HIM helpless! Weak! HUMAN! . . . And that's exactly what I *have* done you know.

This last was delivered in a tone so matter-of-fact and complacent that the seven people at the foot of the mast were momentarily taken aback. And then Steve Vanier came pounding up the after companionway ladder and emerged on deck with his brain bursting with horror. He shouted: "The Keoghs—both of them stabbed to death in sick bay! And she must have gone into the cabins that weren't locked—" Crimson images tumbled from his mind. Helayne's manic laughter pealed in the cloud-wracked sky.

Nanomea Fox kept the spotlight steady on the swaying figure. Helayne called out in a crooning voice, "Walter! Come up, dear. Help me. I promise I won't jump if you come." The force of her coercion was an irresistible siren call. Walter, blank-faced, started for the mast as Fox and Marchand stood helplessly by.

"No, Walter!" Patricia screamed. And then the mental tentacle coiled about her own will, commanding her to climb, and Roy, and . . .

Jeff Steinbrenner whipped the carbine from Laroche's paralyzed hands and fired without aiming. There was a sizzling report and a bloom of light like St. Elmo's fire. Something seemed to take wing, uttering a final sound like a seabird's cry. Fragments of wood and metal and severed rope rained onto the deck.

They all looked up at the broken, empty crow's nest, and then braced themselves to go below.

As the dark armored form materialized on its improvised cradle, the docilated man sitting in the dark corner of the hold finally broke his silence. "Commodore's gig approaching! Bosun, your pipe! Mister Kramer, hoist the swallowtail of the Rye Harbor Yacht Club!"

"Shut up, Alex," said Patricia Castellane, "or I'll phase in the algetics at max, so help me God."

Alexis Manion subsided, but a sly smile played over his lips. He got up from his chair and strolled closer as Gerrit Van Wyk pulled the helmet hoist into position and Jordan Kramer monitored the divestment.

When Marc was free of the armor he said, "The stasis held perfectly for three hours thirty minutes. I think I've got it licked. How did it look on this end?"

Kramer said, "Perfect. No sign of anomalous field-warp or bilocation phenomena. We'll have Manion do an analysis in depth, but it looked mighty good in overview. How far out did you go?"

"Eighteen thousand six hundred and twenty-seven light-years. To Poltroy. Testing my limits and indulging my curiosity."

"Was the translation still apparently instantaneous?" Van Wyk asked.

"Yes," said Marc. "There doesn't seem to be any equivalent of the subjective hours or days spent in the gray limbo by superluminal starship riders. I'd estimate I was in the hyperspatial matrix thirty subjective seconds on each of the d-jumps. It takes longer breaking through the superficies at each end, of course."

He stepped into the miniature shower cabinet and threw out the pressure-envelope coverall. The water sprayed hot, sending steam clouds rising among the cable-draped oaken ship timbers.

"So you went to Poltroy, my beamish boy?" Alexis Manion caroled.

"I'd forgotten that the place was mostly glacial during the Pliocene," Marc said. "Fortunately, the locals took me for a slumming god and lent me some furs, or I'd have had to stay in the armor. It would have spoiled the experiment." Patricia came up with a towel and a dressing gown. "I think I finally have the d-jump program fully assimilated. I expect to work out further refinements, but the technique is quite workable now. I can take the armor with me as a safety precaution against a hostile environment, or leave it suspended in the superficies out of the way, or even send it back home to wait until I whistle,

cutting off entirely from the systems at this end of the warp."
He smiled, trying the belt of the robe. "It's the damnedest feeling, going superluminal without a ship. But it was even spook-
ier actually visiting a world in the flesh that I farsaw on the
star-search."

Kramer asked, "Is there discomfort passing through the hyperspatial boundary, as one experiences on a starship?"

Marc nodded. "I'm meshing with an upsilon-field. No matter whether the thing is generated mechanically or metapsychically, it still hurts to go through it. D-jumping does away with
the extended subspace vector—the subjective time-lag spent
in the gray limbo. But the pain factor seems to have its usual
component—geometric increase with the distance jumped. I
was nearly at my limit with the hop to Poltroy, but teleporting
about the Earth is no more uncomfortable than worrying a
hangnail."

Alexis Manion cocked his head impishly and sang:

> *If this is true, it's jolly for you;*
> *Your courage screw to bid us adieu!*
> *And go and show both friend and foe*
> *How much you dare! (I'm quite aware*
> *It's your affair.) Yet I declare*
> *I'd take your share. But I don't much care.*
> *I don't much care . . . I don't much care.*

Marc surveyed him without rancor. "Let's get you out of that
docilator and put you to work, Alex. I want a detailed study of
this operation."

He slid his powerful redactive faculty into the mind of the
dynamicfield specialist to prevent severe disorientation as the
mind-altering headset was removed. Manion winced, blinked,
then massaged his eyelids with his fingers. The underlying
hatred was there still, but it was masked almost immediately
by a peculiar elation.

He said, "We have a little surprise for you, Marc! While
the cat was away, the mad mouse played."

Patricia hurried to forestall him, running her own high-speed
reprise of the shambles. Manion glowed in perverse satisfaction
while Kramer and Van Wyk stood mutely by, confirming that
Helayne had indeed murdered fifteen people—including Kra-

mer's wife, Audrey, and the former Concilium magnates
Deirdre and Diarmid Keogh and Peter Dalembert—before she
herself had been shot dead by Steinbrenner. A few others had
been wounded by the madwoman, Arkady O'Malley seriously.

"Bon dieu de merde," breathed Marc, his mind glaring bright.

"You could apply for that job on Poltroy," Manion suggested
archly, "but the natives might prefer a less graphic job description."

Marc stood motionless. His face had gone livid and his eyes
were those of Abaddon. Alex Manion's body was lifted into
the air and seized by a massive convulsion. His eyes bulged
and oozed blood from a dozen pinpoint hemorrhages. He uttered an animal scream at the same time that his brain flooded
the aether with agony. Then he was sprawled on the planks,
his limbs racked with clonic spasms, half drowned in vomit,
soiled and stinking in his own voided excrement.

Marc looked down at him dispassionately. "Tu es un em-
merdeur, Alex. It's fortunate for you that I still have a sense
of humor. You aren't seriously damaged. Do the field analysis
tomorrow."

The gabbing pain-ridden thing collapsed, unconscious.
Without another glance, Marc took Patricia by the elbow, steered
her past the stricken Van Wyk and Kramer, and went out to
the after companionway.

"Just say the word," Patricia said as they climbed to his
cabin in the stern deckhouse, "And I'll deep-six that swine
myself. It wouldn't surprise me to find that he was the one
who gave the dope to Helayne, hoping that something like this
would happen. It was his poison that turned her against you in
the first place—and corrupted the children as well! Now we've
lost the Keoghs, our top redactors. And Peter—"

"Poor Keoghs," Marc mused. "Siegmund and Sieglinde. At
least they went in style! But whoever would have thought that
Peter Dalembert would die in his bed?" He opened the cabin
door and held it courteously.

"When we found him, his eyes were open. And his face"—
she projected the vision—"quite calm. A creator of his power
should have been able to shield himself from Helayane's knife.
If he had wanted to."

Marc went to the built-in cooking unit and activated it, then
opened a clothes locker. "I had counted on Peter's devotion to

Barry and Fumiko and little Hope to counterbalance his rather blatant deathwish." His smile was distant as he tossed underwear, jeans, and a jersey onto the bed. "Another of my miscalculations. Obviously, Peter thought that I'd be unable to stop the children without harming them."

Patricia was silent.

"But you never did think much of the forebearance notion, did you, Pat?"

"I'd follow any plan of yours. Do whatever you say. Always. You know that. I don't give a damn about Mental Man any more, Marc. Only you." You are my angel, too terrible to love, condescending to share your life with me, to give me fierce joy even when you have none. Why have you none? Your great scheme is still feasible. We don't need Cloud and Hagen and the other children as long as we have the genes and the brain. As long as we have you, everliving!

"Faithful Pat." He was standing close to her, looking down from his great height, and he had let the dressing gown fall. His contours were still magnificent, but an intricate network of keloid scars, the consequence of a too-brief sojourn in the regeneration tank, covered his entire body below the neck. Only his hands and genitals had been perfectly restored.

She came into his arms and their lips met, tasting salt and honey, setting her whirling into the bright burning maelstrom that had him as its inevitable beginning and end. In the wondrous way of master metapsychics there was a constraint of gravity between them, no barrier posed by garments, no awkwardness in the embrace. The ineffable pleasure spun her to the brink of senselessness, lifted her as on a giant wave to the ultimate conjunction. There the binary star would shine for a small eternity, she in the shouting blaze of fullfillment, he, as always, withdrawn into his abyss.

From the beginning, Marc had warned her that there would be no love. She had willingly agreed, leaving him solitary at the climax. But tonight his curtain had been only imperfectly woven. She had caught a glimpse of what lay beneath the brilliant corona of orgasmic release.

She lay alone on the bed, having surfaced into consciousness. Recollection clamped her heart in ice. Had he been distracted because of the terrible events that had taken place? Or had his subconsious been compelled to give up the secret?

"Marc," she whispered. "Is it true?"

He was fully dressed, staring out the forward window of the sterncastle. The sea had moderated and was star-stippled. The sails had been hoisted by the winching mechanism and the great schooner forged ahead.

He said, "You will tell no one. It could be disastrous to morale. The children don't know, of course. No one did, except the Keoghs—and Manion. Alex has his own reasons to keep silent."

"How . . . how long?"

Since before the Rebellion since her death je suis le veuf à la tour abolie.

"My God! But we thought that the Keoghs had—"

"After Cyndia's death, they restored me completely, just as the tank restored me here." He was calm. "There is no organic dysfunction, only nonviability. My late brother blamed it on a sense of sin. I suspect rather a defect of the will, or the inevitable trauma when falling from a great height." He regarded her steadily from beneath winged brows. "The cure, if any, will be spontaneous—induced by success. We still can succeed. Mental Man will live if we prevent the children from passing through that time-gate. Ideally, we need all of them. At the minimum, my son."

"If you had only told Hagen! Or taken precautions—"

"Precautions were taken—and circumvented. I was too trusting during our early years on Ocala. Later, trying to compensate for my neglect, I was too stern with the children. Hagen is weak-willed. Flawed. He knows it. My attempts to intimidate him merely made him hate me. To reveal the truth . . . would give him a weapon. It's a hellish mess, complicated even more by the children's alliance with Aiken Drum. But we *can* still succeed. If the time-gate doesn't open . . . if I can prove to Hagen and Cloud that I love them, that their destiny is with me . . ."

Patricia rose slowly, pushing the light brown hair back from her face, working to suppress the misgivings. "There are so few of us left to help you. O'Malley may not survive, and Fitzpatrick and Sherwoode aren't strong. If we discount those three, that leaves only twenty-two for your offensive metaconcert. Six of us magnates."

"We'll manage. We have plenty of conventional weapons

to counter Aiken Drum. And the d-jump capability."

"You can't take any weapon with you inside the armor."

He did not respond to that. She went to the cooking unit and took out his meal, then poured cups of tea for both of them. "Come and eat your supper while it's hot," she said, sitting down at the table in front of the windows. "There's ham in orange sauce, and even some of your favorite gamma pea soup."

"I ordered it up thinking that I'd be celebrating a successful long jump." He took a spoon and studied the steaming bowl. "Just three pouches left after twenty-seven years. Habitant pea soup in the Pliocene. A touch of New Hampshire aboard a windjamming bateau ivre!" He shook his head slightly and began to eat.

Patricia drank her tea without attempting to touch his thoughts. After a time she began speaking in a low, urgent voice. "I understand now why you opposed those of us who wanted to counter the time-gate threat with force against the children. You were never really afraid of retaliation from the Milieu at all, were you?"

He made a dismissive gesture. "It was a smokescreen. A necessary deception, I thought. Aimed primarily at the children, and at the more dubiously loyal of our own generation."

"I thought so. So you could listen to all our bloodthirsty talk about killing the children if necessary—even pretend to consider the option—but all the while you knew you'd have to find another way."

"I have," he said. "Destruction of the deep rock formation around the site. It's simple and humane—"

"And Alex Manion says it can't possibly work."

"*What?*" Marc lay the spoon down. She felt the power of his coercion engulf her. Willingly she threw open her memory to show the complex mathematical equations exactly as the dynamic-field specialist had shown them to her.

"Alex calls this the theory of the persistence of temporal event nodes. In essence, you can't destroy the time-gate site here in the Pliocene because we *know* it still exists six million years from now, in the Milieu we all came from. Ergo, your hope of demolishing the formations, upsetting the geomagnetic factors in the tau-lattice, is futile. No paradoxes allowed. Reality is. Past, present, future—"

"—and all held secure in the hand of God," he finished for her, mouth lifted in the famous smile. "Once I believed it."

"I never did! And I don't want to believe it now. But Alexis Manion does, and he was the best dynamic-field theorist in the Milieu."

"Damn him to hell . . . Pat, do you know whether he's spoken to any others about this—this theory?"

She lifted helpless hands. "I'm afraid there's no doubt of it. He probably made use of every moment that he wasn't docilated." She spoke with desperation. "Could Alex be mistaken?"

"No. But he could certainly lie." Marc's face was bleak. "I'll find out tomorrow. But even if he's telling the truth as he sees it, I'll keep that gate from opening!"

"But how?" she cried. "Marc, talk to us about this! Confide in us, as you used to. We all feel lost! You've been so absorbed—first in the star-search, now in this d-jump business. We're loyal and we want to follow you but we don't see how we can deal with this situation. We've waited so long and now there are so few of us left . . ." Help us! We have put all our trust in you. Calm our fears. *Say you won't d-jump to another world and abandon us.*

He reached across the table and took her hand. His skin was warm, the fingers youthfully perfect, and the mental contact invincibly reassuring.

"Abandon you? Never. I have something quite different in mind. Right now, there are still urgent matters that I must attend to. However, I promise to make myself available again—not just to you magnates, but to everyone. We'll have regular conferences, starting tomorrow. And I have good news. I'm gaining the confidence of the masterclass woman, Elizabeth Orme. And I've made a start on Aiken Drum, too. Now that the d-jump is nearly perfected, I can begin pressuring him in earnest. Before he knows it, we'll have Kyllikki moored in shallow water off Breton Island opposite his castle. With our sigmas in place, the ship will be an impregnable threat."

"The children have the big force-shield—the SR-35."

"And we have my battery of X-lasers that will cut through any portable screen ever built! Aiken Drum will capitulate, I tell you. And with him on our side, the children will be checkmated. There are other ways to insure that the time-gate never opens. We can destroy the laboratories, after giving warning so that the children can evacuate them. If I wipe out the schematics and certain irreplaceable pieces of manufacturing apparatus—fleck-etchers, photonic alloying machines, mind-controlled micromanipulators—no one will ever build the Guderian device here in the Pliocene. Eventually the children will come to their senses."

"Marc, they won't want to return to Ocala."

He laughed. "Let them spend a few years as subjects of Aiken's barbarian kingdom, then! We can make d-jump visits on holidays, provided we're in the neighborhood of Earth, and renew our invitation at intervals."

He showed her what was in his mind and she gasped.

"Is it feasible?" she cried. "You could carry *us*?"

"If I can generate an upsilon-field large enough to take myself and three tons of armor plating through hyperspace, it should only be a matter of practice before I'm able to encompass a larger volume and greater mass. For short hops on Earth, I doubt that the passengers would even require life support. Felice didn't."

"But . . . you said we'd go extraplanetary."

"We have the spare CE rig armor I intended to use for Hagen, and we can build more—or simply construct a space capsule. Pat, don't you understand the implications? We don't have to await rescue by another coadunate race. We'll rescue ourselves!" His mood was abruptly serious. "But this is for the future. I'll explain what I've been doing to all of you, tomorrow at the conference. It's the end of our exile. We'll soon be able to lay the groundwork for the coming of Mental Man. All of us! And the children as well, when they realize the truth."

"Yes," she said. "Oh, yes."

She lifted his hand, which she still held, and brushed the back of it with her lips. Then they sat together drinking tea, watching pink dawn stain the eastern horizon. It was, Marc assured her, a certain sign of fair weather ahead.

2

THE FINAL HEM ADJUSTMENT HAD BEEN COMPLETED BY MOOL-
iane Frog-Maid, and now Katlinel stood in the center of the
fitting room modeling the finished creation. The place was
crowded with the little beings who had worked on the dress—
portunes and korrigans and nereides and nimble-fingered
trows—and these twittered anxiously as the head couturier,
Bukin the Estimable, pursed his lips and strode around and
around the Mistress of Nionel. He prodded an errant lace ruffle
here, straightened a gilded wire there, leaned close to scrutinize
a critical seam or a suspect bit of beadwork. Finally he stepped
back, cleared his throat, and announced: "It will do. Bring the
looking glass!"

All the goblin tailors and seamstresses squealed for joy and
clapped their hands, paws, or other tactile appendages. Two
sturdy kobold wenches hauled a three-way standing mirror into
position, and for the first time, Katlinel saw herself in the gown
she would wear as hostess of the first Grand Tourney.

It was cut from a stiff white fabric of a mysterious iridescence that glimmered pink and yellow and pale green, like the
interior of a seashell. The low-cut bodice and long sleeves

fitted closely, as did the slender underskirt. Springing from the lowered waist were wired, tapering panels that curved outward and then in toward the knees, like the reflexed petals of a nacreous lily. Beneath this was an overskirt of delicate golden lace, which flared out below the petals in a bright fluted cone. Gold lace also draped the pearly fabric of the sleeves and formed wide cuffs. The head and decolletage of the Lady of the Howlers was set off by a fantastic high collar, and she wore a delicate golden face-frame. As a finishing touch, the entire ensemble was adorned with crystal beads and briolettes, which reflected the everchanging hues of the fabric.

Katlinel turned slowly in front of the mirrors, a reduplicated vision of aurora colors misted with gold. "The gown is magnificent," she said. "I've never seen anything so wonderful. Thank you, dear friends—and especially you, Bukin." She bent down and kissed the brownie designer on his corrugated pate. A flush rose from his neck to the tips of his hairy ears.

"Gracious Mistress Katy," he said gruffly, "my career spans three centuries. I have in that time conceived many a splendid garment—for you know that our misbegotten folk have no peers in the Many-Colored Land in matters of personal adornment. This creation, however, is my masterpiece—and that of all the artisans gathered about you."

A pixie voice piped, "The pearl lamé is unique!" And another chimed in, "Fashioning that gold lace nearly drove us dotty!"

Bukin shuffled his feet. "This Grand Tourney will be the first time in eight hundred and fifty-six years that our Howler nation has participated in a joint event with our nonmutant brethren. We want to do so proudly. And since we are especially proud of *you*, we intend to glorify you before the assembled multitude. Lady . . . you are a flower sprung from Tanu and human stock, now blooming in a garden that must seem strange and bizarre. But we rejoice to have you with us. You console us with your beauty and kindness. By showing your loving devotion to our Master, the most fearfully deformed of us all, you have brought fresh hope to us. You have seen fit to thank us for this gift, but we are the ones who should thank you."

"Thank you," sighed the monsters.

Then the outer door of the atelier was flung open and a

greenhaired sprite shrieked, "He comes! Lord Sugoll comes to see our Lady!"

Katlinel held out her arms as the Lord of the Mutants entered, tall and terrible, trailed by the human geneticist, Gregory Prentice Brown, who beamed as the lovers embraced.

"I thought to save these gifts until the Tourney Eve," Sugoll said. "But I think it better to bestow them now, in the presence of these devoted friends. Greggy! The casket."

Mopping and mowing like an excited tamarin, Greg-Donnet Genetrics Master held out a sizable silver-gilt box. Sugoll opened it, and as the horde of goblin workers squealed and whistled in astonishment, he removed a necklace of rare aurora-borealis stones. Working dextrously with two tentacles, he fastened it just beneath his wife's golden torc. A third tentacle plucked forth a coronet set with the same strangely iridescent gems. Katlinel took it and settled it on her elaborate coiffure.

"Now you are truly our queen," said Sugoll.

The mob of grotesques cheered and capered about. Greggy made a leg, kissed Katlinel's hand, and murmured, "Smashing. Truly smashing."

"Now," the Howler prince said to his folk, "I would ask you to leave us for a time while I confer with my Lady and Lord Greggy on matters of state."

"Lunch break—everybody out!" cried Bukin. "Scoot, you imps and spunkies and tankeraboguses!" The mutant workers fled helterskelter, and in a moment Sugoll and his wife and Greg-Donnet were alone. The geneticist pulled up two chairs for Katlinel and himself, while the great abomination took his ease on the fitting room floor.

"There are odd doings afoot," Sugoll said. "King Aiken-Lugonn has requested Howler guides for an excursion into Fennoscandia—seeking certain unusual ores."

"Whatever for?" Katlinel asked.

The little old geneticist giggled. "Precisely what we asked ourselves, Katy dear! The minerals in question are gadolinite and xenotime, sources of the so-called rare-earth elements. His Puckish Majesty was very cagey at first about his need for these peculiar substances. That his need was *urgent* became apparent when Lord Sugoll showed no inclination to cooperate!"

"And why should I cooperate?" growled the mutant ruler. "What's he done for us lately? Just seven weeks until the

Tourney, and he hasn't even sent us the first installment of the Tanu share of the expenses. The fribbling little pecht! Probably blew his whole treasury on that shameless Grand Loving spectacle in May . . ."

"Rare earths?" Katlinel, who had been a member of the Creator Guild and a High Table sitter before her defection, shook her bejeweled head in puzzlement. "I know little enough chemistry, but sufficient to say that there is scant use for such materials in Tanu technology."

"But not in that of the Milieu!" snapped Sugoll. "And when I balked, the golden wirling finally had to come clean and tell me why he wanted the stuff. He's building a time-gate machine!"

"Almighty Tana," whispered the Lady. "Not—a portal leading *into* the future world?"

Greg-Donnet nodded with wry solemnity. "It seems he's collected experts from all over the Many-Colored Land and plans to reopen the gate that the redoubtable Madame Guderian slammed shut. The potential for mischief making is formidable!"

"Naturally, given the facts, I pledged our full cooperation," Sugoll said.

Katlinel stared at him, taken aback.

Greggy said gently, "If the Howler people could pass through the gate into the world I came from, there would be no doubt that their deformed bodies could be remolded, their genes engineered to the Firvulag norm once again. I've tried a few feeble experiments along those lines during my stay with you— but my piddling attempts are as nothing beside the scientific resources of the Milieu. Their scientists could do in a few months what it might take me decades to accomplish on my own here in the Pliocene."

"I can't believe that Aiken—" Katlinel broke off, shaking her head. "He's devilishly clever, we all know that. But this doesn't seem possible. He must be hatching some other scheme . . . perhaps using this time-gate ploy to divert Sharn and Ayfa from their warlike designs."

"If so," Sugoll put in, "then Téah send success to the Tanu King! And all the more reason for us to cooperate. I have delegated Kalipin to assist Aiken's expedition, since he has had experience in dealing with Lowlives; and for the technical matters, Ilmary and Koblerin the Knocker, who know more about the minerals of the lands beyond the Amber Lakes than any among us."

"Let us not raise false hopes among the people," Katlinel pleaded.

"Don't worry," Greggy said. "I'll keep on with my own experiments, just as before." He winked merrily. "Actually, the Skin-tank device looks rather promising. I have several volunteers eager to try it."

"When does Aiken's expedition set out?" Katlinel asked.

"The first scouts should be here in a few days," said Sugoll. "From Nionel they sail north to the Big Bend of the Seekol, then cut across the Peneplain to the Anversian Sea."

"It'll take them months to find those minerals," Katlinel said. "If they ever do. And as for constructing a time-gate machine—it's just too incredible!"

"I'm afraid you're right," the geneticist sighed. "But if it *did* turn out to be true..." he grinned at Katlinel and her superlatively hideous spouse. "How I'd love to take the two of you on a grand tour of the Galactic Milieu. You'd love it. Really, you would."

Kuhal Earthshaker sat on a glass bench in a secluded part of the castle garden, waiting until she should come. The evening was alive with sound: chirping green bush crickets, a nightingale warbling his heart out in anticipation of the fall mating season, the chiming of small crystal bells festooning the trees, and as a background to it all there were crowd sounds from the city's Gyre of Commerce, which lay only a few hundred meters down the hill, beyond the garden wall and a narrow greenbelt. During the regime of Kuhal's elder brother, Nodonn Battlemaster, evening markets had been forbidden; but the usurper changed all that in his haste to curry favor with his compatriots, who preferred to shop and carouse after the fierce Pliocene sun had set. Now grays and barenecks wandered abroad freely at all hours, disturbing the peace and making extra work for the rama cleanup crews.

A sturdy crescent moon was rising. Fireflies winked in the shrubbery surrounding the lily pool. Up in the Castle of Glass, the jewel-colored windows were ablaze and a full show of faerie lights outlined the freshly repaired towers and battlements. The

King, having returned triumphant from Calamosk that afternoon, was having a party to introduce the North Americans to the High Table and to the flower and chivalry of Goriah. Kuhal had put in a brief, obligatory appearance and managed to arrange this rendezvous.

And now she was coming.

He rose from the bench as he felt her coolly questing thought. She came out from among the willows, a strangely alien figure in a futuristic diamanté sheath of gray satin, her mind carefully guarded.

Cloud, he said, opening to her.

Then they were standing together, not touching physically. Her redactive probe, soft as a moth wing, worked swiftly behind his eyes. She said aloud, "Well, you're truly recovered at last. Both hemispheres in fine fettle, all your metabilities restored, your bereavement receded to memory, where it belongs. Fighting a losing battle and working off your penance cleaning Aiken's Augean stables seem to have agreed with you. I'd say you were a normal man again."

"Only when you're with me," he said. "And it seems we've been separated forever."

"Less than three weeks!" she said, laughing and drawing back from him. His face was shadowed and his fair hair touseled. For the first time since the Grand Loving, he wore the rose-gold robes of the Second Lord Psychokinetic.

"It hardly seems possible," he said. "So many terrible things have happened."

"Well, your ordeal is over now, and you're reinstated at the High Table—for services rendered." Her voice had gone flat and the mental carapace hardened. "What do you intend to do now?"

"Serve him," Kuhal replied, "as I vowed. He is sending me to collect armaments from Roniah, and to secure Castle Gateway in preparation for the new construction. It's a task fraught with great responsibility."

"No doubt," she said shortly, turning away from him to look out over the pond. "Good luck."

He was bewildered. "Cloud—what's wrong? I thought you would rejoice at this meeting, as I have. Has my submission to the King displeased you? Changed things between us?"

She was wearing a shawl of cobweb wool, which she now

pulled more closely about her shoulders, although the evening was warm. "There's nothing between us, Kuhal—except perhaps a little transference, which is rather common in redactor-patient relationships . . . So you're off to Roniah, are you? How soon?"

"The day after tomorrow. But the task need not take long, and we can find ways to be together—"

"No," she said offhandedly, seeming to be absorbed in the sight of a great white heron that had appeared among the water-lilies, stalking froggy victims. "I don't think we'll see each other again, now that you're well. I'll be staying here in Goriah, helping to keep the recruited scientists in line. A number of them are less than enthusiastic about the Guderian Project. But we must complete the device as soon as possible and I'll have no time for distractions. Your really don't need me any more, Kuhal—and I certainly don't need you."

He laughed, a low and quiet sound, and with the utmost gentleness exerted his psychokinesis. She felt herself lifted a few centimeters above the grass and rotated in midair to face him. He had lowered himself to one knee so that their eyes could meet, but there was no trace of subservience in him as he said, "You lie to me, Cloud Remillard. You with your mind in hiding! I know you *do* care for me, else you would not have had tears in your eyes upon your presentation to the High Table this evening—nor would you have agreed to meet me here."

"Put me down!" she exclaimed angrily. "You great barbarian lout!" Her mind pummeled him, but she was unable to free herself from the humiliating sustention, or to undermine his coercion with her own. After a long moment he lowered her, still smiling into her outraged face.

"You lie," he repeated. "Admit it."

The mind-screen trembled. Anger gave way to a more complex emotion. "Perhaps I do care . . . a little. But since I've been back with my own people, I've had time to think. To analyze our situation in the light of what . . . will happen."

"You mean, in light of your determination to pass into the future world of the Galactic Milieu?"

She cried, "We're going to do it or die in the attempt! There's no way you can understand what we've been through, how desperate we are to escape!"

"I know you didn't hesitate to destroy most of my own race when we seemed to stand in your way."

"Yes," she admitted, and the screen thinned to translucency, showing the flush of guilt overlying resolution. "And you'll never forget that. But that's only one part of it."

"I love you in spite of everything. We'll go together to the Milieu."

She let slip a little choking cry. An image peered from her brain, childishly comical, which she tried vainly to suppress.

"What," he inquired with bemused dignity, "is a basketball player?"

She burst out laughing, and then wept and threw her arms around him as he knelt. "It's a joke," she said miserably. "A vicious, cruel joke. That damned Hagen . . . speculating on what our life together might be—especially if we both went to the Milieu."

"I don't understand," he said, holding her. But his mind sang. She *had* lied!

"We're too different," she said, pulling away, and he saw a persistent dark core of denial in the heart of the brightness. "And for all his brutal attempts at humor, Hagen was basically correct. Sooner or later we'd end up despising each other . . . or worse."

"In Afaliah," he reminded her, "the physical differences were nothing compared to the affinity of our minds."

She drew away, began to walk back the way she had come. "When we were in Skin, we were two wounded creatures in need. Licking each other's hurts. Both lonely. Both . . . bereaved. It was natural that there be an attraction. Inevitable. But now the need has passed. We're finished, Kuhal! I'm going now."

He followed. She went more quickly, almost running, but his exotic legs kept pace with her easily. They came into the shadow of the trees where moonlight was as sparse as a flung handful of coins. He seized her with both hands, looming like some fearsome woodland spirit, and she shrank away from his desperation. "Nothing you've said touches on the real reason for your rejection of me! Why, Cloud? *Why?*"

She said, "Fian."

There was wonder in his voice as he asked, "You would deny me because of my dead twin?"

"He was more than your brother!"

"He was the mind of my mind...and he is dead."

"I won't take his place," she said. "Never!" Her redactive thrust caught him off guard, and when he recovered he was standing alone with only the shawl in his hands.

The King wearied of his party, which if truth be told was not much of a success. The young North Americans cared little for dancing and drinking and the preliminaries to sweet hough-magandy, preferring to talk shop with the scientists and technicians who had been assembled for the Guderian Project. Along about midnight, when things should have just started getting a glow on, the ballroom was half empty and the orchestra playing for itself. Those guests who did remain were mostly human, engaged in depressingly earnest conversation.

"The hell with this," Aiken muttered, and went slouching off into the grand foyer and thence to the courtyard for a breath of air. There he found Yosh Watanabe and Raimo Hakkinen climbing into a waiting calèche.

"Going downtown?" the King inquired. "Can't say as I blame you. No fun upstairs at all." He sighed lugubriously.

"We'd planned to pub-crawl," Yosh said. "But first, we're off to visit my neputa works. I've been out of town so long, the crafters have probably managed to screw things up. Sneak inspections keep people on their toes. Besides, the shop's right next door to our favorite groggery, the Mermaid."

Aiken lifted a hand. "Ah. Well, have a good time, guys." He began to turn away.

Raimo said impulsively, "Aik. Come along! Forget this king shit for one friggerty night."

"I'll cramp your style."

"Just get rid of the royal threads," Raimo suggested.

"Like this?" Aiken asked. There was a subdued flash. His magnificent golden outfit disappeared. He wore frayed khaki shorts, calf-high reefwalkers with tabi toes, and a grubby yellow t-shirt imprinted DALRIADA WINDSURFER RACING TEAM. His distinctive physiognomy was hidden under a ratty straw sombrero and he had a silver torc about his neck.

"Climb in, kid," Raimo said, "and we'll show you the big city." He whipped up the hellad and they were off, clopping over the great glass drawbridge and onto the winding road that

"I love it!" Aiken exclaimed. "Let's go have a dram and celebrate."

"What say we leave the carriage over here, out of the way?" Raimo suggested. They followed the ramas out.

"Sounds good," said Aiken. He directed one of the apes to unbar the main gate and the three men slipped out into the street.

"Way!" somebody shouted. "Make way!" A squad of grays in half-armor and livery of a farsensor violet began pushing pedestrians unceremoniously aside so that a Tanu grande dame mounted on an enormous white chaliko could move along without hindrance. "Way for a Most Exalted Personage!" the captal barked, squashing Aiken back against the wall. Raimo and Yosh, in their gold torcs, rated a slightly more courteous degree of manhandling.

"Veil or not, mind-screen or not, I know that woman," Aiken growled. "It's Morna-Ia—who said she was suffering from positiveion migraine when she packed it in at twenty-three bells up in the castle!"

"Well, it looks like she's catching the second show at the Bijou," Raimo remarked, craning to see the noble lady's destination. "I wonder what's playing?"

"*The Maltese Falcon*," said a bareneck passerby. "Classic 2-D. Black and white, but dynamite!" He vanished in the press.

And then, in the inexplicable way of street crowds, there came a momentary lull. A corridor formed all the way to the Gyre entrance nearly thirty meters away. Aiken saw the raspberry ice vendor and his cart rolling slowly by, and then it paused for a customer, a very tall human with curly gray hair, dressed in the tan shirt and trousers and yellow neck scarf that were the usual mufti of the elite guard. The shirt was a tight fit across the man's shoulders, as though he had borrowed it from a less husky friend. When he had paid for his ice, he sampled it with evident enjoyment, glanced up the side street, nodded in a friendly manner when he caught Aiken's eye, and then disappeared into the teeming Gyre.

"Oh, my God," said the King.

"Chief," Yosh whispered. "Are you okay? You look—"

Aiken took a deep breath, then pulled off his straw sombrero and stamped it very thoroughly into the cobblestones.

"Aik—what the hell?" Raimo blurted.

"It's time to go to the Mermaid," Aiken told his friends through gritted teeth, "and get very, very drunk."

He strode away, leaving Raimo and Yosh to eye each other, shrug, and then tag along.

"How long," Elizabeth asked Marc, "do you plan to stay?"

"Five hours should give us a fair start." He glanced down at the sleeping infant in the basket. "We'll have to see how he reacts to the increased psychic pressure of the redaction. On my next visit, I hope to spend more time with you. But to-night"—he smiled reminiscently—"I made a little side trip before coming to Black Crag. Your Many-Colored Land is an interesting place. I'd enjoy discussing it with you."

She eyed the wet coverall with its metallic function monitors and shunt receptables in an uneasy manner, and then for the first time noticed the linen of puncture wounds above his eyebrows. "There's blood on your forehead. Were you injured on your little side trip?"

He waved a gloved hand airily. "From the brain-piercing needles of the CE equipment. Mere mosquito bites. They'll self-heal in a few minutes... Aren't you familiar with the workings of cerebroenergetic enhancers, Grand Master?"

"They're outlawed in the Milieu now. Considered too hazardous for the operator."

Marc only laughed.

Elizabeth said, rather stiffly, "Perhaps you would like some more comfortable clothes."

"You're kind to offer. At my last port of call, I had to steal some."

Her voice was casual. "Then you can't carry anything along with you on the d-jump?"

"Not yet. But I'm working on it."

Without taking her eyes off him, Elizabeth went to the nursery door and opened it. Outside in the corridor, sitting on a bench and placidly telling his beads, was the rugged old Franciscan friar. He looked up expectantly.

"Brother Anatoly," said Elizabeth, "may I present Marc Remillard." Anatoly got to his feet, stowed his rosary, and stared. Marc bowed slightly. Elizabeth continued. "Our visitor is in need of a change of clothing, Brother. Perhaps you'll be kind enough to find him something, then escort him back here. Oh . . . and we'll want you to attend the redactive session, if you please."

Marc was amused. "Commendable prudence, Grand Master."

Her lips tightened. She withdrew back into the baby's room and closed the door, leaving the two men together.

"You make her nervous," Anatoly observed amiably.

"And you? Or do you feel armored against the demògorgon, wearing your breastplate of justice and helmet of salvation?"

"I ought to be afraid of you," Anatoly admitted, beckoning for Marc to follow, "but I'm too intrigued. I came to the Pliocene three years before your famous Rebellion. When you were still a Paramount Grand Master helping the Human Polity dazzle the socks off the unsuspecting exotic members of the Concilium, who hadn't quite figured us out yet. When you were a hero—the champion of the Mental Man concept."

"And what am I now?" Marc asked pleasantly.

"You're about my size, I'd say. Suppose I lend you my sinfully secular silk bathrobe and a pair of gardening dungarees? Next time you visit, I'll have something ready you can call your own. How about white tie and tails, or a Faustian wizard outfit?"

"What am I, Brother Anatoly?"

Stopped in his tracks by an irresistible coercive hold, the old priest strained to look over his shoulder. "We're almost to my room. Why not hold off on the mind-ream job until we get there? Turning me inside out here in the hallway is a mite uncivilized."

"As you like." The grip turned him loose and they moved on. "What are you doing here on Black Crag, Brother?"

"I'm her confessor." The old man grinned ironically. "She hasn't exactly made use of my priestly faculties as yet, but she hasn't thrown me out, either. I've been waiting for you outside that nursery every day from twenty-one hours until three, for the past two and a half weeks—on her orders. D'you suppose she expects me to exorcise you, or something?"

Marc laughed heartily. "You'll have your chance in a few minutes."

They went up a small rear staircase. Anatoly said, "So you two are going to intensify Brendan's redaction, eh? Do you think the little fellow will make it?"

"One can only try."

The friar cast a shrewd glance at the figure in black that followed him. "And I wonder why you *do* try."

Marc did not answer.

"Is the baby just an excuse?" Anatoly opened a door at the top of the stairs. They came into a spacious suite under the eaves of the chalet, with roof-high windows all along one side. When they were inside with the door shut, Marc said: *Now*.

Anatoly gritted his teeth and stood stiff as a post with his eyes screwed shut. "Make it fast, dammit."

He felt the coercive-redactive impulses lance into him, making his scalp tingle and his closed eyes experience a neural fireworks display. As the drain commenced he lost contact with reality. Then he found himself standing quite relaxed in the middle of the sitting room. There were shower noises coming from his bathroom, where someone was whistling "Le veau d'or." Anatoly hunted up the magnificent scarlet brocade robe and the old faded pants and hung them on the door hook. Then he went out onto the balcony and said the First Sorrowful Mystery under the stars to steady his nerves. Gethsemane. Bloody sweat. What if he does ask? All the Remillards were Catholics. If it's possible, let this chalice pass. *Does this man even know it was a sin?*

"It was no sin, only a failure, Anatoly Severinovich. 'And even if my troop fell thence vanquished, yet to have attempted a lofty enterprise is still a trophy...'"

The priest turned around to face the challenger of the galaxy. "Now that's really interesting. Forty-two years in Holy Orders, you hear all the sins in the lexicon. But angelism—! Now there's a genuine rarey." His eyes fell to the scars on Marc's chest. "And are those another trophy of the lofty enterprise?"

"Not at all. Only the traces of a recent accident. They'll disappear in a few months. My body is self-rejuvenating."

"So you can ignore the vultures nibbling at your liver, eh? Still—it must be a terrible kind of security. Lonely in the long run, too. Well... if you ever need me, I'll be around. I told her that, and the same goes for you."

Marc was expressionless. "Listen to me, Anatoly Severinovich. I can see that you mean well, and you're a kindly man. But don't presume to meddle in my affairs."

"Don't tell me you're so far gone that you'd zap a poor old priest just for praying for you?"

"Save your prayers for Elizabeth. I'm past the need. Now let's get back downstairs." He turned and headed for the door, with Anatoly coming after him.

"Nu, ne mudiy, my son! Your brother Jack would never let you get away with saying that."

Marc paused. His voice was deadly calm. "For a man who came to the Pliocene before my brother's . . . notoriety, you seem oddly knowledgeable about his mind-set."

"It's hearing all those confessions," sighed the friar. "You'd be surprised, the kind of people who've gone time-traveling to escape reality. Or maybe, you wouldn't! I know a lot more about you than my memories told you in the brain-ream, son." He smiled encouragingly. "The loneliness, for instance. Is that the real reason you've come here to Black Crag—hoping to find another metapsychic who'll accept you as human instead of failed angel?"

"A very interesting question," said Marc Remillard. "Let's both try to find out the answer." Carrying his black coverall, he went out laughing.

3

PRAISE BE TO TÉ, IT WAS A BANNER YEAR FOR GIANT SLUGS! Purtsinigelee Specklebelly chortled in satisfaction as he lifted the bark lid off the last tray of stale beer. It was crowded with plump mollusks, amber with gray spots. Each slug was nearly the size of the bananas the Lowlives grew at the plantations down at Var-Mesk—and far more succulent and nourishing. Every tray along the trapline this morning had been full of the creatures. Drawn by the seductive aroma of hops, they crept over the floor of the alpine valley rain forest and up the mossy stumps upon which the trays rested. After drinking themselves into a blissful stupor, the slugs tumbled into the beer and drowned. It was an easy death, and Purtsinigelee, who was a peaceable dwarf, often reflected upon it philosophically as he made his daily collections in the Gresson Vale. Later, after they had been pickled and stored in small firkins, the slugs would not only provide protein-rich food for his family when the winter storms swept down from the Helvetides, but they would also be a valuable trade item. The more sophisticated Firvulag in western Famorel paid a hefty price for prime, season-end mollusks like these. The delicacy might even find its way to the banquet table of King Sharn and Queen Ayfa at this year's Grand Tourney. Purtsinigelee hoped that would happen; he was a stay-at-home sort himself, but it was nice to think that some of his slugs would be relished in the highest social circles . . .

Humming a happy tune, he transferred the final creature to the tote-skin slung over his shoulder. Into it he strained the liquid in the tray, topped it off with more stale beer, and replaced the loose-fitting lid with care. Then he was off for home and lunch, striding along the steep trail with the mist coiling about the green, dripping rhododendron trees and the birds and oreopithecine apes making a great racket down by the river.

After a time he emerged from the densely wooded gorge into more open, rocky country. The fog burned away as the sun mounted and it became a cool and splendid September morning. The meadows were dotted with flowers, the sky was so intensely blue that it made the eyes ache, and along the northern horizon the stupendous front range of the Pennine Alps reared in dazzling majesty. The Famorel Firvulag called them the Goddess Mountains—not only because of their beauty, but also because certain First Comers said that the snow-clad peaks resembled the ancestral territory of the Little People on lost Duat. No mountains on Pliocene Earth were more lofty.

Purtsinigelee's home, like that of many other isolated Firvulag living in caveless terrain, was situated on a commanding height. It sat just below the ridge that separated the Gresson Vale from that of the River Ysez to the east. Pausing for a moment on the trail, he spied the snug little cottage, shaped like a stone beehive, nestled among pin oaks and wind-twisted pines at the edge of a tiny tarn. And grouped around it—

He wailed in dismay and darted behind the shelter of a large boulder. *Machines!* Merciful Té—there were some kind of alien contraptions surrounding his home! He cautiously extended his farsight and spotted fair numbers of people as well. Horror upon horror! The Foe was upon him! He moaned out loud and let the sack of slugs slip squishily to the ground.

"My poor Hobbino—and the children! Goddess preserve them!"

Heart pounding, he crept out from behind the rock, keeping down under a low-growing juniper. There appeared to be seven machines, cartlike vehicles with eight fat wheels along each side. They bristled with appendages of unfathomable function and had many dirty windows that gleamed dully in the sunshine. They were a little over twice his height and perhaps four times as long. Not only Tanu knights in glass armor but also torced and bareneck Lowlives were in evidence, strolling in and out of the open door of his cottage and lounging about the grounds as though they owned the place, the vile miscreants! Té alone knew what atrocities had been perpetrated.

Getting a grip on his palsied nerves, he ventured to call his wife's name on the intimate mode. As he feared, there was no answer. The house walls were thick, proof against all but the most extraordinary telepathic penetration. He considered calling to the children, but his two sons and three daughters were all under ten years of age, totally unskilled at mental screening. They would surely betray his presence to the Foe.

He lay there for some time, his senses whirling, clutching the slug sack in anguished desperation. Then he made an effort to pull himself together. What was the Foe doing here? Tanu never ventured into remote Famorel. Once in a great while a pathetic outlaw human might wander up from Var-Mesk, but none of them lasted very long. Not with the likes of Tatsol Flamespitter and Ryfa the Insatiable lurking among the Maritime Alps! Because the region had always been secure, the Little People had no garrisons. The only trained fighters lived close to the viceregal capital, Famorel City, six days' journey to the southwest.

Purtsinigelee cogitated as he had never done before. More might be at stake here than the survival of his precious family! From what he could make out, the expeditionary force numbered at least fifty. Some of them carried gadgets that were all too likely the futuristic Lowlife weapons that everyone was buzzing about. It was necessary—obligatory!—that he pass along this information via the farshout relay.

Using the utmost caution, he crept backward the way he had come. It was only necessary to go a few hundred meters in order to drop below the line of sight from the cottage. Once he was safe from view he began to run. He reached a fork in the trail and turned south, paralleling the ridge and the river, until he had placed the farsenseproof bulk of Pimple Knob between him and his invaded homestead.

He flopped down and caught his breath. His nearest neighbor was Tamlin the Mephitic, a musk-oil processor who lived a day's journey to the west. Because of the solitary nature of his trade he was the most dedicated telepathic gossip in the entire piedmont. Old Tam would see that the great hero Mimee himself learned of this outrage. Gathering all his mental resources, Purtsinigelee made the call. When he had finished he picked up the sackful of slugs and trudged resolutely back to his cottage without any effort at concealment.

He arrived to find the invaders gone. The only trace of them was a lingering cloud along the northern crest. His wife and children were quite safe, sitting numbly around the kitchen table.

"What *happened*?" he cried.

"They said they're going to climb Big Goddess," Hobbino told him. "They didn't hurt us. They wanted to buy provisions before heading into the high country." She began to laugh rather hysterically, then fumbled in the pocket of her skirt and took out a chamois pouch. "Look!" She undid the strings and tipped a glittering little pile of gemstones onto the homespun tablecloth. "More than we could earn in five years!"

"They emptied the cellar," said the oldest boy. "Took every last firkin and keg."

The youngest girl added solemnly, "But, Daddy—you should have heard the naughty things they said when they opened a keg and saw what they'd bought."

VEIKKO: Hagen.

HAGEN: Right here, keed. Hold on a sec while I freshen my drink.

VEIKKO: Lucky sod. The only liquor we have left here is designated medicinal.

HAGEN: Stick to herb tea or you'll end like your old man.

VEIKKO: Better like mine than like *yours*, asshole.

HAGEN: All right, all right, you win that one hands down. Now cool it and report. It's been too long.

VEIKKO: [Edited replay.]

HAGEN: [Laughter.] I hope Irena's well fixed for escargot recipes.

VEIKKO: Listen, given a choice of climbing that mountain or staying here in base camp eating naked snails, I'll take the

creepies à là mode every time. You should eyeball this
Monte Rosa monster! It's not an isolated peak, it's a whole
bloody range—like the wall of the world's edge, dripping
glaciers. Who would've thought there'd be so much snow
in the Pliocene? And it just shoots up out of the Po Valley
flats: instant Alps—below sea level to nine thousand high
inside of sixty kilometers.

HAGEN: Give me a firm position on your camp.

VEIKKO: 40-50-31 north, 7-48-13 east, 4322.3 meters up. We
must be six kloms from the main summit as the crow flies.
Too friggerty bad we're not crows! I'm gasping like a beached
porpoise from altitude sickness. André fainted three times
this afternoon, and some of the King's Men look like they'd
like to. I think their torcs keep 'em going. But the Tanu
seem to feel fine, and Basil's Bastards are downright perky.
Wimborne calls this place Camp Bettaforca. There's snow
but we're cosy enough in the decamole huts except for the
anoxia. The Bastard quacks say we'll probably get acclimatized in a few days.

HAGEN: Any fresh info on plans for the actual climb?

VEIKKO: The big conference is tomorrow. The climbing party
doesn't actually have to reach the top of the sucker, you
understand. Just kind of circle around to the other side where
the aircraft are parked. The idea is to melt one out, fly it
back here, then ferry up the rest of the folks and shuttle off
to Goriah. It shouldn't be too tough getting the birds operational. After all, they haven't been on the mountain all
that long—just since the end of July. The hard part is
reaching the aircraft with the first assault team. Wimborne
will use a kind of relay operation with support groups to
get the principal climbing party over the top.

HAGEN: None of our people are involved in the climbing, are
they?

VEIKKO: Well, Buckmaster and Collins volunteered. You know
them.

HAGEN: Goddam dipshits! Tell 'em to forget it! None of our
people risk their lives unless there's no alternative.

VEIKKO: Amen.

HAGEN: Who's slated for the principal assault team?

VEIKKO: Not sure. But they'll all be Bastards except for the
boss Tanu, Bleyn, and one of his exotic underlings. Going

along to make sure the Bastards don't nip off with the birds. You should see the boots this guy Nirupam whipped up for the climbing high-pocketers: big enough to boil a chicken in! God, I wish we had some chicken...

HAGEN: While this climbing is going on, the rest of you just sit tight and wait?

VEIKKO: Seems like.

HAGEN: [Doubt.] Listen, Veik. I've got a bad feeling about those Firvulag you contacted on the way up. The ones you bought the slimies from.

VEIKKO: Yeah. You think they might have betrayed us to spook HQ. But Elizabeth is supposed to be watching out for Little People pulling a sneak on us, and she hasn't reported any movement—

HAGEN: I wouldn't rely on her overmuch. These days, she's got more interesting things to do than play wetnurse to your lot. The lady has been entertaining Papa in her chalet!

VEIKKO: ?!

HAGEN: She admitted it to the King, cool as you please. She says she's anxious to reconcile Marc with all of us...

VEIKKO: Some hope! Any more sightings of your old man around Goriah?

HAGEN: Not since the King spotted him sampling the night life a week ago. But we're ready if he tries to attack the project. The castle dungeon is carved from bedrock, so he can't jump in, and all the access points are sigma-wrapped and guarded by armed troops. Cloudie has the mind-idents of every person authorized to enter the restricted area and checks them in and out on the castle computer. Papa won't be able to pull a simple masquerade. The really irreplaceable workers are being guarded as carefully as the component store, so he can't hit us that way.

VEIKKO: How's the materials search coming?

HAGEN: We managed to scare up a lot of good stuff. It looks like the only real sticker is the one we anticipated all along— the dysprosium-niobium wire for the microassembly in the tau-generator mesh stacks. The Little King sent a scouting crew off to the Northland hunting ore, but that could take months. We need those aircraft, Veik. And not just for mineral scrounging...I tried to talk the King into flying out over the ocean and blasting Kyllikki out of the water with his wonderful psychocreative powers. But he turned the suggestion down flat. I *knew* there was some trick to the way he zapped us!

VEIKKO: Is Kyllikki still coming strong?

HAGEN: Sailing fair in the westerlies, about halfway between Bermuda and the Azores. She'll be here in nineteen days at the earliest.

VEIKKO: [Fear.] With the X-zappers charged and ready. We sure better bring the birds home to Goriah before then.

HAGEN: How right you are. They're looking more essential every day. For instance—with Papa on the loose, how could we ever hope to carry the Guderian device to the gate site *without* air transport?

VEIKKO: Tell the truth, I was surprised you didn't just build the dingus there at Castle Gateway.

HAGEN: I pushed for it but the King vetoed. He wants us under his thumb, of course. And Goriah is a superior manufacturing locale from a security and logistics standpoint, aside from being too close to the sea. The real problem with Castle Gateway is that it's been pretty well abandoned since the Flood. Last winter a Firvulag raiding party got in past the skeleton guard force and did a lot of damage. The place is being fixed up now, ostensibly as a kind of hostel for travelers bound for the tournament that they're having up north at the beginning of November. The King sent Cloud's Tanu boyfriend off last week to oversee the Castle Gateway rehabilitation.

VEIKKO: Hard luck for her.

HAGEN: Um. She *says* she and Kuhal are finished. But I notice they still keep fairly regular head-skeds. No doubt having serious discussions about the meaning of life and suchlike dreckola.

VEIKKO: How's Diane?

HAGEN: Giving me a hard time, if you must know. Suddenly she has qualms about the kind of reception we might get in the Milieu. Because of Gibraltar. Because of . . . who we are. She's half convinced herself it would be better to stay here.

VEIKKO: God! After all we've been through?

HAGEN: And a way to go yet . . .

VEIKKO: She might be worrying about her father.

HAGEN: Alex can take care of himself. Now that Papa's started d-jumping, he needs Manion more than ever. Still—have you tried to farspeak Walter in Kyllikki recently?

VEIKKO: It wouldn't have been much use, with us camping in valleys every night to keep out of easy farsense range of the Firvulag. Would I try for Walter when I couldn't even raise you?

HAGEN: Well, do it. Now that you're parked halfway up the highest mountain on Earth, you might have a chance of making contact.

VEIKKO: All right. If my brain cells haven't blunk out from oxygen starvation. Anything specific you want to know?

HAGEN: Morale conditions aboard ship. Whether the magnates still favor snuffing us. Whether Papa still leans toward the steel-fist-in-velvet-glove approach. Hints on how he plans to use the X-lasers. On his d-jumping itinerary and maneuvering with the King and Elizabeth . . . Would Walter tell you the truth about any of that?

VEIKKO: Jeez, Hagen, I don't know. He wants us to get away just as much as Alex does. But—

HAGEN: Uh-huh. I'd be more inclined to trust him if he wasn't driving that schooner so efficiently.

VEIKKO: I'll try to farspeak him tonight. In the wee hours of the morning, that is. He usually took the midwatch in the old days. But don't get your hopes up. I'm not the farspeaker Vaughn Jarrow was.

HAGEN: You're not the fucking idiot Vaughn was, either. Do your best.

VEIKKO: One other thing.

HAGEN: ?

VEIKKO: Now that we're camped in an exposed position, we're liable to be spotted by more than Firvulag . . . Hagen, what if Marc shows up here? I know he can't carry weapons. But he wouldn't need to. If those mountain climbers are mushing along in a tricky place, just one little push—

HAGEN: God, yes. At that conference tomorrow, warn Basil and the others of the possibility.

VEIKKO: And?

HAGEN: Don't take any chances. If Papa comes onto that mountain, kill him on sight.

* * *

Irena O'Malley carried a fresh load of steaming plates out of the cook-hut, plopped them onto the buffet table, checked the coffee urn, then decided to take a short break from her chores to see how Veikko was getting along. She climbed the slope above the camp to where he was sitting, alone on a flat rock in the sunshine, among scattered patches of old snow. He was still immured in misery, his slight body hunched in an untidy lotus posture while he seemed to contemplate the precipitous foreslope, which reared above them like a petrified tsunami wave crested with hanging glaciers. To the east was the huge Gresson Icefall; and beyond it, the cloud-plumed summit of Monte Rosa.

"Headache still bad, sweetheart?" Irena inquired. Veikko responded with a wan smile. She gestured at his nearly untouched breakfast. "Didn't you care for the squiche?"

"It tasted great, Rena. Really. I'm just not hungry. Altitude, maybe."

She knelt beside him among tufted alpine plants, a tall and robust young woman with glossy black hair done up in nononsense pigtails. Laying a solicitous hand on his shoulder, she tried to slide her redaction into his mind, only to come up against the same barrier of mysterious grief that had frustrated her earlier attempt at comfort. "If you'd only let me in, I could help! What *is* it with you this morning? And don't you try to fob me off with rubbish about altitude sickness."

He bit his lip and refused to meet her eyes. As she put her arms around him, he shed the last vestiges of self-control, struggling like a trapped wild creature. "Tell me," she insisted.

He had shut his eyes, and now tears forced their way beneath trembling lids. "I'm sorry. I'm so sorry. But you'll have to know sooner or later. They all will!"

"Veikko, *tell* me."

"Last night I finally managed to farspeak Walter on Kyllikki. He told me—something terrible's happened. Helayne Strangford went over the edge. Turned violent. Ten days ago, she—she—Marc was away d-jumping and none of the others on board suspected what she was up to. You know what a clever screener she is. And—she killed people."

Irena's fingers dug into Veikko's shoulders. "Who?"

"Barry Dalembert's father. And the two Keoghs—not that

Nial will give a damn, that coldhearted swine!"

"Shh, baby . . . who else?"

Veikko buried his head in her breast as his mind tolled the list of casualties: Frieda Singer-Dow, mother of Chee-Wu Chan; Claire Shaunavon, mother of Matiwilda; Audrey Truax, mother of Margaret and Rebecca Kramer; Isobel Layton and Alonzo Jarrow, parents of Vaughn Jarrow; John Horvath, father of Imre; Abdulkadir Al-Mah-moud and Olivia Wylie, parents of Jasmin Wylie; Eva Smuts, co-mother of Kané Fox-Laroche; Ronald Inman; Everett Garrison; Gary Evans; and . . .

He was weeping now. "I'm sorry, Rena. Arky, too. He was one of the injured ones. Steinbrenner did his best, but he's not as skilled in surgery as the Keoghs were, and there's no regen tank set up on Kyllikki. Arky died three days ago."

His mind opened at last and she melded, pouring psychic balm on his supersensitive emotional structure, rocking him to and fro while the equinoctial sun warmed the southern flank of the mountain.

She said, "It's strange. I dreamed about Daddy—then. It was a long dream, full of details. Probably a recapitulation of stories he used to tell me when I was small, and the books and the Tri-D cassettes we shared. In the dream, we traveled all over the Milieu. We visited the human colonies of Volhynia and Hibernia first to see how our ethnic kin were taming the wilderness, and then we rested on the cosmop world of Riviera, the vacation place. From there we toured exotic planets. We met funny little Poltroyans and repulsive entities that dripped green, and tall hermaphrodites with enormous yellow eyes—all coadunate metapsychics, in spite of their odd appearance. We saw the Krondaku, who aren't quite as scary in person as they look in a holo; and had a kind of séance with the Lylmiks, and learned that their race is so ancient that it might date from the previous universe. Finally we came home to Old Earth, to New Hampshire in America, where the O'Malleys and the Petroviches worked in the paper mills and had little farms early in the twentieth century. We saw Mount Washington, where the Intervention started, and the old Remillard house in Hanover. Arky and I saw it all together: our grandparents' place, and the schools and churches and stores and restaurants and other landmarks of the real world . . . He was a nice old villain, Veikko. He liked you, too, even though he tried hard not to show it. He kept asking when we were going to have a child."

"Not here."

"I tried to explain. Why we couldn't believe in Marc or his starsearch any longer. But he refused to understand. Now he's dead, and all those others."

Veikko wiped his face on his sleeve, found a comb and ran it through stringy fair hair. His face was thoughtful. "Not too many left now for Marc to manipulate, are there? Let's see. Six magnates, not counting Manion. Those are the minds we really have to worry about. Only Kramer and Warshaw have any children left alive, and the old lady's hard-assed as they come where loyalty to Marc's concerned. I'm not so certain about Kramer. He might balk if it really came down to zorching Marge and Becky along with the rest of us. Secondary grandmaster minds . . . eighteen. Quinn Fitzpatrick and Allison Sherwoode are weak sisters, but the others are concert-fit. And that big stud Boom-Boom Laroche is worth a mind and a half in anybody's roster."

"Surely Walter wouldn't—"

All persons please assemble immediately under the large canopy.

"The conference." Veikko climbed to his feet. As they made their way back to the small village of huts and parked vehicles, he said, "Don't delude yourself about my father, Rena. Walter's like a lot of other ex-Rebels. When he's outside of Marc's aura and thinks for himself he can understand our position and sympathize with us. But put him back within coercive range of the Angel of the Abyss and he's caught in the old spell—just as all of *us* were until Alexis Manion showed us how to escape."

"And paid for it," Irena added. After a minute she asked, "Are you going to tell the others about the murders?"

"Not until I get Hagen's okay. Maybe not even then. Let him break the news once we're all safe in Goriah. If ever."

They took their places on decamole benches facing an improvised rostrum, where Basil Wimborne waited patiently until the last stragglers were seated. Inevitably, the group was tripartite: the ten North Americans, the twenty Bastards, and the King's Men—twelve Tanu and twenty human golds—gathering together in distinct cliques. Only Basil himself and the cheerful little Bastard factotum, Nirupam, had circulated freely during the journey from the Rhône Valley.

Now the former Oxford don tapped the lectern three times and fixed his audience with a gaze of magisterial self-assurance. The babble of thoughts and voices faded to silence.

"We have successfully completed the first leg of the expedition," Basil began. "Thanks to the skill of our drivers and the good offices of the Grand Master Elizabeth, who surveyed our route, we have managed to traverse the four hundred and ninety-six kilometers between Darask and Camp Bettaforca without misadventure. Our journey has taken fourteen days, a most commendable pace under the circumstances. I have been asked by the Deputy Lord Psychokinetic, Bleyn the Champion, to convey to you all the warmest felicitations from King Aiken-Lugonn, who has kept us all in his heart and farseeing eye. His Majesty is fully confident that the second phase of our operation will proceed as successfully as the first."

This sentiment was delivered with a decidedly ironic tone. Most of the Bastards responded with arch grins, while Bleyn and the Tanu preserved a stately solemnity.

"The actual assault upon Monte Rosa involves, as most of you know, my own team of—uh—Bastards. Those expedition members remaining at the base camp will have other matters to occupy their attention, however. Lord Bleyn was advised by Elizabeth early this morning that a force of approximately two hundred ogres and dwarfs has set out from Famorel City and is marching north up the Ysaar Valley. We can only presume that they will follow the river eastward, cross over the Little St. Bernard pass into the Proto-Augusta Valley, and thence seek to clobber us."

Exclamations of astonishment and dismay broke out. Lusk Collins, the young North American ATV wrangler, said, "I warned you to kill those Firvulag we got the slugs from."

"Sparing them was a calculated risk," Basil averred primly. "Aside from humane considerations, may I remind you that we were instructed to avoid bloodshed. Technically, a state of armistice exists between the Tanu and Firvulag kingdoms."

"Remind the Famorel spooks, not us!" exclaimed Phronsie Gillis. "So we fight. What the hell! How long before the little hummers get here?"

"Elizabeth estimates six days," said Basil. "We are well armed, and there should be sufficient time to—uh—dig in and secure the position. Lord Ochal the Harper will coordinate the defensive measures and I will not discuss them further at this time. My province is the mountain, and I believe that it—not the Famorel Firvulag—will prove to be our most formidable opponent."

"Hear, hear," said Mr. Betsy.

Basil rummaged about in the pocket of his shirt and took out a small piece of paper, scrutinizing it before resuming. "The primary objective of this expedition is to secure the twenty-seven rhocraft situated on the other side of Monte Rosa and deliver them to the King at Goriah. I have been instructed to be extremely judicious in the risk of our personnel—especially the pilots. But risk is—er—inherent in the conquest of a peak such as this one, especially since we have so few experienced climbers and only improvised equipment. Needless to say, I plan to take a primary rôle in the operation. Before coming to the Pliocene, I arranged to have my body modified specifically for—uh—high-altitude mountaineering ventures. And since it was a whim of mine that led to the aircrafts' being parked on Monte Rosa in the first place, it's only just that I participate in the most hazardous phases of the retrieval. Unfortunately, I am neither a pilot nor do I possess the technical expertise to—er—fire up the engine of a craft that has been in cold storage for two months. You must also understand that scaling a great mountain such as Rosa is of necessity a team effort. Support groups must set up a string of camps with equipment dumps so that the ultimate assault can leapfrog to the top. I will lead both the support and the assault teams."

"And love every miserable minute of it," drawled Mr. Betsy. He looked more anachronistic than ever with a swansdown vest and pompom balaclava topping off his Elizabethan finery.

Basil continued. "At my request, Lord Bleyn's caravan brought from Goriah certain items such as power winches, rope and cable, vitredur hammers and ice-axes, medical supplies, and warm clothing. We have numbers of the excellent auberge-furnished backpacks with their decamole shelters and ladders, cooking gear and heaters, plus an adequate supply of concentrated food. Nirupam has been busy fashioning vitredur crampons, as well as pitons, ice screws, and other—er—hardware. We have no oxygen equipment, but I believe we can do the job without it, since only the strongest of us will be climbing."

He turned to indicate the gleaming rampart of the mountain

behind him. "Monte Rosa rises 9082 meters above sea level. Fortunately, it will not be necessary for us to scale the summit—although I, personally, would sell my soul in order to be permitted the attempt."

The Bastards smiled knowingly at one another while the rest of the expedition regarded Basil with fascinated horror.

"What we will do is cross over the West Col, that saddle-shaped region to the left of the peak. This lies at an approximate altitude of only 7800 meters. Elizabeth has studied the potential routes with her keen farsense and transmitted to me mental pictures, from which I have roughly plotted our climb. Moving out from Camp Bettaforca, we first cross that frozen expanse you see immediately above us, which I have named the Gresson Glacier. The ice is old, dirty, and rotten; we shall have to be very cautious. Upon reaching the escarpment with its hanging glaciers, we must choose which icefall to ascend, Unfortunately, we face Hobson's choice. The three falls on our left and the easternmost fall are nearly vertical, as are the rocky walls. We are left with the so-called Gresson Icefall, which ascends at a relatively comfortable fifty degrees. I say relatively. The route up this huge tumbled mass is very likely the most perilous section of our climb. Once at the top, we begin to move westward. Note the three massive ridges, like the tines of a monstrous fork, upon the mountain's southwestern flank. We must cross both the Middle Tine and the West Tine—and the pristine, snow-clad glaciers between them—in order to gain the West Col. A minimum of three advance camps will be set up along the route. I have selected a support team of nine persons to serve as—uh—Sherpas. The group includes Nirupam, who is a genuine member of that ethnos, Stan, Phillipe, Derek, Cisco, Chazz, Phronsie, Taffy, and Clifford. After they establish the camps, their work will be done and they can retire to well-deserved rest here at base."

"Just in time for the fight with the Firvulag," Stan Dziekonski sighed.

Basil continued imperturbably. "The eight-person assault group will be divided into two independent teams, traveling an hour apart. Since they will be burdened with heat-beam equipment and aircraft tools, they will make use of power winches and preset anchors, hauling their gear and themselves up the mountain wherever the terrain is compatible with such—er—

unsporting maneuvers. Upon attaining the West Col, the assault teams will proceed downhill to the aircraft side, which lies at 5924 meters on the North Face."

Irena O'Malley asked, "Why two assault teams?"

"Attrition," said the don.

There was dead silence in the audience.

"We may hope," he continued, "that at least one complete team will attain the objective. This would include an experienced mountaineer as leader, a pilot, a technician, and—"

"A Tanu," put in Bleyn the Champion. "By order of the King." His mental tone was entirely good-humored. "Since Lord Aronn and I are both psychokinetics, we might even prove worth our keep."

Basil said, "The number One assault team consists of myself, Dr. Hudspeth, Ookpik, and Lord Bleyn. Number two includes Dr. Thongsa, who is pilot, mountaineer, and physician—"

"All rolled into one insufferable little scuzzbag," Phronsie muttered, glowering at the Tibetan, who pretended not to notice.

Basil swept on. "Nazir will serve as Technician and Bengt as principal pilot—"

"And enforcer!" Phronsie appended. "Any little slanty-eyed folks start thinking again about running off with aircraft, ol' Bengt's gonna whup their ass six ways from Shangri La."

"Lord Aronn will complete the second team," Basil said. "Under ideal conditions, both teams will reach the aircraft and we will have three pilots, not just one, available to fly ships back here to Camp Bettaforca. Our ATV specialist, Mr. Collins, assures me that the fourplex vehicles can be disassembled into their original smaller modules for loading onto the aircraft. We hope to evacuate the entire camp and transport it in toto to the North Face. Even if—uh—Fata obstant and we have only a single ship available for shuttle work, it will still be able to airlift all personnel to safety in a single trip. Once the aircraft have power, they are capable of concentrating an enriched atmosphere. Sensitive individuals will reside on board while a sufficient number of ships are prepared for the first trip to Goriah. Subsequently, only the technical personnel and their Tanu supervisors will have to remain on the mountain to salvage the remaining machines . . . The task we face is difficult. Some of us may lose our lives in the attempt to retrieve these aircraft. But we know, nevertheless, that they may be crucial not only in the reopening of the time-gate but also in the defense of the Many-Colored Land against powerful enemies. At the risk of belaboring a point, I will end by quoting a peculiarly apposite verse from Kipling:

> *Something hidden. Go and find it.*
> *Go and look behind the Ranges—*
> *Something lost behind the Ranges.*
> *Lost and waiting for you. Go!*

If there are any questions I will now answer them."

"When do you plan for us Sherpas to start slogging?" Stan asked.

Basil said, "Tomorrow Nirupam, Ookpik, and I will lay out a route over the Gresson Glacier to the icefall. Support teams will begin carrying supplies to a dump at the icefall foot on Wednesday the twenty-fourth."

"And how long," inquired a worried-looking elite gold, "before the birdies get home to the roost in Goriah?"

"We've got nineteen days," said Veikko distinctly, "whether you realize it or not." And he told them about Kyllikki's estimated time of arrival with the X-zappers, and when the uproar over that had died down, he got around to mentioning the really bad news about Marc.

4

MARY-DEDRA DRIED HER LITTLE SON'S INFLAMED SKIN, THEN
dusted him with velvety spores by squeezing a dry puffball
over his body. He emerged for a moment from the terrible
stupor and his mind smiled. *Like*, he said.

The mother crooned to him through her golden torc: Soon
you will feel better much better soon Brendan. She said aloud
to Elizabeth: "Brother Anatoly suggested this substitute for
baby powder. He said it was an old Siberian remedy. The
fungus does seem to soothe the blisters better than salves."

The baby's eyes with their enlarged pupils fixed on Elizabeth. The feeble glow of pleasure was snuffed out by apprehension. *Hurt me? Hurt again?*

Elizabeth said: Yes Brendan. Hurt to make all hurt go away.
(And you must fear me, poor baby, not love the hurter, lest
the mind-circuits become confused and you mistake the pain
for joy.)

Dedra kept up her own flow of telepathic reassurance as
she wrapped the child in a light blanket. But when she handed
him to Elizabeth he broke into hopeless wails, and Dedra cried
out, overcome with guilt and reproach.

"We're very close," Elizabeth told the mother. "It could be tonight."

"But he doesn't seem to be any better... You say the treatment is going well, but I haven't seen any improvement. Except in his communication with me, telling me how it hurts."

"I know. I'm sorry, but it's inevitable. If we keep him below the pain threshold during the redaction, he won't be able to assist us. But he *is* better, Dedra. Believe me. Unfortunately, the modifications to the brain haven't yet manifested themselves in the rest of his body. When they do, improvement will be dramatic and abrupt. We're well into the multimodal thalamic nuclei—a primary integrative area. The job is nearly done."

"Will you work all night again?"

"Yes." Elizabeth held the sobbing baby against her shoulder, then triggered a massive release of endorphins so that Dedra would at least see him smile before she left... in case this sight of him was the one that would live in memory. "Dedra, there's still a danger. As always."

The mother kissed her baby's head, feverish beneath gossamer-fine curls. *Love Brendan love.*

Brendan loves Mother.

"I know how hard you've worked," Dedra said to Elizabeth. "You and—that man. I'm grateful, whatever happens. Believe me."

Elizabeth placed the quiet child into his basket. "You can send Marc in now. Tell Brother Anatoly to wait outside with you tonight. We can call him if we need him." For the Blessing of Departure.

"Very well."

Dedra went out of the nursery and Elizabeth turned away from the basket, going to the window to take a few breaths of cool air. A harvest moon rode above the silvery undulations of the Montagne Noire. The aether was apparently tranquil all over Europe.

It seems, she thought, that the only dread and unease in the world are here on my sad crag, and I am very much afraid. Not of personal failure. Not even of facing Dedra's grief. I'm afraid of him, and the energies he will channel through me into the mind of this dying child. He has come here faithfully for the past ten days. He has been a superlative assistant, never making the slightest attempt to seize control or even question my direction. Even his socializing has been formal. And still I am threatened . . .

"Good evening, Elizabeth."

She turned from the window and he was there, standing beside the child's basket, as usual wearing the crimson silk robe that Brother Anatoly had gladly relinquished.

"We'll attempt the finalization tonight," she said. "Since it will be hard on all three of us, we'll go at it in brief stages and give the child ample time for synpatic recuperation as we impose the new circuitry. Are you ready?"

"In a moment." He held out a closed fist toward her, turned it over and let the fingers open. In the palm of his hand was a small white star. "I went exploring today and brought you a souvenir."

In spite of herself, she reached out. It was a flower with a central cluster of golden buttons, surrounded by fleshy bracts clothed in fine white wool. She studied it in some perplexity.

He said, "Edelweiss. Shall we begin?"

Hold. Quickly halt that surge!
    Done.
    YesOgood see the holonet react burn it HARD yes enough. Now brainstem input. *(SleepBrendansleepbabysleepnow.)* Disengage easy . . . comeout Marc and rest.

They sat in their chairs on either side of the cot, heads bowed as they caught their breath. As always, he recovered first and went to the nearby tabouret for the carafe of fruit juice and glasses. After he had poured, he bent down and picked up something from the floor.

"You lost your flower," he said, smiling.

She took it from him and tucked it carefully into the breast pocket of her jumpsuit so that the fuzzy asterim formed a decoration. "My award for valor," she remarked. "If we succeed tonight, I may cherish it forever."

He lifted his glass to her and drank.

"In the Milieu," she said after a time, "the edelweiss plant grew wild only in high mountains. In the Alps."

"It's the same in the Pliocene." He drained his glass and poured another. "And a somewhat perilous memento, as it turned out. Fortunately for me, young Jasmin Wylie is a wretched shot with a Matsu carbine."

"You found the Monte Rosa expedition!"

"It wasn't difficult. I tried to be circumspect in my observations, but it's obvious that I was expected—and unwelcome. I confess that I decamped without attempting to probe the markswoman's motivation. Did the shoot-to-kill order come from Aiken Drum?"

"I—I'm afraid it was Hagen's decision. The King concurred, however. He's determined to have the aircraft."

"Let him have them."

She was surprised. "Don't you intend to oppose the salvage operation?"

"Why should I? You must reassure Hagen and the King, tell them that I don't intend to revisit Monte Rosa in the foreseeable future." His shadowed eyes held an enigmatic glint. "Nevertheless, I'm glad to have been able to bring you the flower."

The realization was upon her with spine-chilling suddenness. "You brought it back with you on the d-jump."

"My first effort. Completely enclosed in my gloved hand, of course, which is almost cheating. But one must begin somewhere. Perhaps you'll pass the information along to my son."

Harderharderharder MORE thrust MORE energy Odamn! DAMN . . .

Elizabethlinkcreative/coerciveafferentQUICKLY! IseeyesNOW . . . okaythankGodalmostlosthim . . . Bring up the brainstem input again. He's all right for moment with bypass. *(Sleepbabysleep.)* JesusGod let's get out . . .

They looked down at the small body, pale now against the white coverlet, the chest rising and falling almost imperceptibly. "There's no more pain," Elizabeth whispered. "But he almost slipped away from us, Marc. We went too far, pushed too hard."

"But it *worked*."

"Yes," she said dully. They rested for a long time, not speaking.

He said, "There's still the torc-circuitry cutoff—the moment of truth. And then the boost to operancy."

She covered her face with her hands, deep in self-redaction.

When she lifted her head the lines of strain about her mouth
and brow were erased but desolation looked from her eyes.
Her voice was calm. "Marc, I can handle the abscission—but
not the boost. Your energies exceed my capacity in this conformation. I'm too finely tuned in the redactive mode, and
Brendan needs brute thrust to break free of the latency."

"Let me take the executive, and we can do it."

Stark terror blended with rage fountained from her mind.
"I *knew* it! This is what you've been waiting for all along, isn't
it? The chance to take control of me!" Youwon'tyoucan'tdamn-
youneveragaincontrolGrandMastersprogrammedterminateulti-
mateviolationprevented—

"No, Elizabeth. I would not take advantage of you, Please
trust me."

Her control reasserted itself. "I can't risk it. Brendan will
be a normal person without the torc, even though he remains
latent. We must settle for that."

Marc leaned over the basket. The long, perfect fingers of
his right hand caressed the top of the child's skull, palpating
the anterior fontanelle where the brain was protected only by
fragile skin, the bones not yet fully knit together. "He could
have so much more if you could only bring yourself to trust
me."

"Aiken trusted you," she said. "You gave him a metaconcert
program to use against Felice, intending that it should kill both
of them."

"Nonsense."

"Do you know what frustrated your scheme? Let me show
you!" She projected the events that climaxed the fight at the
Río Genil. "It was Felice herself who saved Aiken, in spite of
the cost to herself, so that her beloved Culluket wouldn't be
annihilated together with the King. When it was all over and
Aiken had recovered, he analyzed your metaconcert program
and removed the mental booby trap. He can use it against you
now without danger to himself—and he will, if you try to stop
the reopening of the time-gate."

"My children must not pass into the Milieu. They don't
realize what they're doing."

"If you're concerned about your personal safety and that of
the other ex-Rebels, we can give assurance that if you behave
peaceably—"

"There can be no assurance if my son leaves here—but that's beside the point."

Elizabeth cried out, "*All* this is beside the point! The only thing that matters here and now is this child. Will you work with me in the coercer-inferior conformation to complete the redaction, or won't you?"

He inclined his head slowly. One side of his mouth lifted in that smile of peculiar sweetness. Compelling trust, offering to light and rule.

"Follow me," she said, and they began again.

ComebabycomeBrendan. Let go. Come this way not that.
AFRAID.

Let go baby. Try the new way steep but better leading to good things soon to be easy very easy.

NO. AFRAID.

(Now Marc push.)

NO [anguish] NO!

(HarderMarcharder burn behind him so he must use the New Way.) Seebabysee yes O yes come along now Brendan. (Almost ready...) Just try baby try once only then (CUT OFF!) *yes*.

[WONDER.]

I told you it would be good.

[WONDER.]

Yes baby yes.

[Joy. Release. Growth.]

Yes. (Wrap up the premotor cortex Marc while I hold. Ah. Then it's done God done. He's latent but safe. Remove torc...whatareyouDOINGMarcwhatare—*NO!!* STOP STOP ABADDON STOP DEVILBASTARD STOPSTOPSTOP—)

Let me lead. You need not die. And so...

[ECSTASY.]

...it is done. And so easily.

You—you let us go?

Poor Elizabeth. of course.

Later, he said, "I'm profoundly sorry that I had to use force. But it never again would have come so easily for him as it did at that moment. He was ripe, ready; and I felt the end justified the means. I knew I wouldn't suicide. Your unconscious realized that I was no threat, even if your panicky conscious tried to tell you otherwise."

"You devil," she said, nearly paralyzed with revulsion.

"I'm only a man, as *you* are only a woman." His tone was level, almost scolding. "And one, au fond, more comfortable in the subordinate mode, as your late husband Lawrence undoubtedly realized. You might keep that in mind as you ponder your personal predicament."

"No wonder your children hate you! And the Milieu..."

Wearily, he turned away, moving toward the window. "Neither you nor the baby was harmed. And he's operant."

A syntactical probe gave her confirmation of the diagnosis. The infant lay sleeping, his mind cycling in bright dreamlessness. His skin was a normal rose-ivory color; the only traces of the fierce blistering were tiny bits of dry crust about the torcless small throat.

Elizabeth sank back into her chair and let her eyes close, fatigued to the uttermost depths of her soul. She heard Marc say:

"Children... You and Lawrence thought your work was more important, and learned your mistake too late. I never intended to have natural children, either. Not after bioengineering of the normally sited human brain was proved impracticable. Not with my heritage! The vicissitudes overcome by the saintly Jack must have their place in the history texts of your post-Rebellion Milieu. But I doubt whether you know the truth about me and the others—Luc and Marie and poor damned Madeleine, and the stillborn ones and the teratoid abortions, and Matthieu, who would have killed me before birth if I hadn't anticipated him and struck first. Oh, we were a little less than the angels, we Remillards, if the truth be told. One saint and a myriad of sinners! And all except the lucky one, chained to our weak flesh, distracted by its needs, afflicted by the chemical reactions we call emotion. And doomed like all the rest of humankind to evolve only through endless, slow, pain-filled generations—until I thought I had found the way to force evolution's hand. I foresaw a billion human minds released, free and immortal: all of them my children. Engendering Mental Man would have been fatherhood enough for me..."

There was silence. She saw him standing in front of her,

dressed again in the familiar black, but with a golden circlet fastened about one wrist. Brother Anatoly's brocade robe was like a puddle of blood on the floor at his feet.

She said, "But you did father Hagen and Cloud."

"Cyndia wanted children, and I loved her."

"But you couldn't love *them*?"

"Of course I did. And do. I brought them to this place, knowing they would grow up flawed, less than I, because it was impossible to abandon all that I had left of my dream. My children still have the potential within them—and not only Hagen and Cloud, but all the others as well. If they'll only follow me."

"You don't understand at all why they want to escape you!" Her voice was tense with loathing.

"Their vision is limited, like their minds."

"Marc—they simply want to be free!"

He said patiently, "When they were younger, they accepted their destiny willingly. But there were problems on Ocala, attrition among the weaker-minded of my old associates, and I was away on the star-search too much of the time. The children were seduced from the ideal, primarily by a man named Alexis Manion, who had once been my closest friend."

"He's in the history texts, too. The one who attempted to disprove the Unity concept."

Marc uttered a brief laugh. "You'll be interested to know that he changed his mind."

"He discovered the truth, you mean! The Unity is the only way humanity can continue to evolve naturally. You and your followers were mistaken in thinking that it threatened individuality. Evolution toward a Galactic Mind is an inevitable consequent of intelligent life. Coadunation doesn't shackle our minds, it sets them free! It's our nature to need others, to move toward universal love. All the races of thinking entities realize this, even those that are premetapsychic. That's why your children seem to have instinctively perceived the truth of what Manion told them. Why they reject your plan that seems such a logical shortcut to perfection."

"It would *work*."

"It's too draconian, too devoid of any semblance of love. It would have resulted in an isolation of humankind from the rest of the Galactic Mind. Your scheme has a certain objective grandeur, but its artificiality is just as much of a dead end as the golden torcs of the Tanu."

"We could transcend the human condition," he insisted, "giving every human mind what Jack had!"

What Jack had. Finally, Elizabeth understood.

For the first time, she reached out and took Marc's gloved hand. "Don't you see? With Jack it was the other way around. Your brother never embraced his inhumanity. Even though his terrible mutation set him irrevocably apart, he insisted on belonging with all the rest of us. You saw Mental Man as the ideal human—but *he* was too wise to make that mistake. That's why he had to oppose you, even though he loved you. Why he and his wife laid down their lives to end your Rebellion."

"Leaving me widowed, immortal, and damned." He spoke lightly, and his fingers transmitted a faint pressure to underline the jest. Then their hands fell apart. The baby was awake and cooing. "It's time I left, and time you took Brendan to his mother."

He went to open the door for her. At the slight sound, Debra and the priest, who had been sleeping propped up against each other on the bench, sprang to their feet. The mother burst into tears, and Brother Anatoly prayed a thunderous blessing that roused the entire household. As the corridor filled and jubilant bedlam prevailed, Marc slipped back into the nursery.

A towering robed form waited for him. "My name is Creyn. I am Elizabeth's friend and guardian. So the work with the child is complete?"

"You saw," said Marc shortly. "And no harm was done to Elizabeth. Stand away from that window so that I can go."

"You have raised Brendan to operancy. Now do the same for me."

"God—you can't be serious!" The man in black levitated and hovered, silhouetted against the dawnlit sky. A nimbus of spectral machinery formed about his body. His hair stirred like water-borne tendrils and he winced as a line of tiny dots stitched across his shining brow.

"If the little one could survive the procedure, so could I," Creyn said. "I entreat you."

The transfixed head regarded him with blind eyes. *You fool. Do you know who I am?*

"You are the Adversary, fated from all time to provoke our

people. I know what you did in your future world and I know what you did here for the child. I also know what you must do during the aeons between. Help me and I will help you."

I need no help.

"You do. I know where you are to go, and what the work is. You do not. And my Guild is the custodian of the mitigator, which not even the science of your Milieu possesses. Transform my mind. Raise me to her level and I will give it to you, along with the truth."

The new-risen sun glanced off the small golden torc clasped about Marc Remillard's wrist. The molecules of his body were attenuating into the upsilon-field and he had become as transparent as water. He seemed about to speak but transmitted only a wisp of perplexity, then disbelief.

Creyn said, "I do not lie. Perhaps we will talk next time."

The shadow shrugged and extinguished itself.

When his experience warned him that Elizabeth was on the brink of some explosive reaction, Brother Anatoly took her away from the celebration to the chalet's kitchen, all dim and warm from the night baking and quite deserted.

"The child's healing is a great excuse for a party," the friar said, "but you need peace and quiet now."

He made her sit down at the big trestle table while he prepared a quick breakfast—scrambled eggs and ducks' livers and new bread with strawberry jam. As she ate, he encouraged her to talk about the mental feat that she and Marc had accomplished, even though her detailed explanation was all but incomprehensible to him. Nevertheless, Anatoly was able to infer that Brendan's cure was both gratifying and unprecedented. He also strongly suspected that Elizabeth's own life had somehow been at risk during the procedure, even though she refused to confirm this.

"That aspect doesn't matter, Brother," Elizabeth said. "What matters is that it's done—and done right. God! I can't tell you how marvelous it feels to do the kind of work I was trained for, preceptive redaction, instead of mucking around incompetently the way I seem to have been doing ever since I came to the Pliocene."

The friar was at the stove making coffee. "I wouldn't call Aiken Drum's personality integration an amateur effort."

"He accomplished most of his healing himself. All I did was guide. But this child was another thing altogether. How can I explain? It was teaching rather than operating! The kind of work I did professionally back in the Milieu. The thing I'm good at. Even Marc saw—" She trailed off, frowning at her plate.

"What did he see?" Anatoly asked.

She poked at her eggs, then put down her fork and began to slather jam on a slice of bread. "Marc was good at preception, too," she said, in a puzzled tone. "Whoever would have thought it? A man like that. A world wrecker."

"Is that how you see him?" Anatoly found two big glass mugs and filled them with the steaming brew. He pulled a silver flask from under his scapular and laced Elizabeth's coffee with the contents. "Martell Réserve du Fondateur. For heaven's sake don't tell Mary-Dedra I've been treating it so cavalierly." He thrust the cup at her. "Drink!"

Elizabeth laughed helplessly. "You're almost as impossible as Marc." The fumes of the cognac brought tears to her eyes as she drank. "How else would I look upon him, except as a fanatic who would have destroyed the Unity? And all those people who died because of his obsession—"

Anatoly said, "You must remember that I came to the Pliocene before his Rebellion. I never knew him personally, of course, but he was a public figure for many years, a magnetic leader whose ideals were by no means self-evidently evil. He was a great man, widely admired. The debacle came only when he felt constrained to use force. And a great many good people sided with his Rebellion—not merely the human chauvinists."

Elizabeth emptied her cup and sat back limply, eyes closed. "I must admit, he was different . . . from what I expected. After we had worked together, I found it hard to reconcile my impressions of him with my preconceived notions."

The priest laughed. "How old were you at the time of the Rebellion?"

"Seventeen."

"No wonder you thought of him as Satan incarnate."

Elizabeth's eyes opened. Her tone was bitter as she said, "He's still proud as the devil—and determined to have his own way." She told how Marc had taken over the final stages of the redaction, forcing her into the subordinate mode of the mental linkage. "He had me utterly within his power. He could have killed me, could have kept me subservient. But he didn't. That's even stranger than his original desire to assist me with the baby's healing! Brother—what does he *want*?"

"God knows," said Anatoly. He emptied the last of the cognac into Elizabeth's mug. "Drink."

She did, savoring the redolence that rose from the still warm glass. "Marc has searched the stars for twenty-seven years, trying to find a single planet with minds at the coadunate level. But when I asked what he intended to do if he found such a world . . . he only laughed."

The friar shook his head. "I'm only a poor old Siberian priest without a metafunction in my skull. How should I know what motivates the likes of Marc Remillard . . . or you?"

Elizabeth eyed him for a moment in silence. He was smiling modestly into his half-empty coffee mug. "It's a shame," she said at last, "that you never met an old friend of mine named Claude Majewski. The pair of you would have got on famously. He was another sly old codger with a wide streak of low cunning."

"Funny, Sister Roccaro mentioned that, too." He gave the brandy flask a futile shake, then capped it and put it back in the pocket of his habit. "I certainly hope there's more of that Martell hidden away in the Black Crag cellars. Beats Lourdes water all hollow. You want to go to confession?"

She started. "No!"

He lifted his hands, palms up, the little smile still in place. "Easy does it. Just thought I'd ask." He headed for the kitchen door. "Anytime, though."

"Why don't you ask *him*?" she shot out.

"Oh, I did. Three or four days ago, after I'd stolen his coverall, thinking it would prevent him from leaving the chalet via his infernal machine."

"You *what*—"

Anatoly paused with his hand on the latch. "A futile gesture, as it turned out. He doesn't need the coverall to d-jump. It's only a monitoring convenience. So I gave it back to him."

"And your offer of spiritual assistance?"

The friar chuckled, went out the door, and shut it behind him.

5

"I BESEECH YOU TO RECONSIDER," OLD MAN KAWAI SAID.

He stood on the stoop of Madame Guderian's cottage, holding a tawny little cat in his arms. Three kittens tumbled groggily about his feet. Occasionally one would essay a tentative growl at the two riders on chalikos who loomed in the gray mist of the dooryard.

"You are the one who should reconsider, Tadanori-san," said Chief Burke. "Any day now, the Firvulag are likely to attack Hidden Springs—no matter what Fitharn Pegleg says. He's friendly, but he's only a single individual. And Fort Rusty was the straw that broke the hippy's back. We simply can't trust the Little People any longer. Sharn and Ayfa have lied too many times."

"It was the Iron Villages that the Firvulag King and Queen wanted to destroy," the elderly Japanese said. "Because they constituted a threat. One that is now removed."

"Eighty-three died at Rusty," Denny Johnson said. "Couple hundred more slaughtered in dribs and drabs over the months we've been slowly forced out of the other iron settlements on the Moselle—and at least that many wounded or missing. This

222

neck of the woods is just too close to the hostiles, Old Man. Ol' Sharn's been saying 'Hop frog' to us for a long time now. We just finally clevered up and decided to jump! And you will too, 'less you're ready to die. Nobody's asking you to go on the Roniah raid. You can join the caravan heading for Nionel. Lowlives are welcome there, bless the Howlers' ugly hearts."

"I cannot go," Kawai said, stroking the cat. "I understand why the rest of you wish to leave this place, but I must stay."

Burke leaned down from the saddle, proffering a Husqvarna stungun. "At least take this for self-defense."

Kawai shook his head. "You will need every weapon for the infiltration of Roniah. Besides, if the Firvulag know that I am defenseless, why should they molest me—a half-blind octogenarian with a cottage full of cats? No, I will stay and be a caretaker for this good home of ours that sheltered us for so many years. I will tend the gardens, and keep the pathways free of grass, and see to the water mill, and secure the buildings against the encroachment of vermin. Some of the liberated livestock also linger—goats and a few chickens, and the big gander that Peppino could not entice into a pannier. I will feed them. And, who knows? Perhaps some day, when the troubles have resolved themselves, human beings may wish to return to Hidden Springs."

"I'd stay, God knows," Denny Johnson said, "if I thought we'd be left in peace. But you know what Fitharn said."

Kawai frowned. "You believe his tale of a coming Nightfall War?"

"Old Man, I don't know what to believe anymore. But one thing's for damn sure: I didn't know when I was well off in the Milieu singing for my supper at Covent Garden. They let me go back through that time-gate, I don't care if I have to play Iago in whiteface."

Kawai smothered a giggle in the cat's fur. "Well—umaku iku yo ni, dear friend. Good luck!"

Johnson returned the sentiment, then said to Burke, "We gotta ride now, Redskin, 'fore that caravan gets too far ahead of us on the trail."

"You go along, Yellow-Eyes, while I give a last bit of legal advice to this stubborn old carp."

As the other rider melted into the mist, Chief Burke climbed down out of the tall saddle and stood with his fists on his hips before the diminutive Japanese. His scarred mahogany face was impassive, but his voice broke as he said, "Don't do it. Please."

The old man sighed. "Her spirit is here, and I will be safe."

"She'd be the first to tell you what an idiot you are!"

The cat jumped from Kawai's arms and hastened to retrieve one kitten, which had gone off to challenge a prowling toad.

"Listen to me, Peopeo Moxmox. I am proud of the life I lived here in the Pliocene. A life close to nature, full of danger but rich in simple satisfaction. I never yearned to be bushi as you did, only to become a competent craftsman like my ancestors. Here in this village I made looms and grinding machines and paper and ceramic ware and shoes. I taught my homely skills to others. In a time of need, I even helped to lead our Lowlife people. It was all very good. Even the loss of Madame and Amerie-chan and the others was bearable, taken in the context of the wheel of endless change and eternal sameness. But I feel very tired now, Peo. Even though you and I are very close together in years, I have become truly old while you still retain your vigor. So I will stay here, as I have a right to do. I will pray that you and the others succeed in stealing weapons from Roniah, since you have decided that they are necessary if you are to negotiate with the King. I myself feel that you could use more diplomatic means to insure safe passage through the time-gate—but I can understand your wishing to have a power base for bargaining. But this is not for me. Not anymore. My own wheel has nearly turned full circle, and you must forgive me if I am silly enough to want to stay here, in the place I am so proud of."

"You aren't silly, Old Man." Burke bowed from the waist. "Good-bye."

"I will not say sayonara to you, Peo, but rather, itte irasshai, which means only 'farewell for now.' Please tell the people who are going to Nionel to remember me and visit me here when they can. And if you should change your mind about the time-gate, your wigwam will be waiting for you. I shall put a new roof on it before the rains come, and repair the hide-stretching frames."

"Thank you," said Burke.

The old man bowed deeply, and when he straightened, Burke was back in the saddle. The Chief lifted one hand, then spurred the chaliko and galloped away down the streamside trail.

Kawai pursed his lips and gave the undulating whistle that called Dejah and the kittens for their morning collation of fish and goat's milk. He had a frugal breakfast of his own and spent some time pottering about the cottage.

When the mist had burned away and shafts of sunlight stabbed down through the pines he went outside to tidy up the rose garden. The weeds had flourished and the mastodon-manured bushes were in need of pruning. Many were coming into their fall bloom, filling the garden with perfume. After he had labored for nearly three hours he rested on a rustic bench and watched the cat teach her kittens to stalk grasshoppers. Then what to do? "I will bring her flowers!" he decided impulsively. He selected a jar from those on the shelf of the garden shed and filled it at the spring basin. Then he cut a bouquet of the barely unfurled buds of Precious Platinum, lushly scented and deep red. "Red for martyrs," he told the cat. "And they were a favorite of Madame, as well."

In order to show proper respect, he went to put on clean clothing, shutting the animals inside the cottage before he left so they would not be a distraction. He walked slowly through the deserted cluster of dwellings, crossed the central brook that received the waters of the scores of hot and cold springs that had given the village its name, and continued downstream for half a kilometer along the main trail until he came to the burying ground. A hiss of chagrin escaped him as he noticed how here, too, just three weeks of neglect had allowed the jungle to begin its invasion. Everyone had been too busy with leave-taking preparations to give any thought to the dead.

"Restoring this will be my first priority!" he vowed.

All at once he stood very still, listening.

Over the birdsong and the chatter of a drey of giant squirrels came another sound, deep and rhythmic, that seemed to emanate from the soil under his feet like the earth's own heartbeat. This was joined by a rolling murmur that intensified and revealed itself to be a sonorous contrabasso chant, sung by inhuman voices. Kawai had heard it before. It was the marching song of the Firvulag.

He stepped back onto the main trail and looked toward the foot of the canyon. His dim eyes perceived an inky shimmer, shot through with barbaric flashes of colored light. The drum-

beats throbbed and the deep musical humming began to re-
verberate off the narrowing walls of the gorge as the invaders
approached. Kawai saw effigy-topped standards hung with
golden blobs, squat marchers armed in obsidian, black-trapped
chalikos bearing the ogre officers.

Still holding the jar of red roses, he stood in the middle of
the trail and waited.

With dreamlike indifference, the goblin horde advanced.
The foot soldiers bore serrated pikes, peculiar new crossbows,
and lances tipped with a metal that could only be iron. As the
four-abreast column reached him it divided, flowing on either
side of him as though he were a rock in the middle of a dark
stream. The chant droned on. Not a single Firvulag took note
of him. He was rooted in the dust, too astonished to be afraid.

When the corps of mounted officers and cavalry reached
him they reined up. The infantry marched inexorably on toward
the village. Kawai stared at a single gigantic rider, clad from
head to toe in glittering plates of black glass that were ornamented with spikes and knobs and jeweled excrescences. The
massive helmet bore a crest of milk-colored crystalline horns.
The left gauntlet of the apparition was also of white glass. He
carried an enormous gem-crusted shield, and at his side hung
a sheath, from which protruded the handle of some formidable
twenty-second-century weapon. Halted behind the leading ogre
were two others of less splendid appearance, together with a
dwarf officer who looked rather ridiculous perched on the back
of a huge gray charger. The company of Firvulag cavalry flared
out on either side of Kawai and took up a stance. At an unspoken
command they drew laser carbines and solar-powered blasters
from saddle scabbards and trained them on the old man.

Kawai bowed gravely to the officers. "Good morning. Welcome to Hidden Springs Canyon. Under terms of the Armistice
attested by King Sharn and Queen Ayfa, you are my honored
guests."

He held out the bouquet of roses.

The Firvulag leader lifted the visor of his helmet, revealing
a grotesquely creased visage knit in a ferocious glower. "I am
Betularn of the White Hand, Champion and Great Captain and
First Comer and Scourge of the Foe!" he declaimed in a grating
bellow. "Pray to whatever puny gods you acknowledge, Lowlife!"

"I have already done so, thank you," said Kawai, stepping close to the monster's chaliko. "Your flowers, Lord Betularn." He thrust up the roses, smiling and insistent.

There was a rumble from the other officers. The one with the pouter-pigeon cuirass unhelmed and turned out to be a frizz-haired female, who grinned broadly at her superior. "Well, he's got you cold, White Hand—although how a Lowlife ever tumbled to that obscure geis, Té only knows! Take them."

The white gauntlet claimed the flowers. Miraculously, the weapons were lowered. The other two officers opened their visors and looked down upon Kawai with bemusement. One of them made a gesture to the mounted troopers, who trotted away toward the village.

"So the gift of flowers has meaning among your people as well as our own," the old man remarked suavely.

Betularn ignored that. He cocked his head as though listening, then gave a grunt of surprise. "Gone?" he exclaimed. "What do you mean—gone?" He peered down at the old man. "Where are the rest of the Lowlives?"

Kawai composed his features in an expression of formal regret. "Go-men nasai, Lord Betularn. They have all gone away. You see, we have suffered so many misfortunes during the past months. Marauding forces acting contrary to the wishes of your Monarchs attacked our peaceful settlements, killing many people. It was decided that these lands are too perilous for human occupation. All of the Lowlives except myself have gone to Nionel, to accept the hospitality so generously offered by Lord Sugoll and his consort, Katlinel the Darkeyed."

"Well, that's one less tiff to distract our lads and lasses," the female officer said. "On to the main event!"

"You shut up, Fouletot," snarled the Great Captain. He asked Kawai, "When did your folks take off?"

"Oh, ages ago. They must be nearly to the Pliktol headwaters by now."

Betularn chewed his grizzled mustaches and tugged at his beard. "Damn . . . we'll have to sidetrack to check this out."

"It's only a week until Truce!" shrilled the dwarf officer.

"You shut up, Pingol!" roared Betularn.

"Remember our orders," the second male ogre said.

"You shut up *too*, Monolokee! Té blast me to a cinder— let me think for a moment."

Kawai said softly, "I can offer you only meager hospitality, good neighbors. However, the spring house contains cold beer, which might be refreshing after a hot ride, and I have a rather large crock of strawberry jam."

Betularn fixed the smiling little human with a piercing eye. "If this is a trick . . ."

Kawai spread his hands in a protestation of submissiveness. "I am all alone. Surely your forces have confirmed the fact by now. Please—follow me. You are most welcome, I assure you." He turned about and began to walk toward the village. *Dear Amerie-chan*, he prayed, *your roses accomplished half a miracle. You wouldn't want to blow it now, would you, daughter?*

Behind him, he heard monstrous laughter, the creak of harness, the slow plop-plop of clawed feet in the dust. "That damn beer better be cold," muttered Betularn.

"Oh, yes!" Kawai grinned over his shoulder. "Just come along. It's not far."

"Are you certain that you want to go ahead with this?" Greg-Donnet inquired.

The single blue eye in the center of the Howler woman's forehead was unblinking. "If I had looked like a human, he would have loved me. My illusions were not good enough. Having once worn a silver torc, he had insights superior to those of the other Lowlife husbands."

She removed the last of her garments, handed them to the female laboratory assistant, and stood shivering slightly beside the expansive array of the tank apparatus and its directive console. Her mutant body was slender, scaly, with a light pelt like that of a blue fox growing about her shoulders and down the midline of her thorax. "I am ready. What do I do now, Melina?"

"Step into the tank," the technician said, "and we'll just wrap you in the Skin. Then Dr. Prentice Brown and I will apply the monitors and attach your life-support equipment. It will feel like you're going to sleep. You'll never know when the tank fills."

"Will I dream?" The question was fearful.

"Good dreams," Greggy reassured her. "Perhaps of him."

The little creature smiled. "I know there is a chance that I will die, or emerge from the tank more deformed than ever.

But I do this thing gladly. If he should come before I wake, you will tell him that, won't you?"

"Certainly," said Greggy. "Now in you go—and think positive thoughts! It's very important to initiate your self-redactive impulses voluntarily."

He and his assistant went to work, swiftly wrapping the mutant woman in transparent membrane and attaching the ancillary equipment. They closed the tank, did a final scan of her functions, and let the great crystal container fill. The body floated free and assumed a horizontal position, tethered by the Medusa-cap that would soon begin feeding regenerative commands into the sleeping brain.

Greg-Donnet touched his golden torc as he watched the changing readouts on the console. "Are you asleep, lambie? Can you hear me?"

Brainwaves cycled slowly on the monitoring screen. A single word crossed the threshold of consciousness before the mutant's mind surrendered to the Skin-tank and its healing oblivion:

Tonee.

6

THE EIGHT UNITS OF THE BRAVE NEW RATVC, FRESHLY PAINTED in plum and gold, charged out of the surf and onto the sandy Breton Island beach. From the whip antenna of the command vehicle streamed the digitus impudicus banner of King Aiken-Lugonn, who was himself at the controls. He was in a high humor because, for a change, all the news was good. The Alpine Expedition had mapped a route up the tricky Gresson Icefall and had set up the first supply camp. The Famorel force marching toward Monte Rosa, on the other hand, had been hit by a fortuitous landslide in the Tarentaise, losing a day's march and more than thirty troops. In Roniah, Kuhal Earthshaker reported that the stockpile of Milieu-style arms was more extensive than they had dared hope. He was packing the bulk of the armory for shipment to Goriah via the roundabout but safe southern route. It was deemed unwise to risk shipping the weapons directly along the Western Track, even during the Truce. A heavy guard of Tanu stalwarts would bring them down the Rhône, overland to Sasaran, and then via riverboat down the Garonne, where the Royal Fleet could sail them to Goriah.

Feeling frisky, Aiken leaned on the ATV's klaxon and sent a fanfare of *oogahs* ricocheting off the grassy dunes. Sandpipers and godwits scattered and the King laughed. He was, along with certain of his courtiers and fourteen of the young North Americans, on his way to the formal opening of the Royal Siderurgical Establishment up in the Breton highlands, which was ready to go into full production at long last. The castle caterers had packed an outstanding lunch, the ATVs rolled smartly on a well-graded track made to accommodate heavy traffic from the new forges, and the cobalt sky was piled with cauliflower clouds.

"Much too nice a day," Aiken remarked to Dougal, "for a coup. You probably imagined the whole thing, old son."

The counterfeit medievalist, who sat in the co-pilot's seat, gave a great sigh. "Such welcome and unwelcome things at once, 'tis hard to reconcile! It is the bright day that brings forth the adder; and that craves wary walking . . . And if the wight plans no harm, then why rides he with the Children of Rebellion?"

"Vilkas goes where his boss goes," said the King reasonably. "And Yosh is checking out the course-director robotics of Hagen's ATV. Seems there's some kind of minor glitch."

"I am but a poor lackwit," Dougal said, "but I have told you truly what I heard this morning as the caitiff North Americans assembled in the castle base-court. (They pay no attention to me because I'm mad.) The import of their scheme was clear, Sire. They know of your mental disability through information supplied by the malefactory Lithuanian, and plan somehow to use you treacherously this day."

The King's eyes were black glittering slots beneath the brim of his golden hat. "Vilkas and Yosh and the other lad *were* there in Calamosk when I pulled my trick. But what could be Vilkas' motive for betraying me?"

"He thinks too much. Such men are dangerous! And he is of a sour and grudging temperament, and bitter because he was not torced with gold."

Alberonn Mindeater, who sat with his wife Eadnar in the navigation seats at the rear of the cockpit, now leaned forward radiating anxiety. "If treason is afoot, High King, we should turn back to Goriah at once. You have none too many stalwart minds accompanying you on this excursion, nor have you seen fit to wear your mechanical screens."

"I find them stuffy," said Aiken. He revved the turbine as the trail became a straightaway. Soon their ATV outdistanced the other vehicles in the pack, tearing through the open woodland at nearly 90 kph. The windscreen ionizers had broken down again, and the King squinted through the bug splatters, deep in thought. When they came to the new suspension bridge over the Proto-Oust he eased the throttle so that they crawled sedately across. None of the other vehicles was in sight.

Aiken pulled to a stop and waited. The terrain-survey display showed the smeltery buildings less than three kilometers ahead. He said, "And you're certain they were cooking up something for today, Dougie? Not just indulging in a bit of foolish lèse-majesté?"

"Foolery, Sire, does walk about the orb like the sun; it shines everywhere!" The zany underwent one of his lightning changes of persona and added cogently, "Fourteen of those junior Rebels along on this outing. Only Miss Cloud and the three scientific whizzes stayed home. Plenty of brainpower there for a nasty little coercive metaconcert. And I heard the foxy-faced one, Nial Keogh, say that an iron foundry offered unique opportunities."

Alberonn and Eadnar threw out simultaneous thoughts: Bloodmetal in amplesupply! Your stalwartdefenders mostly Tanu&vulnerable!

The other seven vehicles now approached the bridge, led by the one bearing Hagen and his confederates. Aiken studied it through his farsenses and perceived nothing but innocent merriment within. The repair job on the autopilot had evidently been accomplished, and now the North Americans were plying Yosh, Vilkas, and Jim with jugs of the undistinguished but plentiful muscadet wine that the commonalty of Goriah had dubbed Poodle Pee.

Aiken zinged Yosh with a trenchant inquiry: Important. Think! Could the glitch in robotics be deliberate fabrication excuse get you & assistants into Hagen ATV instead of another?

Well hell Chief . . . it's possible. Why you ask?

Nevermind Yoshilad just keep alert for mischief.

"There's such divinity that doth hedge a king," Dougal reassured Aiken, "that treason can but peep to what it would."

"You think so, do you?" Aiken bestowed a bleak grin on the big ginger-beard who had become his court jester through an uncanny sort of insinuation. "Your divinity better look slippy if I have to fight Hagen and his gang as well as Marc Remillard! Here I thought I had the young Rebs on my side—and now it seems that they were just biding their time, waiting for the chance to launch a royal screw. They've probably decided I'm a burnt-out case after what Vilkas told them about the Calamosk chicane."

"They should know better," Alberonn exclaimed, "having seen you direct the metaconcert maneuvers of our forces!"

"Ah, but a director doesn't have to be a personal hotshot," Aiken observed. "As long as he has the right program tucked away in his noodle, mental strength isn't nearly as important as adroitness and the ability to channel energies. I think Hagen might be afraid that I'd be unable to handle Marc in a one-on-one confrontation, without a concert to back me up. He's a supercautious young prick, you know. He doesn't much care for my freewheeling style—going blithely about without three sigma-shells and a full suit of cerametal armor to safeguard my royal ass from sneak attack. The kid could be worrying that his old man might simply grab me. And use me."

The other ATVs rumbled over the span, one at a time. Hagen's breezy thought addressed Aiken on the intimate mode: *Sir you left us all in the dust didn't you? You're a better driver than any of us! Would you like us to form up for a parade entry into the Establishment? I could even broadcast some snappy bagpipe music over the loudhailer—*

Aiken's thought was wry: *Just follow Me.*

"He would," Dougal said softly, as Aiken started up their own vehicle. "He'd follow for expediency's sake, provided that you demonstrate once and for all who is vassal and who is King." And he tapped the lion's head embroidered in gold on his knightly surtout.

Aiken cast a sidelong glance of surprise at the medievalist, who wore no torc yet so often seemed to know his thoughts. He noticed for the first time that the leonine charge now wore a crown, and this tripped a half-forgotten memory from his misspent youth on the planet Dalriada. But the thought slipped away before the press of immediate matters and he said, "First we must make absolutely certain that they're planning a coup.

It's never a good idea to waste your shots. Especially when you don't have all that many in the old quiver."

The Iron Master of the new Royal Siderurgical Establishment was a tough old bareneck named Axel, an early defector from the Lowlife Iron Villages in the Vosges. With the King's carte blanche on materials and personnel, the technician had organized a far more sophisticated setup on Breton Island— one that was, moreover, secure from virtually any kind of attack short of aerial bombardment. The mine-workings, which yielded siderite, were entirely underground. Ore was removed with a minimum of human labor by four compact mining machines liberated from the Goriah contraband cache. The initial smelting was done in an adjacent blast furnace equipped with a pair of huge water-powered bellows.

After a brief stroll through the mine and a look at the roaring furnace, Aiken and his party were taken to a catwalk about fifteen meters above the main floor of the enormous smeltery structure. There they watched molten pig iron stream spectacularly from the crucible into a great bucket-shaped charging ladle. This container was three times the height of the scurrying workers, who attended it dressed in silvery reflective garb that protected them from the heat and flying sparks. When it was full, the ladle came trundling along a track to an even larger, egg-shaped vessel with an open top, tilted on its side ready to receive the unrefined liquid iron.

"We use metal straight from the crucible for arrows and lance heads and other simple applications," Axel explained to the King. "Or cast it into pigs for conversion into wrought iron in the hammer shed next door. But that process is as noisy as the bells of hell and not too interesting. I figured you Exalteds would rather watch something livelier—so we're going to do the first blow of the new Bessemer converter for you!"

The King said, "That should be fun."

"I wanted to build one of these up in Haut Furneauxville, but our supervisor, Tony Wayland, overruled me." Axel grimaced. "He wanted something sophisticated—as if we needed fancy alloys or squeaky-pure iron for stabbing Firvulag! Wayland never did get his electric furnace into operation. We couldn't salvage the proper power supply from Finiah."

The King was listening intently. "This Wayland—in your opinion, was he a topnotch metallurgist?"

The Iron Master's lip curled and he tipped his head toward Dougal. "Better ask him. He was Wayland's keeper. All I know is, we can process a hundred times as much steel in my Bessemer converter as we would have been able to do in Wayland's electric dipstick oven. You'll see!"

The charging ladle poured white-hot metal into the converter's wide mouth. Alberonn remarked, "How the Firvulag Foe would quail, could they but see this abundance of blood-metal being refined to their destruction..."

"They *will* see it," Aiken declared, "because I'm going to display some useful steel thingummies at the Grand Tourney, just to let Sharn and Ayfa know that it didn't do them any good to knock out the Lowlife Iron Villages. Then we'll find out if the Little Folks are still keen to start the Nightfall War."

Axel peered down at the workers. One silvery form clasped gloved hands above its hooded head in a sign of readiness. The charging ladle rolled away and the great egg loaded with molten iron began to tilt up on its trunnions. For a moment the mouth faced directly at the group of observers and they shrank back involuntarily from the view of the white, glowing interior. Then the converter was vertical, and finally came to rest canted slightly to the rear, so that the mouth could blow against a curved shield that protected the building's wooden wall.

"Everybody gather round!" Axel cried, bubbling with show-biz fervor. "I'll explain what's going to happen."

Aiken had been closely hemmed by Tanu members of his entourage, and the North Americans and most of the human retainers were scattered along the railing. The King suddenly told the exotics, "Now, then, Exalted Brothers and Sisters! Where's your sense of hospitality? Make a place for our North American guests up here close to Me so that they can hear what Axel has to say. And you, too, Yosh! Come over here and bring your assistants. This steelworks is only partially automated, and you might get some useful notions on how to improve production."

The samurai gold-torc bowed. "As you command, Aiken-sama." Sunny Jim pushed up eagerly to take a front position, but Vilkas hung back with a diffident air.

"Come along, man," Aiken urged. "We're ready for the big show. Don't you want a front seat? There's plenty of room next to Hagen and Nial."

Young Remillard and his thirteen associates stood in a loose group at the King's left. Axel beamed delightedly at them. A human chauvinist to the core, the Iron Master was secretly proud that these important young people were barenecks like himself. They had listened with flattering attention to his little lectures on the tour, and several were particularly impressed by his surreptitious explanation of why blood-metal was the ultimate weapon against both exotic races.

Now Axel addressed the gathering with growing excitement. "The Bessemer converter is as simple as it is dramatic. You will note that there is *no* means of externally heating the chamber—and yet, within a few minutes, the temperature will rise, converting certain impurities into glowing gases and others into slag! We do this by forcing a mighty blast of air through nozzles in the converter's bottom. It comes not from a simple bellows but from a solar-powered compressor! The injected oxygen causes carbon still trapped in the iron to ignite. The converter contents boil like a volcano! Undesirable elements belch forth in a display of fireworks that is as awesome as it is efficient!" He hauled out a bandanna handkerchief and swabbed his dripping face. "Any last questions before we let 'er rip?"

"Is there no hazard in the coddling of this devil's egg?" Dougal asked sternly. "After all—you did say this was its maiden blast-off."

"No danger, none at all," Axel insisted. "Lordy, we're fifty meters away from the thing, and it's pointed the other way!"

"Let's get on with it," Hagen said. "We're not afraid. It should be very interesting." He turned a cool blue eye on Aiken. "What do you say, Your Majesty?"

"Carry on," said the King.

Axel leaned over the railing and gave the bandanna a vigorous shake. One of the silver figures waved and hurried to a big wheel valve in the pipes entering at the right trunnion. As he hauled the thing open a hissing scream manifested itself and a monstrous tongue of flame howled from the converter mouth. Sparks erupted in a dazzling shower, bouncing off the protective steel-ceramic shield on the rear wall. A wave of heat swept over the onlookers. The entire building quivered to the foundations. Multicolored smoke roiled into the roof beams to escape through ventilation slots.

"Just wait!" yelled Axel. "It gets better!"

The valve operator was admitting more compressed air. The roaring heightened in pitch until the converter seemed to scream in triumph. The smoke glowed a peculiar brownish scarlet and elongate lances of incandescent gas thrust from it, flickering purple and pink and orange. Drops of molten slag arced through the air like meteorites. The silver-clad workers down on the floor were jumping up and down ecstatically, while on the catwalk, the group gathered about the King was engrossed in the spectacle.

Slowly, the flame spurts became bright yellow. The smoke cleared as the purification of the iron continued and silicon burned. Unobtrusively, Hagen and his people edged away to the left, with Vilkas trailing after. The Lithuanian in his festive ashigaru outfit was open-mouthed; his eyes darted back and forth between the King and the fire-spitting egg across the building. The North Americans stood shoulder to shoulder in a compact knot ten meters away. Their eyes, amazingly, had closed.

The flames of the converter turned from orange to purest white, spraying a diamond glitter and writhing like braided star-stuff. Carbon burned now; the incandescent gases were at their hottest, blasting the shield so that the firebrick cladding became a shining bullseye.

The converter began to rotate on its trunnions.

Axel screamed, "*No!*"

The stupendous jet moved off the shield as the flask pivoted and ignited the wall timbers in a split second. Down below, workers scattered. One heroic figure could be seen wrestling impotently with the air valve. Like a colossal blowtorch, the flames roaring from the egg swept a scorching three-meter path across the entire roof and down the wall immediately behind the King and his stunned retinue.

Then the open mouth blasted directly at them and they were engulfed in white heat.

Vilkas gave a moan of terror. The catwalk was in flames and the entire building filled with thick smoke. He began to run, and reached the wooden stairway only to stumble and nearly pitch headlong when a gust of smoke choked and nearly blinded him. He sobbed out loud, clung to the railing, howled, "Help, somebody, for God's sake!"

He heard the roar of the converter cut off. Then the snap of burning timber rustled away to nothingness. There came a great wind that drove the smoke upward, out of the roof vents, and for a brief moment the embers of the quenched wood glowed brightly again before subsiding into dead charcoal.

Vilkas pulled himself upright, tears streaming from his stinging eyes. The great egg-shaped converter was motionless, tipped at an approximate forty-five-degree angle with its mouth aimed at the place where Aiken and his group were standing. They were safe inside a shimmering globe of psychocreative force that the King's mind had generated, gathered upon a length of unscorched catwalk that apparently hung unsupported in midair.

Gently, the bubble floated to the furnace-house floor. The section of walk came to rest on the pounded earth as the sphere evaporated.

Axel fell to his knees before Aiken and burst into tears. Vilkas could hear the King's reaction very clearly through his gray torc.

"Don't fash yourself, guy. It wasn't your fault and we're not hurt." The little man in the golden suit tilted his head to regard the fourteen young North Americans, now motionless near the end of the devastated mezzanine. "And it seems our overseas chums also survived the disaster! That's kaleidoscopic. We'd be hard put to build the time-gate and defend the Many-Colored Land from your dear parents without your help! Of course, if some terrible accident deprived us of your company, we'd manage to muddle through somehow. But working together would see us all to our goals more handily . . . Or don't you agree, Hagen Remillard?"

"I agree, High King."

Not looking at the people up on the catwalk, Aiken strolled over to the looming Bessemer converter and considered the cooling dribblets of slag depending from the lip. "With a little adjustment—and some new safety measures installed—this thing will serve us well. Safety measures can be installed on people, too. I'd really hate to do it, though, since some folks have such an adverse reaction to torcs. I haven't the faintest idea whether silver ones could be locked onto non-coadunate operants without blowing the circuitry of the collars—or the brains. I'm not anxious to experiment along those lines unless I've no alternative. Do you understand *that*, Hagen Remillard?"

"I understand, High King."

The King resumed his walk, waving a forgiving hand at the workers, who had pulled off their silvery hoods and gathered in an apprehensive little clutch. "Tush. Think nothing of it, lads and lasses. All's well that ends well—as my crony Dougal would say . . ." He spun about and faced his Tanu and human subjects. "Nonetheless, there have been rumors floating around. It's been said that my royal powers were weakened, that I was no longer fit to be King of the Many-Colored Land." His coercive power settled over them like a bright net. "What do you say to that?"

"Slonshal, Aiken-Lugonn!" they all cried.

The King was humming a ditty that might have been "Hail to the Chief." He came up to Vilkas, who stood at the foot of the catwalk stairs. "And here's another one who was lucky. Or was he?"

Vilkas uttered a strangled groan. The furnace building seemed to fade from view, then rush back to surround him with abnormal clarity. Agony flooded his skull.

Aiken clucked in sympathy. "I hate to be so crude in the mindream, but it's necessary to make sure. Ah. What a shame. And it was all because you thought you deserved gold? You poor gowk. If you'd got it, you'd only have found something else to brood on—and perhaps another logical reason to betray those who trusted you."

"Please, High King—" Vilkas began. And then he gave a single shattering cry and seized his torc with fingers that crisped and stank of broiled meat. The gray metal around Vilkas' neck glowed like the yellow molten steel still smoking inside the Bessemer converter. He fell to the earthen floor without making another sound.

"You wanted gold," said the King, and turned away.

7

Tony Wayland poled his dinghy through the vast marsh below the Lac de Bresse, trying to maintain a compass course that would take him north to open water. He was having a sticky time of it. The dank morning mist permitted only a few meters' visibility, and the swamp was alive with leeches that were ready to drink his blood if he happened to brush against their hiding places among the dense, dripping reeds.

He had been moving northward for more than three weeks since his escape from Bardelask, most of the time traveling on foot along the Great South Road that paralleled the Rhône. He had encountered no Firvulag at all in the West Bank country, where the widely scattered Little People were secretive and inclined to give the Foe-infested river corridor a wide berth. The principal hazards Tony had suffered were vipers in the dry campsites and wild boars in the bottomlands—and unexpected perils from members of his own predatory species. He'd had a very close call when a band of bareneck outlaws ambushed him on a back trail as he tried to avoid a large fort. It had been necessary to shoot two of the buggers before they gave him up as a bad job.

Coming up on the metropolis of Roniah, Tony had run afoul of a different sort of menace: the Royal Recruiting Service. King Aiken-Lugonn was combing the bushes and byways for personnel of every sort, intensifying his earlier efforts as war with the Firvulag seemed more and more inevitable. Tempting perquisites were offered to volunteers who would accept gray torcs, and there were rumors that out-and-out conscription among the displaced persons had already begun. Tony, of course, wore gold. But the contrast between his Exalted neckware and his shabby accouterments was in itself cause for official suspicion. He'd been careful to hide the torc with a neck cloth on the few occasions that he was forced to purchase supplies or mix with fellow travelers along the road.

The Recruiting Service had artfully spread its net on a tree-less savanna where the Great South Road ascended to bypass a precipitous gorge of the Rhône. Up there on the windswept heights, one could see for scores of kilometers in almost every direction; any traveler who attempted to leave the main thoroughfare could be spotted at once. Tony's first clue to imminent danger was a cheery billboard:

> WELCOME WAYFARERS!
> THIRSTY? HUNGRY?
> FREE FOOD & DRINK AHEAD!
> HILLTOP HOUSE R.R.S.—6 KM

The afternoon when Tony hiked that stretch had been a hot and dusty one, and he viewed the sign with elation. But then a caravan of hellads pulling carts of chaliko fodder to Roniah overtook him, and one of the teamsters gave Tony a lift. His name was Wiggy and he was quick to explain the true nature of the establishment they were approaching.

"Friggerty crimps' nest, that's wot it is! You watch your arse there, pilgrim, or they'll have you gray-chokered and off to Goriah as a raw ree-cruit in the King's Shitkicker Brigade."

The drivers, well known to the recruiting team and off limits because of their gainful employment, nonetheless were accustomed to pig out on the free refreshments every time they passed. There was nothing Tony could do but face up to jeopardy with a stout heart. He tramped inside with the rest and soon they were sitting at long tables drinking cold beer or sangria and munching on snack foods. It was obvious that the teamsters were old acquaintances of the presiding captal and the squad of soldiers who ran the place. Tony felt his innards churn as the officer jokingly referred to him as a "live one" and promised that Wiggy would receive a nice bounty should Tony sign up.

"Thanks awfully, but I've been sick," the metallurgist said. "I'm not the type you're looking for at all. You want brave people for the King's army." (The late Karbree's elephant rifle, concealed in a rancid rawhide sheath, had been left outside the wagon with Tony's other duffle.)

The recruiting captal's eyes twinkled. "Plenty of other good bunks available in the royal service! I can tell you're an educated man—not spook fodder like the rest of this gang of helly-patoots." The drivers, drinking and eating fast while the game lasted, guffawed and elbowed one another. "If you're got a technical skill, we could sign you up for the new Scientific Corps that the Creator Guild is instituting. It's headed up by good old Lord Celadeyr, a real Tanu gent if there ever was one. Loves human beings just like a genuine mensch and passes out silver torcs like carnival kickshaws to scientific mavens who cooperate nicely."

"Well—uh—I'm more of a humanities student," Tony mumbled.

"Brains is brains," said the genial captal. "You'd like it in Goriah. All the women you want, good food and liquor, night life—shoot, I'd go myself if I could."

He whipped out a parchment scroll crowded with fine print, a ball-point pen, and a handsome blue-velvet bag that contained something circular, lumpy, and about sixteen cents in diameter.

"Just sign here, guy, and you'll never regret it. We can have you off to Goriah by express caravan tomorrow . . . after an evening of fun and games in Roniah down the pike that you'll never forget! What say?"

The teamsters sitting around the table with Tony and the captal giggled like lunatics and all of them except Wiggy urged him to sign. As a final inducement, the captal opened the bag and dramatically took out a gleaming gray torc. The laughter and joking were instantly quelled. The necks of all the drivers were bare.

The captal pushed the torc across the table toward Tony. Its knobbed catch was open. The twisted metal was hollow, incised with small openings to ventilate the psychoelectronic components inside.

"Take off your scarf," the captal suggested to Tony. "Just try it on." He touched his own gray necklet. "These things are wonderful. They *do* things for you, y'know? No more headaches or sore feet or feeling blah or tired or scared. And that's not the half of it. If your boss is a gold or a silver, he can program pleasure for you through the torc. Give you a rush like you never had from sex or dope or even buzz-heading. Make you forget all your troubles in the wink of an eye, this magic collar will. *Sign.*"

Four large troopers materialized behind Tony's seat. He half rose, then dropped back, with sweat streaming from his head and soaking his neckerchief. "I—I'd rather not just now."

The teamsters downed the dregs in their tankards, snatched up a last cookie or handful of nuts, and drifted toward the door. Wiggy had a shamefaced look.

"Sign," urged the captal, his eyes locked onto those of the panic-stricken metallurgist.

"Sign!" chorused the quartet of bruisers, grinning like wolves.

Tony tried to push his chair back. It wouldn't budge. The captal had risen and taken up the torc. He came around to Tony's side of the table, twisting the thing farther open on its rotating hinge, poising it above Tony's head.

"Goddammit, *no!*"

Tony's mind triggered the pleasure-induction circuitry of the recruiting team through his own golden torc, hitting their brains with the maximum orgasmic load. All five of the soldiers dropped to the floor as though they'd been poleaxed.

"Holy shit," breathed Tony's teamster friend. Several other drivers peered over his shoulder and gaped.

Pushing the table back, Tony negotiated the bodies, faced the teamsters, and ripped the scarf from his neck. There was a gasp.

"Enough is enough! Now I've got to get out of here. These fellows won't remember a thing when they wake up . . . I don't think. But in case they do, I want to be far away." Tony summoned his most imperious glare. "Will you drive me to Roniah or won't you?"

Wiggy touched his forehead, smirking. "Your carriage awaits, Exalted Lord."

Tony grabbed the gray torc and advanced upon the man with it. "I have a good mind to collar you, to be quite sure that you keep your word."

"No!" the teamster shrieked. "No!"

Tony gave a nasty little chuckle. "So you do know what overindulgence in Tanu delights can do to a chap! Very well. Just so we understand one another. Now let's get moving."

He was about to discard the torc when he thought the better of it, replaced it in the velvet bag, and took it along.

That evening in Roniah, he sold the device on the black market for enough money to buy a completely equipped chaliko, a new outfit of clothes, a decamole boat and cap hut, and a suspect but very flashy parure of rubies that would make an appealing peace offering for Rowane. He had plenty of money left to insure that he would travel the rest of the way to Nionel in style, and the next morning he was on his way.

Once again, fickle fortune thumbed its nose at him. The chaliko turned out to be a lemon that went permanently lame 40 kloms north of Roniah. If he returned to the city to complain or procure a fresh mount, he stood a chance of being picked up for committing mental mayhem upon the Royal Recruiters. He was in the midst of country that teemed with hostile Firvulag, many no doubt eager for a last hit before the Truce, which began in five days. Northbound traffic had dwindled to military trains and poor straggling refugees, bound like himself for the Promised Land of Nionel. There seemed little chance for Tony to hook a ride, but proceeding on foot in his expensive new outfit would make him a sitting duck to human and exotic marauders.

There remained the option of travel by water. The Saône at this point was broad and sluggish, readily navigable by sailing dinghy; or he could simply row along in the placid lagoons. He tried this, and it worked. Progress was by no means rapid, but once he was in the Lac de Bresse it would be clear sailing to the trailhead of the Western Track—and then, on to Nionel! . . .

Thus Tony found himself poling through misty canebrakes that 27th of September, ever alert for falling leeches. His farsight was useless in the featureless swamp and he had to continually orient himself by means of his wrist navigation unit. He cursed himself for not spending the extra money on a course director with a bleeper earplug, back in the Roniah black market. But who would have thought he'd need it? When he finally reached an area with twisting creeks he gave a sigh of relief. It was the end of the leeches, at any rate. Then the sun came out, and with it mosquitoes and midges. He smeared himself with bug repellent and endured.

Occasionally he passed small low-lying islets. As the time for elevenses rolled around he beached the dinghy on one of these and brewed up coffee under a taxodium all hung with moss. He had a decamole table-and-bench combo that inflated in a jiffy and a good selection of leftover pastries to eat. A pair of black-and-red anhingas watched him from a nearby tree, craning their snaky necks. A small aquatic rodent paddled in an adjacent pool, leaving a languid wake. There were waterlilies. The sun was warm and the bugs went away. Tony Wayland felt at peace.

Rowane . . .

With his eyes dreamily closed, he left his farspeech call to her. She was more than 300 kilometers away, but perhaps yearning would give strength to his feeble metafaculties. He said:

I'm coming back to you little bride. Your Tonee is on his way with a new golden to keep his spirits up! From now on there'll be no stopping us. Wait for me Rowane. Wait.

He dozed a bit—then woke to the sound of paddles chunking.

Who's there? his mind called involuntarily. He started up from the table, spilling cold coffee and scaring off a tiny harvest mouse that had been foraging among the crumbs.

The reeds across the pool parted and a big decamole canoe daubed with camouflage colors glided into view. It carried five human men and a woman, all impressive physical specimens and all armed to the teeth. Another war canoe was bow-to-stern with the first and bore a second woman and three more men, along with a number of freight packs. The bow oarsman in the lead craft, an enormous Native American in jungle fatigues, lifted a zapper and took aim just as Tony made up his mind to try a dash to his dinghy.

"Stop right there," said Chief Burke.

Tony fell back with a sullen glower, hands high. The canoes landed and the desperados disembarked. One of the women began going through Tony's gear while the others loafed about, vanished discreetly into the bushes, or tinkered with the coffee-making apparatus. The rummaging woman, who was a stocky Latin type with arcs of blue mascara above her large eyes, gave a whoop of excitement when she uncovered the Rigby elephant gun.

"Madre! Will you look at this cojonudo piece? Two barrels—and a shot from just one would blow any of you poor cagarrutas clean in half!"

Burke subjected his prisoner to a deep scrutiny. "Don't I know you? What's your name?"

"Bill," said Tony, his eyes shifting. "Bill—Johnson."

A big black man standing behind the Indian laughed richly. "Hey—could be my long-lost little brother! Wonder if he can sing tenor?"

"His name's not Bill," the Latin woman called. She waved something. "Not unless he's got a thing for yellow-silk boxer shorts and a matching hanky with 'Tony' embroidered on them in love knots."

"You leave those alone, dammit!" Tony howled. He thanked heaven that the rubies were in a hidden money belt.

The woman clucked at him in mock pity. "Ay! Hoy tiene mala leche—no?" She held up a slender book-plaque. "This is all we need right here, Peo. I thought the guy looked familiar." She came over and handed the book to Denny Johnson, who studied the title display.

"*Technic of Metallurgy*—presented to one Anthony Bryce Wayland by the Alchymist Society of Manchester University." Denny stepped forward ominously. "So! Our absconding straw boss from the Iron Villages. You all remember Tony Wayland, who betrayed our people at the Vale of Hyenas! Shall we hang him now—or wait till later so's not to spoil our lunch?"

Tony pulled aside the scarf he still wore at his throat. Gold gleamed. "Don't touch me!" he cried, fingering the necklet. "I can mind-burn you or zap you to death anytime I want to!" A very small gout of psychoenergy flew from the extended fingers of his other hand and zorched the damp moss in front of Chief Burke's boots. "That's just a sample, Redskin! Now drop that gun—and don't any of the rest of you get cute, or—"

Tony Tony Tony.

A sprightly little ring of flames danced about Tony's own feet. Chief Burke unbuttoned the top of his green blouse and said:

As you can see I've got a golden torc too. And that means I can see your metapsychic aura. It's *very* small. I might even call it piss-poor . . . or roughly equal to mine in the aggressive metafunctions. Unless you want to chance a fast weenie roast you lose your bluff.

"Oh, bloody hell," said Tony in disgust. "Hang me and have done with it."

Burke shook his head. "You're more valuable to us alive. The aether has been buzzing about you for several weeks. It seems King Aiken-Lugonn is very anxious to make your acquaintance."

Tony perked up again, then caught a certain look in Burke's eyes and slumped again. "What have I done to *him*, for God's sake? Sometimes it seems that everyone in the whole Many-Colored Land is out to nail my hide to the wall."

"You're trading-goods," Burke said succinctly. "That's all you have to know." He turned to Denny Johnson, handing him the photon gun. "He's your prisoner from now on, Yellow-Eyes. Take damn good care of him if you ever expect to do Baron Scarpia again at the Garden."

"Take him on the *Roniah* operation?!" Johnson exclaimed. "Are you out of your tomahawking mind, Peo?"

"We don't have to invade Roniah looking for arms," Burke said. "It's no longer necessary to use force to insure fair treatment for Lowlives, or our own passage through the time-gate. We'll go into Roniah openly and the King's High Table deputy, Kuhal Earthshaker, will welcome us and give us whatever we ask for."

"Because of *him*?" cried one man.

The Chief nodded. "Wayland is a turncoat and an informer and an all-around consecrated twerp. But he's also our ticket back to the Galactic Milieu."

The gathering of desperados murmured and whispered. The Latin woman cried out, "But Orion Blue and Karolina and the two others died because of this puto! And Basil's people were betrayed! I say he must hang!"

"It's no use, Marialena," said Burke. "Tony Wayland's got his reprieve right from the drumhead Supreme Court."

She shot a murderous glance at the metallurgist. "Well, you don't get the shorts back," she hissed. Then she turned to the others and declared, "Now I will make lunch."

MARC: Cloud. Daughter.

CLOUD: *Papa*! You shouldn't have come—there's danger—

MARC: I'm only present in simulacrum. Like the sendings of your friend Kuhal. The garden is secluded, but Aiken Drum has fed the scanners my mental signature. I know better than to d-jump into the Castle of Glass.

CLOUD: You've been watching me as I come here?

MARC: Watching, not listening. Believe me.

CLOUD: . . . What do you want?

MARC: Your help. With Hagen.

CLOUD: It's too late.

MARC: I deserve to be rejected by both of you. I was negligent, distracted by my work. Unfeeling toward you. Impatient with his weakness. Harsh. The incident with the tarpon was unforgivable. But I want to ask his forgiveness. He can't help being what he is, no more than I can. But he must understand that I was not being capriciously cruel. It was misguided therapy.

CLOUD: It was a calculated act of violence. You know he's always been afraid of you. You thought to break him, and instead he gained strength for escape . . .

MARC: He mustn't, Cloud. I must have a chance to explain to him—to both of you—why you mustn't go.

CLOUD: We won't let the Milieu authorities come back through the gate—

MARC: I know. That was never a serious worry. There's a far more important reason why you mustn't return to the Milieu.

CLOUD: What is it, Papa?

MARC: Let me meet with both of you, in person. I'll explain everything.

CLOUD: I'm willing to trust you, but I'm afraid Hagen never will. Tell me what you want to say to him. I'll transmit your message.

MARC: It won't work that way. I have to talk to you face to face—

CLOUD: To coerce us? Oh, Papa.

MARC: My dear, what I have to ask of you can never be gained through coercion. That lasts only as long as the coercer's grip holds. I need your free cooperation, your commitment—

CLOUD: Papa, it's too late! Years too late! We've made our choice. To be free.

MARC: But that's just it. You wouldn't be free in the Milieu. Not truly, any more than I was. You are my children, with my heritage. There are things you don't understand . . . that I had not intended to tell you until the star-search succeeded. For your own peace of mind. But now you've forced my hand.

CLOUD: Papa, for God's sake! *What?*

MARC: I must tell you both. Face to face. Everything I've done was for your good. You must believe it.

CLOUD: I—all I can do is tell Hagen what you've told me. But he's afraid, Papa. And now . . . so am I.

MARC: You need not be. Not with me. If you only have courage, your future can be wonderful. I'll tell you everything if you'll only meet with me.

CLOUD: I'll tell Hagen what you said. We'll talk about it.

MARC: Thank you, Cloud. I love you.

CLOUD: I love you, too, Papa, but—

MARC: Please.

. . .

MARC: Cloud?

. . .

8

As HE VANISHED INTO THE DEPTHS OF THE GREAT CREVASSE, Basil's thought maintained its usual laconic tone:

Falling. Everyone self-arrest.

Chazz, who was Number 2 on the rope, shouted an obscenity. He fell on his face, ice axe dangling impotently at the end of its keeperstrap, and was dragged through harsh, granular snow with arms and legs floundering. Derek, the Number 3, drove his axe into hard white ice simultaneously with Nirupam, the tail-man, just as Chazz reached the crack's edge. The rope went taut with a muffled *twung*!

Nirupam said: How you Baz?

Basil said: Dangling upside down like a snared hare. A moment while I shed my pack . . . ah. Over we go. Good heavens I just missed pranging into a rather bad shelf. Good show on the arrest even if a bit tardy. Is Chazz in the hole too?

Chazz said: Right on the mothering lip.

Nirupam said: Please don't move anyone. Derek are you belayed good and fast?

Derek said: I wouldn't bet on it.

An echoing yelp came from Chazz and he screamed aloud:

"The damn rope's cutting into the crevasse edge like a knife into cheese! I'm going over—"

Basil said: I shall cut my rope to ease the strain.

"Don't do it, Baz, don't!" the man above cried. The image of Basil's body tumbling into a bottomless blue crystal chasm flooded his mind and was broadcast by his gray torc to the others.

Basil said: Easy my boy. I *told* you I was just above a shelf. There. I'm down.

Nirupam said: Terrific. Everybody just hang cool or whatever while I drop anchor. Soon as I unpack a bit of gear we'll get the Death-Defying Baz & Chazz Rescue Act rolling.

Deep in his roofed canyon of blue ice, Basil moved cautiously along the shelf a few meters so he was no longer directly beneath the severed climbing rope, to which his pack remained clipped by a lighter line. Showers of soft snow dribbled constantly from overhead as Chazz was slowly winched back to safety. Then abruptly, a chunk of snow as large as an ATV module cracked from the lip and crashed onto the shelf, disintegrating into a sugary cloud.

Basil said: Not to worry. I believe I'll try walking out.

The others exclaimed: *What?*

Basil said: The shelf rises and the crevasse is closing as I move northward. Hello. The ice is warping up here and the snow cover getting very thin. I believe—can you see me?

He had poked his arm up through the snow crust and waggled it. A moment later his entire upper body was at the surface. He laughed to see the expressions on the others as he traced a curved path back to the winch-belay.

"Will you look at the man?" Derek exclaimed. "Cool as the proverbial gherkin. My God—when I saw you drop out of sight and Chazz go sliding after, I thought you were both on the way to join poor Phillipe in Valhalla!"

Basil's pack came slithering over the snow, drawn in by the solar-powered donkey engine. The classics professor and the three technicians hunkered to enjoy a fast cup of tea and a bar of chocolate algiprote.

"Crevasses needn't be lethal," Basil said, "as long as one isn't injured in the fall—or, in the case of Phillipe, drowned in meltwater. He was unlucky enough to fall into a moulin, a kind of drainpipe crevasse in the rotten ice of the glacier snout. With the tortuous nature of the fissure and the fast-moving water, there was no helping him—not even with Lord Bleyn's psychokinesis."

"My memory still retains his final mind-shouts," said Nirupam softly. "How ironic to die on the very first day of our support operation."

Chazz was smearing his abraded face with ointment. "Sure taught the rest of us grunts to stick to your flagged trail—even to take a leak. Beats me how you and Basil and Ookpik can tell where crevasses are hiding under the snow."

"We do miscalculate occasionally," observed the don. He took a tiny monocular from his anorak and studied the Middle Tine Ridge, toward which they had been trekking.

"Found us a fast route?" Nirupam inquired. "Time's getting on. We'll have stonefall in the gullies as the sun heats the frosty rock, and that ridge has some ugly-looking little snowfields that might be thinking about going avalanche before supper."

"It's a straightforward slog across the rest of this glacial tongue," Basil said, handing over the scope. "Just a small randkluft moat where the ice falls away from the ridge wall. Then we must pick and choose among the couloirs for the ascent. I rather fancy the darkish one, shaded by that second spur. It promises to hold tight longer than the others."

Nirupam squinched his Mongoloid features. "Hold tight, all right. It looks like it hasn't had any sun since the Miocene! Sharp and deep and probably black ice from top to bottom, as tough as cured solicrete. Our ice-axes will bounce right off it. Unless we melt steps with the blaster, we could be five hours gaining the ridgetop. I'm for one of the more open chutes. We can stay well to the shady side and keep alert. The third couloir north of your black beauty is steep enough to avalanche regularly. It can't have much snow buildup. I'd try that first." He gave Basil the glass and waited as the don considered the suggestion. "Well? You like?"

Basil sighed. "Very well. I christen it Darjeeling Gutter in your honor, if you will forgive the—er—ecumenical usage."

They finished their tea, repacked the equipment, roped up, and were on their way.

Taking advantage of a brilliant waning moon and clear weather, they had begun the day's trek at 0300 hours, departing from the supply dump at the base of the Gresson Icefall when that unstable jumble of séracs was at its most quiescent. Basil and the experienced Indian climber each carried forty kilos and Chazz and Derek took twenty-eight, and the bulk of that was left at Camp 1, newly established at 5585 meters. At dawn they had set off again to reconnoiter a route to Camp 2, taking flagged wands, a bivouac kit, the winch, and plenty of rope. Ideally, after they had gained the crest of Middle Tine via one gully or another they would scout about until they located a good spot for a "flywalk" winch-belay. Once the machinery and ropes were permanently emplaced, other climbers could simply latch on, signal the faithful donkey, and be drawn up the rocky ridge flank with minimum effort.

The pioneering team, however had to do it the hard way.

It was nearly 0930 when they reached the moatlike randkluft that was the western edge of the Tine Glacier. Late in the afternoon, the half-rock, half-ice corridor would be perilous with running meltwater. But now it was frozen solid and almost like a staircase to their crampon-shod feet. They ascended easily to the base of Darjeeling Gutter, crossed the miniature bergschrund where its cascading snows joined the main glacier, and began to creep up the sixty-degree slope of dazzling white. They bore as far to the left as possible in order to avoid the deadly warming effect of the sun, trigger of rockfalls and avalanches. It was about 900 meters to the top. Over most of that distance the couloir was a constantly changing patchwork of hardened snow, opaque and brittle ice formed by the daily thaw-and-freeze cycle, tough "live ice" that resisted the glass fangs of crampons and ice-axes, and rare patches of powder snow.

At first they moved briskly, but after an hour or so, Chazz and Derek weakened. Only amateur climbers, they had to use the easily learned but tiring crampon technique called front-pointing—digging the horizontal toe-points of the crampons into the ice as they hauled themselves along with the aid of their axes. Basil and Nirupam, using the more efficient flat-footed technique, found that they had to slow their pace drastically—then begin to belay their fatigued rope-mates and even cut steps over the worst stretches of live ice.

The sun climbed and the gully became a heat trap. They all wore sun goggles but the light was blinding. Chunks of brittle ice began to zoom down the chute. They were not large and the climbers had hard hats, but the psychological effect was harrowing.

Above the halfway point the slope eased and the two amateurs regained their spirits. Lunch was a scratch affair taken hurriedly on a small rock cleaver that split the snowslope. Chazz's scraped face was swollen and raw. But it had become so warm that the thought of even a lightweight silk mask-bandage was intolerable, so he simply smeared on more antibiotic goo.

They had been climbing again for less than half an hour when Basil's telepathic voice signaled a halt just above a tiny ledge.

He said: Niru oldman don't much like looks of this pitch.

Nirupam said: Getting late snow deep enough to be slabby.

Basil said: It could go.

Nirupam said: Alternative traverse couloir go up rock southside. Hell scramble take us twice long we could still make the Gutter work not even 1400 hours yet.

Basil said: Risky.

Nirupam said: You boss. But Chazz running on ballpower small disaster you shrugged off back at crevasse got to him maybe delayed shock on top sore face & nearly blind.

Basil said: Chazz oldman we're going to move you to Number3 on rope. It be safer for all incase I come cropper leading.

Chazz said: Sorry to be the crock of the flock guys.

Derek said: Spare us bouillabaisse goodbuddy. Just switch with me. Snap on safety lines? Okay. Easy! You stomp me with tackety boots they hear my screech in basecamp!

Basil said: Please be very quiet all of you . . . even if stepped on. The consequences of sudden noise this point could be lamentable.

Chazz said: He means avalanche could be set off by your bigmouth Derek.

Derek said: Or your clumsy feet.

Basil was looking down on the pair, who had unsnapped their harnesses from the main rope. Both were maneuvering carefully on the tiny ledge of compacted snow, Chazz linked to Derek by a light safety line and Derek ready to refasten them to the rope as soon as the position switch had been accomplished. Nirupam, the low man, was keeping a sharp eye on the two amateurs, offering advice and encouragement. And then there was a distant crackling sound. Nirupam caught sight of a small wisp of white blurring the dazzle of the upper ice field. A jagged blue line spread across the high face of the chute and opened like a fanged mouth before disappearing behind a foaming cloud of snow.

"She's coming down!" Nirupam yelled. "Hold! Hold!"

His cries were smothered in a musical rumble, as if someone had trod upon the pedals of a great organ. A cascade of broken thin crust came jangling and hissing ahead of the snowslide. The climbers cringed, hugging the slope and drawing their heads down between their shoulders. Basil whipped his tube-pointed hammer from its holster and sank the second tool into the ice with his left hand, clinging to axe and hammer with all his strength as the avalanche rolled over them.

He said: Hold on boys *hold*!

Chazz's mind spoke first, incredulous, refusing to admit that he was cartwheeling through opaque white air instead of clinging to a slope by the tips of his toes and an insecurely anchored axe. Derek was torn screaming from his place by a forty-kilo slab of snow that slammed into him like a skating chunk of sidewalk. He flailed out with his axe in a futile attempt at self-arrest and cut the rope linking Nirupam to Basil. The Indian mountaineer, struck by Derek's body, tumbled helplessly as the strap of his dropped ice-axe banged about his ankles. The tool was still tethered to his harness, but he could not haul it up because his neck was broken and the motor nerves of his arms refused to function.

The rushing snow passed Basil by. He dared to lift his head and look down, in time to see the avalanche reach the base of the couloir and make glittering puffballs as it buried the bergschrund. Chazz spoke a last telepathic curse and Derek simply said: Goodbye. Nirupam was serenely reciting a Buddhist prayer as he expired from a severed spinal cord. Basil called the names of all three men telepathically and out loud, and then he hung there facing the ice and let tears course down his weathered cheeks. It was sunny and very quiet.

After a while he summoned the long-range faculty of his farspeech and bespoke Bleyn the Champion in Camp Betta-forca. No, he said, he would not turn back. Since he still carried the winch and cable, he would complete the climb up the now avalanche-free slope and see to the installation of the apparatus, so that Camp 2 might be set up easily by the next support team. It would be a simple matter for him to return to Camp 1 by nightfall by winching down and then following the marked route across Tine Glacier.

Reluctantly, Bleyn agreed to this. And for some time he watched the dogged human creep upward, and heard with his mind's ear the tag that spun endlessly through Basil's mind, to be broadcast inadvertently into the aether:

> I, demens, et saevas curre per Alpes,
> ut pueris placeas et declamatio fias.

The Tanu knew that Basil was quoting from a human poet again, as he had done when delivering his orientation speech at the start of the climb. The verse from Kipling had appealed to Bleyn's native bravura; but this one, oddly enough, seemed to come from Basil's own unconscious:

> Go, madman, and hurry over the cruel Alps,
> that you may delight small boys and inspire
> feckless adulation.

Humans, thought Bleyn the Champion, were a paradoxical lot.

9

AIKEN WAS ALONE ON HIS BALCONY IN THE CASTLE OF GLASS, watching Kyllikki with his farsense. Although it was night in Goriah the sun had just set in the region of the Atlantic just north of the Azores where the great schooner plowed along in a fair breeze. Her solar-collector sails gleamed like bronze in the warm light. She sailed on a flaming sea with the evening star over her shoulder and deep night her destination.

Aiken called: Elizabeth.

Yes. How are you dear?

Cultivating lionheartedness. I've been watching Kyllikki and drinking Laphroaig and stuffing myself with Scotch eggs. There are three portable sigmas all charged and ready to hang around my royal neck when I decide to go to sleep and I can't help thinking how a beam from an X-zapper could slice through those shields like a sgian dhu through a goddamn clootie dumpling...I don't suppose you know where Marc is?

No. When he left us on Wednesday after the baby's cure he gave no indication when he'd return here. Shall I do a scan of Goriah for you?

Please.

   . . . All clear unless he's put up a mental umbrella.
Are you *sure*?

   Aiken I can't farsearch for him as I would an ordinary person. Once he pops through the superficies into normal space he's free to disguise his aura or even wipe it out so that not even a Grand Master can track him. But I know he isn't able to carry anything large along with him yet. Only small objects that would fit inside the armor. Certainly not an X-ray laser. You're safe from him wearing your sigmas. And I really don't think he'd try to kill you . . . yet.

Not like his darling son Hagen you mean? Well that one's cooled down nicely! All the same he won't get any rides in those aircraft—granting Basil and the boys manage to bring them back. Both Hagen and Cloud are staying with me on tight leash until further notice. Let 'em work on the Guderian device with old Celo breathing down their necks watching for a false move.

   How is the project coming?

Well enough I guess. They've taken apart half the gadgets in my contraband store cannibalizing components and materials.

   Have you thought further about whether you'd return to the Milieu?

All I can think about is confronting Marc. Get the damn thing over and done with.

   He'll pick his own time and place. Unless you do as I suggested.

Meet him at your place? . . . Not on your life! He'd have *both* of us right where he wanted us.

   He had the chance to dominate me already when he took over the executive during Brendan's redaction. And he let me go: I don't think you understand Marc—

!YouthinkYOU do?!

   Better than you. I've worked with him and I've also done a deep memoreview of some Rebellion history materials that I studied a long time ago. Marc is a man with his own strange code of honor. If he agreed to confer with you on neutral ground with me as monitor he'd do you no harm.

Ha! I'd wallop *him* without blinking a fewking eye—truce or not!

> No you won't. Not if you give your word to me. I know you.

Damned if you do Woman! This matter of Marc toting things around with him on the d-jump really tears it. When he gets the program squared away what's to stop him from plopping Kyllikki herself right down in the castle courtyard?

> Listen to me Aiken. Try to understand. Once Marc becomes capable of that sort of psychotransport *he has no motive left for opposing the reopening of the time-gate.* I want to get the two of you together to be sure you realize this.

? . . . You mean the Milieu fuzz would be no threat to Marc if he could hop all over the planet—with his geriatric villains and their gear tucked under his metaphorical arm?

> Exactly.

[Elation.] Woman you could be right. [Dejection.] Oh-oh. We're forgetting a complicating factor. Those bloody Rebel kids. And I use the sanguine modifier with deliberate precision.

> Any resolution would have to involve them. Marc doesn't want to let them go.

[Perplexity. Anger. Dichotomous potentialities. Fatigue.]

> I know dear. Nothing can be done immediately anyway. I'll be too busy watching the situation on Monte Rosa and advising the people there.

You think the Famorel Firvulag will attack tomorrow then? When the two assault teams try to take off on their big push over the top?

> It's only two days until Truce—and the Famorel Little People are more traditional-minded than Sharn and Ayfa. They'll quit fighting and go home at dawn on October first.

I watched them creeping around the base of the mountain today. Damn! If only I could do something! But I barely managed to queer the Bessemer converter coup. The drain left me too pooped to fly—although Hagen and his crowd don't know that.

> You'll regain your strength more quickly now that the integration of your personality is proceeding. Eventually

you'll be even stronger than before.

No doubt. If I live so long. But I've an uncanny feeling... Do you know we're the only two Greenies left?

?Group Green?

All of them gone. Except the two of us. And now daft Dougal blethering on about Aslan and his noble sacrifice, and the Tanu on my High Table deciding it's Marc Remillard who's the Adversary that will set off the Nightfall War. Then the only one left will be you.

Aiken dear. You've been drinking too much malt whisky. You're maudlin—and you're wrong. Stein's alive.

I've looked for him. Never found hide nor hair nor horned helm.

... You *are* a bit squiffed. I'll show you him and Sukey and little Thor if you promise me that you'll never try to make contact with them or interfere with them in any way.

They had a kid—? Aw. I promise. On my honor as Nonborn King. Why should I drag them into my troubles? But wait... are they happy?

Happy as can be.

[Sentimental satisfaction.] Then show me. Please.

Wait. There. [*Image: River island half-moon rushlighted window reflection black water cypresses live oaks cinnamons log house jetty clinkerbuilt dory crocodile fence silvered garden plot thorn-guarded yard thatch roof stick chimney. Open bead-screened summer room work shed main cabin glass windows wide hearth planked floor* A MAN A WOMAN HOLDING A CHILD.]

A boy named Thor you say? How old?

About two months now. He's a lovely strong child.

Sukey looks fine. Stein looks... older. How do they live?

He hunts and fishes and traps. Sometimes very rarely he goes down the Garonne and sails to Rocilan to trade. Sukey is starting to pester him to take her and the child but he puts her off afraid she would want to settle near the city. Near Tanu and other humans who would find out.

How Stein helped Felice at Gibraltar?... Does that bother him?

He remembers. He thinks it was necessary but he remembers. It would be much worse if you were to come back into his life. Stein must be let alone like a healing wound. Look. [*Image. Baby placed in cradle cries Father takes him holds against massive deerskin-vested shoulder pats tiny back expertly dips fingertip in honeypot Baby suckles Father cuddles yellow-bearded ferocity smiles.*]
He makes a pretty good dad.

 Your unconscious thought so.

. . . A weird thing that and one I never would have anticipated.

 The unconscious uses what it must.

And why Mayvar for my mother figure—and not you?

 She was *right*. You loved her and him too power&vulnerability stature&puniness maturejudgement&childishimpulse. In both. In you. Their child is father of your man. You choose your parents and gave birth to yourself.

I love you too!

 Sisterly. I'm the Ice Queen remember?

[Quiet laughter. Contemplation of slowly fading image.]
Funny. I haven't been interested in that sort of thing lately.

 You will be. Don't worry about *that*.

Save my energy for the real problems . . . One piece of good news today amidst the encircling gloom: We've located Tony Wayland that metallurgist we need for the Guderian Project. Would you believe? Chief Burke and his Lowlives nabbed the guy and offered to barter him to us! All they want in return is free passage back to the Milieu and a fair shake for their bandito buddies. Of course I agreed. The Chief will be coming into Roniah tomorrow to work out details of the swap with Kuhal Earthshaker at the City-Lord's place.

 Hm. I haven't been in touch with Peo since before young Brendan's redaction. Strange that he should be willing to deal with a fellow Lowlife as a commodity.

Tony was eager to be sold down the river. The alternative was being hanged for high crimes and misdemeanors.

 Good grief.

Good night Elizabeth.

* * *

Walter Saastamoinen came onto Kyllikki's bridge punctually at midnight to relieve Patricia Castellane at the helm.

"All peaceful, I presume," he remarked, thumbing the key pad of the course director and studying the replay of first-watch performance events. "You're doing very well at manual for an apprentice, Pat. The director only overruled you once in the entire four-hour trick."

"It's a relief to be able to do something besides those miserable psych-up exercises," she said. "My metafunctions aren't going to get much stronger through mental muscle flexing. More likely weaker, with my dirigent formation. But try to tell Jeff that." Her mouth was taut with resentment.

Walter moved to the wheel, disengaged the autopilot, and let the soul of the great schooner come into him. *Oh, you beauty!* "Sailing Kyllikki is good for what ails both of us. I wish we could just keep going. Alter course to the south . . . touch in along the coast of Africa . . . round the Cape of Good Hope and go up into the Indian Ocean to see Pliocene Asia. Marc would never let us range out, after the Antarctic tragedy. But now there's no real reason why we shouldn't."

She was making them coffee at the dispenser and now handed a mug to Walter, frowning slightly. "I don't understand you."

"The Milieu coppers aren't going to be able to nab us if Marc succeeds with this new d-jump thing." He twiddled with the atmospheric analog unit next to the binnacle. "As I understand it, he should be able to take us *all* extraplanetary once he gets the thing mastered. We could cruise around until he does. Forget about fighting with the kids over the time-gate. Surely they'd be willing to delay the opening until we got safely away."

"Would they?" Patricia's voice was flat. "I can think of at least one who might not."

Walter ignored that. "I'm not sure I trust this little weather analoger overmuch," he said, frowning. "It's wishy-washy about the deep trough below Rockall. Doesn't want to commit itself on trend. We may have to ask Marc to do a deep scan of the system. If the storm drifts our way we could be in for an uncomfortable couple of days that could be avoided with a course change, given the proper trend data."

Patricia was not to be distracted. "You know Hagen hates

Marc. The boy is looking forward to setting the Magistratum on his father! We'll have to use force to keep that time-gate closed. Nothing else will suffice. Unless *you* convince the children of their danger, Walter."

"I like sailing along the moonpath, don't you? It doesn't often happen that it works out just right that way—but when it does, it's magic."

She slammed her coffee cup down on the chart console. "Stick your head in the sand, then! Keep dreaming that we can solve this terrible mess with sweet reason and kindly intentions. But Cordelia Warshaw and I know better—and it won't be long before even Marc has to face the truth."

Walter's lips compressed into a hard line. He stared straight ahead, adjusting the wheel with delicate movements.

Patricia said, "I was talking to Jordy about the teleportation of external mass. In order for Marc to carry objects situated outside his CE rig, he'll have to expand the upsilon-field generated by his mind. It means jacking up the input power to the rig—putting a greater and greater stress on his brain. He can't do it abruptly or he'll risk overload. Kramer's not even sure that Marc has the capacity to encompass an area large enough to be practicable. Then there are the passengers. Will they need life-support gear for jumps on Earth? All we have is the spare suit of CE armor, three more tons of mass for Marc to carry. The testing will take time . . . But I hardly think Hagen or Aiken Drum will delay opening the time-gate while Marc solves his teleportation problems."

"We could ask them to," Walter said.

Patricia was at the wheelhouse door. "We will. With the X-lasters behind us, and all the concerted coercion we can lash together!" Then she was gone.

Walter tracked her briefly to make certain that she had retired to her cabin, then scanned the rest of his shipmates. They were all either asleep or occupied with their work—except two. Marc was gone on the jump and Alexis Manion was unexpectedly at large, wandering about the main deck, pausing from time to time to swab at the bright work with a polishing rag. He was under the influence of the docilator. No one had thought to send him to bed, and only the magnates had the requisite command code. Subsidiary Grand Masters such as Walter were forbidden to interfere with the potentially dangerous Manion.

"Poor devil," Walter muttered. The dim figure disappeared behind the night-shrouded forward deckhouse. For some time Walter brooded about Manion, whose crime had been revealing to the children the truth about their elders. Then it was time to farspeak Veikko, and Walter forgot the dynamic-field specialist as he sent his mind ranging eastward to the Alps.

WALTER: Hey, boy.

VEIKKO: I'm here, Walter.

WALTER: How are things going?

VEIKKO: One of the climbers got a touch of pulmonary edema and another has frostbitten feet. But we progress. Camp 3 was stocked today. The assault teams leave here for the big push tomorrow. Basil is still on the mountain leading the support group down, and by rights the assault party should wait until he gets back. But we're expecting Firvulag company, so they're jumping the gun. Basil delegated a Tibetan medic named Thongsa to lead the other six assaulters in a single group until they connect up with him. Then they'll split into two smaller teams as originally planned and Basil will lead them to the aircraft.

WALTER: Sounds like this Basil hasn't had much rest in the last week.

VEIKKO: He's led just about every other support group. I can't believe the guy is seventy-two. Rejuvenated, of course.

WALTER: That makes him a year younger than Marc. And a couple of years older than me.

VEIKKO: Well, we all know bloody Marc's immortal. But you look—I mean—

WALTER: The Ocala regen tank was getting a bit obsolete. I didn't make much use of it. I'm sure this Basil is a product of more sophisticated Milieu technology if he's the climbing superman you say he is.

VEIKKO: It must be quite a place... the Milieu, I mean.

WALTER: You'll see.

VEIKKO: ... Walter, are you sure you still want to try it?

WALTER: You kids have got to have your chance.

VEIKKO: Oh, God. But Marc might kill you.

WALTER: It's possible. But he might think twice. Suppose the course director autopilot broke? It's not too tricky maneuvering Kyllikki in fine weather. But given a storm—and there might be one lurking out there—this big four-poster is a bitch-kitty to steer manually.

VEIKKO: I remember the gale in the Ross Sea! . . . So you think that even if you—you think Marc won't dare—

WALTER: I'm going to try it, and hope that Marc won't kill me when he finds out. But whatever happens, happens. I don't know when my chance will come, but when it does, I'll grab it. The things are locked up tight, but I'll figure some way to neutralize them.

VEIKKO: Oh, Walter. Oh, Daddy.

WALTER: See that you and Irena don't get yourselves killed by the damned goblins or whatever they are. If anything happened to you, I don't think I could go through with this.

VEIKKO: We've got the base camp all dug in and there are plenty of weapons. We'll be fine. But you—when—

WALTER: When I can. Don't worry. Call me tomorrow if possible. Otherwise, on Tuesday.

VEIKKO: The Tanu with us say that the Firvulag will probably quit when their sacred Truce begins at dawn on Wednesday.

WALTER; Well—that's something. Take care, son. Someone's just come into the wheelhouse and I'll have to let you go.

VEIKKO: Good luck . . .

Walter thumbed the autopilot and turned smiling from the wheel. "Hello, Alex. Come in."

"A wand'ring minstrel I," Manion sang, "a thing of shreds and patches." He began to rub industriously at the port-frames with his polishing rag.

Walter said distinctly: "Alex. Stop that. Come here and listen to me."

The docilated man obediently lowered his cloth and stood before Kyllikki's captain.

"You're the best PK-head of us all, Alex. And not too shabby a coercer either. I wonder if you're strong enough to get past the docilator. I wonder if your coercion can push down the command-set if I give you the proper inspiration. Listen Alex: *I know how you and I can help the children!* I need your help. Do you understand?"

A broad smile spread slowly across the ravaged face. Manion sang softly:

> *Am I alone, and unobserved? I am!*
> *Then let me own I'm an aesthetic sham!*

Walter grasped him by the arms. "Can you do it? Have you been picking away at it from the inside? You know I can't turn the docilator off."

Alex sang:

> *This air severe is but a mere veneer!*
> *This cynic smile is but a wile of guile!*
> *This costume chaste is but good taste misplaced!*

"Good man! I want you to go down to the forward hold with me—and break Marc's fancy lock."

Alex whispered:

> *With catlike tread upon our prey we steal;*
> *In silence dread our cautious way we feel . . .*

"I'm going to sabotage the X-lasers, Alex, so that Marc can't use them against the children. He'll still have the other weapons, of course. But the kids' sigma-shields can turn them aside. And there's a fair chance that our metaconcert potential has dwindled at the same time that the Little King's has been growing. When Marc finds out what we've done, he might kill us. But he needs you badly, and nobody can sail this tub as well as I can—so there's a chance. And if we make it to Europe, who knows what might happen? Marc might even change his mind about using force against the kids if the hell-zappers aren't an option anymore."

Alex sang:

> *When a felon's not engaged in his employment*
> *   (his employment)*
> *Or maturing his felonious little plans*
> *   (little plans),*
> *His capacity for innocent enjoyment*
> *   (-cent enjoyment)*
> *Is just as great as any honest man's.*

With tremulous slowness, one eyelid drooped shut, then opened again. Alexis Manion had definitely winked.

"Marc's out jumping and the rest of them are asleep or busy," Walter said. "Let's go do it right now, shall we?" He took the physicist by the hand and led him away like a happy child.

10

BETS! WAKE UP GUY! WAKE UP IT'S TIME TO MARCH!

Mr. Betsy stirred. A manicured hand crept from the interior of his silk-and-swansdown sleeping bag and hooked over the opening of his balaclava, which had ridden up to the vicinity of his receding natural hairline. A finger pulled the pink knitted helmet down so that a single green eye peered from the woolen slot and read the illuminated digits on the inturned wrist chronograph: 0216. The gray torc tingled, banishing sleep.

Mr. Betsy's telepathic voice was surly: Good grief Ookpik it can't be starting time I just went to *bed*!

Bad news. Elizabeth sent word our Tanu farsensor that Firvulag coming up fast on Bettaforca. Also Basil on mountain says weather looking iffy. We can't wait until dawn to start climb. Ten minutes.

Betsy said aloud, "Oh, friggerty fudge."

Ookpik said: And don't forget your gun.

Growling feebly, Betsy levered himself upright and hopped across the hut like an acrobatic caterpillar enveloped in its cocoon. He lit the hut lantern and knelt in front of the oven of the cooking unit, where his boots and outer clothing had spent the brief night toasting fifty degrees Celsius. He checked the outside

268

temperature and was surprised to find it hovering just above freezing. Right. Never mind the down pants and jacket for now: on with the breathable grintlaskin wet-wind gear over his layered woolies, snap on the boots, then the snow gaiters and climbing harness. To extract the perspiration from his sleeping bag, he stuffed it into the oven for a few moments and let the busy little microwaves do their work. Then the bag and down clothing went into his pack. He pulled on his mitts and grabbed ice-axe and Weatherby Magnum blaster.

Six minutes. Mr. Betsy allowed himself a satisfied smirk as he stepped out into the alpine night.

A warmish wind was blowing from the west and the fresh-fallen snow of yesterday had gone slushy. The camp was blacked out as a safety precaution, but Betsy saw dark shapes moving among the huts of the gold-torc soldiery. A fuzzy half-moon lit Monte Rosa with wan, greenish radiance. The massif was crowned with an unusual double cloud formation, a smooth cap curving over the highest elevation, surmounted by an elongate, eastward-trailing plume.

After a quick visit to the latrine, Betsy came into the climbers' staging hut. Ookpik was the only one there as yet, hunched on a bench next to the grub buffeteria, drinking tea and nibbling slugs Villeroy.

"I'm glad somebody in this outfit is quick on the aufgesprungen," the Eskimo remarked wryly. "The rest of the team are still stumbling around looking for their socks—and that includes our redoubtable leader, Dr. Thongsa. Have some tea, Bets. The French-fried slimies aren't too bad. You see that cloud on the mountain?"

"Yes," said Betsy shortly. He dropped his gear and shucked his mittens. "Lord Bleyn was doing his best to put a good face on matters yesterday. I might have known we'd never get out of here so easily! Those Firvulag must be able to conceal their movements somehow if they've managed to come so close without Elizabeth farseeing them. They weren't supposed to arrive until late tomorrow. A night start over the glacier snout in warm weather like this could be extremely hazardous."

Ookpik scrutinized a gasteropod fritter before popping it into his mouth. "That's not the only waktoo hitting the fan, good buddy. I farspoke Basil myself. Couldn't sleep."

Betsy ladled a big dollop of honey into his tea. "I thought you couldn't broadcast more than a few hundred meters?"

"I've been practicing. You'd be surprised how sheer panic jacks up the old cerebral output... Anyhow, Stan's worse."

"Oh, my."

"He's a rugged old walrus, but pulmonary edema's nothing to fool around with. Getting him down to Camp Two eased his condition a little, but he's still a bagger. Basil and Taffy will have to hump him all the rest of the way on the decamole sledge."

"How's poor dear Phronsie?"

"Her feet are responding to the torc-induced circulation boost. She can walk, but not very fast. She wants Baz and Taffy to leave her at Camp Two and press on down with Stan. She says she thinks she could make it back here on her own, given a couple days' rest. Or we could send a rescue team."

"If the Firvulag don't wipe out Bettaforca first," Betsy muttered. "Rescue team—? The only climbers left down here after we take off will be Cliff and Cisco Briscoe, and neither one is very strong." He pulled a dubious face and replaced a half-eaten slug on the platter. "Attrition is thinning the ranks of Basil's Bastards rather rapidly. We really *don't* need a premature Firvulag attack and a storm on top of everything else."

The hut door opened, admitting three exotics and Kang Lee, the gold-torc officer of the watch. The Tanu climbers Bleyn the Champion and Aronn looked almost like outsized humans in their alpine clothing; but Ochal the Harper was an eerie sight, a white anorak and pants pulled over his brightly glowing amethyst armor.

"The others are coming immediately," the farsensor said. "We'll use this map for orientation rather than attempt a mind-meld." He spread a large sheet of durofilm on the table in the center of the hut. More people came stomping in—Bengt Sand-vik and Nazir of the second assault team, and the nonclimbing physician, Magnus Bell. Last of all, smiling and imperturbable in the face of the others' coolness, came the little deputy assault leader, Dr. Thongsa.

"Now let the briefing commence!" he ordered. Somebody snickered.

Ochal's mailed finger traced a path across the map, leaving

a lingering bright mark on the plass. "It seems the Foe has done the unexpected. With their forces diminished by the landslide back in the Tarentaise, no one suspected that they would dare to split what was left. Nevertheless, this is exactly what they did. After crossing the Little St. Bernard Pass and marching into the Proto-Augusta Valley, they arrived here." He indicated a point on the river some 40 kilometers east of the pass. "About one hundred Firvulag continued to move east along the Augusta in a straightforward manner to the Val d'Ayas, which is their most logical corridor of access to Camp Bettaforca. This was the force Elizabeth tracked."

"And the rest of them?" Ookpik asked.

"The force she did *not* perceive," Ochal resumed, "consisted of some seventy of the more stalwart Foe, those able to exercise strong shielding functions. After these troops broke away from their fellows, they went through the steep gorges of the Valpelline, where even a Grand Master would have the utmost difficulty farsensing them. They traveled northeast and then east across very rugged terrain, then curved back southward. They will fall upon us from the head of the Ayas instead of the foot, probably attacking from that ridge to the northwest."

"The storm's coming in from that direction," Ookpik noted brightly. "Might slow the bastards down."

"We must be off at once!" piped Thongsa, prodding the air with his ice axe spike. "Once we reach the glacier, the Firvulag won't dare follow—and at least *we'll* be safe!"

An embarrassed silence greeted this gaffe.

Ochal said gently, "We think that the Foe are poised to attack Camp Bettaforca, and our people are armed and ready. But you must understand that another possibility exists. The Firvulag nation were anciently born and bred in the high snowy mountains of Duat, our native world. Even a thousand years in the Many-Colored Land will not have diminished their craftiness in such terrain—and the Famorel Little People are even more mountain-wise than their kinfolk of the northern realm. They are keen farsensors. They undoubtedly know the locations of our advance camps on Monte Rosa."

"Surely not!" wailed the Tibetan physician.

"The Firvulag objective," Bleyn the Champion reminded him, "is to deny us the aircraft. Attacking Bettaforca with its strong defenses isn't nearly so tempting as going for us climbers. Besides—the second force of Little People will be in a better position to attack the base."

Thongsa's black eyes darted like terrified beetles in his flat bronze face. "We must postpone the assault until the enemy is defeated!"

Bleyn was implacable. "The Foe may win. The King commands that we begin the high climb at once."

"But we may have to fight our way up the entire South Face!" Thongsa cried.

"*Now* you have it straight, darling," said Mr. Betsy comfortably. He hoicked up his pack, fastened the buckles, and adjusted the hood of his anorak over the pink pompoms of his balaclava. "Shall we be off?"

"Wait!" exclaimed the Tibetan wildly. His voice was drowned by the rumbling agreement of the others, who began putting on their gear.

"Feel like guiding a rookie today, Bets?" asked Magnus Bell. "I'm mooching along with you guys—part of the way, at least—to cope with the sickees, help haul them back down. Mountaineering-wise, I'm dumb but willing. In the tough pitches, I expect to be dragged."

Thongsa was fairly hopping with fury. "This is madness! When I agreed to lead the second assault team, I never anticipated it would involve a running gun battle! I resign forthwith!"

"Go right ahead," said Aronn gloomily. He was a horse-faced Tanu with an air of perennial disillusionment, not above using his PK talent to cheat at craps. He had muscles like a bull gigantopithecus. "You may back out of the leadership if you choose, Lowlife, but your alpine expertise and piloting ability are irreplaceable. You go with us if I must carry you by the scruff of the neck."

"This is insupportable," Thongsa whimpered.

"Isn't it, though?" agreed Betsy. His dainty goateed face thrust close to that of the rebellious pilot-physician. As other hands lifted Thongsa's pack to his shoulders, Betsy latched it on. "Think of the aircraft, darling. Think of the time-gate that the aircraft will help to build! Think of yourself going through that time-gate. Don't you want to go back to the Milieu?"

Tears stood in Thongsa's eyes. "I did not think so before. But now . . . yes. Yes! *YES!*"

They crept across the rotten ice of the Gresson Glacier, divided into four-man parties and firmly roped in spite of the fact that the trail was marked with flagged wands. All around them were the sounds of running water and the squeaks and groans of settling ice. At long intervals they heard thunderous crashes as séracs calved from the four great icefalls. The moon had a ring around it and the summit of Monte Rosa wore a spectral caul.

The two Tanu kept in constant telepathic communication with the base camp at the same time that their farsense scanned the expanse of ice for signs of the advancing Foe. But nothing happened. For more than two hours, until the gray light of dawn smudged the sky behind Rosa's right flank, they picked their way across the glacier. Thongsa went first, probing with his long-hafted axe, leading Nazir, Bengt, and Aronn. Then came Ookpik leading Betsy, Magnus, and Bleyn the Champion. No one fell into a crevasse. No one even lost his footing. The torcs helped them to see in the dark. Thongsa's route finding was a model of conservative ice travel: painstaking, safe, and very, very slow.

They saw the storm sweeping toward them as they approached the supply dump at the foot of the Gresson Icefall. At the same time Bleyn announced:

Elizabeth regrets that a combination of meteorological interference thoughtresistant rock formations and Firvulag screening makes it all but impossible for her to pinpoint the location of the northern force of the Foe. The southern force is easily farsensed 8 kilometers south of Bettaforca in the Ayas Valley apparently bivouacked . . .

Sleet struck them. The aether rang with epithets as they paused to seal shut the scabbards of their weapons and pull down their hoods. Then they slogged on through the gloaming, with Aronn's farsight helping Thongsa to locate the wands as the storm intensified. Sometimes they were ankle-deep in running water and their socks quickly became soaked. But it was possible for the two Tanu overlords to step up circulation in the extremities of the gray-torc wearers, so their wool-clad feet remained warm, if slightly chafed.

Magnus said: All the same we're sure to get blisters unless we dry out soon.

Bleyn said: I faresee the supply dump tents less than half a league ahead.

Ookpik asked: How much is that in honest meters?

Aronn said: I know not but you puny-leggers will take at least another hour to get there unless you crank it up.

Nazir said: Subhan'llah I think I'm sinking guys!...*I am!*

Thongsa said: Belay Bengt I am fast.

Bengt said: Got him.

Nazir said: Bloody hell I'm waist deep...

Thongsa said: Can you lift him Lord Aronn?

Aronn said: Upsy-pupsy little man.

As if he were on an elevator, the Arab technician levitated from the mush-filled crevasse that had threatened to swallow him. The psychokinesis of both Aronn and Bleyn held him in midair, then tilted him carefully to spill water from various parts of his clothing.

Bleyn said: It storms too hard to do a proper job drying you Nazir. I can banish discomfort until we reach the dump. Satisfactory?

Nazir said: Carry on.

The sleet storm moderated somewhat with the coming of dawn. Monte Rosa's snowfields slowly took on a sanguine tinge and the sky turned to purplish crimson, strewn with fast-moving little black clouds.

"I know it's 'red sky at morning, sailors take warning,'" Magnus quoted. "Does that hold true for mountain weather as well?"

"Probably," said Betsy, with cheerful pessimism. "Look there! The wind's blowing open the mist ahead. I see the icefall—and the tents."

The humans all cheered. The shelters of silver decamole were virtually invisible against the ice, but they bore banners of streaming orange silk, and seemed not more than 150 meters away.

"We will rest well, dry out, and prepare a substantial meal," Thongsa declared. "It's obvious that the Firvulag were more prudent than we, doubtless spending the night in some cosy, stormproof shelter. Come! Let us make haste!"

He strode forward with his axe held at a jaunty piolet-canne and his glass crampons clinking against the water ice. The photon beam that killed him instantly was undoubtedly a mistake. Some impetuous Firvulag stalwart had bungled and fired too soon from the tumble of broken white blocks to the left of the tents. The ragged fusillade that followed was delivered from extreme Matsu range, and was hopelessly fouled by a sudden blatter of sleet that swept across the glacier.

"Get down!" Bleyn shouted. "Behind that ice ridge!"

They broke away from the flagged trail just in time. The storm was giving its last gasp, and as the air cleared, the laser beams zapped with increasing efficiency, chipping great hunks from the ridge.

They unroped and wormed away eastward. The ridge, though not very high, was adequate cover, leading them to an outcropping of verglas-sheathed granite, where they regrouped and considered the situation.

It was now full light. They were more than 300 meters from the tent site and somewhat farther from the hiding place of the Firvulag. The Foe had concealed themselves in a pile of house-sized sérac on the righthand margin of the icefall and now commanded the only route up the mountain.

"Somebody using his noggin among that lot," Ookpik observed. "Still, things could be worse."

"And would be," Betsy muttered, "if one spook hadn't got itchy trigger finger."

"Is it the entire gang?" Nazir asked. "The seventy-odd sods Ochal the Harper estimated?"

"I am counting," Bleyn said grimly. "At such close range, I can pick them out, even if they are screened."

"Pity you didn't earlier," murmured Betsy.

"I was unforgivably careless," the Champion admitted. "Such scrunity requires intense concentration, and my attention was divided. Even a High Table member may nod—Tana curse the luck!"

"Things could be worse," Ookpik said again. He seemed unaccountably excited as he extracted a monocular from his pack with some difficulty and peered through it.

"What ho?" Bengt asked.

"They don't call it an icefall for nothing, cheechako," said the Inuit engineer.

Aronn said, "It hasn't moved since we first came to the mountain."

"Needed lubrication," said Ookpik.

"You'll have to hit the trigger point just right," Nazir said dubiously. "I mean, we can't fart around for hours peppering the fall, or the spooks will wise up."

"How can I estimate these angles if you keep yapping?" Ookpik complained. Everyone was still for several minutes. Then the Eskimo asked, "Any of you Tanu fly?"

"No," said Bleyn. "I have a mental block and Aronn has never been able to assimilate the program."

"But you can move things at distance?"

"I'm no Kuhal Earthshaker, but I can fling about eight times my weight. Aronn's good for half that much."

Ookpik did a rapid calculation. "Better than ton. Ho-*kay*. You could move something over on the icefall?"

"Well—" Bleyn hesitated. "We could try. But just tossing about, mind you. No sustained lift. And we have to have a line of sight on it."

The Eskimo's eyes were glittering. "Just give me a few more minutes."

They relaxed behind the ice-covered rocks. Soggy footgear was dried by Aronn's creative power. Betsy helped Nazir change his clothing. Magnus brewed hot chocolate. From time to time the Firvulag opened fire on their position, but the only result was the removal of most of the ice-rind on the north side of the outcropping and minimal damage to the granite.

"I count sixty-eight of the Foe," Bleyn announced. "The entire northern wing must be dug in behind those enormous glacial blocks."

"They seem to be mostly Matsu-equipped," Betsy said. "I've noted only two or three blasts of a different color. Possibly Mauser solar-powered. Nothing to match our Weatherbies and Bosches."

"I found the spot," Ookpik said at last. "Perfect. A little higher than I'd like, but what the hell—momentum's momentum. So what if we have to scout a new route up the fall? We can rest in the dump first, maybe give Basil a chance to get down with poor Stan."

"We don't know that this will work," Betsy said grimly. "Let's not plan *too* far ahead, darling."

Ookpik had the monocular to his eye. "Tune in on my optics, everybody. See that sérac shaped like a sideways Coke bottle?"

"What is a Coke bottle?" Aronn asked.

"*That* one," Ookpik clarified. When everyone had identified the key ice-block, the engineer explained what had to be done. They all took up their weapons and aimed carefully at a designated point. "Remember, you two Exalteds," Ookpik told the Tanu, "as we zap 'er, *lift*. We've got to send it tumbling down, and then with any luck the whole lash-up will collapse. Ready? . . ."

Fire.

Three green beams and four blue-white ones lanced out. There was a bloom of steam and pulverized ice. The two psychokinetics exerted their mental power. The sérac shuddered but stood fast.

"Rock it!" yelled Ookpik. "Fire again!"

The photon weapons sang. Bleyn and Aronn stood shoulder to shoulder, their handsome faces distorted by the effort. The cloud halfway up the icefall expanded. A grating sound reached their ears. Aronn cried, "it's going over the edge!" And then the trough of giant ice-blocks seemed to shimmer in the strengthening light. The farsenses of the Tanu locked onto the sight and broadcast it to the gray torcs of the humans. They saw the face of the looming frozen cascade heave and ripple. Blue-and-white masses flew up and outward as if in slow motion, then tumbled end over end with facets gleaming and projections fracturing like cloudy glass. A stupendous roar filled the air. Loose snow, shaken from the tumbling blocks, exploded in great clots, and crystal whirlwinds sparkled at the fringes of the monstrous avalanche.

In the aether, there were inhuman cries.

When it was over, the Gresson Icefall looked very little changed, for one chunk of ice is not very different from another. But the apron of the fall, which had been dirty gray, was now pristine—and extended nearly halfway to the rocks where the climbing party had taken refuge. The Firvulag redoubt was buried beneath at least sixteen meters of icy rubble. The supply dump tents were only buried ten meters deep.

Ookpik looked at the others with a resigned expression. "You win a few, you lose a few. But I guess we'd better start climbing. It's a long way up to Camp 1."

11

Shackled with glass gyves, sullen but resigned, Tony Wayland stood beside Kuhal Earthshaker on the balcony of the Roniah City-Lord's palace and addressed the King's simulacrum, which appeared to be seated cross-legged in the limpid afternoon air just the other side of the balustrade.

"Well, Your Majesty, you have to work the niobium in an argon atmosphere, for starters. That's the biggest part of your problem. As for alloying it with dysprosium, I'm afraid I haven't the foggiest."

"But you could experiment?" Aiken leaned forward anxiously, his hands braced on the knees of his golden pocketsuit.

"Oh, I suppose so." Tony's manner was barely civil. "Given sufficient quantities of the stuff to work with. But you say you don't have any of the pure element. Do you realize how difficult it's going to be extracting the Dy from ores? I mean, even when you manage to coax the yttrium complex out of the crud, you'll have a devil of a time sifting the Dy out in any kind of pure state. I suppose you couldn't substitute some other paramagnetic substance?"

"No," said Aiken. "We have a gadget called an ion concentrator that might help with your refining problem, however."

"It might," Tony snapped. "But the problem's yours, not mine."

Kuhal Earthshaker cuffed the metallurgist lightly, sending him to his knees. "Remember to whom you speak. Lowlife! Your survival hangs by a thread!"

Tony only laughed. His golden torc and relatively fragile psyche would protect him against the more subtle manifestations of mental violence—as he knew very well from his years in Finiah. "Go ahead and beat me!" he sneered. "Fat lot of good I'll be to you if you crock up my cortex!"

Aiken nodded agreement. "It was always friendly persuasion that kept you turning out the barium, wasn't it, Tony?"

"Damn right."

"I want to be your friend, too," said the King winningly. "I won't have Lord Kuhal replace your golden torc with a gray or silver one if you give me your word of honor to work with us in a spirit of goodwill. I'm afraid you'll have to be kept under house arrest for the duration of the project, but that's more for your safety than anything else. You'll have free run of the Castle of Glass outside of working hours and whatever goodies your heart desires. When we get the Guderian device into operation, you can ask for whatever reward you like."

"All I want," said Tony forlornly, "is to go home to my wife in Nionel."

The King unfolded his limbs, stood up and stretched. "You help us make this gimcrack wire that we need, and you could be gazing into her loving eyes by Grand Tourney time."

"Eye," Tony corrected him. "Oh . . . very well. I'll give it my best shot. You have my word."

"Send him out with the convoy tonight," Aiken ordered Kuhal, and vanished.

The Earthshaker steered Tony toward the stairway. "We'll leave the shackles on for safety's sake. They're not too uncomfortable. I wore them myself for a while."

"No shit?" said Tony listlessly. Glass links extended from each wrist to a ring fastened about his torc. The chains were more symbolic than confining; nevertheless, the humiliation quotient was sizable. He brooded as they descended into the lower regions of the palace and made their way to the courtyard, where chalikos waited to take them to the Roniah docks.

"But at least I'm free of that band of Lowlife cutthroats who caught me in the swamp," Tony remarked as he settled into the saddle. "I presume they were showered with the royal favor."

Kuhal said, "The High King was pleased to grant their requests. They asked for free passage back through the time-gate, should it be reopened, and the opportunity to take with them such of their fellows who also yearn to return to Elder Earth."

"Huh!" Tony was contemptuous. "Good riddance, I say."

Kuhal flashed him a sudden smile. "I think the High King shares your sentiment, Creative Brother."

A pang of remembrance went through the metallurgist's heart. Creative Brother... The Tanu in Finiah had called him that, and now this High Table member nonchalantly reaffirmed his adoption. Tony thought: I might be temporarily déclassé, but at least I have great expectations!

"I really meant it when I said I'd cooperate," he said in a low voice.

"I know." Kuhal was entirely amiable now. "And the knowledge gladdens me. I myself am one of those who would pass through the time-gate into the Galactic Milieu."

"You!" Tony cried, incredulous.

"If you do your work well and quickly, many people will owe you gratitude. There are portentous events in the offing that you know not of, and your destiny may be crucial to that of thousands."

Tony was struck dumb. They rode out of the palace grounds and through the Tanu quarter of Roniah. The city was ruled now by Condateyr Fulminator since the death of Bormol in the Great Flood, and the population was somewhat diminished. But for the most part, Roniah had scarcely been touched by the turmoil visited upon so many other parts of the land. Ramas scuttled about delivering packages, sweeping the cobbled streets, and tending the flowerbeds. Fountains tinkled into silver basins in the cool, tree-girt plazas. Roniah was not so baroquely magnificent as the City of Lights had been, but it was splendid enough, with its filigree arches of frost-white marble, its dazzling buildings with their stained-glass windows, and the roofs of gold and blue tile punctuated by lacy spires.

Tony and Kuhal rode down to the esplanade. All around them were the Tanu and human inhabitants of the city, strolling or going about their business in the drowsy afternoon heat.

"I'd forgotten how nice a Tanu city could be," the metallurgist said. "After Finiah fell, the Lowlives had me trapped up north in the Iron Villages. God, it was squalid. I ran away."

"And came to Nionel?" inquired the Earthshaker.

Tony grinned. "Right at Grand Loving time. I never expected to get married. After I was, I couldn't bear to stay, even though I loved Rowane. They'd cut off my silver torc and . . . well, you know. But after I left and got into all sorts of trouble, I realized that I had to be with Rowane again. I just had to. It's very odd, really. We had very little in common. Rowane is a Howler." He projected her astonishing mental image, all softly haloed, and studied the reins of his chaliko. "Strange thing, love. One doesn't pick and choose."

"I understand, Brother. Better than you know."

"I don't suppose—" Tony hesitated, then said, "Would the King consider letting Rowane come to Goriah? If she'll forgive me for deserting her, that is?"

The beautiful, melancholy face of the Tanu was full of regret. "There must be an incentive for great tasks, Brother. The King would say that Rowane is yours. But surely you will communicate freely with her. Through your golden torc, your hearts may meet across the leagues."

"I've tried," Tony said wretchedly. "But I wasn't torced when we were together, and I guess I'm just not up to farspeech on the Firvulag mode. I'm really not very good at it even with our own people at long range."

"Then you might ask help from the Lady Katlinel."

Tony brightened. "Could you let me have her signature?"

"Willingly," said the Tanu. And he projected the image while Tony labored to commit it to memory, vowing to attempt contact with the Lady of Nionel that very night.

In a mood of easy companionship, they rode along the river, where there was a green pleasance with willows and flowering shrubs. Human and exotic women were there with their gold-torced children, and an ancient bareneck wandered about with a hurdy-gurdy and a costumed monkey on a chain. Tony's mouth tightened at the sight of the captive beast, but Kuhal's thought slid into his mind:

Your only true freedom is with your adopted people. Soon the shackles will be removed and everything will be better than before. Only help them build the time-gate generator.

You really must be eager to go!

She will go and I must follow.

Oh. Well it's a funny place the Milieu. But good luck.

They were approaching the main dock area, which was thronged with workers. Carts full of goods and hellad caravans added to the congestion on the quays. The slips were nearly all occupied by pneumatic craft in the process of being off-loaded.

"Supplies for the Grand Tourney," Kuhal explained. "Fortunately, the plantations of the upper Rhône have been spared Firvulag depredation. Perhaps the Little People are shrewder than we know and did not wish to risk a shortage of refreshments at the games."

"So the King's really abolished the Combat, then?"

"There will still be ardent competition, and doubtless some loss of life. But the scoring no longer is based upon heads taken." He sighed. "The Peace Faction are most gratified and have declared their intention to participate. Perhaps the events will not be so tame as some traditionalists fear if Minanonn the Heretic enters the jousts."

They came to a large pier that had been cordoned off from the others. Some twenty large craft were being loaded by gray-torc stevedores rather than ramas. Tanu knights in full glass panoply bearing Milieu weapons stood guard on the boats and near the piles of sealed crates that still remained on the dock. Squads of grays in bronze half-armor patrolled the perimeter, shooing away curious onlookers.

"You will sail down the Rhône, then go overland to Sasaran and the River Baar," Kuhal said. "You may be interested to know that you accompany a cargo that is perhaps the most valuable ever to be shipped from this city. The Lord of Sasaran himself will escort you."

"Oh? Treasure?"

The Earthshaker shook his golden head. "It's better that you do not know. But be assured that you and the cargo are both extremely precious to King Aiken-Lugonn."

Kuhal rode up to a blue-crested captal of the guard and saluted by placing his fist against the counterchanged Janus-face emblem on his rose-gold tunic. "My compliments to the Most Exalted Lord Neyal the Younger, and tell him to come collect his passenger."

"At your service, Exalted Lords," the captal said. "His baggage has already arrived and been put aboard." He helped Tony to dismount and the metallurgist stood there uncertainly.

"Well, I'll say goodbye—" he began.

A loud hail, both vocal and telepathic, rang out from the far end of the pier. Waving a clipboard and bounding toward them broadcasting waves of geniality came Sasaran's City-Lord, helmetless but otherwise attired in sapphire coercer harness all chased with gold and amber zircons. Neyal was so tall and thin that he could only be called gangling. His hair was like wheat stubble.

"Shaker! I meant to see you when the caravan got in, but they put me right to work on these Tana-forsaken boats!"

Neyal exchanged cordialities with his fellow High Tabler, beamed on Tony like the spirit of Harvest, and proffered a gauntleted hand.

Tony took it with some trepidation, but the greeting proved to be discreet.

Kuhal said, "May I present out Creative Brother Wayland-Velkonn, who wears the symbols of Tana's peace only until he is given into the custody of the High King."

Again Tony experienced the feeling of déjà vu. No one had styled him with his honorific of Velkonn since the City of Lights went up in flames so long ago . . . or was it long?

"A year ago today," said Neyal, going somber. "And as some think, the prelude to Nightfall."

Kuhal's opaque blue eyes held warning. "Those who think so should keep their thoughts to themselves."

Neyal shrugged. "Come aboard with us and hoist a jar," he invited Kuhal. But the latter declined, saying he had to hurry back to Castle Gateway.

"I was only summoned to Roniah to act as the King's negotiator in securing the services of Lord Wayland-Velkonn," the Earthshaker said. "With the Truce upon us, I must make sure that the platform for the time-gate is completed inside Castle Gateway before sports fans come north in great numbers for the Tourney. All manner of spies are abroad these days, and the King wants the site secured."

Tony looked surprised. "But surely you'll build the Guderian device outside the castle, where the Milieu side of the warp opened . . ."

Kuhal said, "I would have thought so myself. But the King sent to us one Dimitri Anastos—late of the outlaw cadre called Basil's Bastards. This worthy seems to have spent his days in the Milieu designing upsilon-field equipment, and he presumably knows something about the theory of temporal plication as well. At any rate, he cautioned us that our device would not work unless there was no possibility of interference from the Milieu device. Our gate must debouch into empty air on Elder Earth."

Tony looked wise. "Right. I see. Just as this end has you materializing half a meter or so in midair above the open rocky place fronting Castle Gateway."

"It seems," Kuhal added, "that the tau-field will operate more or less anywhere within the environs of a certain futuristic city in the Rhône Valley. The original machine was even moved about by its inventor. But if one selects a site where the—uh—shipment would materialize inside an obdurate mass of matter, then the Guderian device simply will not work."

"Fail safe," Tony noted. "It would be depressing to emerge from the warp into solid rock. Or even partially embedded in the wall of a French provincial cottage."

Kuhal said, "This Anastos picked out a suitable spot inside Castle Gateway. We're building a platform on it, to take into account the way this region has risen slightly in the six million years between now and then."

"You will be there at the games, won't you, Shaker?" Neyal asked. "Our Sasaran lads are ready to put on a good show at shinty, but we'll need cheering on."

"I'll be there," Kuhal said, "unless our friend, here, does his work very quickly. In which case I have a previous engagement."

Neyal laughed uncomprehendingly. "Well, see you anon. You come right along, Velkonn. We'll be casting off straightaway." He whacked his fist to the nine-pointed star on his cuirass in a farewell salute and beckoned Tony to follow.

"I—I *will* do my best," the metallurgist said again to Kuhal. "Good luck to you and your lady." He turned away and went slowly down the pier, threading his way through bustling porters. Lord Neyal was arguing with a truculent silver foreman, waving his clipboard, and seemed to have forgotten about his passenger. Tony sat on a mysterious crate for a while, unmolested and unremarked. Finally the captal of the guard told him he was to be quartered on the endmost boat, so he ambled on board. The cabin with his baggage was tiny and drab, so he went out into the open stern, which projected out toward the mainstream of the Rhône. The inflated fabric formed a comfortable bench, and it was pleasant to sit in the sun and watch the other river traffic. Lord Neyal's promise of an imminent departure turned out to be a typical Tanu piece of over-optimism. An hour passed, then two. Tony fell asleep.

He woke to an ironic telepathic voice:

Nu if it isn't the prize shlemiel!

He peered groggily about. At first he saw nothing but the broad river, streaked with maroon and ochre from the sunset, and the twinkling lamps along the curving esplanade, and the big torchères flaming in the twilight at the head of the pier.

Eh! Out on the water shmuck! Upstream eighty meters.

Tony strained to focus his farsense. His eyes made out a dark narrow blob, some kind of rivercraft. His mind-sight, still muzzy from sleep, sorted out a rough-hewn figure leaning on the gunwale and watching him.

Tony said: Chief Burke.

Burke said: The same. I thought you'd be sold down the river by now.

Tony said coolly: Any hour now. This bunch is about as efficient as you Lowlives.

Burke said: Touché bubi. But you don't have anything to worry about you know. I made sure Aiken Drum would treat you right before I even agreed to bring you into Roniah. Not that I could tell the rest of my people that.

Tony said: I hope you held out for more than a string of wampum and a return ticket to Utopia Limited in exchange for me.

Burke said: We also got this powerboat plus all the weaponry we could carry. Now we're on our way to Nionel where the rest of our Hidden Springs folks have gone to escape Firvulag raiders.

Tony said: *Nionel*?

Burke said: Not many Lowlives left in the Vosges. Or anywhere else in the Firvulag stamping grounds. Nionel is about our only alternative to joining up with Aiken Drum . . . until the time-gate reopens.

Tony said: Well ta-ta and don't bother to write.

Burke said: No hard feelings?

Tony said: Number 10 on Moh's Scale will suffice.

Burke said: Nasty nasty. And I was trying to be Kemosabe.

Tony said: Burke . . . my wife's in Nionel. I left her. I was an ass. I'll try to contact her but if anything happens will you tell her I'll try to come back somehow? This is what she looks like [Image.] Her name is Rowane.

Burke said: I'll tell her. She looks like a sweetminded little lady. Shalom bubi. Keep out of trouble for a change.

Tony didn't bother to answer. He sat with his head down and the world blotted out, sequestered in the golden solitude of his torc. Two more hours passed. Lord Neyal's minions, having finally finished the loading, were now obliged to hunt out the riverboat crews among the taverns and knocking shops of the waterfront. The guard on the pier was assiduously maintained.

Tony was roused from his reverie when something sharp jabbed him in the breastbone. He opened his eyes with an indignant squawk and saw a heavy-set man dressed in outlaw rags at the other end of an iron-tipped lance.

"Keep your trap shut, Lowlife," came a harsh whisper. "If you move or farspeak, I'll skewer you like a broiled lark."

Some kind of rude boarding ladder had been hooked over the stern. The ruffian climbed up and was immediately followed by a dozen or so comrades. Two had Matsu carbines and the rest carried iron weapons.

"How many people on this tub?" inquired the leading rascal.

"I didn't see anyone but the knight guarding the gangplank," Tony replied. The spear shifted to his Adam's apple and began to prick. "For God's sake believe me! I'm only a bloody passenger. A prisoner!" He held up the glass chains. "Most of the soldiers were out on the dock when I came aboard. That was hours ago."

"Search the boat," ordered the spearman.

There were soft splashes out among the other moored vessels. The moon was not yet up and the Rhône, swatched in mist, was nearly pitch-black just a few meters off the sternrail. Sounds of music and jollity arose from the region beyond the cordon, and Roniah's faerie lights were all turned on, spangling the buildings with amber and blue. It seemed likely that the city was prematurely celebrating the Truce, and the departure of the convoy had been postponed in spite of royal orders to the contrary.

Most of the boarding party had gone off to investigate the inner reaches of Tony's boat. "You're making a big mistake, you know," he hissed urgently. "You Lowlives don't have to steal from the Tanu cities any more. There's an amnesty. I suppose you're after weapons."

"Smart little nipper, isn't he, Pingol?" observed a hulking villain armed with a zapper.

"Too damn smart." The iron lance drew a gentle semicircle from one of Tony's ears to the other, snicking his golden torc en route. "On the other hand, his metapsychic powers are pretty pitiful, as any fool can plainly see, and he's a fucking coward to boot. So why is he wearing gold? To say nothing of the Goddess's holy fetters?"

The tall Matsu carrier leaned forward, face nearly concealed by a great mop of greasy dark hair. The outlaw's breath made Tony reel. "What's your name, squeak-poop?"

"I'm Lord Velkonn!"

The lance tip hovered in front of Tony's left eyeball and the spearman spoke in tones of silken menace. "Your *human* name."

The words tumbled from Tony's lips. "Tony Wayland. But you shouldn't be doing this, I tell you! Chief Burke got a load of arms in exchange for me. He's off to take them to your people in Nionel. If you carry out this raid, the King might be so pissed that he cancels your amnesty! As for me, they'll never get the Guderian device built without any help, and if you harm me, your Lowlife mates who want to return to the Milieu will have your sweetbreads on toast!"

The tall invader drew back and exclaimed, "Tony Wayland?!"

"Té in a tapdance, what're you all shat up over?" the spear-man growled to his companion. "Let's snuff this bloodless turnip and—"

One of the outlaws who had gone forward came dashing to report. "Captain Pingol! Captain Fouletot! Great tidings. There was but a lone Tanu knight guarding the vessel within, and she succumbed to our blood-metal. The other vessels at this pier seem to be similarly neglected, although there are nu-merous grays patrolling the esplanade. Shall I signal the other boarding parties?"

"Deliver the command in person," said the spearman. "No farspeech, lest the Foe overhear." His features now shone with a foxfire luminosity and there was something curiously insub-stantial about his form.

Tony took a shuddering breath. "You aren't Lowlives!"

The pair chuckled in malevolent unison.

The dwarfish bearer of good news added gleefully, "We opened a crate in the cargo compartment. Praise be to Té, it was as our spies foretold! The crate was full of Milieu weap-ons!"

"Advise the Lord Betularn White Hand at once," said the spearman. He and his compeer were changing before Tony's horrified eyes, throwing off their Lowlife disguise and resum-ing their natural shapes. One was a gnome and the other a female ogre. Both wore the obsidian mail of officers in the battle-company of King Sharn and Queen Ayfa.

"And also tell Betularn that we have in our power the in-famous Tony Wayland," said the ogress Fouletot, "the same who murdered the Dreadful Skathe, my valiant kinswoman, and the hero Karbree the Worm."

The messenger saluted and clambered back over the stern, to disappear in darkness.

"What are you going to do with me?" Tony asked faintly.

"Trade you to King Aiken-Lugonn for our sacred Sword," Pingol replied with a leer. "Eventually."

12

"HAPPY NAMEDAY! HAPPY NAMEDAY! SLITSAL TO YOUNG Smudger!"

The great hall in High Vrazel rocked with applause as the seventeen-year-old eldest son of the Firvulag royal couple was led onto the dais by his Sponsor-Brother, the hero Medor. To mark his promotion from the estate of infant to that of youth, the child was outfitted in a miniature suit of glittering jet armor, adorned with green crystalline spikes and knobs. His helmet was crested with an emerald wart-biter with wings aggressively spread. He peeped from the open visor rather apprehensively as the tumult died down and the mob strained forward in anticipation of his First Manifestation.

"Doesn't he look wonderful?" Ayfa whispered to her husband, wiping away a tear. They were concealed behind a stalagmite so that the sight of them in their regal paraphernalia would not increase the child's nervousness. "Our firstborn! And what a marvelous present for *all* of us on his Nameday . . ."

"Hush," said the King. "Medor's beginning."

"Battle-companions, stalwart youths, and infants!" declaimed the hero. "We gather here tonight to celebrate the passage by ordeal of one of our number from the state of noncombatant dependency into the ranks of Warrior Youth! Here he takes his first step along our sacred Way—the path to glory commanded by our Goddess of Battles from time immemorial. As all fighting candidates do, he will find the Way an arduous one. He will spend his young strength in mind-bending study and martial-arts training. He will serve his elders with a humble and loyal heart. He will carry out the commands of his Sponsor-Brother even to laying down his life . . . so that in Té's good time he may himself be admitted to the Battle-Company of the Firvulag Nation!"

The crowd howled the ritual query: "Who is he? Who is he?"

Medor's towering black form and the lad's small one stood with hands linked. "I knew him from his cradle days—as I knew his father and his father's father before him. We have seen him at play with his brothers and sisters in the coverts and byways of High Vrazel. Of late, we have welcomed him to feasts and ceremonies. Some of us have been his teachers and ordeal coaches. Others have admonished him when infantile high spirits temporarily distracted him from his duties."

The other children in the hall giggled. The adults clamored: "Who is he?"

"For six years we have called him by his baby name, Smudger. But tonight he sets that aside forever, along with the other insignia of infant dependency, and takes on his one, true name." Medor stepped behind the boy and placed his hands on the small shoulders. "With confidence and love, I call him: *Sharn-Ador! Stand forth and manifest!*"

"Here it comes," Ayfa whispered tremulously. "O Goddess, don't let him muff it."

Medor drew back, leaving the armored boy alone at the front of the platform. Sharn-Ador lifted his hands high and began to shine with a pulsating green light. His body lost its humanoid form and shape-shifted into the aspect of a trans-lucent emerald locust with rainbow-tinted wings and fierce, clashing mandibles. He grew until he was quite as tall as the ogre behind him.

The crowd roared: "Sharn-Ador! Slitsal! Slitsal! Slitsal!" And then they fell silent as the psychoamplified voice of the boy echoed through the cave.

"I stand before you as a youth. And to thank you for your acclaim, I have the honor to announce a great triumph of our Battle-Company! The hero Betularn of the White Hand and his deputies, Fouletot Blackbreast, Pingol the Horripilant, and Monolokee the Scunnersome have won a signal victory in the Foe's city of Roniah!"

The audience gasped, then broke into a bedlam of shouts and cheers. The illusory grasshopper bounded exuberantly up and down, up and down, barely dodging the captive banners and gilded skulls that dripped from the multicolored rock formations of the cavern roof. "We beat em! We beat 'em!" the shape-shifted lad chirped. Then he settled back onto the dais, recouped his dignity, and announced: "Not one hour ago, our warriors attacked a superior force of bloodthirsty Tanu knights and destroyed them utterly! And loot—! I mean, the spoils of victory included a whacking big collection of crazy future weapons!" Joyous bellows greeted this, but the child persisted: "Wait, wait, that's not all! We also put the snatch on that turdling butcher Tony Wayland! Right this minute, Fouletot and Pingol are getting ready to zorch off the brute's arms and legs and make him eat his own barbecued privities!"

Aaaaah! exulted the vengeful minds of the mob.

The child reassumed his own natural form and bowed modestly. "And I don't mind saying, I don't think anyone ever had such a terrific Nameday as me."

"Slitsal, Sharn-Ador! Slitsal! Slitsal!"

"My baby!" cried Ayfa, going all misty-eyed.

But the King had gripped her arm suddenly. "Great Goddess!" he barked. "Look there!"

The plaudits of the crowd gave way to expressions of stupefaction. Young Sharn-Ador stood transfixed with dismay, staring toward the unoccupied twin thrones at the rear of the dais, before which a patch of scintillating golden fog now coalesced.

In the midst of it stood a small figure in a suit all covered with pockets. A jeweled baldric and powerpack harness was fastened about his shoulders and waist, and he had a great diamond-bladed Sword in one hand. With the other he beckoned to the paralyzed child.

"I've got one more present for you, kid."

Sharn, Ayfa, and Medor rushed out onto the platform, weapons raised and minds roaring fury. Serrated obsidian blades smote the golden manikin—only to pass through thin air and clang upon the flags of the platform, cutting the carpet to ribbons. Aiken stood unharmed.

"Idiots," he said. "I'm a mental projection."

The two monarchs and their Great Captain fell back in confusion. The spectators were mute and motionless. Little Sharn-Ador piped up: "*What* present?"

Aiken brandished the Sword.

Oooooh, crooned the monster horde.

Aiken said, "I want Tony Wayland and you want the Sword. You can do business—but only if Wayland is completely unharmed. You'd better farspeak your flunkies in Roniah and see to it."

King Sharn glowered, but his mind was simultaneously communicating on the intimate mode.

Queen Ayfa said, "It may be true that the murderer Tony Wayland is now in our custody. If so, we will consider turning him over to you in exchange for our sacred Sword."

"*And* the ten boatloads of weapons you managed to get away with," Aiken demanded, "before the patrols and Lord Neyal's stalwarts got their asses in gear and chased your gang of sneak thieves across the river."

"We know nothing about any boats or weapons," said Ayfa blandly. "We have heard that Roniah was attacked tonight by Lowlives. But the Firvulag Nation holds to the Armistice, as always."

"So that's the line you're going to take, is it?" Aiken's simulacrum twirled the heavy Sword, filling the mountain hall with dancing prismatic lights.

"That's it, Aik," Sharn said. "You want Wayland, he's yours. You fly the Sword personally to Betularn tomorrow, the first day of the Truce. He'll meet you on the Northern Track two leagues above Roniah. He's leading a peaceful exploration party in the Hercynian Forest at the moment. That's where Wayland was captured."

"Tony told Katlinel the Darkeyed another story," Aiken said.

"Lowlives are such liars," said the Firvulag King.

Ayfa said, "We only deal on a no-questions-asked basis. Wayland for the Sword. Take it or leave it."

"Oh, I'll take it," said the little man. "Tomorrow then. Around sunset. And no tricks, or you'll regret it."

Ayfa's face assumed an expression of cynical solicitude. "Are you quite sure you feel up to flying all the way from Goriah with that heavy Sword? We wouldn't want you to strain yourself, dear."

"Your concern is touching," Aiken replied earnestly. "But I guess if I can sustain an astral projection through a kilom and a half of solid rock, I'll be able to muddle through on the flit. See you all at the Grand Tourney." The golden figure began to shimmer, then abruptly resolidified, strode over to young Sharn-Ador, and tapped him briefly on each pauldron with the flat of the Sword. "Almost forgot. I hereby dub thee an honorary Tanu knight. Stride boldly, Lord Ador the Wart-Biter! Come and see me sometime, kid—and happy Nameday."

With that, the Tanu King disappeared.

The assembly of Firvulag all began to shout at once, some in triumph, some in indignation at the brazen behavior of the regal Foe. The child in armor turned to his parents with a shining face.

"Father! Mums! Did you see what he did?"

Ayfa and Sharn's eyes met above their son's head. "We saw," said the King bleakly. He knelt down, grasped the child, and exclaimed: "You will repudiate the base accolade! Aiken Drum is the Foe, destined to fall before my sacred Sword in the Nightfall War, and you are a warrior youth, not to be distracted from our glorious Way by idle gestures! Do you understand? Say that you repudiate him!"

"I do," cried the child. "I do." And he turned and ran from the dais with his visor down to hide his woe.

VEIKKO: Walter! Walter!

WALTER: . . . Oh, son. Are you all right? I tried to farspeak you earlier but there was no reply, and I was so worried.

VEIKKO: We had a lot going on around here to keep us busy. The Famorel Firvulag attacked Camp Bettaforca around 1900 hours. Another bunch of them ambushed the climbing team this morning. One of the climbers was killed but the others are all right. They've rendezvoused with Basil in Camp 1 and plan to start out for the summit at first light.

WALTER: Never mind them! How are you and Irena? Your thoughts are so weak—

VEIKKO: Well, it's nearly dawn here and Old Sol is starting to hash me out. But I'm fine and so is Rena.

WALTER: Thank God. Tell me about it.

VEIKKO: [Event replay.] It was only bad at the start of their attack, when they were using the tight metaconcert to shield themselves and direct the psychoenergetic blasts. The elite golds and the Tanu knights got the worst of that. Four humans and one exotic killed. But then the spooks let mental discipline slip and went one on one. Our people mowed them down like sawgrass in a hurricane with the heavy blasters once they let the multiple mind-screen slip. None of us kids was even singed. The action was over at least two hours ago, but I was feeling a bit rocky—reacting to the violence, I guess. It's taken me this long to pull myself together so I could bespeak you. I'm sorry you were worried.

WALTER: It's all right. Just so you're safe.

VEIKKO: We must have killed 60 or 70 Firvulag. The rest just ran away.

WALTER: Any chance of further attacks?

VEIKKO: Our Tanu leader, Ochal, says the Firvulag won't fight now that their Truce has begun. We'll be safe from here on in, I think.

WALTER: Wonderful.

VEIKKO: . . . Daddy? Did you do it?

WALTER: Yes. Alex Manion and I wrecked every one. We took Boom-Boom's cutting torch from the shop and burned the EM pulsars to slag. Melted down the spare parts, too. You can tell the Little King that he won't have to worry about being attacked with X-lasers. I just wish we could have got the rest of the weapons. But they're stored too near the CE rig's hold. Too many sensors about.

VEIKKO: Did—did Marc find out yet?

WALTER: Don't worry about it, son. I broke Kyllikki's autopilot after we finished the job on the zappers. There's a whole chain of storms brewing along our path. Marc's not about to kill me and chance having the ship sink. Not with the CE rig's powerplant on board.

VEIKKO: Marc could do worse than kill you. I still remember how he turned Hagen into a fish and played him!

WALTER: He didn't really.

VEIKKO: So it was an illusion. But Hag still has the scar on his mouth from the barb. Psychosomatic. That's even *worse*.

WALTER: You said that the climbing party is ready to leave Camp 1. How long before they can reach the aircraft?

VEIKKO: If everything goes well, about three days. I'll keep you posted. Now . . . tell the others the great news . . . when I think of the risk . . . worry . . . how you . . .

WALTER: You're skipping out, son. Catch you later. I'm gone.

Walter Saastamoinen let his eyes come back into focus and flick momentarily to the wind-trend readout, then to the marine scanner. Ominous high cirrus clouds streaked the northern horizon, but otherwise it was a beautiful sunny morning on the North Atlantic.

"Congratulations on the survival of your son," Marc said.

Walter nodded. "I don't suppose you happened to d-jump in on the little scene and help the kids out?"

"The base camp was adequately defended. They didn't require my assistance. Earlier, I did help to precipitate an avalanche down around the ears of the other Firvulag force—the one menacing the climbing party."

"That was kind of you. I wonder why you bother, though?"

"It takes guts to tackle that mountain. I have a certain admiration for those with unmitigated gall."

Walter smiled, watching the sea. "Is that why you let me live?"

Marc did not reply.

"But you made an example of me, nonetheless. I'm curious. Is there a reason why you chose . . . this particular form of discipline?"

"We're on shipboard," Marc said, "and I was reminded somehow of the tale of the Little Mermaid. She insisted upon abandoning her own kind and paid a severe price for it—as you have. The mermaid wanted legs rather than her fish's tail, and her wish was granted. But whenever she walked, it seemed to her that she trod upon invisible knives."

The bridge door opened and Steve Vanier came in. "Eight bells and all's well! I relieve you at the helm, skipper. How're you, Marc? Ready to take one of us along with you on the jump?"

"Not quite yet, Steve. I want to minimize the risk factor."

Vanier was studying the instrumentation. He frowned. "I see George is down again."

Walter said, "I'm afraid so, Steve. Just maintain course on manual."

"Aye-aye, sir."

Marc said, "Would you like me to give you a hand to your cabin, Walter?"

"Appreciate it," Kyllikki's master said. Leaning heavily on Marc, he limped toward the door. He was wearing only heavy woolen socks on his feet, and he left a trail of dark stains on the deck behind him.

At Vanier's horrified exclamation, he grinned and said, "Bit by a goddam mermaid. Wake me if the wind tops thirty knots, and don't bother asking Arne-Rolf to try fixing the autopilot. When I break a thing, it stays broken."

13

ANOTHER STORM STRUCK MONTE ROSA ON THE THIRD DAY OF the principal assault. Fortunately, the climbers had been given ample warning of its approach by Elizabeth, who tracked them almost constantly with her farsight. Led by Basil, the seven-man party pushed off from Camp 2 before dawn and moved up the spur of Middle Tine in deceptively perfect weather. Aside from the altitude sickness that had begun to afflict both Tanu, the trek was uneventful. The climbers traversed the upper Bettaforca Glacier as awesome cumulonimbus clouds reared above the alabaster Breithorn to the west. Static electricity charged the air, making the scalp crawl and the torc sing odd, buzzing melodies as a counterpoint to the tympanic rumbles of the approaching storm.

No sooner had they settled into the two decamole huts of Camp 3 than a titanic lightning bolt, pink in the gathering murk, blasted Monte Rosa's summit. The polycell structure of the decamole was an excellent insulator—a fact they gave thanks for during the next hour or so, when a pyrotechnic display of stunning violence seemed to shake the massif to its roots. Then hail rattled down, followed by thick snow, and the wind howled up a hurricane.

But Camp 3 was nestled snugly in the lee of a rock cleaver at 7039 meters, and the seven people inside were safe and warm. Farspoken reassurances from Ochal the Harper at base camp told them that Taffy Evans and Magnus had finally brought Stan and Phronsie to safety. The reduction in altitude had eased Stan's edema, and Magnus seemed confident that the former starfleet officer would recover in time to pilot a flyer back to Goriah. Phronsie's frostbitten feet were responding to treatment. Dr. Thongsa's body had been retrieved and interred in a rock cairn. The assault party was encouraged to proceed with all dispatch, since even the pickled slugs were running low in Camp Bettaforca's commissary.

Late that night, when the storm had nearly blown itself out, Elizabeth bespoke Bleyn the Champion in Camp 3.

ELIZABETH: Do you hear, Bleyn?

BLEYN: Yes, Elizabeth. I was not asleep, nor is Aronn. But the humans fill the second hut with their snores so as to drown out even the roar of the tempest.

ELIZABETH: [Mind-smile.] They are well, then?

BLEYN: Basil is a prodigy of strength. Ookpik, Bengt, and Nazir are weary but fit. The one called Mr. Betsy complains vociferously at every opportunity but seems second only to Basil in stamina.

ELIZABETH: And you Tanu?

BLEYN: [Malaise.] Both Aronn and I suffer greatly from headache, shortness of breath, and muscle weakness. Basil thinks our large exotic bodies have not acclimatized to the high altitude as readily as those of the humans. We are trying to consume additional fluids and redact one another through the night.

ELIZABETH: [Concern.] Wouldn't sleep be more therapeutic?

BLEYN: You know that we Tanu naturally require less sleep than your race. We are far more comfortable awake, when we can maintain our respiration at a higher rate and alleviate the effects of anoxia.

ELIZABETH: Well . . . be careful. I understand that mountain sickness can afflict the strong as well as the less rugged among humans. This is doubtless true among Tanu as well.

BLEYN: Tomorrow we reach the high point of our journey. We will endure . . . Do you have the route selected for us? I have the chart ready to mark.

ELIZABETH: [Image.] It seems that the snowy ridge above Camp 3 still provides your best access to the Col. After the storm the snow will be deeper and you can expect soft and slow going. Tell Basil there are dangerous cornices that have formed within the saddle of the Col, so he can no longer count upon using that route. You'll have to traverse the hard-frozen snowfield at the foot of Rosa's West Face. It means an additional climb, I'm afraid, but only about 400 meters total gain.

BLEYN: To 8210! Goddess sustain us. The breath burns in my lungs at the very thought.

ELIZABETH: But from then on, it's downhill all the way—and in good weather. You should have clear blue skies for at least three days.

BLEYN: Tana willing, there is a good chance we may even reach the aircraft tomorrow. Did the storms bury them?

ELIZABETH: They're still quite visible. Only slightly hidden in drifts.

BLEYN: Something hidden. Go and find it. Something lost behind the Ranges . . . [laughter].

ELIZABETH: [Anxiety.]

BLEYN: No—It's only a silly poem that Basil quoted to us, a human glorification of adventures such as this one. I find the poem, and the attitude it celebrates incomprehensible. Yet of the five humans in our party, only Mr. Betsy had the good sense to despise and abominate our travels through this terrible place. The others are thrilled at the prospect of the mountain's conquest! . . . Tell me, Elizabeth. Is it true that in your future world, humans climb peaks such as this purely for sport?

ELIZABETH: Quite true.

BLEYN: How will we ever understand your race!

ELIZABETH: If I told you, you would never believe it.

In the morning, Bleyn and Aronn felt better. Basil decided to revert to the original climbing configuration of two parties. He, Betsy, and Bleyn led the way, with Ookpik, Bengt, Nazir, and Aronn following some fifteen minutes behind. The snow on the ridge was knee-keep, and very soft after the early morning sun went to work on it. Basil's team plowed ahead breaking trail for three tedious hours; then Ookpik's group had their turn. In some places, the humans floundered nearly waist-deep, but it was the long-legged Tanu who seemed most depleted by the effort. Aronn, especially, had gone ashen-faced and sluggish. He seemed confused by Ookpik's simplest orders and found it difficult to keep up the modest pace set by the humans in the team.

By noon the climbers had nearly attained the elevation of the West Col. Basil decreed a lunch halt in a sheltered snow hollow.

"Do you see that foggy glitter ahead?" He pointed up the slope. "It's wind, blowing through the Col, and it means the end of this beastly soft stuff. However, I'm afraid we'll have to—er—lean into it a bit crossing the snowfield on the upper slope. The traverse will be short, but possibly rather grim, until we get down onto the northern flank and out of the venturi-effect wind. What we need now is good hot food, and plenty to drink. Soup and sweet tea. Dehydration is one of our deadliest enemies now. It aggravates the fatigue and hypothermia and mountain sickness and other stresses on our bodies."

"The worst stress I suffer is when I look into a mirror," Mr. Betsy complained. "My poor nose and cheeks are sunburned to a frazzle!"

Ookpik thrust a portable stove and a large decamole pot at him. "Go melt snow and spare us the bitching and I'll let you have some of my rhinoceros lard. It's only a little rancid."

"Ugh!" cried Betsy and flounced off.

Basil beckoned to Bleyn and led him apart from the others. "I'm quite worried about Aronn. His condition seems to be deteriorating."

"I have noted it." The Champion's eyes turned to his Guild Brother, who sat apathetically in front of an infrared heating unit, holding an untasted chocolate bar in one mittened hand.

"We'll have to go roped on the slope," Basil said. "There may be some steep pitches of ice and the wind will be severe. I'm afraid it's out of the question for Aronn to continue as tailman to Ookpik's team. If he should fall, his great weight would tear the other three loose. They would slide down the slick chute into the lap of the Col, perhaps more than a thousand meters."

"Very likely," said the Tanu.

"I have seen other climbers with Aronn's symptoms," Basil went on. "I must tell you that there is a chance of your friend becoming irrational. He could panic, even become madly euphoric and decide to throw away his ice axe, or go dancing about the slope. Will you be able to control him through your golden torc?"

"I can coerce him, certainly. But Aronn is a stalwart psychokinetic, and if he becomes crazed he may override my compulsion. When persons of my race suffer mental disorder, it is redaction and not coercion that they require—and my brain, impelled by self-preservation, concentrates this faculty willy-nilly to my own benefit. There is another problem. Even though I am normally Aronn's coercive superior, his powers may at times exceed my own when he is stimulated by aberrant mental impulses."

Basil said, "We cannot leave Aronn here and we cannot turn back. Once we get across the Col, we can put him into a decamole sledge for the downhill slog. But somehow, he's going to have to make it across the snowfield. I propose that we transfer Betsy to Ookpik's rope. You and I will be Aronn's ropemates. We will lead the way, and I will provide—uh—bombproof belays all the way."

"Aronn weighs nearly one hundred eighty of your kilos. Would this not put you at considerable hazard? I myself am greatly weakened. I do not think I could sustain Aronn with my psychokinesis. It would have to be done physically."

"We could put him between us—"

"And if all three of us should fall," Bleyn said starkly, "who will lead the others to the aircraft? Ookpik, I will remind you, is not nearly so experienced in alpine mountaineering as was the late Thongsa. My orders from the King command me to retrieve the aircraft at any cost."

"We will not abandon Aronn." Basil was firm.

"No," Bleyn agreed softly. "But *you* will lead the others in a five-man team, and I and my Guild Brother will follow, roped together. We will trust in Tana to sustain us. If we fall, it is her will."

Basil said, "If you fall, we humans will come to the aircraft with no Tanu overlord to compel us! How do you know we won't abscond with a ship and fly to freedom? Neither you nor the King could coerce us at long distance."

"There is no need to coerce you. I have said that humans are impossible to understand—but I was wrong. I understand you well enough, Basil, to know that you will do as you have promised, whether or not Aronn or I survive."

The don gave a diffident nod. "That's all right, then. Shall we get on with it?"

The wind screamed. Its chill factor, Basil estimated, was probably better than minus sixty Celsius. He felt his face congealing inside the rime-coated fur ruff of his anorak hood. His fingers grew more and more numb with the cutting of each step in the tough white ice. He sank an ice screw, made fast, and said: Belay on! Climb away.

Ookpik said: Climbing. He scuttled quickly across the freshly cut foothold, then anchored himself in turn. Meanwhile Basil was chopping, chopping, cramponing along, with Ookpik belayed and braced against a possible fall of the leader. As the line of slots extended across the steep slope, Bengt followed on the rope, then Nazir, then Betsy; and ten meters or so in the rear and dropping farther and farther behind came the two Tanu.

Basil swung his axe in time to the rhythm of his laboring heart. His lungs strained to extract oxygen from the thin, frigid air and the pain drove him to greater effort. Faster. He worked out to the end of the rope that Ookpik had secured, chopping ice with as much speed as he dared; for speed was the only thing that would bring them out of the screaming wind that was freezing them slowly to death. Basil knew it and Bleyn the Champion knew it. The others were too weak and miserable to care.

Basil said: How Aronn doing Bleyn?

Bleyn said: Weak very weak halfstupefied but no mania Tanabethanked he responds my coercion.

Basil said: We angling down now. Steep steep pitch but near end perhaps 200 meters farther to safe shelf. *Do you all hear?* Not far now!

A few minds responded with formless transmissions.

The wind screamed.

Basil cut steps.

The line of five small figures and two larger ones now slanted downhill on the shining white slope above the Col. The air was brilliantly clear. No cloud marred the azure sky. High above them, Monte Rosa formed a monolith of heart-wrenching purity. Almost all of her western face had been freshly plastered with snow by the late storm and she stood pristine.

A virgin mountain! Basil thought. The virgin queen of mountains, perhaps the highest Earth has ever borne. You will be mine. You will.

He cut steps.

Suddenly they were again in a region of swirling light snow, approaching a rock wall topped by a curling snow cornice. The wind scream diminished to a howl, to a moan, to a sob. Basil took a final step off the perilous forty-five-degree slope onto crunchy level ice, thinly snow-clad. The cornice overhung him and looked as solid as white plascrete. Gray rocks coated with transparent ice jutted from its base. By moving a couple of meters farther on, Basil was able to see around the shoulder of the outcropping down the North Face of the mountain.

The Inner Helvetides, the Pliocene Alps, fell away in serrated waves to the horizon. From here, they would go down.

He said: Belay on! Come across! We've made it chaps!

There were feebly jubilant mind-shouts from the humans. Ookpik appeared out of the sparkling surface blizzard, and then Bengt, grinning broadly. Nazir moved with agonized care to safety, breathing a prayer of thanks to Allah. Then there was Betsy, whacking sturdily at the final step with his axe to improve the crumbling foothold.

Basil called: Bleyn?

I am here.

Basil said: Come along. Can't be 10 meters.

Bleyn said: I regret most deeply.

Through their torcs the humans saw an image. A great body half kneeling on a slanted, glaring whiteness. Cramponed feet wedged insecurely into two small holes. Arms stretched overhead gripping the shafts of implanted ice axe and sharpnose hammer. From the belt of the harness a taut rope. At its end, five meters below, another form supine on the ice-slick, sliding lower centimeter by centimeter as the sustaining hands of the man above slipped from the shafts of his tools.

Basil cried: Mindstogetherall! COME BLEYN. HOLD.

They all wished it, compelled it: COME BLEYN. HOLD.

Bleyn's flexed knees stiffened against gravity, against the pull of Aronn's dead weight. His nerveless hands gripped the tool shafts. He forced himself up.

COME BLEYN. HOLD. HOLD.

Slowly, one arm bent, wrenching the poorly anchored axe free. *Chink!* Bleyn swung, reembedding the pick. He held.

Basil said: Wraprock Ookpik belayme *strong*. HOLD BLEYN I COME.

The others said: HOLD BLEYN HOLD.

Ookpik said: Belayrockfast. Gogogo.

Basil said: Climbing climbing. HOLD BLEYN.

Bleyn said: I regret most deeply. I cannot hold.

Ookpik said: Gotem Basil gotem? Fast? HOLDHOLD-HOLD ...

Bleyn fell.

Basil screamed: *Holdholdhold!*

He fell.

The three bodies hurtled down the ice, gathering momentum, then arrested with a crashing jar as they came to the end of Basil's firmly clipped rope. The don lifted his bruised head and grinned up at Ookpik. "They both seem to be unconscious," he called, "but I've got them quite securely."

"And I've got your rope fast to the winch cable," said Mr. Betsy in triumph. "Ready to haul whenever you are, darling."

Basil said: O God *now* you fucking idiot!

"Tsk tsk," Betsy chided, switching the mechanism on.

After they had rested and recovered a little, they began the descent. It was cautious at first, with the two Tanu lashed to sledges. But then they found a broad avalanche runnel that had already dumped, and Basil said: "All aboard for the short cut!" He showed the others what to do, each man according to his expertise, and sent them skidding and otter-sliding and tobogganing down more than a thousand meters of slope, whooping and screeching. And when they were safe he came down himself in a rooster-tailing glissade, schussbooming on the soles of his boots and broadcasting a great mind-roar of joy into the aether that reached not only Elizabeth and their colleagues on

the other side of the mountain, but even the King in faraway
Goriah.

And Aiken said: Well done.

After a long interval, Basil said (this time via Elizabeth's
relay): Thank you sir.

Aiken said: I understand that Bleyn and Aronn had to be
carried down.

Basil said: They are recovering inside one of the reactivated
aircraft High King. Its environmental system is providing sea-
level oxygen concentration. They should be fully restored within
a day or two.

Aiken said: Good good. So you lit up a flyer without much
trouble?

Basil said: Several are easily accessible. Their powerplants
must be recharged with distilled water of course and there will
be labor involved in freeing some of them from the snowdrifts.
No serious problems are foreseen.

Aiken said: Kaleidoscopic! It's all right then . . .

Basil said: Yes.

Aiken said: Name your gratuity.

Basil said: One day's rest. Then while the others get on
with the ferrying and reactivation I wish to climb to the summit
of Monte Rosa. Alone. If I have not returned after three days
you will assume that I have perished in the attempt. No one
must risk his life or these aircraft in futile rescue maneuvers.
This is the only personal request I make of you.

Aiken said: It is granted.

Phronsie Gillis set aside her book-plaque of *Grey Lensman*
and stared out of the flight-deck port of Old Number One at
the thickening blizzard. "Sweet chariot, just look at that snow.
If it's coming down like this on top of the mountain, poor
Basil's quickfrozen by now. He hasn't got a Chinaman's
chance."

Miss Wang looked up from her fêng-huang embroidery and
said plaintively, "I wish you would use less offensive meta-
phors."

"Honey," Phronsie retorted, "I got insults for every race,
ethnic group, religious faith, and sexual orientation. Nothin'
personal."

Miss Wang hung her head and sniffled. "Basil was a good leader. I shall miss him."

"We all will," said Stan Dziekonski. He slapped his cards on the navigator's tank. "Gin."

The three other cardplayers tossed in their hands gloomily. "Can't you catch anything with your farsight?" Ookpik demanded of Bleyn.

The Champion shook his great blond head. "It's the storm. If Elizabeth is frustrated in her attempts to locate Basil, how shall I hope to succeed? And there is no response to our telepathic calls."

"We have already waited longer than the specified time," Ochal the Harper told them. "We'll have to go."

"Damn the specified time!" Phronsie shouted, whacking the console of Old Number One with her book. "You go off with Stan and Ooky in Number Two, Lord Harper, and let us hang on here another day. Bleyn won't mind—will you, Champ?"

Bleyn said, "Both ships must go, Phronsie. We are the last, and it was Basil himself who laid down the conditions."

"He did," said Miss Wang in a small miserable voice. She wiped her nose on her sleeve, took the pilot's seat, and began the preflight very slowly. "Phronsie, please take the power readouts."

There was a collective exhalation of breath from the others. Stan said, "Well, guess Ooky and Lord Harper and I better slog back to Two."

"Yes," said Bleyn. "See you in Goriah."

The departing trio pulled up hoods, zipped anoraks, and stuffed their hands into mittens. They shuffled back to the belly hatch. When Miss Wang cracked it open, the blizzard moaned a dirge.

"Rho-field generators looking good," said Phronsie. "Environmentals go. Hatch secure."

Miss Wang stifled a sob. "R-power to the external web. Wings back full. Ready for lift."

Phronsie spoke into the RF com. "You guys safe in Two, come back?"

"Affirm," said Ookpik. "And Harper did another scan while we were outside. Zip to the nth. But Basil's where he wanted to be."

"Damn muffer could have planned it that way," Phronsie growled. "It wouldn't surprise me one little bit . . . Oh, for God's sake, get us out of here, Wang!"

On the pinnacle of Monte Rosa, Basil sat secure in his snow cave until the hurricane roar of the wind died away. Then he plied his vitredur shovel and tunneled out. The sky above was velvet black, dusted with subtly colored stars. A vast cloud deck blanketed the world below 8000 meters. Off to the west, two purplish streaks like dying meteorites arced out of sight behind the Proto-Matterhorn.

Basil sat down on a compacted pile of snow, stretching his legs with extreme caution. There were crackling sounds from the left tibia and the right ankle. Stars not of the cosmos danced momentarily before his eyes and he gasped out loud. The torn knees of his grintlaskin outer pants and down trousers were black with frozen blood. He had stumped up the last two or three hundred meters after the fall. It had been rather easy, actually; but the granular snow had torn his clothing like broken glass, and he'd had to dig in precipitously before the blizzard struck.

He swiveled slowly about, surveying his world. His breath made frosty nebulae that drifted off into the void, one puff following another at short and shorter intervals. The warming band of constriction about his chest tightened with each filling of his lungs. He was very happy.

The overwhelming cold lanced at his unprotected eyes and so he closed them and felt immediately warmer. He said: "Vulgo enim dicitur: iucundi acti labores."

Cicero, isn't it?

"Quite right. 'De Finibus.'"

The good fathers in New Hampshire had heavy going pounding the Latin into us, but I think I can still manage. "It's commonly said that accomplished labors are delightful." An appropriate sentiment, but one I couldn't swear to myself.

Basil opened his eyes and saw a dark mass, very tall and approximately man-shaped, standing on the snow in front of him.

"Hello, there," said the don. "I suppose it is you? As opposed to an hypothermic hallucination, that is."

The thing slid closer, seeming to exude a chill even more

profound than that of the high alpine night.

You must excuse me if I stay within my armor.

"Perfectly understandable. I presume you've been observing our efforts."

Yours, especially.

"Ah. Well, I'm done now."

You propose to die here?

"There seems little alternative."

I could offer one.

"How very curious," Basil murmured. "Tell me about it."

I've been experimenting with my d-jumping faculty, learning to carry things outside this armored mechanism that encases my body. It's a matter of mentally generating an upsilon-field, you see.

"Like a superluminal starship?"

Exactly. I've raised my capacity to about 75 kilos of inert mass. Now I'm ready to try teleporting something alive. I could use an animal, of course.

Basil nodded judiciously. "Or you could use me."

There is considerable risk. I've not yet had the opportunity to translate any living thing in the external field. You would be riding outside the starship, as it were. In theory, it should work.

"What must I do?"

If you could manage to stand upright, and come as close as possible to the apparatus without touching it.

Basil groped about and found the shovel. "I shall have to balance on my broken ankle. The left leg is compounded. You'll have to be quick at it, for I shan't last long.

Come.

He sank the blade into the snow and heaved. The pain came in sickening waves and he cried out. Then he was standing, wobbling slightly before the dead-black monstrosity.

"I'm ready," he said, and the gray limbo claimed both of them.

THE END OF PART TWO

PART III

NIGHTFALL

1

RAIN DELUGED THE ARMORICAN NIGHT. GORIAH, ON THE northwestern horizon, was an indistinct blob of light all but lost amid the lightening flashes. Secure inside a bubble of psychocreative force, Elizabeth and Minanonn flew through the storm.

"It seems more like January than early October," Elizabeth observed.

Minanonn said, "Four great tempests, one following the other! The weather reflects the perverse spirit of the times. In my stronghold in the Pyrénées, the snows have already sealed the high passes. This has never happened so early in the season during my five hundred and sixteen years of banishment. It's enough to make one believe in Nightfall! Our legends say that the Terrible Winter precedes it."

"Then we should be safe from war until spring," Elizabeth said.

"I wish that were so! But *winter* was an ambiguous term on Duat. Because our planet has no axial tilt, the seasons are not clearly defined. To us, therefore, winter is any prolonged period of bad weather."

Elizabeth did not comment on this. Instead she asked, "Will the mountain snows prevent members of the Peace Faction from attending the games?"

"Those who could not resist the lure of Aiken's novelty left last week, on the first day of the Truce. They are already in the lowlands. I fear that most of them will have to spend the next half-year there unless the weather moderates—and I blame myself not a little for their predicament. If I had not accepted the King's invitation to participate, my Peaceful Folk would not have been so attracted to the spectacle."

Rather undiplomatically, Elizabeth asked, "Whatever possessed you to accept?"

The Heretic uttered a rueful laugh. "I could rationalize the decision, saying that thus I affirm Aiken-Lugonn's sublimation of the ancient bloodletting of the Grand Combat. But why not be honest? In my heart, I was fired by the prospect of once again joining in on a whacking great row! My intellect may abjure violence and contention—but the Battlemaster of old still lurks within me, whether I will or no. Sometimes this drives me to despair. But at other times, when I am philosophical, I bless Tana for having let me know myself as she must know me... while still steadfastly holding me in her loving hand."

"Don't you ever curse yourself for giving in? For letting your family get the better of you?"

The Heretic's face had a lambent glow in the stormy darkness. "Tana did not make us perfect, it is said, for then there could be no growth through triumph over pain and adversity, no supervening transcendence. Not for the individual, and especially not for the Galactic Mind."

"I was taught that," Elizabeth admitted. "Long ago. But the idea easily slips away from one. Especially when we're forced to confront suffering and evil. One becomes impatient with mysteries, and despairs of waiting for good to come out of one's own weakness."

They began to descend over Goriah. Minanonn showed a momentarily youthful grin. "Nevertheless, I *still* plan to fight in Aiken's Grand Tourney!"

The King himself came to greet them as they landed in the courtyard of the Castle of Glass. Only guttering oil lamps and torches lit the scene. In the shadowed area next to the garrison buildings, more than twenty of the dark, birdlike aircraft stood shrouded under high-slung canopies.

"Great to see you again in the flesh!" Aiken said to Elizabeth. He stood on tiptoe and planted a light kiss on her cheek. Minanonn rated only a sardonic tip of the royal hat. "What say we go inside so I don't have to strain my meager faculties keeping the rain off us?"

"We wouldn't want you to exert yourself unduly," Minanonn said. "You must conserve your strength for the Grand Tourney. So far, the storms have bypassed Nionel, but if this unseasonable rain continues, the field of Gold may require metapsychic roofing. In bygone days, Kuhal and his late twin, Fian Skybreaker, performed the sheltering office at the arena in Muriah. But I fear that Kuhal's solitary effort would not prove adequate to the task of covering the tournament grounds. The job would fall to you, High King."

"Or you, Brother Heretic," the King retorted. "Kuhal's not fighting in the lists. If you gave him a psychocreative hand, the pair of you could umbrella the Field of Gold against a cyclone. What d'you say? It's a peaceful enough manifestation of power."

"I'll think about it," said Minanonn, rather glumly. They came into the castle portico, with its twisted pillars of bronze metal and purple glass, and tall, gold-gleaming torchères.

Elizabeth put a casual question. "Is that all the aircraft you managed to salvage—twenty-one?"

"Observant, aren't you?" Aiken remarked. "No, we retrieved all twenty-seven. I sent six off to Fennoscandia right away to join the prospecting team." He eyed Elizabeth speculatively. "I thought you'd know that already, All-Seeing One."

She shot him an irritated glance. "I have to rest sometime. And after monitoring that assault on Monte Rosa—"

"Excuses, excuses," the King scolded waggishly. "Some Pliocene dirigent *you* are."

"I'm not the dirigent!" she snapped. "Nobody appointed me to the office. Not Brede—and certainly not you."

Aiken raised one eyebrow. "Most of us took your assumption of the rôle for granted, lovie. Isn't it a bit late in the game to tell us you never intended to play?"

"I—I never said I wouldn't do my best to help you. And

the others. But my position is only informal, advisory. I'm not competent to direct, and I have no power. I don't *want* any—"

"Oh, lass." The King was grave. "Still flying high above us all, are you? Looking down on all the scrambling Lowlives and feckless faerie folk? . . . And do you have a bit of company now? A kindred proud soul to share your noble melancholia?"

Elizabeth said, "Don't be a bloody idiot." Her mind-tone was desperately weary.

"Where is he, anyway?" the King inquired. "I haven't been able to farsee hide nor hair of him for nearly a week. And with these storms one right after another, even the schooner's dropped out of sight. I was thinking about sending one of the flyers out to reconnoiter—in spite of danger of it getting zapped by Marc's shipmates. But now that you're here, we won't have to risk lives. Will you come up to the tower with me right now and do a fast scan?"

"It's not necessary," Elizabeth said. "I know where Marc is. That's what I've come here to talk to you about. You and Hagen and Cloud."

"Ah," said the King. "So that's the way the wind blows." They were walking across the great entry hall. Even though it was still early in the evening, there were few people about. Only the patient gray-torc soldiers of the palace guard were ubiquitous, still standing station in their gleaming bronze half-armor and violent cloaks, but bearing Milieu-style weapons instead of the traditional glass blades.

"Marc is at Black Crag," said Elizabeth. "I'm here at his behest."

"So!" exclaimed the King. "Is he feeling more peaceable now that the scales are tipping my way? It must have been quite a blow to his plans, losing those X-lasers."

Elizabeth said, "Aiken, Marc brought Basil Wimborne to us from the top of Monte Rosa. Via d-jump."

The King stopped dead in his tracks. "Christ!"

Elizabeth regarded him in silence. The flippant insouciance had vanished.

"Is that what you came here to tell me?" Aiken demanded of her. "That Marc's ready to close in, and we should abandon the Guderian Project?"

"No," she said.

"What then?"

"Marc has a proposal for you and Hagen and Cloud. I'd like to discuss it with the three of you together."

Minanonn said, "I think you'll be as safe with the King as with me, Elizabeth. If you'll excuse me, I shall visit with the Farsening Lady Sibel Longtress. In times long gone she and I shared many a diverting hour—debating the merits of peace." He went off, leaving Elizabeth smiling.

"Quite the protector, isn't he?" Aiken's tone was sour.

"He approves of you and your reign thus far."

"Well, hoo-rah," the King drawled. "Pity he's not willing to fight for his high principles! I need every stalwart mind I can get these days. You know about my having to give Sharn and Ayfa the Sword—and what that could mean."

She nodded. "The Firvulag couldn't initiate the Nightfall War without their sacred weapon—and now they have it. You've taken a big gamble."

His black eyes were snapping. "Maybe not." They stood at the entry corridor to the castle's west wing, which was barred by a great bronze grille and guarded by elite gold troopers holding the leashes of spike-collared amphicyons. "I could call Hagen and Cloud up to the royal presence chamber to meet with us, but perhaps you'd fancy going down to them. I'll take you on a fifty-pence tour of the Guderian Project laboratories—and I wouldn't mind one bit if you told Marc just how we were progressing."

She said, "I'd be very glad to take your tour. To tell you the truth, I've been quite curious."

With a certain swagger, Aiken commanded the guards to unbar the gate. Then he led the way, pointing out the various security measures protecting the installation. Sensor systems ringed the entire wing where the young North Americans and the technical personnel resided. Elites were on duty inside, and the parapets were patrolled by heavily armed grays and silvers, programmed to report to their Tanu overlords any attempts to break out or in. The precincts about the single stairwell giving access to the modified dungeons, which had once held the "general store" of contraband and now housed the laboratories, were guarded by Tanu stalwarts under the command of Celadeyr of Afaliah. The foyer was hedged with booby traps, both mechanical and metapsychic, in addition to electromagnetic barriers of increasingly lethal potential. If one managed to negotiate these hazards, there still remained the last bastion: the great SR-35 sigma-field, with its airlock that would only pass those whose mental signatures were on file in the royal computer.

"You *are* on file now, sweets," Aiken told Elizabeth with a wink. "But just for today."

The mirrorlike wall at the end of the airlock dissolved before them at the King's gesture, and they entered the laboratory anteroom. Elizabeth watched the dynamic field re-form behind them and tapped the pseudoslippery interface with one fingernail. "So this is the impregnable sigma that Marc hoped to breach with his X-lasers."

The King's jovial mien shaded off into grimness. "It is. The kids brought it from Ocala. As long as we keep the project under it, we'll be safe. Hagen says it's proof against a psychoenergetic attack to the five-hundredth degree of magnitude. Felice might have been able to mind-blast her way in here— but Abaddon hasn't a prayer. Not with the handful of minds he can muster in metaconcert these days."

"You can't use the Guderian device here in Goriah," Elizabeth pointed out.

"No," the King conceded. "Bit of bad planning on my part, that. I should have set up the labs at the Castle Gateway site in the first place, and devil take the inconvenience. But it's no use crying over spilt milk. The SR-35's no good for aerial operation, but we'll work out something when the time comes to move. You can tell *that* to Marc, as well as all the rest of it."

They passed through a seemingly endless series of small workrooms where components of the tau-generator were being assembled and tested. Aiken knew what was going on in every chamber and greeted the technicians and senior scientists and their North American supervisors by name. The laboratories were crowded and deceptively chaotic in appearance. Much of the assembly was being done under micromanipulators, and to the uninitiated observer it was rather unexciting. The chemical engineering rooms were slightly more dramatic, full of burbling gadgetry and elusive stenches as critical materials were cooked up, then sent out on the manufacturing units.

In one of the larger workrooms of this type, Tony Wayland accosted the King.

"I'll need at least three more diamonds," he said, "twelve carats or better. Also an industrial laser that can drill holes five to forty microns in diameter, a cerametal whisker grower, some Canada balsam or an equivalent syn-resin, another bottle of argon, and a new room-mate. That miserable Hewitt snores like a sawmill."

"Anything else?" inquired the King mildly.

"Some news about my wife!"

"Lady Katlinel is making inquires. There's some problem. Your Howler in-laws are a bit miffed that you ran out on their little girl, and are disinclined to cooperate. Lady Katy counsels patience."

Tony threw up his hands and stomped away. The King and Elizabeth moved on. When they were safely in the next room, she said, "My redactive faculty detects a whiff of level-two dysfunction in that man's psyche. I gather he's been through some rough times. I shouldn't let him get too highly stressed if I were you."

"He wants to work," Aiken said. "That's the best thing for him now. It'll distract him from this business about his Howler wife."

"I'd be glad to have Minanonn fly me to Nionel. Perhaps I could mediate with the irate parents-in-law."

"Thanks, Elizabeth." Aiken was glum. "But I lied to poor Tony back there—partly for selfish reasons and partly because it seems the kindest thing to do at this point. You know Lord Greg-Donnet, who was King Thagdal's Genetics Master?"

"The one they called Crazy Greggy . . ." She nodded.

"He went to Nionel with Katy when she married Sugoll, and now he's pottering about with a scheme for alleviating the deformities of the mutants. Talented man, Greggy, in spite of his little quirks. Well—it seems he worked up an experimental thingummy, a sort of cross between the healing Tanu Skin and a Milieu-style regeneration tank. He thinks this Skin-tank might help restore the really grotesque Howlers to a more normal Firvulag appearance. He asked for a volunteer. Guess who he got."

"Oh, dear," said Elizabeth.

The King said, "Tony's wife, Rowane, thought he dumped her because she was a monster. Greggy's experiment looked like a golden opportunity to her. So there she floats, switch-off, for at least another four weeks, while Greggy and the Howler equivalent of redactors remold her protoplasm. Rowane might come out worse than before, she might die, or the experiment could be a great success. But I think we're wise to stall Tony."

"I agree. It's pathetic . . ."

"Aren't we all?" said the King. He led the way into a sizable chamber where a skeletal glass structure stood upon a platform. It was a latticed box strung about with metallic cables that intertwined its vitreous members like multicolored vine stems. Many more of the flexible lines lay about on workbenches with their innards exposed to the probing attention of the workers. Monitors, testing equipment, and a confusion of installation machinery crowded the platform.

"And there it is," Aiken announced. "The Guderian device—more or less."

"I hadn't remembered its being so large," Elizabeth said.

"We expanded it a trifle. Our tame dynamic-field boffin, Anastos, said it wouldn't hurt. That's him cursing out the fleck installer. The scrawny dark haired fellow. And of course you recognize the disapproving duo looking over his shoulder."

"I've farseen them. Is there some place we could speak in private?"

Aiken led her into an unoccupied window-sided cubicle that apparently served as a workers' lounge. There were soft seats and a table, and a few spartan refreshment amenities. Then he delivered a polite telepathic summons to Hagen and Cloud Remillard. The brother and sister came into the lounge, closing the door behind them. Their curiosity at the presence of the untorced female visitor was imperfectly concealed. Both of them wore white coveralls not much different from those of the other workers. Their hair was the same reddish-gold color, but otherwise they were not particularly alike. Cloud had a high, rounded Celtic forehead that appeared almost polished, and nearly invisible brows. Her eyes were deep-set, of a piercing greenish blue, and fringed with sooty lashes. Her skin was transparent, lightly freckled, and her nose curved slightly, like a small, delicate blade. Seeing her in the flesh, Elizabeth could strip away certain characteristics inherited from Marc and perceive the ghostly image of a woman long dead. Hagen Remillard had his father's aquiline profile and powerful build, but there was something raw, almost blurred, about his features. His aura was one of suppressed rage, without a trace of Marc's magnetic urbanity. At the brief, hot touch of his mind, Elizabeth felt both pity and apprehension. From Cloud, in contrast, came open empathy. Then the mental walls shut down, and the pair of them stood with empty smiles waiting upon the King's pleasure.

"May I present the Grand Master Redactor and Farsensor Elizabeth Orme," Aiken said. "She is an honorary member of my High Table and serves as de facto dirigent of Pliocene Earth."

Hagen and Cloud responded formally. The King bade everyone be seated and served them tea and biscuits with his own royal hands while asking brief questions about this or that aspect of the project. The young Remillards replied with terse competence. They expressed hope that the geological expedition would be successful in tracking down the critical ores.

"The aircraft should rendezvous with the land party tomorrow," said the King. "Now those prospectors can comb Fennoscandia properly, from the air, without having to constantly keep on the lookout for trolls and Yotunag."

"Well, they'd better get a move on," Hagen said. "We've managed to cannibalize the niobium we need from other devices, but there's no way we'll get the rare-earth metal except through ores. Half the damn gazebo cables have cores woven of niobium-dysprosium wire."

"Once you have the wire, how long might it take to complete the device?" Elizabeth asked.

Hagen gave her a penetrating look. "Thinking of joining the exodus, Grand Master?"

Elizabeth flushed. She said levelly, "I had considered it, yes."

Hagen chuckled. "Then I hope you use your good offices to stave off Marc—or I'm afraid our chances of reentering the Milieu are rather slim."

She looked at him in silence for a moment. "I'd forgotten you were born there . . . But the others of the younger generation are all Pliocene natives?"

"And all at least three years younger than Hagen and I," said Cloud. She gave her brother a reproving frown. "To answer your question, it might take us a month or more to complete the device, given the core wire. We have the most talented scientists in the Many-Colored Land at work here, with manufacturing equipment of every description. It's incredible what some time-travelers thought to bring to the Pliocene! And, of course, we ransacked Papa's store of matériel before we left Ocala—"

Hagen interrupted her. "The Grand Master knows that, Cloudie. She knows *all* about us."

There was a pregnant pause. Hagen faced Elizabeth defiantly. "Would the Milieu let us in—knowing who we are?"

"Yes," said Elizabeth.

"Knowing what we helped Felice to do?" the young man added softly.

"If you hope to be embraced by the Unity, you'll have to pay your debt. The circumstances were extraordinary, but your act was still a crime."

"Not against free human beings," Hagen said. "Against exotic oppressors and their corrupt minions!"

"Nearly fifty thousand people perished in the Gibraltar Flood," Elizabeth said. "Many of them were entirely innocent."

"We only intended to kill the exotics. It's not as though they were human beings—"

"Both Tanu and Firvulag will contribute to the Homo sapiens stem," Elizabeth said. "I have reluctantly come to the conclusion that remnants of both groups persisted on Earth almost into historic times, mating with human stock just as they have mated with time-travelers here in the Pliocene. Our myths and legends and the other heritage of the collective unconscious confirm it."

"But that's impossible!" Cloud cried. "There are no fossils, no other concrete evidence—"

Elizabeth was unperturbed by the shocked reaction of the Remillards. She noted that Aiken seemed similarly equable. "Have you any idea," she asked them, "how scanty the fossil evidence is for the supposedly well-known races of early hominids? For Ramapithecus? For Homo erectus? For the Neanderthaler race of sapiens? . . . A pathetic handful of fragments for the first. Only scattered skulls and broken bones for the second. And fewer than eighty specimens of Neanderthal Man left of the millions who must have walked Pleistocene Earth!"

"You'd think at least one specimen of Tanu or Firvulag would have turned up," Hagen protested.

"Anomalies have been found," Elizabeth told him. "Many of them. And not only skeletal remains. King Aiken-Lugonn's computer library has admirable references that I've been able to consult over the past few months. But since the atypical finds didn't fit in with more acceptable data, they were dismissed. Other explanations were put forth to account for the anomalies, so as not to discompose the scientific establishment." A mischievous expression came over her face. "It's one of the more tempting motives one could have for returning to the Milieu. To watch the cat among the paleontological pigeons."

Cloud was somber as she returned to the serious matter at hand. "But we *would* be punished for helping Felice."

"The world you wish to enter is very different from the one Marc and his Rebels left. There's still crime and there's still punishment. But for those who are genuinely sorry, the atonement consists largely of reeducation and public service."

The brother and sister looked at Elizabeth dubiously. Aiken said, "No statute of limitations? Extenuating circumstances? Non compos mentis?"

"It would be up to the forensic redactors to determine individual culpability," Elizabeth said.

"And they'd *know*?" asked Hagen.

"Oh, yes," the Grand Master replied.

"But after we—atoned," Cloud said. "Then they'd accept us into the Unity?"

"I'm certain of it," said Elizabeth.

"There you are, kids!" Aiken vouchsafed the pair a bright smile. "If we take our licks, we get to join the grownups. Still think it would be worth it?"

Hagen was bland. "Do you, High King?"

"Who knows what I'll do?" Aiken replied airily. "You haven't built the time-gate yet, and Night may not fall."

"And Papa may still figure out some way to use that brain-roasting CE rig of his to blast us all to kingdom come," Hagen said.

Elizabeth's concern embraced the three of them. "That's

why I came here tonight to speak to you. Marc's d-jump faculty now includes the ability to transport significant quantities of matter in a field generated outside of his cerebroenergetic enhancer. He's transported a living man without harming him, and before too long he'll be able to do considerably better than that." Hagen barked a bitter obscenity and she held up a monitory hand. "You know that Marc has always maintained his love for you children. He also professes no malice toward Aiken. He's asked me to act as his emissary and mediator, so that we can resolve the present crisis peaceably. He'd like you to meet with him in my chalet on Black Crag."

"Not on your life!" Hagen exclaimed. "We told him once before—he can farspeak any deal he has in mind. I'm not getting within three air kloms or a twenty-power sigma of dear Papa. No more coercing!"

"He gives his solemn word that he won't try it," Elizabeth said. "And he let me probe him, so I know he spoke the truth. In any case, if the King attends the meeting, his coercive ability would be entirely sufficient to neutralize Marc's."

"I can believe that," Hagen muttered.

Cloud said, "But nothing has really changed. Papa and his confederates will never agree to our opening the time-gate."

Elizabeth said, "Marc asked me to tell you that he has something completely new to discuss with you. He said—and I confess I have no idea what he means—he said it concerned the answer to your old question about your genetic heritage."

"God—he said that?" Hagen's voice was hoarse. His mind engaged that of his sister on the intimate mode and both Elizabeth and the King perceived the agitation of the exchange. Hagen and Cloud were desperately afraid—and at the same time, fascinated.

"Elizabeth," the King asked, "do you know whether or not Marc can use that CE device on more than one metafaculty at a time?"

"I can answer that!" Hagen exclaimed. "God—can I! Papa instructed me thoroughly enough in the damn thing's operation. He was ready to chain me to a backup suit of armor he had all ready when we escaped from Ocala—"

"Pull yourself together." The King's barely leashed coercion hovered about the young man. "This is important!"

Hagen swallowed. "The rig can enhance only one metafunction at a time. For instance, when Marc performs a d-jump, the rig is locked onto his upsilon-field-generating faculty. When he was doing the star-search, it enhanced his farsight."

"And when the bunch of you got together with Felice to zap Gibraltar," Aiken interposed, "he was augmenting his creativity?"

"That's it," Hagen agreed. "When he's phased into the thing—when the needle-electrodes are in his brain and it goes white-hot—he has only a single preprogrammed superfaculty. The others are in peripheral mode. They're there, but only in his usual barebrained order of magnitude. He'd have to jump back to the directive computer if he wanted to switch."

"That's all right then," Aiken said, considerably relieved. "I was afraid he could use the rig to mind-zorch us in Black Crag."

"Not possible." A twisted smile spread over Hagen's face. "He won't be able to pull *that* off until he's capable of teleporting the whole CE setup around with him—power supply, auxiliaries, and all. Ten tons of junk."

"Then we've got time," Aiken said. "I say we go see what Marc has to say. If he's barebrained, I'll take a chance."

"Could you burn *him*?" Hagen asked quietly.

"No!" cried Cloud.

Elizabeth said, "All of you must give me your solemn word to keep the peace—and let me probe you redactively now and at Black Crag to be sure you mean it."

"Agreed," said Cloud at once.

Hagen took a bit longer, but finally he nodded his head.

Elizabeth looked inquiringly at Aiken. He screwed up his brow in a mock attitude of deep thought. "If I did mind-zorch Marc—just supposing I could beat him in barebrain combat—it would save all of us a lot of potential grief."

"I want your word," Elizabeth insisted. "And an open mind."

The shoebutton eyes sparkled wickedly. "I could promise. I could believe it, so your redactive ream showed I told you true. And I could change my mind. You just never know about Me!"

"Oh, yes I do," Elizabeth said.

The little man shrugged his golden shoulders. "When shall we leave for Black Crag? Tomorrow? You can tell Minanonn he'll have to carry us all. I'm not flying that far on my own steam. I haven't been well."

Across Pliocene France in the Montagne Noire, where the latest storm was still many hours away, Marc and Brother Anatoly sat on the chalet balcony under the stars, drinking up the last of the Martell cognac and discussing the theological aspects of imputability and unconscious motivation. They were deeply engrossed and Marc only excused himself once, to do a rapid farscan of Kyllikki, to be sure she was bearing well to the north of the new depression menacing the west coast of Armorica. When he saw that the schooner was safe, following the course he had given Walter Saastamoinen, he took up once again the fascinating topic of his own damnation. It was piquant to serve as Devil's Advocate to one's self.

2

THE FIRVULAG KING AND HIS NOMINAL VASSAL SUGOLL RODE
out unattended to the Field of Gold to await the arrival of
Betularn with the treasure. The day was gloriously sunny and
hot.

Side by side, the two white chalikos trotted onto the new
Rainbow Bridge over the River Nonol. The former rickety
suspension structure had been replaced by a fine cantilevered
arch engineered by the Lowlife adoptees of Nionel. The bridge
was colored like its namesake, topped with ornate bronze rail-
ings and lamp standards, and wide enough to accommodate
twenty chalikos abreast.

"Magnificent structure," Sharn commented heartily. The
Lord of the Howlers accepted the praise with his usual equa-
nimity, bowing his handsome, bald-pated head. Sugoll wore a
flowing silver-tissue caftan over an illusory body that may or
may not have been humanoid. Sharn was dressed in kidskin
riding breeches of Lincoln green, jackboots with bejeweled
high heels and spurs, and a balloon-sleeved shirt of fawn-
colored georgette, open to the navel to show off the regal chest-
pelt and ventilate the regal armpits.

When the two rulers reached the center of the span, they paused to pay tribute to the view. Behind them was Nionel, a vision of El Dorado in the shimmering heat. Below rolled the broad river, its right bank bordered by gargantuan ash trees and spicy thickets of cinnamon, sour-orange, and willow. Ahead of them lay the flowering steppe where the Grand Tourney would be held, with its grandstands and fair buildings and other structures now almost completely refurbished by the industrious gobling emigrés. The field itself was a brilliant green, powdered with buttercups.

"I'm surprised to see the place looking so verdant," Sharn said, "since the countryside hereabouts has escaped the storms plaguing more southerly regions."

"The woodlands are indeed overdry," Sugoll said. "But we have taken pains to conjure a sprinkle every third night so that the Tourney grounds will be kept in good condition for the festivities. By game time the entire flat will be blanketed with sun-daisies, and golden rockroses will adorn the marge and the campgrounds back among the tall trees."

"Conjure a sprinkle—?" Sharn was clearly nonplussed. "You mean, *make it rain*?"

The mutant nodded innocently. "It's a small matter to herd together suitable clouds if all the people put their minds to it under proper leadership. Or haven't you found it so?"

"Uh," said Sharn.

"We would be remiss hosts indeed if a parched field were all we could offer for this first Grand Tourney."

Sharn was trying to suppress his astonishment. "Cousin, do your people then make it frequent custom to mesh minds? To act in what the Lowlives would call metaconcert?"

Sugoll considered. "I don't suppose we do it any more frequently than other folks. It does take organizing, after all. We do weather modification when it's necessary, and certain large construction projects like the bridge and the polishing of the city domes when we first moved in . . . and back in Meadow Mountain, there was a certain amount of blasting. But that never involved more than fifty or so of the folk at once, and they didn't require my direction."

"When you direct their minds—do they accept your leadership without question?"

Surgoll was puzzled. "Most certainly. Don't your people?"

Sharn sighed gustily. "Cousin, we must speak of this later, at some length. In your long isolation from the mainstream of our Firvulag race, you have suffered certain deprivations. But the merciful Goddess has also blessed you with an extraordinary recompense!"

"Well," said Sugoll modestly, "she did make us rich."

Sharn ground his teeth. "That, too. But I was really speaking of your facility for mental teamwork. I must confess that my nonmutant subjects have only recently begun to forsake their independent bloody-mindedness in favor of cooperative effort."

"You're fighters," Sugoll said bluntly. "We're not. We've had to cooperate in order to survive."

Sharn spoke eagerly. "And now I invite you to cooperate with the rest of us . . . in the most noble enterprise in the history of the Many-Colored Land! This inspection trip of mine was only an excuse to come and tell you about it, to enlist you and your people in the great venture!" With a sudden dramatic gesture, he pointed up the river. "Look there! Here comes Betularn, as I promised, and you'll never in a million years guess what he's bringing—courtesy of the Shining Jackanapes of Goriah!"

The Howler lord smiled in a noncommittal fashion. "While we await the hero's arrival, perhaps you would care to take a closer look at some of our renovations."

Together they rode off the bridge and along a broad, yellow-sanded way to the enormous twin grandstands of carved lime-stone. These had nearly fallen to ruin during the forty years of disuse. Now mutant workers were everywhere, tuckpointing and painting and redecorating. The structures were freshly decked out in many shades of green, with honey-colored pillars and balustrades. Later there would be straw-filled amber cushions for the spectators, and green-and-yellow striped awnings shading the stands. The central royal enclosures had green serpentine columns, staircases painted a vivid gamboge that led down to stages at the sidelines, and quaintly peaked roofs with golden tiles and effigy-topped spires. The crest adorning the Firvulag loge combined King Sharn's crystal scorpion with Queen Ayfa's horned moon. The Tanu spire bore a gilt representation of Aiken's impudent finger.

Reminiscence mellowed the Firvulag monarch. "I'd forgotten how nice and sturdy the structures were on our Field of

Gold. Much more impressive than the flimsy pavilions the Tanu used to set up on the White Silver Plain—and a hell of a lot cooler, too. You've done a spiffing job of renovation, Cousin. What're those barricade things down around the award presentation stages?"

Sugoll explained some of the more novel games that would be featured at the Tourney, and the safety precautions that the new spirit of good-fellowship called for.

Sharn grinned, showing lustrous pointed teeth. "We'll get in a few licks against the Foe just the same. The jousting and the steeplechase events have great possibilities for mayhem. And the hurling, of course. Imagine the foe resurrecting that old romp! My father told me of hurley being played on Duat, and with enemy heads."

"The Tanu call it shinty," Surgoll said. "We'll use a large white ball with black spots as a substitute for the skull." He glanced toward the river. "The great hero Betularn is about to arrive. Shall we meet him?"

They rode down to the water's edge, where bleachers for the boat races were still under construction. At the docks were eighteen large inflatable craft, jammed to the gunwales with armored regulars and crated cargo. White Hand, caparisoned in full obsidian harness and carrying a purple-leather box nearly as long as he was tall, leaped from the lead boat and strode up to Sharn. He dropped to one knee before the mounted Firvulag King, proffering the great case. His visor was open and tears streamed from his pouched eyes.

"Your Appalling Highness!" Betularn croaked. "Sovereign Lord of the Heights and Depths, Monarch of the Infernal Infinite, Father of All Firvulag, and Undoubted Co-Ruler of the Known World—into your hands I commend our Sword."

Sharn vaulted from the saddle, seized the purple container, and ripped off the lid. The huge diamond-bright weapon flashed in the sunshine. The studs on its hilt were gems of several colors. Its cable was neatly coiled, and the powerpack showed full charge.

"Goddess!" cried Sharn. "At last!" He lifted the photon weapon reverently. Betularn and all of the Firvulag still on the boats stood at attention, mailed fists against their hearts. Sugoll slowly dismounted, reassumed his natural appearance, and squatted in enigmatic abomination as the nonmutants raised the Firvulag song.

When its last deep-noted echo had died away across the river, Sharn said, "Gird me."

Betularn buckled on the jeweled harness and slung the powerpack at the King's waist. Sharn's face wore an expression of exultation. "Bid your troops to take their ease, White Hand, and come walk with me and our mutant cousin." He thrust the Sword into its belt loop and strolled off along the yellow pathway leading to the grandstands. The torrid breeze off the expanse of grassland had a redolence of spiced tea.

Betularn cast a disapproving eye on the Lord of the Howlers. "Your long absence from our Firvulag Court has atrophied your piety, Cousin Sugoll. One hopes your allegiance has not suffered a similar decline."

"I am ever the Goddess's good servant," the Great Abomination rumbled, "and a faithful vassal to the High King."

"Now, White Hand," Sharn said amiably, "let's not have any snipping on this historic occasion."

"I'm only zealous in defense of your honor," the old warrior growled, "and you know my heart is loyal to you until earth be torn asunder, and high heaven, and Nightfall follows upon the cleansing flame!"

Somewhere out in the Field of Gold a meadowlark trilled. The Firvulag King, the veteran general, and the Prince of Monsters stepped off the blazing sandy path onto green coolness strewn with buttercups.

"So it is true," Sugoll said.

"Yes," Sharn said. He clasped his hands behind his back and watched his boots flatten the little yellow flowers as they walked. "But you must not be dismayed by Betularn's overliteral interpretation of the racial myth."

"I do not understand," said the Abomination.

"Neither do I!" White Hand's voice was rough with shock. "Is it to be the war that ends the world, or not?"

Sharn held up a soothing hand, smiling as he kept his eyes on the ground, then let his fingers rest on the control studs of the Sword. "Let me explain to you both, as I'll explain to all the Little People. Ayfa and I have done a careful study of the sacred traditions since coming to the Throne. The signs and portents and the business about the Adversary, and all the rest of it. Our researchers have convinced us that the Nightfall War doesn't have to be a conflict of mutual annihilation at all. The traditions can be given a more positive interpretation, with the rebirth of a new and more glorious world following the destruction of the old order—and a single race victorious over all. Us, of course."

"What do you youngsters know of the old Way?" Betularn cried. "Your idea is a travesty! Your Atrocious Great-Great-Grandsire who fell immortal at the Ship's Grave must be puking before the Seat of the Goddess to hear such blasphemy. Nightfall is the end, everyone knows that. The end of everything!"

"It isn't," Sharn insisted, "for, whatever we do here, Duat survives and all her daughter worlds—and would have done, had Firvulag and Tanu fought to Nightfall at Void's Edge."

"Heresy!" spluttered Betularn. "No, it's worse! *Casuistry!*"

Sugoll said, "You maintain, Royal Cousin, that Nightfall's taking place in the Many-Colored Land would initiate the New Heaven and New Earth of our traditions here—in space and time—rather than on the higher plane of reality?"

"Precisely," said Sharn. "And we Firvulag as precursors of the whole glorious affair! The foe are in a fatally weak position, diminished in numbers and strength. Their ruler is an alien usurper who pads his puny battle-company with homesick fellow Lowlives who can hardly wait to skip back through the time-gate to their drab future world! We're stronger than ever before, with a stock of high-technology weapons in addition to our new metapsychic fighting tactics. And now we have the Sword."

He paused, drew the great glass blade from his belt, and held it aloft with both hands. He said softly, "Night falls for the Foe, but for us it will be a new dawn."

He thumbed the lowest stud, the power-setting for ritual combat, and blasted the golden digitus impudicus emblem atop the Tanu royal enclosure to a puff of glowing plasma.

"Goddess!" cried Betularn. His face mirrored the turmoil taking place in his mind. "I was willing to put an end to it, to bow to the omens. But now . . . Sharn-Mes, laddie, you've got this old soldier snorled to a fare-thee-well. I just don't know what to make of this."

"Trust me," urged Sharn. He turned to Sugoll. "And how

about you, Cousin Howler? Are you confused, too?"

"I think not."

Sharn winked. "Reserving judgment, though. Is that it?"

The terrible crested head made a slight gesture of affirmation.

Sharn flipped the caplock from the upper power-settings of the Sword. "May I recall to both your minds that our sacred weapon is a many-splendored thing. The Golden Asaleny's got himself a fleet of aircraft, which he thinks give him an upper hand in the arms race. But our Sword was designed not only for rituals, but also for defense when we were getting our asses harried from planet to planet back in the old galaxy."

A flock of pied swans winged westward from the river, and Sharn, lips thinned in a foreboding smile, took fresh aim. "Shall we see what effect the highest power-setting will produce? Yes, let's!"

He thumbed the top stud.

Nothing happened.

Mounting incredulous blasphemies, the King tried the other three superior settings. None worked.

"That treacherous bastard! That conniving little trickster!" Sharn punched the lowest stud. A green flash obliterated a single swan. The rest of the flock scattered, terrified by the concussion.

"The Sword is still entirely adequate for its legitimate purpose," Betularn noted austerely, "and its symbolic value is unimpaired. The Foe has been extremely clever."

Sharn choked back his rage. "I suppose you're right. But to be cheated in this flagrant way! It's—it's—"

"Typical of the times," said the Lord of the Howlers in a calm, sad voice. He reassumed his humanoid shape. "The heat becomes most oppressive, my liege. Shall we return to the peace of Nionel?" Sugoll bowed slightly to Betularn. "I offer you and your troops our hospitality as well, White Hand."

"My thanks," said the general, "but we may as well get on with making camp here in the Field, in anticipation of the games. I'll come by for supper after I get the lads and lasses squared away."

Sugoll nodded. "Only a few guests are in the hostel buildings as yet, but the facilities are quite ready for occupancy. Or have you brought your own equipment?"

"Everything we could possibly need," Betularn replied, "plus a little bit more."

WALTER: Do you hear, son?

VEIKKO: Dad! At last. Jeez, you're loud. You must be awfully close.

WALTER: Less than 300 kilometers north of you there in Goriah, up in the gulf of Armorica.

VEIKKO: ! How?

WALTER: All those storms. We ran before 'em.

VEIKKO: You ran . . . in Kyllikki? Oh, my God. You must be out of your mind! Or were you doing your best to—

WALTER: What do you think?

VEIKKO: Marc didn't realize?

WALTER: He hasn't been here that often, and he's never voyaged aboard Kyllikki before. Remember that back in the Rye Harbor Yacht Club, the most boat he ever had under him was a 10-meter Nicholson. Nice craft, but it doesn't clue you to the whims of a four-poster schooner. Besides, I played it straight, conned her the best I could. If we'd taken the plunge it would have been kismet. Actually, Marc was rather gratified at the turn of speed I managed. And our keeping inside the storm track must have played hob with attempts to farsense us.

VEIKKO: Nobody in Goriah has the faintest notion where you are. Hagen was out of his mind. He got me to try farsensing you. [Chuckle.] Somehow I just couldn't get a fix . . . Then he wanted to send a flyer to hunt and zap, but the King nixed that. Something funny's going on, Walter. This morning Cloud, Hagen, and the King took off with Elizabeth and some hot-shot Tanu stooge of hers. Body-flying, for chrissake, when we've got these perfectly good aircraft. Nobody here knows—

WALTER: It's Marc.

VEIKKO: ?

WALTER: His final appeal to you children.

VEIKKO: You mean, if Hagen doesn't agree to stop work on the time-gate, it'll be no holds barred from now on?

WALTER: That's about the size of it. You realize, don't you, that Marc has been the voice of sweet reason all along, refusing to harm you if there was any possible alternative.

Castellane and Warshaw and most of the other magnates favored hitting you kids with the full load, at the first possible opportunity.

VEIKKO: You evened the odds for us, Walter. You and Manion. I told Diane what her father did. She wasn't surprised. Hagen was.

WALTER: He would be, poor devil.

VEIKKO: . . . What shall I do now? I can't target you for the King, Dad. I *can't*.

WALTER: Now that we're near the mainland, it's going to be tough for anybody to farsense us. Ragnar Gathen and Arne-Rolf Lillestrom wired up a psychoelectronic fuzzer during the voyage. Crude, but probably effective enough to defeat long-range peeking. Has the King got any mechanical scanners?

VEIKKO: An IR with a range of about 70 kloms, and the aircraft have some kind of ground-combers. Can't you get *away*?

WALTER: Don't worry about it.

VEIKKO: But I do . . . You know I do.

WALTER: If Marc's proposing to tell Hagen and Cloud what I think he is, you may find all our problems solved.

VEIKKO: ? !! . . . No matter what Marc promises, we're going to build the Guderian device.

WALTER: Possibly.

VEIKKO: We're all agreed, Dad. Well . . . most of us. And the King's on our side.

WALTER: Wait, just the same, until you hear the proposal.

VEIKKO: Walter, you're not switching to *his* side? God!

WALTER: I'm on your side, Veik. Always. Now listen. Don't try to contact me again unless you *do* agree to Marc's proposal. It'll be too dangerous for both of us. You're almost within Castellane's tracking range now, and if she told Marc what we were doing . . . Well, I still might be useful to you if I stay alive. Dead, I'm only useful if I take Kyllikki with me.

VEIKKO: But what'll I—

WALTER: Wait. It can't be much longer. Goodbye, Veikko.

VEIKKO: Goodbye, Dad.

3

BASIL OPENED HIS EYES TO BLURRED OBSCURITY. THERE WAS red illumination overall and superimposed upon it, subtly writhing, an intricate branched pattern like veins. He heard the soft, regular hiss of surf. He heard a muffled cardiac drumbeat: dum-*dum* (skip) dum-*dum* (skip) dum-*dum* (skip). His memory furnished a tune to fit—"Zwei Hertzen in Dreivierteltakt." He thought: No, it's only one heart in three-quarter time. Mine. In an artificial womb. Constatne?

"Quite right, old friend."

A pale-colored blob hovered above eye level. The haziness was abruptly clarified as something crackling and transparent, resembling plass membrane, was stripped away from his face. He saw an El Greco angel wearing a golden torc. He said to it, "Well, hello, Creyn. Have I been in Skin?"

"For two days."

"I feel comfortable," Basil said. The light brightened a bit and took on a more normal spectrum. He was aware of other Tanu standing in the shadowed recesses of the chamber. The carved timbering, stucco walls, and baroque window shutters were certainly those of the Black Crag chalet. "So he brought

336

me here. How perfectly splendid! . . . But surely my bones can't have knit already?"

"We'll see." Creyn continued to unwrap him, stuffing the used Skin membrane into a scarlet pouch. He said over his shoulder, "Lord Healer, will you do the microscan?"

A taller Tanu, dressed like Creyn in red-and-white robes, stepped closer. His eyes with their pinpoint pupils were faded blue with glints of other colors, like certain opals. Except for deep lines about the mouth, his face was youthful. He had hair like fine-spun platinum.

"Remarkable," said Dionket at length. "The accelerated tissue-repair program of the Adversary has restored the ankle completely. The tibia still has some incomplete regeneration about the medullary cavity but appears quite adequate for normal load-bearing function."

Five Tanu minds intoned: Praise be to Tana.

Basil appended fervently: In saecula saeculorum!

He felt some kind of frame withdrawing support from his body. Then he was standing on his own two feet and realized he was stark naked. He stepped down from a sort of pedestal.

Creyn smiled at him. "Do you feel weak?"

"Not a bit of it, old chap. Just ravenously hungry."

Creyn helped him into a white-cotton robe and slippers. "These healers who have helped you are Dionket, once President of our Guild of Redactors, Lord Peredeyr Firstcomer, Meyn the Unsleeping, and Lady Brintil."

Basil said, "I thank you for your—er—professional ministrations. I'm amazed that you could do the job so quickly. I thought that Skin treatment for injuries such as this took considerably longer."

"It usually does," Dionket said, "when traditional redactive techniques are employed. But we used an experimental method on you—a concerted, intensive operation involving five healers rather than one."

"Mm," said Basil. "Glad I was able to take advantage of it."

Dionket and the three touched Basil's mind briefly through his gray torc, then filed out. The don said to Creyn, "I must also thank my rescuer for bringing me off Monte Rosa. I don't suppose Remillard is still here?"

Creyn's face showed no expression. "He is. It was his modification of the Skin program that we used to heal you."

"Judas priest! Then I owe him double thanks, don't I?" They came out of the infirmary and mounted an open stairway that led to the first floor of the lodge. "I don't mind telling you it was a shocker, having him show up on the mountaintop, all armored like some archetypal god of the machine. I didn't see anything of the man himself. The prospect of seeing him face to face is a trifle unnerving... the challenger of the galaxy, the metapsychic paragon who became the deepest-dyed villain our race has ever known..."

"He eats mushroom omelettes and popcorn with Brother Anatoly," Creyn said. "And puts his feet up on the hearth fender to warm them on stormy nights like this. And forgets to put the lid down on the toilet."

Basil laughed. "Point taken. One of us after all, eh?"

"No," said Creyn. "But I think he would like to be."

Basil paused at the head of the stairs. His eyes met those of the Tanu who had become his friend on the long exodus from drowned Muriah. "There were hints dropped by Bleyn the Champion while we were on our expedition: that Remillard has actually been working mind to mind with Elizabeth. Is it true?"

"Together, they cured the chalet housekeeper's baby of the black-torc syndrome. More than that—they raised the little one to full operancy. Torcless metafunction."

"Good God. And when Remillard brought me here—"

"The Adversary was intrigued when we proposed putting you into our healing Skin. He had never seen the psychoactive substance in use. When Dionket Lord Healer demonstrated our customary redactive program the Adversary conceived this new technique, which he described as a spinoff from the more elaborate procedure used on the infant. Elizabeth bade us follow his instructions, saying he had been a paramount designer of metaconcert programs in your Galactic Milieu. The result was your accelerated healing."

They came into a small sitting room where there was a fire. Basil said, "That name you apply to Remillard: the Adversary. Would you care to explain its significance?" He touched the gray metal at his throat. "I catch odd mental overtones from you, old chap. Just how deeply has Elizabeth become involved with this bastard?"

"I'll tell you everything I know, as well as the conclusions I've drawn and confided to no one . . . Basil, you and I have both loved her without hope. We have seen her self-doubting and tempted to despair, not knowing where her destiny lies. Now she fears this Adversary, at the same time that she is drawn inextricably into his orbit. We may be able to help her."

"For God's sake, how?"

Creyn helped him into a chair, drew up a footstool. "Rest here for a while. I'll be back directly with some food for you—and a golden torc."

Heavy rain sluiced against the French windows at the lodge's grand salon. The slow-burning oak logs in the great fireplace did little to dissipate the chill.

Marc said to Brother Anatoly, "They have arrived."

The lanky old friar arose from one of the settees and brushed crumbs of tetraploid popcorn from his scapular. "Then I'll be off to bed. You won't want me cluttering the family reunion. I don't think I can wish you good luck."

"I wish you'd stay. You might find yourself coming to appreciate my point of view." Marc knelt beside the wood rack, selecting some billets of stone pine. "So might the children. None of you have all the data. When you do, perhaps you'll finally understand. Cloud and Hagen don't realize that they're absolutely vital to the Mental Man concept. Neither do most of my old associates who accompanied me to the Pliocene. If the children had never been born, I would have been content to die in my failed Rebellion and that would have been the end of it. But they *were* born. Call it providence or synchronicity or whatever. Now they have no choice but to fulfill their destiny."

"No choice?" Anatoly flared. "Ne kruti mne yaitsa, khui morzhoviy! A choice is exactly what they do have!"

Marc fed the fire, smiling. "God, you have an ugly mouth, priest."

"I know. It got me in trouble a lot back in Yakutsk. Lack of charity, the besetting sin of my life . . . It could be yours, too, you Paramount Grand Master tinkling cymbal, if you persist in treating your children like specimens in some breeding experiment!"

"You have no notion of the importance of the Mental Man concept."

"Maybe not. But I do understand human dignity—and your children's right to a free choice."

"The birth of transcendent humanity is more important than the rights of two individuals, no matter who they are! Hagen and Cloud can't be permitted to withdraw. Not now, when I finally have the means to bring the project to fruition."

"Then make them believe in you," Anatoly said. "Convince them. Convince yourself! Prove that the Milieu's verdict on you was a mistake!"

The flames were building as the resinous wood caught. Marc said, "The human race must fulfill its great potential. This can't be evil!"

"So," said the friar in a voice ominously quiet. "Instead of my reforming your erroneous conscience, you want to reform mine! One poor old zalupa konskaya tells you it wasn't a sin after all, that makes it all right? It's not me you have to justify yourself to, Marc—it's Hagen and Cloud."

Firelight shadowed Abaddon's eyes. "You'd better pray that I can, Anatoly. Because all I really require is their germ plasm."

There was a knock on the door.

Elizabeth's mind said: We've come.

Marc sprang to his feet and stood with his back to the fire, a silhouette in a black polo-necked sweater and black cord trousers. The salon's double doors opened. Four people were there, all wearing Tanu storm-suits with the hoods thrown back. Elizabeth stepped aside. Cloud and Hagen, both in white, stood there together. Behind them was the King.

Cloud said, "Papa!" Marc opened his arms and she ran to him. Their minds embraced and she kissed him, and he held her bright-haired head against his chest until she stopped weeping. Then she looked up at him with a plea naked in her eyes, moved away, and waited for Hagen.

The young man stood a full four meters off, at the side of Aiken Drum. His hands were still gloved, stiff at his sides. He ignored his sister's invitation and Marc's, keeping his mind tightly barricaded. He said, "I'll hear what you have to say,

Papa. That's all." The heavy raindrops clattered against the windowpanes.

"Will you sit down?" Marc's voice was mild. "It won't take long." He deliberately turned his back on them to poke up the guttering fire.

There were three large settees grouped around a low table. Brother Anatoly said, "Come on, son. You'll be safe. who'd connive at brainburning on a night light this, with popcorn and mulled wine? Have some. I was just leaving." Touching Elizabeth's hand in passing, he started for the door.

Marc commanded, "Stay here."

The friar stopped dead, then went to a chair far back in the shadows and sat down.

On the table by the fire, the crock of spiced wine steamed. The corn puffs were also hot, and glistening with butter. Aiken, all aglow in gilded leather, helped himself and said, "I don't mind sharing a little snack with you, Remillard. I brought my long spoon." He plumped down on the couch farthest from the hearth. After hesitating, Hagen sat beside him. Cloud took the seat near her father. Elizabeth sat alone on the lefthand couch.

"I said I would tell you children about your heredity," Marc said without preamble. "You know my own body is self-rejuvenating. Except for my recalcitrant hair, my appearance hasn't changed very much in thirty years. I'm a mutant, like all the children of Paul Remillard and Teresa Kendall. The rejuvenating character is genetically dominant, as are most mutations. Both you, Cloud, and you, Hagen, are also virtually immortal."

"I knew it!" Hagen leapt to his feet. "But you wouldn't tell us the truth before, would you, Papa? No—that would have weakened your hold over us and diminished your stature in the eyes of the others. You had to be unique! So you fobbed us off, warned us not to have any kids of our own, hinted there was a chance we carried horrible genes like Uncle Jack's—"

"What you were told," Marc interrupted, "and what you were not told were for your own safety and peace of mind. You have supravital alleles for self-rejuvenation and high meta-function . . . and you have others. The infamous patchwork heritage of the Remillards. You would have found out about the immortality eventually, of course."

"But what about the rest?" Cloud asked, bewildered. "Were you afraid we wouldn't be able to bear knowing the truth?"

"*You* might have borne it," Marc told her. He was still facing the fire. No one spoke for several minutes. Hagen subsided back onto the couch.

Finally Elizabeth said, "Marc, you must tell them why they were brought to the Pliocene."

"Because you are the parents of Mental Man," Marc said.

Hagen and Cloud sat as though turned to stone. Then Hagen said, "You censored the library flecks back on Ocala, wiped out all details of the real motive behind your Rebellion. All we had were hints, and the fact that Mama tried to kill you herself to prevent the plan's success. For God's sake, Papa— what was the Mental Man project? *What is it still?*"

His mind showed them.

Overwhelmed by disbelief, they sat with mental barriers fallen.

Elizabeth said to Aiken: Keep your guard up now if ever.

Aiken said: Lord Woman he's not coercing can't you *see*?

Marc still did not face them. He had his palms flat against the mantelstone and his head bowed. Flames outlined him with a burning corona. He said, "Until I conceived this project, long before I met your mother, I looked upon my immortality as nothing but the bitter jest of a whimsical evolution. Have you ever thought what physical immortality really might mean? An operant mind shackled to a weak, emotion-tossed human body! It was more a curse than a blessing in a world populated by fearful, short-lived fellow humans and self-righteous exotics already suspicous of human genetic potential. Our whole family had the trait—more or less. Much good it did us . . . And then Jack was born. The rest of us watched his very special combination of sublethals run its course. It was terrible and it was grand and it was the *answer*. He personified the ultimate trend of human evolution: the disembodied brain capable of wearing any material form it chose. Or none. But we discovered that le bon dieu had played another cosmic joke. Poor Jack was not immortal. The marvelous brain was doomed to break down slowly. It would die in less than eighty years . . . Then I had the revelation, the idea for Mental Man's artificial engendering. Some members of my family and some magnates of the Concilium who would appreciate the dream helped with the early experimentation. We used my seed, since I represented the culmination of the immortal strain, and female gametes from the most genetically favored women involved in the project. It was all done artificially and in secret because of the controversy the idea had provoked. We seemed to be succeeding. And then the difficulties began; there was sabotage, disloyalty. The debate concerning the morality of the whole Mental Man concept became an ideological battleground between the fearful and the far-sighted. Was it beneficial to the Galactic Mind to permit the acceleration of evolution by such radical means? Human thinkers were divided. Exotics universally condemned us."

"And Mama," Cloud said.

"And Cyndia," Marc agreed. "Marriage and natural children had never been part of my life-schema. All I wanted was to father Mental Man in vitro and in cerebro. But there was Cyndia. For a time, she even seemed to favor the project. You see, she thought the developing nonborns would be allowed to keep their bodies . . . She insisted that we have children of our own, even though I told her of the family problems. Finally, I couldn't deny her. You two were born, ostensibly perfect. But I knew you would never be able to attain your full potential, any more than I had, unless—"

"Unless you included us in the Mental Man project as well," Cloud said.

"And that's when she tried to kill you!" Hagen shouted, surging up. Aiken's fingers closed about his wrist like steel bands and he sank back with a groan. "And when Mama bungled it, you killed *her*."

Marc turned toward them at last, calm and implacable. "Cyndia's first intent was not to take my life. After the disaster struck our secret laboratories in the early days of the Rebellion, she thought that sterilizing me would be sufficient to put an end to Mental Man, and to the war. She had a small sonic disruptor, a very sophisticated device. She did what she set out to do and narrowly missed killing me. My mind struck her down in self-defense."

"Jesus," said Aiken. "Then all you had left were the kids."

"Oh, Papa," Cloud said in a dead voice. "That's why you said it was *necessary* to bring us to the Pliocene when your Rebellion failed. Why you want to keep us with you now."

Marc said, "The Milieu will not permit you to reproduce

our strain. You have the dangerous strengths and weaknesses of both your parents. In my day, the Human Polity eugenicists were more free and easy in such matters. It was fairly easy for the powerful to circumvent the restrictions. But even Jack was born illicitly, as you know. He should have been aborted, with his overwhelming quotient of so-called lethal genes."

"And if he had been," Elizabeth said, "you would have won."

Marc only smiled his famous smile.

Hagen's thoughts were chaotic, imperfectly screened. "But you could have been restored in the regen tank, back in the Milieu or even here. God—you *were* restored here, after Felice fire-flayed you! And your self-regenerating faculty—don't tell me it balks at rehabilitating zapped gonads!"

"The body doesn't balk," Marc said. "Only the mind."

Taken aback, Hagen could only repeat, "The mind?"

Marc's steady gaze turned to Elizabeth. "Ask the Grand Master why she receded into metapsychic latency after her accident, even though her brain was perfectly restored."

"We restore ourselves," she said to Hagen. "In any healing process—whether ordinary or extraordinary, tank or Tanu Skin or specialized autoregeneration—the restored body cells must be reintegrated into the whole. Accepted and directed to function through the subtle redactive process of the mind."

"And . . . you can't?" Cloud asked her father.

"No," said Marc.

"But, *why*?"

"Perhaps Brother Anatoly knows," said Marc lightly. "We've been considering at some length the heart's sly subornation of the intellect. What I should do, I do not! Je suis le veuf, without a star left on my lute. For me, there is only the abyss . . . You children must take up the engendering of Mental Man in a place safe from the interference of jealous exotics and puny-minded humans. But there's no need for a star-search any longer. We don't have to wait to be rescued. Before too long I'll have the ability to d-jump all of us anywhere in the galaxy. There are at least three worlds I know of with high-technology civilizations that could foster our project. None has true operant metafunction or even superluminal transport as yet, but we could deal with that easily enough once we took control of a planet." Marc displayed a mental image.

"We." Hagen eyed his father with misgiving. "Then the other children are still to be included somehow in the project, just as you told us back on Ocala?"

"All who still accept the Mental Man ideology may join us. An adequate pool of genes from operant human stock is essential to offset the sublethal alleles of the Remillards. My old colleagues have known this all along. What they did *not* know was that you two were the only sources left of the immortality strain. They assumed—as I did—that I would be able to restore my fertility eventually. Most of them still think I have done so. It was the better part of prudence not to disillusion them during the early years of our exile. The times were unsettled. I was well able to take care of myself, but you children were vulnerable."

"I'm surprised," said Hagen caustically, "that you didn't bank specimens of our germ plasm."

"I did. The Keoghs, who were our chief physicians and knew the truth, took one ovary and one testis from you while you were still very young children. The only other person who knew, my closest friend and confidant, destroyed them at about the same time that he began poisoning your minds against me."

"Manion!" cried Hagen, and he began to laugh uproariously.

"Why does Alex want us to go back to the Milieu, Papa?" Cloud asked. Her brother's laughter choked off.

"He wants Mental Man—and you—subordinated to the Unity. He's a deluded fool."

Hagen brushed this aside. "So you really do need us after all. We're the priceless raw material for your Mental Man stud farm—is that it?"

Marc cut him off. "You and Cloud will be the principal administrators of the project. It will be yours. I'll subdue the host planet for you, give you every assistance. But the responsibility would be yours. Think very carefully before you refuse it. Nothing comparable awaits you in the Galactic Milieu. On the contrary." And his mind displayed a panorama of alarming scenarios that caused the two young people to gasp, then turn incredulously to Elizabeth.

She shook her head. "I don't know. Certainly not the more drastic hypotheses. The Milieu would never be so unjust. Ultimately, your fate would probably depend upon you. Your mind-set and response to the Unity—"

"You mean, we'd have to take our medicine," Hagen said, "and swear to be good little neurons in the Galactic Brain."

"It's not like that!" Elizabeth protested. "The Unity is love and fulfillment and an end to loneliness. Manion was right when he told you you'd find peace with your own kind."

But Marc said, "There's no room in the Milieu for persons whose dreams diverge from the norm—much less persons whose mental potential exceeds the narrow course predetermined for humanity by the exotic races. You are Remillards. You'd be a threat. And unless you submitted to the domination of the Unity you'd be dealt with . . . as I was."

"And don't forget Me," said Aiken.

"I'd never do that," Marc replied smoothly. "Elizabeth told me your history. In spite of our vast latent metabilities, the Magistratum was prepared to dispose of you. I invited you to be here at this meeting precisely because I saw you as my ally, one who would plead my cause to Hagen and Cloud once you understood the truth. I'm not afraid of having Milieu agents come after me through the time-gate. Why should they bother? The past *is*. They know I can never return. I stand condemned. But you, High King . . . What kind of reception would you have if you should go back to the Milieu? Are you ready to subordinate your mind to the will of your inferiors in the Unity? And if you stay here, and a two-way warp is established, are you ready to welcome busybody reformers from the future, backed by the enforcers of the Magistratum? Your rule is hardly a model of enlightened democracy! And the third contingency: closure of the gate after the disaffected have fled the Pliocene. At the very least, you stand to lose many of your most talented subjects. There are even uglier possibilities."

Aiken grinned. "Including the one that all this havering may be moot, if the Firvulag are right and Götterdämmerung is about to fall."

Suddenly the little man in gold was on his feet, holding Hagen's wrist with his left hand and Cloud's with his right. All three of them were inside a shining envelope of psycho-creative force.

Marc tensed. He stepped forward, his eyes alight with fury. He said: *It is not your decision to make!*

"I've made it mine." Aiken was no longer smiling. "Do you care to dispute the point?"

The aspect of Abaddon faded as quickly as it had appeared. Mare shook his head with apparent unconcern.

Aiken drew Cloud and Hagen toward the tall French windows that still streamed with rain. He said to Marc, "We'll think very carefully about what you've said, and then we'll give you our decision. But not now. We need time."

"You may have two days," Marc said coldly. "No longer."

The windows were flung open, admitting a howling blast of wind-driven water. Aiken and the young Remillards were abruptly hooded, unrecognizable, ready to fly. The King asked, "Will you wait here at Black Crag for the answer?"

Marc said, "If I'm not here, Elizabeth will know how to find me." His mind reached toward his masked son and daughter. *I know that what I've told you has been shocking. Frightening, even. But all that will be taken care of in time. You'll understand everything . . . in time. Don't let Aiken stampede or coerce you. You carry a priceless potential, an enormous responsibility. Let me help you fulfill it. Don't turn away from me. Forgive me for the mistakes, for hurting you. I only meant it for the best. I do love both of you. Believe me . . .*

The golden figure and the two white ones vanished into the storm. The window-doors slammed shut.

Marc and Elizabeth had completely forgotten Brother Anatoly. He hauled himself up from his isolated seat with a wheezy sigh and came sloshing through the puddles on the floor. At the fireside table he busied himself ladling out three cups of the still-steaming mulled wine. He gave one to Marc and one to Elizabeth, then stood muttering under his breath for a moment. He said, "You're going to need all the help you can get. Take it and drink it. You know what it is. For your good and everybody's."

Elizabeth's eyes went wide with shock. "I can't. What do you think you're *doing*?"

"Of course you can," said Anatoly comfortably. "Look at him. Are you that much worse?"

Very carefully, Elizabeth set the cup of wine down on the table. "Amerie must have been out of her mind to send you," she said, and then she rushed out of the room.

Marc raised a bemused brow over the rim of his cup.

Anatoly drank his, then took Elizabeth's. "I do believe she's scandalized. She has terrible scruples, you know. And despair.

It's difficult to deal with. In her way, she's even prouder than you. And unfortunately, damnation will always be a matter of choice."

"I still don't concede guilt."

"You're an arrogant, invincibly ignorant bastard, and your subconscious *does* concede, and ego te absolvo." He finished Elizabeth's wine and set down the empty cup. "This new thing, on the other hand, is a different kettle of borscht. It's wrong and you know it. No psychological bullshit about it, Remillard. You force those kids or mutilate them again and you make your own hell. For keeps, this time."

"I know," Marc said. "I'm trying to decide if it's worth it."

4

THE STORM ENGULFED THEM; BUT BEFORE HAGEN AND CLOUD could articulate a single thought, the King's mind spoke irresistibly:

Sleep. Put it all aside now. All fear all anxiety all decision. There is only the dark and the water and the wind. The world sleeps invisible below and you on high are secure and guarded. Sleep . . .

They awoke totally refreshed, seated side by side on a glass bench in a starlit garden. The faint tinkle of tiny bells in the trees and a partial glimpse of a tower delineated in yellow and violet sparks told them that they were back in Goriah, in the castle grounds.

Hagen pushed off his hood and looked at his wrist chronometer. It was only a little after one in the morning. "My God, it took that Tanu, Minanonn, nearly four hours to carry us to Black Crag. The King's flown us back in less than ninety minutes!"

"With a detour to Roniah," said a deep exotic voice from the shadows.

Cloud was on her feet, straining her farsense. "Kuhal," she whispered.

The Second Lord Psychokinetic stepped out onto the silver lawn. There was a human woman with him.

Bewildered, Hagen managed to say, "Is that you, Diane?"

"The King sent us both," said the daughter of Alexis Manion. "He said—and I quote—'It's been a long time since any of you had a fun-break. Go downtown and play. Tomorrow you can come back to the castle and we'll discuss the future.'"

"Did—he tell you where we'd been?" Hagen asked.

Kuhal said, "He told us everything. He said he had his reasons."

Cloud nodded and spoke as if to herself. "We're not to be allowed to keep it secret."

A breeze blew up from the Gyre of Commerce, carrying the eerie skirling of an electronic bagpipe. Kuhal drew Cloud aside. "The King may not have realized, when he arranged this meeting, that you and I had agreed to set a wall between us. He knew we still farspoke one another over the leagues and shared out hearts' troubles. He saw that we were friends—"

"And mistook it for love," she said.

"It has always remained so, on my part."

Cloud moved away from his touch. "And so you have been brought here to influence my decision. And Diane to sway Hagen."

"I think you misjudge Aiken deeply. His motive was kindness, not machination."

"Perhaps you're right."

They walked along the shrub-bordered path, leaving the other couple behind at the lily pond. Mushroom-shaped glass lamps lit the way to an obscure gate in the garden wall that opened into the town green-belt. Cloud kept her mind veiled. She still had the storm-suit hood covering her hair and the taut skin made her slender figure almost sexless, a glimmer of white moving along beside a demigod in barbaric High Table vesture.

"Through all the turmoil of the last month," he said, "you farspoke me from this very garden."

"Papa watched us," she said. "He says he didn't listen."

"What matter if he did? The guilt owing to the Flood is his as well as yours. He might have gained insight, as you did."

Cloud laughed, a sad, quiet sound. "Papa has enough guilt of his own to make the Flood deaths seem irrelevant. I doubt that he thinks of the event from a moral standpoint at all. We children asked his help in an expediency, and he condescended. But the crime was ours."

"You are sorry," Kuhal said.

"Most of us are," she admitted, "now. Now that we perceive you as real people instead of inconvenient abstractions standing in the way of our great undertaking. Yes, we're sorry . . . but remorse isn't really enough, is it? Sterile brooding over the wrongs we've committed doesn't *help*. Not when the wrongdoing was so appalling."

His mind reached out in empathy, only to strike the mental shield.

She said, "As we flew down to Black Crag, I mind-spoke at some length with Minanonn the Heretic, asking him how he had found peace after realizing the futility of the battle-religion. He told me that a change of heart isn't really sufficient recompense for a great sin. It had to be affirmed by some kind of repentant action or the mind can't purge guilt, and if we try to deny this, then the soul finds its own penance, as Papa's has tried to do. But in his case, where he consciously rejects atonement, there will never be any true peace . . . Hagen and I and the others don't reject the idea of recompense, as Papa has. But we don't know *how* to atone for what we did to your people."

"Your father has offered you one possible course of action," Kuhal said. "Mental Man could be a force for wisdom and goodness in this galaxy."

Her mind-veil parted briefly, letting irony escape. "It could— if Papa and Hagen weren't part of the scheme. But I know my father better than anyone. He says that Hagen and I would be the administrators—but he'd never let us be. Not while he lived. And if my brother killed him—as he would, inevitably— Mental Man would carry the mark of Cain, just like all the rest of the human race."

"And mine," Kuhal said.

Her mind flashed a smile. "You do understand."

"We understand each other, Cloud. And I think you speak of this now only to bolster your courage, for you know very well what you must do, what decision you must make—and convince your brother to share."

"Hagen's going to be terribly afraid, Kuhal. Back on Ocala, when Alexis Manion first began to talk to us about the Unity as an alternative to Papa's plan, Hagen was almost paralyzed at the very notion of defiance. As much as he feared Papa and wanted to escape, the thought of confronting a Galactic Mind in the Milieu—becoming a part of it—frightened him still more. We're a self-centered lot, we Remillards. Jealous of our individuality."

"Don't I know that!" The yearning insufficiency reached out to her. The need. "And love does mean a surrender of some part of the heart's sovereignty. But not subordination, Cloud. Not in real love. And not in this Unity we must all join, either, if it is as Elizabeth's mind shows it. Your father's rejection of the Unity was part of his greater rejection of love in favor of power."

"You're wrong! Papa does love us. And he loved Mama to the point of unreason. He's passionately concerned with the welfare of the human race—"

"In the abstract, perhaps. But not the untidy, bloody-minded verity of real people."

She refused to respond to this.

Kuhal said, "I understand very well why your father was called the Angel of the Abyss. The Goddess leads and teaches her children, trying to bring them to maturity, and weeps over their obtuseness. But Abaddon would force his offspring into perfection."

Cloud's mind smiled. "You don't know how lucky you Tanu are to have perceived deity as a goddess. Mothers are much more inclined to let their children grow up at their own pace."

They came to the garden gate. The lights of the city twinkled through the open woodland and they heard crowd noises. The sound of music was much louder, the pipes wailing some restless chase tune.

"Do you think you'll have much trouble convincing Hagen?" Kuhal asked.

"I'll have most of the others on my side, with the principal exception of Nial Keogh, who's a vicious little power seeker. Some of them, like Diana Manion, are simply timid about going to the Milieu and more inclined to accept the devil we know rather than the one we don't. But I think I'll be able to handle things. You'll help, won't you? Thanks to your advice, I was able to do a pretty good job smoothing over the mess after that stupid attack on the King's life at the iron foundry. No doubt you'll be able to suggest some ploys for dealing with this situation as well."

"Politicking," he said whimsically. "Why shouldn't I know the game? I've been at it for more than four hundred years."

She started, then laughed. "Yes. You have, haven't you? You Tanu live so long. How long do you live, Kuhal?"

"It's been said that we seldom see three millennia out, the perils of the battle-company being what they are, and the shortage of Skin practitioners. I was most fortunate to have you as my redactor."

"You began to love me even then," she accused him. "That's what made your healing so effective. Boduragol said so."

"It was mutual."

"It wasn't! We simply have mental affinity. We're very close, but that's not the same as love."

"It's a beginning," he suggested.

"You'll always be my dearest friend. But—"

"You don't wish me to follow you through the time-gate? My presence would be an embarrassment to you? . . . Very well. I will stay here."

"No!" she cried. For the first time she let her barriers down. "I don't really love you—but what would I do without you?"

His mind responded with a formless outcry, human in its joy born of desolation. He held both her hands and she felt the electric warmth of his life-force flow through their clasped fingers and set every nerve ending in her body ablaze. Joined in a single aura, the stately robed figure and the small white-clad one filled the dark corner of the garden with rosy gold light. It lasted only an instant. Then they walked hand in hand through the gate.

"But it solves everything, darling—don't you see?" Diane Manion was desperately eager. "This way, there'd be no worry about the Milieu treating us as criminals, no fear of being punished or possibly ostracized because of who we are . . . You say Marc lied to you. But only about inconsequential things! The really important matter—that all of us children should share in the creation of a grand new race of ultrametapsychics— was true! It's what Marc has said all along. What we learned from Falemoana and Dr. Curtis and Trudi when we were little children. But now your father's dream isn't far off in the future, or dependent upon some altruistic race coming to fetch us off this godfosaken planet. It's *now*! We can leave here and begin the work! You and I can have an army of super-Cubs of our own, Hagen! I wouldn't mind the other. I mean, it would be all test tubes and artificial nurture, just like the nonborns in the Milieu colonies, so I couldn't possibly be jealous. I'd be proud! Darling—*you* are the key to this whole glorious idea—not Cloud! If what you say is true, then your sister has only a single ovary. Perhaps one hundred thousand gametes if they all proved viable, which they wouldn't. But you—"

"Lucky me." Hagen laughed softly. "I'm a male, and I could sire millions and millions. With banked sperm and a little tissue culture, Mental Man could propagate for aeons even if I should die. Accidentally."

He was standing at the shore of the garden pond, not looking at her. The night-blooming waterlilies gave off a pineapple fragrance. Diane had been almost totally unaware of his mood, so thick had been his mental screening. He had simply confirmed the report that Aiken had given Diane about the meeting with Marc, then asked her for her reaction. Now he had it.

"It's not as though we wouldn't have children of our own," she protested.

"And how will you feel when it comes time to take the babies' bodies away?"

"Bodies . . . away?"

Hagen whirled about, seizing her by the arms, crushing them through the light fabric of her Tanu gown. "That's part of it, you little fool! Not just for the artificially engendered children—for all of them! They're to be bodiless, like my sainted Uncle Jack, to force them to utilize their full mental potential. Naked brains that conjure up psychocreative disguises to hide their inhumanity! But better than Jack—oh, I'll hand Marc that! They'll be immortal, and able to hook themselves into cerebroenergetic enhancers whenever they please, without being inconvenienced by primitive appendages such as arms or legs or hearts or guts. Brains without faces! Without lips to kiss hands to touch each other. Neat, efficient brains with needle-electrodes in them, glowing white-hot with great thoughts! What will they think about, Diane? Will they dream? Will they find things to laugh at? Will they love each other? Will they love us and thank us for making them that way? Will they, Diane?"

His mind opened, showing a black thing roughly humanoid in shape, self-contained, armored against the world, divorced from its unnecessary body, its ultrasenses prowling the galaxy on a never-ending search for other minds like itself—and finding none, resolving to make such minds. *Don't cry, Hagen. Don't be afraid. It's only Papa . . .*

Hagen said, "He's got a second suit of armor there in Kyllikki, ready for me."

Diane screamed.

He folded his arms around her then and held her to his breast. The white antelope skin of the storm-suit was soft, warmed by the living flesh inside, faintly redolent of wax and tanning compound and human sweat. The face that looked down at her was haggard, wet with tears, in need of a shave, the jaw trembling with tension and still scarred on the left side with the psychosomatic stigma of the hook. A face that was almost Marc's.

"He won't let us go," Diane whispered in terror.

"With Aiken Drum on our side, we can give him a damn good run for his money," Hagen said. "And if the old wolf starts getting too close to the fleeing sleigh—well, I can always make Marc a present of the other nut. Then he'd have his Mental Man and we'd be free of him forever."

She burst into tears, and then she was laughing with him, and then the laughter was smothered in their kisses. He said, "Come on, babe," and led her to the starproof shadow of a flowering daphne. After they had coupled they lay on their side, face to face, and body to body, clinging to one another. The turf was dewy and none too soft and a chill breeze stole over the pond, but still they lay together sharing warmth and breath.

"I wish we could have made Mental Man tonight," he said. "Damn that implant."

"I'll ask Becky Kramer to take it out tomorrow."

"The kid will be born in the Milieu," Hagen said, "or we'll just fly away, babe. The three of us. Okay?"

"Yes."

They held each other more tightly and let the mental images drift from one mind to the other. Fears. Elizabeth's reassurance. Dangers. The possible failure of the Guderian Project. Alexis Manion's persistent reassurance last winter in Ocala that they would only find fulfillment in the Unity . . . as would their child.

"And it'll be immortal, like you," Diane whispered tremulously.

"Self-rejuvenating," Hagen corrected her. "And in case you're fearful of losing your endearing young charms, let me remind you that some of the time-travelers in our lab went through four refit jobs in tanks back in the Milieu, and would likely have kept up the good work indefinitely if they hadn't hankered for the primitive life here in the Pliocene."

Diane giggled. "Can't you imagine the consternation among all those sensible stay-at-home Milieu folks when we pop through the time-gate and tell them we have the grandson of Mental Man in embryo?"

Hagen made an indelicate noise. "That'll be the *first* shock. If this thing works out, we'll be lucky if the whole exile population doesn't come along with us. Cloud and her faerie prince aren't the half of it."

Diane was quiet for a long moment. "Hagen—she wouldn't stay, would she? She says she doesn't love Kuhal. She wouldn't be tempted to sacrifice herself for the rest of us, would she?"

"For Papa's sake, you mean? Don't kid yourself! In the first place, you were all too right when you noted that in the Mental Man game, the male of the species has natural advantages over the female. Papa wants me. Why do you think he let Cloud go to Europe with Elaby and the others, but kept me there in Ocala? I'm to take *his* place."

"Cloud has the genes," Diane insisted. "Marc could use her."

"She wants Unity more than any of us! Cloud and Elaby were the first ones to be convinced by Alex that rebellion was the better part."

"But Elaby's dead, Hagen, and Cloud says she'll never fall in love with anyone again and risk the pain—"

"My cerebral sister wouldn't know love if it bit her on the ankle. No matter what she says, she and Kuhal will follow right along with the rest of us . . . and if you think our offspring will rock the Milieu, what about a Tanu-Remillard cross?"

"We Manions have our hidden marvels, too. Let me show you one."

There followed a good deal of laughter and other pleasantry. But all too soon the stars dimmed and disappeared behind an overcast. As the first drops of rain from the next storm fell upon them, they helped each other to dress and had a last kiss. Then Hagen spun a small psychocreative umbrella and they walked under it back to the Castle of Glass, intending to give their decision to the King.

Aiken was not at home.

Neither was the Guderian Project laboratory, its personnel, the giant sigma-generator, or the twenty-one aircraft that had been parked in the castle courtyard.

There was pain of translation and then he hung in the gray limbo, not for a subjective instant as during his former d-jumps, but for an excruciating quarter of an hour, since he was experimentally transporting three tons of inert matter in addition to his regular armor. He endured while the stubborn fabric of space bent to his mind's command and the hyperspatial catenary was executed: a nonline drawn through a nondimensional region by a nonforce.

Imprisoned inside the refrigerated and ultrapressurized CE rig, the supercharged brain was deprived of all normal and all metasensory input. Hyperspace was without form and void. He was fully conscious and self-possessed within its matrix, as though he rode a superluminal starship; but there the analog ended. If he had been on a ship he might have slept or read or taken light exercise or eaten or amused himself in any number of ways, trusting to the ship's crew and machinery to translate him across more than 14,000 light-years of interstellar space.

Instead, he was the ship.

He had no artificial guidance system, no computerized routefinder such as a starship captain had, no engine powered by fusing nuclei to energize his passage. The equipment worn by his brain served only to assist in puncturing the superficies. It let him enter hyperspace via an upsilon-field gateway; but once inside the gray limbo, there was only the mental program to provide direction and impetus. It was a wondrous program, purchased at great price, and its use was not for the fainthearted. Seeming to move along an invisible cable hung between two worlds, the d-jumper did not dare to relax his concentration for an instant. His attention must not falter, must not be distracted from the goal by a single vagrant thought. The goal alone was life. If his mind relinquished it for the millionth part of a second, he would be lost.

He held fast through the endless and horrific minutes, knowing only the goal. It was a star: G3-1668 in his catalog, a sun he had never bothered to name when he farsensed it more than seven years ago and rejected it because the people were pre-metapsychic and apparently useless for his purposes. Now, however, of the three star systems that were potential cradles for Mental Man, he judged this one to be the most promising. So he named the sun Goal, and filled his mind with it in order to forget the events that must be taking place back on Earth...

In time he reached the terminal superficies. His brain flared, drawing heavily upon the cortical augmentation reserves to suck in more energy. He spun the upsilon-field, thrust the three tons of ballast rock through it, and then followed himself. He knew hideous agony and uttered a cosmic groan. Then he hung in space, surveying the scene with his mind's eye.

A yellow star lit half of a white-swirled blue marble. It was the fourth planet of the Goal system, home of the indigenous race. He studied it with his farsense for several hours, savoring the respite from pain, then wished himself and his cargo to the surface. This time the d-jump took less time than an eye-blink and caused less discomfort than a plucked lash. The teleported rocks, for whose sake he had risked his life, lay in an undistinguished heap. Some of them were still crusted with frozen mud from the Seine estuary.

Marc forgot them. He emerged from his armor, rendered himself invisible, and walked among the unsuspecting exotic people for two days.

They were bipeds, approximately humanoid in form and approximately saurischian in derivation. They were intelligent, peaceable, and had a birthrate that was probably too low ever to admit of their attaining the "magic number" of ten thousand million living minds, the normal minimum required for coadunation. The planet had an advanced technoeconomy that kept its people prosperous and healthy. Its biomedical establishment was sophisticated enough to support the Mental Man breeding program. It was an attractive world, with an ecology as congruous to human life as any colonial planet of the Milieu. The people were a hardworking and worthy lot, with a psychosocial index that would suggest rapid adaptation to a benevolent despotism.

It was a world, he thought, that would do nicely. Here, under his aegis, Mental Man would burgeon and flourish and expand His bright dominion from star to star through the aeons to come, the all-conquering and immortal Mind.

And in six million years, there would remain not a trace of Him.

He could not pray for the desired outcome. It did not exist and would not. He wondered: Can I *will* it?

After two days of observation in the Goal star system, depressed to the depths of his being, Marc d-jumped back to Kyllikki. He farspoke Elizabeth on Black Crag and said:

Tell me.

She said: The children gave me their response and asked me to relay it to you.

Very well.

[*Image: Daughter and son stand before hilltop stone castle rain lush grass path bordered white stones flat rock surface with Square.*]

' Hagen: This is Castle Gateway Papa. We're standing on the site of the time-gate leading from the Milieu to the Pliocene. The gate we all came through. We've thought about your proposition. Both of us. We've spoken to all the other children as well and conferred with the King but the decision was ours. We've decided to go back to the Galactic Milieu. Back to the world that we were born in back to the mind-family that can help us find peace. We'd never have that with you. Mental Man could never be happy in the form you envision. Not unless each mind was a saint like Uncle Jack was. And saints aren't that common Papa! You aren't one and neither are Cloud and I. We'll need a lot of help from our friends to make a success of life and so will our children. That's who Mental Man really is Papa . . . our children. They're going to be human beings like their parents with bodies as well as minds. Not angels. They'll be frightened by their immortality just as you are . . . and we are. But they'll be linked to billions of other minds who'll offer love and support and good counsel. We think that will suffice.

Cloud: We can't go your way Papa. Your vision is flawed. Deep in your heart I think you know it. There were so many times you could have stopped us compelled us to submit to you even killed us and taken the genes. And yet you didn't. Find out why and perhaps you'll be able to resign yourself to letting us go. Look far back into your past Papa! Understand why you cast Mental Man in this inhuman mold and tried to force yourself and your children to conform to it. I think we are beginning to see the reasons why. Eventually we'll be able to forgive you and you must do the same for us. We'll take good care of your dream and see that it's nurtured in the Unity where it belongs. It will all be for the best. Trust us Papa . . .

[*Image: Son and daughter gesture walk up path rain falls on louring stone castle barbican gate opens glimpse inner courtyard people machinery weapons SILVER HEMISPHERE FLASHES INTO BEING enveloping entire castle Golden Manikin appears.*]

Aiken: I've moved the entire Guderian Project from Goriah to Castle Gateway. One of my loyal subjects has hooked up the big SR-35 sigma generator to a pair of SR-15s that I happened to have stashed away—and now Cloud and Hagen are safe inside the sigma-field with all the others. The psychoenergetic equivalent of the stacked screens is over 900 now. You don't have enough watts to break through even if you push your creativity to the limit with the enhancer and mesh all your old cronies into the metaconcert. There isn't a weapon in the Pliocene that can puncture that silver bubble Marc. Not even my photon Spear. Not even Felice could crack it! And the only one who can activate its airlock now is Me. . . . You're checkmated Marc. Your children told me they'd rather die than go your way. But they aren't going to die. I've taken them under my protection. They're going to finish the Guderian device and go through the time-gate into the Milieu. Right there inside Castle Gateway under the sigma-umbrella if need be. The device will work in there. Ask Alexis Manion if you don't believe me . . . I don't want to fight you Marc. I want to resolve this mess peacefully if I can and tend to some other urgent business. But if you insist on attacking the Guderian Project be assured that I'll defend it—and so will the minds that work in metaconcert with Me. Thousands of them all meshed nicely now under my command in the program you gave me down at the Río Genil . . . I know that the schooner carrying your CE-rig power supply is somewhere in the Gulf of Armorica or the Seine Delta. You've got her camouflaged

with some kind of farsight fuzzer. But if you try to fight me
I'll find Kyllikki one way or another and I'll nail her and nail
you . . . But wouldn't that be a tawdry way to end it now?
Wouldn't it be more your style—and mine!—to let the Truce
prevail? Sail Kyllikki right up the Seine all the way to the Field
of Gold—white flag up and screens off. You and your Rebels
are invited to be my guests at the Grand Tourney! Watch the
games then kiss your kids goodbye and sail on back to Florida . . . Think about it Marc. You have a lot of things to think
about. [*Fading image.*]

Elizabeth said: That's the entire message. Aiken's told you
the truth about Castle Gateway. He did move the Guderian
Project there—in a single evening. He's regained his strength
and integrated the powers of Nodonn and Mercy as well. Don't
challenge him Marc. You'll only destroy the Many-Colored
Land to no purpose. Yield. Please!

Marc said: They've made their decision. Now I'll make
mine. It may take some time.

The farspoken voice died away, and all that was left in the
aether were reverberations from faraway lightning bolts and a
faint rustle of mental static.

Elizabeth sent her tightest farsight beam arrowing along the
path of Marc's communication. But at the extremity there was
only wind-riffled water where a great river met the sea, and
starless night.

In the stern hold of Kyllikki, Jordan Kramer and Gerrit Van
Wyk lifted the heavy casque from Marc's head, then helped
him from the body armor. The other surviving magnates were
there waiting: Cordelia Warshaw and Ragnar Gathen and Jeff
Steinbrenner and Patricia Castellane. Off in a corner on a stool,
with eyes strangely lucid in spite of the docilator, sat Alexis
Manion. They waited.

Marc said, "The children have declined my offer. As you
know now, there can be no Mental Man without them. Cloud
and Hagen and the others are at the time-gate site on the Rhône
River. Aiken Drum transferred the entire Guderian Project there,
and shielded it with a nine hundred-power sigma. My son and
daughter have said they would prefer death to cooperation with
me in the engendering of Mental Man. They intended for Him
to be subordinated to the Milieu."

Alexis Manion smiled.

Patricia cried, "You can take their genes!"

"I don't know whether I can or not." He stood there in the black pressure suit, soaked with the amniotic fluid of the enhancer, blood from the electrode wounds flowing thinly down his brow and cheeks. "At the moment, I can't think of any way to break through their defenses. I'm not even convinced I should try." One side of his mouth lifted gently. "I find myself precariously tempted to virtue."

"But, if you give it up—it's the end!" Patricia exclaimed.

Alexis Manion said distinctly:

> Mon front est rouge encore du baiser de la
> reine.
> J'ai rêvé dans la grotte où nage la sirène . . .

Marc nodded in agreement. "And the siren still sings and holds out the promise, and I'm addicted to the kiss of the vampire-queen."

Patricia said, "You're exhausted. You should sleep. Later you can consider what might be done."

The other magnates added a murmur of half-voiced thoughts. All of them hid behind thick mental walls.

Marc said to Ragnar Gathen, "We'll sail up the river. I've been told that it's navigable for several hundred kilometers. How are the solar impellers holding up?"

"Very well," said the former starfleet strategist.

"Have Walter take us up at a modest cruise speed, then. We're in no hurry. Maintain the camouflage—and be sure it's dense enough to foil aerial surveillance as well as farsight scan."

"We'll be secure enough," Gathen said, "unless one of the King's people actually eyeballs us from the riverbank."

"We ought to make certain no stray thought betrays our position," Patricia said, glancing at Manion.

"I'll count on you to take care of that," Marc said.

Cordelia Warshaw asked, "Do you have any further orders for us?"

"Relax," Marc told them all, the famous smile overriding the desolation in his eyes. "I myself intend to go fishing."

5

DURING THAT TRUCE BEFORE NIGHTFALL, IT SEEMED THAT almost everyone in the Many-Colored Land was on the move.

The Tanu had always flocked to the games; but this autumn, the King issued an extraordinary proclamation, commanding that every human—even those who customarily remained at home caretaking the cities and plantations and other establishments—must attend the Grand Tourney. So they all came out to enjoy the holiday, people torced in gold and silver and gray, and the lowly bareneck serfs as well. The cities, with the exception of the capital and Roniah, which hosted the travelers, were left almost deserted but for the faithful ramas. The King's invitation was extended to outlaw humans, too, and they came trickling out of the Spanish wilderness, the high Helvetides, and the Jura. The royal word reached into the swamps of Bordeaux and the Paris Basin and the haunted forests of darkest Albion. Drawn as much by the prospect of fun and free food and drink as by curiosity over the import of the King's decree, more than 45,000 human beings set out for Nionel and the Field of Gold—virtually all who resided in Pliocene Europe. Of them, perhaps 1500 were operant golds and twice that number were torced with the precious metal but lacking in significant mental powers. There were 4200 silvers, some 8500 grays, and under 20,000 barenecks who had willingly accepted Tanu servitude. The free Lowlives numbered about 8000, but more than half of those were already residents of Nionel.

Tadanori Kawai was among the few who heard the King's proclamation and politely demurred. He wished to husband his failing strength, and there was considerable work to be done preparing Hidden Springs for the rainy season.

Stein Oleson heard the proclamation and ignored it. His Viking intuition told him what the Fimbulvetr presaged, and he knew that the Field of Gold was no place for him or his family.

Huldah Henning, away on the Isle of Kersic, never knew of the royal announcement at all, nor would she have accepted its invitation. She was in her eighth month, and the tri-hybrid son of Nodonn Battlemaster rode turbulently in her womb.

To his metapsychically operant subjects King Aiken-Lugonn sent a more somber message: Attend the Tourney, ready to cooperate in metaconcert, or risk the Foe's conquest of our land.

The response was one of overwhelming fealty. Every gold-wearer in the kingdom who was not at the threshold of Tana's Peace or in Skin set out obediently for Nionel: some 2400 pureblooded Tanu and less than 500 hybrids. Together with the operant human golds and silvers, the minds pledged to the King's service in the event of Nightfall totaled just over 13,000.

Not counting the Howlers, there were more than 80,000 Firvulag.

On a day in mid-October, when the Roniah Fair was at its height and the air quivered in thirty-five degree heat and thunderheads skulked about the flanks of the steaming Mont-Dore volcano, the fearsome prodigy appeared!

Travelers on the Great South Road craned their necks and came to a standstill, peering into the dazzling afternoon sky. Their minds and voices uttered cries of amazement, surprised recognition, or near panic—according to whether the observer was Tanu, human, or Firvulag. Chalikos, hellads, and the motley collection of hipparions and half-tamed antelopes that the Little People rode or drove spooked as they caught sight of the thing. The highway, the Roniah fairgrounds, and the adjacent campsites were thrown into an uproar of plunging beasts, laughing humans, bemused Tanu, and outraged Firvulag.

It looked at first like a dark, floating fish. It had stubby fins and a needle nose and seemed to swim down through the heat-thickened air with sinister deliberation, becoming more and more enormous as it neared the earth. Purple strings of fire, like a dimly glowing net, enshrouded it. (And revealed to the former Milieu citizens that it had to be none other than a rhocraft, albeit one of highly unorthodox configuration.) A terrified dwarf shot a bolt of psychoenergy at the thing hovering overhead, and his countrymen wailed aloud, fearful of retribution.

All that happened was that a vent in the thing's belly opened. It seemed to lay thousands upon thousands of buoyant yellow eggs, cascading them over the crowd like a hen-salmon strewing her redd. The aircraft glided to and fro, discharging its bounty; and a different sort of cry arose from the throng when it became clear that the spawn of the sky-fish was nothing more than balloons. Each one, when popped, yielded candy or cold fruit or a petit four or a liqueur-filled sugar shell. (And a few of the Tanu whispered, "Mercy-Rosmar!" remembering her gentle manifestation of power at the last Grand Combat.)

The cynosure of all eyes then lifted its pointed snout to the zenith and hung stock-still in midair, not more than 150 meters above the mobbed fairgrounds. It appeared to be gargantuan, like a flanged broad arrow, black beneath the violet flickering. From the open belly hatch now came a flood of balloons like lustrous grapes. They seemed to be self-animated, and darted and swooped and soared in the sky like frenzied protozoa.

The aircraft proceeded to shoot them down. A blue-white ray lanced from its nose, while green, red, and yellow beams spat at a dozen different angles from the leading edges of the fins. There were sharp detonations. The people screamed. Puffs of multicolored smoke dissolved to wraiths of perfume and a shower of confetti glitter.

The upright dark thing began to change. Its stubby fins expanded into wings and it tilted so that all the observers could see a glowing golden emblem on its underside, the hand of King Aiken-Lugonn. Then the emblem also changed. The impudent digit gave way to a hand fully opened and apaumy, with the fingers together in the dignified gesture that most humans recognized as the greeting between operant citizens of the Milieu.

The aircraft began to rise swiftly then, and there was applause from the King's subjects and scattered mental cries of "Slonshal!" But then they all fell silent, for the ship emblazoned with the golden hand took its place at the point of a V-formation of others identical to itself that came gliding up from the south at an altitude of several thousand meters. There were twenty-seven flyers altogether, small against the sky like a flight of wild geese. They stayed in view of the Roniah multitude for five minutes before going full inertialess and vanishing in a thunderous sonic boom.

Dougal, sitting in the copilot's seat, vented a bemused sigh. "I might not this believe without the sensible and true avouch of mine own eyes . . . Just how the devil *did* you manage that caper, my liege?"

Aiken laughed. "Creativity, lad. Sleight of mind. An illusion here, a genuine manifestation there, a scary black cerametal machine that's all too real, and a spot of royal markmanship to dazzle 'em with science at the finale."

"Extremely gaudy," said Mr. Betsy, making a prissy face. He lounged in the navigator's station of the flight deck, attired for the occasion in a mauve flying suit all slashed with gold zippers, a bouffant red wig, and a discreet little diadem with cabochon amethysts. "A great bluff, that's what it was."

"I prefer to think of it as a show of strength," said the King. He grinned over his shoulder at the Flight Instructor Royal.

Betsy said, "The eighteen pilot recruits were pushing their luck just to carry off a straight level flyby, and you know it. We'll be doing well to whip them into a minimally competent check-out state by Tourney time—much less teach them aerial combat technique."

"I have every confidence in you," the King said. "Look how well you taught Me!" He picked up the RF com and said to his squadron, "Thank you very much, ladies and gentlemen. Our air show was a great success. Let's hope it heartened our friends and discombobulated the Foe. You may now return to Goriah base and take the rest of the day off."

Mr. Betsy adjusted the exotic sky-sweep scanner to watch

the departure. He sighed. "What an abysmally sloppy peel-away. It's those wretched wings. Only a *very* decadent technology would put wings on a rhocraft."

"Yet thus equipped," Dougal said, "they are the more fearsome of the miscreant eye . . . and the wings are also a damn good place to mount the secondary zapper arrays."

Mr. Betsy gave a scathing snort. "Guns, dear zany, are only useful when you have competent gunners. May I remind you that Stan and Taffy Evans are the only persons with the appropriate training, while the other six Bastard pilots and I are as hopelessly noncombatant as the recruits. I doubt if any of us could hit Mont-Dore at point-blank range—and Miss Wang goes into hysterics at the mere thought of a fire fight."

"If the Firvulag host gets between her and the time-gate," Aiken noted dryly, "she may find her backbone stiffening." He twiddled the controls and the sky outside the flyer turned from cobalt to star-spangled black. "There's hope for you duffers, though. Yosh Watanabe is putting together some robot target locks for the weaponry. As long as the spooks don't mount a Flying Hunt, the targeters should take most of the worry out of air-to-ground zapmanship."

"Only one thing will do that," Betsy said. "Aircraft force-shields that *don't* have to be neutralized at every salvo!"

"I'm sorry," the King said uncomfortably. "All we have left are small sigmas. The weaponry we have available just isn't compatible. You'll have to turn the shield off before firing. I'm trying to work out a method of metapsychic shelter—assign several creative stalwarts to each ship. But I'm afraid that if war does come, I'll need every strong mind I can scrounge for my own metaconcert. In an all-out attack, the Flying Corps may have to do the best it can with conventional weapons and screens."

"Blow, wind! Come, wrack!" Dougal declaimed. "At least we'll die with harness on our back!"

"Why don't you stuff it, you anachronist booby?" Betsy hissed. Then he seemed to notice for the first time that they were high in the ionosphere. The expanse of the Northern Peneplain spread out below like a brown and ochre map of low relief, veined with dark green watercourses. "Where are you taking us?" he asked the King petulantly. "I'm not really in the mood for any joyrides."

"No joy," muttered the King. "Now that I can fly one of these birds with medium incompetence, I thought I'd better have a cautious look-see at the River Seine. It's been four days since Marc got the bad news from Elizabeth, and still not a squeak out of him. So it's time for an aerial survey."

"God's death!" snared the incarnation of Good Queen Bess. "What if the brute tries to zap us?"

"We're out of range of the 414 blasters. Hagen says that there's nothing heavier on Kyllikki, now that the X-lasers are out."

"Remillard could d-jump on board!"

"He doesn't know we're here. We're too high to see, and he's got no reason to be farsensing up here. Now quit your chuntering, man, and get on that ground sweeper. Comb the river starting at the estuary."

Grumbling bitterly, Betsy did as he was told.

The King relaxed in his seat, staring pensively at the daytime stars. After a while he said to Dougal, "I hate to admit it, but I've about given up trying to figure out what Marc Remillard will do next. I guess I didn't really expect him to reply to my invitation to the Grand Tourney. He's hardly about to abandon his scheme after so many years, just because his kids run out on him. Elizabeth said it was a long shot, though, that he might pack it in. And I saw for myself that the guy really does love his children."

"Love is not love," Dougal murmured, "when it is mingled with regards that stand aloof from the entire point. As you should know."

"I like enemies I can pin a label on," Aiken complained. "Sharn and Ayfa! Nodonn! Even Gomnol, damn his dead eyes. But Marc's a different breed. So bloody charming . . ."

"One may smile and smile and be a villain."

The King seemed to be talking to himself. "I can't let Remillard put the wind up me. I've got to carry on with my royal duties, even if it means he might nail me when I least expect it. But if I could find where he's hiding . . ." He called out to Betsy. "Any sign?"

"Negative," growled the counterfeit Elizabethan.

"The King's will," Dougal said, "is not his own. He may not, as unvalued persons do, carve for himself, for on his choice depends the safety and health of the whole state. So then, my liege, be bloody, bold, and resolute! Be lion-mettled, proud, and take no care who chafes, who frets, or where conspirers are—for if 'tis true that doomsday's near, then die all, die merrily!"

He placed both hands upon the crowned lion blazon on his knightly surcoat.

Aiken stared at the golden charge. "Perhaps I should have taken the lion for my emblem instead of the hand." His brow creased. "Dougie, I've seen it before. Back on Dalriada, when I was just a juvenile delinquent disturbing the peace of the other haggis-wallopers. What does the lion emblem mean?"

"It is Aslan, of course," said the madman, "and an ancient badge among our Scottish kinfolk as well, with its motto *'S Rioghal Mo Dhream*—Royal Is My Race. It's the crest of Clan Gregor."

Aiken drew in a sharp breath. "And that's your family name?"

"No. I was born a Fletcher—a sept of the clan. But the one I sought so long is a MacGregor unknowing. Father'd he is, and yet he's fatherless." The mad knight smiled at the King.

Aiken sank back in the pilot's seat and began to laugh. "First it's born and then it's rooted! Priceless!" He opened a leg pocket, took out a white handkerchief, and wiped his face. "Thanks Dougie, I needed that."

The medievalist said softly, "My liege, receive what cheer you may. The night is long that never finds the day."

"If you can get control of yourself," came Betsy's acerbic interruption, "you might care to take a goggle at this. Your Majesty. I've scanned the entire river from the Gulf of Armorica to its confluence with the Nonol just below Nionel. The only remotely anomalous object I can pick up on this barbarian peep-scope is here—a little over one hundred kilometers inland."

The King frowned at the display. "Jack up the magnification. No, that only makes it fuzzier. And look how the damn thing keeps hopping about, skipping up and down the river like a will-o'-the-wisp."

"I told you it was anomalous," Betsy said. "It could be some obscure gravomagnetic effect, or a glitch in the imaging cir-cuitry. After all, the poor scope's at least a thousand years old. On the other hand—"

"You don't get this gremlin in any other part of the river?"

"No. We could descend to a lower altitude, of course, or

probe it with a detector beam or your farsense."

"I don't think we'll risk that," said the King. "If it is Kyllikki, they might feel the tickle."

"The better part of valor is discretion," Dougal quoted.

"And I have a High Table meeting at Castle Gateway in an hour," Aiken added. "If Marc wants to play coy, I'll let him. For now."

There were other travelers abroad in the land besides those headed for the tournament Field of Gold, and Mary-Dedra, chatelaine of Black Crag Lodge, came to tell Elizabeth of the latest batch.

"Six more got in just after lunch. On foot, without supplies, and they'd sent back their escorts before setting out on the last leg of the climb today. That's twenty-two all told. Nine humans, the rest Tanu."

"But there's nothing we can do," Elizabeth exclaimed. "Didn't you tell them that?"

"They're not taking no for an answer."

"Oh, dear. I suppose I'll have to deal with them myself." Elizabeth pressed fingers against her aching temples, trying to call up a self-redactive impulse. But she'd been at the farsensing too long, hoping to discover where Marc and the schooner might be concealed, and the fatigue and some perverse mental block frustrated healing. She sent out a plea to Creyn on the intimate mode, then said to Dedra: "You'd better bring them all up here—*without* the children—and I'll try to explain things as kindly as possible."

The human farsensor nodded and left the suite. Elizabeth sat in a chair by one of the large windows, which stood open to the breeze coming out of the north. The heath had begun its second bloom, brightening the dusty green slope with patches of carmine and delicate pink. Brother Anatoly pottered in the kitchen garden below, and cerulean doves cooed in the rafters of the rambling chalet.

Creyn closed the door softly behind him. She sent him a wordless appeal and he strode to her chair and spread his hands above her head. The throbbing ceased.

"Thank you." She let her eyes close. The hands descended to rest lightly on her hair as he stood behind her.

"Have you found anything?" he asked.

"Not a trace. Marc must be using some kind of artificial screen. Not a sigma—that would stick out like a beacon—but something absorptive that swallows my mental beam instead of reflecting it. I never had much to do with such mechanisms back in the Milieu so I don't have counterprogramming. Most of my farsensing was communication, bespeaking other teachers and exchanging information among the worlds of the Human Polity. Hunter-searcher farsensors operated in an entirely different sphere." Aware that she was babbling, she fell silent. After a few moments had passed, she said, "Perhaps Marc's done the unexpected after all. Gone away to another planet and taken the others with him."

"I doubt it. He's been deprived of his life's objective—or he will be if he accepts the rejection of his children. He will not be satisfied until he discovers the new work that is to take the place of the flawed dream. I would have told him—even given him the mitigator program that would have made the work possible. But I was a fool and tried to bargain with him."

Distracted, Elizabeth had no notion of what he was talking about. In the courteous way of metapsychics, he opened the deeper level of his mind in explanation, reprising the memory of his last meeting with Marc. The request. The refusal.

Bewilderment clouded Elizabeth's comprehension. "A *new* work for Marc?"

Creyn nodded. "The Goddess has been pleased to give me the insight. But I was wrong not to pass it on to him freely. My only excuse is that I was a man desperate."

"You wanted Marc to apply Brendan's redactive program to your mind?" She was incredulous. "But it would never work! You're fully adult, burdened with the habitual thought-patterns of years—centuries! Oh, my dear, I'm sorry. You thought . . . but even if such a redaction were possible, it could never change things between us."

"I know that now." He smiled reassuringly. "Another insight vouchsafed by Tana, although tardily. And I had not then visualized your own role in the work, nor appreciated the significance of the inevitable duality. Again my emotions clouded my thinking."

She frowned. "You're speaking riddles, Creyn. What work?"

He showed her.

"My God!" she cried. "Are you mad?" Horror and revulsion

poured from her mind before she sent her walls crashing into place. She collected herself and said in a calm voice. "Your deep disappointment has affected your judgment even more seriously than you realize. I think you'll understand this yourself in a little while. But I must ask you—I want you to promise—you must *never* speak of this idea to anyone! Most especially not to Marc. Please, Creyn. If you care at all about me, you must promise."

His barriers lowered as a warrant of sincerity. "I promise. It's enough that you know."

"The entire notion is futile. Besides, we both know quite well what Marc will decide to do. As for the rest of it—" She shook her head. "You've been infected by the Shipspouse's lunatic prescience, not touched by Tana's wisdom."

"Perhaps." He turned away. "Forgive me if I insulted you. But as a solution, it displayed an elegant inevitability—"

"Don't mention it again. God knows I have enough to worry about."

There was a knock on the door, and Dedra's leading thought. Elizabeth rose as the door opened and steeled herself to meet the mothers of the black-torc babies.

6

AIKEN CAME INTO THE DARK COOLNESS OF THE RONIAH CITY-
Lord's sanctum, where the High Table members had gathered.
Of those that had served the Thagdal there remained only Kuhal
Earthshaker, Bleyn the Champion, and Alberonn Mindeater.
Celadeyr, who had been raised to the Table on the battlefield
of the last Grand Combat and then attainted for his role in
Nodonn's treason, was now finally adjudged worthy of rein-
statement. He stood with the seven newly chosen Great Ones
ready to take the pledge of fealty.

AIKEN: It's fitting that the High Table should be complete at
this first Grand Tourney celebration so that our High Kingdom may present a unified face to the Foe. To this end I
have nominated a full slate of Great Ones . . .
ALL: [Surprised murmurs.] But two seats are unfilled!
AIKEN: A full slate, I say. But before receiving your oaths I
command your commemoration of those High Table Members who have passed into Tana's Peace since our last con-
vocation at the Grand Loving: Aluteyn Craftsmaster, Second
Lord Creator; Artigonn of Amalizan, Second Lord Coercer;
Armida the Formidable of Bardelask.

ALL: To them be Tana's Peace.

AIKEN: And in compassion let us commend those who fell from My favor and forfeited their seats through treason: Thufan Thunderhead of Tarasiah; Diarmet of Geroniah; Moreyn Glasscrafter of Var-Mesk.

ALL: To them also be Tana's Peace.

AIKEN: [Pain.] And the late Queen Mercy-Rosmar.

ALL: Peace to her.

AIKEN: Peace to her. And my most noble antagonist Nodonn Battlemaster.

ALL: Peace to him.

AIKEN: And finally, let us commend one who does not rest to the mercy of the Goddess, that in her good time she may give him peace: Culluket the Interrogator, Lord Redactor.

ALL: [Dread.] Tana grant him release. [The Song.]
      (Silence.)

AIKEN: Now let the sitting Great Ones reaffirm fealty.

MORNA-IA KINGMAKER + SIBEL LONGTRESS + BLEYN THE CHAMPION + KUHAL EARTHSHAKER + CONDATEYR FULMINATOR + ALBERONN MINDEATER + EADNAR OF ROCILAN + NEYEL OF SASARAN + LOMNOVEL BRAINBURNER + ESTELLA-SIRONE OF DARASK: Slonshal to the Shining One, Aiken-Lugonn High King of our Many-Colored Land.

AIKEN: And to you Slonshal ... Let the nominated Great Ones here present pledge fealty. Celadeyr of Afaliah, Second Lord Creator.

CELADEYR: I swear by the torc.

AIKEN: Boduragol of Afaliah, Lord Redactor, and Lady Credela, Second Redactor.

BODURAGOL + CREDELA: We swear by the torc.

AIKEN: The city-lords Ochal the Harper of Bardelask, Parthol Swiftfoot of Calamosk, Ferdiet the Courteous of Tarasiah, Heymdol Buccinator of Geroniah, and Donal of Amalizan.

OCHAL + PARTHOL + FERDIET + HEYMDOL + DONAL: We swear by the torc.

AIKEN: And now I will fill the last two seats.
      (Speculation. Wonderment.)

AIKEN: We live in terrible and portentous times, greatly outnumbered by our ancient Foe and beset by outlandish menaces as well. Yet we are not without friends, some of whom are unable to publicly declare themselves. These friends

have given Me good counsel and deserve to sit among the
Great Ones by reason of the love they have for our land,
the goodwill they bear toward its King, and their own sovereign dignity. They must for now sit at our Table in secret.
Let them manifest themselves in simulacrum to take their
pledge.

(Stupefaction.)

KATLINEL THE DARKEYED AND SUGOLL: We swear by the
love we bear one another and by our love for the land
and its people that we will uphold King Aiken-Lugonn in
all noble-minded endeavor. We vow our alliance in battle
in the event of the Nightfall War, and repudiate our erstwhile vassalage to the Firvulag Throne. And thou, Teah,
witnesseth.

AIKEN: Slonshal and Slitsal to one and all.

(Uproar.)

AIKEN: Does anyone dispute My right to seat these two?

(Silence.)

AIKEN: Brothers and Sisters, desperate times call for desperate
remedies. Sugoll and Katy have told me how King Sharn
openly boasted of a scheme to touch off Nightfall at the
climax of the Tourney.

CELADEYR: I knew it! And they called me an antiquated death-
wisher!

AIKEN: Sharn has been drilling his stalwarts in metaconcert
technique for months. And Ayfa's contribution is dinging
the brains of the stubborn ones who cling to the old indi-
vidualistic Way. The Little People have new tactics and new
weapons. They use cavalry and captured Milieu weapons—
and even the blood-metal, since they're not as sensitive to
iron poisoning as Tanu are.

DONAL OF AMALIZAN: But this is monstrous! Sharn and Ayfa
must be insane to think of precipitating Nightfall. They're
both young, with children, and Nightfall means the doom
of both our races!

CELADEYR: Only according to orthodox Tanu belief, son. The
Firvulag have convinced themselves that Nightfall will bring
victory to one faction: themselves. And there is a dim jus-
tification for the notion in our sacred writings, given a fast
and loose interpretation.

KUHAL EARTHSHAKER: Trust the Firvulag to do just that.

OCHAL THE HARPER: We have confidence that the Shining One will forestall Night!

AIKEN: I'm going to do my damnedest. We're outnumbered, but we've got discipline in our metaconcert—and a much more efficient program that yields more watts per mind. We've also got the Spear, a good supply of sophisticated weapons, and the Royal Flying Corps—which you saw in action this afternoon.

(Admiration.)

SUGOLL: Are *all* the flying machines armed, as was your flag-ship?

AIKEN: We're working on it. Refitting a rhocraft is tricky be-cause of the reticular field that covers the skin. With luck, most of the fleet will be zapper-equipped by tournament time.

MORNA-IA KINGMAKER: Woe! O Goddess forfend! That I, a First Comer, should live to see a renewal of those dread hostil-ities from which Brede Shipspouse sought to save us!

CELADEYR: A pity *we* only have Elizabeth . . .

AIKEN: You have Me.

ALL: Yes.

SUGOLL: And there is also the time-gate.

(Consternation.)

CELADEYR: No true warrior of Tana's battle-company would turn tail and flee the Foe!

AIKEN: There are worse perils than the Little People. [Image.]

KATLINEL THE DARKEYED: In my veins runs Tanu and human blood, and my heart is linked to the Firvulag race of my husband. Well do I recall the words of that spokesman for peace, Dionket Lord Healer, when he bade Sugoll and me to be a bridge. We will willingly undertake a mediation role, and pursue it from now until the Grand Tourney. If Tana wills, we may move the hearts of the Little People, dissuading them from war. Night may not fall.

SUGOLL: But if it should, our people claim the option proffered by King Aiken-Lugonn in exchange for our fealty: If doom cannot be averted, our Howler and human subjects will seek sanctuary in the Milieu.

CELADEYR: Galloping Goddess—what if the damn time-gate device is finished *before* the Tourney?

AIKEN: Not fewkin' likely. There's a snag. I'm going to look into it later today.

KUHAL EARTHSHAKER: Sisters and Brothers, let us gratefully accept the offer of the Lord and Lady of the Howlers to mediate with the Firvulag, their kin. At the same time, let us prepare for the worst, marshaling all stalwart torced minds under the executive of the Shining One, following him without hesitation or question. This has not been our Way in the past, for we are a proud and stiff-necked people, loving turmoil and glorying in contention. Now we must act in concert or perish. And I remind the pious that if Night falls, it will be the hand of the Adversary that rings it to pass rather than Tanu or Firvulag. *He* is the true Foe.

(Silence.)

AIKEN: Thanks for meeting Me here today. I'll see you all in Nionel, at the games.

Swollen by the heavy rains in the jungles to the south, the River Nonol ran deep and swift beneath the Rainbow Bridge. Upstream the watercourse was crowded with small boats, carrying sports lovers of three races to the landing stages at the Field of Gold. But the tiny dock at the foot of the bridge's right-bank abutment pier was deserted except for a laden decamole canoe that strained at its painter and two people standing in the afternoon shadows beside it, their minds linked by the fellowship of the golden torc. One was a splendidly dressed hybrid woman, Tanu in every feature except for her brown eyes. The other was a massive Native American with straggling iron-gray hair, wearing only a breechclout, moccasins, and an elaborate wrist navigation unit.

Misgiving tinged the hopeful mind-veneer of Katlinel the Darkeyed. "I wish we had one of the sigma-field devices to give you in addition to the weapons, Chief Burke."

He smiled, radiating ironic reassurance. "If it's really Marc Remillard in that schooner I'm hunting, a little sigma-shield would be about as much protection as a sheet of durofilm. Not to worry, Lady Katy. Us Redskins are just naturally adept at lurking and sneaking—and my training as a lawyer makes me wilier than most. I'll take care that the gang on Kyllikki don't spot me, assuming she is sailing up the Seine."

"The King thinks it most likely. He did an inconclusive scan from his aircraft."

"I call it weird," Burke said, "that with all the high-powered minds and contraband gadgetry at the King's disposal, he can't track this boat except with a pair of tired old human eyeballs."

"Nevertheless, that seems to be the case. It does seem terribly unfair that you must undertake this scouting mission now, risking your life and perhaps your chance to pass through the time-gate . . ."

Burke shrugged. "If Remillard has his way, there won't *be* any gate. No—the King's arguments were very persuasive, and he sure as hell picked the right man for the job. With the river up the way it is, I should be able to comb the entire five hundred odd kilometers between here and the sea in a week to ten days. I'll farspeak the King on a regular sked all the way. If the schooner's not there, I'll have had a nice excursion to liven up my last days in the Pliocene."

"And if you find it—"

"I'm no Crazy Horse. All I do is report her position and haul my tush on out of there full speed ahead. From the mouth of the Seine to Goriah is about a week's journey by sea. A little mazel, I won't even have to miss the Grand Tourney!"

He untied the line, jumped lightly into the canoe—which barely rocked as he settled onto his haunches—and lifted his paddle in salute.

"Tana guide you," said the Lady of the Howlers.

Burke lifted his instrument-equipped wrist. "And the Messrs. Plath."

"Well, what's the hoo-ha?" the King asked Tony Wayland.

The metallurgist thrust a sealed bottle containing a silvery rod under Aiken's nose. "This. It's taken the prospecting team all this time to locate a suitable dysprosium ore, what with dodging renegade Howlers and having the Norwegian locale turn out a bummer. And now that they've settled in to refine thalenite instead of the xenotime and we finally *have* an abundant source of ore, the bloody idiots are sending down dreck like this."

"What's the problem?" The King controlled his impatience.

"Contaminated," said Hagen gloomily.

"Simply lousy with holmium," Tony said. "And any sort

of impurity in the dysprosium core screws up the resistivity factor of the wire something chronic—I mean, quite badly."

"Is it the fault of the equipment, or what?" asked the King.

"The machinery we sent up should be able to do the job," Tony said. "They have a high-speed Ramsgate extractor for the ion separation and a nice little electroliser for production of the metal. *I* think they're skimping on quality control somewhere. Perhaps in the beginning stages of the ore feed."

"I sent up Candyman, our industrial chemist," Hagen said, "but he couldn't spot the problem. He's really an organic specialist. The crew on the job are experienced mining engineers. They ought to be able to—"

Tony glowered darkly. "You remember that I expressed certain reservations about Yobbo Ruan and Trevarthen when I first learned they'd been put in charge. They may have done well enough mucking about the Amalizan gold mines, but rare-earth refining demands finesse."

"The niobium-dysprosium wire is vital to the project," Hagen said. "This fuck-up means delay at best, and failure if we can't lick it."

The King studied the bottle with its pencil-sized ingot. "You can't complete the purification process here in the labs at Castle Gateway?"

Hagen said, "We'd have to take the extractor away from the mining crew, and we only have the one. Since, we need forty kilos of the stuff, and the basic run-through will take three weeks—"

"Oh, for shit's sake," said the King irritably. "You know there's only one answer to this. Get properly refined metal from Fennoscandia in the first place. Solve the problem at the source."

Hagen nodded. "I want to be sure you appreciate the risk, though. Some species of gigantic Howler lives up there. Yotunag, they're called, and they're outside Sugoll's sway. We've already lost Stosh Nowak and John-Henry King in raids on the mining camp. I wanted your personal authorization before we risk Tony. After all, you paid a high price for him."

"Coo!" cried the metallurgist in vast alarm. "Now wait just a damn minute!"

The King fixed him with an icy gaze. "*Could* you see that the refining is done properly if we send you to Fennoscandia?"

"I'm needed here!" Perspiration started out on Tony's forehead. "I'm at a critical stage in the setup of the cladding device—the gizmo that'll actually make the wire!"

"Answer my question," Aiken demanded. "Could you get the pure metal, or couldn't you?"

"Probably," Tony admitted sullenly.

"Right," said Aiken. "Start packing." He turned on his heel and left the cubicle, with Hagen trailing after.

Hagen said, "One of my people, Chee-Wu Chan, will be able to finish up the cladding device easily enough."

"Good," said the King. "As long as I'm here, I'll do a quick inspection. See how you've settled in here at Gateway." The door closed.

"Oh, bloody hell," Tony moaned. He clutched his golden torc in both sweaty hands, seeking solace. "Here I go again."

In the cool of evening, the fisherman trolled for giant catfish from a dinghy being towed far astern of Kyllikki. The catfish were hardly the fighting fools that the Florida tarpon had been; but they routinely weighted in at 200 kilos and measured better than four meters in length. They were scrappy enough when their stomachs were empty at the start of a night's feeding cruise, and as a bonus, they were excellent eating.

Catfishing was a quiet occupation, which suited the fisherman very well. With his small boat trailing out from under the thoughtproof screen, he could let his unaugmented farsight range about the Many-Colored Land. There was also ample time for contemplation of his personal quandary, away from the increasing tensions aboard the schooner.

The matter had to be faced. Morale among his old associates was deteriorating rapidly, as was inevitable once he let his own resolution waver. Too many of the Rebels found it difficult to recast the vision of Mental Man around Cloud and Hagen, rather than around Marc himself. It had been decades since the dream was fresh, inspiring fanatic loyalty. Instead, it had assumed the status of a familiar religion, a dogma that had been accepted without question—until the prophet himself turned skeptic. Now only Patricia and Cordelia Warshaw remained unswervingly committed.

And what about me? he wondered. Am I really to be seduced by the promises of a simple-minded old man? In my heart, did

I reject the vision even before I saw it? And if it's finished, what is the use of a life without end?

The line tugged gently. He sent his deep sight under the murky water and saw that he had only hooked a snag. A touch of PK released the hook. He reeled in to afix fresh bait.

Was there no way to convince the children in spite of everything—to win them to his side? The gate. If it could never open. If the Guderian Project were doomed to failure...

He cast far astern, paid out line, and adjusted the depth of the troll. On either side of the oil-smooth Seine, dessicated jungle had become matte-black walls separating starry sky from luminous water. The forest belt was noisy with the calls of insects and monkeys and prowling elephants, a narrow oasis amid an inhospitable moorland.

Force, he thought. The only alternative to persuasion was force. Once he would not have hesitated.

A farspoken voice called: Marc.

Elizabeth? (And quickly erect the personal diffuser, so she cannot track.)

Thank God you've finally answered. I . . . we need your help.

?

Mothers with other black-torc children have been coming to the chalet. I suppose I was naive not to have realized that the news would leak out. There are more than 20 of them here. I've tried to explain that Brendan's redaction was a special case. That you . . . worked with me only for reasons of your own. But they won't go away Marc. They say they'll stay here hoping waiting if necessary letting the babies die—

Elizabeth there are other matters demanding my attention. I'm sorry that you're caught up in this predicament. But I must resolve one of my own.

I know. But I was thinking. About Basil's healing. You modified our program so that several redactors could accelerate the Skin treatment. Would it be possible to do a similar adaptation of the black-torc redaction? A metaconcert with groups of coercers and redactors in place of just you and me?

. . . It's a nice problem.

In the Milieu no one was your peer in metaconcert design.

You are mistaken.

Oh . . . yes. But will you think it over?

Certainly. But I can't promise anything . . . I presume that the Tanu Dionket represents the top redactive potential of his race and the other minds with that metafaculty predominating are of lesser stature.

That's correct. And Minanonn would be the best coercer available. Aside from Aiken of course.

Of course.

Well. Thank you for agreeing to try. Goodbye.

Adieu then Elizabeth.

. . .

He sat in the dinghy, the big rod socketed in the transom cup, and tried to farsense his children. But there was no trace of them in the environs of Roniah, and he came inevitably to the mirrored hemisphere that covered Castle Gateway. If it were only possible to break in! If he only had minds enough at his command . . .

During the Rebellion he had commanded millions. Now there were just twenty-four, and he was no longer Abaddon but enfeebled Anfortas, fishing in the Seine while his last hope of victory hid beneath an impervious silver bubble.

Through his farsight, he saw an aircraft rise from behind the moon-gilt sigma-field. The King, no doubt, heading home after his busy day. The ship's occupants were concealed by a smaller sigma, unidentifiable. Marc watched idly as the flyer went inertialess and arrowed off to the northeast at 12,000 kph. Odd. At least Aiken wasn't coming around to spy on *him* again; but where was he going? To the uttermost Swedish boondocks, for a fact! There was a human settlement of some sort, tucked into an obscure valley where one would never have noticed it. Curiouser and curiouser!

The aircraft landed. Five minutes later it took off again for Goriah, heedlessly overflying Kyllikki en route. But Marc paid no attention to it. Instead, he listened in astonishment to an incompetent gold-torc human thought-projection emanating from the lonely outpost in Fennoscandia. It was a cry from the heart that combined yearning for someone named Rowane with sundry curses upon the rare-earth element dysprosium.

Abruptly, the thought was cut off.

And a great catfish swallowed Marc's hook and set the reel to screaming.

7

BROTHER ANATOLY PICKED THE LAST OF THE MANGETOUT peas in the Black Crag garden and Elizabeth sat on a bench beneath a twisted stone pine, reweaving a hole in his brown-wool scapular. They waited for Marc, who for reasons unspecified had asked to be met outdoors, and quarreled over the friar's scandalous absolution of the arch-Rebel.

"Only a sentimental innocent would think that Marc Remillard repented of the Metapsychic Rebellion," Elizabeth said. "He'd do the same thing all over again without half a second's thought."

"I keep forgetting what a great mind reader you are," Anatoly said.

"And to absolve him when he didn't even confess—!"

"Why do you think he made me stay there and listen to what he told his children? You expect a man like that to go down on his knees and say, 'Bless me, Brother'? So he did what his pride allowed him to do, the poor khuy, and if you were any kind of a psychologist you'd know he's been sorry for twenty-seven years without knowing it."

"Poppycock!" She jabbed at the fabric with the big needle and narrowly missed impaling her finger. "You might as well

383

talk of reconciling Adolf Hitler or some other infamous monster."

"Look who strains the quality of mercy—Miss Scrupulosity, who wore out Amerie's ears and patience, the one who's afraid to trust anybody but herself!" Anatoly popped a handful of crisp peapods into his mouth and chewed ferociously.

"We're not discussing me," she snapped, "we're talking about a man who instigated an interplanetary war, who was responsible for the deaths of four billion people and who nearly destroyed the Milieu because of his twisted ambition. How you could even *think* of offering him forgiveness—"

"Nu, the Prodigal Son would get a chilly welcome at your place!"

"Don't be ridiculous."

"What's ridiculous is a high-and-mighty pizda trying to put limits on the pity of God."

"If you think," she said coldly, "that you can avoid lack of charity by calling me vulgar names in Russian, let me remind you that any metapsychic can—"

The words died in her throat. Anatoly whirled around to see an apparition forming at the far end of the garden, where there was a graveled drying yard. Not one but two black cerametal hulks materialized, their great mass pressing down the stones with an ominous crunching sound. Behind them stood a large computer console and a collection of instrumentation cabinets that occupied most of the yard.

"Bozhye moi!" whispered the priest.

The righthand suit of armor seemed to go momentarily transparent. Then Marc was standing outside it and the cerametal was as substantial as before.

"Good morning, Elizabeth. Brother."

The friar offered a lame grin and a wave. Elizabeth simply nodded.

Marc indicated the twin CE rigs and the auxiliaries. "The other suit is empty. This is by way of a demonstration, to show you my progress in teleportation. I can't quite manage the power-modules yet."

"Is this—demonstration the only reason you asked to meet with me?" Elizabeth asked.

"Of course not." Marc flashed his smile. "I've brought you the adaptation of Brendan's program."

She gave a joyous shout, dropped the scapular and sewing kit, and ran toward the black-clad figure. Then she suddenly pulled up short and her arms fell back to her sides. Marc's smile faded.

Anatoly hoisted the basket of peas, grabbed the fallen scapular in passing, shot a disgusted "V'yperdka!" at Elizabeth, and stomped off to the kitchen.

Elizabeth flushed. She said to Marc, "I'm sorry if I appeared ungrateful."

"It's quite all right. I understand. And Anatoly is a churlish old peasant, isn't he? If it's any consolation to you, he's called me much worse names. It seems to be his customary spiritual counseling technique: the tough crust over the creamed ham pie . . . He worries about you, Elizabeth."

The two of them sat down on the bench under the tree and Marc drew off his gloves. The pressure suit was completely dry and there was no trace of the usual brow wounds. His mind bore an impress of profound excitement.

Elizabeth said, "When we didn't hear from you after a week had gone by, I assumed the solution to the redactive problem had eluded you."

"I'm sorry it took so long. I was distracted by other matters, and the adaptation proved to be quite a challenge. I wanted to shorten the time of the operation as well as spread it among members of a manageable metaconcert. This is what I did." And he displayed the construct.

"But it's so simple!" she exclaimed. "The way you've elided the tedious backtracking and shoring maneuvers . . . and incorporated the operancy resultant into the ongoing redactive trend. Why didn't I think of that? Of course, every great solution looks simple in retrospect, doesn't it? Marc—thank you. It's magnificent."

The elegant mental edifice seemed to hover between them. She enfolded it in her memory with meticulous care, and then Marc rose.

"No doubt you noticed," he said, "that the metaconcert does not include you."

She looked away. "That's for the best."

"Are you so very anxious to return to the Milieu?"

His voice and mind carried a warning flavor, and she suddenly felt her heart go cold. "You're going to oppose us after all! You've found some way to keep the gate from opening!"

His coercion compelled her to face him. "I must."

Her mental voice cried: Anatoly I told you so . . .

He had taken her by the hand, and before she realized what had happened they had walked together to the other end of the garden. The noon sun was harsh and the two suits of armor, enveloped in heart-shimmer, loomed facelessly over her.

She heard him say, "I could show you another world where you would be truly needed. An educative work that would never pall. Challenge without end."

"No, Marc." Her voice was steady. She pulled her hand away.

He said, "I'll win, one way or another. You must tell Anatoly that the temptation was too great."

"Yes, I know," she said.

He took a step backward into blackness and in a moment the graveled yard was empty.

Jordan Kramer came onto Kyllikki's bridge with obvious reluctance, closed the door behind him, then gave a curt exclamation of surprise as he spotted Alex Manion standing behind the chart table, out of casual view from the quarterdeck.

"Dammit, Walter—what's *he* doing here?"

"We both want to talk to you, Jordy," Saastamoinen said.

"I should be back in the stern hold with Gerry. Marc will be back soon from Black Crag—

"That's why we want to talk to you now. Time's running out." He thumbed several studs of the autowinch unit. "Half a mo', though. Little headwind coming up and we're sheet-heavy. Liable to drag anchor. One disadvantage of solar-collection sails."

Manion, the docilator headpiece firmly in place, fixed intent eyes on Kramer and said, "Marc . . . ordered . . . batteries . . . recharged . . . max. He's . . . ready . . . to . . . flit."

"Jesus, he can override the docilator!" Kramer cried.

"But it's hard on him," Walter said. "Let him out, Jordy. You've got the keying sequence."

"Are you out of your mind?" the shocked physicist asked.

Manion said, "*You* . . . are . . . if . . . you . . . think . . . Marc . . . plans . . . let . . . kids . . . live." He drew a shuddering breath. Sweat poured from his head and stained his light knit shirt.

"Do . . . you . . . love . . . Marge . . . Becky . . . more . . . than . . . Marc . . . or . . . not?"

"What have my children got to do with this?" Kramer had gone white. "Walter—what the hell are you two up to?"

"Not just us, Jordy," said the skipper. "The whole damn fo'c'sle gang. And now we want you and Gerry. Van Wyk doesn't have any kids, but you can pressure him into cooperating. With threats, if nothing else. Unhook Alex. He's not going to attempt coercion. A coerced mind won't fit a meta-concert."

"It's a goddam *mutiny*, isn't it?" Kramer said.

"Very astute deduction. Precipitated by Marc's order for the express battery charge before he went jumping this morning. He's made up his mind to go after the kids and force them to submit—kill Hagen and Cloud if necessary, and any others that stand in the way. He'll take Mental Man's genes from the dead bodies of his own kids and coerce whatever survivors there are into going away with him to the Goal world. He only needs seven or eight live ones for an adequate reproductive pool."

"You can't know what his plans are!"

"The big power requirement can only be for one purpose, Jordy. Marc is ready to teleport the entire CE complex off Kyllikki, to some safe hiding place where he can make his moves without having to worry about our fizzling loyalty. Do you think he's been blind to the mood on shipboard during the last two weeks? The only ones who are still committed to Marc and Mental Man are Castellane, Warshaw, and Steinbrenner."

"You're not making me out a traitor," Kramer blustered. Then his expression changed. "Do you mean to tell me that Ragnar Gathen is in on this conspiracy?"

Manion said, "Elaby . . . was . . . among . . . first . . . to . . . accept . . . my . . . insights."

"And Ragnar's with us for the sake of his son's memory—and for Cloud," Walter said, "just as you have to join for the sake of Becky and Marge. Marc's hatched some new scheme, I tell you. Boom-Boom Laroche came on him in the library studying the specs of the Guderian device. And he made a casual remark to Ragnar two nights ago about farsnooping the Firvulag at this tournament gathering upriver. Something to do with the gnomes making droll, inefficient efforts at metaconcert. Do you realize what implications that could have?"

Manion said, "Eighty . . . thousand . . . Firvulag."

Kramer's eyes darted from one man to the other. "This is all pure speculation—"

Walter leaned closer, fury blazing from his weatherbeaten face. "Listen to me, Jordy! Once Marc teleports the CE equipment off the boat, we'll be helpless to stop him. We have to act now—put together a mind-meld strong enough to overpower Castellane and the other two, and then sabotage the power-modules."

"Trap . . . Marc . . . in . . . gray . . . limbo."

The pair of them stood back, quietly waiting. Kramer had his hand on the doorlatch. His teeth bit his lower lip and a whirlwind of conflicting thoughts seeped through undermined mental defenses. "Let me think . . . God, you can't expect me to make a decision like this right off the top of my head!" He tugged at the door. It remained firmly closed.

Alex Manion sang:

> What though the night may come too soon,
> We've years and years of afternoon!

"We need you, Jordy," Walter said. "You're a magnate, the last unit we need in the offensive combo. We can't hack it without you, and it's got to be done right away."

A farspoken thought impinged upon all three of their minds, a call from Gerry Van Wyk down in the stern hold, broadcast with typical sloppiness on the declamatory rather than the intimate mode:

Jordy get down here man. Marc's at superficies.

"Well?" Walter said to Kramer. "We're ready to act the very next time he d-jumps. If you're with us."

Kramer took a deep breath. He came away from the door and stood in front of Alexis Manion. With a complex signal he keyed the docilator shutoff, then supported the surfacing mind until it was in full control of its faculties.

The bridge door opened by itself. Walter said, "Thanks, Jordy."

"Set it up," said Kramer, and hurried away.

Manion massaged his temples and blinked. He did not attempt to remove the headpiece and his eyes were as mild and unfocused as ever. "When it's safe," he said to Walter, "find out from Jordy when Marc plans his next excursion. I'll see that the others are ready."

Because the exhaust of the electroliser unit was outside the five-meter diameter of the little sigma-shield, Tony Wayland and his fellow captives, Kalipin the Howler and Alice Greatorex, a middle-aged chemical engineer, could pass the time turning dysprosium chloride into the pure element. Outside the force-field, the mob of Yotunag ogres gnashed their bloody tusks impotently and howled inaudible epithets.

"Eventually they'll get tired and go away," Kalipin predicted. But he'd been saying that for nearly three hours now.

"When we miss the eighteen-hundred-hour sked, the King will send help," said Alice.

Tony gave a hollow laugh. "If the battery on this puny sigma doesn't go flat first! And with my luck—"

The timer on the electroliser pinged. Tony opened its small hatch and removed a pencil-sized cylinder of metal with a pair of forceps. Alice held out an open bottle. He slid the ingot inside, tossed a deox packet after it, and snapped on the lid.

Alice numbered the bottle and set it with the other four. "You guys realize this is our two-hundred-fifty-eighth slug of Dy? Only fifty-five more of these little suckers and we can pack up and leave beautiful Fennoscandia and its quaint native peoples."

Outside, the devastated mining camp was dimly visible, as through a one-way mirror. A fresh group of deformed monsters came loping up from the direction of the diggings and joined their mates in whacking at the slippery surface of the force-field with granite hammer-axes.

"Persistent," Tony commented. "You think they could have finally done for Amathon and the other Tanu trapped in the tunnel?"

Kalipin screwed his illusory face into an expression of resignation. "My savage kinfolk usually stick to a job until they finish it." He emptied the dross from the electroliser and began charging it for the next batch. A faint tange of chlorine wafted about their imprisoning hemisphere before slowly diffusing out through the semipermeable field. "The feathers do resemble those on the crest of Lord Amathon's helmet. Coercer blue. And since he was the stoutest mind among those cornered in the shaft, I fear for the worst. You might also note the fresh stains on the hammers of the newly arrived Yotunag."

"I'd rather not, actually," Tony said. He turned on the little electric furnace and sat back in his chair. Outside, flames licked up in one corner of the ruined lab shed. After a few minutes the display on the electroliser went dead. "Shit! There goes the power line."

"Now you can be glad the sigma's on battery," Alice said comfortably.

Kalipin watched the spreading fire with apprehension. "Will we remain safe inside this shelter?"

Alice said, "Safe as in your mommie's lap, little friend. When the lab floor burns through we'll settle down a bit, that's all."

The blaze was becoming quite brisk. Some of the Yotunag hurled burning brands at the frustrating sigma bubble, to no effect.

"Damn them," Tony muttered. "They can't see us. Why the devil do they keep up the siege? For all they know, we've skipped out from under."

"They farsense our presence," Kalipin sighed. "The force-field is as you noted, a rather puny one."

Alice fingered her golden torc with fatalistic good humor. "But quite strong enough to keep us from farshouting out." She checked the small sigma generator that sat in the middle of the cluttered lab bench. "You guys interested in knowing how much bumbershoot juice we have left?"

"No," growled Tony.

"I think the fire's accelerating the drain. It's going to be one of those days, I'm afraid...And I was really looking forward to going back to the Milieu and thumbing my nose at NAICE. How about you, Wayland?"

Tony was unloading the electroliser, replacing the dysprosium salts in their canister. He said dully, "I hoped to live here in peace with my wife. She's in Nionel."

"Tough," Alice said. "Woops—the floor's starting to go. Hang on to the equipment."

The flames stretched high and the broken walls of the lab building crashed all around them. As the conflagration dwindled they had a clear view of the camp compound. The shuttle aircraft that had landed shortly before the Yotunag onslaught was a smoldering ruin. A few mutant bodies lay about, but there was, ominously, no sign of human or Tanu remains.

Alice cuddled the small sigma generator solicitously while Tony braced the electric furnace and Kalipin saw to the safety of the bottled dysprosium. The lab bench bucked as the floor subsided. Small tools and the chloride canister went flying. The chairs fell over and a taboret dumped. The monsters outside, sensing the disturbance, capered and yawped and smote the crumbling floorboards with their hammers to accelerate the process of disintegration; but the sigma held, and eventually those inside stood on a stabilized wooden cutout, surrounded by smoking debris.

"Fire doesn't seem to bother the ghoulies much," Alice remarked to Kalipin.

The Howler shrugged. "Their feet are tougher than horn, and it's said they commonly use wildfire to harry game here in the northern wastes. The Yotunag are the most terrible of our mutant brethren. Not even the Howlers of the Bohemian mountains are so cruel and intractable. These creatures laughed to scorn my Master Sugoll's invitation to join him at Nionel, and they even dared to devour certain Ingathers who attempted to pass through their territory on the way south from the Amber Lakes. Oh—Yotunag are rotten through and through! No doubt about it. And as crafty as they are ferocious, as the stealth of their attack today proves. It's not easy for Howlers to go invisible, you know."

"Why the hell couldn't they leave us alone?" Tony whined. "We weren't doing any harm."

Kalipin held up the handful of glass vials with the dysprosium. "We were taking something from the earth. A commodity useless to them, it's true, but one that was nevertheless their property. Ilmary and Koblerin the Knocker and I tried to explain to the man Trevarthen that we should pay for the stolen minerals with gemstones valued by the Yotunag. But he refused to listen, even when John-Henry and Stosh were ambushed and killed. His response, and that of King Aiken-Lugonn, was to mount more gray-torc guards with Milieu weapons around the camp. Well—we saw what happened as a result of Trevarthen's bad judgment."

"He's past caring now," Tony said, "along with all the rest of them caught outside the sigma."

Alice studied the display on the force-field generator. "And so will we all be—in about ten minutes, rough reckoning."

The monsters raged, circling amidst the smoke. There were forty or fifty of them, waving bronze-bladed spears and hammer-axes with stone heads the size of bed pillows. Great glee was manifested when a squad of brutes laden with bulging leather bags came shuffling over from the area of the diggings. The bags, emptied on the ground, proved to be full of roasted refreshments for the battle-company. The Yotunag fell to with a will, from time to time flinging bones or other grisly leftovers at the sigma bubble. Tony and Alice turned green and Kalipin settled down to recommend his soul to Teah's mercy.

Then Alice exclaimed, "Hey—look over there!"

They saw blue-white flashes beyond the shell of the primary refining shed. Two large trolls came rushing pell-mell around the ruins, only to be downed by dazzling blasts that left them incinerated skeletons.

"Sweet shit," Tony said. "There's somebody back there with a Bosch 414 or some other heavy-duty blaster! Don't tell me the Marines have landed—"

The besieging monsters all went charging off in the direction of the renewed hostilities. Numbers of them went invisible. They were met by a fusillade that nearly blinded the sigma captives in spite of the screening effect of the dynamic field.

"See how our rescuer shoots even the invisible Foe!" Kalipin cried. "Thanks be to the Goddess!"

It was true. Once the visible ogres had been zapped, the hidden marksman set to work potting unseen targets. Inside of five minutes the yard between the wrecked lab and the refining shed was thick with calcined exotic bones and blackened metal accoutrements.

The firing stopped.

The sigma-field fizzled and died as its battery was exhausted.

A tall human being came strolling into the open, carrying

his weapon jauntily over his shoulder and waving in an encouraging fashion. Tony and Alice and Kalipin stepped off their wooden island and ran to meet the rescuer, emanating farspoken cries of relief and thanks.

"Think nothing of it," the man said. He raised a protective visor from his deepset eyes and perched it on top of curly gray hair. He wore a tight-fitting black coverall studded with metal receptacles. "It was nervy of the creatures to anticipate me. I should have kept a closer eye on things up here."

"Mother o' pearl!" Alice said softly. "It's Remillard himself!"

She and Tony made simultaneous attempts to farscream. When that failed, they tried vainly to run. Only little Kalipin confronted the challenger of the galaxy with resolution. "So. Do you save us from the Foe only to destroy our minds, human?"

Marc laughed. Then his tone became adamantine. "I have no time to waste. Your King will be making his regularly scheduled evening call shortly. Where is the dysprosium?"

Tony was helpless under coercion. "Five rods, all we managed to refine today, in Kalipin's pouch."

The Howler handed over the bottles without a word.

"And the concentrate?" Marc demanded. "And the ion extractor?"

"There's one can of $DyCl_3$ back where we were hiding under the sigma. The rest is in that undamaged building over in the trees. The extractor's there, too."

Marc said to Alice and Kalipin, "Get the machine and the salts and bring them here." Deprived of volition, they rushed off. Marc asked Tony, "Are there any other high-tech extraction devices available to the Guderian Project workers?"

"Not as far as I know," the metallurgist said listlessly. "You scarper with that one, the project's had it. I couldn't care less."

Marc lifted a surprised eyebrow.

Tony licked his lips, looked about to be sure the others were well out of earshot, then said, "Listen! I'm no ally of the King or his bunch of North American fanatics. I was dragooned into working on the project. Check my mind and you'll see I'm telling the truth! All I want to do is get back to my wife in Nionel. I—I don't suppose you'd consider letting me live?"

Marc said, "It seems the better part of prudence to deprive Aiken of your unique talents. There are other ways of processing lanthanons."

Tony's eyes misted over. "B-but it'll take months to sift out the Dy by ordinary chemical techniques, and the King wouldn't need me for that. All you have to do is destroy the ion extractor and the accumulated concentrate, and the project is hopelessly stalled—"

"I would rather keep my options on the matter open." Marc smiled in satisfaction as he saw Alice and Kalipin emerge from the building back in the trees. The Howler was trundling a loaded wheelbarrow and the woman had her arms full of canisters. "However, you needn't worry about me slaughtering you out of hand. The dysprosium and its manufacturing equipment will go back to my ship with me, via d-jump. And so will you."

Tony's world reeled. An enormous dark-colored mass reminiscent of a deep-sea diving rig was materializing behind the rebel leader. As if in a dream, Tony heard Kalipin and Alice being ordered to stack the materials close to the suit of armor. Then a voice in his own brain said:

Stand very still. It would be best if you held your breath and closed your eyes although our translation through the gray limbo will occupy only the merest fraction of a second.

Tony screamed: Don't! Don't take me! I don't want to die in hyper-space! JesushelpmeOGodRowane . . .

Zang.

Tony felt the appalling pain attending penetration of the superficies, familiar from many a superluminal voyage between Milieu worlds. For the merest instant he felt frozen, suffocated, on the verge of having every body cell explode.

Zung.

He sprawled on hands and knees, opened his eyes, and saw Alice and Kalipin goggling in astonishment. A smoky Fennoscandian landscape. Scattered bones. Charred rubble. A towering suit of black armor with a Bosch blaster leaning against it. Purloined equipment and containers and Tony and all—right back where they had started from!

Zang.

GodGodGodnooooAAAAAGH! Ooh.

Zung.

Dusty stubble covered with soot and ash. A severed human pinkie (not his) with two flies crawling on it. Babble from the Howler and Alice's mind screeching for the King on the distance-spanning farspeech mode. Much nearer, a sepulchral metallic roar.

Quel putain de gâchis what are they playing at back there?... Rubberband effect... try it this time without the external load—

The armored form disappeared, leaving Tony and cargo behind.

Trembling and sobbing, eyes screwed shut, he waited to be snatched back into the gray limbo and the pain. But nothing happened. He lifted his head and saw sweet old Alice, who knelt beside him radiating a mishmash of horror and tentative relief. She said, "I think he's gone, baby. But if he pops back out of the hype, I'll cook him in his own can." She hefted the Bosch. "I bespoke the King. He's sending a flyer with help."

Tony gently lowered his face to the ground and began taking deep breaths.

Within the matrix of gray negation, the mind clung to the all-important pseudolocus and concentrated on the far end of the catenary. It terminated properly. He had not miscalculated the curve nor the coefficient of penetration. He completed the jump, attained the superficies, and willed the generation of the upsilon-field that would form an aperture into the normal universe.

Nothing. It would not open. *There was no field*.

Rubberband back! Attain the antiterminus will the u-field the u-field the u-field!

Nothing. There was insufficient energy. The incandescent brain felt itself cooling; emergency life-support modules operating independently of the enhancer circuitry and its transdimensional power source kicked in, sustaining him. He would not freeze, drown, smother, or decompress for at least five days, until the armor's internal resources were drained.

Barebrained, he slid back along the catenary to the Kyllikki end. The path seemed to glow faintly in the pervasive gray. He poked and thrust at the stubborn interface but it would not yield.

He was trapped in limbo.

* * *

The full moon rising above the sea of dry grass was almost like another sun—swollen, slightly flattened at top and bottom, and an awful reddish color in the thick haze.

Chief Burke used his paddle for a rudder as the canoe swept around a wide bend in the Seine, bearing north now instead of east. The trees here were sparse and almost leafless from drought. There were no land animals except the ubiquitous crocodiles, and very few birds. He knew he would have to find a safe campsite soon; but something urged him to continue on for just a bit more, to come fully around the bend so he would have a clear view of the waterway the next morning...

Then he saw it ahead, riding the bloody water: a huge argosy with a full spread of gleaming golden sails, moored fore and aft in midstream.

Cursing, he angled the canoe to the right bank, where a partially undermined tree leaned branches into the water and provided a thin screen. It had to be Kyllikki. He pulled out his monocular and studied her. She was less than 200 meters away, motionless in the evening calm. There was no hint of any mechanical or metapsychic barrier around her. The decks seemed deserted.

Burke slipped the little scope back into its case, touched his golden torc, and called:

Aiken. I've found her.

...Thanks Chief I'm on my way.

Inside the barricaded stern hold of the schooner, Patricia Castellane's voice rose in a despairing scream.

"They've cut him off! He's trapped! Help me, Jeff— Cordelia—give me everything you've got. They haven't broken anything yet, only opened the CE main at the redundant terminal in the power room. I can bridge it! Just feed me— feed me to overload, dammit!—everything you've got. Marc, come through! *Marc!*"

The hold that had gone pitch-black with the power failure flared as three bodies appeared suddenly clothed in writhing discharges of psychic lightning. A triple mind-shout knifed the aether. Reactivated display panels and telltales showed that the equipment was on line again. A black phantasm flickered and solidified on its customary wooden cradle.

From the loudspeaker of the computer clanged an inhuman voice:

YOU IN THE POWER ROOM. STAND AWAY OR DIE. I COMMAND RECLOSING OF CE POWER MAIN NOW.

Jeff Steinbrenner and Cordelia Warshaw fell to the deck. Patricia supported herself with difficulty against the computer console and whispered, "It's all right. The power's back. You're safe, Marc..."

A simulacrum of his face smiled at her from the blind black helm. "Thank you, Pat. Dear Pat."

One hand was raised toward him. "Go. You'll have to teleport everything away. All the others—turned against us. Escape, Marc. Then it was worth it."

For the last time, the mind shone with a dirigent's creative-coercive power; then all thinking was extinguished and her body lay beside the two others on the rough oaken planks.

Marc's amplified voice echoed through the hull:

LEAVE THE POWER ROOM. ALL OF YOU.

Outside Kyllikki there was a tremendous sonic boom. The schooner rocked.

He sucked in energy, heedless of the risk, absorbed a greater input than he had ever attempted here in the Pliocene exile. Yes! Fully powered, he spun the upsilon-field and made the hyperspatial gateway enormous. His mind designated the pieces of equipment to be translated: the entire CE complex, some weapons, supplies, more than eleven tons of mass altogether. How easy it was to lift! How nonchalantly he pushed the load and himself through the gaping superficies—and slammed it shut in the Golden Adversary's frustrated face.

Zang.

...A perfect place to hide, farseen weeks ago.

Zung.

The materialization down inside the deep, dry watercourse would have been visible to the naked eye for less than a second. Then the absorptive camouflaging mechanism that had formerly sheltered Kyllikki clicked on, twisting the moonbeams to form an illusion that, viewed from above, roofed the gully with apparently solid ground.

After several hours the camouflager was turned off, and the gulley seemed to be as barren of life as ever. But the little cave where Madame Guderian and Claude Majewski had hidden was now greatly enlarged to accommodate a new tenant. He came out briefly after midnight and sat beneath the old acacia tree that slouched at the canyon lip, looking at the force-field hemisphere that shrouded Castle Gateway just up the slope to the south. A few hares and other night-prowling creatures ventured to creep up and inspect him—but they fled soon enough at the cold, terrible touch of his mind.

8

MINANONN THE HERETIC OPENED THE DOOR OF THE FORMER feasting hall of the chalet, which had been converted into a nursery for the black-torc babies. The room was lit only by clusters of red faerie lights. He saw a double row of small cots with ten redactors seated on stools before them. The mothers were ranged behind the infants, observing. Dionket stood at the side, directing the operation, faintly veiled in carmine luminescence. Basil Wimborne played a quiet melody on his recorder and an aura of healing prevaded the chamber.

It's going to work, Minanonn thought. The new program is beginning to help the poor little things even now, before the coercive segment of the metaconcert is phased in. They'll be cured, whole-minded again, inside of a week or so. And not only that, they'll be operant: the first of the new generation Brede the Shipspouse had foreseen.

They must not be left to perish in Nightfall! Fortunately, the King's suggestion provides the perfect solution . . .

Minanonn waited. He caught sight of Elizabeth seated in a dark corner, her mind detached, her face covered by her hands—unneeded. Then the preliminary session came to a close; the

399

young minds were awash in soothing endorphins and the pain was in abeyance. Basil absently mind-sang the human lullaby as he played his flute.

> *Joy will come to us at morning,*
> *Life with sunrise hope adorning,*
> *Though sad dreams may give dread warning,*
> *   All through the night.*

The last notes of the song died away. Dionket and the redactor company looked at one another and smiled, and then the healers rose and filed out. Minanonn's urgent summons brought the Lord Healer and Elizabeth to him, and they left the chalet by a side door and went into the twilit rock garden where the full moon was just rising above the hills.

"There have been important developments," the Heretic said. "I didn't want to interrupt the work. Here is a message sent to me by the King within the last half hour." He displayed a picture of the portentous events that had taken place on the Upper Seine.

Elizabeth's mind darkened in dismay. "Then Marc's at large with his mind-enchancing equipment!"

"But deprived of his base of operation and his confederates," Dionket said. "Surely that's encouraging news. Even with his infernal machine, the Adversary is unable to break into Castle Gateway. And the King will surely take precautions against any renewed attempt against the dysprosium miners."

Elizabeth frowned. "I wonder if the Guderian Project is vulnerable to any other indirect attacks?"

"The King declared it was not," Minanonn said. "Save for the one critical element, the workers have all the raw materials and manufacturing equipment safe in Castle Gateway. A few more days will see the completion of the Fennoscandian operation. According to the King, the time-gate device should be completed sometime during Grand Tourney week."

"How appropriate." Elizabeth's mind was once again curtained and unfathomable. "The Field of Gold isn't too convenient to Castle Gateway—but of course there are the aircraft..."

The three of them came to an ornamental grotto, a shallow cave with a spring trickling out of it, surrounded by ferns and night-fragrant plantings of damewort and mignonette. An oil lantern dangling from a tree cast warm light on the surrounding rocks and a pair of rustic benches. They sat down.

Dionket said, "Brother Heretic, you hold something back from us. What was the rest of the King's message?"

The former Battlemaster's attitude was one of dejection. His massive shoulders slumped and he picked up pebbles from the pathways and tossed them into the little stream. "The King captured the Adversary's large sailing ship. He interrogated the twenty-two surviving North Americans aboard, those who mutinied against Remillard. A certain Rebel named Manion believes that the next phase of the Adversary's scheme may involve the Firvulag. As participants in an offensive meta-concert led by Remillard."

Dionket burst out laughing. "The idea is ludicrous! The Foe would never permit any human to direct them—much less *him*."

"I call to your mind certain traditions," Minanonn retorted. "The Adversary is no mere observer in Nightfall."

His confidence shaken, the Lord Healer said, "But the Little People aren't fools! Subordinating themselves to Remillard in an Organic Mind setup would be to risk permanent mental slavery. As it is, Sharn and Ayfa command a mind-force that may very well be superior to Aiken's. They require no assistance from this human interloper—"

"Not if the Firvulag really know how to make metaconcert work," Elizabeth said in a low voice. "If they can put the structure together so that the whole is greater than the sum of the small parts—the comparatively weak individual mind-units—and keep the thing working efficiently under their direction. But we've already had plenty of hints that Firvulag mastery of the orchestration technique is far from complete. They tend to fall apart, go every mind for itself, when they're backed into a corner. That was the point Sugoll and Katlinel hoped to pound home in their conciliation efforts, warning Sharn and Ayfa that they'd never be able to match Aiken's disciplined and efficient counterforce. But if Marc comes along promising to reorganize the Firvulag metaconcert in return for their helping to break the Castle Gateway defenses..."

"This is what the King fears," Minanonn said. "All the Adversary need do is bide his time. Make his offer known.

Suggest ways that the royal pair might work with him while still maintaining independence. Wait for the inevitable flaws in Firvulag mental cooperation to manifest themselves. In time, Sharn and Ayfa will find his temptation to be irresistible."

"Irresistible," Elizabeth repeated. She stared at her hands, at the small diamond ring that had been the symbol of her profession back in the Milieu. Lawrence had worn its twin. Now the stone's sparkle was forlorn in the lamplight.

"What are we going to do?" Dionket asked.

"Flee," said Minanonn flatly.

"To the Milieu?" Elizabeth laughed. "Marc's collusion with those eighty thousand Firvulag minds will dispose of that option, I assure you. He won't even need the Little People on the scene at Castle Gateway. He can channel the psychoenergy from a distance—from Nionel—just as he did when he smashed Gibraltar and put down Felice."

"I didn't contemplate fleeing through the time-gate, Elizabeth," the Heretic said. "I asked the King, in the name of the Peace Faction, for the great ship Kyllikki. He agreed to give it to us, subject to his removing most of the armament. A prize crew of Tanu stalwarts and armed humans are taking it at full speed back down the Seine. It will be provisioned at Goriah for a return voyage across the ocean to the Blessed Isles. The surviving North Americans have asserted that they will cooperate fully and accept the Peace Faction's governance."

Elizabeth was speechless.

Dionket slowly raised both hands. "The Isles! Of course. The sanctuary of our ancient legends . . . the Land of Youth! We can complete the work on the black-torc infants in the week remaining before the Tourney, and take them with us!"

Minanonn said, "Our Peaceful Folk can be diverted from Nionel to Goriah, traveling the Western Track and then boating down the Laar. There is still time. I will petition the King for a flying machine to evacuate those confined to the Pyrénées by the snows. And we here on Black Crag—"

Elizabeth finished ironically, "Can slip away quietly, while Aiken fights the Nightfall War and Marc Remillard destroys his own children."

"The King thought the plan a most excellent one," Minanonn protested. "He told me he would be heartened, knowing that you and the children and the Peaceful Folk would be preserved against the fall of Night. If anyone can save this poor Many-Colored Land, he can. Nevertheless, he seeks to repay what he considers to be his debt to us three, in gratitude for saving his life at the Río Genil and his sanity at Quicksilver Cave."

"I'm not going with you on Kyllikki," Elizabeth said.

"But you must!" Dionket exclaimed. "We'll need your help to raise the newly operant young ones to their full potential."

She had shut herself away from them. "Lord Healer, I don't have the courage to begin all over again in your Fortunate Isles. I've had enough of exile. I'll teach you and Creyn as much of the preceptorial material as I can—the educational shortcuts, the special mind-expanding techniques that you can't infer or deduce yourselves. The children won't grow up Milieu-adept, but they'll do well enough. And with Marc's adaptation of Brendan's program, you'll be able to modify the brain of each newly born baby so that the torcs will never be needed again."

"But we need *you*!" Dionket exclaimed.

"You don't," she retorted. "Why won't you understand? Is it because you refuse to? Must I show you my self naked before you'll accept what I tell you and let me be?"

Minanonn said, "Elizabeth, we love you and want you with us!"

"So does Aiken," she said. "I've decided to stand by him, to give him whatever help I can in the war."

"He hasn't asked this of you," Dionket said. "This doom-seeking choice of yours is born of despair, not love for your friend."

"And what if it is?" she shot back. "It's my life, isn't it? I've tried to do my best for all of you—God knows I have. But I can't bear any more! I want to help Aiken precisely because he hasn't begged me to. He knows I'm not some maternal abstraction, some all-wise personification of your Goddess sent to light and guard and rule and guide. I'm just his friend. And I'm going to sit beside him at the games and forget about Nightfall for a few days, and not think about anybody but myself!"

"Elizabeth, reconsider," Minanonn begged her. "You could be such a great help to us. It would be satisfying work—"

"Oh, yes?" she said quietly; and before they realized what was happening her barriers had fallen to show the cocoon of fire. "I've tried that, friends. Done my very best—just as I promised you when I left Redactor House in Muriah after the Flood. A little of what I accomplished lifted me, but the fire was always just out of sight, waiting for the pendulum to swing to the failure side again. You wanted me to be Brede, but I was only a misfit—just as out of place here in the Many-Colored Land as Marc Remillard was in the Galactic Milieu." And like me he could have done so much good his dream his power his immortality all wasted why wasn't he Jack why was I separated from Lawrence why am I too weak alone why is he too determined to be strong alone why if God lives does he let the misfit minds suffer so misunderstand themselves so refuse touch refuse love why was I afraid even knowing he was sorry reaching gratified by Brendan why couldn't I have touched him even at the last told him the answer his real work (Creyn knew!) helped him find it in spite of fearing now it's too late he's lost I'm lost let it pass let it all pass let me go friends if you care let me go let me fly away . . .

"Don't!" they both cried. But she had run off down the garden path into the night and her mental admonition not to follow seemed to hang in the air, written in anguish.

"So Creyn was right after all," said Minanonn. "How very singular."

Dionket sighed. "I've had a hard day, and tomorrow will be even worse when I have to phase in you and the rest of the coercers. Don't worry about Elizabeth. She won't do anything rash tonight. I'm going to bed. Take my advice and do the same."

The two of them went back to the chalet. Somewhere a flute was playing.

9

It was almost dawn. The First Day of the Grand Tourney was about to begin.

"I can't do it!" she protested to the Genetics Master. "I'm not worthy of such an honor."

But he said, "Don't be an idiot, girl. You're my guest—and my triumph!—and you'll ride at my side and you'll love it."

And she did. And here they were, passing through the western gate of Nionel under the ritual overcast of the pearly sunrise, all in a great procession heading for the Rainbow Bridge.

Sugoll, as host of the games, led the way riding a white chaliko and wearing milk-colored armor chased with silver. Behind him came Katlinel in her auroral gown; and riding on her right hand were Sharn and Ayfa in jewel-lavished obsidian mail, and on her left Aiken-Lugonn the Shining One with Elizabeth, who wore Brede's black-and-scarlet robes and glittering mask. After the royalty, flanked by marching Howlers wearing their most attractive illusory bodies and carrying chains of flowers, rode the members of the High Table and the Gnomish Council in alternating double files. They were followed by the

Howler Great Ones (and she and Greg-Donnet in the midst of them!) and the high nobility of the dimorphic race ranged four-and-four abreast, knights and noncombatants in colorful array. The rest of the Howler commons marched solemnly in the rear, carrying green branches and flower sheaves bound onto ribbon-topped poles. There were no skull-topped effigy standards in evidence, no martial battle-pennons, no unsheathed arms.

The air was alive with a deep humming, the Firvulag commonalty in the packed grandstand across the river voicing their traditional overture to the Opening of the Sky. In previous years, on the salt flats of the Tanu-dominated Grand Combat, the sound had been bitter and mindprickling. But here was no sterile expanse of sea bottom but rather a green meadow, and thousands of birds sang their dawn chorus in a cheerful descant to the portentous drone. Even the Firvulag nobles found themselves smiling as they crossed the Nonol and entered the Field of Gold, that scene of past glories, and noted that the Little People jammed their grandstand and overflowed onto the sidelines, whereas the other seating structure that accommodated Tanu and humanity was only three-quarters filled.

"How strangely bright everything looks!" she exclaimed to Greg-Donnet. "And so clear! It seems I can see every little flower in the festoons borne by our folk, and every gem adorning the armor of the Great Ones, and every decoration on every banner topping the two grandstands!"

"Binocular vision, my dear. Two eyes are much better than one. And, of course, you are happy."

The Royals were mounting the central dais before the twin stands, taking a position facing the eastern range of hills behind Nionel.

"I'm happy—and thankful to you, Greggy," she said. And then she peeped sidelong from beneath the ruby-studded bridal headdress. "Am I really beautiful now?"

Greg-Donnet kissed his fingertips in an extravagant gesture. "More than that. You're *splendid*."

Her mind still held a shadow of uncertainty. "Oh, Greggy, if only my Tonee were here to see. How will I bear the waiting?"

"Just a few days," he soothed her. "The King told me that Tony's job will be finished soon. He'll be able to join you before the end of the Tourney . . . Now watch the Kings open the sky together. This is something new, to symbolize the bogus Armistice." He gave a sad giggle. "A nice sentiment, at any rate."

The small figure in golden armor and the gigantic one in sharply faceted black lifted Spear and Sword. The photon weapons sent emerald beams slanting skyward and the clouds parted as they had for countless millennia on lost Duat and for a thousand years on Pliocene Earth. As the entire assembly exerted its creativity, the mist rolled away and a shaft of sunlight shone upon the two monarchs. Tanu and Firvulag and Howler and human voices combined in the Song.

There is a land that shines through life and time,
A comely land through the length of the world's age,
And many-colored blossoms fall on it,
From the old trees where the birds are singing.
> *Every color glows there, delight is commonplace,*
> *Music abounds on the Field of Gold,*
On the Sweet-Scented Field of the Many-Colored Land,
On the Field of Gold to the north.

There is no weeping, no treachery, no grief,
There is no sickness, no weakness, no death.
There are riches, treasures of many colors,
Sweet music to hear, the best of wine to drink.
> *Golden chariots contend on the Plain of Sports,*
> *Many-colored steeds run in days of lasting*
> *weather.*
The host range over the Field of Sport,
It is beautiful and not weak their game is..

There will come at sunrise a star of morning,
Lighting up the land, riding the wave-beaten plain,
Stirring the sea until it turns to blood,
Raising the armies before the Singing Stone.
> *The Stone sings a Song to the host;*
> *The music magnifies as all sing together.*
Neither death nor the ebbing of the tide
Will come to those of the Many-Colored Land.

Elizabeth said to Aiken, "The words were different."

He said, "Morna-Ia Kingmaker said they were the ones we should sing this year." He gave her an enigmatic smile. "Look— here come the Firvulag artisans with the new trophy, the Singing Stone. Carved from a single huge aquamarine. Rumor hath it that the thing is already programmed to the aura of Sharn and Ayfa. How do you like that for impudence?" ·

They were sitting in the Tanu royal enclosure watching the preliminary events. A lavish breakfast buffet had been spread and most of the High Table members and their guests were partaking heartily. The King only nibbled an unbuttered crois-sant. Elizabeth, whose lower face was still hidden by Brede's heavily gem-encrusted respirator, ate nothing.

She said, "The line in the Song about a 'star of morning' hit a trifle too close to the bone for my taste."

Aiken shrugged. "Marc's probably out there in the mob right this minute laughing himself sick at that cutesy-poo Firvulag folkdance routine going on around the Singing Stone. Florida was never like this."

"I don't suppose he tried to contact you?"

"About making a deal?" Aiken shook his head. "I'll give him credit for that much class. Not a peep. No ultimatum about me opening the Gateway sigma in exchange for his canceling Götterdämmerung."

"He knows you wouldn't betray the children once you placed them under your protection. He seems to have his own notion of honor."

"Not that it wouldn't be a simple solution to this crock of shit," Aiken said brutally. Tearing a chunk from the pastry, he chewed it in silence for a minute. "All I can do is hope that Hagen and his crew finish the Guderian device before Marc talks the Firvulag around. Once the kids are through to the Milieu, our homegrown Lucifer is euchred. I'll take my chances fighting Nightfall with the Firvulag just as long as Marc isn't leading them in metaconcert."

She said, "Whatever happens—I want to help you. You know I'm blocked against aggressive action, but there's still my farsensing function, and I can heal—"

She broke off, tears spilling from her eyes. The little man in the gold-lustre armor took both her hands in his own. "Why won't you go on Kyllikki?"

She looked away, shaking her head, trying to free her hands. The King only gripped her more tightly.

"I don't want you here, Elizabeth. I want you safe. Kyllikki sails from Goriah tomorrow night. I'm going to fly you there and put you aboard with the others."

"No! I want to stay here and help you . . . and if there's a chance of the time-gate opening—"

"So you'd go back to the Milieu if you could?"

"Wouldn't you?" she demanded hotly, her eyes glaring at him above the diamond mask.

He released her suddenly and she fell back in her chair. There was a roar from the crowd and a storm of laughter and applause. With the pompous formalities concluded, a troupe of Firvulag comedians were putting on a turn, making perilous mock of the Singing Stone and the upcoming factional rivalry for it. Almost everyone in the Tanu royal enclosure was watching the fun. Nobody paid any attention to Aiken and Elizabeth.

He answered her question. "I'm the King and this is my land and I'll stay here until I die."

"Let me help you," she begged. "I want to very much, Aiken."

"All right." His agreement was abrupt. "If you'll take off the mask."

"No," she said stubbornly. "These people want me to symbolize Brede, and so I'm going to do it in full fig. Two-faced, just like her."

"Take it off." His black eyes were irresistible fonts of coercion. "Do you think I don't know what's in your mind? You don't want to be Brede, you want to be Saint Illusio the Martyr! And I'm a little slow on the uptake, so I've just begun to figure out why. But you're not going to get away with it, lass. You'll be no good to me playing weird little games: metapsychic hide-and-seek. If you're for me, it's going to be on my terms. Do you understand?"

"Yes." She reached up and unfastened the straps of the jeweled respirator, lowered it, and smiled at him in obvious relief. "It was getting very hot," she admitted. "I don't know what possessed me. It just seemed to be an appropriate gesture. Comforting. I suppose I was subconsciously hiding."

"That's right." He poured iced wine into a crystal goblet and held it out for her. "And when you discover what you're hiding from, you'll be home free. Now drink this and relax. I'll see you later. It's time for me to be off and get things ready for our own half of the preliminary fun and games."

There were 900 knights in the precision-riding maneuver team, and they came proudly onto the field in Guild formations, led by the golden-armored King on his unique black steed. The chalikos of the company had their coats dyed in heraldic colors and were trapped in gem-studded garniture. Unicorn spikes adorned the mounts' chamfrons and they trailed gauzy lappets of gold or silver to match the floating capes and banner-topped lances carried by the riders. Following Aiken-Lugonn in the place of honor were the violet-and-gold knights of the Farsensor Guild; though few in number, they had been the first to take the King to kin. Then came the combatant redactors in ruby and silver; and the more numerous psychokinetics blazing rosy gold; and the bold sapphire chivalry of the Coercer Guild; and finally the creators wearing lustrous and changeable sea-hues— cyan and beryl and olivine and deepest ultramarine glass armor. The Shining One took up a position in the middle of the display ground, and the riders maneuvered about him to the music of curling glass horns and thunderous kettledrums. The gorgeous clawed beasts marched and countermarched and wheeled and curvetted. They performed flashy caracoles and leaps, dancing in ever-changing patterns of color about the motionless King. Flowers bloomed, rainbow stars exploded and were metamorphosed into abstract swirling designs, and the Tanu and human spectators cheered and ooh'd at each fresh display of equestrian virtuosity.

"Very pretty," sneered King Sharn, "if not particularly impressive from a martial arts point of view." He quaffed the beer in his skull-cup with a mighty gulp and gestured to a dwarf servitor for a refill. "Freshen your lime squash, too, Cousin?"

"No, thank you, Awful King," Sugoll said.

"Tarting up the chalikos with those dye-jobs is a fairly recent innovation you may not have seen before, Cousin. Lowlife golds introduced it at the Muriah games about thirty years ago, when they'd helped the Foe cement their domination of the Grand combat. But you folks never bothered much with the ritual fighting, did you?"

"It was the reason we originally separated from the main

body of Firvulag in my grandsire's day, and retreated to the hinterlands. The annual slaughter of the Combat had begun to seem meaningless to us."

In a low voice, Sharn said, "Don't mention it to the farts on my Gnomish Council—but Ayfa and I felt the same. War's good for one thing: putting yourself on top!"

"As it happens," Sugoll said, "I did attend the games in Muriah once. Last year, and incognito. I had been told that human scientists in thrall to the Tanu might have the technology to alleviate the deformities of my people. Thanks be to Teah the All-Merciful, this has proved to be true."

Sharn tipped a wink at the mutant. "If little Rowane turns out to be a typical refit job, you'll have to beat off Firvulag swains from your girlies with a stick at next year's Grand Loving! I suppose you'll be a candidate for the Skin-tank yourself now, eh?"

"I will be the last, as is fitting."

Sharn studied the foam in the goblet. "Oh. Well, of course. But you know, after we win the Nightfall War, we'll have lots more of the Skin you can use. And we'll save the noncombatant redactors to help with your healing if they promise to behave."

Sugoll's illusory eyes regarded the King calmly. "As Teah wills."

"We need you on our side in Nightfall, Cousin. Are you with us?"

"I must do as the Goddess prompts me."

Sharn leaned forward. His face had become ominous in the ornate black-glass helm. "She wills that we conquer, Cousin—and you'd better consider carefully if you think otherwise! Oh, I know what your Lady's been up to. Working on Ayfa, badmouthing Firvulag prospects in the war, saying we won't be able to hold our shit together when the Golden Futterbug comes against us in metaconcert... Well, I'm bighearted, and I'll make allowances for Katy. She's a Tanu-human hybrid, after all, and probably a secret Peace Faction member to boot. But *you've* got a Firvulag soul, Cousin, no matter what shape your body is. You belong with us!"

Sugoll said, "We are all children of the Goddess, all of one blood in the great mystery, folk of Duat and folk of Earth fated to share each other's destiny."

"Bosh!" cried Sharn. "Boondock mysticism! While you lot

were off in the wilderness thinking noble thoughts, the Tanu crushed our spirits with the help of their human minions. Now it's our turn! We've got the advantage and we're going to win!"

"Look," said the Howler Lord, pointing out onto the tournament field. "Aiken-Lugonn directs the finale of his demonstration."

"A Flying Hunt," Sharn growled. "It figures."

The Firvulag monarch and the mutant stood side by side watching. Out on the golden sand, the small figure on the black chaliko was the center of a vortex of iridescence. The jewel-colored knights on their faerie charges were rising in a great spiral above him, mounting high into the clear blue sky as the blaring horns and the drums rolled to a crescendo.

"Nine hundred knights," Sharn said bitterly, "and he's hoisting them all himself, too, not phasing in a metaconcert."

"Aircraft are approaching," Sugoll noted.

Twenty-six dark flyers with the openhanded golden blazon arranged themselves in a vast diamond pattern about the inverted cone of levitant knights. The rhocraft descended vertically until they floated a scant two hundred meters above the grandstands. The crawling purple network of the force-fields negating gravity's pull could be seen clearly, enveloping the birdlike shapes.

Suddenly, the music stopped.

The small golden manikin dismounted from his chaliko and stood with his arms raised high. The spiraling knights halted as though frozen in the bright transparent air. The spectators uttered a low sound, then were utterly silent.

The rho-fields clothing the fleet of aircraft winked out— and still the dark birds hung in the sky.

"Great Goddess," whispered Sharn.

Softly, the horns sang the Song of the Stone. Then it was finished, and the ships were cloaked again in violet fire and wafed away like a drift of leaves. The Flying Hunt reversed its spiral, swiftly returned to earth, formed ranks, and marched away to a quick-beat of drums.

"Are you still confident of victory, Awful King?" Sugoll asked in a mild voice.

The ogre took a hasty swallow of beer. The dwarf with the pitcher came trotting up, a hesitant expression on his apple-cheeked face. "Majesty, I don't like bothering you . . . but he won't go away."

"Who?" snarled the King. "What're you blithering about, Hofgarn?"

"A Lowlife requests audience, sire. A straping sort of rogue with a very insolent manner who styles himself Star of Morning. He seems to think you're expecting him."

"I believe," Sharn said very slowly, "that I am." He turned to Sugoll. "Thank you for attending us, Cousin. I hope to see you after lunch, at the animal races, and at the Goblinade celebration tonight, together with your gracious Lady. You have my permission to withdraw."

The mutant arose, bowed his head, and moved away to join the others at the front end of the enclosure. Sharn beckoned for more beer in a peremptory manner. He took off his heavy glass helmet, ran fingers combwise through his sweaty hair, and said to the dwarf, "Bring the Lowlife to me now, Hofgarn. And see that we're not disturbed."

Late that evening, after Minanonn had farspoken the base at Goriah telling Commander Congreve that the healing of the black-torc children had finally been accomplished, a single aircraft came to evacuate Black Crag. It stood in the garden, long-legged beneath a gibbous Halloween moon, flight deck inclined like the head of a bemused crane, while the excited mothers carried their babies aboard. They were followed by the small teams of redactors and coercers of the Peace Faction, dead-tired but radiating profound satisfaction, and the chalet staff, and the few other residents who had stayed behind after Elizabeth's entourage went away to Nionel. Basil supervised the loading of the last pieces of luggage while Minanonn went through the shut-up lodge on a final tour of inspection.

When the Heretic returned to the garden he found Creyn and Brother Anatoly waiting with Basil at the foot of the boarding ladder. Mr. Betsy stuck his bewigged head out of the belly hatch and said, "Step lively! I can't wait all night. I've missed half of the Firvulag barbecue at the Field of Gold as it is, twiddling my thumbs while you finished mind-scrubbing these urchins."

Creyn said to Minanonn, "We know that you plan to body-fly to the Grand Tourney, then join Kyllikki later when she is at sea. Anatoly and Basil and I wish to accompany you."

"I asked that pigheaded durachoka to take me with her," the old Franciscan muttered. "Told her I wouldn't harass her. But she went off and left me." He grinned slyly. "As it turned out, it was providential."

Betsy called down waspishly, "Are you coming or *aren't* you?"

Minanonn lifted a great hand. "Off you go. We four seem to have other business to take care of."

Betsy sniffed. "Stand clear, then." The ladder withdrew and the hatch slammed shut. The two Tanu and the two humans moved back as the aircraft powered up and acquired its eerie coating of reticulated light. Wisps of acrid smoke came from the charred areas around the landing-strut pads. The bird seemed to lift its head and look skyward. A moment later it lofted straight up into darkness.

The garden was quiet except for a single chirping cricket and the wind in the pines. Minanonn said, "I'm going to the games because I'm an unregenerate old thrill seeker. Somehow, I suspect you three have a rather different motive."

"We love Elizabeth," Creyn said, "and we want to save her from herself. And perhaps forestall the war in the process."

Minanonn's aura of good humor vanished. "Redactive Brother, I won't see her badgered—no matter what noble intentions you may have!"

"We won't say a word to her," Anatoly declared. "It's Remillard we're after. We want to track him down—he's bound to be there—and make one last appeal to his better judgment." The priest's eyes flicked to Creyn. "Based on new information received."

"Are you out of your minds?" the former Battlemaster exclaimed.

Creyn was patient. "The three of us probably know Remillard as well as any people in Black Crag—excepting Elizabeth. We're not afraid of him."

"And what we hope to tell him," Basil said, "is hardly likely to provoke—er—adversarious wrath. On the contrary. It just may compel a change of heart."

"For the love of Tana, what is it?" Minanonn asked.

Anatoly lifted his shoulders in Slavic declension. Once again he indicated Creyn, whose mind was closely shuttered. "We can't tell you unless Elizabeth releases this poor besotted lozhn'iy from a rash promise he made."

"But obviously," Minanonn said to Anatoly and Basil, "you two share the secret."

The priest waved a bony forefinger. "Creyn told Basil before he made his promise to Elizabeth. As for me—"

The redactor said, "I sought counsel from Brother Anatoly to ease my conscience when it seemed that larger considerations outweighed the promise Elizabeth extracted from me. His judgment—and we three have pondered it at length—is that I have an obligation to give this information to the Adversary."

"All's fair in love and war," mumbled the old Franciscan, "and this is both, dai Bog!"

Minanonn looked from the redactor to the friar to the alpinist with growing exasperation. "If I were not a man of peace I'd coerce the three of you to quivering jellyfish and get to the bottom of this."

"Just take us to the Grand Tourney," Basil said. "We'll find Remillard somehow."

Anatoly said, "Both Creyn and Basil knew his mental signature, and I'll get by with Siberian guile. They'll finger him and I'll make the overture."

"And he'll kill you," Minanonn said, "as easy as squashing flies!"

"He's not a demon out of your Tanu legends," Anatoly told him. "He's only a man. He wore my clothes and worked with me in my garden. We talked . . . about some of the damnedest things. I tell you there's a chance we can change his mind."

The Heretic regarded them bleakly. "You're a trio of lunatics, but I'm going to have to give you the benefit of the doubt. Let's fly. It's a long way to Nionel."

10

ON THE SECOND DAY, THE RIVALRY BETWEEN TANU AND Firvulag sharpened and bookies had a field day among the human sports fans, who threw their money away like there was no tomorrow. Inconspicuous among the throng, the tall man in the white duck pants and black t-shirt spent the morning watching coracle races on the river (won handily by the Firvulag), the kite fights (a draw), and the first round of the enduro chariot races (top points to Kuhal Earthshaker's team). The man smiled as he caught sight of Cloud up in the royal enclosure, disguised as a Warrior Maid in coercer harness, cheering her hero down the stretch.

In the afternoon there were hammer throws and caber-tossing events, dominated by the thicker-thewed Little People; and a stylized free-for-all between the ogresses and the female Tanu knights, fought on foot, which saw the first Grand Tourney fatalities.

After wandering through the refreshment pavilion the man returned to the riverside bleachers to watch more water sports. The windsurfer races, although billed as one of the minor events, attracted an unusually large cheering section of gorgeous Tanu ladies, who applauded madly when the Deputy Marshal of Sport

416

introduced a silver-torc contestant named Niccolò MacGregor. This personage, with all the panache of a bantam rooster, demolished the dwarfish opposition and finished the winning heat handstanding on his surfboard while the exotic women showered his rig with yellow rosebuds.

"It's the King, of course," said a voice at the tall man's elbow. He turned slightly and saw a lanky old friar in a brown-wool habit sitting next to him on the bench, nibbling a tournedos Rossini.

"That looks good," Marc said.

"Vendor's just around the rear of the stand. Be glad to get you one." Anatoly jingled a shabby purse hanging from his cincture. "I'm flush. Made a killing at the chariot races."

"Thank you—but no."

The priest smacked his lips. "Got real truffles and foie-gras on it. Fantastic! Sure you don't want one?"

"Quite sure." Marc sat at ease, watching the pseudo-Niccolò being carried off in triumph by a squad of statuesque beauties in pastel chiffon. "So the King participates in the games, does he?"

"Not officially—and not using his metapsychic powers, of course. Nobody's supposed to use mental strength until the big tug-of-war on Day Four and the no-holds-barred hurley game that climaxes the Tourney."

"Not even in the jousting?"

"Especially not in the jousting."

"Will the King be a contestant tomorrow?"

"It's rumored he'll enter the pogo-stick leap. To help promote the peaceful uses of iron, you see."

"And will he go anonymously into the lists?"

Anatoly's eyes twinkled. "I guess we'll just have to be there tomorrow and see. Coming to the Japanese lantern parade and the Ground-Star Ball tonight?"

"Unless other matters demand my attention."

Anatoly finished the tidbit and licked his fingers. Out on the river, course attendants were setting up a large ring of white floats. The Deputy Marshal announced the next contest, something called a kelpie randan. The priest said, "So the Firvulag King turned down your offer, eh?"

Marc gave him a sharp look. The tip of a coercive-redactive

probe stroked Anatoly's brain, making his cheeks bulge and sweat start out on the back of his neck.

"Did Elizabeth send you here to spy?" Abaddon inquired softly.

"She doesn't even know I'm at the games, dammit! Don't ream me—I'm only the advance man. The one you have to talk to is Creyn, waiting down back of the bleachers with Basil. He'd welcome your turning his mind inside out. He has important information for you."

The probe retracted minimally. The coercive hold tightened. A roar went up from the crowd as a team of grotesque Howlers prepared to face a human squad of the King's Elites in a wild variant of water polo. Marc was on his feet, herding Anatoly toward the exit steps.

"You seem to be telling the truth, Brother. I believe I'll listen to what our friend Creyn has to say. And on the way out, perhaps we can do business with that tournedos vendor after all."

The royal flagship, with Aiken at the controls, landed close to the perimeter of the silver hemisphere and seemed to contemplate its distorted reflection in the gaudy sunset light. Bleyn and Alberonn, armed with big actinic blasters, stood by as the twenty-two metapsychic Rebels who had mutinied against their leader came down the aircraft ladder, followed by the King. Aiken transmitted an indecipherable mental command and an airlock door opened in the surface of the force-field. He watched the others pass through, then came after and resealed the barrier behind him.

The Children of Rebellion were waiting there in the barbican of Castle Gateway, ready to say goodbye to their parents for the last time.

WALTER: Veikko! Son . . . you look fine, and Irena, too. God, this is wonderful. I can't believe it's happening.

VEIKKO: You're limping.

WALTER: It's nothing. The Tanu redactors say they'll be able to fix me up. But you—! Have you kids really done it? Really built the Guderian device?

IRENA: It's not quite finished, Walter. Perhaps by tomorrow.

VEIKKO: The cables need to have their micro-guts tuned up a

skosh, that's all. There are problems with the core-mesh of superfine cladded wire, the damn stuff that's given us hell all along. But once the technical people get it squared away we power up, do a fast test, then just . . . go.

IRENA: Hagen and Cloud will be first, of course, because of Marc. Once they pass through the gate, the rest of us should be safe.

VEIKKO: Cloud pulled a fast one today. Her Tanu lover, rather. He told the King he wouldn't do his thing in the big chariot race unless Cloudie was there watching. Boy, was Aiken Drum pissed! But he finally caved in and took her with him to the royal enclosure and guarded her like a hawk.

IRENA: Kuhal won the race, too.

WALTER: I guess you kids know about this Peace Faction going to resettle Ocala. And why they're leaving Europe . . .

VEIKKO: The Nightfall War may never happen, Dad. Cloud got the latest poop from Kuhal. The King and Queen of the Firvulag don't trust Marc to direct them in metaconcert. They think they can lick Aiken and his Tanu army on their own. And maybe they're right.

IRENA: We're all so glad *you'll* be safe. Whatever happens to us.

WALTER: You'll get away! I know you will! You're so close!

VEIKKO: Sure we will. Good guys always win. And I guess we're good guys . . . [Doubt.]

IRENA: If we get to the Milieu, we'll make up for everything somehow. Some of us have been thinking about it. Planning—

WALTER: I hope you can. God, I hope so.

VEIKKO: We're scared.

WALTER: So am I. But it's different now, isn't it?

VEIKKO: We stood up to him—us kids, and you, too. We'll see that they know in the Milieu, Walter. Especially about you and Alexis Manion—

AIKEN: *Come*.

WALTER: It's time. Kyllikki sails on the evening tide. Good luck, you two.

VEIKKO: Bon voyage, Walter. Wherever.

Elizabeth danced with the King, not knowing or caring what the music was, content to let him lead her, resting in his strength.

The enormous paper neputas were ranged in a circle about the dancing ground, softly gleaming. Their sides showed every sort of scene, every sort of creature and being characteristic of the Many-Colored Land, ironically executed in classic Japanese style in translucent colored paints. Behind the great lanterns were the ancient trees of the bottomland forest, where a myriad of yellow, green, and pink fireflies had been gathered by some Howler art to evoke the theme of the Ground-Star Ball. Overhead, the real stars of Pliocene November flamed more palely as the tardy moon rose. The constellation of the Trumpet, hiding the Duat Galaxy behind its mouthpiece star, was at the zenith.

Aiken said to Elizabeth, "You're happier. I'm glad."

"It's good being with you again, dear."

"Funny," he said, "the way I feel about you. No sex at all. Not brotherly, either. I don't know what to call it. You want me to control you and I want to do it. Like a father and a very little girl."

"Hermes Psychopompos," she said lightly. "The soul guide. A very rare archetype indeed. I presume my subconscious knows what it needs."

"I'm not really the one, though, am I? But I wish—I wish you could be my Queen. I could love you and never be afraid."

"You'll find her someday, Aiken. You're very young."

"But growing up fast," he said, laughing.

Their minds disengaged and for a while, they simply let the dance own them. It was, Elizabeth realized to her surprise, almost a foreshadowing of Unity . . . And then he said:

"I want you to trust me. Let me into the hidden part of you for just a moment. Let me look behind the real mask you've always worn. Will you?"

She stiffened in his arms and there was a fearful chilling. "Why?"

The mind spoke, enclosing her, vast and familiar and strong: Trust me. Let me look. For your sake and for all of us. Please.

I can't—

Please, I must know the truth.

There's fire—

I know. Poor Elizabeth. You're so proud and afraid. If you'd only learn to trust.

Brother Anatoly wants me to trust God—

Just trust Me. Let me come. There . . .

She was suspended in silence, all alone. The blackness around her was not mental. She knew that somehow. It was a remote part of the physical universe, intergalactic space, void of stars, without even a wisp of glowing gas. There was only a single object for her mind to fasten on, one respite from everlasting Night.

A pinwheel of bluish-white sparkling haze, tiny and exquisite. A whirlpool of suns isolated from other clusters of galaxies. A barred spiral she might reach out and touch, and move.

She opened her eyes.

She was dancing with Marc Remillard.

"Creyn broke his promise," she said. "He was not to tell you. The vision is his, not mine. Impossible."

"I agree. And yet—appealing. If only I were not committed to my own challenge, and so close to realizing it again. The years have been bitter, Elizabeth. I can't resist trying."

"I know." She did not dare look at him again. He was not dressed in exotic finery as the King had been but wore almost archaic tropical formal wear, a black dinner jacket and a ruffled shirt. She let her head rest on his breast, submitted to his lead, but without surrendering as she had to the King.

"You have three very persistent and brave friends, Elizabeth."

"I told them not to come here. They have no right to interfere. And Creyn promised!"

"He told me more than his Duat vision," Marc said. "Creyn told me that you loved me, Elizabeth—and so did Aiken. Is it true?"

"It's impossible," she said, from behind the flames.

"I think so, too, but your friends are more stubborn. Basil has climbed the mountain and Creyn has helped make black-torc children whole and operant and Anatoly—experienced a temporary triumph at my expense. As I said, they're stubborn. They'd like to think nothing is impossible."

"We know better, Marc."

"Yes," he said, and they danced in blackness unrelieved. Then it was Aiken who held her under trees starred by fireflies, and the music slowed at last and stopped.

11

Shortly after Dawn on the Third Day, with the King and his entire High Table and Elizabeth standing by as observers, the haggard workers on the Guderian Project gathered in the inner courtyard of Castle Gateway for the initial power-up of the tau-generator. Even the five tiny children of the North Americans were present, drowsy and solemn-faced, but more interested in the spectacularly costumed Tanu Exalted Ones than in the device that might transport them to the Galactic Milieu.

The apparatus was somewhat larger than the original machine built by Théo Guderian. It still bore an uncanny resemblance to an old-fashioned latticework pergola or gazebo draped in vines. In order to compensate for the rise in terrain that would occur over the six-million-year time span, the device stood on scaffolding slightly over two meters in height. Its frame was of transparent glassy material; at each joint was a nodular component of black, having obscure scintillations dimly visible within. The "vines," actually heavy cables of multi-colored alloys, emerged from bare ground under the platform and crept in and out of the lattice. At a point fifteen centimeters above the gazebo roof the cables seemed to vanish, then reappear in a mysterious fashion to twine down again through the rear framework.

"What are you going to send off first?" Aiken asked Hagen.

The young man held out a small box carved from rock crystal, lifting its lid to show a thin wafer of metal with a blue-black tarnish.

"Potassium. After it makes the round trip, we run it through an ordinary kay-ay dater to be sure it's picked up twelve million years. According to theory, the focus of the time-gate is fixed. If the machine works at all, it should take its cargo to the grounds of l'Auberge du Portail on the synchronous Milieu date of 2 November 2111, then whisk it back here as the tau-field recycles."

"Right," said the King. "Let's get on with it." He reached out and took the hand of Elizabeth, who was standing beside him, her face lacking expression and her mind inaccessible.

Hagen mounted the scaffold steps. One of his associates handed him an ordinary four-legged wooden stool, which he positioned in the precise center of the gazebo. He placed the crystal box on the stool and then withdrew to the front row of spectators, to stand with Diane Manion, Cloud, and Kuhal Earthshaker. He said to a young woman seated at the control console, "Do it, Matiwilda."

She said, "Going away."

There was no sound as the Guderian device was activated. The power-drain was so minimal that the spotlights positioned around the castle yard never faltered in brilliance. The gazebo seemed to shimmer; then its interior was hidden, as though mirror panels had suddenly sprung up inside.

"I know the translation's supposed to be instantaneous," Aiken said, "but just give it a minute."

The two hundred people watching held their breath.

"All right," said the King at last.

Matiwilda threw the switch and the mirror effect winked out. In a cometlike leap, Aiken was on the platform squatting before the entrance to the booth. Inside were two truncated pieces of wooden stool fallen to each side of an ash-covered crystal box.

"Suffering Christ!" the King said. "The tau-field only formed a beam yea-wide! Will you look at this, Hagen?"

Cursing, young Remillard rushed onto the platform. The other onlookers buzzed and groaned and sent out a hodgepodge of telepathic execration.

"Anastos, get up here!" Hagen bellowed.

A swarthy man with an authoritative air pushed out of the crowd. After inspecting the gazebo he went to confer with the woman at the control console. Somewhere a childish voice piped, "Does that mean we can't go, Daddy?"

Aiken handed down the crystal box to Bert Candyman, who was standing by with the radio-dating analyzer. The chemist pried open the container gingerly, disclosing a circle of dirty white powder. He offered the King a crooked smile. "Well, it's been *somewhere*, Your Majesty!"

More technicians came onto the platform to inspect the fiasco, then chaffer earnestly with Hagen, the King, or the dynamic-field engineer Dimitri Anastos. Cloud Remillard and Kuhal Earthshaker watched Candyman do his analysis. The King demanded the immediate presence of Tony Wayland via a mind-rocking summons on the declamatory farspeech mode. The metallurgist, wearing a haunted look, was drawn into the consultation.

After perhaps a quarter of an hour of wrangling, there was an abrupt resolution. All the technical personnel retired from the platform, leaving only the King standing beside the gazebo. He held the two chunks of the stool in one upraised hand and the empty crystal box in the other. His mind commanded:

Silence.

A child whimpered. Somebody coughed and somebody else stifled a sob.

"It's only a temporary setback," Aiken informed them. "Here's the good news: Bert says that the potassium wafer traveling in this little box checked in with an approximate age of eleven point seven eight plus-or-minus zero point two million years. That's as close as damnall to being right on the proverbial time button. We have a gate to the Milieu."

Everybody gasped, then there were feeble cheers.

The King flourished the remnants of the doubly guillotined stool. "But it's a very *small* gate—so far. Instead of filling the entire gazebo, the tau-field is being generated in a narrow slice a little over a handspan wide. It's a glitch, but we think we know what's causing it. It's probably a single cable with a faulty core, and it'll be unzipped and put through bench-testing immediately."

Resigned groans. A child asked, "Can we go tomorrow, King?" Tense laughter.

"I hope so, Riki," Aiken said. He looked over his shoulder for a moment at the gleaming latticework machine before tossing away the bits of wood and stowing the empty crystal box in the hip pocket of his golden suit. He walked to the platform edge. The royal forefinger pointed uncompromisingly at Tony Wayland, who stood stiff at the foot of the steps. The metallurgist gaped in horror as the King transmitted a mental image to him on the intimate mode. Aiken said softly, "Eighty thousand Firvulag, Tony—plus the Angel of the Abyss. You *will* do your very best with that core, won't you?"

Clutching his torc, Tony Wayland managed to nod.

He d-jumped directly into the shadowed inner recesses of the nearly deserted Firvulag royal enclosure. The only one who saw him materialize was young Sharn-Ador, banished for an obligatory nap in the middle of the hot afternoon.

"Father! Mother! The Foe!" screamed the boy, tumbling from his camp bed and scrabbling among the pieces of his discarded juvenile armor for his ceremonial sword.

Sharn and Ayfa came charging back, minds exuding metaphorical fire and brimstone. But they burst out laughing together as they identified the intruder.

The Queen reached down to hug her son. "It's only our Low—our human friend, Smudger. He's no Foeman. No danger to us. Go back to sleep."

Wide-eyed, the child gushed profound suspicion from his mind. "But he came out of thin air! Not from being invisible— he *really* came!"

Marc Remillard laughed.

"It's one of the things he can do," King Sharn said drily. "Now obey your mother, or you don't get to watch the Assent Encounters."

The royal pair led Marc to the chairs at the front of the box. Sugoll was there, and the revered dwarfish artisan couple Finoderee and Mabino Dreamspinner, who were noncombatant members of the Gnomish Council; but all the rest of the Firvulag nobility were down in the lists, either getting ready to enter

the High Affray themselves or giving support and encouragement to those who were.

"Too bad you didn't come earlier, Remillard," Sharn said
heartily. He directed his guest to a seat and signaled Hofgarn
to replenish the food and drink. "You missed some lively jousts."

"Seventeen Foe fairly maimed and a dozen clobbered on
points," dear old Mabino cackled. "The tally's tipping our way
at last."

Ayfa poured sangría for Marc herself and offered it with a
gracious smile. Out on the Field of Gold there was a flourish
of trumpets. The stentorian mind-voice of Heymdol Buccinator,
Marshal of Sport, announced the upcoming contest and the
rules of scoring.

"This may be fun," the Queen said. "The participants must
hack off the helmet-crests of the opposition to make points. I
wouldn't be surprised if there were low blows."

Lady Mabino tittered.

Sugoll, wearing his illusion of a handsome bald-headed
humanoid, said, "Perhaps our guest, like so many humans,
finds mayhem repugnant."

"I've been responsible for my share," Marc noted, drinking
deeply of the spiced wine punch. "Even in the Galactic Milieu,
we humans were a rough-and-ready lot—to the scandal of more
civilized races... As it happened, I was off visiting a very
civilized world just this morning, testing a gift someone gave
me yesterday."

Sharn and Ayfa concealed their stupefaction, but the two
noble dwarfs gaped unashamed. Finoderee squeaked, "Té's
teeth—you mean you flew to another planet, Lowlife?"

Marc gave a brief mental explanation of the d-jumping
metafaculty. "And since I was recently given a mitigator program—a technique that does away with most of the pain that
usually accompanies the crossing into hyperspace—I was eager
to test it on a long-distance hop. I went to a world that I call
Goal, fourteen thousand light-years distant."

"Goddess," whispered the Queen.

"The mitigator worked perfectly," Marc said. "I was given
it by a Tanu. An attempt at bribery. He said that it was a part
of the Firvulag mental heritage as well, a legacy of Brede's
Ship that brought all of you to Earth a thousand years ago."

"That was before our time," Sharn said.

Wizened Finoderee bobbed his head, lost in introspection. "*We* remember, though—don't we, Mama?" Mabino's lips trembled.

Marc said, "The Goal world is the place where I hope to take my children . . . after you join me in subduing our mutual Foe, who keeps them captive in Castle Gateway."

Sharn knit his brows, pursed his mouth, and formed a steeple with enormous, spatulate fingers. He did not meet the hypnotic gray eyes of the Adversary. "I'm still taking that matter under advisement, Remillard. You know, we're very impressed by you. Perhaps a trifle too impressed—ha! ha! We Little Folk are only a simple barbarian nation, though, and all this high technology of yours is a radical pill to swallow."

"Our idea of wild innovation," said Ayfa, "is using domestic animals for transport."

"And captured Milieu weaponry for . . . self-defense," Sugoll put in blandly.

Marc seemed unperturbed. "Our alliance could be very profitable to you. In return for a single act of cooperation, I would make you a gift of a highly sophisticated offensive metaconcert program five times more efficient than any you could engineer by yourselves. Your creative potential would be over the thousandth order of magnitude with the proper direction."

Old Finoderee gave a bark of confident laughter. "With eighty thousand of us linked for the zap, Aiken Drum will know he's been hit with more than chopped liver."

"We do appreciate your offer," Sharn said, deeply earnest. "And we're thinking it over very carefully."

Marc's smile tightened. "There may not be much time left. If Aiken's scientists at Castle Gateway reopen the time-gate, there'll surely be a fresh influx of human time-travelers from the Galactic Milieu. They could bring additional armaments to Aiken. There may even be operant metapsychics coming through who could oppose us mentally."

"It's a serious matter," Sharn agreed. "And I don't mean to doubt your word. But there have been rumors that this time-gate device is going to be used as an escape hatch by the Golden Pismire. If he hauled his shining little scut out of here, it would suit us fine."

"If the time-gate opens," Abaddon said, "it will finish you."

"And you," Sugoll appended. He leaned over the rail of the

enclosure, watching the mêlée that was taking place on the yellow sands. "The Tanu look to have the advantage. That last charge à travers by the human fighters under the Bottle Knight wiped the floor with Pingoll's dwarves."

Marc's mouth lifted in bemusement. "The Bottle Knight?"

Sugoll pointed out a bizarre combatant riding a grayish zebra-striped hipparion. Instead of the usual glowing glass armor he was harnessed in a species of scale-mail that appeared to be pieced together from the bottoms of variously colored bottles. His limbs were encased in roughcut cylindrical sections, crudely joined with wire. His helmet looked like nothing more than a sawn-off carboy, with a tuft of broom-straw stuck in the neck for a crest and a snoutish visor made from a wine-magnum riveted to the facial region. The Bottle Knight carried a very long glass lance of no-nonsense design and a slick tilting targe with a peephole and a righthand aperture to accommodate the lance during the pass. This Bottle Knight, Sugoll informed Marc, although torced in mere silver and of unimpressive stature, had cut a wide swath through the four earlier jousting matches. Following the rules, he challenged only the dwarfish or human-sized Firvulag. And he always won.

"We think he's the King," Ayfa stated. "Look what a runt he is. And who else would have the effrontery to come onto the field in such an outlandish getup?"

"Aargh!" Finoderee groaned. "He's taken our Shopiltee Bloodguzzler!"

"He doesn't fight fair," Lady Mabino whined. "He should be cutting off the crests with a sword—not unhorsing our lads and lasses and yanking the crests out by the roots!"

"There's nothing in the rules against it," Sharn growled through gritted teeth.

"Look at that scoreboard," Ayfa wailed. "We're ahead in the stalwart category, but that little puke-ort's killing us in the lightweight division. And since we fielded twice as many gnomes as ogres—"

"Yaaak!" mourned Finoderee. *"He got Mimee of Famorel."*

"Sweet Té on toast," cried the disgusted Sharn. Glass carnices blew a musical blast, ending the match. The Tanu grandstand exploded as the semifinal totals were posted on Yosh Watanabe's huge electronic display board.

"Close," Queen Ayfa muttered. "Too damn close. The Foe

have a whisker's worth of an advantage, but they're sure to run away with the game in the Assent Encounters."

"What are those?" Marc inquired.

Sugoll said, "Bravura performances by the champions of the previous matches. They may be challenged individually by any fighter in the appropriate category."

"They're carrying Mimee off," the Queen moaned. "That wretched Lowlife mountebank snapped poor Famorel's left clavicle like a lark's wishbone. None of our other gnomes will dare face the Bottle Knight."

"May only full-blooded Firvulag enter the lists under your banner?" Marc asked.

The King and Queen stared at him.

Sugoll said, "Technically, any human subject of my city, Nionel, also qualifies as a Little Person. However we are a peaceable folk—both Howler and human citizens alike—and as hosts of the Grand Tourney we have refrained from most of the contests in order to attend to the duties of hospitality."

Marc stood with hands on hips, looking down on the pageantry in the arena with a rakehelly grin. "I don't suppose you'd nominate me an honorary citizen of Nionel, would you, Lord Sugoll?"

"Damn right he will!" Sharn cried. Then his enthusiasm faltered like a half-inflated balloon. "Do you think you could lick him? No metapsychic powers allowed. But you do look pretty well built—"

"Big-game fishing. And this jousting seems fairly simple. One merely calculates the appropriate vectors and kinetic reactions. I presume the contestants may mind-control their mounts."

"Oh, yes," said Sugoll. "That's permissible." He indicated a neat stack of translucent glass, lustrous as moonstone and silver-chased. "If you wish, you may use my armor and steed."

Still smiling, Marc bowed. "À la bonne heure."

"And I'll be your squire!" the Firvulag King enthused. "Let's go sign you up! You'll need a fictitious name, of course."

"Jack Diamond will do," said the Adversary.

Marc dismounted from his blowing, foam-stained charger, threw down his buckler and lance, and pulled the brave tuft of broomstraw from the ridiculous helmet of the fallen Bottle

Knight. The Firvulag spectators filled the air with jubilant cacophony.

Aiken doffed his headpiece, sketched a sardonic salute, and
said, "Well smote, White Knight. God, what a klop! I feel like
I've been in a head-on collision with an impacting asteroid."

Marc raised his visor. "Applied mathematics." He held out
a gauntleted hand and courteously hauled his vanquished opponent upright. "I'm afraid the temptation was irresistible."

"I hoped it would be," the King replied.

Marc's right eyebrow rose a millimeter.

Aiken said, "You see, I had to fight in the jousts. Morale.
However, it would never do for Me to get physically creamed
by one of the Foe, would it? But a big hulking human is
something else." The Trickster's eyes glittered. He gestured at
the eruptive horde of gnomish fans who cheered the victorious
Firvulag chivalry. "See how happy and confident you've made
them feel? They're on top of the world. Invincible! Positive
they can whip us Tanu to a fare-thee-well without hardly trying.
And without any help from talented but possible perfidious
Lowlives."

Abaddon sighed. "Very clever." He retrieved his borrowed
equipment and remounted to join the winners' parade. "But
the time-gate is still closed, isn't it?"

"Wouldn't you like to know!"

"What events are scheduled for tomorrow?"

"The biggie is the tug-of-war," Aiken said. "With minds.
No chance for hanky-panky. We'll have to play it straight. At
least I will."

"Then the advantage is still to the ungodly," Marc said.
"Tomorrow then." He lifted high his lance, with the crest of
the Bottle Knight spitted at the tip, and rode away.

12

THE RUMOR MILL HAD BEEN GRINDING AMONG BARENECK AND gray-torc attendees ever since the Grand Tourney began, with two topics uppermost in the minds of the unprivileged human attendees: the possibility of imminent war, and the possibility of a time-warping escape hatch to the Milieu. It was not until the start of the Fourth Day that the hearsay, innuendo, fear, and suspicion began to find anchorage in undeniable fact.

Item: Twenty-five rhocraft of the Royal Flying Corps took up permanent hover station 4000 meters above the Field of Gold (*Fresh rumor:* A hotshot gray scanner technician maintained that the ships' guns were trained smack on the Firvulag grandstand!)

Item: The encampment of Little People among the trees on the north side of the field, which had welcomed Lowlife visitors during the first three days of the Tourney, was now cordoned off by smiling but resolute ogres. (*Fresh rumor:* Howlers as well as humans were being denied entrance because of their dubious loyalty to the Firvulag cause!)

Item: King Aiken-Lugonn was absent from the royal enclosure after the first round of duels in the Heroic Manifestation of Power. His lack of regal courtesy did not prevent Bleyn, Alberonn, and Celadeyr of Afaliah from scoring signal victories over Galbor Redcap, Tetrol Bonecrusher, and Betularn of the White Hand, thus putting the Tanu far out in front in the point scoring. (*Fresh rumors*: A keen-eyed ex-navigator among the barenecks insisted he had got a fix on the departing flagship of Aiken-Lugonn, and that its vector was a veritable beeline for Castle Gateway! The time-gate was about to open! The time-gate device was hopelessly glitched! The King was getting ready to flit to the Milieu! There was not now nor had there ever been a Guderian Project working on a new time-gate!)

Item: The Howlers had "withdrawn with the greatest reluctance" from participation in the crucial tug-of-war game scheduled for that afternoon, pleading the press of duties in overseeing the equipment that would be required for the culminating sporting event of the Tourney. (*Fresh rumors*: The Firvulag royals were livid with rage at the defection! Human citizens of Nionel hinted at a secret pact between Sugoll and Aiken-Lugonn that pledged the mutant minds to the Tanu cause! The Hurley/Shinty Game to be played on the Fifth Day was nothing more nor less than an exotic version of Gaelic-Rules Football—and any civilized sports fan knew that such contests invariably degenerated into bloody free-for-alls! It was going to be the Nightfall opener!)

Item: The reclusive mystery woman, Elizabeth Orme, sat in the royal box at the side of an unknown human. (*Fresh rumor*: The fellow was none other than Marc Remillard, instigator of the Metapsychic Rebellion, the fabled Adversary in the flesh!)

The morning's events reached their climax, the final match of the Heroic Manifestations of Power. The Howler field attendants pumped up the bellows, making the fountains of fire stretch sky high and pour forth commingled black and rose-colored smoke. The monstrous iron chevaux-de-frise in the midst of the flames glowed white-hot. Glass trumpets sounded a fanfare, kettledrums thundered, and then the Marshal of Sport made his amazing announcement:

"The Tanu hero Kuhal Earthshaker, scheduled to contend in this final Manifestation against the Firvulag Battlemaster Medor, has withdrawn."

A mighty roar of disappointment arose from the Tanu partisans. The Little People cheered roundly and the bookmakers scrambled in a frenzy to cope with the last-minute scratch.

The Marshal declared: "By consent of the Committee of Referees, Lord Kuhal's place will be taken by Minanonn the Proud, also called Heretic, former Battlemaster of the Tanu."

Now tumultuous jubilation seized the Tanu and human spectators while the Firvulag hooted, hummed derisively, and shapeshifted into obscene illusory forms to express their vexation. The points at stake in the contest were sufficient to return the overall advantage to the Little People if Medor should win—and he had been an odds-on favorite over Kuhal because of the latter's status as a precariously healed invalid. Now, however, Medor faced not a convalescent but one who had been the premier metapsychic warrior of his race before retiring to voluntary exile.

The smoke from the central pyre changed. Blue and green smoke gushed up together with the clouds or rose-red and black. The two heroes entered the field. Medor was armed in plates of jet studded with orange diamonds and wicked topaz spikes. Minanonn wore a magnificent panoply embodying his triple coercive, creative, and psychokinetic metafunctions. The triskelion was chased in gold upon his massive cuirass and a golden-winged dolphin crowned his helm. The Firvulag champion and the Tanu took up positions on opposite sides of the surging bonfire. Howler officials handed each contender one end of a stout chain of pyrostatic glass, which passed through the center of the flaming fountain and the incandescent iron hedgehogs that lurked at its heart. Then the Marshal signaled, the crowd howled, and the finale in the Manifestations of Power began.

In the Tanu grandstand, the two of them watched with unseeing eyes and minds distracted.

She said: It was thus between Lawrence and me.

He said: This is the way it was with me and Cyndia.

They agreed: Such perfect soul-consonance may surely be achieved but once and any attempt at reprise is doomed to futility. If this is true even among the small-minded how much more invidious an effort between the grandmasterly. And thrice hopeless when both are proud and untrustful.

Exerting both metapsychic power and physical strength, Minanonn and Medor hauled at each other. At first their pull on the chain was steady. The Firvulag hero found himself dragged closer and closer to the inferno and the two bristling contraptions of blazing blood-metal within it. The Tanu and the humans in the audience whooped in anticipation of a quick victory. But guileful Medor suddenly let himself be yanked wholly into the flames. The crowd shrieked. Minanonn had to shift balance in order to regain purchase lost when the chain fell unexpectedly slack.

Medor gave a mighty leap backward at the same time that his mind slickened the sand with ectoplasmic ichor. The Tanu hero staggered and slid. His own creativity strove to cancel the manifestation of his rival. Medor hauled back with savage, abrupt jerks, intent on preventing Minanonn from regaining a fair grip on the slithering chain. (If the Heretic let it slip out of hand, the match was lost.) Inexorably, the former Tanu Battlemaster was drawn into the fountain of fire. Now his metapsychic strength was divided between shielding his body from the terrible heat and pulling back before Medor managed to bring him up against the white-hot spikes of poisonous iron.

The two humans never noticed.

She said: We lived and loved in Unity. We worked hard formed the strong young minds laid secure foundations of mature function. It was so good. He fulfilled me.

He said: I spawned the inhuman thousands and steered the great scheme and she seemed to relate in loving concurrence. And for love of her I begat the Children of her body and sowed the seed of love's death.

They agreed: Such memories form an insuperable rampart between us.

Minanonn flattened the flames. He clutched the tag-end of the glass chain and gave a herculean wrench. Medor was pulled off his feet. The Heretic grasped the chain more securely and let the fire rise up around him, as it also did around his antagonist. Medor uttered a farspoken howl, which was echoed by his countrymen in the stand. Both heroes were totally engulfed, but it was Minanonn who stood firm and the Firvulag who was hauled closer and closer to the glowing metal points.

The man and woman were oblivious.

She said: We feared even amid happiness knowing that life would not be worth living if we were separated. Surely a loving

God would know this and take us together. We trusted. In the crash I lost my metafaculties and the Unity. He was killed. I died the worse death.

He said: In the very act of love she betrayed me. Murdering Mental Man she wept and said she did it for love of me and all humanity. He is dead in me forever and only the Children can resurrect Him.

They disagreed.

Minanonn, holding the chain fast in preparation for the fatal pull, cried out with mind and voice: "Yield, Medor Battlemaster! Yield or impale yourself on scorching blood-metal, gaining Tana's peace but the obloquy of the Little People as you deprive them of a great leader."

Medor let the chain slip from his hands.

The flames died. Minanonn stood in discolored, soot-filthy armor, holding the entire length of glass chain above his half-melted helmet crest. The Tanu throng cried his name again and again and gave him a shattering accolade of slonshal.

The two up in the royal enclosure were aware only of themselves.

She said: Your vision that you cling to so obstinately is evil. This is not merely my judgment or Anatoly's. After twenty-seven years the consensus of the Galactic Mind was unanimous. If you can't see that Cyndia was right and you were wrong you're just what Anatoly called you: arrogant and invincibly ignorant but still wrong wrong wrong.

He said: And what about you? At least my flaw is grand while yours is merely pathetic. You evade responsibility deny commitment out of simple cowardice. You pretend to noble despair when you are merely whimpering and self-righteous. You condemn my ignorance and arrogance when your own is equally great . . . and you say you can never love and you lie lie lie.

She said: What does a heartless monster like you know about love?

He said: Let me look into your mind. Then say you don't love me.

She said: Never! It's impossible.

He said: Then so is the rehabilitation of the Duat Mind.

They agreed.

* * *

"Well, Medor?" bellowed the Firvulag King.

Aides, trainers, and hangers-on fled from the dressing room of the defeated champion as they felt the scourge of Sharn's wrath. But when he was all alone with his Battlemaster the monarch doffed his robes, helped slather soothing ointment on Medor's blisters, and sprayed them with a painkilling Milieu medicament that was said to be nearly as efficacious as Tanu Skin.

"I did my best," the woebegone general said. "But I knew I was cooked as soon as Heymdol announced that the Foe were entering the Heretic as a ringer. No one but Pallol One-Eye was in Minnie's class." After a moment, he appended diplomatically, "Except you yourself, of course, High King."

Sharn mouthed curses through clenched teeth. "We're not out of the woods yet, either. I lodged protests with the stewards; but there's no valid reason for keeping Minanonn or any other Peace Faction member out of the games, assuming their precious consciences tell them that the Grand Tourney isn't ritual warfare but just good clean fun. The Heretic's banishment was a matter of politics. If Aiken wants to accept him on the Tanu team, there's not a damn thing we can do to prevent it."

"Is Minanonn participating in the tug-of-war metaconcert this afternoon, then?"

"I think it's a foregone conclusion," said the King. He helped Medor into a fresh suit of padding and new armor. "But cheer up, old son. In the tug, it's strictly minds, not muscles, that'll cut the mustard. And there's still only thirteen thousand of them—and eighty thousand of us."

Both Elizabeth and Marc saw the flagship land on a hastily roped-off area just behind the Tanu grandstand. Not long afterward the King came to the royal enclosure seeking Elizabeth. He was accompanied by Creyn, Basil Wimborne, Peopeo Moxmox Burke, and Brother Anatoly.

"I'm afraid you'll have to miss the rest of the games, lass," Aiken told her. "We're taking you for a little ride."

She jumped up from her seat. "It's—it's ready?"

The King only said, "Come along."

Marc lounged back with an unconcerned smile. He was

wearing, with considerable style, the smart plum-and-ochre dress uniform of the King's Own Elite Guard, complete with golden torc and commander's insignia. He said, "The time-gate is not yet operative, Elizabeth. The King is merely antic-ipating. Or possibly thinking wishfully. If the Guderian device were in working order, the entire Many-Colored Land would know it."

Aiken only repeated darkly, "Come along."

"You'll hurry back, I hope," Marc said. "Your heroes missed you during the Heroic Manifestations."

"But won all the same," Aiken snapped. "And now we're leading in the point scoring."

"It wouldn't do for you to miss the tug-of-war, though. Not even for . . . strategic reasons. Your subjects would never stand for it. I'm really looking forward to seeing how your meta-concert technique stacks up against Sharn and Ayfa's."

"Planning to enter the tussle on the Firvulag side again?" Aiken inquired sweetly.

"I wouldn't dream of it. You taught me my lesson very effectively."

The King herded Elizabeth and the others to the exit. He said over his shoulder, "Nothing personal, Marc—but when I get back I'd better find you gone. We've about come to the end of the line in this friendly enemies routine. Fair warning."

Marc nodded. "En garde, then, Little King." And to Elizabeth: "Au revoir."

The true disparity between the Tanu and Firvulag numbers became evident as preparations for the mental tug-of-war neared completion. Emptied of all nonmetafunctional humans, the Tanu grandstand had ominous expanses of empty seats, but the ac-commodation of the Firvulag was jammed to overflowing.

Greggy and Rowane had been banished from the royal en-closure of the Little People along with the rest of the nonpar-ticipant Howlers. But rather than joining Sugoll and Katlinel on the sidelines, they sneaked down to the booth between the stands that housed the control room of the Staging and Prop-erties staff.

"Rank *do* hath its privileges," the Genetics Master crowed to his awed protégée. "And down here, we'll see not only the dragons but also the monitoring panels showing which minds are faltering and ready to drop out of the metaconcert."

"Ooo!" said Rowane.

Out on the Field of Gold an astonishing contrivance had been erected in place of the morning's fiery fountain. Its base was an artificial hill as wide as the paired grandstands and fifteen meters high. It was roughly conical in shape, with large cavelike apertures on the right and left flanks and a summit crater.

The sham mountain harbored monstrous twin serpents.

The one on the righthand Firvulag side was glistening black with fangs and eyes as red as carbuncles. Its opposite number had golden scales, and eyes and teeth of bright amethyst. The heads of the snakes protruded from their respective lairs with jaws agape. It seemed that somewhere in the depths of the mountain their bodies met, entwined, then reared upward from the central crater mouth to form a great knot high in the air. From this sky-knot the tails of the serpents curved down in identical arcs, the black tail apparently being swallowed by the golden serpent and the golden tail by the black. The overall effect given by the huge stage prop was that of an enormous wheel, half golden and half black, mounted in an upright position and partially embedded in the base of imitation rock.

"I call it the double Ourobouros," the senior of the two human technicians in charge of the spectacle informed Greggy and Rowane. "But old Lars, over there at the grandstand grounding monitors, likes Siamese Mithgarthsormr better."

"Will you explain its functioning, Master Baghdanian?" Rowane requested. "You must pardon my simplicity, but I am not quite able to grasp how such a device is to be used in a metapsychic tug-of-war."

"I'm all at sea, too!" Greggy giggled. "My golden torc's honorary, you know. But I must say, the gadget is *madly* impressive."

"Wait till you see the electrostatics in action," Lars offered with a grim smile. "I just wish the voltage was high enough to fry these exotic sonsabitches instead a just making their brains twinge."

Baghdanian gave his colleague a resigned look. "Just ignore Lars' xenophobia, folks, and observe instead the displays in front of him that monitor the Tanu and Firvulag grandstands. Red lights for Little People, amber for the Tanu and human torcers. Intensity of light roughly proportional to cerebral wattage."

"The twinkling yellow jobbie on the Tanu display is our Shining Hope, Aiken-Lugonn himself," Lars said.

The senior man listened to some message coming through his comset headpiece. He thumbed a few switchpads, checked out something or other, and said, "We'd better make this quick, folks. We're almost ready to start. Okay . . . all the people in both grandstands are incorporated into the game's electrical circuitry just as long as they keep their seats. They stand up, that means they resign the game. Got that?"

"Mm," said Greggy, suppressing a snicker. "Fundamental antagonism!"

"You know about mindpower, metafunction having electromagnetic components?" the technician asked rather dubiously.

Greggy sighed. "In my less irrational moments I am a doctor of medicine, of genetic science, of philosophy, and of humane letters (honorary)."

"Right," said Baghdanian. "Now just take a careful look at the snake setup out there. What we've really got is a gigantic ring, standing up like a skinny Ferris wheel. The tails of the snakes going into the mouths make a complete circle through the inside of the mountain and also through the knot up top. The central twisty-twiney part just disguises the frame that supports this big scaly ring made of electroconductive material."

"The whole ring's not conductive," Lars interrupted.

Baghdanian gave him another look. "As I was about to say, the conductivity of the ring is broken by insulating material—glass—in two places: up inside the knot where you can't see it, and just inside the jaws of the two snake heads. The entire arc section through the central mountain is nonconductive at the moment. *But!* If the ring rotates—say, to our right—it'll look like the black Firvulag serpent has let the golden tail of the Tanu serpent slip out of its mouth. At the same time, of course, the Firvulag serpent's bod would go deeper and deeper into the gold snake's mouth."

"But really into the mountain." Greggy nodded sagely.

The technician's eyes had an odd glint. "Inside the hill, we have multiple arrays of Van de Graaffs—electrostatic generators similar to the ones in the old Frankenstein movies. If your snake's tail gets gulped just a little, you'll feel a small mental shock. But the farther that tail goes down the enemy gullet, the more intense the mind-zap."

"Merciful heavens!" Greggy exclaimed.

Baghdanian said, "Notice the large jeweled cuffs that clasp the tail of each snake about three meters away from the enemy teeth. We call those the bracelets. Those are the places where the minds have to grip—and pull. The more powerfully our team hauls away on the tail bracelet of your snake, the deeper the tail of the other team will be swallowed."

"And the more agonizing it is for the opponent to hold on," Lars added.

Greggy shuddered. "What a perfectly beastly piece of ingenuity!"

Baghdanian gave a modest shrug. "Twenty-two years in the special-effects department of Industrial Light and Magic."

"How is the winner known?" Rowane asked.

"The guys who get their bracelet devoured," Lars said, "not only lose, but end up with skulls full of half-fried neurons."

Baghdanian wore an abstracted look as he listened to his comset, watched a digital clock, and monitored the occasionally flickering patterns on the Tanu and Firvulag grandstand monitors. "Two minutes."

"Start praying," Lars told Greggy and Rowane. "If the Firvulag lose big, maybe they'll call off the Nightfall War. Then us humans will be free to go home through the time-gate and forget we ever saw this crazy place!"

"Not all humans want to leave," Rowane protested uneasily. "Some hate the future world and have loving ties to this one."

"Don't you believe it," Lars scoffed. "Show any sane human being a time-gate leading back to the Milieu, he'd take a running jump. Even King Golden Britches himself! Stands to reason." He pointed rudely at Greggy. "Wouldn't *you* go?"

"Well—er—" the geneticist mumbled.

"My Tonee wouldn't go!" Rowane cried. "He wouldn't!"

The chief technician said, "ESGs on full. FX crew stand by with the pyrotechnic intro. Music track go! Tanu metaconcert established. Firvulag ditto. On your mark...get a grip...*heave ho!*"

Out on the Field of Gold, the colossal twin serpents seemed to coil amid a thicket of bramble-branched lightnings. The maws of the fabulous reptiles belched luminous clouds of green smoke that rose up into the low-hanging overcast that now made an eerie roof over the tournament ground. Another ten centimeters of black tail went down the golden weasand.

"Hold, Tanu, hold!" yelled the sidelines crowd, humans and Howlers together. The mutants no longer bothered to pretend that they were on the side of their Firvulag cousins.

Up in the enclosure of King Aiken-Lugonn, the combined aura of the triumphing Great Ones was a solar flare, the subordinate minds sleeving it in a golden swarm of blazing bees. This astral arm appeared to grip the bracelet of the Tanu serpent and haul firmly upwards.

The Firvulag royal enclosure was deep in a nimbus of scarlet anguish. Its dense cluster of supporting mentalities pulsed in irregular rhythm, slowing and then quickening, and flaring up here and there in nervous coruscations of vermilion and angry white. The Firvulag astral arm was much larger than that of the Tanu, but its color shone dull carmine.

"The Little People falter," Katlinel observed to her husband. Her face was troubled, in contrast to the jubilant Howler subjects that capered about.

Sugoll said, "It is as we expected. Having lost the initial advantage when Aiken phased in his unexpected subsumed faculties, they are on the verge of panic. The pain unnerves them and metaconcert is still too unfamiliar a discipline for them to have confidence in their superior potential...Hark! Can you hear the desperate confabulation taking place on the racial submode? They fear they are done for. But Queen Ayfa proposes a bold plan. She will take half the linkage and transfer to the Tanu bracelet and *push*, while Sharn's force continues to pull."

"Firvulag have ever been dubious about following female generals," Katlinel remarked. "I wonder—"

The spectators screeched. The Firvulag astral arm split suddenly into two. But the Tanu responded with violent, wrenching tugs that had the Firvulag bracelet sliding to within a bare half meter of the golden serpent's shining amethyst fangs. The secondary Firvulag arm groped impotently for the base of the Tanu bracelet.

"The blunderers!" Sugoll cried. "The increase in the pain burden causes them to lose heart. Many of Queen Ayfa's force desert her, rushing to help Sharn pull the black serpent's tail away from the rival's punishing jaws! The Queen's ploy is ruined. She retires in disorder."

The second astral arm commanded by luckless Ayfa petered away into falling sparks and the Queen hastened to reestablish the mindlink with her consort. All over the Firvulag grandstand, gnomish minds were giving up the struggle. Tiny red embers winked out as people climbed to their feet and resigned.

Aiken and his team made a flooding sunburst. With a last mighty movement, the golden arm pulled the tail of the black serpent through the Tanu worm's jaws. The dark-jeweled bracelet disappeared behind glittering purple fangs. A final enormous bow of lightning haloed the twin serpentine bodies. Then the black snake seemed to catch fire, devoured in yellow flames. Its head withdrew into the mountain. Its twisted body writhed, disentangling itself from its victorious antagonist. The burning black snake fell to ashes and only a golden circle was left, poised on the artificial mountain base like some huge, upstanding Tanu torc.

"Your people will need some hours to recover their strength," Marc said to Sharn and Ayfa. "We can use it productively. My metaconcert program will not be too difficult for you to assimilate if you both subordinate yourselves to my coercive function and let me force-feed the data."

"Submit to you?" Sharn exclaimed in horror. "I knew it! You intend to enslave us!"

"What good even the Nightfall victory," Ayfa wept, "if in the end, the Adversary rules over all?"

"Fools," said Abaddon. "Haven't I told you that I have no interest in this miserable world? Once your minds help me to break into Castle Gateway, I'll set you free—and good riddance! No strings attached. You'll have my metaconcert program, the ability to exert firm control over the undisciplined brains of your rabble. And I'll have what *I* want . . . secure on a world fourteen thousand light-years away from you. Now choose!"

The co-monarchs stared numbly at the dark armored mass that lurked at the back of the now-deserted royal enclosure. The thing's inhuman mind opened to them, showing a tantalizing glimpse of complexity, beckoning.

Together, they passed into the abyss.

13

It was past 0400. Only Cloud's redactive faculty now sustained Tony Wayland as he made continuous manual adjustments to the faulty cladding device that spun gossamer-fine niobium-dysprosium wire.

"You're doing fine, Tony," Cloud said. "Only another five hundred meters to go. You can do it—"

The cladder's spec-variance alarm went off. He croaked, "God—not again!"

Respool. Cut off the strand at the slub and clear the aperture. Make microscopic adjustments to the fouled vaporizing chamber. Smear more balsam sealant on the leaking nipple gasket.

"Work, damn you, work!" he shouted. The watchers standing about the messy cubicle in the Castle Gateway cloister had blank faces and barricaded minds. Cloud. The thunder-browed redskin, Chief Burke. Kuhal Earthshaker. The incompetent amateur engineer, Chee-Wu Chan, whose screw-up had produced the faulty batch of wire in the first place. "Work!"

Finger the restart. Set tolerance $\pm 0.005\mu$. Feed. *Go!*

He moaned, "Now stay there, you perishing fucker." Cloud caressed his fatigue-poisoned senses. A vision of sweet Rowane

444

seemed to float just beyond the laboring machine, slender scaled arms outstretched, single eye weeping tender tears.

Chee-Wu caught a fresh bobbin as the machine spat it out, and rushed it away to the core-spinning team. Hagen Remillard stuck his head into the cubicle and said to his sister. "Aiken's deep-sight has spotted an anomaly just outside the castle, standing on the old timegate site. Impermeable, two hundred thirty cents high, mass congruent with Papa's CE rig."

"We can't hurry this," Cloud said. "Go flog the other workers."

"We're going to stack all the small sigmas that the King brought with him around the inner ward," Hagen said, "get everybody under the umbrella up next to the Guderian device and the fix-it benches. We'll activate just as soon as you finish the last spool of wire. With luck, there'll be enough time left to complete the last cable repair."

Tony gave a manic chuckle. "Some hope! You have Jonah himself jinxing your escape, kid! Disaster tracks old Tony Wayland like hyenas trailing a wounded buck. You're not going to get away from your father. None of us have a chance! The black Night's closing in and the demon horde is ready to strike—"

The cladder ejected the final spool of wire.

"Grab Tony!" Hagen told Kuhal Earthshaker. "Everybody out into the courtyard!"

"We'll try a psychocreative shield," Aiken told the crowd gathered about the gazebo platform. "It might give us a last-second edge after he cracks the big dome and the improvised sigma-stack. But I can't go the limit defending the time-gate. The war that's coming up has to be my first priority. You understand that, don't you?"

Hagen and Cloud gave simultaneous mental assent. They stood, together with Kuhal Earthshaker and Diane Manion, inside the gazebo of the Guderian device. Every person in the silent assembly knew that once Marc Remillard's children were beyond his reach, the battle would be over. But if Hagen and Cloud failed to escape...

Elizabeth said to them: You have fully assimilated the extremity defense?

Cloud said: Yes. And we'll use it. Papa won't take us alive.

Hagen said: I wish there was some way we could destroy our bodies!

Aiken said: He'll be able to stop that—if it reaches that point. I'm sorry. Elizabeth's snuff sequence is your last bastion.

Kuhal and Diane said: And we are in tandem.

Elizabeth said: Fortunate ones. In the Milieu such consolation would be refused for the greater good of the Unity.

Anatoly said, "And rightly! Poor children. But God understands lovers and forgives. Those who refuse to love are another matter."

Elizabeth cried: *How can you hear us? How dare you?*

"He hears through my mind's ear," replied the King. And he said to her on the intimate mode: Death is not the children's last defender Elizabeth. You are.

Outside the castle the armored shape stood ready in starless dark. Its body was set aside, suspended from life-process in refrigerated stasis. Its brain blazed as the needle electrodes charged it with energies too great for unsupported flesh and blood to bear. It was fully empowered in the aggressive psychocreative faculty. Far away in Nionel, the obedient cells of the Organic Mind, 80,000 strong, awaited its command.

It struck the dome of force capping Castle Gateway. The great sigmafield drained away into bedrock via a hundred metapsychic grounding channels. There was a profound roaring noise and the earth heaved. As the low-hanging clouds reflected the blue-white corona of the conquering Adversary, Castle Gateway rocked, broken by the tremors that shook the plateau, and crumbled slowly into piles of rubble. At its heart was a lesser silver hemisphere, steadfast in the midst of destruction.

The incandescent brain laughed as it transposed its energies to the d-jumping function and teleported into the dusty ruins. Then it struck again, hammering the stacked lesser sigmas and the internal metapsychic shield generated by the King. The shelter attenuated like frost melting from a windowpane.

The brain perceived the two familiar minds, caught them as they hovered on the brink, forestalling their suicide, claiming them.

Now, it cried. *Now!*

The armored black form gave way to the body of a living man. Dismissing both his Firvulag minions and the artificial energies of the enhancer, he stood on the platform in front of the Guderian device, looking at his paralyzed son and daughter. One side of his mouth was lifted in a gentle smile. Then he turned to Elizabeth. She knelt on cracked flagstones next to the control console, surrounded on three sides by motionless workers. Aiken lay unconscious in front of her.

"As you see," Marc said, "I've won. You knew I would."

Elizabeth lifted the King's head and smoothed his disheveled hair. "Another ten or fifteen seconds and they would have been gone. The machine is ready. If only Aiken had let me operate the controls." She was very calm. "I should plead with you, Marc."

"Open to me instead."

Her eyes widened. He only nodded. Aiken's heart beat again and the currents in his brain had the steady cycle of dreamless sleep. She kissed his brow and laid him softly on the stones. Then she stood facing Marc. "Very well."

Her mental walls dissolved. There was no fear, no submission, only a passage of free entry and a dropping of a fiery mask.

Marc said only, "Ah." He stepped to the control console over Aiken's body, activated the tau-generator, and sent the four people inside the gazebo through the gray limbo, into Madame Guderian's rose garden in the hills above Lyon, in the France of the Galactic Milieu.

Dawn came to the Field of Gold, and the squad of Howler referees staggered as they held up the huge leather ball filled with sand. It was white with black markings, and in the fitful overcast of the lurid sunrise it looked like a misshapen skull all smeared with blood.

The Marshal of Sport intoned: "Grand Tourney contestants! This event, called variously hurley or shinty, marks the culmination of this first year's games. As you know, the winner in this contest will also be proclaimed victorious in the Tourney as a whole, and be awarded the Singing Stone. The game will be fought in a single ten-hour match, beginning as the sun lifts above the horizon and concluding as it sets. The playing ground is the entire Field of Gold, sixteen square kilometers. The Firvulag own the north goalposts and the Tanu own the south. Both physical and metapsychic prowess may be employed, but no weapons. The team with the greatest number of goals wins. There are no other rules or restraints...Now let the team captains salute their noble opponents."

A bedlam of cheering greeted Sharn and Ayfa, marching out to the face-off circle at the head of their phalanx of stalwarts. Then the Tanu Great Ones sallied forth—leaderless.

Heymdol Buccinator proclaimed: "Inasmuch as King Aiken-Lugonn is presently unable to take the field, the Tanu team will be captained by Bleyn the Champion."

Groans arose from the human and Howler spectators and delighted catcalls from the ebon host of Little People, who now rushed helter-skelter onto the sandy expanse in front of the grandstands like a swarm of glossy black beetles. Suddenly there was a flash of amber light and an earsplitting sonic boom that made the ground tremble. A flyer emblazoned with an open hand hovered above the Rainbow Bridge. From its open belly hatch plummeted a sizzling little golden comet.

Bleyn said: "I gladly yield the captaincy of the Tanu team to King Aiken-Lugonn!" And the mind-shouts of the humans and mutants drowned out the Firvulag's furious hoots.

Landing, Aiken strutted to the face-off circle and raised the visor of his golden helmet. "Morning, Ayfa. Morning, Sharn. Ready for our little bash?"

"You should be dead!" they cried.

The Shining One lifted his bejeweled pauldrons in a rueful gesture. "The Adversary had other games to play. Are you two ready to get on with this one?"

The ogrish mates grinned then, showing white pointed tusks. Sharn remarked, "So Remillard's gone, eh? Well, he left us a nice souvenir that we'll take great pleasure in demonstrating to you."

"You might call it a winning game plan," Ayfa added. "And you're going to be quite impressed with the postgame festivities, too!"

Aiken held up one plated finger. "Let me make just one little announcement." And his mind-voice rolled and echoed over the Field of Gold, silencing the tumultuous audience and the impatient teams.

I speak to the humans, Aiken said, *and to those other persons of goodwill who seek to live in a world of peace. The time-gate leading to the Galactic Milieu is now open.*

Sensation! Sharn and Ayfa gaped at each other, thunderstruck.

All throughout this Fifth Day of the Grand Tourney my aircraft will shuttle back and forth between here and the time-gate site. They will transport any who wish to go. You may take with you only what can be carried in one arm and nothing that belongs to Me. I myself intend to stay and rule this Many-Colored Land as High King after seating Myself in triumph upon the Singing Stone at the end of today's play. I invite those who love this place to stay also.

"Lowlife!" Sharn raged. "Upstart jackanapes!" screeched Ayfa.

The titanic ball rose into the air, impelled by the psychokinesis of Sugoll, Katlinel, and the Howlers. When it reached an altitude of about forty meters, the Marshal of Sport commanded: "Play ball!"

Crash! The heavy spheroid fell to earth. The opposing teams surged forward, the audience shrieked, and the final contest of the Grand Tourney began.

Ten persons per trip, twenty trips per hour.

After the young North Americans had been translated, and those of the Guderian Project who wanted to return to the Milieu, the time-gate exodus settled down into a fairly routine operation, organized and supervised by Chief Burke, Basil, and those of the Bastards who weren't doing pilot shuttle duty. The commandant of the Roniah garrison, a cheerful little Walloon PK-head named LeCocq, helped maintain order with a small force of loyal grays.

Tony Wayland was caught trying to sneak off to Nionel on a returning aircraft. Burke frogmarched him back to the gazebo and gave him into the charge of an armed guard, with orders that Tony was to stay with the skeleton staff of gazebo technicians who had agreed to stand by in case the apparatus broke down again.

"But the King promised I could go to my wife!" Tony protested.

Burke picked him up by the scruff and dangled him nose to nose. "I still remember the Vale of Hyenas, White Eyes, and for two bits I'd give you a round trip in that time-machine and use your ashes to polish my tomahawk! Now sit there with the others and wait, dammit!"

Tony waited.

That first morning, the aircraft coming from Nionel were only half-full, carrying only the most homesick of the Pliocene exiles, those who had yearned for years to return to Elder Earth. As long as King Aiken-Lugonn and the Tanu put up a good scrap in the hurley-burley, there seemed no need to rush into making the big decision.

Then, some time early in the afternoon, Sharn and Ayfa finally sorted out the fine points of Marc Remillard's meta-concert program and began to use it efficiently. Not only did the Firvulag come up from behind in the scoring, but they began to inflict serious injury upon members of the Tanu team, singling out stalwarts such as Celadeyr of Afaliah, Lomnovel Brainburner, and Parthol Swiftfoot, who had been especially skilled ball carriers. The three were savagely red-dogged and had to be retired to Skin.

With the tide of fortune turning toward the Little People, the mood of the human spectators darkened. They recalled the rumors of impending war—no mere brushfire action such as had taken place at Burask and Bardelask, but a conflict that might involve the entire continent. Pondering their somber options, the Lowlives watched rampaging waves of Tanu and Firvulag surge about the devastated turf of the Tourney field like a living maelstrom. Nightmare illusions were everywhere. The aether throbbed with a hellish din. Mind-bolts, nauseating psychic eructations, and quasi-material missiles were flung in all directions. Frenzied ogres sought to tear their outnumbered Tanu opponents to pieces. Herds of stampeding dwarves stomped fallen torced humans into the bloody dust. Tanu redactors and the scuttling little cadres of Firvulag nurses could scarcely haul away the injured without being mortally endangered themselves.

The tally of Firvulag goals mounted more and more rapidly. By 1400 hours the Little People led 50-33. An hour later their lead had increased to 87-36. The sky grew ever more lowering and oppressive, charged with noxious positive ions, ozone, and a distinct odor of sulfur in addition to the hash of sinister vibes.

Fresh rumors flew about the thinning crowd of spectators:

Mont-Dore was erupting! (But only in a minor fashion.) Thunderstorms had ignited grassfires on the tinder-dry prairies to the west! (But the nearest conflagration was twenty kloms away.) The time-warper was running out of steam! (Bullshit. The thing drew most of its energy from telluric currents in the planetary crust itself. Its power-drain would be very low.) King Aiken-Lugonn was ready to throw in the towel! (Oh, yes? Well, there were still forty-five minutes left to play—and anything could happen when the Shining One was part of the fracas!)

AIKEN: Elizabeth.

ELIZABETH: Yes, dear.

AIKEN: Gads! I'm surprised to find you still here, babe . . . You decided not to waft away after all?

ELIZABETH: Marc and I are discussing things.

AIKEN: I had a sneaking suspicion you might be . . . Babe, that metaconcert program he gave the Firvulag is killing us. We're going to lose this ball game—and the Little People haven't even begun to focus their full mental potential on us. I think they're holding back the terminal zorch for the clincher—the signal for Nightfall.

ELIZABETH: Oh, Aiken! But if it becomes plain that the assault is of lethal intent, you'll be free to use your weapons and your aircraft—

AIKEN: By then, we may be goners. Or I may be—which amounts to the same thing. If I were Sharn and Ayfa, I'd funnel the entire psychocreative load at Me just before old Heymdol blows the Last Trump.

ELIZABETH: Marc—can't *you* do something?

MARC: I promised the Firvulag that I would never use my destructive potential against them.

ELIZABETH: The metaconcert then—!

MARC: I can't rescind it, nor is it susceptible of sabotage. I played fair with the Little People as I did with both of you.

AIKEN: I was afraid you might have. Well . . . I guess that's that. Thanks for the memories, you two. Think about Me as you work out your little penances for the next six million years.

MARC: Just a moment. Are you restricted as to your garb in this game?

AIKEN: ? We wear our usual Grand Combat regalia, but I suppose anything goes. What's this got to do with the fending of Ragnarok?

MARC: I'll show you.

All but hidden in smoky haze, the sun dropped toward the western forest horizon. But the game was rocketing madly in the opposite direction, toward the Rainbow Bridge and Nionel. Aiken Drum and his depleted band of defenders, englobed in a mental shield, were running away with the ball.

Outraged gnomes and ogres trampled through the concession stands, blasted aside the flimsy riverside bleachers, poured in a demonic torrent through empty picnic areas and pleasances, and charged the Tanu stalwarts blocking the approach to the bridge. The spectrum colors of the great arch had a preternaturally brilliant glow. A single low-angled beam of sunlight broke the cloud cover and illuminated gold-domed Nionel.

Out in the middle of the span was the King's protective bubble—and on top of its flexible surface bounced the enormous ball, insolently inaccessible in spite of the combined mental power of the Firvulag seeking vainly to snatch it away.

"Pull it down!" Ayfa entreated her husband. "What's wrong with us? How can that little scoundrel be countering our concerted effort like this?"

"He's getting help!" Sharn gasped. "From somewhere on the other side of the river. Té's Tonsils—it's the *Howlers* lending him their minds!"

"Perfidious misbegottens!" raged the Queen. "There's nothing for it, Sharn. We'll have to hit him with everything we've got. Right now. Before the Last Trump."

"We'll burst the ball—lose the game by default!"

"And win the Nightfall War, you great blockhead!" she screamed. "Order the offensive metaconcert in its ultimate configuration as the Adversary taught us. Now!"

"Wife, wife, our Sacred Way forbids—"

"Do you want to lose? If we cannot take him suddenly, before the game's end, the aircraft with their Milieu armaments will come at us from all directions! Will we have the skill to fend them off—and cope with Aiken Drum at the same time? Call up the offensive!"

Sharn did as he was told.

* * *

In the middle of the Rainbow Bridge, Aiken felt the psychic tension begin to mount, perceived the terrible coherence of the Foe-mind gathering back on the Field of Gold.

He said to his people: Slonshal to Us! It was a grand game after all.

Then he saw the two black armored forms materializing inside his mental bubble, side by side on the deck of the bridge. From the right-hand CE rig came Marc Remillard, shimmering through the impermeable cerametal as though it were the insubstantial projection of a Tri-D. The other suit of armor abruptly split open and the blind helm lifted to show that it was empty.

"Hurry!" Marc told him. "Get inside. The coverall isn't necessary and your own armor will fit within the shell. I'll not oppose them directly, but I'm willing to show *you* how to use the cerebroenergetic enhancer yourself. There will be pain. Pay no attention. Now hurry!"

Without thinking, Aiken dived for the gaping lefthand rig. Marc's simulacrum had vanished back inside the other. As the body halves closed over him, Aiken levitated to keep his head above the neck seal. Something deep inside the armor stabbed him on both sides of the groin. He felt his legs growing cold, his entire body numbing, disappearing...

It's only the femoral circulatory shunt and the start of the refrigeration. Are you keeping your protective bubble up?

Yes. Aagh! It hit my jugular!

Carotid arteries. The primary shunt. Here comes the helmet. Don't panic. Have your people hold fast as best they can. You'll be out of it for the next few seconds.

Descending darkness. Clang! Liquid rising, filling mouth, nose. I'll drown! I won't...I'm cold, not breathing. God—no—lasers drilling my skull—my mind sees the crown of needles plunge into the helpless brain, sprout filaments, hurt me as the energies pour in—Marc make it stopOstop-OGodmakeitstop no no...??? Jesus.

Can you see now? Farsense?

Yes. O yes. YES!

Find the enemy executive. Your farsenses will stay in peripheral mode. As normal. You're power-phased only for psychocreative metafunction. Now quickly—this is the way to augment the faculty with the enhancer. Let me monitor...merde alors you are a strong little bugger aren't you?

*Christ they're winding up to strike! Have you the fix on Sharn
and Ayfa? Hurry for the love of God Aiken hit them hit them
now forgetmetaconcert Boyhitthemyourselfyourownpowerhit-
hit—*

He did.

Oh, it was so good. He hit, and the Foe burned. The encroaching Night was thrust back by the intensity of the fire.
Was the game over? Had the horn blown? Was the sun down?
He didn't know. The Rainbow Bridge seemed to be tumbling
down, and golden onion domes and lacy spires. He was aware
of minds fleeing and minds dying and minds whirling like
sparks in a hurricane all around the central fire of the Shining
One. Let my Brain shine on! This is the way it should be. This
is the way I win, I conquer it all, engulf it in my furnace and
feed upon it!

Never let it stop.

It stops now. And just in time I think . . .

Aiken woke. He was lying on smoldering turf, wearing a
stained and soggy suit of armor-padding. Big Dougal sat beside
him, raising his head and proffering a cup of lukewarm muddy-
tasting water. It was extremely dark except for a dull red glow
all along the northern skyline.

"The wildfire is past, my liege. How fare you?"

Aiken tried to sit up. A pang of agony shot through his head
and he saw multicolored stars. Then he got hold of himself and
managed a puny beam of farsight. He and Dougal seemed to
be the only ones alive in the midst of a scorched plain strewn
with bodies. "No!" he whispered. "No no no!"

"Take heart, Aslan. Many of our people live. They are
beyond the blasted bridge, receiving aid from those who lately
fled. It was said that you had perished in the dire combustion
but I knew it was not so. I sought you out and found you, and
now we will go to a small boat I have waiting, and thence to
an aircraft that will carry you home."

"Sharn . . . Ayfa . . ."

"They are dead, and more than half their host. The rest fled
before the wildfire that your mind enkindled, into the north
and the west and the southern jungle. But none dared cross the
Nonol to our sanctuary, and none dared dispute when the de-

parting Adversary named you High King."

"Gone. Marc's gone." Suddenly, Aiken had to grin. "Oh, that was a narrow escape! Small wonder those rigs are outlawed in the Galactic Milieu."

Dougal had with him an oil lantern that had long ago burnt out. With feebly reviving creativity Aiken engendered a wee faerie light to sit in it and cast a meager radiance to show the way. Arm in arm they limped toward the river. Their progress was very slow. Gradually the eastern sky acquired a tentative gray sheen, silhouetting the broken masses of the twin grandstands and the blackened snags of trees down by the shore. Wraiths of smoke drifted here and there, given substance when the lantern light caught them.

Then they saw something else—a harder, brighter gleam in the midst of a great tumble of Firvulag bodies. They came close and discovered a thing like a backless throne, exquisitely carved from translucent greenish stone and ornamented with silvery metal. Its cushion had been burnt to ashes, but otherwise the Singing Stone was unharmed.

Dougal lifted the lantern high and marveled. "Would you seat yourself upon it, High King?"

Aiken uttered a weary laugh. "Maybe some other time." He turned away from the trophy and let his farsight range, mourning the lost splendor, the wasted lives. And now to begin all over again for the third time! Could he do it? Did he even want to try? Or should he simply turn his back on the entire mess and follow the ones who had surrendered, returning to the security of Elder Earth?

There was a definite tinge of dawn in the east. "Who knows what I'll do?" Aiken said to Dougal. "It looks like the Night is almost over. Let's go find that boat of yours and see what's on the other side of the river."

Tony Wayland had managed to escape the vigilance of Chief Burke when the terrible news from the Field of Gold reached the time-gate site. Wild with fear for Rowane, he secreted himself on a shuttlecraft returning to Nionel. He spent the remaining hours of the night searching futilely among the huddled mutants who dozed in small groups around dead campfires in the eastern meadow. It was not until the sun was full risen that he found Greggy beside a tiny brook, leaning against the trunk of a willow tree, the head of a sleeping woman in his lap.

The Genetics Master giggled softly. "Well, well! Back at last, are you? We'd given you up, you know. Poor Rowane cried herself to sleep."

Tony demanded, "Where's my wife? What have you done with her?"

"Why, she's here," Greggy said slyly. He let one fingertip caress the eyelids of the little beauty who nestled against him. The eyes opened. Saw Tony. He stood there as dumb as a stick of wood as she rose and stood in front of him, lips trembling, hands clasped together. "It's really her," Greggy said. "She went through my new Skin-tank. The very first case. I'm so proud."

She said in a low voice, "I hope you like me. I hope you'll stay now."

"I loved you the way you were," he said brokenly, and then he touched his golden torc. "I loved you too much. I wasn't strong enough then. But now I have my torc and it'll be all right, Rowane."

"But you *do* like me as I am now?" she pleaded.

"I love you. You're beautiful. The most beautiful thing I've ever seen. But it wouldn't have mattered if you'd stayed the same, Rowane. Believe me."

"Not everything about me is changed," she whispered, and then gave a little teasing laugh. Tony gulped, but only held her tighter. She said, "I wonder if the baby will take after you—or me?"

Looking over her shoulder, stunned, Tony saw Greg-Donnet Genetics Master wink at him. "Don't fret, son. Don't give it a second thought."

Deep in the Paris Basin swamps, the boy woke as the paddles splashed and the inflated craft pushed through rattling reeds to an open pool. He saw the kindly face of Lady Mabino Dreamspinner looking down on him. When he struggled upright he caught sight of old Finoderee snoring back in the stern and two rugged dwarves in obsidian half-armor stretching and scratching mosquito bites and taking long swigs from a drinking skin.

"Mother? Father?" the boy called. And then the memories returned and he gasped with the renewal of terror and cried, "Where are they? And my brothers and sisters? What's happened?"

Mabino bestowed a reproving look on him. "Behave yourself, Sharn-Ador. You aren't an infant but a Warrior Youth. We believe your siblings are safe enough with Galbor's wife, Habetrot. But since she's not very adept at farspeech, we'll—"

"Where are my Mother and Father?" the boy asked in a tight voice.

"They are secure in Té's Peace, having traveled the Warrior's Way. We are all very proud of them. Now you may weep for a short time, as is fitting."

Later, he lifted his reddened face and looked across the sunlit marsh. Mallards were swimming there, and immature graylag geese, and one enormous cob swan who dominated the others. "He is their king," the child said, dashing away his tears. He watched the black-and-white bird cruise about with neck proudly curved and wings lifted above his back. "I'll be a king, too, someday! Did you save my armor and sword?"

The stalwart dwarves guffawed and bent again to the paddles. Mabino tightened her mouth in pretended disapproval. "It's in the back of the boat. But don't go crawling over Papa Finoderee and wake him. He's just managed to drop off to sleep after a very bad night."

"Yes, my Lady," said Sharn-Ador. He settled back against the boat's pneumatic gunwale and watched the swan until it had vanished from sight astern.

The Heretic seemed to fly out of the heart of the rising sun and along the wake of the great schooner, to land on the afterdeck, where Alexis Manion greeted him without surprise.

They introduced themselves. Alex said, "I've tracked you for three hours. Welcome to Kyllikki."

"Farsensed me into the sun?" Minanonn let his astonishment show. "That's no mean feat. You must be a power to reckon with."

Alex chuckled. "I was, but that's ancient history."

"Funny, you could say the same for me."

The man who had been Marc Remillard's closest confidant during the Metapsychic Rebellion looked up at the former Tanu Battlemaster. "You like coffee, high pockets?"

"Don't mind if I do, shrimp. You Lowlives are a hopelessly corrupting influence."

"It seems to me I've heard that line before." Alex turned around and beckoned. "Right this way to the galley and let's talk. Enjoy the peace and quiet while you can. When the women and children wake up, this damn ship turns into a floating circus."

Basil Wimborne looked at Chief Burke and Chief Burke looked at Commander LeCocq, who shrugged.

"That's the last?" Burke said, without believing it. "The very last one?"

"So it seems," the officer said.

"How many?" Basil inquired. "I lost count after the third day."

"A total of eleven thousand and three hundred and thirty-two," LeCocq replied. "Rather less than we anticipated. And only a handful of Howlers and Tanu." He allowed himself a superior smile. "Most of the returning humans were bareneck, of course."

"Which leaves the four of us," said Burke. He looked up at the gazebo, which was now sheltered beneath a striped tent fly.

Over at the control console, Phronsie Gillis yawned. "Anyone got a ticket to ride better hop it. It's been a long, long trick and I'm ready for some rest and recuperation. Especially the latter."

Basil studied the Guderian device, frowning thoughtfully. "I could write a most amazing book if I went back."

Burke said, "I suppose young Mermelstein would take me into the old law firm in Salt Lake City."

Basil said, "But Commander LeCocq says there are some really remarkable peaks in the inner Pyrénées. One or two may exceed eight thousand meters."

Burke said, "But who needs the last of the Wallawallas

shmoozing around the office, boring the pants off of everybody with fantastic stories that couldn't possibly have happened? And the kid doesn't even speak Yiddish."

"Shut it down, Phronsie," said Basil. "It looks as though we'll stay after all."

"Shall we see if Mr. Betsy's willing to fly the lot of us down to Roniah to my place for high tea?" Commander LeCocq suggested.

Phronsie flicked off the power on the Guderian device, extracted the electromagnetically encoded glass key, and handed it to the officer. "Hell, I think ol' Bets will be tickled pink at the suggestion!" She thought for a minute. "Pink—or maybe puce."

He said: We approach the superficies for the last time.

She said: Thank God. Seven of these giant steps and each one worse than the last even with the mitigator . . . how Brede's Ship ever managed the entire journey in a single leap is beyond my comprehension.

He said: Not mine. Brede's Ship was attempting to avoid capture. Under the circumstances one is inspired.

She said: The Ship . . . it knew all along. About Earth and its people. It may have been instinctive for it to seek a world with compatible germ plasm and a similar metapsychic pattern but perhaps it really knew.

He said: Anatoly would say it was led. But his philosophy is rather simplistc. Appealing though and definitely anxiety-calming.

She said: Anxiety? You?

He said: Even me. As your friend Creyn noted the challenge rather exceeds that of my Mental Man vision: reorientation of an entire Galactic Mind condemned to a dead end of mental evolution because of the golden torcs. It should occupy our attention for some time.

She said: Will we have it? Time?

He said: I trust so. Both of us.

She said: You're leaning toward the simplistic.

He said: Jack often remarked on it. But the mind-set of one's youth is not rejected with impunity. We were both taught to trust. Shall we Elizabeth?

She said: Yes. Yes Marc . . .

He said: Come then. I'll support you as we make the penetration. Have courage. It's the last step.

She said: The first I think.

They emerged, and the Duat Galaxy swirled around them—smaller than the Milky Way, but still enfolding more than eleven thousand Duat daughter-worlds in its far-flung starry arms. The two suits of black armor hung in space and the enclosed brains saw a nearby expanse of nebulosity that glowed red and royal blue from the double star forming within its heart. Those two stars were still without planets, mindless. But in every direction lay suns with living worlds, of a number too great to count.

"Listen!" Elizabeth cried. "It's not true Unity, but they're close, Marc. Really very close. Perhaps it won't be so hard after all."

"It will be hard, but we'll manage."

He called.

The star-strewn sky was suddenly alive with enormous crystalline creatures and the aether rang with Song.

THE END OF THE ADVERSARY

Thus concludes
The Saga of Pliocene Exile.
There are others,
most notably the Milieu Trilogy, which tells
the root-tales leading to this one,
in books titled
JACK THE BODILESS, DIAMOND MASK,
and MAGNIFICAT.
Gaudete.

APPENDIXES

Map of Northwestern Europe
During the Pliocene Epoch

Map of Western Mediterranean Region
During the Pliocene Epoch,
After the Gibraltar Rupture

Map of the Monte Rosa Massif
During the Pliocene Epoch

Some Aspects of Hyperspatial
Translation and D-Jumping

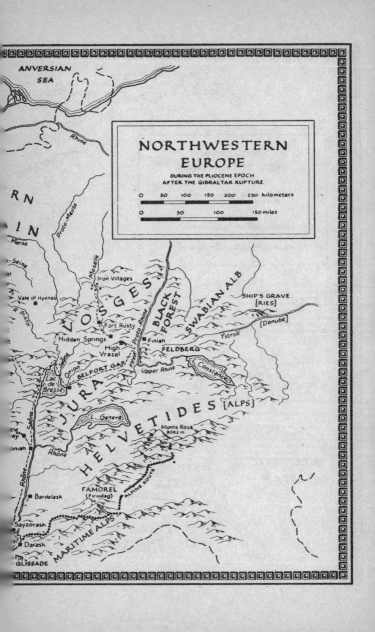

ANVERSIAN
SEA

Rhine

NORTHWESTERN
EUROPE

DURING THE PLIOCENE EPOCH
AFTER THE GIBRALTAR RUPTURE

0   50   100   150   200   250 kilometers

0   50   100   150 miles

RN

AIN

Marne

Seine

Proto-Meuse

Moselle

Iron Villages

Vale of Hyenas

Proto-Rhine

Proto-Saône

Onion

Fort Rusty

Hidden Springs

High
Vrazel

Finiah

VOSGES

BLACK FOREST

SWABIAN ALB

SHIP'S GRAVE
[RIES]

[Danube]

Ystroll

FELDBERG

BELFORT GAP

Lac
de
Bresse

JURA

Upper Rhine

Constance

HELVETIDES [ALPS]

Geneva

Monte Rosa
8082 m

Rhône

Saône

FAMOREL
(Firvulag)

ALPINE ROUTE

Bardelask

MARITIME ALPS

Sayzorask

Darask

GLISSADE

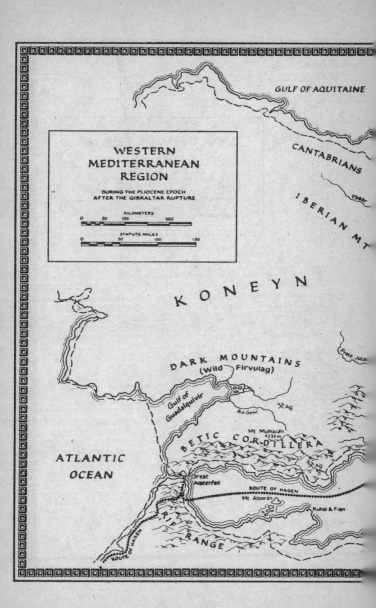

WESTERN
MEDITERRANEAN
REGION

DURING THE PLIOCENE EPOCH
AFTER THE GIBRALTAR RUPTURE

KILOMETERS
0   50   100   200

STATUTE MILES
0   50   100   150

GULF OF AQUITAINE

CANTABRIANS

IBERIAN MT

ybaar

K O N E Y N

Proto-Jucar

DARK   MOUNTAINS
(Wild Firvulag)

Gulf of
Guadalquivir

Rio Genil

Ag

Mt Mulhacén
4233 m.

BETIC COR-DILLERA

Ag

ATLANTIC
OCEAN

Great
Waterfall

ROUTE OF HAGEN

Mt Alborán

Kuhal & Fian

ROUTE OF HAGEN

R
I
F
RANGE

ROUTE OF HAGEN

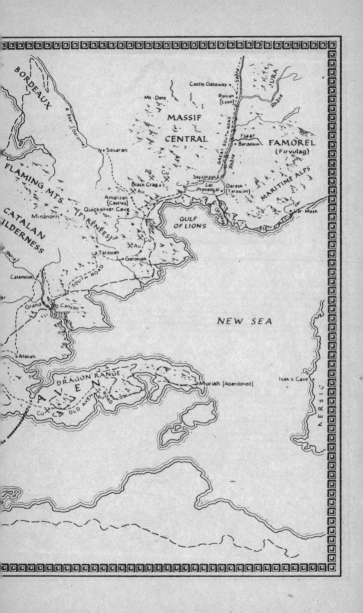

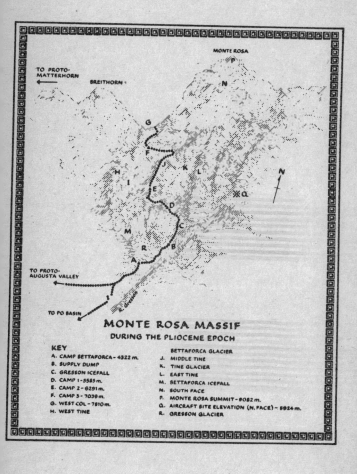

MONTE ROSA MASSIF
DURING THE PLIOCENE EPOCH

MONTE ROSA

TO PROTO-
MATTERHORN

BREITHORN

N

TO PROTO-
AUGUSTA VALLEY

TO PO BASIN

R. Gresson

KEY

A. CAMP BETTAFORCA - 4322 m.
B. SUPPLY DUMP
C. GRESSON ICEFALL
D. CAMP 1 - 5585 m.
E. CAMP 2 - 6291 m.
F. CAMP 3 - 7039 m.
G. WEST COL - 7810 m.
H. WEST TINE

BETTAFORCA GLACIER
J. MIDDLE TINE
K. TINE GLACIER
L. EAST TINE
M. BETTAFORCA ICEFALL
N. SOUTH FACE
P. MONTE ROSA SUMMIT - 9082 m.
Q. AIRCRAFT SITE ELEVATION (N. FACE) - 8924 m.
R. GRESSON GLACIER

Some Aspects of Hyperspatial Translation and D-Jumping

IN THE GALACTIC MILIEU, *SUPERLUMINAL TRANSPORT*, OR FASTER-than-light travel, is accomplished through the "warping" of normal space by means of an *upsilon-field*, one of the primary manifestations of reality. The field can be mechanically generated by a device called a *superluminal translator* (u-field generator, etc.) or—very rarely—by a metapsychic individual possessed of the "teleportation" faculty.

In a typical trip, a starship generates a u-field to break through the *superficies* (boundary) between normal space and the *hyperspatial matrix*. The latter is also called simply hyperspace, the "hype," subspace, the matrix, or the gray limbo. Sentient creatures experience varying degrees of pain during translation.

Once into the hyperspatial matrix, the starship's navigation equipment programs a *hyperspatial catenary*, or subspace vector (vulgarly called "limbo track," "slice of the hype," etc.). For a period of subjective time, the ship and its riders can be said to move along the catenary. Their position at any specified subjective moment is called the *pseudolocus*. Ships are quite capable of halting within the matrix or changing the catenary (with certain limitations) en route. When the catenary is fully described, the starship has effectively reached its destination and once again breaks through the superficies into normal space. A power breakdown during the hyperspatial portion of the trip strands the ship in the matrix. Similarly, a person attempting a d-jump might be stranded if his concentration failed to maintain the correct vector, "visualizing" the intended goal. The *rubberband effect* is a complex phenomenon that must be neutralized, either mechanically or through mental programming, if the starship or d-jumper is not to be pulled back to the point of origin at the completion of the translation.

Starships utilize superluminal translators of varying power. For slower-than-light, or *subluminal*, transport—and invariably within the atmosphere of inhabited planets—the ships switch to *inertialess drive*, made possible by *rho-field generators* operating on gravomagnetic principles.* The upsilon-field is not usually generated within a planetary atmosphere. The "large aperture" u-field necessary to admit a starship into hyperspace generates collateral electromagnetic phenomena, especially ionization, that may constitute a nuisance or even an endangerment to civilized entities and their delicate contraptions. The much smaller u-field generated by a d-jumping individual mind would have a negligible effect upon the environment unless large numbers of people engaged in the activity. Since the faculty is so rare, the contingency is moot.

When a starship captain undertakes a voyage he must consider (a) How far am I going? (b) How fast do I want to get there? (c) How much pain am I, or my passengers and crew, willing to tolerate in the process?

A "slow" translation or *deep catenary*, takes the longest subjective time to accomplish and causes the least amount of pain in the breakthrough. A "fast" translation, or *tight catenary*, (called also the "fast track," "tight leash," etc.) gets one to the destination more quickly, but at the expense of wear and tear on the nervous system. Hotdog spacers who habitually *schuss* must make use of medications or other anodynes to deal with the severe pain. Such stout hearts refer to slowtrack travelers as *bunny-hoppers*.

---

*The rho-field is still another primary manifestation of reality, which according to Milieu theoreticians consists of twenty-one "fields," or dimensional lattices, that interact to generate space, time, matter, energy, life, and mind.

On very long trips, the ordinary passenger-carrying starship would reach its destination via a series of slow jumps. The *displacement factor* (df, "speed," "warp factor," "push," etc.) along the hyperspatial catenary deemed acceptable to non-professional space travelers is about 40 df. This is equivalent to 40 light-years traversed, per subjective day spent in hyper-space. Thus the CSS Queen Elizabeth III might take two sub-jective (and actual, to the Larger Reality outside the hype) days to travel to a star system 80 light-years distant—or 300 days to travel 12,000 light-years. At each incremental jump, the riders would suffer pain.

Individuals have differing tolerances to the pain of trans-lation. Exotics generally have a higher threshold than humans. (The stolid Krondaku withstand 370 df, considered about the upper limit for Milieu races.) Richard Voorhees took 250 df for 136 days on his longest schuss, to Hercules Cluster (M13 or NGC6205 in contemporary catalogs). When he traveled to Orissa many years later, he was pushing his luck to endure 110 df for 17 days in succession.

Obviously, both the time-elapse factor and the pain factor limit the range of superluminal transport. In the Milieu, the exotic races have already mapped and explored most of our Milky Way Galaxy (with the exception of the perilous Hub); and with more than 1000 potentially colonizable planets located within 20,000 light-years of Earth, there is little practical in-centive for extremely long-range translations. Extra-galactic travel is virtually proscribed. The Andromeda Galaxy, our clos-est neighbor, is 2.2 million light-years distant; it would take the hardiest human starship voyager some twenty-four years to get there—and another twenty-four years to get back. Even in an era of multiple rejuvenations, such a trip would have little appeal except to the incorrigibly wanderlustful. A few souls have tried it, with uncertain results.

The exotic beings known as Ships, one of whom, Brede's mate, brought the Tanu and Firvulag from the remote Duat Galaxy to Pliocene Earth, have an extraordinarily high df en-durance. The Ships use a *mitigator*, a special mental program that makes bearable the horrific pain of *ultraluminal*, or "very high speed," translation. Ships teach their passengers, who travel within their bodies in a capsule the size of a conventional starship, how to generate individual mitigator programs of their own. This means that flight within the Duat Galaxy would be all but pain-free for Ship passengers. In addition, the Ship is able to d-jump routinely at very tight catenaries. Most points in its galaxy are reached in minutes, or at the most, a few hours. The d-jump is a single movement, never a series of shorter hops such as those taken by "slow" starships. It should be noted that Brede's Ship fatally strained itself in making the jump from Duat to the Milky Way Galaxy, 270 million light-years distant. Even the most highly talented minds have their limitations.

In making his d-jumps, Marc operates almost exactly like Brede's Ship. His short jaunts about Earth are virtually instantaneous and do not involve more than a split second of subjective time spent in the gray limbo. (The process of breaking through the superficies at either end can take considerably longer, however.) As he d-jumps about the Milky Way, Marc is protected by the armor of the cerebroenergetic enhancer, which holds all portions of his body except the hyperenergized brain in the equivalent of suspended animation. The pain factor remains approximately what it would be in mechanical translation via starship. He stated that he had just about reached his normal-function limit in making the jump to Poltroy. This would put his personal df threshold somewhere in the 18,000 range.

The mitigator is theoretically applicable to ordinary starship travel, provided the riders were metapsychics trained in use of the program. Extremely powerful superluminal translators would be required to "push" the craft to ultratight catenaries. There seems no reason why *ultraluminal starships* could not be built. Milieu models are limited in range by the fragility of the minds carried, not by any mechanical factor.

ABOUT THE AUTHOR

JULIAN MAY's short science fiction novel, *Dune Roller*, was published by John W. Campbell in 1951 and has now become a minor classic of the genre. It was produced on American television and on the BBC, became a movie, and has frequently been anthologized. Julian May lives in the state of Washington.